Strike, Stay Your Hand

Anton Brinza

Deserted Home Press

Copyright © 2024 by Anton Brinza
All rights reserved.

No part of this book may be reproduced in any form or by any electronic or mechanical means, including information storage and retrieval systems, without written permission from the author, except for the use of brief quotations in a book review.

The story, including all names, characters, and incidents portrayed in this production are fictitious. No identification with actual persons, places, buildings, and products is intended or should be inferred.

Certain historical figures and events appear throughout this novel. These characters, the times they came from, and their cultural beliefs are portrayed according to commonly held historical scholarship. However, the portrayals of these characters and events are entirely fictitious.

Quotations from the *Bhagavad Gita* were taken from The Project Gutenberg ebook translated by Sir Edwin Arnold (2000). The selected quotations have been altered.

Cover photograph: Martina Rigoli/iStock
Back cover photograph: Gréta Erdei/Pexels
Spine photograph: Brett Sayles/Pexels
Interior illustrations: Gyubin Song
Cover design: Arturo Palomo

ISBN 979-8-9915061-0-6 (ebook) / 979-8-9915061-1-3 (print)

Published by DESERTED HOME PRESS
An imprint of Ludovico Treats Publishing LLC
www.ludovicotreats.com
www.antonbrinza.com

For Gyubin Song,
my muse

Contents

Prologue ... 1

Part One
1. The Driver ... 7
2. The Graceful Soldier ... 13
3. The Digger ... 16
4. The Noisemaker ... 27
5. The Journalist ... 33
6. A Form of Prayer ... 49
7. Flight ... 56
8. Blood, Again ... 66
9. The Horse ... 73
10. The Deserter ... 90
11. Whereto the Creek Leads ... 96
12. The Cave ... 103

Part Two
13. The Full Moon ... 113
14. The Lullaby ... 127
15. Mirrors ... 134
16. Paradise ... 156
17. Repetition ... 161
18. Miracles ... 169
19. The Scrap ... 172
20. Sweet Everlasting ... 186

Part Three
21. The Closed Door ... 193
22. Into the River ... 204
23. The Dogs ... 210
24. To Scale a Mountain ... 226
25. Seduction ... 230
26. Giant Dog Sickness ... 247
27. The Labyrinth ... 252
28. The White Serpents ... 261

29. The Summer Blossom	269
30. Reflections	284
31. On Pain of Debt	288
32. The Voices	298

Part Four

33. The Debt Collector	305
34. Resident of Nowhere	328
35. The Disciples	337
36. The Medicine Man	352
37. The Hunters	358
38. The Tide	373
39. The Betrayer	380
40. Penance and Reconciliation	394
41. The Horned Goat	403
42. The Cost of Loyalty	432
43. The Weight	438
44. The Visitor	450

Part Five

45. Loss	459
46. The Missionary	469
47. Guilt	478
48. The Open Door	506
49. Fear	516
50. The Saint	535
51. Jo's Last Stand	546
52. The Carnival	558
A Note on Digging	567
About the Author	571
Also by Anton Brinza	573

"The cardinal directions are lost, and so are you, disorientation reigns now as King."

—Dunmore "Sonny" Judson

Prologue

October 3, 1840
The Community of Man, Indian Country

THEY MARCHED AGAINST THEIR WILL, SOME AT THE MERCY OF bayonets, others under the weight of their failure—all of them, their arms linked to repel the constant threats of illness, fatigue, mishap, and loss. Without a thought spared for worldly possessions, they traveled empty-handed, for the trail forgave no excess. How they suffered, rounded up like so many cattle, unprotected from the elements, lacking the energy to resist or complain, swallowing their laments along with meager rations of cornmeal and rotted pork strips. Their tears fell in an eerie hush and pooled in the footprints, their own and those of their fallen brethren.

Always at their side, I held them when they stumbled. I tended their wounds and coerced them to accept white medicines. I dried their tears and dabbed their foreheads with a cool cloth when they were taken with fever. Sitting around small fires, we ate with our hands and could not spare a drop of water to rinse away the filth. I read Scripture on the Sabbath to distract them from their misery, and I told tales to lift their spirits, to quell the coarseness of reality, because if those eight hundred miles hold any clues to the true nature of men, then we are—all of us—better off residing in dreams.

Since 1830, I have ventured numerous times into the West, seeking out prophets and miracles. But small parties of strong, healthy men differ from entire societies dragging chains of defeat. It is the ill, the aged, and the children who break first, and then the strong are broken by an ultimate loss. The trail where we cried, *Nunahi-Duna-Dlo-Hilu-I*. I traveled that woeful road alongside them, but I had a choice. It was my choice to return time and again, walking that treacherous path three times in just two years and spreading my own strength so thin that by the end, I, too, nearly broke. I have chosen a wandering life, but they desired nothing more than to inhabit the lands of their fathers, to hunt the game that their fathers hunted, to forage in the mountains where their fathers gathered wood and herbs and roots, to farm the valleys where their fathers harvested corn and beans, to bathe in the rivers and streams where their fathers bathed.

The final detachment arrived in March 1839. I was among that group, and as we stepped into Fort Gibson, I squeezed the hand of our leader, the noble leader of all Cherokee people, my dear friend Chief John Ross, whose wife we were forced to bury in the frozen ground amongst the hills of the Arkansas Territory. With our hands clasped together, we shared a weak smile, grateful that we had survived the journey but fearful of what lay ahead.

This land the American government has allocated to the Cherokees is flat and a thousand times more expansive than the eastern allotments. The communal lifestyle that once dominated Cherokee society and held their customs intact is already fading. Families isolate themselves. Ideas of possession and ownership have infected them, along with an array of white men's illnesses.

Idle moments prove most challenging, and they are plentiful. Too many have forgone the efforts required to rebuild, to plow forward in aim of an admirable life. Once-able-bodied men have succumbed to lives of idleness, in destitute forfeiture of traditional values they once held dear, and yet never for a moment taking their eyes off the departed past. As a man of the cloth, it has for many years been my duty to prostrate myself in contemplation, hours upon hours in prayer. However, the pleasure and reassurance I used to experience through worship have been replaced by horrifying, sorrowful recollections. My bones retain the freezing temperatures of long days beside the Mississippi, waiting for the ice to clear so we might safely cross. My joints often ache with the memory of digging the frozen ground so that I might bury a member of the party. Hunger pangs sting my stomach still, even following a full meal, in remembrance of a week without a single solid morsel, as there was never enough to go around. The image of two adolescent twins being crushed to death simultaneously—she beneath a frightened horse and her brother under the wagon wheel as he leapt to save his sister—this vision will never be swept free from my immediate consciousness. I still hear the sounds of endless rain and wind, the continual coughing, vomiting, and moaning of a dozen different diseases.

Each day, new struggles abound, troubles particular to this dry, barren prairie. There is little consensus on how to govern these lands and minimal knowledge regarding how to farm them. Poor soil yields little sustenance. Coyotes terrorize our livestock. Families are drawn into solitude, ashamed to face their neighbors. Fathers and sons alike turn to whiskey for healing. Children are robbed of the traditions that define their heritage, as few adults possess the strength to recount that heart-rending story. A few of us attempt to educate the young, but more often than not, our efforts are squandered by their extreme hunger, lessons terminated by a summons for the children to work the fields or gather wood from a forest several miles distant. Even less time is granted them for those innocent enjoyments of youth—play and mischief.

My faith in God, admittedly never as fervent as it ought to have been, has staggered. Collapsed upon itself, it now lies buried along those trails, covered beneath the soiled earth along with the bodies of friends and family, of children yet virgin to the sins of this world, sacrifices to man's greed, his selfish contempt for fellow man. I have grappled with my work as a missionary out of compulsion and, as my mentor before me, an indolent acceptance of the simplest route through this life, fate's arbitrary dictations upon the soul. The act of forsaking my own name was born of weakness, a shipwreck victim's panicked thrashing about in the open sea, and yet it was that very act which has now delivered me to the threshold of my life's purpose. Many years ago, a hideous old crone rescued me from the brink of death, and while nursing me back to health, she admonished my feeble trust in God. Now, after all these long years, I finally understand the wicked tones of her laughter that day, and I am resolved to correct my mistakes.

Following our arrival, my wife and I wandered this land of broken souls for a full year, seeking out familiar faces and new friends alike, hearing their stories, comforting and mending their wounded spirits. I have shared their sorrows, listened to their personal accounts of this misfortune, lured out their deepest wishes and truest fears. There is no longer hope to be gleaned from Scripture, nor is there benefit in converting an injured and helpless people. Strength and resilience must first be coerced to return, followed by solidarity, collectiveness, and community. I shall lead them to rediscover those elements so integral to life.

Such elucidations came to me with the help of a man I have long wished to meet, the same man who prompted my previous journeys into the frontier. Many claimed he was dead, yet rumors lived on in each place I visited. My search proved fruitless for many years, but some months ago, I finally tracked down the Shawnee prophet known as Tenskwatawa, living a lonesome life at the furthest reaches of the territory. Many years of solitary contemplation have elapsed since the remarkable events that shaped his life. He is now elderly, frail, and peculiar. But his voice has not lost its urgency, and his wisdom has shed light upon a path I had given up to darkness.

Regardless of tribe or religion or political loyalties, all who have settled here share one trait—the eyes. One glimpse reveals the distant gaze of scarred and weary travelers lost on their way home. They have been vilified in their own fatherlands and imprisoned in this wide-ranging desolation. Futility directs their aimless stares. Loss haunts their every waking hour. Each night, the horrors of the trail resurrect in their nightmares and, likewise, in mine.

Not today. This day brings new light. Promises. Hope. A future not simply to behold but to share. A new journey. I have recruited more than fifty loyal friends from all corners of Indian Country. They represent a blend of tribal affiliations, rogue Spaniards from the nearby Mexican territories, and disillusioned American frontiersmen. Early this morning, we broke ground alongside a small but pleasant creek as we laid the foundations of a dream I have long contemplated. Locating the Shawnee prophet has hardened my resolve. With his counsel and the bond of friendship, I have found the courage to implement my dream in truth. This is The Community of Man, a celebration of life that culminated today with an unexpected arrival, the greatest of gifts.

A new dream unfurls at our feet, gracing us with the joyous cries of birth and blessing this expansive prairie we shall henceforth call our own. Today, every member of The Community was present to offer their support and love as my wife brought our daughter, Josephine, into this world.

Part One

Harmless Games of Youth

Chapter 1

The Driver

Lying concealed amongst the riverside foliage, Johannes Metternich loses himself in the slow crawl of morning mist, the gentle shimmer of dew as daylight intensifies. But there is no smell of spring here, not spring as it smelled on the mountain. The odor of diesel and rust rises from the parking lot while sewage floats buoyant atop the river current. As the glow of dawn begins to spread over the water, the chill of morning really sets in, burrowing past his shredded outer layers right through to the bones, the dawn hour never failing to bring the coldest time of day.

Johannes and the trucker had hardly shared a word since he'd jumped in somewhere outside Columbia. But as they lurched into the lot, the downshifting of gears had startled him awake, along with the trucker's coughs and gruff, gravelly voice.

"Gotta fend your way from here, pal. This is the place."

"What..."

"Place you been whinnyin' about. You been dozin' in and out but mumblin' this whole time. All crap and hot air, far as I could tell. Kept on about the water, the fallin' water, some kinda stream or river ridge. Only thing I really made out, though, was this here."

"This...where?"

"Name of this place. No-Show No-Go. Some name. Yer lucky it's on my normal route, otherwise how in the hell'd I have known? There's yer river right there. Grand ol' Missouri. Bit of advice though, buddy. When we stop to pick up hard-worn thumbers like yerself, we do it for someone to talk to. Like to hear a story or two on the road. Ain't no mobile motel I'm haulin'. Go on, then. They got showers inside. Trust me, you need one. Go on. And have a good life..."

And so Johannes has been outside the truck stop diner for an hour or more, delaying the move indoors as long as he can hold out, far from the path of truckers coming and going, fighting the cold and staring out across the Grand ol' Missouri, the diner's neon sign humming somewhere behind him. He feels as though he's been here before, but other than the name, it's no different from the other diners he's found himself stranded at over the past week. According to road signs, he's made it as far as the outskirts of Kansas City. Not that it matters where he ends up each day. Over a week on the move now and all the towns are like other towns, the roads like other roads, truck stops and waysides like all the rest. In every one of them, he has felt like he's been there before, but he never remembers.

Avoiding eye contact with patrons and staff alike, he takes a stool at the end of the bar. The waitress approaches, making no attempt to disguise her disgust, coughing, snorting, waving her hands to disperse the smell. Two, three, four weeks since he last scrubbed the grime from his skin, untangled the knots from his hair. Longer still since he bothered to wash his tattered clothing in the pool at the bottom of the waterfall. When she finally asks for his order, she's covering her mouth and nose with her apron. He only shakes his head and asks for water. A few patrons take up the stools beside him before vacating to distant corners of the restaurant. As the sun rises and more customers arrive, he's left with a wide berth all to himself. At shift change, the red-eyed waitress whispers to her chipper replacements—a middle-aged platinum blonde with exquisite skin and a flamboyant twenty-something with tattoos up and down his arms.

The young waiter kickstarts the morning shift with obnoxious energy. His rowdy greetings and optimistic small talk slowly rouse the dreary-eyed diners. He stands at the opposite end of the bar for a long time, chatting with an older man who must be a regular. They laugh and clasp hands, grasping each other by the shoulders while indiscreetly staring and commenting in Johannes's direction. The waiter brings a pitcher and says something as he refills Johannes's glass with ice water, but Johannes doesn't understand the question. After a few seconds, the kid waves toward the far end of the bar to the old man, who stands and makes his way around. The waiter follows with the man's coffee and then hovers over them while the man settles in.

"Been waiting around here some time now." The man blows into his mug. "What would you like? Toast? Coffee?"

Johannes scratches his beard, glances at the man, and nods.

"Get him a mug, Graham," the man says. "On me, of course."

"Your wish, my command." The kid giggles as he turns away.

The man makes himself comfortable, groaning an old man's groan as he leans his elbows on the counter. His hunched, private presence is calming, and he treats Johannes unlike anyone else that Johannes has encountered on the road. The man is himself weathered by time and circumstance, unconcerned with Johannes's appearance, the stench, the maniac hair and beard. In fact, the man seems intrigued in a passive, detached sort of way. Like he's seen it all before, seen worse.

The clank of the mug and saucer sets Johannes on edge. He's more used to being kicked out of places by this point, not served.

"Regular or decaf?" The waiter's nose scrunches like a confused child's as his eyes shift between Johannes and the man.

"Regular's alright, I imagine," answers the man, turning toward Johannes. "Looks like he needs a good strong cup, doesn't he?"

The waiter fills the mug with a flourish. "Enjoy. Anything else, Dunny?"

"Not just now. I'll let you know."

"Pleasure's all mine, of course. Wish you'd come around more'n you do. It's been a trip having you around like this, what's it been, little over a week? And now this sudden, abrupt curtailing of our conversations. A sad day, unfortunate soul am I. Once a week ain't gonna be enough for our talks. You're one of a kind, Dunny. More help than you could possibly know."

"Like I said, kid, all jobs come to an end eventually. Gotta get used to it. And anyhow, spring's here, which means summer business is just around the bend. You can bet I'll be passing through more and more."

"Gotcha. Well then, you give my regards to that lovely family of yours. I do hope to meet 'em someday."

"Sure thing, kiddo."

A fly circles around Johannes's head. This small familiarity, a comfort. He already misses the chorus of insects in the forest. But the coffee smells other-worldly, the warm scent of a distant past knocking to be let in from the cold. He can't recall his last cup of coffee. He often blended tea with forest herbs, berries, and roots that he gathered. On a few occasions, he had ground up acorns from the oak tree to attempt a kind of coffee, and each time it turned out a waste of good acorns.

He places his hand above the mug to absorb its warmth, tilts his head, and inhales. The steam raises a hint of his last cup of coffee, but no memory materializes.

"Nice, isn't it?" The man slurps his own. "Try it."

Johannes lifts the mug. His hand trembles and coffee burns his thumb as it sloshes over the brim. He steadies the mug with his free hand and lowers his face instead.

"Yes..." says Johannes, carefully setting down the mug. "Good..." His whiskers glisten, and a dark droplet falls to the counter.

"Sometimes I'll be damn near falling asleep at the wheel, and the only thing that keeps me awake is the thought of this here java. Better than anything you get in the city."

Johannes takes another sip.

"Long ways to Chicago. Always thought this here made for the perfect rest stop. The No-Show No-Go. Prophetic, ain't it? Take a piss, freshen up, bit of talk. Out of the way, sure, but worth the loss of time. That where you're trying to get to? Chicago? Sure looks like you been away a long time. Any idea? How long?" The man watches Johannes, studying him as the waiter arrives with a plate of eggs, toast, and hash browns. "The food here ain't too bad, either. You hungry?"

Johannes's eyes are trained on the steam rising and dissipating. The warm scent hints at something, a past which he is uncertain whether to reach out and touch or turn his back on.

"You have some troubles, son. You can tell me. It helps to talk. How about a meal? What do you say?"

Johannes shuts his eyes, accepting the chance that a memory will arise—the enjoyment of a long-forgotten cup of coffee floating there in the darkness, details gradually fleshed out. A well-lit cafe with a book and chatter from all directions. Sitting with a special someone around a neat and quiet dining table, dim and intimate. But whenever he closes his eyes—to sleep, to meditate, at times to cry, yearning to remember, or shying away from the truth—he is met by the reality of his one and only memory.

The mountainside caves in upon itself, collapsing down the steep grade, calling out his name.

"It only took...a moment..."

"What's that now?"

"And then...it was gone..."

Johannes's hoarse voice has drawn the man closer. He nods along, but then, suddenly, he goes stiff, losing the easygoing carelessness he'd displayed, now drawn up with caution, the alertness of animals on the mountain once they catch whiff of an intruder.

"That moment is...still...still now...even here...here...where...where am I?"

"What was gone?"

"Everything, swept away, dust..."

"Dust, you say? I see. You know, it happens to the best of us. Only thing to do is to keep at it. Keep on truckin'. I hear that every day on the road, in places like this. But as I was saying...Chicago is, it's a bit of a hike. That where you're trying to go? Not heading back there myself, not anytime soon. But I could. You trying to get to...where exactly?"

"I don't...I don't know..."

"Got a direction, at least? Which direction you heading?"

"What?"

"Look, do you want a lift or not?"

"Huh? Yes, I need...would you?...west...I think..."

"Hey, your lucky day, then. In a bit of a hurry myself. Tired as all hell. I can take you as far as a little town at the other end of Kansas. Might be difficult to catch another ride from there. If you're planning to go further, that is. You must be trying to get to, what, California or someplace, I'd bet. Sunshine 'n beach bunnies? That's what you ought to be doing at your time in life. Of course, you don't exactly fit the description of a beach bum, do you? You're a mountain man, you are. More at home in the woods, ain't that right? Higher elevations. Off to chase them ski bunnies in the Rockies, perhaps? I don't blame you. Half the fun is in undressing them. You may have missed the season, though. Spring's already in full swing."

"Mountains?"

The man stares at Johannes a moment, looks him up and down. "It's obvious. You smell of the mountains. They have a unique aroma, the Smokies do. Dead leaves, rotting wood, wild animal shit. It's all over you. You reek of it, friend. Same as a man can spot a dog owner or an alcoholic with the ol' nostrils alone. Abraham took his boy Isaac up the side of a mountain. Guess which one you resemble, son. Better off with them beach bunnies, if you ask me."

"What is it...called..."

"It's called the prime of a man's life!"

"The town..."

"Ah," the man chuckles, "Creek's Ridge. The town is Creek's Ridge."

Johannes spills his coffee.

"How's that? You know it?" asks the man.

Johannes had fled the mountain knowing only to follow the sun, a ghostly recollection without certitude or reason. A town, somewhere, nothing but a blank for a name. And, too, a face, a friend without features and no name himself. Johannes had begun to wonder how long he'd have to wander, east-to-west, west-to-east, an endless trail, circling round and round the base of the mountain, never to find his way out and never again to summit the peak.

"Creek's Ridge? That's it..."

"No kidding?" The man eyes Johannes without emotion. "Find that hard to believe... It's barely a speck of dust on the map."

"What's his...name..."

The man leans in close. "Pardon me?"

"What?"

"You need to speak up, son. Mumbling is for the timid, the weak."

"No..." Johannes steadies the coffee mug, tries not to reveal the pounding of his heart. "I'm...looking for someone...I think..."

"This someone got a name? If he's there, I'll know him."

"I don't...I don't know. I don't remember..."

"How about you, son? Got a name?"

Johannes slurps his coffee, looks away, grabs a napkin, examines its folds and creases, wipes his tangled whiskers. "No...no mountains..."

"Flat as can be."

"Okay."

"Okay what?"

"I'll have eggs."

The old man's eyes squint and then brighten. "'Atta boy. Hey Graham, another order up over here. Straighten you out. Get you back into your own skin in no time. Been a hot minute, by the looks of it."

"Just...no mountains."

"No mountains, huh? Yeah, well, no worries there. But that's no kind of a name. So how about I just call you John for now? John Doe, alright? Leave it at that? There are those who prefer to remain nameless for a time. To disappear. But I tell you what, some things cling to you like your shadow. Best not stray too far, lest it betray your secrets. Anyhow, this town, Creek's Ridge, it's got nothing in the way of mountains. Bit of a history, that's about it. Nice place, though. Peaceful, basically."

Chapter 2

The Graceful Soldier

August 14, 1816
San Agustín, La Florida

EARLY THIS DAWN, THE SHORE OF NEW SPAIN APPEARED LIKE A shadow upon the dark horizon. As we crept closer, waves surged against the hull, and it was the land that seemed to swell and recede rather than the water—the patient inhalations of a long, slender reptile displaying no signs of aggression but quite clearly awaiting its meal.

I sit now on the edge of a mangrove swamp, beneath palm fronds and amongst coconut husks, sipping a most fragrant coffee served by a lovely Spanish widow while the trials of my first Atlantic passage are relegated to the hazy memory of history. Her two young children are, at this moment, chasing each other around the wooden building that serves as both their home and their livelihood. A dirt path leads back toward the port of San Agustín, and a little further on lies the Cathedral Basilica, which I took the opportunity to visit with Father Jimenez the moment we made land. Alongside the cafe is a wide, wooden pen. Its sturdy walls rise up to my shoulders. Housed within, three enormous and menacing lizards are sunning themselves as the final rays of sunlight trickle through the treetops. The widow tells me they are called alligators and that they live here in abundance.

Two months ago, at the port of Bilbao, I conned my way into the service of Captain Hernando Vasquez and onto the decks of his ship, El Soldado Agraciado. Since I could not provide papers of identification, he was reluctant to take me on, but a tale of my juvenile sister's flight to

New Spain with the man responsible for destroying my family's wealth and reputation in Madrid was all it took to shake his resolve. The look in his eyes informed me that similar misfortunes had led him into a life at sea, his inflated desire for vengeance reason enough to empathize with my cause. The story of a runaway sister, though true, was borrowed. I had heard it only a couple weeks prior while traveling with a group of bandits in the Pyreneesian foothills, and I concluded by increasing my age to twenty-three, the fiction of those five additional years a tumor, perhaps, chipping away at my destined lifespan upon this earth.

Captain Vasquez sails under direct orders from King Ferdinand, who currently struggles to maintain an influential presence in the New World. El Soldado Agraciado has carried a veritable army of priests and missionaries tasked with stiffening the King's control over the peninsula of La Florida, spreading Roman Catholicism and the Spanish tongue amongst the native peoples, gaining their trust, and guaranteeing them autonomy and Spain's ongoing friendship at a time when they receive nothing but hostility from the United States. A few of the priests will remain with the ship until we reach Cuba and then Mexico, with a view to reinforcing Spain's standing in the Gulf, after which we will continue south with a purely economic function to Buenos Aires and then back through Puerto Rico before returning to Spain.

For a boy who entered manhood scavenging for food on the streets of Madrid, the past eight weeks have been utterly detached from reality. For a boy who often slept beneath the arches at the Church of San Isidro el Real or beneath stars in the valleys of the Sierra de Ávila, who often fled into Guadalajaran beech forests to escape persecution from the law, who at times sought protection and friendship with Franciscan monks along the Douro, who at other times lived with rebel groups in León organizing resistance against the monarchy—for a land-bound Spaniard such as I, barely grown into manhood, these past two months at sea have elicited a blend of fantasy and nightmare. When I close my eyes, the ground still sways and buckles. Though the sea's voice is now reduced to the sound of the surf gently stretching up the beach, I can still hear her dangerous undertones, her moans and groans, her erotic warnings. And now, here I sit, not without admiration for the incredible and magical feats that have delivered me to foreign soil. I have been seduced by this land's wet and tangy scent. Ever since escaping the orphanage at the innocent age of twelve, I have enjoyed a type of freedom, but this is the first moment I have felt truly unshackled. This small port town survives on its own, all but cut off from Spain. Ships such as El Soldado Agraciado bring wine, brandy, fabrics, spices, news, and Bibles, but such things are not necessities. Thousands of churning miles lie between me and my rogue life, a life I never wanted but was forced to partake in. That unkind lance of fate does not reach me here. Symbolically, I feed that life to the alligators—

The reptiles fight playfully over the scraps of bread and the fatty strips of pork belly I tossed into their enclosure. Their mouths are caverns, their teeth the jagged granite that tears you open on the way down. I asked the proprietress why she keeps them—does she not fear for the safety of her children? She told me that the children have an innate respect for the creatures. She says it is safer to capture the beasts and keep them cooped up and that her children know what to do when they see one roaming wild.

"What's that?" I asked.

"They run," said she.

Smart kids.

Chapter 3

The Digger

"Metternich?" Grant Cagniss squints and lifts both hands, a blend of surprise and greeting in the gesture. Mostly surprise. "Christ almighty, you're rough and haggard. What happened?"

"It's you... Grant? You are, too...dirty..."

"Shit. Good to see you though." Grant has just appeared from behind the house. Johannes stopped out front when he heard screaming, then he saw someone hauling ass through the backyard. When the man spotted Johannes in the street, he hid and peeked around the corner. Now, he walks through the yard with a natural, fearless stride and a lingering exhaustion. "Been a while, hasn't it? How long?"

"A long time." Johannes remains in the street, anxiously gazing along the empty boulevard, unsure whether to stay or keep moving. "I don't remember when...the last time..."

"How could you forget?" Grant has a deep laugh. He approaches, scrutinizing Johannes's face. "The last time? We were at that titty bar in Topeka, remember? Right before you took off for the Smokies. We had a fight. A proper one, fists and all, bruised and bloody. Then you had a twelve-hour whiskey nap on that rusty park bench. You remember. I felt bad kicking you out of the hotel room like that, but that stripper, Jesus...she was perfect. Nothing any man can pass up. Besides, I gave you the rest of the Jim Beam and fifty bucks, too, I think. Every time I go through Topeka now, I look for her. She's gone, probably. The next afternoon, I found you on that bench with two snake bites and plenty of curious onlookers. Not venomous, apparently." He laughs again but with less certainty this time. "Nothing memorable. Hey, man... You look like shit."

Grant's words spill and pile upon one another, quick and confused, blending together, indecipherable. Johannes's eyes wander over Grant's face and body, completely covered in dirt, sticky and dark with sweat. Muddied streaks stretch down his temples, neck, and forearms. While Johannes doesn't recognize Grant in the proper sense, the strongest quality in Grant's features could be called familiarity. All that Johannes recollects is an imageless shape, a friendly essence. But Grant's broad shoulders, his prominent forehead and trim dark hair, the natural scowl beneath agitated eyes—they fit with unexpected ease into Johannes's preconceived mold. On the mountain, Knecht had filled this role of friendship, providing all that Johannes could not procure for himself. But Knecht, he remembers. He can still close his eyes and visualize every detail of Knecht's features, whereas Grant seems brand new, a freshly conceptualized mockup of a long budding idea. Somehow too real to be real, his physical body slipping precisely, almost too easily, into the mental apparition Johannes has been chasing, even though he hadn't been able to remember the name—Grant Cagniss—until hearing Grant's voice and seeing his face, watching as Grant stepped closer and became a living, breathing memory with no place in any past other than the current moments as one by one they tick by.

"You know," Grant erupts, "I thought about you not too long ago."

"What?"

"No, it was nothing. Just a wandering thought, six months or so."

"Six months?"

"Six months ago. Or so."

"You said...not long ago."

"Is that long? I didn't think so. Not in the grand scheme of it all. It may have been a year ago. And it might've been yesterday. Does it matter? You entered my thoughts. I figured that'd be enough. What? You never thought of me? Out there in that big bad wide world?" Grant rubs his hands together and slaps them on his pant legs, knocking loose a few crumbs of dirt. "No need to overthink a good thing, right?" He steps forward, holding out his hand. "Sorry, this should have come first."

Johannes glares uncertainly at the hand, then searches Grant's face again. Without expressly willing it, he lifts his own hand, and Grant grabs hold. His strong grip brings on a sharp pain that spreads from the center of Johannes's palm until his entire hand is throbbing.

"I would hug you..." says Grant, "I would, but Christ, you're filthy. You stink like death."

Johannes pulls his hand free, wincing as he looks away, up and down the main street, toward the house behind Grant and the expansive yard surrounding it, suddenly wondering where he is and what the hell he's doing here.

"Is this yours?"

"What?" Grant notices flakes of dried blood transferred onto his palm and fingers, and he watches Johannes cradling his wounded hand. Then, he looks up and turns around, following Johannes's eyes. "The house? Of course it is. It's always been mine. Since I moved here. What? You don't remember?"

"Always? No, I...vaguely, I don't know..."

Grant hesitates, laughs, and peers at Johannes. "What do you mean? You stayed here with me for, what was it? A couple of months, at least. Sleeping on the floor like the bum that you are. Looks like you've had a time of it out there. What the hell, man?"

"Out where?"

"Wherever the hell you've been. How should I know?"

"Actually, I was hoping you could...help me..."

"With what?"

"With...that... Just that."

"Oh, no. Nope. You've got the wrong man. I'm good for moral support and fighting. And finding things. I've recently taken up digging."

"Digging? For what?"

"The usual, I guess."

"Digging..." Johannes slowly opens and closes his right fist, still throbbing and cradled close to his chest. "That might be just what I need."

"Yeah, maybe. Not right now, though. We've got a major dilemma here, buddy. Goddamn strangest thing..."

"Back there? What were you running from?"

"What? I wasn't...where?"

"There...the back..." hazards Johannes, questioning his ability to recall even the past couple of minutes. He points at the house. "You ran out from the backyard just now, didn't you? Screaming?"

"I wasn't screaming." Grant steps forward, their faces only a few inches apart. "How long have you been here?"

Johannes thinks it over. "I've been walking for...a couple hours, I guess. Just walking." He turns and sweeps his arm to indicate the main street, allowing Grant to catch sight of the wound on his palm. "My internal clock is...not reliable. And I didn't know...I didn't remember any of this. But I heard a scream, so I walked toward the sound. Here. Then I saw you running in the backyard."

"It's my horse..." Grant says as he grabs hold of Johannes's wrist. He examines the wound but shows no trace of concern or worry, more like fascination. After a few seconds, he lets go, his eyes glassed over. "She's gone."

After emerging from the previous weeks of hell, Johannes should feel graced by luck at a moment like this. But the sensation he's now having is much the same as during the landslide. The urgency for immediate action stonewalls him, incapacitated by the very necessity that drives him forward, like falling from an incredible height when all he can do is count the seconds until impact. Johannes knows he would have tumbled over that waterfall if the landslide had dragged him into the river, and it surely would have had it not been for his sole friend on the mountain, Knecht. Or else, in the aftermath, if he'd possessed the courage to jump into the river himself, as he'd wanted to do at the time. With every ounce of his being, he had wished for that. And, had he been able to, he might have spared himself this disappointing repetition.

Grant exhales a loud moan.

"Where have the years gone, amigo? Look at us. We're nearing middle age." Grant grips Johannes by the shoulder and leads him down the street. Johannes resists a moment and stares back at the house before giving in.

"Where are we going?"

"You said you were having a walk. I could use one myself. Gotta catch up, don't we? Come on."

"But, wait—"

"Can you believe it?" continues Grant. "One day, we're running wild through the forests of the U.P., throwing rocks and sticks at each other. Building gigantic bonfires. Two city boys climbing trees, hunting squirrels, torturing bats, chasing chicks. Next thing you know, here we are— grown, broken, guilty. Where are those harmless games of youth, huh? Thirty-some-odd years in the can. How many left, I wonder..." Grant's eyes flit here and there, and he keeps turning to gaze back at the house.

"Thirty years..." muses Johannes. "Has it been that long?"

"Unbelievable, isn't it? Can't be certain of which point we became aware of each other's existence, of course. Surely, the infant years don't count for much. But proximity has got to be worth a few pennies at least."

Grant's pace seems to be increasing. Now and then, he glances over his shoulder, silently urging Johannes to keep up. Johannes is distracted by an odd sense of safety, a surety of step. Even after walking the town all afternoon in a haze of recognition and doubt, he's still sure of nothing other than the town's name and a general awareness of place. If not quite attachment, then comfort. Acceptance, perhaps.

Most of the buildings are situated along the wide main street with large swaths of land separating them. Side roads cross the street and lead to dead ends or secluded structures—specialty shops, farmhouses, barns—though a few paths continue into an empty distance. Others are mere dirt tracks that disappear into the grass or are cut off by the creek that weaves in from the northeast, running south along the entire length of the town. Yet another road leads to a quaint schoolhouse and playground, and across the street, a long squat warehouse, each bristling with midday activity. Homes old and new, small commercial complexes, and family businesses all dot the roadside. An impressive steeple rises to the south, but it is inordinately far from the rest of the town, and Johannes hadn't bothered to walk all that way. All the buildings are in a state of charming disrepair. The residents seem to represent every walk of life, and they had each remained perfectly at ease in the way they regarded Johannes's defeated, beggar's appearance. They greeted him with, at worst, curiosity and, at best, indifference. A boisterous group of old men sitting around a cooler outside the grocery store had waved without halting their conversation. A large woman in an apron had yoo-hooed him from afar and then hurried into her diner, The Borderlands, only to re-emerge and hand him a fat slice of warm carrot cake with a wordless smile. It was altogether a different world from the disgust and mistrust he'd received everywhere else between the mountain and here.

"Grant? How long...have I been gone? Out there?"

"What am I, your goddamn secretary?" Grant peers at Johannes and recoils slightly. "I guess it's been...about seven years, hasn't it? A little more, maybe. Why the hell are you asking me?"

"I don't..."

"You mean you don't know?"

"Seven...? And I was here? With you? Before I went to the mountain?"

"You haven't been in the mountains all this time, have you?"

Two small boys come bounding toward them from across the road. One trails behind, distracted by something he's holding out in front of him. The boy in the lead squeals with delight.

"Hi, Captain!"

"Hey there, kiddo."

The first boy skips past, feverishly happy with that same sense of childhood freedom Grant had spoken of. The boy's expression is distant, untouchable. Johannes watches, unable to relate, wondering when he last saw anyone boasting such carefree playfulness. And then he glances at Grant, wondering why they hadn't, after all this time, glowed so brightly upon encountering one another again. *Seven years...?*

Johannes and the second boy collide, each startled out of a daze. The boy falls onto his back. White knuckled, he clutches a turtle shell for all that life is worth. Grant and the first boy curl over in laughter while the alarmed boy on the ground stares alternately between Johannes and the shell. As the dust settles around them, Johannes is tossed back to an abstract past. Sacrifice. Heartache. Promises of steel and promises of wax. And then, movement. Legs emerge. A head pokes out cautiously from its dark cavern. The legs wriggle for a few seconds before the turtle is struck by glaring sunlight, and all at once, its limbs retreat into safety.

Grant's laughter trails off. "Help the kid up, you shit."

Johannes makes no move to help the poor child, who wobbles, ironically, on his back, unwilling to set the turtle down in trade for his life. Grant squats to lift the boy onto his feet.

"Thanks, Captain..." The boy averts his eyes. "My mom says hi."

The two boys run off together, giggling and never once looking back.

Grant watches them until they're far down the street, obscured in the dust they've kicked up. "Once upon a time," he says, then he turns and stares at Johannes. "I see you're still some son of a bitch."

"Why do they call you Captain?"

Grant nudges Johannes and they're on their way again. "It's nothing. New line of work. Don't worry about that yet. We've got other things to discuss."

"What? I've only just—"

"Is discuss is the wrong word? Reminisce? Reminiscing is better, yeah? Start by reminiscing, and then down to business. But business is pressing this year."

"We can't reminisce walking like this. Grant, slow down. Hey, Grant! Hold on a minute."

"What?" Grant barks, glancing back but still moving forward.

"Look, I'm exhausted. I was hoping to lie down and rest awhile before anything. Where are we going? I need to...straighten myself out. It's been hard...all of this..."

Grant hesitates and finally stops. He looks Johannes up and down again, then shakes his head. "No way. I'm not letting you near the house looking like that."

"You're almost as dirty as I am."

"Well...that's relative. But that's what I mean. I'm not allowed inside either."

"But it's your house."

"And neither of us should be caught dead wandering dreamland like this."

"Why not?"

"Neverland. Whatever the hell it's called."

"What?"

"Have you seen your clothes?"

"I know, but—"

"Eh...I suppose you're basically dressed as a Lost Boy. Beard's a dead giveaway, though."

"Grant?"

Grant stops, squinting as he stares at Johannes, but he keeps looking away, shifting his stance, looking up and down the street and then back to Johannes. "It looks as though something's been eating them. Slobber and mud and blood. A shower and a shave are in order. The beard looks good, by the way. It suits you. Maybe give it a trim and a wash, even it out. You need some bandages, too. You're scratched all to hell. And what in the hell happened to your hand? Jesus, that's infected, you know. What? You were mauled on the way in? Those Kansas City whores couldn't get enough of you, huh?"

"But they're my clothes. This is all I've got left. There's nothing else."

"Don't be such a prick. Those are rags."

A car horn blasts as an engine thunders up behind them. It's the same red pickup that Johannes hitched in on, slowing as it passes while the driver from the diner sticks his hand out the window, waving and shouting inaudibly. Johannes and Grant both raise their hands in greeting.

"He's going to give us all heart attacks one day," says Grant. "What kind of goddamn magician can sneak up on someone driving a machine like that?"

As the truck accelerates on its way, the goat stands in the truck bed and looks back at them over the tailgate. Johannes wonders whether he should have taken the goat when the driver offered it. The animal might have provided a cool balance to counter Grant's impatient mania.

"I take it you've seen him already?" Grant barges into Johannes's contemplation.

"Seen who?"

"Pa Sonny."

"Who?"

"That was Sonny," Grant huffs and points at the receding pickup.

"The driver of that truck. That look you gave him...recognition without recognition. You lunatic."

"The driver...no, yes I...I just met him. We didn't talk much."

"Huh." Grant's step slows. "What do you mean?"

"What?"

"You just met him?"

"This morning. I ended up at this diner, and he offered me a ride. Someplace outside Kansas City, I think. Seemed like an alright guy. But I sat in the back. With the animals. I don't think I ever got his name..."

"Diner?" Grant laughs under his breath and mutters silently to himself.

Small plumes of dust billow around their feet.

"You mean you didn't recognize him?" Grant asks. "I can understand why he wouldn't recognize you. You look like hell itself shit you out. But he doesn't look any different. A little older, I suppose. Packed on a few pounds, maybe. And he's sober..." Grant is expectant, amused as he watches Johannes. "You really don't know?"

"Know what?"

"Who that is?"

Johannes shakes his head. "Somebody I met here? Last time?"

"Fuck, man..." Grant stops again. He checks his watch, then turns away and stares down the road. He turns to Johannes, gives a curious smile, and splutters a hesitant laugh. "Get the fuck out of here..."

"How could I know him?"

"Fuck off. It's Sonny."

Sifting through the murky past will yield no memories. Same as the coffee, the names of town and alleged friend, the imprecise period he spent on the mountain, the reasons he was there in the first place. Johannes has a go at it anyhow and comes up empty. He reaches up to touch his face, holds out his arms to look at his filthy, blood-encrusted hands, and then cranks his neck downward to see his stained and shredded clothing, catching a whiff of his stench.

"Sonny...?"

"It's Pa Sonny," repeats Grant. "Our old pastor."

Long, deep valleys have formed on Grant's brow, creases around his eyes. Johannes remembers the driver, hunched over the diner bar and sipping his coffee, his curious side-glances and confidential tone, the seemingly careless airs he exhibited, as though landslides were petty annoyances and everything was sure to work out in the end.

"Our pastor? How could you expect me to remember him? That was...ages ago."

"Shit, what's wrong with you?" Grant studies Johannes, just now finally showing genuine interest. "You're a real wreck, huh? And him, too. What's wrong with him? Has everybody suddenly gone and lost their goddamn minds?"

"I've lost a lot more than that."

"That right? Well, now's not the time, but we'll figure it out. Come on." Grant pats Johannes on the shoulder as they resume walking. "Here, I'll give you a mental nudge. Pa Sonny quit the Church...about ten years ago, I guess. He was wasting away back home, the life of a barfly, remember? So when I moved to Creek's Ridge, I wrote to him, told him about the place, and asked if he wanted to come and check it out. Not so different from you, actually, except he already knew about the town, somehow. His mysterious past, apparently. And after he came to see me, he just stuck around. Now, he's lived here almost as long as I have. Just about nine years." Grant stumbles over a broken chunk of concrete. He picks it up and tosses it to the side of the street. "You used to drink with him. All coming back to you? I'm sure it is, but never mind that for now. We'll juice that old memory muscle up with a cattle prod. Right as rain in no time. We're here."

They cross the street toward a two-story brick office building. Grant reaches into the mailbox mounted beside the main entrance, pulls out a set of keys, and fumbles through them before realizing the door is unlocked. "That asshole," he grumbles and shoves Johannes inside. "At the end, on the right. I'll be right in."

The corridor is wide and crammed with stacks of tattered boxes on both sides. Cobwebs hang from the high ceiling. Old paint chips litter the floor, along with scraps of paper and various layers of dirt. Johannes glances back and realizes Grant has not followed him inside. A glass door at the far end of the hall provides a view of the barren field behind the building. The glass is tinted, and a wide awning shelters it from the outside, so it serves up a clear reflection as Johannes approaches. But before he can recognize his own image, Grant suddenly swings the door open and storms past into the office on the right.

"Oh—" Grant announces with a start. "You're here?"

Johannes squeezes in beside Grant to see a man reclined at one of several desks, his feet propped on top, head hung back over the chair, hands folded peacefully at his belt. A thick book rests on the man's chest, open and perilously close to slipping off. The man slowly lifts his head, his eyes barely opening, and glances from Grant to Johannes.

"Of course," the man slurs.

"When'd you get in?" asks Grant.

"Last night, I suppose. What time is it?"

"What did I tell you about the doors?"

"Never meant to doze off like this..."

"Didn't I tell you to leave them open when you're around?"

"Look here, you've been away from the big city a while now, but we don't do it like that. Rule número uno—Trust no one, amigo."

"Jesus, Amondale." Grant stomps to a row of lockers in the corner and rifles through them. "Nobody around here's going to come in to filch your unfinished manuscripts or fondle your marbles."

"Whoa-now, wouldn't mind if they did." Amondale grins at Johannes, his eyebrows bouncing playfully and a conspiratorial wink. "Some pretty young thing. Maybe what's-her-name from the grocery. Or how about that one you're always sneaking around with...the married one, husband's never in town, young but not so young?"

"Shut up. We need to air the musk out of this place if we plan to rent out the rest of these offices."

Amondale sits up and shifts a few papers around the desk. "I know you've got big plans for this building, Sergeant. God knows what they might be. But all that dust outside funnels right down that there hall and into this here office. Does a nasty number on my allergies. It's not pretty, I'll tell you that. You find me a working door for this little workspace, this so-called station of yours, and then we can talk business. Don't know why you don't get yourself a real one."

"I told you, I don't need one." Grant maneuvers around the room, digging through desk drawers and rearranging things as he goes. "Don't have the budget for it anyway. Besides, you're the one who said you'd move into one of your own."

"The publishing game is like a slow crawl through hell. And back. Just waiting to strike gold, pardner." The man nods at Johannes, "Looks like he is, too."

Grant snorts as he goes through one of the lockers again. He slams the door and pulls a few things from a third desk by the far wall. "John, this is Amondale," he says. "Amondale, John. Take care of him for five minutes, alright?"

"John?" says Johannes as Grant disappears into a bathroom. The sound of running water fills the silence.

"What the hell does he mean?" Amondale examines Johannes without masking his repulsion. "You need help tying your half-Windsor?"

"How did he know that?"

"Know what?"

"The driver...this morning at the diner...he called me that too... John...John Doe..."

"I don't know who you are or what you're talking about, but you sure as hell look like a John Doe to me." Amondale grunts and leans back in the chair, kicking his legs onto the desk again. "You know, we have that same argument every time I come here. He could just bring any door from his house and it would all be settled. It's not as though he uses them." He folds his hands over his belt and shuts his eyes. "The only other chair's all busted up. I'd say sit on the desk, but you've got a stink on you worse than the slums of Port-au-Prince. You wouldn't mind waiting out in the hall, eh? Here," he slides the book across the desk. "Take this. Right up your alley, by the looks of it."

The book is *Don Quixote*. Johannes takes it into the hall, noting the odd certainty that he has read it before, even though he recalls nothing about it. He flips through it, closes it again, feels its heaviness and a dangling curiosity. But he's distracted by the reality of his situation, which is finally resting its full weight upon him—he has reached his destination.

Beyond the glass doorway, a monotonous field stretches to a flat horizon and a distant tree line. No dip or rise in the land, absolutely level. No mountains here, no landslides forthcoming, no waterfalls over which to tumble and break. Nothing to run from and also nowhere to hide. And in the glass, he catches sight of his reflection again. He steps back a few paces to view himself, head to toe. It's been years since he's seen himself like this. Over the past week, he'd caught fragmented glimpses of himself on the road, in rear- and side-view mirrors, spectral visions reflected off shop windows or the cracked and grimy mirrors of wayside bathrooms, but he hasn't yet seen the sum-total like this, all pieced together.

Something is different here and now. He's no longer on the road, nor is he in the wilderness. He is no longer alone.

And Grant is right—he looks like shit.

When Grant bursts out of the bathroom, he's already shouting incomprehensibly at Amondale, who has dozed off again. He buttons up a clean shirt, water still dripping from his hair and arms, glistening on his face. He runs a comb through his hair and drags Johannes back into the office, handing him a towel with scissors and a razor balanced on top.

"Here. Take your time. You need it more than I did." He's searching through drawers and boxes again. "Hey, Amondale, do you know where the bandages and disinfectant are? Do we have any gauze? John's hand is..." He notices Johannes watching him from the doorway and yells, "What are you doing? Get in there. Hurry up."

Chapter 4

The Noisemaker

Lalawethika lay on his back in the center of the wigwam. The old man, Penagashea, was pacing around him and fingering a strand of dried beans that reached the ground. Sometimes he halted to chant sacred words in his deep, raspy voice, and then he would step over Lalawethika's body, brushing his toes across the protruding belly. The medicine man's circles gradually constricted until he was walking right up against his motionless subject, the beans hanging down and tickling Lalawethika's flesh. This portion of the purifying ritual continued for a long time, arousing the sensation of insects scaling the bulging mounds of his midsection. Outside, they could hear the clamor of the hunting party returning.

"Your brother," said the medicine man, positioning himself directly above Lalawethika's face. "We shall eat well tonight."

From his previous experiences being subject to this ritual, Lalawethika knew to neither close his eyes nor divert his gaze. Unblinking, he stared upward at the medicine man's flaccid penis and testicles dangling free behind his breechclout.

"Do not move," the medicine man growled. "Do not make a sound."

A sharp sting struck Lalawethika's upper abdomen. The next blow landed firmly across his groin. The beans rattled as the old man whipped them through the air, raining a long series of uninterrupted lashes upon Lalawethika's body. With each lash, the medicine man grunted a single word, words of the old language or of a foreign tongue. Though Lalawethika was supposed to be reflective in this moment, it was difficult to concentrate beyond the pain. Lalawethika watched the medicine man's testicles swaying back and forth as he spun the strand to gain momentum before unleashing them again. Just as the pain became unbearable and Lalawethika's jaw ached from clamping it shut to hold back his screams, he noticed the shaft of the old man's penis begin to acquire girth and stiffen.

Dusk was already falling over the village when the medicine man completed the ritual. They emerged from his wigwam to a cool northern breeze that soothed the welts upon Lalawethika's body. Penagashea commanded Lalawethika to fetch wood for the fire.

Penagashea sat close to the fire pit, perched on the stump passed down to him from his predecessor. Lalawethika stood nearby. No other Shawnees were permitted to sit around the medicine man's fire.

"It is not as you think," the old man lectured. "Your medicine is strong. But your mother, Methoataske, when she left, it was a poison to you. As a weak river freezes when the snows come, her abandonment froze your medicine. A child left out during the cold season becomes numb, cannot feel the touch of the Great Spirit. Such a child grows without nourishment into an empty husk. Lifeless, as a branch or stone we find on the forest floor. A tool, neither good nor bad. But how we use tools can have consequences. This tool you have been granted, it was no choice of yours. Unfortunate, yes. But it is yours to behold, to utilize however you see fit, should you choose to do so. This empty husk, day after day you fill it with the white man's firewater. There is intense warmth in that drink, yes, I know it. A tool for the white man, then? This, the road you choose to follow. But the white man's firewater cannot melt your medicine. Only the Great Spirit's fire can do that. Come, step closer. Feel the heat. Touch it..."

Lalawethika stepped forward and lifted his hands toward the flames. Penagashea had not once removed his eyes from the fire while he spoke, but now, shaking his head, he lifted his gaze to Lalawethika.

"Do you not desire access to your own medicine? Do you not seek communion with the Great Spirit?" Reflections of the flames played in his pupils. Then, the loose flesh of his cheeks and neck trembled as he erupted with rage. "*Coward! Touch it!*"

Lalawethika wailed as the flames licked his fingers. He tore his hands back and fell to his knees. The medicine man stood and grabbed Lalawethika by the hair, dragging him away from the fire pit. He raised his medicine staff and struck Lalawethika repeatedly, shouting his name as an insult—

"*Noisemaker! Noisemaker!* Your mother was also a noisemaker. She was a whore whose howls rode the night winds over the hills and through the forests to every corner of the Shawnee Nation. She left you to rot and ruin with the other bastards she left behind. That was how she honored your noble father. He died a warrior's death, defending our people, and then she opened her tent, crouching on all fours and souring the air with her foul odor, offending the Great Spirit of our people with her wicked cries. She abandoned you and your bastard brothers, leaving you to wander the village begging for food, begging for attention. The final insult on your father's grave. Look at you now. This is no man she left behind. This is a filthy dog."

Sunlight faded quickly from the world, but the heat of summer would last throughout the night. It was during these humid, sticky summer nights that he struggled most with the voice that had for so many years plagued his existence, the vice that poisoned his spirit. He walked alone through the forest, feeling sorry for himself and regretting that he had ever approached the medicine man for help. He came upon a stream and dipped his blistered fingers into the water.

Muffled sounds from the village drifted through the brush. The women would be hurrying to finish their work so they could join the men who had returned from the hunt. The elders would congregate around the huge communal fire, examining and commenting on the animals the hunters had brought home. The children would be drawn away from their idle games to clamber all over their fathers and brothers. And the hunters themselves would be laughing, relating stories of the hunt as they gutted and skinned their haul.

For as long as Lalawethika could remember, hatred had budded within him. Just as he had done since boyhood, he attempted to direct that hatred unto others. Now, he aimed it at the medicine man who was supposed to be curing him. But no different from his poor skill with a bow, he missed. Penagashea understood—Lalawethika had been neglected by the Shawnee people because his mother had abandoned him and his siblings. Only his elder brother, Tecumseh, had grown up with renown, known as the son of their father, the great warrior. His brother had excelled as a huntsman from an early age, had proved himself in battle, and stood poised to become a fit leader for the Shawnee Nation. Lalawethika, on the other hand, was still forced to wander the village seeking handouts so he could feed his wife and children. And yet, Tecumseh did not deserve Lalawethika's hatred either.

Within the tribe, even amongst his other siblings, Tecumseh was the only person who had always treated Lalawethika, if not with respect, then at least with kindness.

Lalawethika's earliest memory was of a sunny afternoon when he was four years old. He was playing in a field with his twin brother, Kumskaukau, when Tecumseh came running through the tall grass, calling out their names. The twins poked their heads up and then went about crawling on the ground, hiding under the misapprehension that their elder brother had come to play with them—a rare and exciting occurrence for the two young boys. But when Tecumseh tracked them down, he pinned them to the ground, scolding and embracing them with a ferocious affection he had never before bestowed upon them, and then they realized he was crying. For a long time, he wept and whispered of things they could not comprehend. Finally, he explained in simple language that their mother had left the village, that they would never see her again, and that they must be strong. They mustn't cry or howl as he had done. But Lalawethika shrieked and hollered for his mother, so Tecumseh had to beat him until he was quiet before they could head back to the village. This was the only memory Lalawethika had of his mother—after she had already gone.

A voice accompanied the darkness of night as it crept into the forest, a voice Lalawethika had been expecting, half in dread and half in anticipation. He clutched his head and moaned. His fingers rolled roughly over his right eye socket, the source of so much suffering. The scar was thick and fleshy, the lids pursed permanently shut with the look of lips clenched in pain, half the world constantly blanketed in darkness and mystery. He rocked on his haunches and his moans intensified. He clamped his mouth over his forearm to stifle the oncoming scream as he lost control of his boiling animus. It morphed and twisted and turned on him. He knew what the voice had to say, to where it would call him, and he shook his head in resistance. He bit hard enough for his teeth to break flesh, and as soon as his own blood wet his tongue, he was drowned in a memory of shame and fear.

Although he fell unconscious for only a matter of seconds, this was time enough for the voice to fill volumes. A persistent, uninflected voice that had long ago wormed its way into the very fabric of his being, that whispered to him throughout each day and bellowed from the shadows come nightfall, droning seductively when his hatred rendered him defenseless to fight. But its provocative summons also promised comfort, a temporary reprieve from the shame and ridicule he was victim to within his own tribe. It propounded the advantages of his loud, braggart ways, demanding he live up to his epithet. Lalawethika—

The Noisemaker. A proud voice, it often retold the story of his first taste of the white man's firewater, intoning that if he could convince the white men of his worth, then surely he could convince his own tribesmen. And after the voice distracted him from his self-loathing, it no longer mattered that he knew the voice to be a trickster, a manipulator, an expression of his own failure—it already had him shackled to that unquenchable thirst, set his saliva churning with desire, drawing a direct line from that first intoxicating sip so many years ago to the present moment.

A stronger man, like Tecumseh, might have silenced that voice without much trouble. But Lalawethika was nothing like his brother.

As he lifted his face off the dirt of the forest floor, every insistent word the voice had uttered remained with him, just as the dirt clung to his cheek and the feral taste of blood still wet his lips. He sensed he was not alone, so he rose to display his full size before whatever man or beast dared to stalk him. No rustling issued from the surrounding brush, no scurrying of paws or hisses of agitation, but the sensation became stronger until Lalawethika was certain. Someone or something prowled nearby, and it was different from the voice that had just taken him, that hounded him always. A more significant creature, agile and breathing the same air as he.

He stepped cautiously amongst the brambles lining the stream, thinking he would kill for a mouthful of firewater if this intruder should have any.

With hatred and greed blooming anew, Lalawethika peered into the shadows across the stream and leaped into the shallow water to startle the illusive other out of hiding.

"Show yourself!" Lalawethika tried to inflect his voice like his brother's, forceful and resounding. "Step out from the darkness, you cur!"

A breeze cut through the grove, animating the branches with sluggish, ghostly reflexes. Lalawethika stepped backward out of the water, slipping on the muddy bank but maintaining his balance.

"If you knew who you shared this wood with, you would not hide so gracefully. You would befriend the wind and flee from this place. I am the son of Puckeshinwa, fearless warrior and leader of the Kispokotha Shawnee. My ax has crushed the skulls of men of all colors and beasts of all sizes. A single whoop from my throat would summon two hundred bloodthirsty warriors upon you before you had withdrawn a single step. I carry and distribute the medicine of all my people. I decide the life and death of my tribesmen as well as those who tread in my path. My will is that of a felled tree. I am the thunder and the cougar's roar. Announce yourself, or be ruined."

The mysterious other approached as though from a great distance and from all directions at once. It bore down on Lalawethika, making itself known by commanding absolute silence. All sound disappeared from the forest, including the gallop of Lalawethika's heart, and he wondered whether he had gone deaf, or worse. A breath hit Lalawethika's neck and spread across his back, extending along his limbs and saturating his insides with fear. He spun around, choking for air and flailing his hands.

There was no one there. But he heard a chuckle of derision, and then—

You are nothing.

Though little more than a whisper, the effect rang like cannon fire, a thousand-strong volley. A sensation felt as much as heard, burrowing through every pore to the seat of his soul. The One who had spoken, faceless and formless, had in those few short words disproved all the lies Lalawethika had ever told while at the same time claiming them for itself. And then, the Other left just as quickly as it had come, not a trace remaining except the tingling of Lalawethika's flesh, proving unquestionably the reality of what he had just experienced. The other voice—the voice that demanded firewater each and every day—had receded. It became as meaningless as the indistinguishable clatter of geese hidden behind clouds high overhead.

The woods were now suffocated by darkness. Lalawethika reoriented himself by following the sounds of the village until he was close enough to see their great blazing fires through the branches. All thoughts of meat and firewater had been replaced with a singular compulsion to seek out Penagashea, a desperate urge to tell the medicine man what had just occurred.

Chapter 5

The Journalist

"I'm sick and tired of all this concrete and steel. God, I envy you. I'd love to live amongst real mountains, real valleys. Nature pristine. I tell you what, Johnny Boy, I've been working too damn hard."

"What steel?" says Johannes.

"Ahh, the mountains. That air, fresh and pure... What? New York, Chicago, Mexico City, Miami, Lisbon, Paris...big city life, you know."

"This isn't...you don't live here?"

Amondale seems not to have heard him. Johannes rests his chin in his good hand and gazes into the bar's dim corners. He had decided against using the razor and only trimmed his beard with the scissors. The bristles are uneven and itchy upon his palm, scrubbed raw to remove the layers of grime.

After Johannes had emerged from a long shower, Grant had already gone. He told Amondale to dump Johannes's soiled clothing in with the combustibles. Amondale prepared some of his own clothes as replacements and then helped Johannes clean his wounded hand with alcohol and wrap it in gauze, after which Amondale announced that he needed a drink. He led Johannes here to the local tavern, talking while they walked and explaining the deal that he and Grant had made for the clothes. Without fully understanding, Johannes pieced together only that Grant had bargained some sort of interview for an hour of Amondale's time helping with some questionable project, the same project that Johannes was apparently already involved with but knew nothing about.

"Uhh...well, it's only an office. But I sleep in there, you know."

Amondale pours the rest of the soda from the bottle into his glass and twirls it around. The fizzing orange drink releases a sickly sweet scent. He nods at Johannes's beer bottle. "Drink up. You want something else? On me today. But, no, I shouldn't say that. It's more than an office. More like a regional outpost, really. I haven't had a permanent residence in years. I mean, I have several abodes, in various locales. This is one, but my time is divided. I'm a wanderer by trade. Not that I wouldn't love it, of course."

"Love what?" As Johannes shifts his gaze, he catches unrecognizable glimpses of himself above Amondale's shoulder and every other which way he looks, reflections from the tall mirrors that line the walls of the bar.

"To settle up my bills with life. Cash in my responsibilities, a bit of peace and quiet. You know what I mean. But I'd get bored eventually. I'm a thrill seeker, vicariously. No danger if I can avoid it, heh heh." Amondale leans over the table and beckons Johannes to do the same. "So, how does this little dive fit your tastes?"

Johannes stares back at him. "I'm sorry?"

"This bar. This joint. This establishment whence we now sit. What else? It's changed since you last visited, I gather. Still called Jo's Last Stand back then, no? So how do you like its new face?" Amondale's mustache twitches and a sour glow bounces off his teeth.

"What's it called now?"

"What's that got to do with it? Either you like it or you don't."

"Fine." Johannes sighs. "It's fine. It's just been so long."

"So long, heh heh..." Amondale slaps the table and then looks hard at Johannes. "What do you mean, exactly? Since you were last here?"

"No, not here. Since...anywhere. Any place like this." He lifts the bottle of High Life, looks at it, takes a sip. "Since I've had a beer. Or spent time with people."

"Yes, well, you're certainly dressed for it. Looking sharp in those... they fit alright? Comfy enough? Looks stunning, if I may, not to sound... I meant the clothes, of course. Not you. But them Stacies on your booties—two hundred'n fifty bones, clear. Blessed are the Freddie Freeloaders, heh heh heh." Amondale finishes his orange soda and glances around the bar. "Theo, old man! Bring us another orange and cream, will you? And a glass of The Carnival for my friend here."

"What about you?" the barman yells back. "I ordered eight crates worth and you're never around to drink it."

Amondale ignores the barman and swipes the beer bottle from Johannes, sets it on the next table over. "The beer he stocks in here is literal dog's piss. I've ordered you a glass of the finest, quote, Scotch whisky. Unquote."

Johannes nods. He's ill at ease—the borrowed clothes, the bar's stuffy atmosphere, this forced conversation. But this man, Amondale, has a certain skittish charm that provides a welcome relief from Grant's unpredictable intensity.

"Sorry, but do you know Sonny?" hazards Johannes. "Pa Sonny?"

"Of course I do. I know everyone. I may not be here year-round, but I'm resident enough. I'd estimate Creek's Ridge claims fifty percent of my time. Forty, to be sure. Definitely the majority. It's just the place to get some honest work done. Why? You've already had a sit-down with him?"

"With who?"

"With the good pastor. Sonny."

"No. I mean, not exactly."

"Good thing. That old drunk will pull all the juicy bits out of you before I ever get the chance, the vulture. Pick the corpse clean. Grant guaranteed me an exclusive."

"I don't really know him, not very well. An exclusive?"

"Don't you start bullshitting me before we've even begun. Who do you think you're dealing with?"

"I'm not—begun what?"

"Look, I know all about your history with Grant. And with Sonny. Not only that, but I can tell you every shade of booze that colors his canvas. Hell, I can tell you his brands of choice over the years if you'd like. But we're not here to talk about Sonny, are we?"

"What are we here to talk about?"

The barman walks over with their drinks. "And when you do come around, you're drinking pop. You know I stock this for the kids, don't you?"

"I've got more youth left in me than you've ever had, old man. Ah, beautiful." Amondale is already pouring the soda into his glass, but he tilts his eyes at Johannes. "I hope that you are, in fact, a Scotch man."

"Like I said, been a long time."

"Fine, fine. It'll loosen you up a bit. You were tense as a brick wall back there in the office. And there you have it. Scotch is a perfect example."

"What?"

"What was I just saying? For Sonny. Painting a picture. Scotch was his go-to just before he went rogue from the Church. He had two labels under his coat then...let's see...Chivas was the norm. No money, you know, in preaching. But at times, he did claim a windfall, and then he'd spring for something like the Dalwhinnie. Not the absolute top of the shelf, but a man can only pilfer so much from the donation trays before someone takes notice, yeah? Some woman parishioner with money, too. She'd make him a gift of a bottle now and again. Have to buy our way into heaven somehow, heh heh. Got the best of him, though. He won't touch upon the topic, not with a whaling spear. But some years back, I met Grant's folks and they leaked these juicy bits without remorse. Actually, I sensed fondness in the way they told it. I doubt anyone ever held anything against the man. At least not his parishioners. He wasn't a sloppy drunk until he came here, you know. The entire congregation, that whole community, they must have known he was a drinker, but it never bothered anyone because Sonny was there when they needed him. He gave them the heart-and-soul that he preached was inside all of them. He could actually prove it existed by delivering it, on his word, sober or not. Until that infamous Easter Sunday when he walked out in the middle of the service. A wonderful story, that. Just up and stopped sermonizing right in the middle of the resurrection, then walked right on up the aisle and out of the building. The congregation waited in the pews. Some of them waited over an hour, until one of the acolytes returned and said he couldn't find Pastor Sonny anywhere. Sonny bummed around the country a bit after that. But people would find him home at times, or at the dives around the corner from your old church. They pressed him for explanations, but Sonny knows how to seal his lips. Around a bottle of booze, heh heh heh. Of course, by then he'd moved on to tequila, but we can get into the tequila escapades some other time." Amondale pauses, about to take a drink, though only staring into his glass. "But why should I tell you all this? If anything, you should be spilling beans for me, some juicy details that have so far eluded my discovery, being a once-upon-a-time member of that selfsame congregation." He sets down his glass. "Now, where were we? You've not yet answered my question."

"Yes?"

"Yes."

"About this bar?"

"What? No, that's immaterial. About the mountain."

"What about the mountain?"

"What was the name of the mountain?"

"What mountain?"

"This mountain where you've been living. You still lodged up there, or what? Taking a vacation into real life? Or moving out of the middle ages and into middle-age with the rest of us lot? Where is it exactly? Sierra Nevada? Grand Tetons? Appalachia is lovely, but it gets damned cold up north. Spent a lot of time there myself, as a boy. Love to get back someday. But alas, here I sit. Dawdling when I ought to be—"

"How do you know about that?"

"I have my channels."

Johannes glares across the table and then away into the mirrors.

"Grant, obviously. How else? All that fellow is good for are the facts."

"I don't want to talk about the mountain."

"Of course you don't." Amondale's face flushes. His mustache twitches erratically as he produces a baby-blue handkerchief to wipe his brow. "Would you rather we reversed this? You want to do my job for me? You want this story to bloom according to your blueprint, game plan, mapped-and-scripted God's will? Then here," he removes a small, worn notebook from his inner breast pocket and produces an inch-long pencil from somewhere, pushes them both toward Johannes. "Ask away, Jack."

Johannes examines the strange markings carved onto the notebook's cover. He rolls the pencil over in his fingers, uses it to pick at a frayed strand on the bandage wrapped around his right hand. "I never agreed to an interview."

"Grant's word is as good as yours. Better, I'd assume."

"What's that supposed to mean?"

"What do you think? I know how to do my job, alright. I didn't win the double-J-double-A-SCP Award five years ago for nothing. My methods are my methods because they work the way I need them to work. Would you rather I asked why you foolishly left the world and expected nature to adopt and care for the sick and the fallen? I'm not sure what happened to you out there. But I tell you what, buddy, your face speaks of the trip." Amondale heaves loudly and sits up straight. He lifts his glass as if to drink but sets it down again. "At least that natty beard shrouded you in mystery. Now that it's trimmed, your pain is as evident as the sun at daybreak. Pa Sonny is a successful cheat because he wears no emotions, keeps them in his bottle. Leave me to my methods, and I will treat you likewise."

Amondale trembles, his face gone cherry-red. He gulps down his soda and stares into the empty glass. Johannes recalls the howling of coyotes and passionate owl calls just before dawn.

"Where do you come from?" says Johannes.

"Actually, I've just returned from Death Valley. Following up on a story, you know. Bred and raised in Chicago, though, like yourself. But I've claimed New York as my own since my university days. When I blossomed."

"So, where are your homes?"

"Here, there, everywhere. East Coast mainly. The American West was never meant for habitation if you ask me. Not for people of my temperament, anyway. A region for explorations and vacations, that's what it is. Settle down there? No thank'ee. I've always thought we should have given that whole half of the country over to the Native Americans. Not exactly an even trade for swiping their homes out from under their feet, but it would've been a better outcome than the eventual state of things. Once they were herded into this here part of the country—which was called Indian Country in those days, for Christ's sake—and then after the Mexican-American War, we'd have done right to make the Natives a gift of everything west, from Indian Country straight through to the Pacific. Should have let them form their own nation, or nations, and then stayed the hell out of their business forever. Or let the free thinkers of the time, like the founder of this here town, Emil of the Woods, have a real crack at their social experiments."

"What?"

"You know, The Community of Man."

"I don't..."

"Well you should. A fascinating history, that. The blooming, the withering, Christ... Planning to write a factual narrative of it myself. Somebody's got to. One of several projects I'm currently tangled up in. Better to educate the oblivious public, like yourself, on the world we might have had, or just missed out on. However you like it. Allies are better than dead bodies, I say."

"Huh?"

"There's a joke about it, fitting for our occasion, here and now. A prophet, a priest, and a saint all walk into a bar."

"Why?"

"Salvation's in the bottle, obviously, heh heh. It has to do with the Native American raids. Nearly wiped Creek's Ridge off the map, out of the public consciousness, to be sure. Took place, oh, twenty-three years after the town was founded by the very same Natives who would turn around and ransack the place. Founded in conjunction with the Natives, that is. They were integral to the concept of the Community of Man at the start. A sort of all-inclusive frontier resort. How things change in just a few short years, huh? I'm sure you can attest to that..."

"Me? I haven't even had a chance to—"

"Some blame them three, the prophet, the priest, and the saint. Hell, some folks still blame them for the way things are now, the way things turned out. But, of course, the whole damn country was in a state of confusion at the time. The Civil War raging out east, all reason and order on the brink. They were just doing their damndest to survive."

"The brink?"

"Yeah, the brink. Of a precipice. An upheaval. What you will. I'm not claiming to have all the answers, who started it, who ended it, who's at fault, who suffered needlessly or righteously. The writing's on the walls. Only it's illegible, faded over time."

"I don't get it."

"What are you? Some kind of simpleton? What am I talking about? The Community of Man, the raids, the legacy."

"But what's the joke?"

"It's all a joke. That's what I'm saying. But some jokes are not to be taken lightly. Now where were we? Your home. No, my home. Home sweet home... Well, to be perfectly honest, I only have one home that's all mine and...homely. The rest are like my office here, convenient and reliable places to put a roof over my head. I only wish I could spend more time at my one true home. It's just not feasible for a working man."

"Me too."

"Cheers, compadre. You gonna drink that or what?"

"As far as I know," says Johannes, "the mountain has no name."

"Well..." Amondale perks up and leans forward to search Johannes's face. "Where was it?"

"Eastern Tennessee."

"The Great Smokies?"

Johannes nods. "Blue Ridge Range. But it wouldn't matter anyway."

"What? What wouldn't matter?"

"If you asked why I left normal life behind. I can't tell you."

"Why not?"

"Because I don't remember."

"No shit? That's the most interesting thing you've said yet..." Amondale leans back in the booth with a deep exhalation. For several moments, he remains silent, staring up at the ceiling. "Then, Sonny too? You really don't remember him?"

Johannes nods.

"What about Grant?"

Johannes looks away and the mirrors on the wall throw his gaze back at him.

Amondale's face returns to its natural pallor as the corners of his lips twist upwards, a conman who's just found his sucker. Suddenly, he sits up, gaping at the empty tables around them. He checks his watch and taps it before shrinking back into the wall.

"Son of a bitch, I'm late." Amondale digs out a few singles and throws them on the table. "We'll have to put the thought on hold... resume it later...at another juncture. Great start, though. Really. I have to catch the five-twenty-eight from Mitchell or else skin the cat. Damnit, give Grant a message for me, alright? Tell him...tell him to go to hell. Till next time, Johnnies."

Amondale reaches for his hat and grabs the notebook and pencil off the table. He yells something at the barman, who offers no response but only watches him run out the door.

Light momentarily floods the bar. Johannes's shadow stretches across the table and up the back of the bench opposite, filling the seat Amondale has vacated. If there's relief at Amondale's departure, there's also a dread of the unknown. Johannes, alone again. Just himself and his shadow—witness to everything he has done and experienced. Keeper of the mystery. But the door closes, and the bar's darkness creeps in to absorb the shadow and the secrets before an inquiry can truly begin.

The barman is lost in his thoughts, his arms crossed over his chest, an unsteady rise and fall. A grimace stretches between unshaven cheeks on which stubble conceals ancient acne scars. He seems to be at peace in this moment, if not persuaded into peace by some remembered pain. The recognition of distance from past hardships offers the greatest of blessings, a standstill on the edge of the flow of time, the ability to scour the mind clear of all activity for a short interval. This is the drinking-den version of Johannes's own daily meditation regimen underneath the oak tree. It's been weeks since he last meditated, and he needs it now. But the bar reeks with musky, human odors. His chair wobbles on unbalanced legs. The table is chipped and discolored. He runs his hand along the table's edge, fraying his bandage on the wood where the lacquer has been worn away by countless hours of elbows and hands rubbing against it, innumerable spilled drinks. The glass of Scotch perspires in the warmth of evening, as does his forehead, although his face and arms are chilled. An old jazz standard plays through the speakers. The male vocalist sings about loving someone forever, no matter what unforeseen circumstances might occur. A few feet from Johannes rests the recipient of the barman's unfocused stare—an upright piano tucked into a corner, blanketed in shadows. Johannes wants a closer look but refrains from disturbing the temporary calm. Except for the street-facing wall with its huge frosted windows, the mirrors surround Johannes. They stretch from the ceiling down to the burgundy stained trim, and below are long matted benches. Each mirror measures a foot wide, spaced at intervals of two inches around the entire bar. None of the mirrors are flush against the wall. They're tilted slightly at irregular angles, inverting the room upon itself, an effect which could be almost magical if they weren't so smeared and dusty. It's not clear whether the offset of the mirrors was intentional or not, whether there's supposed to be a pattern, but from certain points around the bar, they create a delusive, infinite regression to which the bar's poor lighting adds a trace of the ominous. The barman's reflection floats within the mirror-world, far beyond the piano, more like an apparition, a haunting presence impossible to either confirm or deny. Johannes struggles to pull his gaze away. This dazed apprehension has persisted since he fled the mountain. Details of the world have been unreal—fleeting, distorted, and copious. People, with their speech habits, their indecipherable gestures and expressions. The shapes and layouts that form cities and towns, as well as the colors, textures, smells, and sounds that lend them depth and immediacy. The construction of buildings and the rapidity of advertisements. The exchange of money and merchandise. The speed of vehicles on the roads and the option to go anywhere he chooses, so long as he befriends the right people. It has all converged to create a vivid turmoil too frenzied to decipher.

Johannes envies the barman's ability to capture tranquility in a place like this, something that had been so easy for him to do on the mountain, his sanctuary. Harmony always at hand.

Standing now, he scans the room and takes a few hesitant steps, following the trail of mirrors and expecting to be greeted by his true reflection, a more faithful reflection than he'd seen earlier in the glass door at the office. Instead, directly in front of him, he's met by a messy array of cracked glass, questionably held together. He searches the fissures, then looks deeper, trying to focus between the cracks, or beyond them.

Cracks ripped through the mountainside, too, just before the landslide came. His shack, torn apart and crushed, dragged into the rapids by violent thrusts of the land.

The music has stopped. Only the crackling of the record remains. Johannes grips the side of the nearest table, tense and quivering from the unwanted memory, sharp and focused but limited to that single fractured instant. He looks away from the broken mirror. A deep breath escapes him as an odd sensation descends, the sound of leaves rustling in the wind when all the leaves around are motionless. He lifts his glass and peers into the murky liquid, its scent stinging his nasal cavity. The revelatory scent of coffee from that very morning returns as an olfactory memory from a lifetime ago.

As Johannes walks over to the bar, the barman's concentration shifts away from the piano and onto Johannes, though he makes no friendly or servile gesture. He only follows Johannes with his eyes. Johannes takes a sip and sets his glass on the bar.

"You don't happen to serve coffee, do you?"

"Fresh out."

"Too bad. I had one this morning...craving one now. I'm worn out." Johannes risks another sip. "And this is some terrible drink."

The barman smiles. "The worst. It's Portuguese."

"Portuguese Scotch?"

"Well, Brazilian, to be precise. Distilled someplace outside São Paulo, but the owners are Portuguese, I believe. So, who knows, really. I've had to order crates of it for him. I've tried to tell him—"

"For who?"

"Oscar. He's the only one who drinks it." The barman laughs when he notices Johannes's blank stare. "Your companion there. Oscar Amondale, the famous journalist. Although his fame is debatable."

"I don't really..." Johannes takes a larger sip and then lifts himself onto a barstool. "I only met him a little while ago."

The barman has turned around to change the record. Crackling resumes from the speakers, followed by the slowly broiling string section of an orchestra.

"That's much better," says Johannes.

"The drink? Getting used to it already?"

"The music."

"Better than Trane and Johnny? Just a few years ago, I might have fought you tooth and nail for even suggesting it. Nowadays, though, I tend to agree with you. Anyway, I've told him a hundred times that Brazilians can't legally make Scotch whisky. Forget about distilling methods or international borders, it's not even the right goddamn hemisphere." He leans his elbows on the bar top across from Johannes. "Ignoring all standards and practices...and you would not believe the import taxes on something like this. But he insisted that I order it. Says he came across it while living with this Brazilian gal in New York. So, now I got six-dozen bottles in the cellar, and they're not going anywhere because that damned sissy quit drinking for the time being. Plus, he's hardly ever around. Can you believe that? So you go ahead and drink up, I guess. On the house. Ain't doing no good rotting down there. Rather just free up the space. Last time I listen to a journalist..."

"I haven't had a drink in...seven years. At least."

"Down off that wagon, huh?"

"Something like that."

"Everyone does, eventually."

Johannes sips again, choking as the drink scratches down his throat.

The barman chuckles and tops off Johannes's glass, then he takes a shot himself, directly from the bottle. Johannes finds something comforting in this. He reaches for the bottle to get a better look. *The Carnival Scotch Whisky.*

"Does anyone ever play that piano back there?"

"Once upon a time. Used to be a man around here, name of...what was it now? Reynaldo? Big Ray, I think they called him. Big-someone-or-other. Hasn't even been that long, only a year or two. Shit...the faulty memory of old age...anyhow, big black fella. He'd lug his old upright bass in here when he came around to drink bourbon. After a few shots, he would stand up with that bass and start walking up and down blues scales. One of them nights, that big bastard got so piss-assed drunk he fell into that mirror over there, the busted one, with his bass. Never saw him again. Heard he skipped town after that for some reason or another. On those nights, though, I'd sit down and we'd riff off each other damn near till the sun came up. The piano, well, I haven't touched it since. Haven't had it tuned, either. Must sound like hell." The barman gives an approving nod as he stares longingly at the instrument, his eyes flickering at memories drifting past. "I miss that. Used to have a local fellow, Grant, help run the bar those long nights."

"Grant?"

"You know him?"

"He's the reason I'm here. Old friends."

"That right?"

Johannes sips his drink. "When no one's around like this, don't you ever sit and play?"

"You wanna play? Have a go at it."

"No," Johannes turns to the instrument, "I don't...I just like to hear it. I think."

"Same here," says the barman. "I can only play for people. Playing music has never done anything for me on its own. It's for people to enjoy. I'm not people. I'm only one."

"I'd like to hear you sometime. Hearing these records, I don't know... It feels like music means something to me. Or did. But I've forgotten what it is."

"Not today. If there're no people, there's no emotion. That's not music. I'd need a room that's bubbling with activity. A pulse pumping the rhythm of life." He picks at the label on the bottle, peeling it back slowly, then pressing it down and repeating, a little further with each pull. Then he lifts the bottle and looks at it before tilting it to his mouth.

"I tell you what," says Johannes. "How about nights? Does it get busy?"

"Sometimes."

"I might be around for a while. One of these nights, I'll come in and tend your bar. Then you can play."

"What? You're looking for work? Can't pay you much. Tips and drinks, that's about it."

"That's enough. I'm looking for something. Music might help, somehow."

"Looking for what?"

"I'll let you know when I know."

The barman makes no reaction. He stares at Johannes with noncommittal eyes, a trace of sorrow. "What's your name, son?"

Johannes hesitates.

"Well?"

"Sorry. Johannes...Metternich..." These sounds, distant, disconnected, now reflected, bouncing from mirror to mirror.

"Johannes..." The barman gazes over Johannes's shoulder, his head bobbing. Then, surprised, he looks at Johannes. "You're Grant's friend?"

Johannes nods.

"You must be the fella who went off to live in the mountains. You're John."

Johannes manages what he hopes is a friendly smile, but it's laced with panic.

"Grant talks about you sometimes. Alright then, Johannes. You got yourself a deal. Under one condition. You promise to come in here on at least two occasions—once to tend my bar and once to tell me a story."

"No..."

"I like to hear people's stories. It's the reason I ditched my former trade and bought this place. Don't feel singled out. I require it of everybody. Anyone who asks a favor of me has to sit right there and pay up, in words. A story for a story. Or, in this case, a couple of songs for a story."

"What story?"

"Any story you like. I've heard a lot of god-awful ones and a few worth remembering. Trouble is that I only remember the god-awful ones. But I've got a suspicion that, somewhere inside you, you've got the best story I haven't heard yet."

"You don't want me to tell you about the mountain?"

"The mountain? I don't give a damn. Just a strong, simple story. Could be about a hunting party or a tea party or sci-fi rocket ships for all I care. Just a story, that's it. Anything you like."

"I'm not sure I know any…"

"Ridiculous," the barman laughs. "Any idea what my name is?"

"Theo? He called you Theo."

"Who? Oscar? Don't listen to him. He's a bastard when it comes to names. Doesn't give them much notice unless he's writing them down in an article or a book. And even then…nominal liberty, he calls it. He calls me Thelonious for kicks, after…no, never mind that. My name's Ernest. And my last name? Have a guess. Think famous Ernests."

Johannes only stares back, waiting, and finally shakes his head.

"Hemmings. My name is Ernest Hemmings." The barman raps his knuckles on the countertop, expecting a reaction. "Used to get two dunderheads a day, minimum, asking me if I'm the one who wrote the story about the old guy and the fish. Two per day! It doesn't seem like a lot, but that's sixty dolts a month asking me the same goddamn ludicrous question. More than once, it made me want to put the muzzle of a shotgun in my own mouth."

Johannes realizes he's supposed to understand something implicitly, but he can only manage a soft laughter in response to the barman's exasperation. He raises his glass, "Nice to meet you, Mr. Hemmings."

"Sure," replies the barman, lifting the bottle. "Do you follow me with this, Johannes?"

"I don't. Not at all."

"I never discovered myself until after I'd shed that connection to a famous name. Know how I did it? I stopped leaving home. Stopped going on the road. Had to stay put, some-one-place. Creek's Ridge won the figurative lotto. Quit playing music, quit meeting people. Stay in a place where everyone knows you and the wells run dry. The questions have already been answered, the jokes gone stale. I hardly ever leave my bar. It's give and take, though. Inspiration runs dry, too. Any creative impulse, really. You must know what I mean. And so what about you? Is it John or Johannes?"

"It's Johannes."

"Better fit, I'd say," nods Ernest.

"Do you enjoy it here? This life?"

"It's not ideal. I miss some things. But it is peaceful, practical, and lucrative enough. And I hated being confused for a genius more than anything. That's why I need people's stories. Because I never could write one. Not even if I wanted to. And believe me, I did. I do."

Ernest keeps his pain concealed behind these mirrored walls, torturing himself by always glaring into the ugly truth. In this, Johannes recognizes something of himself, the confused fear he faced when he ran down the mountainside, leaving his home, not by choice or overflowing with hope, but only with the guilt and shame that bloom from true fear. The landslide had destroyed not only his home and way of life but also the peace he had found within himself, his trust in the world around him.

Johannes chokes down his Scotch. As Ernest moves to refill him, he's interrupted by the startling metallic sound of things falling and crashing at the rear of the bar.

"Grant?" calls Ernest.

"Jesus Christ, Ern..." Grant shoots in from around the corner near the bathroom. "Why'd you pile all that stuff on top of the trash bin? Right in front of the door?"

"Too much trouble moving it down into the cellar. My back. And no one uses that door but you."

"Have you seen a..." Grant notices Johannes sitting at the bar and comes at him. "You. What the hell are you doing here? What's taking so long? It's been three hours. You were supposed to come directly to my place. What happened to Amondale? Where is he? Come on. We've got work to do. The sun's going, going, gone in a heartbeat. We have to crack this nut before dark."

"It hasn't been three hours, has it?" Johannes looks at Ernest, who only shrugs. "He told me you were meeting us here."

"Who?"

"Amondale."

"That's not what we agreed. Goddamnit, John. Let's go. Sorry, Ern, I gotta take him home. He gets all...wishy-washy when he's drunk. Not the day for that."

"No matter," says Ernest. "The hounds'll come wandering in soon enough. See you boys again. And don't think about it too hard, Johannes."

Grant shoves Johannes out through the main entrance, slamming the door behind him but not following him out. A few moments later, he comes round from the back of the building, whistles at Johannes, and starts off almost at a run. His hands, arms, and clothes are all covered in dirt again. Johannes follows but doesn't even try to keep up.

"Hey, Grant..."

"Don't think about what? What did he mean?"

"What's the hurry? What are we doing?"

"I've been out there alone. What did Amondale tell you? He promised to bring you straight back to the house. We were supposed to talk there, all three of us, and map out a strategy. That was part of the fucking deal. I had to go and see Pa Sonny about something, and then... But when you assholes didn't show up, I couldn't wait any longer. I started hearing fucking voices. So I went out to dig again. I couldn't help it. Only thing I could think of to shut them up. But it's not there. You were supposed to help. How in the fuck did you lose Amondale?"

"I didn't lose him. He left a while ago. Said he had to catch the five-twenty-something. From Mitchell."

"The what? A bus? There are no buses here. Asshole..."

"He mentioned something about a project, but he didn't tell me anything about it. And he said to tell you to go to hell."

"Your memory seems fine to me..." Grant keeps glaring back and pausing to wait for Johannes, but as soon as Johannes catches up, he takes off again.

Johannes's legs are sore, his body aches, his mind is fatigued. But the conversations with Amondale and Ernest have done him good. The calm that descends at the end of a long journey. Tranquility is equally prevalent on the surrounding streets, the entire town at the mercy of its own slow rhythm, its humble quietude and unvarying flatness. In the distance, the sharp rise of the steeple is brilliantly lit by the golden hues of a fading sun.

"Why does that church seem so far away?" says Johannes.

"St. Josephine's?" Grant finally slows to match Johannes's leisurely stroll. He watches the sun sinking in the west as he waits for Johannes to catch up. "Because it is. A bit of a trek. Nothing else over there. I don't know why it's separated. That's just where they built it. A lot of local lore behind the place. Something about a mad Indian, a mad missionary, and a mad saint."

"Do you know the joke?"

"Sure. Everyone knows it. But nobody gets it. It's just one of those things that people repeat without really knowing what they're saying."

"What is it?"

"They go into a bar and what do you think? They get liquored up and lose track of themselves. Apparently everyone went nuts in those days. But how would we know? We're all nuts ourselves. The borders, too, they're all out of whack. Nothing I can do about it. Beyond my reach of influence. Though they say the Saint was a real head-turner. Smokin' hot. Desired by anyone who laid eyes on her, sought after by every man within two hundred miles. That's how she became a saint, by standing her ground. Rejecting them all. So they say."

"Who says?"

"They. The legends. I don't know. You'll have to take a walk over there someday and have a look around. At times, it can be soothing. It's like stepping into the past. The priest is a solitary guy, but he's friendly. Good for a chat. Just don't ask Pa Sonny to go with you."

"Why not?"

"He despises the place."

They both admire the steeple against the sky's deepening shades, a long, beautiful transition from yellows and oranges to pinks and purples, transforming the face of the town as this comforting blanket is laid out.

Grant sighs, not a sigh of misery or frustration, but the gradual release of disquiet and agitation.

"So," Grant says through a tight grin, "did you ask Ernest about *The Old Man and the Sea?*"

"What?"

"Didn't he tell you his name?"

"Yeah, but I—"

"Of course he did. I thought you'd get a kick out of that. You always placed those books on such a high goddamn pedestal. Always." Grant laughs, shaking his head and lowering his gaze toward the ground. Suddenly, he stops and grabs Johannes's arm. "What? You forgot that, too? For shit. You were reading *For Whom the Bell Tolls* and *Green Hills of Africa* when the rest of us were reading fairy tales. The fucking Hardy Boys. And what was that one enormous book you used to tote around with you? Everywhere we went for two straight years? Some boring brick of a thing about the stars or mythology or something? Constellations, wasn't it? Anyway, I call him Mr. Hemingway all the time. Give it a try. He pretends to hate it, but I know he really eats it up. It's as close as he'll ever come to fame again. Just try it, you'll see. His face flushes red as raspberries, and he'll start pouring sweat. Fumbles the glasses. Spills liquor all over the bar. His breathing gets short and erratic, and he'll pick and tap at things. You know, nervous ticks. But he always holds his head a little higher and straighter, too."

Chapter 6

A Form of Prayer

August 15, 1816
San Agustín, La Florida

ALL MY LIFE HAS OCCURRED AMIDST CASTILE'S PLATEAUS AND mountains. My earth has never moved as the sea moves, seductive and foreboding. In all the stories I heard from rebels and merchants, in all the writings I read with the monks, nothing had prepared me for the sea's surreal swollen girth. What twists and turns of destiny brought me to Bilbao? One day, I am pursued by the King's army, the next day, I am pursued by bandits, and still the next day, I have become the bandit. An empty stomach contorts the fabric of even the strongest-willed of men. Other days, I walked with leisure, attentive only to dramatic landscapes, blissful in my solitude or the companionship of my fellow wanderers, until this blue behemoth suddenly appeared on the horizon to instruct me in the true meaning of both solitude and companionship. What I saw as I trounced into Bilbao was an impossible embellishment on the grand tales those folks had shared with me. Instinctually, that body of swirling, agitated water seemed unnatural. What's more, I had never harbored the desire to witness this frothing monstrosity. I never meant to feel its saltiness upon my skin, upon my tongue.

But mere thoughts and idle desires cannot measure up against true confrontation. The devil appears and offers the forbidden fruit, and though the voice of God admonishes against such foolishness, you take it, instinct always at war with curiosity, and you bite down. Thus was I bound. The moment I beheld the limits of my country and the vastness of the unknown, I was helpless to choose.

Several times each day, I vomited over the side of the ship, after which I would rinse my mouth and then resume my duties. After a week, these bouts of seasickness ceased. I maintained an orderly and clean below decks and distributed food to the priests and sailors. Daily contact with the priests made it natural for me to get to know them. There exists an unspoken division between men of the cloth and seafaring souls. At first, the priests welcomed me with bemusement, a sort of hesitant embrace not befitting clerics. Later, they conducted our conversations with an unconcealed condescension, defensive as if I were out to ensnare them. Apparently, it is not uncommon for sailors to approach them on these journeys in search of carnal release right there in the ship's hold. Or, more unsettling still, to attempt bargaining for the honor of young native girls. Some representatives of the Catholic Church do not shy from bartering in morals. I met their disdain with impartiality and a willingness to volley their unfounded suspicions with jabs of wit, eventually winning them over. They came to recognize my honest interest in the nature of their missionary work, the genuine awe I feel at the strange and noble lives they lead. Then, they began to speak candidly with me, recounting stories of their roaming lives and diverse homes, of their successes and failures in Africa and the Far East. Many of them were bound for the Americas for the first time. And a few of them never warmed up to me, though those types never seemed to warm up to anyone.

More slowly than with the priests, I learned to get on with the sailors as well. Indeed, the most grueling task aboard that ship was drilling through the thick skin of those—I regret to admit it—ignorant seafaring men. Most of them grew up in fishing villages. San Sebastián, Getaria, Mutriku, even as distant as Vigo and A Coruña in Galicia. They have spent their entire lives at sea and know the ship as an extension of their limbs, but sadly, they know little regarding men or the ways of the world. They display minimal awareness of the scope of their travels, the thousands of miles they've sailed, the unbelievable lands they've shored upon. As far as I could gather, they live daily with the sole desire of surviving each passage in order to lay anchor at so-and-so destination port, where they might have a few days to taste the wines they transport and the local spirits, as well as a sampling of the local women. Captain Vasquez prohibits the consumption of drink aboard his vessel—wisely, I believe. However, he would set a better example if he concealed his own consumption of wine and brandy more effectively. Better still if he held fast to his own restrictions. Several inventive men, driven by the

Captain's periodic lapses, have perfected undetectable methods for extracting wine from the wooden casks. I, too, on occasion, partook in this pilfering.

The sailors taught me to raise and drop sails, to load and fire cannons, and to interpret the waves. By then, I had gained their trust, and they considered me one of their own, treating me like a brother. During downtime, I continued to visit the priests. I borrowed books from them and listened as they spoke of their previous missionary appointments. For this, the sailors chided me endlessly, and they would assign me menial tasks to keep me separated from their *human cargo*—a sickening epithet they deliver with odd mirth. Perhaps it is naivety, maybe it is my nature, but I cannot find it in myself to adhere to such arbitrary distinctions.

It was during one of many long, wistful spells of confusion, rendered immobile as I gazed over the mighty ocean with equal parts hope and horror, that I finally recognized the difference between such men. Whenever I entered this state, the sailors would pat me gently on the back, forgoing their usual wisecracks and deck antics as they nodded solemnly with lowered eyes. I knew the sailors understood my volatile emotions because I often caught them similarly struck, glassy-eyed and incommunicative, hypnotized by the waves for hours at a time. But when I later questioned them about this common spectacle, they told me that they thought of nothing during these spells. Nothing at all. They said that the sea, in all her majesty and beauty, wiped clean their thoughts, worries, dreams, desires, and fears. A form of prayer, I pointed out, to which they readily acceded. But for me, this was not the case. For me, these were not welcome respites from consciousness but rather the knowledge of our human fragility bearing down upon me, squeezing with a pressure one might expect at the bottom of the sea, where, at those moments, I became convinced that I would meet my end. My instinctual desire to flee flared up, while at the same time I apprehended that there was no possible place to escape to.

But the priests understood the meaning of the terror in my eyes, and I then understood why they rarely appeared above decks.

All peculiarities aside, the sailors are, each and every one of them, good men. A warmhearted, strong-willed, peaceful lot who have found and embraced their rightful places on God's earth. Their respect was hard won, and for it, I am infinitely grateful. I am proud to have earned their trust, and I rest easy knowing that I can trust any of them with my life.

By turns, Captain Vasquez has come to trust me as well. From the start of our voyage, I believe he suspected I was a fugitive, never entirely convinced by my lies and often watching me with vigilant eyes. He would loom nearby while I conversed with the priests. When speaking with me in private, he would pose questions about my past, which I always answered in line with the story I had given him at the outset, but my responses were nevertheless met with misgivings. This continued until one calm, clear night during the final week of our voyage. I was privileged with the night watch—a quiet, uneventful, contemplative duty. For a long time, I admired the oily heavens, seeking out old friends, the constellations whom I had always confided in during cold nights on Castilian plateaus. I then lit a candle and studied a small volume borrowed from Father Alvarez. I heard footsteps as I read a few verses of Latin poetry aloud. The Captain tore the book from my grasp and scolded me about the flame, for we had entered the domain of pirates. I blew it out as the Captain examined the book and questioned me about the words I had been reciting. I told him the truth, that I had learned some Latin during my upbringing but that most of my knowledge had come from the Franciscans, who offered generously to wanderers like myself in trade for labor. They used to say that the betterment of the soul is an aid to the entire community. Sometimes I tended their land or animals, but I could generally be found in their libraries. The Captain handed the book back to me and, in a softer tone, requested that I save such noble activities for the daylight.

As we entered port yesterday, Captain Vasquez presented me with this journal as a token of promise between us. When our journey recommences, he means to relieve me from duties of strenuous and filthy labor. He is adamant that my unique skills and unorthodox education will be more beneficial to him in the ship's log. He wants me to learn bookkeeping for the final leg of the voyage, and he has offered to train me in the art of navigation, should I so desire.

———

August 16, 1816
San Agustín, La Florida

Captain Vasquez believes that men are not equal, that those of higher rank or esteem need not mingle with the crude classes. This is precisely the attitude that drove me to leave Madrid. There is no reason, as I told him when last we spoke, why I cannot undertake the bookkeeping and the ship's log, acquire the art of navigation, and learn to conduct business transactions at port, all while still maintaining my place amongst the ship's men and pulling my weight on our shared passage over dangerous waters. My sweat and blood are neither more nor less worthy than theirs. I did not battle to earn their high opinion in order to isolate myself at the soonest opportunity, to spit at their shoes and then demand they wipe clean the stains. The Captain, though, is as stubborn as the tide. If only he realized that this is a quality he has in common with each member of his crew.

Although I succeeded in my sailor's initiation, those long hours spent in contemplation of the sea have chipped away at my resolve to explore a world of such magnitude. As I prepare once more to embark upon the seas, doubt has become an unavoidable part of my daily routine. The ocean's size is staggering. Its scope, majestic. But with such majesty comes a power that men cannot harness. Nor should any man desire such power. The sea speaks an indecipherable language—the language of chaos. Our voyage occurred without incident, but there was never a moment aboard when I did not feel helpless, at the mercy of some great will that might become disgruntled on a whim. I was—no, we were, the entire ship was—but a tick of the sort I often found crawling over my skin in the woodlands of Guadalajara. Once discovered, I would pinch the bastards off, cursing them as I tossed them into the fire or crushed them into non-existence.

I can appreciate the fascination men like Captain Vasquez experience in tempting such a fate, though I do not feel it myself.

The Captain intends to rest through the week here in San Agustín before we depart for Havana. Father Jimenez has kindly invited me to join him inland, where I might pass the time and obtain a more faithful introduction to this expansive continent and its people. For the time being, I have had my fill of the sea. In opposition, this strange land calls out in a language I can understand. This is God's song, whereas the sea sings eternity's laments.

August 18, 1816
St. Johns River, La Florida

Before departing yesterday, I went off in search of Captain Vasquez. I meant to inform him of Father Jimenez's invitation to explore the Seminole village and ensure him of my intentions to return with ample time to prepare the ship. Instead, I found Friar Hector Ruiz Ruiz gorging alone on a feast the likes of which I have only seen in dreams. Friar Ruiz, like Father Jimenez, hails from Valencia. However, Friar Ruiz is a round, gluttonous, ornery cleric with hardly a kind word to share and little more than complaints and discomforts to grumble about. On the rare occasions that he spoke with the other priests, his remarks contained no benevolence. There is little Godliness about the man. It is no wonder that Spain fails to woo the distant peoples of the globe if the Ruiz Ruizes are among those representatives we send forth.

Ruiz's trunk sat unattended nearby. Petty theft for the purposes of survival has never affected me adversely. So it was without remorse that I helped myself to a sack of sunflower seeds and almonds, a small flask of brandy, his rosary, and his Holy Bible. Along with my few personal effects, I bundled it all into one of his spare habits, tying off the habit and slinging it over my shoulder. I could not find the Captain, but one of the deckhands suggested he might be found in the house of a certain local woman of ill repute and that he would most likely be occupied. The agreed-upon hour had arrived, so I decided against interrupting the Captain's amorous pastime and left to reconvene with Father Jimenez and his Seminole friends.

Father Jimenez is sixty-eight years old, but he moves with the grace of a much younger man. He is tall for a Spaniard, which caused him great difficulty aboard the ship when coming or going from below decks. It has been thirty-two years since he first set foot in the Americas, having taken a post the same year the Britons returned La Florida to our nation, and he has made his home with this same tribe of Seminoles for thirty of those years. This past voyage to Spain was his last. He knows he will not evade death much longer, so he wished to lay eyes on his country of birth one final time while he still had enough strength to appreciate its beauty.

The tribal lands are situated some distance inland along the St. Johns River. As we set off, the sun's rays rained upon us like so many nails. We were drenched in sweat before we even embarked from the town center. The Natives who led us through the fields and swamps wore nothing but decorative paint and simple leather garments to cover their genitals. They spoke and gestured excitedly along the way, recounting the events of the past few months for Father Jimenez in a blend of Spanish and their native tongue. It was an exercise in restraint to stop myself from stripping away my clothes. The stony valleys of the Sierra de Ávila brought similar, albeit drier, heat in the summers, and I often ran from stream to stream bare-assed, unashamed to flaunt my natural state. Here, however, I take my cues from Father Jimenez. In full dress, he betrays neither fatigue nor discomfort, accustomed as he is to this climate. We arrived after dark to find the entire tribe gathered in celebration of the Father's return. The Father was overcome with gratitude for having survived these two final Atlantic passages, for returning safely to his adopted home, and for once again embracing these Natives, his adoptive family.

Exhausted though I was, I remained awake through the night, in pleasant observation of these happy people and marveling at both their uninhibited kindness and their fearless use of my native tongue. When sleep finally took me, it was a sleep I have never known. A sleep in which the morrow is not a question but an exclamation. This morning, waking to the heat and exotic smells of this foreign land, my mind is at peace for the first time in as long as I can recall.

Chapter 7

Flight

"But why don't we use the door?" Johannes lifts himself over the windowsill and stumbles onto the living room floor.

"This is faster. Trust me." Grant hoists himself inside and gestures toward the front door, lined top to bottom with locks of all varieties. "The guy who owned this place before me, he was some kind of paranoid nut. Apparently had several reasons to be. Still, he may have gone overboard. Most of the keys are missing, or else they have combinations that were never written down anywhere. Couldn't use the door even if I wanted to. And I just never bothered, you know..."

"What?"

"To remove them."

"But why wouldn't you?"

"A lot of hassle for nothing. Bad luck, brother. Remember? Avoid front doors at all costs. And black cats, cracked mirrors, ladders, blondes who used to be brunettes. Come on, you used to hate my guts for that kind of thing when we were kids."

"I don't...what about the backdoor? And, but, where's the window?"

"Took it out. Ease of access. And escape. More fun this way, don't you think? C'mon, I thought you'd be impressed. You know, like camping year-round. Keeps the air circulating and also acts as a sort of invitation to intruders. But no one fucks with me here. Back in Chicago I fought off burglars once a week, at least. In Miami, the same. But here...this is...it's a dull life."

Rectangular patches of fading light cover the wooden floor of the living room. Thick shadows shroud the furniture, carving the room into skewed blocks of light and dark. A heavy dust lingers, perpetually hanging in the final weak rays of sunlight.

"What about animals? Don't they get in, too?"

Grant grunts as he walks away. "I just let one in."

The kitchen has wood-paneled walls, a stained and sticky tile floor, a stack of dirty dishes near the sink, and a sour trace of food gone bad. Grant pulls out a chair and directs Johannes to sit at the table. He peers into an empty glass beside the sink, fills it from the tap, and hands it to Johannes. A window looks out over the backyard. Grant opens it and leans his elbows against the frame.

Sounds from Creek's Ridge drift through the house, the general affairs of life progressing at its sleepy pace. A car passes. A lawnmower chokes as it's shut off. The steady rhythm of a hammer striking its target. Kids congregate and then separate, seeping throughout the community. A door slams. A dog barks. Grant pushes a button on a small wall-mounted radio. The sound is tinny, so he adjusts knobs until the oldies become background noise, a strange, solitary blanket of sound that cancels out all those other discernible sounds of a moment ago.

The water is tepid. Johannes slouches, unsure of what to do or say. Grant remains hunched over with his head and shoulders thrust out the window. He sighs as he pulls his body back inside, turns around, and looks at Johannes like he's forgotten someone is there.

Although the dining table is family-sized, there are only two chairs. Grant slides the other one around so they're both on the same side of the table and sits down facing Johannes.

"You showed up at the right time," Grant taps his fingers on the tabletop. "We might never have seen each other again. I've been thinking of moving along, too. Finding something else. You know? Getting out of this place. Pulling a runner." Grant glances over his shoulder, out the window again. "Pulling a Metternich, as we say."

Johannes leans over and tries to look past Grant to see what he keeps looking at outside. Nothing but an empty yard, a featureless flat prairie.

"As who says?"

"Everyone. Except my dad. You remember what he says, don't you? Going to the John." Grant lets out a short, loud laugh. He closes his eyes, tilts his head back, and rubs his face. "Eh...wasn't the first time. It's only...no one was sure this time, you know? Myself included. Whether you would come back or not, I mean. That was the second time in my life I was set to follow in your footsteps. And here you turn up. Out of nowhere. On the eve.

I've always envied your travels. Why couldn't you let me have mine?"

"Don't let me hold you back."

Grant shakes his head. "I can't leave Pa Sonny. He's got nobody else. He... I'm worried about him. He's different since he quit drinking. Secretive. Solitary. Like he's hiding something."

"He seemed friendly with me."

"Did he? Well, he's always been that. Kind, good with people. But I don't know what it is. It's something different. Something's off."

"Sure it's not you?"

Grant stares at Johannes with something like shock.

"I'm not sure why I'm here," says Johannes, "but I wouldn't have made it here if it weren't for him. This town, you... It was the only thought in my head, the one place I had to get to, and I didn't know how to find it. I didn't even really know what I was looking for until I got here. Even now, I'm not sure I know. And it's only luck that I made my way here at all."

"Luck..." Grant snorts. "So, you really did go to live in the mountains, huh?" He leans forward, elbows resting on his knees as he searches Johannes's face.

Johannes nods.

"And you've been there this whole time?"

Johannes nods again. "Yeah."

"Jesus..." Grant's eyes wander toward the living room and what little light still finds its way in from the west. He leans back again, slouching like Johannes but cradling the back of his head with his hands. "I always imagined you were off doing something more...interesting. Still moving around. Or that you'd met some broad? Shacked up with her? Nothing like that?"

"What?"

"Then, so...what's your plan?"

"Plan? There is no plan. Never was."

"Yeah, I suppose..." Grant smirks, his eyes lose focus, then he shrugs it off. "Anyway, it's good that you're here. Something to keep me grounded. I don't need to be running off to any goddamned who-knows-where right now. That's the last thing I... Just got to put it all behind us, I guess."

"What's behind us?"

"You've changed, too, you know that? I'm not sure I can say how. Not yet. I don't suppose you've talked to anyone, huh? Nobody knows you're here?"

Johannes shakes his head. "Who?"

"I don't know. Your sis, your mom, your cousins. Professors. New friends, old friends. David or Lenny or Joe. Inez?" Grant changes positions so it's easier for him to keep one eye probing out the window behind him. "Figured you must have kept in contact with someone."

Johannes remains silent, shaking his head when Grant turns toward him again. Then, "I've been...alone."

"Yeah, well, I should've guessed. At least Sonny knows you're here. Pa Sonny... He did recognize you, you know that? He told me so, when I stopped over by his place. Good thing, too."

"Why?"

"Because it means he still has a sense of humor. Clearly threw you a curveball. Kind of a mean trick, but a good one. Too good. You really never caught on? Didn't recognize him at all?"

"No, I..."

"He did seem a little unsettled by the encounter. Thought you'd maybe turned the gag around on him or something. Rubbing his face in his own shit. But anyway, don't worry, he won't tell anybody. He doesn't talk to anyone anymore, either. Cut ties from everyone and everything. Been two and a half years now since he gave up the booze. I don't think he's counting, but I am."

"He offered me the goat."

"Huh..." Grant considers this, inching forward like he's about to stand up. "What goat?"

"The goat in his truck. It was in the back. Staring at us."

"Didn't notice."

They sit without speaking for a while. When Johannes looks away, Grant examines him, noting the changes in his friend's appearance since they last met. Thinner, to be sure, but somehow healthier. And when Grant looks away, Johannes does the same thing. But Johannes is still trying to dredge up a more fleshed-out memory with which to compare the man he has found. Occasionally, their gazes cross paths.

"You mentioned a horse earlier?" says Johannes.

"The horse..." Grant sighs. His eyes wander, avoiding Johannes. "That's what you and Amondale are supposed to be helping me with right now. Wasted days...Christ... Glad you're here for it, though. Your timing is dead on. Bullseye, as usual. But I have a feeling Amondale won't hold up his end. I only started this afternoon, before you popped up out of...hmm... But it wasn't supposed to take more than a couple of hours. Shouldn't be a difficult thing to do. Not some fucking riddle."

"What horse?"

"My horse."

"That's not all that's bothering you, is it?"

"No...maybe...I don't..." Grant looks away, straining to sort out the problem. "I don't know. It's this town. The charm is dying. These last few years, it's gone from peaceful to lifeless. No longer providing what I came here for. I'm bored. I took this new job expecting a surge of excitement, but there's none. And the people, they're...they're fine. Alright, in their way. But sometimes I wish Sonny would go back to drinking. Or preaching. Something. The way he is now...he's no help to me this way. Not like he used to be. I shouldn't have waited so long, John. I should have just followed your lead. Gone someplace. Maybe when you leave again, I'll...I mean, if you... How was your soul-searching journey, anyway? What were you doing out there? Christ, seven years, man..."

"Why do you keep calling me that?"

"What? Christ?"

"John."

"What do you mean?"

"Since I arrived, you've only called me John."

"Yeah?"

"So did he, the driver...Pa Sonny...at the diner this morning. He called me that, too. John."

"Did he?"

"John Doe."

"John Doe!" Grant's laughter fills the house. "He didn't tell me that. Well, what? It's your name, isn't it? John Metternich?" Grant stands up and leans forward, squinting and playfully scanning over Johannes in a mocking pantomime of curiosity. "Yup. That's you alright. John Metternich. Jesus...you really did a number on yourself. And Sonny really took you for a ride—John Doe, that's a good one. You'd better be careful, you know. The two of us together...could be a volatile combination. Two goddamned madmen. Most days, I can't even see straight. One eyeball's looking this way while the other's trying to look that way." Grant points in opposite directions with unsteady hands. His breath staggers as he looks hard at Johannes. "And now, on top of everything else, this fucking horse. Unbelievable..."

The orange glow from outside has disappeared, twilight fading to pale dusk. Now, it's Johannes averting his eyes, staring over Grant's shoulder and through the window, where the outlines of a few distant trees stand solitary against a gray sky.

"It's too dark to do any more digging tonight," announces Grant. "We'll have to start in the morning. First thing. At dawn." Grant's body melts into the chair, his anxiety almost visibly dissipating. His expression has returned to one of friendship, of concern. "Only two people I ever knew of who called you by your real name. You never... When did you... Seriously, what the hell happened to you out there?"

Johannes couldn't have been tortured into telling any more than he told to Amondale, Ernest, or any of the drivers who had driven him halfway across the country. But there's a latent intimacy in Grant's presence, something proper and deserving about the present moment, as though he owes Grant on some defunct wager.

"There was this oak tree," Johannes starts, unsure of what he's about to reveal or even what he's capable of remembering. "A white oak. Three-quarters of the way up the mountain, where it leveled out before a sheer rise to the peak. The trees thin out at that elevation. Mostly scrawny things, a lot of low-lying bushes. But there was this thicket of hearty trees, and this one oak had thrived. Two men to wrap their arms fully around that trunk. I built my shack there, in the shadow of the oak. Every night, I looked forward to morning, when I could gaze out over the surrounding mountaintops. And every day, I looked forward to nighttime, when I could study the stars. Appreciate them. Lose myself in the constellations. Converse with them. In a certain sense, there was no hiding up there. Maybe that's what I wanted, life at a perfect balance, everything out in the open. But I don't remember. I can't remember anything from before. It's like my whole life took place on that mountain. I worked the land. I gathered what I needed from the forest and bathed in the water from a natural spring on the other side of the peak or at the bottom of the waterfall. The stream wove its way down and around the peak, past the oak and my shack, and eventually over this huge rocky drop that more than once nearly took my life. I was at one with that place, with life there. I spent long days in meditation, searching deep within myself and every facet of the ecosystem. The meaning and significance of life was evident there, inescapable. I only wanted to decode it. To understand it. And it seemed simple enough. To walk in there and set myself up, not as a resident but as a functioning part of it. Equal to the oak tree. To the stream and the waterfall. The mountain lions and mice, spiders and bats. The sun, the moon, the stars, the rain, and the wind. To be at one, with all of them. To be at peace. That's all I wanted, I think. I had no intention of ever leaving. And at the end, I had no recollection of having arrived, never a thought about my former life. Never. Like I'd always been there, been a part of that. And the oak tree—I named it Knecht. I can't remember why, what the name meant, or where it came from. You asked about new friends? Knecht was my friend. And the stars. Boötes the herdsman, Orion the hunter. There was a pine tree, too. And others."

"Those aren't friends," says Grant. "You what? Spoke at them? Hung out together? Let loose and shot the shit?"

"On any clear night, I could lay and look up at the constellations, and my mind became as clear and light and free as if they were talking to me. Showing me the way. They could empty my mind and fill it at the same time. I meditated beneath Knecht. Its scent became...an addiction. It protected me, it comforted me, it fed me. Its acorns made up almost half of my diet. The shape of its canopy is seared into my mind. The angles and curves of its branches are, to me, the contours of a friend's face. These are the only memories I have. And I miss the reality of it. It was my paradise. Until a storm. I'd seen countless storms up there, and I made events of watching them. They're amazing at that altitude. Have you ever...?"

Grant is staring at the ground, shaking his head.

"This one started like any regular spring rain. But the rain kept on falling, hour after hour, faster, louder, heavier, wetter. It never stopped growing fiercer."

"Sounds like a good romp with—" Grant looks up and is startled by the weight of Johannes's expression.

"It was midday with the sky black as midnight on a new moon. The wind howled louder with each gust, and the gusts became physical attacks. By noon, the stream had swelled up the bank, right up to the walls of my shack, and it churned and splashed like furious rapids. It was the only time since I'd been there that I felt true danger. I knew a man and wife living at the base of one of the neighboring mountains, but now I can't even...I don't remember their names. They run a small roadside shop. They have a dog. Huge, terrifying."

"The dog? Terrifying?"

"And I knew of a few small caves nearby, but by that point, it was impossible to trek down or up or anywhere. Worried that my shack wouldn't withstand the winds, I remained outside, exposed, underneath the oak tree as I watched the world dissolve around me. I'd never seen lightning so abundant or heard thunder so deafening. Something inconceivable and absurd was happening, not just around me but to me. The world coming to its inevitable end, and me stuck right at the center of it. Have you ever...been hunted by a starved wild animal?"

"Can't say I have."

"That's what it felt like. And then it began. A huge chunk of the mountain above my shack—the whole southern ridge of the peak—cracked and shifted. It held still for a moment, or what seemed like a moment. It could have been longer. Impossible to tell. Time loses all boundaries. I heard the roar before I realized the peak was tumbling down, coming straight for me. I was inches from being crushed, swept away and buried. But Knecht was raised up on a steep mound, so as the land rushed at me, it was funneled away, redirected right into my shack, destroying it and dragging it into the river. The fear I felt for my life was so powerful and precise that I still feel it. It's still with me now. The landslide is still happening, at every moment."

"Jesus... Why didn't you tell me? First thing?"

"Because I didn't... Do you know what I remember most vividly? When it was finished, when everything I had in the world had been washed away and the torrent still hadn't abated, I felt that my path had been laid out. That the only choice was to throw myself into the river. Sick and tired of the rain and the wind and the cold, better to just submerge myself in it. The only way out. Sort of what I had set out to do from the beginning anyway, as far as I can figure it. And while I struggled to accept and act on this realization, a great horned owl approached. A huge bird. It circled above in wide, graceful arcs, arcs on their own plane of existence, totally independent and unaffected by the wind or the rain. Beautiful enough to make me forget about the storm. To forget those desperate thoughts and collect my disparate selves. I stepped out from beneath Knecht to watch this bird—the only thing that mattered anymore, its utter perfection. Before I made it two steps, a gust of wind struck me and I slipped. That's how I cut my hand. Caught myself on Knecht's exposed root, which saved me from falling into the raging stream. And I remember how the wind manipulated the fat raindrops as they fell. A mesmerizing chaos of motion, terrifying in its unnatural fury. But that owl just floated through it. Slow, steady, composed, defying every law of physics. At least the raindrops were controlled by something. The owl eventually perched on Knecht, on the long branch that reaches out over the stream. And it sat there, an extension of the tree that nothing could shake loose. Its head swiveled to examine the entire scene of destruction—carefully, calmly, almost appreciatively—while all I had left was my fear. Failure stings like guilt. And now, here I am. World-weary, defeated."

"Shit, man," Grant lets out a long, slow breath. "I mean... I could tell something had happened. Something big. But I didn't think it was anything like that. That is... I don't know what to say. You should have told me right away. What were you...? You're right about one thing, though. Failure hurts. I know. Sounds to me like that owl saved your life."

Johannes's lips form a tight smile, his first in a long time. He nods and sighs a tone of acceptance. But their faces are obscured by shadows.

None of the lights are on in the house, and the darkness of night is nearly complete.

"Then you don't remember what happened with us? Before you..." Grants starts but trails off.

"What I just told you, that's what I remember. That's it."

"So, through all of that..." Grant pauses to clear his throat, "...that circus, did you at least find what you went searching for?"

"Maybe. If I did, then it's gone now." Johannes exhales, the air crushed out beneath this excruciating epiphany. "When the mountain crumbled, everything I had and everything I had gained was lost. I think I almost found it, but I can't be sure. Honestly, all I remember is my long, peaceful existence in that place and my sudden, violent eviction. That's it. My entire life has been compacted into just that. If he...if Pa Sonny hadn't been at that diner, I don't know where I would have ended up. I never would have found my way here. I didn't know where I was going or why. Everything's gone. Shelter, possessions, memories. My bearings and my grasp on what's real and what's not. My cat. My understanding of self. Everything." Saying this aloud, Johannes senses a peculiar weightlessness.

"What was its name?"

"What?"

"Your cat..."

"I don't know. I don't remember that, either. Now, even my clothes are gone. And my name, it seems."

"No, no," Grant is shaking his head. "There's got to be more to it than that. Look, Pa Sonny knew you'd be there. At that diner. He'd been waiting for you almost a week. He told me."

"How? How could he have known?"

"He didn't say. But anyway, he doesn't buy it either, your memory loss. Misplaced is all, maybe a bit damaged, some kind of trauma, but nothing's gone. It's temporary, okay? You've changed, but you're still the same John Metternich. Either way, you shed a lot of baggage you were out to get rid of. Too much, in my opinion, but maybe that's what you were after. Not seeking...but relieving yourself. When a dog has to piss, it doesn't piss in its own bed. It gets its ass up and finds a tree. Men, too. We piss out in the bush, on the side of the road. But then we come back. So half your intentions came to light. Fifty percent success. What else can you ask for? Better than most people ever fare. Sometimes, when we're pissing, the spray hits us. A dribble here and there. No big deal."

For all of Grant's wild oscillations throughout the day, he speaks with sense. He levies a small amount of balance, which Johannes needs right now. Johannes doesn't know how he can help to keep Grant grounded, but perhaps the pairing of them together will create a shared density that roots them both into the ground.

"Look," Grant bursts, "I'm glad you're not dead, alright? And I'm glad you're here to help me dig through my current dilemma. This is just the sort of project I need right now. With you involved, it'll be just like the good old days. Our harmless games of youth. And then, after we find it and have made digging experts of ourselves, I don't see why we can't go back to that mountain of yours and unearth whatever got buried out there. The lost John Metternich. Actually, I'm relieved to hear that that's where you've been all this time. Seven-plus years in the mountains and nowhere else. Makes it easier for me...to picture it. And even though it's done, and you're back, it's like a weight fell off my shoulders, too, now that I know where you were. I always thought you'd gone...someplace else. But I believe you. And maybe you're right. Maybe it's better to forget. But I'll tell you one thing, if you expect me to start calling you Johannes now, after all this time, then you can pack your shit, which won't take long, and keep right on thumbing it. Your mom didn't even call you by that name unless she was pissed off. Nobody except those two—Pa Sonny and you-know-who—ever insisted on calling you by your birth name. If that's what you want, then go, but don't ever come back here if you do. I don't want anything to do with that name. Between this horse and you turning up, I've had a lot to think about today, alright? These stupid tricks that fate plays on us. God has to have his fun, I guess. But why is it always at our expense? Puzzle pieces kicked around in a fit of rage. And so what? As long as we're still alive and of sound mind, we can find our place in it all. Remembering the perfection of a past when the pieces were arranged as they're meant to be. Much too complicated for us to understand, let alone solve the damn puzzle, but if we can figure out a way to cheat the system, to skirt another encounter with God's clumsiness, then why not? Where's the harm in that? Sonny's right. He's always been right. Why do I need the Father, anyway?"

"Grant? What are you talking about?"

"Nothing. Forget it."

"It's so dark in here," says Johannes. "I can hardly see your face."

"All part of the immense beauty of life, isn't it, brother? One can never be sure if it's painted with sincerity or clownishness. No matter how bright it is, shadows always loom to conceal the truth."

Chapter 8

Blood, Again

LALAWETHIKA PAUSED AT THE TREE LINE TO OBSERVE HIS KINSMEN. A festive atmosphere pulsed at the village center. Children clung to their mothers or gathered near the elders to hear tales of the old days. The unmarried women had already begun packing excess meat into dried horse bladders for storage. Drums and flutes appeared around the fires, and the skilled musicians were giving lessons before they began to play for dancing that would continue well into the night. The communal fires were larger than usual, the air thick with the scent of venison. Lalawethika knew that when he showed his face to receive his share, he would be scoffed at, scolded, and questioned. *Where had he been while they gathered wood? How many nights had he spent in the wilderness, on the hunt? How many animals had he slain? How much corn had he ground? What, exactly, had he contributed?* If he was lucky, Tecumseh would intercede on his behalf, and if not, then he would defend himself until vile words sprayed in every direction. Soon after that, half the tribe would be against him. He would be driven to dangerous lengths to obtain a spot of firewater, and he would disappear from the village for two or three days, hiding out in a nearby cave or in a shed near the white man's town, where he could slip out under cover of night and break into a cask. Eventually, he would return with hunger pangs like lances splitting his side, boasting of a grand adventure with perilous scrapes. But none of his tribesmen would even have noticed that he had gone missing, and even his wife would greet him with a bothered sigh, a turned shoulder. It was this pathetic repetition that had induced Lalawethika to seek help from the medicine man.

He remained skulking in the shadows of the tree line until he spotted Penagashea moving across the grass with his head lowered, his string of beans swaying rhythmically when he stopped to examine antlers that had been sawed off an enormous buck. The medicine man commented on them, but the hunters ignored him. He continued toward the next fire and held out his hands for a few more strips of meat. The youngest hunters, fresh off their first hunt, stood and hailed insults unto Penagashea. They kicked dirt at his feet and danced crude versions of the medicine dances he had taught them as children.

Lalawethika leapt from the shadows and barked at the young hunters. They cried out and hopped back in fright. One of them reached for a spear and aimed it at Lalawethika with trembling hands.

"Your screams are still high and piercing," roared Lalawethika. "Like women's shrieks. These are yet but children, without the earthy voices of men, without experience of hardship, without the knowledge of time passing swiftly through their bodies." He stood over the boys, glaring down at them and projecting his voice outward for all the village to hear. "And we will allow them to disrespect their elders? Their holy men? This is a dishonor to our entire tribe, our history and our future. This is the behavior of vermin."

The boys squinted at the dramatic figure towering over them. One by one, they realized who chided them so—Lalawethika, The Noisemaker. They regained their composure and watched Lalawethika curiously until, with fading attention, they resumed their tasks, ignoring both Lalawethika and Penagashea.

One of the elder hunters had been watching the entire exchange. He stepped forward and ordered the youngsters to apologize to Penagashea and to give him his meat. They picked out a few small, fatty strips, but the hunter told them to give Penagashea what good meat was left. Only the poor strips remained. The hunters, both young and old, sniggered as they handed them to Lalawethika.

The hunter told the boys to continue cleaning off the bones. Then, he turned to Lalawethika.

"It is not your place to punish our young," he spoke low and turned his back so the young hunters would not hear. "Next time, come and inform me or one of the other warriors. Better still, seek out your brother. That one, there, he is the Chief's son. Should the Chief learn of this, he will—"

"I know who the rodent is. I know them all. It is not only my right but also my duty to uphold Shawnee honor and traditions. Am I not a member of this tribe?"

"Not if it were up to me." As the hunter walked away, he added,

"The next time you visit the white man's town for your firewater, do us a favor and stay there."

Lalawethika and Penagashea returned to the medicine man's wigwam at the edge of the village, far from the noise and bluster of the feast. Penagashea sat on his log and directed Lalawethika to sit on the ground beside him, close to the fire. Lalawethika protested that he mustn't, but the old man insisted.

"You spoke well back there," Penagashea said. "And you spoke truths. The Shawnee people have failed. Our traditions wither a slow death. The future of our people has been placed into the hands of the warriors, but the warriors no longer fight. They evade battle. They prefer to negotiate with the white man, to sell off our land in exchange for gifts meant to hasten our ruin."

Penagashea handed the rest of his meat to Lalawethika, who promptly resumed his protestations. Penagashea hushed him. They were silent, staring into the fire and listening to the distant murmur of songs, flutes whining, drums rising and falling, a heartbeat under duress.

Lalawethika chewed the meat and sipped from a small bowl of mashed corn. Food brought on the thirst. His mouth watered at the thought of it. He could already taste the firewater, its slick burn slipping down his throat. As though coming out of a trance, Penagashea finally pulled his eyes away from the fire. He watched patiently as Lalawethika shifted around in agitation.

"Have you had your firewater tonight?" Penagashea asked.

Lalawethika shook his head.

"You were gone for a long time."

"There was a voice."

"It is to be expected. I warned you of this. The Great Serpent will never release its hold once it knows how to harness you. Never. You are cursed to a lifetime in converse with that voice."

"I did hear that voice, yes. It lingers still, and always. But there was also another. A different voice. More than a voice, something...other. A presence."

As best he could, Lalawethika conveyed his experience in the woods. He spoke with reserve, surprising even himself with his lack of embellishment. The experience itself had been singular and unsettling enough. No exaggeration could enhance its confounding message.

Penagashea listened solemnly. After Lalawethika had finished, he returned his gaze to the fire and fingered his string of beans. In a hoarse whisper, Penagashea repeated the words.

"'You are nothing, you are nothing, you are nothing...' I have heard those words before," Penagashea muttered, his tone subdued. "Many years ago. When I presented myself to our previous medicine man, Three Stones, I approached him prepared. I spoke of my valor on the battlefield. I offered him samples of the many scalps I had taken from red men, white men, and the dark race alike. I spoke like a war chief, which I was bound to become. I boasted of my active loins, my ten children. I proved my allegiance to the Great Spirit with my knowledge of our origins, showing off my accomplished singing voice and familiarity with the medicine chants. Then, I expressed my desire to participate in the rich history of the Shawnee medicine men. I told him there was no Shawnee better equipped for this honorable post. I, Changing Feathers, would be the next medicine man if he would teach me the way. Three Stones heard my appeal without interruption. He observed my actions and gestures without nodding, wincing, stretching, or blinking. After much time had passed, his vitality returned. He looked me in the eyes as he spoke those same words. 'You are nothing.' No one had ever insulted me before. I walked from his wigwam with a weight on my shoulders that I knew not how to bear. This was a man I respected more than my own father, more than the wisest of our war chiefs, more than the warriors who had saved my life during battle. And he had shunned me with only three words. Me, a warrior who could have ended the elder's life with only three fingers. For several weeks, I did not speak to anyone. Not to my wife, not to my children. The chief requested my presence, and I ignored his summons. I ate little and disappeared into the forest for days at a time. Then, one day, Three Stones sought me out as I sat alone near the river. He sat beside me. We watched the river together for many hours. I had no words for him, so we sat in silence. Finally, he spoke again, three more words for me—'You learn quickly,' said he.

"Noisemaker, what I said earlier about your mother, none of that was true. Methoataske was no whore. She was one of the most respectable women this tribe has ever known. Beautiful, generous, intelligent, and at one time strong. But when your father left this world, she felt lost, unprotected. The white man terrified her, and she feared she would fail as a Shawnee without your father. So, she returned south to her Creek family. We Shawnee have become soft like fresh snow. Easily sullied. But the Creeks are vicious warriors. With them, she will have felt safe all these years. To bring you and your siblings with her would have been a mistake. Without doubt, she was welcomed into the bosom of her people, but you children, all of you, would have been treated as slaves.

"When Three Stones lay dying, he spoke of the death of the Shawnee people. Like your mother, Three Stones was fearful of the white man. He did not fear his own death. He was prepared for it and accepted it, but he mourned the death of our people. The Great Serpent, he said, had unleashed the white man upon us not as a punishment but as a test. And should we fail this test, then we deserve to perish. Already by that time, I wore the headdress of a medicine man, and he warned me that I would be granted one brief opportunity to save the Shawnee people. He said it would be unexpected and I must not waver in my responsibilities. So near to his death, after having said all that remained to be said, he requested to be bled, to purify his body and invite death to his bedside. With a bone blade, I cut along his neck and then turned the blade on my own hand, sealing my promise with blood."

Penagashea held out his left hand for Lalawethika to see. A long scar, smoothed with age, stretched diagonally across his palm.

"Our blood spilled together as one, and I sang laments beside his body for two days before we carried it out to the funeral pyre. Then commenced many years of disappointment as I witnessed the fire within our people slowly extinguish. Many years of delivering warnings, of pleading with them to protect that flame. But I have been tossed aside. You know it, you have witnessed it. I have never been highly regarded as a medicine man, though it was through no fault of my own. The medicine man was once revered with an esteem greater than the Chief's. For fifteen trying years, I shadowed my predecessor, learning the ways and working to gain his approval. And when he died, there was no one better suited to take his place. However, by that time the white man had encroached upon our lands. We received daily reports of skirmishes between other tribes and the powerful, greedy white man pushing west. The Shawnee people gradually shifted their concerns away from spiritual matters. They wished for practical, observable solutions to the immediate troubles arising each day. The loss of wild game. White traders carrying dangerous weapons across our borders in search of pelts or guides. An influx of mysterious and lethal diseases. Delegates to meet with officials from the new white government and strike treaties that balanced peace and separation, and the problem of the white languages. Thus, the Shawnee people came to believe they no longer required a medicine man. I have been forgotten and ridiculed by my own people. I am met with skepticism by those who once relied upon me and on Three Stones before me.

"Noisemaker, I am old. I have waited so long that, at some point, I lost track of what I was waiting for. And, like you, I have developed a fondness for the white man's firewater. Unlike you, I enjoy it in privacy. Though, I imagine that no man in the village cares enough about my habits or vices to raise a hand against me. I had given up on the Shawnee people, on the medicine, on waiting for a sign from the Great Spirit. Until you came to seek my counsel. The Noisemaker. The most reviled man in all our village. The whitest red man. Everyone knows not to touch your lies, for they are poison. You shame us with your penchant for the firewater. Your children look to your brother for advice. Your wife looks to your neighbors for food. The scorn you receive could fill a hollow mountain. But your voice—your voice was the sign I had been waiting for. The sign from the Great Spirit."

"Do you mean...the entity I met in the forest?"

"No," Penagashea was grinding dried berries between his fingers. He tossed the powder into the fire, momentarily producing multicolored flames. "That, I believe, was a message for me. It was your own human voice, back there with the hunters. Tell me, did you notice how everyone was watching you? All the women and children, the hunters and the elders, they all heard your voice and stood to see. To admire. They all know and scorn you, yet your words penetrated their hearts. When used correctly, Noisemaker, your voice manifests both the force and beauty of a sunset. It is not brash and abrasive like your brother's voice. The truth is undeniable when delivered in so passionate a way as you sometimes command. Bring me my medicine pack."

Lalawethika lifted himself and went into the wigwam. He returned with the leather pouch containing the medicine man's most sacred objects, handed it to Penagashea, and stood back. Penagashea beckoned him to come near.

"I acceded to your request for help and guidance because I was bored. I beat and abused you to appease my boredom. Imagine my surprise when I found that my methods had taken root. That you had, in fact, tilted away from the liquid fire. That you had occasionally held your tongue in public. Driven onward by this revelation, I continued. Why should I have ceased when this is the first good deed I have been able to offer our village in so many years? So, I increased my efforts. I sought to draw you out of hiding by tearing down your entire existence. And tonight, my project has succeeded."

Penagashea opened the medicine pack and pulled out a long bone blade, turning it over and over in his hands.

"When the sun slumps into the west, only then do we glimpse the mysteries of light copulating with our world, spawning the infinite sea of colors, the Four Winds engaged in their eternal creations. Only then are we convinced to rest from our labor and sleep with our thoughts through the darkness. And only then are we complicit in the knowledge that, one day, the sun will abandon us."

The medicine man suddenly grabbed Lalawethika's wrist and pulled him closer.

"The voice you heard in the woods this night, it was Three Stones in commune with the Great Spirit. The time for the Shawnee people has begun. This is the final test. And your voice is chosen to lead us. But first..."

Twisting Lalawethika's arm, exposing his palm.

"A promise. Our oath to the Great Spirit. An acknowledgment of our past. We two shall be bound to each other, bound to the future of our people..."

Raising the blade, entreating Lalawethika to offer himself, to witness and accept what must be.

"No...no..." whimpered Lalawethika, clenching his fist. "Not blood... not again..."

"You must face your fears if you are to shoulder the weight of the future. Open your hand. I will have your loyalty or your life. Do not tempt me. Do you not wish to be saved? Do you not wish to be a savior? Open your hand, you coward. And watch."

Lalawethika stifled his voice as the blade pierced his flesh. Penagashea held on tight until Lalawethika fell to his knees, the blood running down his arm. Then the medicine man turned the blade on himself, cutting into the ancient scar on his left palm, reviving the wound, giving himself fresh life and purpose. He dropped the blade and grabbed Lalawethika, lifting him up and forcing him to offer his hand, his blood, to enter into this sacred bond with all of himself present and aware, no chance now for backing out.

Penagashea rubbed their wounds together. Their combined blood fell and pooled below. Lalawethika moaned, not in pain but at the sight of the blood, at the memory it raised.

"Look at it," Penagashea released his subject. "It has begun. We have much to prepare."

Lalawethika looked and saw his life spilled in the dirt and grass at his feet, where it would be slowly swallowed by the earth.

Chapter 9

The Horse

SOMEONE SCREAMS. RUMBLES DISRUPT THE HAZY YELLOW GLOW OF morning. The landslide carves out its path in incessant pursuit. No matter where nor how far he runs, the mountain shakes and staggers, groans its grim portents and patient threats as he seeks out the cover of Knecht and the shelter of his shack. Home. But his shack, his possessions, the grass mat he wove for a bed, everything has already been swept away, replaced instead by neglected furniture—new television and stereo, both unplugged, rosewood coffee table covered with stains and oddly shaped discolorations, Persian rug rife with frays and crumbs, stacks of warped and curled magazines, mud-splattered boots and shoes worn through at the toes. The sofa is stiff and squeaky, like it's never been used, and made with several blended pigments of gray that produce an obnoxious golden shimmer from certain angles. A layer of dust covers it all. An arid heat flows freely through the windowless window frame, bringing with it the scent of dead grass and dog shit. The tumbling of the mountain continues, the roar of the water, the rapids still calling out to him, waiting for him to plunge in by the force of his own volition, history reaching out to correct itself.

"Fuck—"

A dish drops, shatters. The high-pitched crack cuts through these last vestiges of sleep, and he looks up to find the entire room balanced impossibly atop a mountain summit, the peak poking through floorboards as the weight on each side succumbs to gravity, the inevitable rupture, the fissures and the flaws. And he's not alone. Someone stares back from opposite a divide, pale terror plastered upon that face, followed by another scream.

The running water shuts off and the rumbling comes to a clunky halt.

Grant pokes his head around from the kitchen. "You're awake? You alright?"

"What..." Johannes sits up, but he's distracted by the other, not Grant but his own slanted image staring back at him from an enormous mirror leaning against the wall. "Where am I?"

"At home."

"But where?"

"The border, remember?" Grant's head slips back into the kitchen, but his voice continues. "Kansas and Oklahoma. Right in between. The signs say Creek's Ridge, Kansas, but I swear to Christ it always felt more like Oklahoma to me. Less than an hour from the Colorado border, too. All cut and dried straight lines. Except the church...landbound island...that place..."

Johannes looks himself over as consciousness gradually dispels any remaining doubt. All those objects he'd noticed through the dreary haze of dreams are actually there, scattered around the living room. The mirror is leaned against the wall, confusingly placed beside the arched opening into the kitchen. A full-body mirror, wide enough for two or three people side by side, bending and distorting and extending the shape of the room whenever Johannes's eyes pass over it. Grant is sweeping up broken shards, dumping them into the trash can. Then, he emerges into the living room, where Johannes is surprised to see a stiff brown uniform standing frighteningly erect in front of the crooked image in the mirror. The badge on Grant's breast glints from an unknown light source. Looming authority, tried and stolid, with swift, undaunted power hammered into his features.

"You've been screaming like that all night. Scared the hell out of me. Jesus Christ, I haven't broken a dish in years. Bad luck, brother...what? What is it?" As Grant examines a cut on his finger, he notices Johannes's wary glances into the mirror. "You remember this old thing, don't you? Been with me forever. Every time I moved halfway across the country, I swore I'd get rid of it, but I could never leave it behind. Too many memories. You must remember. You helped me mount it on the ceiling at my place on Jackson Street. Right after I met...Inez. Incredible that it hasn't broken yet, huh? All that time..."

"You're a policeman?" Johannes lifts himself up and nearly stands but for a sudden discomfort in his back. He crumples again into a lazy mass.

"I'm *the* policeman. The one-and-only. Sheriff, to be exact. I'm a'runnin this here town. Whole county, in fact." Grant turns and steps up to the mirror. He straightens out creases in his uniform, sweeps his hands through his hair. "But I don't start for three hours, which means we've got three hours to clear up this mess. So you need to get up. Now. Come on. I've got good, strong coffee brewed and waiting. I know you were never a morning person, but I assumed living by nature's clock would've straightened you out."

"My back is killing me." Johannes slinks down onto the floor and stretches out along the floorboards. "Can't you let me have just one decent night's sleep before pulling me into some insane project?"

"You dimwit. Why didn't you pull out the bed?"

"What bed?"

"The sofa bed," Grant explodes. "It folds out into a bed."

They stare at each other, deaf-mutes steeped in metaphysical soporific debate.

"Look, I told you last night that we'd start at dawn." Grant reaches down to lift Johannes up by the arm. "You can see for yourself that it's well past sunrise. Already behind schedule before we've even begun. Either we finish this thing, or I'll have to leave here tonight. For good. Once and for all. Forever. My dreams last night were not of the pleasant sort."

"Neither were mine."

Grant glares at Johannes through the mirror, but when he turns to face him, his expression softens. "I know. I heard."

In the kitchen, Grant pours coffee into a giant mug, hands it to Johannes, then grabs a plate of buttered toast and sausages and heads for the back door. The mug portrays a beach scene—the base coated with real sand, the blue sea curved inward in mock-perspective, and the handle an awkward palm tree with no convenient way to grasp it. A tiny silhouetted couple painted onto the side holds hands as they stare at a sunset reflected off the water. Johannes takes a seat as he examines the mug. He has a sip and moans with pleasure.

"Coffee to go," shouts Grant. "We have to start and finish this today, right now. I'm serious."

Grant's voice wavers, betraying emotions that Johannes cannot immediately recognize, a weakness that clashes with the figure standing before him. An indistinct memory of power-inflicted youth sallies through Johannes's mind, growing and taking shape in this huge neurotic man-child. Clad in the formidable uniform of authority, Grant has become his own oppressor, handing out and carrying out his own sentence, holding his own hand down death row alley as the executioner marches on behind.

Johannes reclines in the chair and lifts the mug to inhale the scent. "Smells nice..."

"Food's coming out with me," Grant growls. "And if you're not out there by the time I've finished eating, then you can get out. Find someplace else to stay tonight. And good riddan—"

The door slams. Johannes sips the coffee, and although he's not hungry, curiosity propels him up and out the door, aromatic beach scene in hand.

The sun shines piercingly from the east, consuming the sparse, sickly trees in the distance. Light encompasses their thin leafless branches, which seem to cower from the harsh rays blasting unintelligible, impossible demands upon them, demands that will renew every morning until their final sinking extinction. Coffee dribbles over the rim with each step and burns Johannes's hand, a jerk and a twitch and then spilling a little bit more. By the time he reaches Grant at the far end of the vast yard, the earth has swallowed half his coffee.

Grant stands next to a low dirt mound, chewing on a sausage and staring at the dirt. Johannes strolls through the dead grass as an odd, seductive freedom whispers the secrets of this first new day. A frontier of unknowns. Life after life.

Mornings upon the mountain hadn't been much different. He always woke early and spent hours walking, admiring the colors and shadows of the forest, the wet aroma of dew and mist, the sun's gentle arc and warm touch. What mysterious links bound him there for so long? Johannes, implanting himself as an immigrant, had latched onto sacred worship and blind faith unknowingly, like a lone Spaniard come to assimilate into Native American culture. But the medicine men had learned where he came from and what his kind were after, so the Great Spirits of those people became displeased and dislodged their loyal tenant with derisive fury. Assuming his life on the mountain had been a form of exile, then what is his current condition? Exiled from exile? At some point in such a regression, the laws and social structures that frame our world must collapse. The gears of existence must unchain and float apart, one act having no impact or link to any other, all adhesive washed away by the rains and swept downriver. Flushed down the john.

Grant hands the plate to Johannes, and Johannes sets both the mug and the plate at his feet, taking the last sausage in trade. He sniffs and bites into it as he joins Grant, who's staring into a shallow, oblong hole dug into the ground. Off to one end lies a shovel, a pickax, and a roughly hewn and twined wooden cross. A few steps past that lies the creek, flowing southward, and on just the other side of the creek grows a patch of tangled thorn bushes dressed with thick brownish leaves and fat buds ready to burst anew.

"It was here." Grant points at the empty depression. "Pa Sonny helped me bury the fucking thing."

Johannes steps closer, scrutinizes the rough-edged hole. "What thing?"

"The horse."

"There's supposed to be a horse in here?"

Grant lifts his gaze to scan the horizon, looking anywhere, everywhere, to avoid looking at Johannes. But eventually, inevitably, his eyes fall upon his friend.

"It was right here," his tone full of misfortune, though not without a trace of comic absurdity. These conflicting extremes lend a certain hilarity to this infantile, pseudo law enforcer.

"So what?" says Johannes, stepping into the pit and kicking the loose dirt around.

Grant is pacing with careful, measured steps, counting them out to himself, and repeatedly returning to the wooden cross near the head of the pit, where he starts again with minor adjustments in direction. Then, he picks up the cross and spins slowly around, surveying the entire yard. "We have to find it. That's what."

"But...why was there a horse buried in your yard?"

"I had to bury her." Grant throws the cross to the ground, then stomps on it as he lifts up the shovel. "She hated me, and I couldn't take care of her. She hated me because I couldn't take care of her. Just like Inez. I couldn't go through it again."

"Inez?" Something about that name, like so many other fleeting memories with nothing concrete to latch onto. "So you...killed a horse?"

"I buried her, my horse."

Johannes searches Grant's pained expression and continues sifting absent-mindedly through the dirt.

"But it was..." Johannes's foot strikes something solid. "Dead?"

"Well, yeah. I mean...I don't think so. I don't know. Maybe."

"You buried a live horse?" Johannes brushes away the dirt with the tip of his shoe. "Sounds like bad luck to me."

"She was unconscious, I think. I hit her...I hit her hard..." Grant is using his fingernail to scrape bits of dirt off the shovel. "It was a long time ago, I don't fucking know."

Johannes nudges the stationary object, loosening it little by little, but never enough. Even after he kicks out a massive chunk of dirt, the object still won't come loose. Johannes grabs the shovel from Grant, and Grant resumes his pacing, empty hands dancing with frustration.

"Did Pa Sonny know? That he was burying a live horse?"

"Of course not."

"Minister, drinker, deliveryman, and gravedigger," Johannes laughs. "No doubt he's an interesting guy. What else does he get up to?"

"He was drunk that night."

"I imagine you were, too."

"Yeah. But..." Grant's gaze takes in the full breadth of the yard, absorbing every square foot in a continuous panoramic sweep.

"But what?"

"What? No, nothing. I was, too. Drunk."

"You didn't dig down very deep," says Johannes.

"We didn't bury it very deep." Grant steps away, stomping on the ground at various points in the yard.

Johannes stops nitpicking at the dirt and places his weight onto the shovel, pushing it deep beside the object. "You've only gone down a foot, foot-and-a-half..." He twists and presses down on the handle before uplifting it with relative ease.

Johannes bends down to grab the unearthed object. He knocks away tiny clumps of dirt still clinging to it. Two feet long, undamaged, perfect. Impulse tells him to continue cleaning it, to keep it for himself, to take it back to his shack and display it on the wall as one of his prized discoveries. Or to fashion a tool from it, a knife or a handsaw. At this size, he could make a machete. But his shack is gone. And this bone, he knows, belongs to Grant.

He steps out of the bunker and holds it out, presenting this offering, but Grant is still wandering and peering around the yard, trying to work out the puzzles of his mind. Johannes steps forward, grasps one end, and swings a healthy blow to Grant's thigh. Grant's leg recoils. He stares at the bone without comprehension. Then he takes it, striving to understand, rubbing his leg, losing his balance, and stumbling backward all at the same time. But as soon as he apprehends the meaning of the thing in his hand, the strength returns to his leg.

"What...?" A series of emotions slowly manipulates Grant's features. "A bone? It's a leg...a femur...you...how did you...you found it...you?"

Reading and reacting to body language are lost skills for Johannes, so all he can glean from his friend's evolving reaction is wavering instability, cracks in a foundation. And then, without warning, Grant drops the bone—a toy that's outlived its ability for intrigue and distraction—and trades it for the shovel as he lunges into the hole.

"Grab that pickax." Grant is already digging in the spot where Johannes pulled up the bone.

As Grant tears into the earth, the teetering instability he's been exhibiting transforms into intoxicating strength, a passion in which everything but a sole pursuit ceases to hold sway over his life. A moment ago, he was a building disintegrating into rubble and dust; now, he is the earthquake bringing about that destruction. Johannes is drawn in, recruited not by Grant's commands but by the motion of Grant's limbs, convinced by the grunts of satisfaction that accompany each shovelful. And just as an infection silently takes hold of a body, Johannes doesn't even notice when he has lifted the pickax and situated himself beside Grant, swinging with equal fervor. Together, they are oblivious to all that was before and all that is to come. Johannes has forgotten the cause. There is no horse, no bone he unearthed. Nothing matters but the impact of the ax-head in the dirt, this kinetic release. Mind separates from body and becomes a storied entity from another life-line. They are left swinging at the spinning duty to survive, the oscillating obligation to traverse boundaries and escape their self-constructed fortifications.

Wordless, they work the earth, sweating beneath the Kansas-Oklahoma sky, prisoners vying for their escape before the warden rounds the corner. As they dig deeper, they each find solace in the other's voiceless companionship, and by the time the crushing truth becomes apparent, they have grown much closer than they were.

Three hours later and seven feet below ground, in a hollow wide enough for a pair of Comanche battle horses, these two deaf-mute convicts exchange a series of caustic glances, each one corroding any faint trace of hope they might retain.

Only when Grant throws down the shovel does Johannes even consider pausing in his work. A short rest brings relief, but aches soon surface throughout his body. Grant is pacing from one end of the hole to the other, taking giant strides and aggressive turns as he stares up at the sky and sucks down gulps of air. With a final exertion of strength, Johannes buries the point of the pickax in the wall. After struggling to lift himself out of the pit, he locates the one piece of evidence they've uncovered, the massive femur, and he sits with his legs dangling into a grave, of which Grant is the sole tenant.

"Goddamnit...doesn't make sense..." Grant whispers.

"What are we doing?" asks Johannes.

"Goddamnit...son of a bitch sucking asshole...fucking shit goddamnit impossible doesn't make sense how could it just...coming and going...to hell to shit to fuck, fuck...how can a...bastard fuck...disappear from the fucking...I know it, I know...even in death...running off again...here it was here it was fucking right here...pulling a..."

"Grant."

"What? You...you were...did you...?"

"Tell me what we're doing here. What is this all about?"

"I already told you."

"You didn't tell me anything."

"You know. You know what it's about. Limping Lady. My horse. We have to...we have to find her."

"Why?"

"It doesn't matter why."

"It does matter. Because we've been digging all morning and there's no horse here. Just this one bone. What do you plan to do? Dig up the entire yard? I still don't understand why you killed it."

"Why do you always need a fucking reason? Huh?" Grant's gaze bores into Johannes. His complexion darkens a shade. "You've spent your whole life questioning. Everything. No answer was ever good enough. You boast of your ability to explore the inner-self, to find the roots or the cause of your identity or some shit, an explanation for everything that happens. But you've never trusted anyone, and you drift, you drift away as soon as you begin to get close to someone, and then you return with more fucking questions and demanding fucking answers, reasons. And then where do you go to find them? Maybe your life in the woods could be broken down into simple questions and answers, but look at where it fucking got you. Nearly killed, for one. And here you are, back from the fucking dead and...and demanding more fucking answers. It doesn't work like that here. Not everything can be explained. There doesn't always have to be a reason to do what we do. There are only reasons not to. When will you learn that?"

Grant glares at Johannes and then drops into a motionless heap sheltered by the rapidly diminishing shade of the eastern wall.

Up above, Johannes looks out over the landscape. It seems more expansive now that the sun is high and offering its full potential. The thorn bushes on the other side of the creek rustle as a bulky shape moves silently amidst them. Its branches tremble—not from the wind, but organically, infused with life and fear, or possibly a fear of life. Johannes gapes on in wonder and recalls the meaningless words he and Grant had shared that led them into the oblivion of digging. The bushes shake erratically. A rabbit leaps out, quickly followed by a large graceful form bursting out from behind and giving chase. Johannes watches this race for survival with the sensation that he has admired or been a part of this event a thousand times past.

"It's huge..." says Johannes.

"What?"

"A wolf?"

"There are no wolves here. Not yet. Is it black or gray?"

"I...I don't..." Johannes squirms on the ledge, prepared to jump up and flee like the rabbit or jump into the hole with Grant.

"What's the matter with you?"

"Black, mostly..."

"Then it's the German shepherd, lives down the road. Coyotes around here, they're a sort of sandy gray."

The dog's strides are chillingly angelic as it bounds southward in pursuit of the rabbit. A cloud of dust grows in their wake, blotting them out of sight until they are nothing but shadows hinted at through the sunlit haze, ghosts straddling the curtain between life and death. Johannes can't take his eyes off them. He feels as though he's there with them, aware of the danger and yet blinded by the dust, wanting to leap in and rescue the rabbit from its approaching fate but too terrified of the dog himself. As the dust settles and the animals blend into the landscape, Johannes's mind drifts back to a single name. A name that, without recognition, he has heard Grant utter several times already, Grant's tone swelling in repetition, the hesitant inflection each time he says it, both guarded and scathing, deepening the impression it carves out. Johannes's memory offers no help, but there's a shadow climbing around in there, formless and fluid like the ghostly rabbit and dog through the dust. There's something revealing in the way Grant says the name, and likewise, something disconcerting about the way it bounces off Johannes like rain hitting a leaf. But, should providence hold true, the raindrop one day manages the long journey through the soil, the roots, back up the trunk, and finally navigating the branches to get where it needs to go.

"Grant? Who's Inez?"

Grant looks up but displays no shred of comprehension. Their eyes meet and they share a brief moment devoid of all significance and worth, an instant surgically lifted from the flow of time. First a shriek, then a harsh bark and a snarl cut through the silence. Johannes looks up to see the dog in the distance, no longer running but prancing in a circle, thrashing its prey against the ground until it stops struggling and moves on from this world. The dog drops it and surveys the landscape before taking the lifeless rabbit in its mouth again and trotting away.

"What's that?" Dark streaks of muddy sweat run down Grant's temples.

"The dog, it...killed a rabbit..."

"Not that...what you said. What did you say?"

"I said, who's Inez? You keep mentioning her..."

"What do you mean?" Grant wheezes. He coughs and spits on the mound of dirt beside him. "Don't do this. Not now. You know...you...you...did you...?"

"I told you," says Johannes, "I don't remember anything. Really. Only the mountain. And the landslide."

"And what about me?" Grant lets his head fall backward. It slams into the dirt wall, and he leaves it there as he stares over the lip of the grave. "Don't you fucking lie to me...no games...not this time..."

"What does she have to do with this horse?"

"Nothing."

A horrible, contagious sadness saturates Grant's voice, his childlike nakedness exposed. The innocence he spoke of the previous day has been manhandled, twisted out of shape by this acute, mature pain. And like the surge of energy that started Johannes swinging the pickax beside his friend, the cool clutch of sorrow and loss is close behind. Grant is down below, protected by the shade, but Johannes is up above, his eyes viewing a world blindingly lit up, wide open and stretching forever, a type of expansive emancipation he never considered on the mountain. But he sees it now. He knows it's real, and it's inescapable. He has already joined Grant, lost in this valley dominated by wounds that weaken and disfigure, wounds that Johannes had once been familiar with, that he'd cleaned and licked like a bitch tending her pups. Shared wounds that Johannes and Grant have confronted before.

But infections and memories alike, they hide. They weasel their way deep below the surface and lie dormant. When they're finally unearthed again, they've metamorphosed, and the world they once inhabited has transformed as well. If nothing remains the same for very long, how do we recognize something faceless and nameless? A wound that should have long since healed?

"Then..." Johannes shields his eyes as the sun's blazing glare shines from behind a feathery cloud. "What happened?"

"With who?"

"I don't know...both?"

Grant's eyes rove the sky, a pained expression chiseled into his features. The details are precise, permanent. He never looks at Johannes, but the question weighs on him, and he succumbs.

"Next month," Grant coughs again, still staring skyward. "It'll already be twelve years ago next month. Can you believe that? It was an incredible wedding. Her parents had money, and short of flying us all down to Mexico City, they demanded the most authentic and extravagant ceremony possible. So, they flew their entire extended family up from Mexico instead. They'd lived in Chicago since they were kids, but their thoughts were eternally south of the border. I never understood that about them..." Grant speaks with the informal, emotionless tone reserved for lonely, reflective monologues. "They planned the entire wedding themselves. Inez and I never had to lift a finger. My mom tried to help, but I don't think they let her contribute much. And it was an unforgettable event. I don't think anyone who attended slept at all that weekend. It's wild that you don't..." Grant finally looks at Johannes. "No. You weren't there, of course. Off traveling Asia or some goddamn place. But I still named you honorary best man. Prodigal best man. That's what we all called you that day," Grant almost laughs. He's staring at Johannes with intense curiosity. "I have since realized that nobody in that family cared a damn for me or the marriage. Each and every one of them was interested only in the party. Half of them never even learned my fucking name, and those who did couldn't pronounce it anyway. *Gharrr-ent*. But we, Inez and I, we were happy. We were young, but it was love. I'll always believe that. And I really, truly care for her, like nothing I've ever cared for before. Or since."

The act of recounting the story seems to replenish Grant's energy. He stands up, pacing the length of the pit again, actively dredging the bogs of his past.

"Less than a year in and she was already getting restless. Things had become strained with her family and some of our friends. We had talked about a move away from Chicago eventually. To Southern California or Miami. Bum the Caribbean for a while. Southeast Asia. The Mediterranean, of course. She wanted to travel...like you. And she had always known those types of desires with immediacy, accustomed to her dad's money, raised that way. I never knew where her family got their money, but they had mountains of it. She claimed that she didn't know how her dad made his money. Said it was complicated. Investments and shit that she didn't understand. I don't know, I never really bought that. The man had a lot of fun, though. And they spent like maniacs. Anything they wanted, anything she wanted. People like us—my family, your family—we never dreamed of buying or doing the things that these people did. Month-long vacations or cruises twice a year. Penthouses God-knows-where. I think they financed a movie once. They had a small fleet of sailboats and yachts in Lake Michigan. An endless cycle of extended family and friends always visiting from Mexico, all expenses paid in full. A couple restaurants, too. And a chain of Latin American grocery stores. Fingers in a lot of different places, I guess. Illegal ventures, some of them, I'm sure of it."

Johannes coughs, bringing up a dark glob of phlegm, which he lets fly off to the side of the pit.

Grant looks up, surprised that he's been speaking to a real live person.

"She could have kept on living that life forever. Her dad never wanted to let go of her. When he brought her down the aisle, he had this look in his eyes. Like it was all an elaborate trap, him just waiting to sick his greasy cousins on me. Take me out right there in the cathedral. But she wanted out of that life. She did. She loved her dad, and she valued what he provided. Only, she wanted independence. Same as when she got her tattoo, the big one. She didn't tell anyone, not even me, until after the first session, the outline of the leaves and petals, and that damned bird. It was a huge secret from her pa because he never would have allowed it. Her first step toward separation and asserting her own life. And the same with us. She wanted us to build our own life, to do it ourselves. It was an obsession of hers, the story of how her dad came to the US and built himself up. She liked the idea of starting from nothing, building it with our bare hands. Together. She worked, but on and off, like you. No job was ever good enough for her. Couldn't stay still for any amount of time. Like you..."

Grant stops pacing, lifts his hands, and stares at them. Dark trails of sweat roll around his eyebrows and down his cheeks.

"It didn't matter. I worked. And she was perfectly happy with our lifestyle, for a time. Domestic. Monetarily restricted. She cooked the spiciest goddamned food. We fucked like rabbits. She was relieved by the ease of that simple life. She liked it, and I relished seeing her happy. The future was wide open, boundless and waiting for us. We discussed our plans for the future constantly. Detailed plans that bordered on fantasy as far as I was concerned. Dreams. That's the thing—they were always dreams for me, but for her, it was just a matter of how soon. Dreams like that require backing, and I didn't have the dough. Simple as that. The world that I came from taught me that dreams are possible if you work your ass to the fucking bone. And I would have done anything for her, so I did. I worked my goddamn ass off. Sixty, seventy hours a week." He launches the shovel out of the pit. "You remember..." he pulls the pickax out of the dirt wall and tosses it over the ridge, "...that was when..." pulling himself onto the eastern wall opposite Johannes, "...I worked construction."

A change has come over Grant—the sheriff returning to do his job, to stand tall and fearless, to intimidate would-be transgressors, to chase convicts into dark corners and abuse them in the shadows before hauling them into the light of the courthouse. He's looking across the pit at Johannes with the grin of a law enforcer who has just witnessed someone slip up.

"No," Grant shakes his head. "Of course you don't."

"So what happened?"

"I tried to explain, to prove to her how I was moving up the ladder at the construction firm. I would have been a goddamn site manager within two years. I was on good terms with the higher-ups, friendly with all the contractors and suppliers, but none of that was good enough. One day, I came home, and she insisted, no, she informed me that we were moving south. I knew it was a bad idea, but I couldn't contain that spark in her any longer. Let it go too long and it becomes a wildfire. I couldn't bear the thought of not giving her what she wanted." A faint smile plays on Grant's face and fades just as quickly. "But, me too. I was distracted in Chicago. And jealous, I guess. Selfish. So we moved to Miami. You had just left yourself, to someplace, so the move is one thing I can believe you might have forgotten. But you knew we'd moved there. We talked, you and I, we still spoke regularly then. When we first got there, we roved Miami Beach for a week. Between the clubs and bars of South Beach and that shitty apartment, we blew a crater in my savings. Took a weekend in the Keys that turned into two weeks. Eventually, I found a job with some piss-ant construction firm building rigged-up bridges, tool sheds, gazebos, piers, that sort of thing. They wouldn't pay me any more than they paid an illegal immigrant. And somehow...in the middle of it all...she began to resent me. I was starting from the bottom of the chain with no opportunities for promotion on the horizon, I made less than I ever made anywhere in the Midwest, and I lived in a ridiculously expensive city with a woman who was slipping back into her high society ways. She wanted the lifestyle back but without her family's help. Whenever we argued about it, I'd tell her she had to hold down a job, that she couldn't go quitting on everything like she did when her dad was behind her. But our arguments would only escalate into explosive Spanish. My Spanish was decent by then, but I couldn't make out more than a word in ten on those nights. So different from her sex-Spanish. A confusing time. For our first anniversary, I planned a romantic getaway—dinner and a beachside cottage—out on Key West. Quiet, peaceful, just the two of us together, like it's supposed to be. And I spent it alone."

The chains that bind people to one another are strong, vexing, and attractive. Although Grant's voice contains no signs of the pain that colored the start of his story, Johannes can sense it, thick as the dirt coating their throats. He wants to hold his friend, if not for the immense ravine separating them. He can't shake the feeling that Grant's suffering is, in some minute way, also his own. That suffering, some would call it the human condition. After all, what would life be without it? A leisurely stroll over a vast, flat prairie? With butterflies and consistent seventy degree sunshine? It's our intrinsic curiosity and boredom that draws us toward mountain ridges and perilous crevasses, that compels us to befriend the snakes and wolves and wasps of the world just as we would conspire with puppies and kittens, with our mothers and siblings. It's not time that drives our lives forward—it's suffering. But suffering, though it cannot be completely released, it must at times be dispersed. It must be eased, or it can trap you, halt life's progress, consume you until the only thing that's left is the pain.

"And then...she left?" asks Johannes.

Grant is out there on a precipice, balancing with his suffering on his shoulders. Johannes wants to help him down, but he doesn't want to touch his friend's suffering for himself.

"I couldn't take care of her," Grant nods. "I couldn't provide. I did everything I could. I wanted to do everything for her. I tried, I did. For months and months, I tried. But nothing I could do was enough. When she left me for good, she was fucking this Puerto Rican. Some DJ. This kid from the slums of San Juan who scammed his way into the exclusive clubs on the beach strip. Couldn't speak a word of English. The one time I approached this fucker, he flashed a fucking ten-inch blade, and then his crew kicked the shit out of me. I got in a few good shots, laid a few of them out. But there were at least fifteen of them, only one of me. The next day, she was gone. Blamed me for everything. I got a few phone calls when she was drunk or stoned, denying everything in a mishmash of crying and raging Spanglish. Soon enough, the legal papers were drawn up. I left. Headed west, wound up in Creek's Ridge. Pa Sonny came out after a while. And then you, too. You were here. A few months. Before the mountains, but after you'd been there..."

"After what? What was before the mountains?"

"No. Nothing. You were here."

Grant wipes his brow with his sleeve, which only smears the dirt across his face. Reversion to a solid rock in uniform, hard-edged and prepared to withstand the resistance of another terrestrial rotation. Not only firm and incorruptible but also perfectly at ease, as though he recounts this story each morning, part of a routine that helps him transition out of the recurring nightmare and into each new day.

"You're like the hunter," says Johannes.

"Who?"

"Orion, the lovesick hunter."

"Who in the hell's that?"

"One of my friends."

"..."

"On the mountain."

"Right, the imaginary friends. Is that what I am, then?"

"..."

"Oh, what the hell!" barks Grant. "Why am I even telling you this? You already know it all, and more. That all happened before you started renouncing God-knows-what. Everything. You know, you come off as a real bastard sometimes. Some kind of friend."

"It helps to talk," mumbles Johannes.

"What?"

"Nothing. Just something he said to me, Pa Sonny, at that diner." Johannes tastes dirt and sweat as they trickle into the creases of his lips. He holds up the horse femur, the morning's one discovery, and he notices a smear of blood spread across its ivory surface. Then, he feels the thick saturation of his bandaged hand. The gauze is stained a deep red, and the fingers on both of his hands are covered in blisters, a few of them already ripped open, the skin torn clear off.

"And what about this?" Johannes waves the bone around before tossing it over the gully to Grant. "When did this horse happen?"

"Almost two years after I moved here. Eight years ago last week. Not long before you showed up. Is that a coincidence? Irony? She was a beautiful animal, Limping Lady. That's what she was called. One leg was shorter than the others. I always think about her come springtime. The season, something about it. But then, like clockwork, I'm reminded of that night. When we buried her. This year, I just...I couldn't handle it. It was too much."

"Grant, I don't get it. Why didn't you just take care of her? Or sell her? Why did you have to kill her?"

A rigid silence settles as Johannes and Grant both strain to find any line of logic in the obvious but murky equation.

"Look," says Grant, "I had been here for less than a week when I found this house. She was part of the original lease, before I bought the place. I signed at a lowball price, under the condition that I take care of the owner's stuff and Limping Lady until he got a chance to come around and claim them. He was in some sort of trouble and needed to disappear for a while, but he didn't want to lose the horse. Or the house."

"Seems alright," says Johannes.

"Better than alright. I was in bad shape after Miami. I'd never even ridden a horse before, so it was something to keep me occupied. I threw myself at the task. I learned how to ride, how to groom and feed her. I did everything for her. The problem was, I gave so much attention to the horse that I neglected to find a job. Limping Lady had become my job, full-time. She really calmed my mind, eased my heart, you know? Then, the guy who owned this place, he got caught in whatever racket he was mixed up in. Some sort of fraud, I think. Received a long sentence. The house went up for auction. So, with some help from my folks, I put down the money and scooped it up. Brand new life, simple as that. It had been more than ten months since I'd been here, I'd grown comfortable, and it felt like home. And then I got the news about Pa Sonny and invited him down. Funny thing was, he already knew about Creek's Ridge. Had been here before, I think, and said he hated the place. But he came anyway. And he would go on and on about the town's founder and the Indians, complaining about the deep past, a hundred and fifty years ago as though it was yesterday, as if it had a direct impact on the sorry state of his life. So now, I had a horse and a broke-ass, drunken, half-delusional pastor to look after. But by then, my bank account was only a shadow of what it had been. It couldn't be done, John. Impossible."

"So you...killed the only thing you cared for?"

"No, I turned and hit the bottle with Sonny. He convinced me it was time to find a job. Fed me this shit about social obligations, moral responsibilities, personal equilibrium. You know, how he always was with us. I started working at that warehouse across from the school. Instant supervisor. Manager after a month. He did, too. Started running his deliveries, bought his house. But all that did was fuel our drinking, as Sonny probably intended. It paid the bills, too, but I lost track of Lil."

"Lil?"

"I called her Lil. She transformed, became an angry horse. I'd already developed a deep fondness for her, more than any dog I ever raised. Christ, more than most people I've known. But she resented me, just like Inez resented me. She would bite and kick, and throw me whenever I tried to ride her. It hit me hard. I wasn't seeing anything straight in those days. Then I received some news. I was let down. Broken again. I loved her. I think I still do."

"What news?"

Grant gazes into the barren landscape stretching all around them. He stands and tosses the bone back across to Johannes, then walks over to retrieve the wooden cross—makeshift headstone for his long-departed equine lover. As he turns it over in his hands, his eyes keep bouncing between different points in the yard. Finally, he rams it into the dirt at the head of the massive grave.

"She wasn't even truly mine. After all, what is?"

"What is what?"

"Truly ours. She was just an animal, I know that. Not a woman, not Inez. But I loved her all the same. And I couldn't watch her drift from me like that. Not again. Not into someone else's hands. A man can only take so much. I always thought that you, of all people, would understand. I guess not. You never did, did you?"

Grant's voice recedes as he retreats. Johannes summons the strength to lift himself up and follow Grant toward the house. A lone cloud creeps in to cover the sun. Johannes looks at the sky, searching that extreme pale purity, the brilliant rays spread out behind the cloud. Everything above is static and beautifully sincere. There are no games up there, no tricks, no mysteries.

Johannes enters the house to find Grant half-heartedly cleaning his uniform. The lawman swallowing gigantic gulps of coffee, washing away evidence of his unsavory pastime and leaving the sink covered with a film of mud, a mound of filthy rags piled nearby. Grant turns critical eyes on Johannes, and for a minute, he doesn't say a word, but his stare lingers like an accusation.

"This isn't..." Grant mutters. "It's not right...this is all...backwards... upside down..." He turns away, motionless, holding himself over the sink. "We're supposed to...we've made so many mistakes... You shouldn't have... Me neither, or Pa Sonny. I never understood why he stayed. He hates it here. I have a reason. He never did. Only said he felt responsible..."

"Responsible for what?"

"For us."

"Creek's Ridge?"

"No. For me and you."

The sound of running water resumes. Steam rises. Grant adjusts the faucet until the steam dissipates, cups his hands below the water, and splashes his face again and again. After drying himself, he emerges heaving for air, running his hands through his hair. He places his hat on his head, holsters his gun, pats himself down one last time. The transformation is complete.

As he's leaving, before he lowers himself out of the front window, he pauses and turns to Johannes.

"John, we have to find the rest of that fucking horse."

Grant J. Cagniss, Sheriff, Morton County, Kansas, USofA.

Chapter 10

The Deserter

August 20, 1816
St. Johns River, La Florida

SINCE WE ARRIVED, A GROUP OF MEN BOTH YOUNG AND OLD HAVE been gathered at the village center. Dressed in an ornate fashion, they sit in a curved row facing east toward the sea. At the center sits the elderly medicine man, Long Grass, named so for his exceedingly long fingers and toes. In between their uninterrupted chanting, they inhale continuously from long pipes stuffed with tobacco. They then release lungfuls of aromatic smoke as though expunging demons from their bodies. Father Jimenez tells me this ritual is intended to protect the village against the violent storms that afflict this region.

August 23, 1816
St. Johns River, La Florida

Tonight, Father Jimenez found me idle when I should have been saying my goodbyes in anticipation of tomorrow's ten-hour trek back to San Agustín. Through observation alone, the Father had long since guessed the cause of my troubled conscience. The Father contains an endless reservoir of sound advice. He has a second sight when it comes to human nature. We conversed by firelight through the midnight hours, during which he helped to elevate me above my dilemma, to observe it as a bird of prey rather than as a quick meal scurrying between fallen leaves for cover.

Apparent to both of us was my dissatisfaction with such a brief stay in this land. But what reason have I to remain?

"That question," the Father stated, "is akin to asking God to provide the reason for life itself. The answer is implicit in the question, but incommunicable and useless."

He suggested posing more direct and fitting questions. *What good can come of indenturing myself to Captain Vasquez? What purpose is there in subjecting myself to the haunting songs of the sea? What reason have I for returning to Spain?*

Something extraordinary happened to me when El Soldado Agraciado left Bilbao and I watched my beloved Spain sink into an unreachable distance. Such an upheaval strikes every individual differently, a culmination of all life's gifts and travails up to that point in their mortal sojourn, not unlike the moments preceding death, I must presume. The peculiarities of my upbringing, as well as the few fortunate escapes from death's grasp already encountered in my short years upon this earth, have all blossomed from the good-natured generosity of others. The orphanage took me in as a hapless toddler stumbling half-naked through a patch of briars, and they raised me at significant cost and risk to themselves until the curiosity of adolescence beckoned me astray. When shepherds found me collapsed from lack of food, they gladly offered me their bread and wine. Monks welcomed me during severe weather and nourished my starved mind with knowledge. Rebels taught me to defend myself, to survive off the land, and to contribute to communal life, while solitary bandits proved that there are no limits to ingenuity where survival is concerned and that trust is a malleable, inconsistent endeavor. Just as I recognized with infinite gratitude the gifts of my varied Spanish families, and just as I always strove to repay them my debts—whether through labor or companionship or criminal complicity —I presently find myself ethically indebted to Captain Vasquez.

Father Jimenez responded with laughter.

"If ethical debts condition our lives," he told me, "then we are—all of us—destitute. How fortunate for you, then, that God does not deal in ethics or economics. These are earthly constraints, harnesses that need not bind your soul. They are human concerns that life itself will alleviate if you allow it to. One can and should give oneself over to the benefit of others, but not at a cost to oneself. There is a reason why true communion with God occurs individually, as opposed to communally. God desires every man and woman—we, his children—to discover and maintain our happiness alone. The path to Him is a lonely road. There is much that a man is capable of, but our time on this earth is brief. Take it from one who has all but used up his allotment. Time spent at sea is limbo. And loyalty is for dogs."

———

August 26, 1816
St. Johns River, La Florida

This afternoon, a group of Seminole traders returned from San Agustín. They informed us that all yesterday and continuing through the night, the Captain's first mate and a small party of sailors roamed the town asking after a young Spaniard matching my description. They were possessed with a sort of worried panic that shifted toward anger over the course of the day, providing endless amusement for our Seminole friends who kept constant, inconspicuous eyes on them. As night approached, their search moved into the taverns, where they became intoxicated and forgot about the missing youngster until sometime after midnight when Captain Vasquez showed up beside himself with rage. The Captain chased them back to the waterfront, his vulgar tirade and public reaming of the delinquent sailors creating quite the spectacle along those sleepy avenues.

Our Seminole friends stood by in the shadows, falling over each other in fits of suppressed laughter, though their minds had been set at ease. Throughout the day, the sailors approached them several times, and although they could have had no knowledge of my recent conversations with the Father or of my subsequent decision, they lied on my behalf. And at dawn this morning, they watched El Soldado Agraciado set sail for Cuba.

Their intuition was keen. They made no error in judgment. I have resolved to make my home here beside the St. Johns River with Father Jimenez and the native peoples of this bountiful land.

———

August 29, 1816
St. Johns River, La Florida

While I am not yet prepared to discount the virtue of all Seminole beliefs, the smoke rituals intended to stave off violent storms have not succeeded. An inconceivable quantity of water has spilled from the sky in the past two days, rivaled only by the terrifying intensity of the winds. On the plateaus of Castile, I was no stranger to sharp gusts strong enough to knock me off my feet. But these winds have felled trees in the swamp. Most of the village structures have suffered damage. Still, the Seminoles smirk in delight at my whimsical terror. In an attempt to console me, the Father explained in his rational and imperturbable manner that these tropical storms pass through every year at this season. Even as the rain batters us from all directions, he assures me this storm is not particularly brutal. With good humor, he adds that if I have brought bad luck, then we shall be hosts to an even crueler tempest before the season ends.

The village has been without fire since the wind and rain began. Dry skin and clothing are but a fleeting wish. I barely sleep at night, as I am tormented by nightmares in which I am tossed about El Soldado Agraciado's deck and pelted with frigid water as a wrathful sea crashes endlessly onto the hull. When I am finally thrown overboard and sent plunging into the pitch-black frothing chaos, I wake, only to find that conditions here on land differ very little.

———

November 14, 1816
St. Johns River, La Florida

I did not know my parents and have never known with certainty whether I descend from a line of Christians. As a Spaniard, I would assume they were Christians. However, the nuns at the orphanage where I was raised were always keen to remind me that they would have been better off had they left me wailing in the forest, for to be found nurturing a bastard child of the religion of Muhammed would have landed them in more trouble than I was worth. I have chestnut hair, though my eyes, I have been told, contain the heavy hues of the Moorish race, and my skin, while not dark, is indeed a shade darker than most Spaniards I have encountered. Without having been adequately educated or indoctrinated in the ways of religion, I have always considered myself to be a Christian, if for no other reason than the circumstances of time and place. Although I have never felt particularly close to Christ or the Virgin Mother, the kindest and most radiant folks I met while wandering throughout Spain were always the monks who took in weary travelers like myself. Also, the curious traveling priests I sometimes encountered never lacked food to spare and could always direct a fellow traveler toward their destination. Those types always knew the appropriate words for lifting hopeless spirits. I learned what I could from such folk, and they earned my respect, so I have always been proud to align myself with their Christian morals. And yet, here I am, in a literal land of heathens by the Roman Catholic standard, and it is me that Father Jimenez seems most intent on converting.

The Father is the type of man who will never fail to greet you warmly, though most often, he greets you without words, merely a nod and a smile. While conversing, he speaks in a disinterested, anonymous tone, and he listens intently, with a penetrative, searching gaze, responding with direct questions that help to clear away the muddle that accumulates when people speak. I have seen him hunched over in conversation with the priests on the ship, with Spaniards in San Agustín, with the Seminoles here in the village, with American and British traders that pass through, and even, oddly enough, with a black snake that lives in the trees at the edge of the village. This particular snake, a dangerous creature to be sure, is believed by the tribesmen to be a guardian and is therefore off limits to harm. They have named it Toklan Nakne Chente because it is nearly as long as two men. It has never once shown aggression toward the tribespeople. When I asked what they would do if it ever attacked one of the children, for instance, I was assured that it never would. Heathens, too, have their faith.

However, the Father's personal disposition differs from his sermonizing. His sermons are delivered with a poignancy of spirit that sets even the Seminole youngsters on their toes. Not a soul is missing during our daily service. None leave to get an early start on their work. They gather punctually at the village center in the cleared-out open-air chapel marked off by four massive wooden posts and a perimeter of stones. Father Jimenez walks freely amongst us, resting his hands on shoulders and heads as he orates. Sometimes, he will lift a child into his arms and adoringly bounce the youngster up and down as he weaves through the packed throng. All the energy he can summon, which on some days is less than others, he transfers to his unflagging congregation, who happily accept his gift and all but sprint from the service to attend their daily tasks with love and devotion. After he has finished, the Father retires to his hut to rest. On occasion, he requests that I accompany him, so I know he does not nap during this time. Rather, he sits with a book—the Holy Bible, the Confessions of the Saint, or a worn copy of Cervantes—but he does not read. He merely opens the book to a desired passage and then proceeds to gaze outside, sometimes for an hour or more, after which he shuts the book and busies himself around his modest home. Should I happen to be present, he will resume our most recent conversation in that same suppressed conversational tone, as though there had been no break in our stream of words.

The content of his sermons remains something of a mystery to me. Father Jimenez says this elucidates the gaps in my faith. I maintain that it is simply a matter of language, since half of each sermon is spoken in the Seminole tongue, and even his Spanish makes me dizzy when inflamed by his Valencian dialect.

Thus, he has made me promise to listen less carefully. "Words and their meanings," he says, "are no arbiters of faith."

Chapter 11

Whereto the Creek Leads

Johannes showers and changes the bandage on his hand. He spends the rest of the morning staring out the kitchen window at the mound of dirt they dug up, going over their conversation by the pit, and ruminating on the events of the past few weeks. For as much as he wants no part in Grant's project, his thoughts return repeatedly to the hours they spent digging. Speaking with Grant and listening to him recount the past has done little to fill the gaping trench of Johannes's memory. Rather, it has provided only fragmentary clues that amplify Johannes's loss, making him more aware of his incomplete nature, drawing out pangs of guilt and the desire to keep moving far from this place.

Squeezed into the metal beds of pickups and farm supply trucks, lifted high into tobacco-stained semi-truck cabs, Johannes had grown accustomed to engine vibrations and the violent jolts of scarred highways and gravel roads. At a certain point, he even began to appreciate it, thinking it wouldn't be so bad to keep up this search for the mystery town indefinitely, until he found it in some distant future when it wouldn't matter so much anymore. Filtered through yellowish clouds kicked up by tires, the landscape had gradually morphed before his eyes. The mountains of Tennessee dipped into vast fog-filled valleys. The valleys led to unassuming hills that later opened upon the Mississippi River, followed by a rapid flattening and drying out of all things, life itself evaporating as he pushed through the Midwestern plains. Trees shriveled before disappearing altogether. The color green withered into feathery brown tufts, endless stretches of dry grass, dirt, dust, and barren farmlands yet untilled for a new season's crops. Motor tremors shook his weathered bones into numbness. All through it, he had to keep reminding himself that he had not left his mountain sanctuary on some whim, some miscalculated emotional upheaval. No, the longer and farther he traveled, the more he wanted to turn around and go back. But he couldn't. He can't.

He had not fled from the landslide. Instead, he had clung to the oak tree, held on for dear life while at the same time prepared for death, there in what he believed to be his rightful place, his home, his end, his destined grave. But it was not his time, nor did he possess the strength necessary to twist the limbs of fate, to carry himself off, weakened perhaps by the wound, master Knecht's rebuke of such feeble human thoughts. How many days had he sat drying his skin in meditative, malnourished delirium? How many weeks had he scavenged and slept curled in a ball at the base of the oak, protecting himself from the cold with a blanket of dead leaves? Nausea, fumes from a putrid carcass reaching a thousand fingery strands to knot and twist an irreconcilable sickness. Days of vomiting cattails, mint leaves, and water from the stream, all the sustenance he could find without straying too far from the scene of his loss, the site of desolation, or the presence of Knecht, his protectorate. Anticipating and awaiting death with calm sternness, his suffering a fit punishment, this drawn-out, painful end, exposed to the elements and the prying eyes of the forest, his sentence for having escaped a swift execution along with his home and everything he owned. The mud swallowed everything he had built, pushed it into the river, and swept it all away, all those things he recognized as his own ceasing to be graspable, visible. Just wisps of imagination. A jumble of past and present slowly and painfully leading into an inevitable future.

On the morning he finally left, it was fear that drove him out. Waking to an unimaginably beautiful dawn sky, unobscured and teeming with pinpoints of starlight just before they faded, then disappeared, until nothing remained but the empty blue and yellow hues of morning —it was then that he fled down the mountain from something unseen, a sensation that rose overnight and took reign over the forest, the mountains, all the things he knew and cherished corrupted beyond hope. Endless hours tripping, stumbling, climbing, crawling downhill as the day advanced, the world illuminated and on display, and then emerging at last, breathless and exhausted, collapsing upon the asphalt of the nearest road, out front of the general store and modest home, that kind young couple—what were their names?—his only neighbors all those years. They had found him lying there and tried to help, but a car drove up before they could even bring him a glass of water. It stopped suddenly, tires squealing as it pulled over, inviting him in. Questions without answers, curiosity without concern, repeated requests for money, then for dope or amphetamines, silence for another twenty-thirty miles, and then *Hey buddy, this is bullshit, just get out—*

The agitation of remembering, the uncertainty of whether to feel thankful or fretful, the stillness and solidity of this kitchen table and the chairs, domestic surroundings at once familiar yet foreign, they coalesce to lift Johannes out of his idleness and around the house for a few minutes, exploring but not yet absorbing, a few small bites from scraps of leftovers in the fridge, and then out into the yard. For a while, he circles around the pit they've dug out, the mound they've unearthed, and he examines the bone, a horse's femur, attempting to contain an unexpected thrust of anxious energy. He sets it down and steps up to the creek, where he dips his hands, calmed by its gentle flow, its cool silkiness wetting his face and hair. For once, he closes his eyes without fear but only the pleasant sensation of recreating the way things used to be, his own placid stream, discharged from the natural spring near the peak, its graceful winding path down past his shack, a refreshing sip, a cool bath, cleanliness unmatched.

The creek wanders in from the northeast and continues along the entire length of the town. Johannes gazes in both directions, as well as back at the house and the mound and the hole in the ground, but his gaze is held by the distant pointed steeple of the church towering above all else, inclining him to follow the creek's temperate southward flow.

After feeding Johannes a light breakfast of eggs and toast at the diner, the driver, Pa Sonny, had led him out to the parking lot. His rusted-out Ford pickup had once been cherry red, he'd said, but he admitted that he had grown to prefer its current earthy tones. The old man had collected a few odds-and-ends to sell or transport, and he offered to move the tractor engine out of the passenger seat so Johannes could join him inside the cab, but Johannes had already noticed the animals in the back and maneuvered himself onto the cramped truck bed. Two piglets cuddled together in a cardboard box, four ducks in a wire cage, and a goat leashed to the tailgate. The ride was smooth through most of the state. The meal had revitalized him, but this also made him more conscious of what he was doing, which made him want to pound on the cab window, stop the driver driving, and start hitching his way back in the direction from which he'd come. He wished desperately to gaze out upon the vistas from his mountain peak once again, such a pleasure and a relief on crisp spring days. The goat nibbled at his clothes, distracting him from a barrage of troubling uncertainties. An ongoing tug-of-war took place, resulting in Johannes losing several sizable chunks of fabric from his already tattered garments. They eventually dozed off together for a short time, Johannes and the goat, before being startled awake by a powerful bump as they turned onto a rough road, soon to pass the town welcome sign before pulling into the service station at the northern border of Creek's Ridge. Something poignant in the town's name tugged at emotional strings that hadn't been plucked in a while. And although Johannes knew he shouldn't cling too tightly to coincidence, he had recognized as unbelievable the fact that of all the people who had offered him rides, the only one to make an honest attempt at conversation had been headed for the same small, isolated town that he'd been blindly hitchhiking toward all along.

"This is as far as I'm going, bud." The driver's wrinkled gray eyes had searched Johannes with the same soft but pointed gaze from the diner. "Likely have to wait a while if you plan to catch another ride from here. Not many folks pass through this way, not without a reason to."

Johannes stood up in the truck bed, waiting for the memories to come flooding back, and explaining that this was the end of the road for him, too.

"Strange place to stop in." The driver patted himself down, releasing a dust cloud from his jacket and jeans. "You been here before?"

"Yes, I...think so..."

"There're worse places to get stuck in..." said the driver, shrugging and nodding casually with a knowing grin. He rested his arm on the tailgate, and they both gazed down the main street to admire the town. It was quiet and calm, nothing out of the ordinary. Far away, they could just barely make out the church's sleepy steeple, keeping its distant, unobtrusive vigil.

"Good luck to you, then...John Doe."

The goat nudged Johannes and sniffed at his crotch, pulling him out of a foggy past and back to the present dilemma of *What now?* Pa Sonny, supposed friend from former days, had simply left it at that, walked into the service station knowing full-well the identity of this vagrant he had just turned loose, but never once exposing his knowledge. Even the name, John Doe, had been part of the trick, a calculated jab, perhaps meant to jostle Johannes back to himself. It hadn't worked. So, left to his own aimless designs, Johannes had simply stared out over the town, knowing he must have been here before but unsure of how long it had been or whether there was still anyone or anything here for him.

When he felt the dry lick of the goat's tongue on his hand, he came to and lowered himself off the truck bed. At eye level, he studied the goat's eyes, its devilish irises. The driver returned and caught them in this interaction, so he suggested Johannes take the goat with him, free of charge. Said it seemed to have an affection for him that it had for no others. Johannes declined, somewhat rudely, and headed for the main street.

"Do you know a man..." Johannes had turned to ask.

"Know a lot of men. You're looking for somebody?"

"No, never mind..."

"Well, if you need anything, anything at all, then you come and find me, alright? I'll be around tonight, but hitting the road again first thing in the morning. Gotta shift these critters before I fall in love...or make mutton of this goat..." The driver indicated a dingy shotgun house across the street, the only other structure in that part of town. "You can find me there as long as I'm around to be found. The sheriff might be of some help, too, if you can locate him."

Johannes had never, at any moment or with any inkling of recollection, recognized the old man, but he had recognized the town's name as soon as the driver said it. Before that, he'd only known, almost instinctually, that the town was west and that there was someone there he needed to find. But when he finally began footing it up and down the main street, in and out of narrow side streets, no distinct memories were upended. By stumbling upon the exact location he'd been trying to reach, he had, in effect, sealed away weeks of doubt and misadventure as relics of the past, only to replace them with a whole new set of troubles.

Following the creek south, he's walking away from the driver's shotgun house and looking up as he approaches the sharp rise of the church's spire. The driver, Pa Sonny, would be gone by now anyhow, off to sell his wares, to find loving homes for the pigs, the ducks, and the goat—or to the slaughterhouse—his knowledge of the town and its past carried away, soon to be forgotten, lost. Would it have been worth it to stick with that man rather than latching on to Grant? To wander the country picking things up and leaving them behind? But the more Johannes returns to the unanswered questions of the previous day, the past couple of weeks, the last seven years, the more he gets used to the idea of being off the road, off the mountain. And with that comes gratitude for a roof under which to sleep come nightfall, the warmth of its walls, protection from any danger that might arise, and even a sheriff to watch over his faltering footsteps.

Johannes passes the last building of the town proper, affording him his first unobstructed view of the church, though it's still another half-mile further along on the opposite side of the road. The building is from another time, gracefully aged and dilapidated, surrounded by a vast and well-maintained perimeter of low bushes and budding trees, a trim lawn, and backed by the stone and iron fence of a cemetery. He continues admiringly onward, but before he crosses the desolate main street, he's distracted, held rapt by a blooming glade of green that grows alongside the creek.

The moment he steps into the glade, his thoughts roam untethered back to his mountain, the welcoming intimacy of the glade surrounding his shack, Knecht and the healthy growth wrapped tightly around them both, balanced and at peace so high above the rest of the world, cradled between nature and the wide open sky, floating between clouds and valley fogs, meditating and navigating his own internal terrain to the very edge, never a fear of falling, of losing his place, until it is swiped away from beneath, in the space of a single breath.

Johannes inhales deeply and sits down atop tough blades of grass, folds his legs and reins in his thoughts, silences all but the one thought that will not be hushed—

Digging.

Only while they were digging had Johannes truly recognized Grant as the friend he needed that day when he ran down off the mountain, and even more on each of those consecutive, mindless days hitchhiking the roads. Unspoken companionship, expressed through the focused rhythm of their limbs swinging together, comparable to years of solitude and meditation, all that time spent inverting himself and searching the depths of his identity, pummeling his organs with abstinence, his body with the elements, studying the intricacies of nature, of the animals, of his own mind and instincts—but now, suddenly, this added bond of friendship, the strength of another, those harmless games of youth, and the confidence that together they can move the earth.

Digging with Grant is as close to an honest memory as he's had since the landslide.

The sun begins to set. The evening's moisture renders the dust heavy, compelling it toward the ground for the night. Johannes has spent the entire afternoon within the confines of the glade near the creek, not meditating but simply contemplating, allowing his tempestuous thoughts to calm and disperse over the landscape.

Dusk settles over Creek's Ridge. Johannes follows the creek back to the house. Grant has not yet returned. Johannes opens the refrigerator, tastes what little there is to be had, but he's not hungry anyhow. So after one more glance at the yard and the mound and the single deep hole they have carved out, he goes into the living room and climbs out the front window. He walks the main street, greeting people along the way until he comes to the bar, where Ernest nods in welcome and pours him a glass of The Carnival before he even asks. Grant shows up an hour or so later, entering not through the front but through the unseen rear entrance, and he sits down, betraying no surprise at finding Johannes there. They stay late into the night, drinking and chatting with Ernest and a few other customers. Grant tells stories of their shared childhood, recounting the trials, mistakes, and freedom of adolescence. He compels Johannes to tell something of life on the mountain, the hardships of surviving on his own, constantly at the mercy of nature and his own thoughts.

And in the morning, they dig.

Chapter 12

The Cave

After Penagashea took Lalawethika under his wing, the two became inseparable. They remained largely away from the tribe, near a cave that Penagashea had long used as a private retreat from the injustices he suffered in the village.

At first, they spent their days in peace. The quiet and solitude of the surrounding forest and the nearby stream never wore thin. They spoke in low, confidential tones, sitting beside the stream or around their small fire. Penagashea related the entire Shawnee history as it had been taught to him—wars and tribal factions, migrations and struggles for power, fruitful harvests and brutal winters. He then spoke of the creation legends and the Great Spirit. After several days of this, he asked Lalawethika to repeat everything back to him, and when Lalawethika had done so, they began again. This repetition continued until Lalawethika had memorized the stories, after which Penagashea instructed him to make the stories his own by blending them, dropping and adding facts at will, interpreting his surroundings and his listeners' reactions. To lead by following, Penagashea explained. To observe and listen while never ceasing to speak, but altering course accordingly. This was the true nature of the medicine—persuasion—the magic that a medicine man must possess.

"There must be a marriage between the unshakable force of a great river and the gentle, yielding, unpredictability of the winds. In this, admittedly, I have failed. But it falls to me to pass this knowledge to someone capable of wielding it. This is my role as medicine man. Your role, Noisemaker, will be much greater."

During lulls in their lessons, Penagashea often glanced toward the cave, but he had yet to allow Lalawethika to enter that sanctuary.

One day, the old medicine man interrupted as Lalawethika recited the creation story in a bold voice, altering it slightly here and there based on Penagashea's subtle expressions. He said that Lalawethika's storytelling had improved but that his voice had lost the savage urgency it possessed the night of the feast. Lalawethika began again, but he was cut short by a blow to the head from Penagashea's medicine staff.

"You filthy bastard," the old man roared. "Your mother spread her legs for every Shawnee male from here to the great lake. She favored your brother Tecumseh with a vile, unnatural motherly love so that he could claim his pedestal within the tribe. She was a beacon for white traders who wanted no furs but hers, which she gave over for fun. Now she is wrinkled and fat amongst the Creeks, and she wanders the southern mountains as the most prodigious whore in this land. And you are not worthy even of her, you weakling. You excrement. You are not of her womb but of her bowels."

He spat and swung his medicine staff repeatedly at Lalawethika's body until Lalawethika, deflecting the blows and protecting himself, chanced to grab hold of the staff. His grasp was stronger than Penagashea's, so he swung the old man loose. Penagashea rolled into the shallow stream and stared up at Lalawethika.

"Now," he heaved. "Tell the story now."

Without thinking, Lalawethika proceeded with the creation story. He told it in flying, grotesque language, with imagery that could not fail to produce discomfort in the most hardened of warriors. He howled like the wolves. He pounded and pointed and slashed with the medicine staff. His voice rolled like thunder, flashed like lightning, and offered hope like the rains.

By the end, Penagashea was spilling tears of both fear and pride. "Now, do you see? Do you understand what is possible? What you are capable of? Come now, to the cave. A reward..."

The cave was not large, but it was full of oddly shaped caverns and crags, many of which concealed earthenware jugs. Penagashea ordered Lalawethika to resume his tales. Lalawethika did as he was told, speaking with the might of an army, the echoes inside the cave amplifying the sound so that his voice became a separate entity, issuing not from his throat but from the walls themselves, from the ground, from the cracks that led deep into the earth. He shut his eyes and became a giant, invincible, interwoven with the fabrics of creation and destruction. When he opened his eyes again, he found Penagashea hunched in a corner, drinking from one of the earthenware jugs. Lalawethika watched the old man in confusion. Penagashea waved him over and gestured for him to sit. He held the jug out to Lalawethika and nodded approval, a pleased grin wrinkling his face. They drank the firewater as they listened to the birds chirping outside and the wind whipping past the cave entrance. Sometimes, a breeze swirled into the cave, producing a low whistle.

The firewater spread its warm, welcoming glow through their bodies. Lalawethika's limbs went loose and limp as he counted the weeks since he last had a taste. Penagashea admitted that he had been coming into the cave by night to steal a few sips while Lalawethika slept by the fire. Together, they noted the sensation of insects bustling just beneath the surface of their skin. Then Penagashea began to heap praise upon Lalawethika—the extraordinary effect of his voice, the speed with which he had learned the Shawnee legends, his creativity and flexibility as a storyteller. How he would one day make a fine delegate and negotiator. How his lethargic, idle gait resembled the Shawnee chiefs and medicine men of old. How his ugly, deformed eye would one day be eternalized in lore as a heroic sacrifice, re-enacted through stomp dances around enormous fires on lands that belonged to the Shawnee people without worry or threat from the white man.

Lalawethika listened, nodding and grunting an accompaniment to the old man's compliments. But the firewater worked on Lalawethika as well, and before long, he interrupted, incapable of holding his tongue any longer—

"A maimed young outcast, exploring the woods alone, stumbles across a group of raucous white men sprawled around a pitiful fire. They spot him peeking through the branches, so they beckon his approach with friendly gestures, laughing all the while. The boy holds himself erect and proud as he approaches. They point at his ruined eye, at the unusual plumpness of this native boy. A few of them attempt to touch him, but he backs away and returns what he believes to be a menacing glare. Their endless laughter renders them unsteady on their feet as they pass around a large container of liquid from which they drink heartily. Some of their language is familiar, but their speech is quick, with a difficult looseness to their words. They speak of the container, pointing at it and at the boy. One of the men grabs it and hugs it close to his chest, refusing to give it up, his anger lashing outward unto his brethren. The others turn their laughter toward their greedy companion. They surround him and take the jug by force, and then they turn to the native boy, offering the jug to him with the jeering and taunting of false kindnesses. They coax him forward and pass him the container. Its scent is of sweetened wood but heavy and sharp, like a dead animal. They watch him, gesturing for him to drink. Elevated by his fear of embarrassment and loneliness, he stares at them as he lifts the container to his lips and tilts his head back, allowing the liquid to flow freely as he swallows. It burns his throat like an inhalation of pine smoke. It seems impossible to hold it down. As a mole adeptly digs through the soil, he feels it churning back up his throat. He knows his face is contorted, but the white men have become silent, and he realizes this is the firewater he has often heard tell of amongst the older members of his tribe. He tightens every muscle in his body, and they stare in amazement. He glares from one white man to the next, silently communicating with them as the liquid settles in his stomach, and then, boldly, he takes another drink. The white men explode into cheers and hurrahs. They crowd around the boy and clap him on the back, all talking at once and laughing again, but now their laughter is joyful and accepting. They entreat the boy to join them around their fire. The rest of the night is spent conversing through simple words and gestures, the jug passed around until it is empty. One by one, the men fall asleep on the open ground around the flames. The boy lies down, too, taking his place amongst his new friends. He looks up at the stars, of which there seem to be far more than there ought. Since losing his eye, this is the first time he has been treated with respect. He imagines the countless things these men can teach him, the unimaginable places they will take him. There is no longer reason to return to his tribe. And for once, he falls asleep happy, eager to ride out in the morning atop one of their huge horses. But when he wakes, the sun is directly overhead, the fire is reduced to cold black coals, and the white men have gone. No offer to ride out with them, no gifts of parting, not even a single word of farewell. They have left him with nothing more than dreams and the scars of their firewater."

Lalawethika paced from one end of the cave to the other. As he finished recounting this memory, he grabbed the jug from the old man's hands and tilted it over his mouth, spluttering, choking, and snarling as it filled his throat, mouth, and nostrils, overflowing and spilling down the length of his body.

"No, no, no more..." Penagashea stuttered. "No more will we be ensnared by the white man's traps."

"This is the white man's trap," Lalawethika screamed, holding up the jug and thrashing it around. His eyes rolled back in his head and his body went stiff. "This poison. This is how they control us. This is how they extinguish our fires and convince us to believe their lies. This is how they beget our fear. That boy I told of is not only me. He is every red man, every rightful inhabitant of this land. From its disgusting orifices, the Great Serpent retched and shat white men into the sea, from where they washed up to pollute our shores."

Lalawethika launched the jug across the cave and it shattered against the wall.

"Continue, continue!" Penagashea leapt around with howls of delight. "More, more!" he bellowed as he crawled over the cave floor in search of another full jug.

"Transformation," explained Penagashea. "We must not allow the Great Spirit or the Great Serpent to behold you until it is complete. Their essence is everywhere, but the cave is protected. Here, you are concealed from prying eyes. Do not move. Relax. Enjoy the fire."

For several weeks, Penagashea forbade Lalawethika from leaving the cave. Penagashea himself rarely ventured into the open air during this time except to gather food, water, and firewood.

Lalawethika was permitted to move around the cave for only a few minutes each day. At times, he was ordered to stand motionless for several hours, chanting and reciting. At other times, Penagashea sat him down so close beside the fire that blisters developed on Lalawethika's knees and shins. Once, his hair was singed by a flame gone rogue in a draft. Penagashea interpreted this as a sign, prompting him to cut off Lalawethika's long hair with a bone knife. Still other times, Lalawethika was directed to kneel atop a bear hide, with Penagashea slumped on a stone nearby and murmuring in low tones. Penagashea denied Lalawethika food and allowed him to drink only small amounts of water or firewater. Lalawethika's energy quickly wore thin. He soon became helplessly lost in exhaustion and delirium, which Penagashea stoked further by allowing him only an hour of sleep at a time, a few times per day. When Penagashea returned from his walks, he would often enter already speaking to Lalawethika, as though there had been no break in his speech.

"Your physical body and your spiritual self. Communication and aura. Strength, health, vitality. Honesty and reliability and wisdom." Penagashea had brought back a handful of long stems, each topped by several double-lipped violet flowers. He removed the leaves and petals, arranging them on a flat stone. "Even deception and trickery. Master all arts, always to maintain an advantage over friends and enemies alike. You must become unrecognizable. To your brother, to your wife and your children, to every Shawnee and every white man, to the animals of the forest. Even to me, to yourself. To the Great Spirit. This, the only way you will earn respect." He tossed the stripped stems onto the fire and used a rock to grind the leaves and petals. "Respect warrants survival. Survival for yourself and for our people, and also for the sacred charge of a medicine man. After you have won their respect, you will hold onto it by showing equal respect to every creature that exposes itself before you, no matter how vile they seem or how insincere your true intentions may be." He wet his hands, scraped the plant paste off the stone, and rolled it between his fingers to form pellets, which he then dipped in water. "Swallow these. It is skullcap. It will sharpen your mind. It will help you to focus your energy inward. You must sift through the shit of which you are made if you wish to open a direct link to the Great Spirit."

Since coming to the cave, Penagashea had also been collecting herbs and roots. While he readied them for Lalawethika to ingest, he would describe their uses and methods of preparation. Lalawethika repeated every word his mentor said. Roots were washed and soaked in boiling water for hours before they could be chewed. Herbs were ground up, like the skullcap, and then mixed with water to be swallowed or rubbed over the skin. Penagashea accumulated a large quantity of one plant in particular but never used it. They only hung it from the cave wall nearest the fire. The greens of this plant shriveled and turned brown, but the tiny white flowers appeared to retain every trace of life, even after the plants had completely dried out. Penagashea called this plant Sweet Everlasting.

Sometimes, Penagashea came back from the riverbank with lumps of red clay. He would thoroughly moisten it with water and then instruct Lalawethika to knead it until it was sufficiently soft. Using his fingers, Penagashea would carefully apply three lines of the paste to his own forehead, three more to each of his cheeks, and a single line down the center of his chin, after which he would proceed to cover portions of Lalawethika's body in thick, solid coats. Then, he would dig a lump of glowing coal out from the fire, crush it, and mix it with water before using a sharpened stick to draw intricate designs with black ash over the red clay on Lalawethika's flesh.

"For many years, our warriors have painted themselves red. Ferocity to the battle. Blood on the hunt. But these are crude ventures." He was using crushed berries to accent the lighter red of the clay. "Red was once a holy color to the Shawnee people. The Great Spirit does not crave spilled blood. The Great Spirit wants us to honor the land, the gravesite of our fathers and the fathers of our fathers. Our souls diffuse through this color. Through the color red, we seek and attain balance with the earth, communion with one another. With red, we purge our spirits of the filth and wickedness that accumulates within us. We observe the sanctity of blood that flows, not of spilled blood. Our warriors have twisted our customs out of fear and greed. They mask their fear as bloodlust, and they convince others of their fearlessness, claiming that their fearlessness alone can defend us from the white man. This is their mistake. For it is our fear that protects us. Noisemaker, you have every right to fear the memory of the blood you lost in your youth. But now, you must embrace it as well. Red is a celebration of our fear, an expression of our desire to survive and flourish as long as the earth and the Great Spirit might allow us. Red shall be your purification."

Early one morning, Penagashea spent a long time examining the plants hung on the cave wall. When he finished, he announced that it would be Lalawethika's final day imprisoned within the cave. Penagashea was going out in search of cottonwood trees, from which they would need the leaf buds for their final ritual. The nearest cottonwood thicket was several miles distant, so he would not return until nightfall. He left Lalawethika with instructions to recite everything he had learned thus far, to speak non-stop with both passion and charisma, addressing all the creatures that had ever walked the earth and perished, convincing them to accept life over the tedium of death. While he spoke, he was to walk around the cave, stretching and returning strength to his limbs, and he was not to rest until Penagashea returned.

Isolated, malnourished, dehydrated, fatigued—Lalawethika should not have had the energy to stand, let alone walk and talk for an entire day. But Penagashea's trials had plunged Lalawethika into a delusional state. His hunger, weariness, and fear were now one and the same. The boundary that segregated the cave from the world outside had melted into an indeterminate shape—a commanding force or a concept, such as justice, rather than just a line separating in from out, light from dark. Penagashea had come to represent something more than just a benefactor, more than a medicine man or a drinking companion or a spiritual guide. He had become something one does not disobey—a father.

So Lalawethika ignored his exhaustion, shed his ennui, and obeyed. Penagashea listened awhile as Lalawethika began to relate the creation myths. Then, he drank the final drops from the jug he was holding and walked out of the cave.

The blinding light issuing from the head of the cave swallowed Penagashea. Lalawethika thought he heard the earth groan, as though from gratitude, so he intensified his speech. He spoke to the powerful light outside but did not dare approach it, remaining instead near the shadows cast by the fire. The fire burned full and strong and tall. Sometimes it moved like a child dancing, other times like an old woman sitting and heaving sighs of sadness.

Part Two

Shall We Dance?

Chapter 13

The Full Moon

The sun has nearly sunk below the western tree line and the air smells of oncoming rain. Mountainous storm clouds lurch in from the north. To the south, the ghostlike outline of the moon slips westward across a wispy sky. A slight breeze cruises the evening streets, though it does little to cool this spring night that has all but been hijacked by the dry heat of an early summer.

The breeze flows off the street and in through the open door. Most days by this time, a few droopy-eyed local drunks are already slumped around the tables, but not today. The bar smells fresher than usual. The lights are bright for once, throwing an inviting glisten over everything, especially the mirrors, where reflections are no longer cloudy specters but clean-cut reproductions. Each one mimics every gesture, none peering from behind films of grime or concealed in shadow, and being hounded by all those replicated eyes is reason enough to make anyone wish for solitude.

One of the reflections trembles silently as the sound of footsteps becomes audible.

"Johannes, goddamnit, that you?" Ernest stumbles at the top of the cellar stairs, his face hidden behind the stack of boxes he's balancing atop a crate. The musical clang of loose bottles continues after he drops the load onto the bar. His face is puffy, his stubble glistens, and his stocky body heaves from the exertion. "Thanks for lending a hand. God knows why I still serve you free of charge. If I had tumbled to my death down those steps, you'd just slip right on out of here as casually as you walked in, wouldn't you? Leave the fat old barman to rot below his own establishment..."

"Not such a bad way to be buried," Johannes says as he approaches the bar. "At least people would know where to pay their respects."

"Respects," Ernest grunts. "No one's coming here to pay any respects. I could be a felon, dangerous, violent, unhinged, and that wouldn't stop anyone from coming in here. It's the booze they want."

"Lucky you."

"Why's that?" Ernest dabs his sweat with a towel, trying to conceal his suspicion.

"We can test your theory tonight. Should we make a wager of it? Twenty bucks? A hundred?"

"I was beginning to think that our bargain was just big talk. You haven't given me a proper story yet. I oughta make you go first. I don't trust you're the sort of fellow who sticks around more than a couple weeks in a town like this."

"Grant keeps me occupied."

"No shit. I took a walk the other day and saw the mess you two've made of his yard. What in the mother-loving hell are you two up to?"

"Digging."

"Digging what? A goddamned lake? The great Kansas catacombs? Laying a foundation? For what? A house? Some kind of hippy compound?"

Johannes smiles. "Just digging."

"I suppose if you're building yourself a house, you might be around a while yet. Clearly, you're not scoping out the market to buy a place. You couldn't even pay for a quarter of the booze you drink in here, could you? And how do you plan to pay me a hundred smackers when you lose this bet? Don't go forging debts you can't live up to. They'll haunt you into the grave. That's one thing I've learned from this life."

"I'll risk it."

"Oh, to be young again," Ernest swoons. "Young and stupid. You see, at least your mind is functioning soundly. It appears that way anyhow, when you move your mouth and words come out. It's your behavior that doesn't make a bit of goddamn sense. Instead of chasing honeys around, you're in here all the time. Or else you're out there playing in the dirt. I might've expected such madness from Grant before you showed up. But even at his craziest, he was always out there chasing women."

"So far, the only peace I've found has been in digging. I'll take whatever I can get. A few days ago, you told me something was wrong with me. You said I needed a cure, and the cure was music—not women."

"Did I?"

"At the tail end of a bottle. But I don't know... Maybe digging is the cure, for me and for Grant."

"Never mind what I said. A woman is the cure. A woman is always the cure. I got news for you—you're not that young. Neither one of you is. It won't last."

"Does Grant really chase after women?"

"Right up until this nonsensical digging of yours began, there was nothing else for him to do but cruise around looking tough in his uniform. Strutting his feathers. What I don't understand is why you don't go someplace where you can dig for real. Nothing wrong with taking up a new hobby. But head into Utah or Montana for some real fossils. How about the Yucatán or the Andes? Find some ancient ruins to wreck with your tooling. What are you gonna do with a bunch of bones from the frontier days? You think it's a big secret, but anyone who knows anything about this town knows that's what you two are looking for. You're not the first. Folks pass through every now and again, asking after the remains of that missionary fellow and his daughter. And Native Americans, too. Tales of some kind of loony cult leader that started it all."

"Started what?"

"This town. Or the idea of this town. I don't know what myself. Story goes that the local Native Americans didn't much like what the settlement was becoming. They felt left out and encroached upon. Again. So, the various tribes came together and raided the place, looking to punish the leader by kidnapping his daughter and slaughtering most everyone else. The town put up a fight, and by the end of it, there were plenty dead on both sides. No clear winner, no clear outcome. Just a whole lot of death and hard feelings. And bones buried all over the surrounding area. A few whispers of treasure, too. Officially, it was all moved to the church cemetery decades ago, a few housed inside as relics, they say. But what's the point? No magic left in a couple of rotting bones, even if the folks who walked around with them possessed something special. If you're interested in the Native American raids, well, then go and flip through a history book like the rest of us. Supposedly some personal journals have survived from that time, still floating around."

"Where?"

"Someplace," Ernest shrugs. "Maybe you'll have to dig them up, too. Anyway, with the amount you've been drinking, I'd say you're finding plenty of peace in these here bottles."

"The taste of dirt clings to my mouth, just about permanent now. Water enhances the earthiness, which brings up bad memories. The landslide. The nightmares. And the flavor of any other drink is tainted. Nothing but The Carnival has stood up to the challenge."

Ernest pulls a new bottle of The Carnival from the crate, twists it in his hands. Families, groups of friends, and lovers shuffle past the open doorway on their evening walks. Sometimes, they dawdle out front, kids playing, couples talking, their voices and laughter swelling like passing cars, with the occasional high-pitched squeal of a traffic accident releasing merriment instead of despair. Ernest gazes mournfully out the door as he pulls the cork from the bottle.

"Well, whatever it is, I'm glad for the help. And the company, too. I was sick to death of drinking this swill by myself. Oscar, that prick. This close, I was this close, I swear, to pouring it all down the drain. That's one thing you've been good for, I'll give you that. Now, you just bring those history books in here with you and we'll really be onto something. I don't know much about the raids, either. Always been curious..."

"Are you ready for tonight?" Johannes settles onto a barstool.

Ernest pours the Scotch into two glasses, his head bowed.

"Will there be enough people?" presses Johannes.

"You kidding? You saw the moon, didn't you?" Ernest glances up as he grabs a rag to wipe down the bar again.

"Barely. There's still daylight."

"Yeah, but you must have seen it last night. The expectation of what that tiny remaining sliver must mean."

"No, I..."

"Some mountain man you are. But there's something in the air, too. Tonight of all nights...no wonder you're so assertive. I couldn't make them go away if I wanted to, not tonight. You know, a lot of folks passing through, newcomers, they don't realize that this part of the country is dry. All the counties surrounding us, on both sides of the border, they're dry counties. All except us. Morton County has survived the test of time on liquor. According to Oscar, it's because of St. Josephine's. Used to be a popular place, especially Sundays, and they could have kept their wine supply coming in with no problem. Only there was a priest here some thirty, forty years back, had a thirst like a whale apparently. He's the one who fought to keep the county juiced." Ernest finishes rinsing out a glass, then he turns around, looking for a place to set it amongst the others. He glances up into the mirrors and their eyes meet. "Even with God's direct intervention, me and George's Grocery are the only licensed sellers in the damn county." A cloud of mystery obscures his mouth in the mirror. They both stare until it fades, and Ernest turns to face Johannes again, reaching for his glass. "Most of my regulars have to drive an hour or more to sit here and have a few. Some people drive three hours to shop at George's just so they can bring home a bottle of rum or bourbon or wine with their groceries. A measly six-pack. Imagine that. When I was a kid in St. Louis, the drunks on the stoops used to hand cans of beer out to us like they were lollipops. Only way George manages to make his alimony and child support payments *and* keep his store afloat is the booze money."

Johannes nods, sips his Scotch.

"It sounds silly," Ernest sips his own, "but full moons really do bring something out in people. I never believed in crap like that until I bought this place and witnessed it firsthand. Nobody's turning into wolves, nothing like that. But they want to. That's why they come to drink, no matter the distance."

"The moon... It did something to the animals, too. On the mountain."

"That's what I'm saying. There'd be a riot if I was ever closed during a full moon."

"Might be something to consider. Give Grant something to do, a bit of enjoyment in his work. The inactivity of that job is driving him nuts. *That's* why we're digging."

"You haven't seen Grant and crazy. Sonny says Grant was never like that before, always level-headed, logical, steady. I guess it began a few years ago. He took that sheriff's position and everything was smooth as cheesecake, until Sonny quit drinking, oddly enough. Sonny went straight and Grant flew off the rails. Like they traded personalities. Then you show up, and it just stops. He's gone back to the way he was. His problem is that he doesn't want to accept the nature of his job. He believes his role is useless because there are no murders, no theft to speak of. He wants to be the sword in the stone people look to for strength. And he is, only he doesn't know it, or it's not good enough. When he took that job, nothing changed except the face behind the badge. Suddenly, it was him that people could have faith in. Something they could admire and pretend to fear. For a long time, he was slipping. Now, with you here, he seems to have returned to his former self. But, I'll tell you, it's a slippery world."

"Have you ever told him these things?"

"Of course I have. But Grant's not always the type to listen when a man is speaking to him. His problem is much the same as yours, I assume."

"What's that?"

"He needs a woman!" Ernest huffs as he reaches for the bottle and refills their glasses. "The last time I mentioned it, he opened the ol' self-pity valves, telling me all about his shoebox full of drugs and his divorce, cheating wives and husbands, brothers and sisters, midnight prowlers, runaway horses, Latin American misfortunes, Midwestern deceptions, and what-have-you. When he gets to ranting, there's no stopping him. He just goes and goes. And then the son of a bitch started a bar fight. He did, himself, right here. Picture that for a minute. The goddamn sheriff instigating the bar brawl. Who am I supposed to call in, then? For backup? Sonny, that's who. Christ. And now this digging—I'm not sure what's worse, to be honest." Ernest takes a sip and points aggressively at Johannes, "You know what people say about the two of you, don't you?"

"Who?"

"Lunatics. They call you lunatics. No one's shy about it, either. Everyone has seen those holes all over Grant's yard, and they talk openly about you two bums. They say you've lost every last marble in the jar. Not that you had any to begin with, living out in the wild like you did. And then here you come to flick away the last few marbles Grant has left. But you know what? They say it with pride. Envy even. It's ridiculous."

Ernest officially puts Johannes on duty for the night and then promptly steps out to grab a bite to eat and pick up a few supplies that have run low. No customers have come in yet, so Johannes steps outside to check on the storm clouds. It still smells like rain, but the clouds have already moved along and stars have begun to decorate the stage. Johannes's eyes rove slowly through the sky, admiring the emerging stars, acknowledging the impending appearance of old friends, when his gaze falls upon the heavy, lustrous full moon, reddish and low to the horizon. It hangs above St. Josephine's, the steeple brought out in stark, unsettling contrast. Johannes is struck, held in awe by the bewitching sight, a beauty he has not yet seen in Creek's Ridge. He hears a noise inside the bar. Wondering if Grant might have gone in through the back, he is drawn away from the sky.

The piano is the only part of the bar that Ernest has neglected to clean, but that detracts nothing from its splendor. Its layer of dust evokes a royal shawl. Intricate carvings string along elegantly curved edges. The side panels are covered by further carvings that Johannes can't make out through the shadows and dust, but the skill involved in creating this woodwork cannot be mistaken. The key-guard is made from a different type of wood than the body, a lighter hue with a more delicate grain. Closer inspection reveals the tiniest, almost invisible etchings, one complete and flowing organic design that seems to bleed over the entire instrument, barely distinguishable from the grain of the wood.

If no one comes, then Ernest won't have an audience, and he won't play. But there are others all around the bar. The reflections, their glassy prying eyes, they follow Johannes. Straight ahead, he singles out and stares into a pair of those eyes. Before long, he's restless, uncertain whether it is truly him doing the staring and not the other way around. It requires effort to unlock his gaze, and the effort runs along his limbs, amplifying the aches from digging all day, every day.

He examines each one, determined to call out imposters. One of the Johanneses in the far corner stands out from the others, better lit and more sharply defined. He steps closer, intimate and peering at the other, critiquing, and when he's satisfied, he steps over to the next. In each mirror, he finds some minuscule imperfection until he comes to the mirror that's cracked and splintered in its entirety, smashed up in a single brutal round with a drunk and his instrument. He hears Grant's warning, *Bad luck, brother,* and he's paralyzed by the image's shocking forwardness. Its deformity poses no threats, yet he stares as one does at a disfigured child, incapable of pulling his gaze away, painfully acknowledging what the eyes of the world hold in store for the poor innocent. Drifting somewhere behind the cracks and chinks in the glass, the image stares back, boldly and unabashedly stating that no, they are not the same, that he is a different, distinct Johannes, untouchable and grateful not to share in this sorry life, to be cut off from the source. It laughs and glares in open disgust, not bothering to question the nature of itself, confident in its own existence, in the safety of its fractured world. Johannes loosens his focus, his vision blurs, and the webbed cracks create a network of glittery pinpoints and dead space, segregating the image into the hundreds of tiny puzzle pieces that contain it. The sound of footsteps suddenly thunders around him. The embedded fragments of mirror quiver to life, a rigid, cynical existence, each razor-like shard its own entity. If a sole shard is dislodged, will the lot crumble to the ground? Scatter invisibly on the floor, littering it with unseen dangers? Will the warped image remain, somewhere?

It used to happen, on the mountain, that an animal would sneak into his hut in the night, alarming him to wakefulness. Half-aware of a presence, he would not see or hear anything other than the pounding from his own chest. And he would stay like that, sunk in the darkness, waiting, listening for movement. Eventually, his fear would succumb to sleep. He would dream easy for the rest of the night and wake a few hours later feeling like a fool, a first-timer to the wilderness. But later, after he got up and started his day, he would find the evidence—a pile of shit in the corner or his food supply raided—exposing the supposed security of his shack for what it truly was.

Anything, even that rightful and acknowledged fear of shadowy intruders prowling around your bed in the night, even that is better than consorting with these strangers, these imposters in the mirrors. So Johannes decides to get away from the suffocating proximity of these walls of glass, their delusional illusion of space, and this congregation of others who may or may not be himself, who may be only accusations and demands. Instead, he'll step outside again, seek out true companionship in the vigilant eyes of the stars, the moon, the steeple, the flat and natural lay of the town. No obstructions, no mountains to climb, always the possibility to escape, should it come to that—true solitude.

Johannes turns around, heading for the door, and slams directly into a body.

"Watch it, pal."

"Excuse me...sorry I..."

"Where in the hell's Ernest?"

"Ernest is...he's out..."

"Well? Are you gonna get me a drink or what?"

―――

Ernest stands at the piano for a few moments before taking out a handkerchief to sweep the layer of dust onto the floor, disrobing its majesty. He lifts the key-guard and glides his fingers gently above the keys, the hesitant caressing of an old scar, facing down memories he would prefer to leave buried beneath the dust of years. A few regulars are spaced around the bar, men who've come in alone and begun their nightly meditations, meditations which, after a few hours, a few drinks, will bleed into each other, drawing out disagreements and forming factions, voices ratcheted up several notches and redundancies flowing like the booze that has brought them to this point—all a part of the reason they come night after night. And so, they are noticeably unnerved by Johannes's presence behind the bar, and they follow Ernest's cautious advance on the instrument with the uneasy curiosity of witnesses to a crime.

The piano sounds like hell. The strings are loose, all the notes at least a register lower than standard tuning. But the keys are in tune relative to themselves, and though Ernest grumbles to himself about the lowest C, D, F-sharp, and A, he takes the awkward tuning as given and adjusts his playing with the ease of a master.

He's only been playing for fifteen minutes—working through a few lounge classics and experimenting with key changes as he establishes his voice in the tuning—when Oscar Amondale walks through the door. Amondale doesn't notice anything out of the ordinary until he gets to the bar and looks up to find Johannes staring back at him. His gaze swivels mechanically around the room, and then, wide-eyed, he raises his hands to Johannes. He proceeds to bumble his way around the tables along the street-side wall as he struggles with the windows, throwing them open and shouting into the night air. He hurries outside, but within a few seconds he's ushering in a group of six with excited whispers, and then he's gone again. Curious groups and solos wander in, drawn off the street by music becoming more lively with each passing measure. For the next half hour, Amondale returns at sporadic intervals, always leading another group inside with the efficiency of an experienced tour guide. Before long, every seat in the place is occupied. People are crowded around the bar, filling the floor space between tables, lined along the walls, rubbing elbows with one another, toes tapping, heads bobbing.

Now, Ernest is really cruising along the keys, and Johannes can no longer focus on the unusual charge of visual and auditory stimuli. The human flood that Amondale has diverted inside keeps Johannes occupied. But Johannes is unaccustomed to this diversity, this variety of human sounds and human faces, not only surrounding him but cornering him, pitching for his attention. It's not like digging, where he can flail away at the dirt for hours on end and it's only more dirt that falls at his feet. He can't sift through the muck that's coming at him, can't arrange it into sensible emotions or react with common sense. Earlier, the hundred Johanneses had hounded him with their threatening silence. Then, he had felt some measure of control, or at least involvement. This is different. Although it's his job to serve and maintain order, he's swept up by the current. But the current is rising, lifting everyone inside to heights unseen. So nobody notices how he screws up their orders.

The bar serves slowly tonight, but no one complains. Johannes has the pages of a cocktail book spread open, consulting ingredients and proportions. New orders come from unknown directions and throw him off. Whiskey Sour, Tom Collins, Scotch and soda, OJ straight-up. He has no recollection of these drinks or their names. He's been drinking The Carnival exclusively, and free, at that. A man he's never met but whom he recognizes as George, the owner of the grocery, orders martinis. Charlie the postman sips shots of bourbon. Mindy, the part-time waitress at The Borderlands, is drinking gin and water. Alonzo, the blind elderly Native American, orders Old Fashioneds for himself and cola for the young man who helps to guide him around town. Greenah Taylor stirs the same Bloody Mary all night long, while Claire Young returns every thirty minutes for a new one. A short, older Asian man curiously examines the bottle of The Carnival, then orders a glass of The Macallan but appears to only sniff it the entire night. A road-weary couple names off several obscure liquors and cocktails, but they settle for draft beer in the end and go through it like water. A group of college-aged kids starts off with shots of tequila, their group growing a little larger and more rowdy with each trip to the bar. Whenever new people come in, Johannes glances out through the door. Sometimes he'll see the German shepherd hanging around out front, not leashed to anything but calmly waiting, or keeping watch, and getting attention from all who pass by on their way inside. Johannes can't shake the feeling that the dog is not on guard to protect those inside but rather to keep them there. He briefly considers making a run for it out the back entrance, but then he might run into Grant, who hasn't shown up yet, and he would only be dragged back into the dog's trap. Amondale occasionally steps behind the bar for another orange pop, cracking jokes and distracting Johannes from the dog and the growing chaos of his job. All the bottled beer looks the same. More than once, Johannes is sent back to the cooler to fetch the correct one. He draws a breath of relief each time someone shouts for draft beer until the keg has to be changed, which is when he finally calls on Amondale for help.

 The top-shelf Scotch whisky runs out near the end of Ernest's first set. Johannes searches through cabinets for another bottle, but people seem to sense that Ernest is waning toward a break. They're making their way back to the bar, waving Johannes down from every direction. When the music comes to an end, Ernest approaches, and Johannes asks what to do about the Scotch. Before Ernest can answer, they are accosted by the mob squeezing against the bar, bickering over stools, calling out orders. Ernest pours himself a drink, smiling and laughing with a boisterous group that keeps patting him on the back and throwing their arms around his shoulders. Every time Johannes looks his way, he's holding a bottle of The Carnival, toying with it, his fingers still working the keys, but he watches Johannes from the corner of his eye and eventually breaks free from the group. He takes an ice cube from the ice tub, rubs it across his forehead, then leans in close and whispers, "Carnival is an important festival, you know." As he backs away, he winks, and his hands mime a pouring motion. Someone waves to Ernest, so he slips out past Johannes, who's finishing up a round of rum and cokes. Johannes sets them on the bar and takes the bills from the young man. The kid is with a large group in the corner and somehow manages to lift all five glasses at once, nodding at Johannes to keep the change.

Voices rise and fall, tremors between one landslide and the next. Johannes gazes into the smoky bar and sees thousands of faces, reflections stretching to the limits of visual perception, foreboding in the dimness behind the mirrors. He hears a voice that sounds like it comes from everywhere, from the mirrors themselves, from the collective voice of that reflective realm.

"Try to enjoy the music," Ernest slaps him on the back. "Speaking of which, how about some tunes during the break? You remember how to work the record player? Or should I get Oscar to do it?"

"Of course I do," Johannes has to shout to be heard. "But what about that Scotch?"

"What? Any damn one. A whole stack of records over there. Take your pick."

Ernest is smiling and rosy-cheeked, happier than Johannes has ever seen him. An elderly black man in a dirty sports coat approaches the end of the bar. He shouts Ernest's name as loud as he can but barely makes a dent in the roar of the room. Johannes nods and gestures over Ernest's shoulder. Ernest lets out a whoop and embraces the man as a brother might.

Johannes flips through the records, his eyes watching through the mirrors as the people behind him call out their orders. He chooses one, sets the disc on the turntable, adjusts the needle, and turns the volume knob on the receiver until the speakers crackle. When he returns to the sink, his foot strikes something, knocking it over. On the floor are two bottles that weren't there a moment ago—the empty bottle of whisky he's been fretting over and an unopened bottle of The Carnival. He squats down, out of sight of prying eyes. At the end of the bar, Ernest nods along and smiles at his friend, but he's still watching Johannes. Now Johannes understands. Kneeling behind the bar, he opens The new Carnival and begins to pour it into The empty Macallan. While he's making the transfer, dribbling booze all over the floor, hidden from the throng and free to breathe easy for a moment, he shuts his eyes and listens to the music he has chosen. A symphonic record, a classical concerto, at once eerie and lively. The swirling string melody coils around him, implementing cohesion where Johannes had thought it impossible. His hands have steadied. The Carnival is empty now, and the empty bottle full again, but he is held stunted as a piano melody takes over the song—a lurching, hesitant waltz that doesn't last long, no more than half a minute, but completely arrests his attention.

As soon as it's finished, Johannes is released from his trance. He stands up and scans the room with eyes that have just been born, disconnected from all the pulsing activity around him, strangers both physical and reflected, as though his skin has clung tighter around his bones, leaving no worries about his skeleton's integrity. No spillage, no leaks. Contained and safe within this body, within this Self, as he has often felt at the extremes of meditation. Or while digging. The unimaginably beautiful transcendence of a spirit synced to its given vessel, balanced in harmony against the world outside.

Johannes places the empty Carnival into the crate and sets the refilled Macallan on the shelf, feeling a curious blend of satisfaction and guilt. Ernest is still standing with his friend, nodding as the man speaks but locked on Johannes with overt, almost prying concentration, the wonder and fascination of magic happening before his very eyes.

Several people stand huddled around the piano, pointing and commenting and admiring the carvings in the wood. The group drinking rum and cokes is playing some sort of drinking game that's drawn the interest of those around them. Laughter circulates from table to table, an amiable virus. Amondale is likewise circulating, listening in or latching onto every conversation in progress. None of the other Johanneses are visible in the mirrors. The festive throng has forced them out. People stand around the bar, talking with their neighbors. No one is in a hurry, giving Johannes this spare moment to himself. Ernest flicks his head to signal that somebody had better take care of the roadblock that's forming. Johannes nods and lifts the bottle he and Ernest have been sharing, taking a swift swig. A few of the patrons at the bar grimace, followed by a chorus of approving shouts. Now they clamor just to raise their glasses to Johannes, to clink off the new bartender's bottle.

Ernest takes the bottle, forcing Johannes back to work. Amondale has appeared out of nowhere to lend a hand washing the glasses stacked beside the sink. Johannes consults the book and measures out proportions with less concern for perfection. By Amondale's recommendation, and also for the sake of familiarity and comfort in this complex environment, he has started sampling each drink before sending them out. Ernest makes a lap around the room to greet his audience, and when he returns, he slaps Johannes and Amondale on their backs, says something that's lost to the noise of the crowd.

Then, Ernest shuts off the stereo, and everyone in the bar falls silent. A path opens for him. As he sits meditatively before his instrument, hushed voices quiver from every corner. The tension of anticipation causes the room itself to tremble. Johannes swears he can hear the mirrors vibrating against the walls, and the short piano melody from the record he chose is still spinning in his mind, reaching him from one of those worlds beyond the mirrors where it never stopped—trapped, eternal, repetitive reflections of itself echoing toward a climax that never comes. But then, as soon as Ernest's hands fall onto the keys, Johannes stops what he's doing and nearly drops the bottle of rum in his hand. He is spellbound by the sounds as they glide and drift and swell and swirl and synchronously link arms with the melody still resounding between his ears. Ernest is playing the same melody that had, just minutes ago, beguiled Johannes—here it is, burst forth from a glass house of reproductions, a reflection come to life.

The first set had been a basic repertoire of recognizable tunes, but now Ernest is inspired. After churning Johannes's melody through a series of variations for twenty minutes, he wanders into a catchy, rhythmic progression that coerces the entire room to stomp their feet in time. For an hour and a half, he flows seamlessly from theme to theme. He hurdles stylistic boundaries without hesitation and without warning, plunging from an obscure jazz standard into a slow blues romp while he whistles an accompanying melody, and then showing his concealed dexterity as he erupts into a virtuosic bombardment of notes. Delicately, he slides into a graceful, melancholic piece and calls on Greenah Taylor to help out with a soulful lyric before building into an avant-garde maze of dissonant chords that unite and culminate in a funky staccato groove. And always, like ghosts lurking somewhere within the music itself, there are the constant melodic suggestions and allusions to the same short melody that had hooked Johannes.

Johannes learns to perform his duties in stride, allowing his mind to absorb each note and melodic shift with narcotic satisfaction. He pours drinks and handles money as he gawks through gaps in the crowd just to catch a glimpse of Ernest's sweat-stained back. The customers have become like trees, sheltering and consistent, which, for Johannes, is more a comfort than a bother. At intermittent periods, either everyone has a drink or no one can wrest their attention from Ernest, which allows Johannes to not only listen but also contemplate the effect of the music. And he's drinking plenty of The Carnival himself, especially during these lonesome lapses when he becomes lost amidst the pathways of the mind, lassoed by the notes and strung along by their implications. Every thought and every breath heightened, ultra-sensitive, lifeblood circulating, propelled by a heartbeat, simultaneously pulled in and drawn away. To his surprise, he likes the feeling, the unsteadiness of it, uncertainty grabbing him, holding him by the shoulders and jerking him around, now sharp, now gentle, like a lover. Nothing like the music of the forest, where such volatility often meant life or death.

Another bottle of The Carnival, empty. Johannes drops it into the crate with the other empties. Ernest pounds on the keys, his ferocity steadily growing. Johannes pulls out another bottle, fills a glass with a handful of ice. The ice pops in the Scotch, and as he's taking a sip, he looks up to see Pa Sonny standing cross-armed beside the entrance. This is the first he's seen of Pa Sonny since the day they drove into Creek's Ridge from that diner, three weeks ago now, and he can't pull his eyes away from the man. Pa Sonny is watching Ernest like everyone else, but his face bears no expression, not even when he shifts his gaze toward Johannes and stares straight into Johannes's eyes.

Ernest lays out a final, ominous chord. The audience convulses with whistles, claps, stomping of floorboards, pounding on tables, drawing Johannes back toward the pianist for this finale. The loose strings rattle muddily, and Ernest allows the pitch to waver while he drops a couple sparse closing statements from the high octave, statements poignant enough to quell the crowd into silence, but only for a moment before they explode again, even wilder and more animated now.

Johannes glances toward the door just in time to see it swing closed and catch a glimpse through the windows as Pa Sonny walks away, highlighted against the dark street by light spilling from the bar.

The bar top and tables are a mess with empty glasses and bottles. People stand around, giddy and chatting as they watch Ernest stride back to the bar. Most everyone speaks in subdued voices, as though Ernest is still playing and they wish to maintain a modicum of etiquette. In another sense, however, it's deafening. Something about the stifled continuous drawl, the mirrors and their dizzying depth, the drone of cicadas, unseen and everywhere at the same time.

Before long, people begin to leave, content and satisfied with the unexpected twists and turns of the full moon. Midnight isn't far off, and the real drinkers breathe a collective sigh of relief that's felt more than heard. Those who remain attend to rearranging the tables and staking their claims. Ernest and Amondale scurry from table to table with wet rags, carrying perilously stacked towers of empty glasses and armfuls of beer bottles back to the bar. And they call for Johannes to snap out of it, to get out of his malingering drunken stupor and help them goddamnit—

But then they both notice the gorgeous woman standing across from him. So, for the moment, they leave him be.

Chapter 14

The Lullaby

March 9, 1817
St. Johns River, La Florida

LATE YESTERDAY AFTERNOON, WE WERE GRACED BY CLEAR SKIES AND a mighty sun after being hounded by storm clouds for several days. It was a mild storm, with nothing like the destruction of the tempest last autumn. Still, by the end of it, everything we possess other than our faith was thoroughly soaked. Having helped the Father move his belongings into the sunlight, I dumped out the contents of my satchel and spread my meager possessions about the ground. When I finished, I stretched myself atop the grass to warm my saturated skin. At once, the Father's shadow fell across me. He held up a dripping priest's habit and glared at me with an uncharacteristic sternness. At first, I did not recognize the garment as my own. Even though I had spread its sleeves over the grass just moments before, I assumed it must be his. "How did you come by this?" he asked.

I stared at it before recognizing my makeshift satchel for what it actually was. I told him that I had sometimes served as an acolyte in Madrid to earn food and avoid being chased from the church's covered promenade on wet Spanish nights—an ingenious and quick-witted untruth, one that might have sufficed for a dimmer man than Father Jimenez. But he was already showing me the name ornately stitched upon the inner breast pocket in golden thread—*Fr. Hector Ruiz Ruiz.*

With a bowed head, I explained my actions. It has been many

months since I first set out through the swamps with the Father, but not until that very moment did I fully realize how attached I have become to the man. I was prepared for the worst. Not for mere chastisement, but to be stripped of his friendship and driven from the village, as minor breaches of trust were generally resolved in Spain. To my surprise, this confession initiated a lengthy conversation on the state of my faith and my future aims for survival in this land.

Like me, Father Jimenez does not hold a favorable opinion of Ruiz Ruiz. His initial anger upon seeing his colleague's cloak arose from the assumption that I had stolen the habit as an act of simpleminded mischievousness, meant for no other reason than to aggrieve poor Ruiz Ruiz. He pointed out that less harmful pranks than that often result in the loss of life in these lawless lands. I raised the objection that we are still under Spanish governance and, therefore, Spanish law.

"My boy," he answered, somewhat cryptically, "we are a long way from Spain."

The Father's bearing returned to its usual lightheartedness as he spoke at length, intoning that he always knew I never intended to return to El Soldado Agraciado. Though I myself may not have known it at the time, I had merely been clumsily improvising a path toward my future survival. However, it will no longer serve me beneficially to falsify my past actions. Rather, I must learn to accept them and radiate the light of my true self to better illuminate the path I intend to tread forward.

The Father speaks in a calm, reflective manner, causing the most trivial matters to weigh heavily upon one's conscience, but he does so with a half-smile always shaping his lips and his eyes constantly roving about your face, which creates the impression that he means to lead you into an elaborate labyrinthine jest. Where serious matters are concerned, the Father expresses wonder and conjecture with the casual ease of a cloudless sky. Still, one cannot disregard the mortal urgency contained within his words. It is a contradictory way of speaking, which I believe the Father takes great delight in, and its effectiveness is undeniable. Only last week, he spoke to me for an hour about a particular species of songbird native to these swamps, and for the next two days and nights, I struggled with my thoughts on the substance of God as revealed through the natural world.

With the Seminoles, he employs the same tone as he does with me, but in their language. I often wonder whether they are similarly affected by the Father's talks, as well as how much he has been reshaped by their beliefs. I presume that a better understanding of their language and customs shall provide such answers. My capacity with their tongue has indeed progressed rapidly, though not nearly as quickly as their mastery of mine.

Following our conversation, I realized that Father Jimenez has developed a warm, paternal fondness for me, and he views it as his moral obligation to guide and educate me while he still has breath in his body. He has vowed to show me how to thrive and leave a memorable impression on the myriad people I am bound to encounter, whether I choose to don the stolen habit or not. I know of no way to express the gratitude I feel toward him. To have a father figure appear out of thin air is a truly religious experience.

———

May 20, 1817
St. Johns River, La Florida

The Father often speaks at length on the subject of his own death, with a detachment that seems better suited to a stranger's passing—or perhaps to the well-known death of Benedict XIII or Cervantes. And yet his choice of words on certain occasions suggests the moment itself is presently at hand.

At such times, I find myself unsettled in his presence. His insight and equanimity constantly hint at the unspeakable distance that separates us. Yet, I sometimes struggle with opposing feelings when not in his company. I experience an intense loss and longing, not simply for him but for those same qualities that repel me when he is near—his wisdom, his calm.

———

July 29, 1817
St. Johns River, La Florida

Time passes with the steady steps of a shepherd tending his sheep, knowledgeable of the hills he treads, surrounded by plentiful sustenance and crystal-clear streams, uneventful and serene, days and nights rolling one into the next. The shepherd sings as he wanders endlessly, but he is never lost, for he trusts in the stars he observes by night and the sun providing strength by day.

The pleasant days and cool nights have gone, replaced by a wet and sticky heat. A minor inconvenience that the Father says I will become accustomed to. I am grateful that it has not affected my sleep. Here, I have discovered what it means to wake fully rested. Even with the heat, I enjoy a deep, peaceful rest unlike any I have ever known. Each day, I accompany the Seminoles, aiding in their daily tasks. My ability to converse in their language continues to improve. Our days are now split evenly between the two languages. Curiously, I have noticed that the Father rarely uses Spanish with them anymore. We always return to the village before dusk and eat communally, talking and laughing and sharing all that we are fortunate to have. While we work during the day, and then again later, as the sun goes down, we sing their traditional songs, the swell of voices a lullaby that never subsides.

November 28, 1817
St. Johns River, La Florida

Before I rose this morning, a messenger rode in from San Agustín and left word from the governor requesting the presence of both Father Jimenez and our Chief at the soonest possible opportunity. Within the hour, they had departed astride our finest horses. I worry for the Father's health. His condition is no longer fit for strenuous riding.

Though I took the opportunity to sleep longer than usual, I eventually roused myself and was surprised to find the tribe gathering at the village center. The children played their games. The adults spoke of everyday matters while the traders attempted to communicate with a pair of Creeks who recently arrived from up north. They came to scout out new lands for their people, as they are fed up with the unjust treatment they receive in the United States. I greeted everyone, as is customary, and we spoke using both Spanish and their Seminole tongue. Now and then, I interrupted the kids' games with silly antics to break their concentration and start them laughing. The Seminole children are deadly serious when they play, competitive to the roots of their tiny souls.

Surprise struck me yet again when, at the designated hour, the tribespeople began to make their way toward our open-air chapel, and it became clear that they expected me to deliver the morning sermon. I protested and tried to disperse them. In light of the Father's absence, I recommended they continue their idle chatter and enjoy the cool morning breeze while it lasted. But they assured me that our morning services refresh them more than any idleness could do. The communal gathering cleanses the mind from the lunatic dreams and nightmares these humid nights give rise to, chastening their souls for another productive day. They also made it known that they were eager to hear me deliver my first sermon. When I asked what they meant by that—*My first?*—they elaborated, speaking of the Father's approaching death and my subsequently filling his role. I expressed my amusement at such an idea, though I could not help but notice the weight of their expressions. Questioning them further, I discovered that not only do they mean it, they are sure of it. They welcome it as a proper and fortunate circumstance, one they have already discussed and unanimously approved.

What followed, after a slight pause while I recovered from my astonishment, was an involved discussion, almost a debate between myself and the entire tribe, in which I laid out my insufficiencies as a purveyor of spiritual matters, and they refuted my claims with bold statements to the contrary. They do not deny my lack of training and experience as a priest, but they believe this lack reinforces my merits. What they really want, they explained, is for Father Jimenez to remain with them here on earth, though they concede that such an occurrence would be grossly unnatural. They have long been resigned to their eventual loss of the Father. In fact, they did not believe he would survive his trip to Spain.

Many priests have visited the village over the years, wandering missionaries who thread through the forests alone, going from settlement to settlement without friends or credence. The Seminoles view such men as vagabonds, runaways lost and out of touch, and consequently untrustworthy. Not one of those men ever displayed the balanced set of qualities that Father Jimenez possesses. Father Jimenez has never seemed quite like a Spaniard to them. In this sense, he has been an invaluable intermediary. His presence and role within the tribe has never stunk of hidden motives, the missions of an inflexible Christian God, or a covetous Spanish monarch. The Father has willingly and sincerely adapted to their culture. He has been the sturdiest tree in the forest during times of great change. He shares in their troubles with the grace of a still lake and offers advice with the reliability of the rising sun. He does not lean on his God for survival, nor does he insist upon conversions amongst the Seminoles. Of the priests they have encountered, too many approach with the aggression of soldiers hell-bent on victory, unleashing their scripture and dogma like a hail of arrows. Father Jimenez has never forced his God upon them, but he has also never abandoned his beliefs. This, to them, is the definition of manhood, the standard of sainthood, the meaning of life itself. While the Father was away in Spain, they decided they would never invite a less worthy priest or foreigner into the tribe. And so, what blessed providence! Not only had the Father returned to live out his final days with them, but he had also dragged in tow this gift out of the blue! This admirable young runt, worthy of their esteem!

At that moment, I realized that I was weaving my way through the others in the same manner as Father Jimenez does each morning, with every pair of eyes fixed on me. To end the debate, I reluctantly led them in the morning prayer. The tribe nodded with satisfaction, leaving me speechless—for it had not been a debate at all. I had engaged them in the very sermon they sought from the first.

The remainder of the day proved extremely pleasant. A refreshing breeze continued throughout the heat of the afternoon, during which I conducted our daily Spanish lessons. For the first lesson, intended as a Bible study, I took the liberty of substituting Cervantes and was amused to learn from the students that Father Jimenez often does the same. The later lessons, for traders, are much more demanding. They proceeded along the usual track until I began to question them about complex terms in the Seminole tongue, to which they happily obliged my curiosity by taking over the lessons for the day.

For me, at least, the matter of my permanence remains unresolved. While the thought of remaining with the tribe for many years to come looms as an appealing option, I do not envision myself capable of the immense influence that Father Jimenez has attained. Nor would I wish to mistreat his legacy with my bungling lapses in judgment. I have much to learn. As a result of today's talks, however, I have obtained a clearer understanding of their spiritual lives. And I am infinitely grateful to know that these pure and wonderful people value my presence amongst them.

December 2, 1817
St. Johns River, La Florida

In these past fifteen months, I have hardly had time to reflect on the life I left behind. The Seminoles express little interest in my distant homeland, and the Father rarely speaks nostalgically, especially not of Spain. But in my private moments, I have dealt with the doubts of a self-imposed exile. The questions and possibilities are endless, and I have been too cowardly to confront them directly. Only now, with my future in New Spain beginning to unfurl before me, can I assess those doubts in all justness to myself. Although my role here remains to be seen, I am secure with the knowledge that my choice to abandon the relative comforts of El Soldado Agraciado, though decided in haste, was not decided in vain.

Chapter 15

Mirrors

"Hi, could I get a..."

At its simplest, life consists of two distinct types of experience. Most are instantly identifiable, merely repetitions or derivations of experiences one has been through before. But then there is the bafflingly new, the unexpected, those rare events that require concentration and energy just to come to grips with. Most of what defines people as individuals is how they handle this latter type.

"Can I just get a..."

The piano bench is empty, has been for some time, so Johannes is trying to work out where exactly the music is coming from, if indeed it's coming at all. He keeps sipping away at The Carnival and squinting at the instrument because this shouldn't be a difficult riddle to solve, and maybe The Carnival can help, as it has helped to settle his mind and settle him into life here, forgetting and remembering, at times fending off the nightmares, drawing a thin veil over the persistent visions of the storm and the landslide, at other times exacerbating them.

"Hello...?"

The very same melody, a record chosen by his own hands and then transitioned seamlessly into endless variations, Ernest's bottomless reservoir. It's not coming from the record player, either. These notes are full-bodied, pure as a songbird's song. People are hunched over their tables, conspiring with one another or with their drinks of choice, speaking in low tones. Not another soul appears to notice this sublime intrusion of music. Perhaps someone—this woman, for example—perhaps she is humming the melody, somehow lilting her voice densely and precisely without opening her mouth. Had Johannes not wished that Ernest would keep on playing the melody for hours and hours? Forever? When riddles seem unsolvable, sometimes it's best to simply give in and join hands with the impossible, to accept the loss and enjoy the mystery.

So, Johannes resigns himself, lets the music take him if it wants him, and follows the notes, their graceful meanderings, peaceful promises, and sly hints. Lost and carefree, the illusive melody wraps him safely inside this loving touch, ascending and descending a mountain with the effortless ease of feathers on the wind, caressed and kissed by each and every note.

"Hey...excuse me...?"

The woman taps her empty glass against the bar again. She's wearing a long, yellow sundress, its vividness standing out against the dark auburn hair falling down her shoulders. Her smile is turning impatient, her stare insistent.

Ernest approaches, observing this one-sided interaction while Johannes stands stiff with a glass in one hand and a bottle of The Carnival in the other. Ernest takes the bottle without rousing a reaction. The woman watches and then wordlessly appeals to Ernest for an explanation. He shrugs and pours himself a glassful before filling hers.

"What's wrong with him?" she asks. They're both watching Johannes now, intrigued and hesitant to break the spell.

"Very strange," states Ernest, taking small but continuous sips, making up for time lost at the helm of his instrument. "Ahh, well, I suppose I should've expected something like this."

"I'm sorry, but...are you, by any chance, Ernest Hemingway?" She sniffs the contents of her glass and winces. "The writer?"

Ernest nods without taking his eyes off Johannes.

"So this is your bar? What about him?" she says, pointing at Johannes. "He's new here?"

"Yes...well...fairly. I mean, no..." Ernest's brow furrows, and he shakes his head slightly. "Something like that. He's new everywhere, really."

"A foreigner?" She hazards a taste from her glass.

"What? No, no..."

"What's wrong with him then?"

"Very strange..." Ernest, now stricken with a similar malady.

"This whole town is strange." The woman slides a five-dollar bill across the bar. "For the drink," she says.

Ernest looks up, uncomprehending. He only snaps out of it when she waves the bill in front of his nose. "Oh, no," he laughs. "This one's on me. And what I meant was just, well, it's so odd, him not recognizing such a beautiful woman on the doorstep—seeking his attention, no less!"

"That's kind of you," she says, almost defensively. She scrutinizes Ernest, but he's drawn to Johannes and doesn't notice. "He seemed fine earlier," she adds. "Responsive, at least."

"Did he? Yes, well, we'll see...of course, he hasn't been the same since..."

"Since what?"

"Since it happened."

"What happened?"

"You'd have to ask him about that," Ernest shrugs and looks around, returning to life once more as he examines the space behind the bar. "But good luck with that. Everything looks to be in order back here. Seems to have done a decent job of it. Could use a lesson in washing up. You say he hasn't been like this all night? You've been here this whole time?"

"I caught most of your performance, and he seemed fine, for the most part. A little shaken up by something, I suppose. The drink he made me was...a bit strong. Is he drunk?"

"Could be, could be... Doesn't really matter, as long as the money's all here."

"Look. He's swaying."

"So he is..." Ernest leans in close. Soon, he matches Johannes's movements, a consistent, rhythmic rocking. "He's swaying in time. It worked. I did it... He's discovered music..."

The woman takes a step back to watch them both. "You're right. He's dancing."

Ernest's face lights up. He belts out something like a war cry, and everyone in the bar looks their way. Then, Ernest grabs Johannes and spins him around, propelling the glass out of Johannes's hand and sailing through the air toward the mirrors behind the bar—

Glass and melody, both are wrenched viciously away, a cruel sense of loss trampling down, as once the landslide did, and the glass's trajectory leads directly into itself. There's nowhere else it can possibly go but to meet its own mirror image—the laws of physics, or some would say of destiny, deem it so. The arching path dips sharply downward just before the collision, then they meet and burst, glass raining down and a complex array of cracks leaping to life across the mirror, as though they've been there all along, just lying in wait for the signal to manifest.

The dance has ended, its beginning indistinguishable from its end. Bar chatter ceases. Shocked eyes take over—whites showing, pupils erratic, blink blink blink, questions formed and retracted, all these silent pinballs.

"That's it," someone remarks through the silence. "Can't take this a moment longer. Get me the hell off this wagon."

"Bad luck, brother..." says another.

The precise moment of impact lingers, a glass explosion billowing outward, Spinoza's death cloud eternal. Shards lie spread across the ground behind the bar. Johannes picks up the thick base of the glass, intact but jagged and sharp around the edges. He stands to meet yet another distorted image peering from beyond the glistening web, wondering who this monstrosity might be—it can't be, no, it's not him—as he cuts his thumb handling the glass. Blood drips along his palm and splatters the shards below.

Subdued bar talk resumes in spurts. Curious eyes flit across the room.

"Goddamnit," Ernest's rage spikes before rapidly petering out. "Every time I touch that instrument..."

"Where has it gone?" murmurs Johannes.

The woman finally takes a seat at the bar. She's drinking her Scotch and watching the disheartened pair. Her silent smile bounces from Ernest to Johannes and back, a reflection trapped, until she catches sight of the gorgeous, shimmering light, likewise trapped in the newly cracked mirror.

Grant and Amondale saunter over, Grant sidling up close beside the woman. She glances at him and says, "Reminds me of one of Beckett's plays."

"Who?"

"Samuel Beckett. The playwright?"

Grant smirks, but Amondale staggers back at the suggestion, staring her down. Grant reaches for the bottle of The Carnival, looks it over with disgust, and then slides it toward Amondale.

"A beer, please, Ern." Grant turns to the woman. "I don't know about that, but bad tidings are definitely on their way now, if they weren't already. Although, I have to admit...it would be a lot of fun..."

"What would?" wonders the woman.

"Smashing the rest of these hideous mirrors. Destruction, pure and simple. Cathartic, chaotic, swallowing whatever bad fortune comes our way in the end. Can't escape it anyhow, so we might as well take part. I say we do it, all of us, right here, right now. Make this place a lot more welcoming. If we do it ourselves, there'll be less room for misfortune to surprise us with our pants down."

"I'm afraid our sheriff wouldn't know who Sam Beckett is, miss," says Amondale.

"Touch a single mirror and I'll haul your ass out into the street," Ernest holds a beer over the counter. "I don't give a damn if you're the sheriff or the president."

Grant laughs as he takes the bottle and turns to the woman. "Did you ask him? What I told you to ask? The great American writer..."

"I did," she says, rifling through her purse.

"And?"

"Not even a reaction. Nothing. Kind of disappointing, in fact. But he's just finished his little concert, so..."

"Little?" spits Amondale.

The woman pulls out a pack of cigarettes, removes one, and uses it to point at Johannes and the mirror. "And then this happened."

"Figures," says Grant.

Johannes looks up, startled at the sight of Grant. He holds out his hand as the slow, steady drips of blood splatter to the floor. Ernest offers a rag to staunch the bleeding, but Johannes is staring at Grant. "Where have you been?"

Grant wrenches the cap off his beer.

"Missed the whole performance," says Amondale. "Missed out again. The bastard just walked in, slipping in through the back like the prowler he is. No one even saw him arrive."

"Maybe I never did."

"A ghost amongst the living."

"Duty calls," Grant shrugs, sips his beer. "While you all waste away in here, the town out there keeps breathing. I'm responsible for it."

"But everyone's here," says Johannes, though when he looks around the bar, he realizes that most everyone has already left. "Then where's your uniform?"

"Stopped at home," Grant, with a scowl. "Just a citizen tonight..."

The woman is watching them, the unlit cigarette clamped between her teeth. "This just keeps getting better," she says. "Any of you men have a light? Sheriff Citizen?"

Grant shakes his head.

"What exactly is so humorous, little lady?" Ernest produces a book of matches from behind the bar and hands them over. He points at the broken mirror. "You know, this is partly your fault. I'm inclined to send you a bill for damages."

"Glad to contribute," she says, lighting her cigarette. "I've been on the road for a month, and this is the first place that's promised any worthwhile distraction. I was starting to lose hope, thinking of just heading home, but... Your playing was lovely, by the way." She slowly exhales a lungful of smoke that remains suspended over the bar. "You've convinced me to stick around. I'm willing to give your little town a chance."

"And the music wins out again," says Amondale. "The nail in the ol' coffin. Look at this, she's embarrassing the rusty old jazzman."

Ernest glares at Amondale, but a smirk cracks through, his cheeks still flushed red.

Other than hushed whispers from the tables still occupied, the bar has grown quiet. Amondale leans his elbows on the bar, tapping out an itinerant rhythm and shifting on his feet. Johannes slowly pulls the rag away from his hand and examines his sliced thumb. Grant watches the woman as Ernest finishes emptying out an ashtray for her. Johannes moves toward the sink to rinse the wound. Smoke from the woman's cigarette settles above their heads.

"You all haven't been introduced," Grant suddenly bellows. "Ern, this young runaway who flatters you so goes by the name of Caryn Pridieux. Miss Caryn Pridieux. That's Caryn with a *Y*, mind you."

"Parents were illiterates?" says Amondale.

"Ain't nothing wrong with a *Y*," rebuts Ernest. "She can spell her name how she wants."

Johannes looks up and follows their gazes to the woman seated across from him. He stares at her for a few seconds before returning his attention to his thumb.

"Ma'am," Grant lays his hand on her shoulder, "this here is the bar's owner and renowned author, Ernest Hemingway."

"Don't you start with that nonsense, boy. Not tonight."

"How many times have I told you, Sheriff?" she says. "My name, it's kuh-*rinn*."

"Kuh-*rinn Pree*-dyew," Amondale lets the name roll off his tongue. "Caryn Pridieux, Caryn Pridieux. I like it, after all. Fantastic name—a lovely stretch in the cheeks. French names can be touch or go. Knew a man once, name of François Beauvais. A barrel-flying prick, if you ask me, but he could hook any fish in the North American sea, heh heh, with that accent *sensuel*..."

"French," Ernest nods approvingly.

"French?" Grant leans over her, scrutinizing her face.

"French?" says Johannes. "That melody, Ernest—it was French?"

"The melody?"

"...known to balance several women at a time, but he liked exotic women best..."

"And I am not a runaway." Caryn peers through the smoke. "I'm too old to be running."

"Shit," says Grant, "John here has been running his entire adult life. Never too old to flee the scene."

"Look at us fools, bothering this poor girl," Ernest grunts. "She graces us with her presence, laughs along at our folly, and here we are picking apart her personal affairs. Never mind it all. Mademoiselle, to your health." Ernest tops off her glass and raises his.

"...violent though, it came out on certain occasions when I drank with him, ridiculous fits of jealousy and fists a'swinging..."

"Nope," says Grant as he finishes examining her. "She's not French. Divorcee, I'd say. One of the many." He winks in response to her cold, accusatory stare, then holds up his hands. "Myself included. We're all in it together, babe."

"Watch it, Sheriff," she says.

"Call me Grant, will you?"

"I don't think so."

"...years ago, university days, then he went back to Paris for a term, apparently befriended the *philosophés* that were in vogue at the time..."

"Mademoiselle Pridieux," Ernest wraps his arm around Johannes and draws him near, "I'd like you to meet our latent bartender, Johannes Metternich." Ernest turns to Johannes, speaking firmly, "Johannes, this lovely young woman was desperately trying to get your attention while you were supposedly tending my bar, and you looked straight through her without an acknowledging glance. She ain't no spit-shine window. This is the finest stained glass. Perhaps you could meet her now? And throw in an apology for good measure."

"Please don't...don't call me mademoiselle..."

"Ernest, that song—it was French?"

"Ah damn, have I mixed it up? Madame, is it?"

"...met Sartre one time and got into it with him, like everybody else..."

"It's not that. Your sheriff is correct, I'm afraid." Caryn stares at the ashtray after smothering her cigarette. "My ex-husband, he's French-Canadian. From Montreal. But I assure you, I'm pure-blooded American. More so than any of you."

"Her driver's license is two months gone," blurts Grant.

"Gone?" says Ernest.

"It's expired," answers Caryn.

"Sure sign of a runner," Grant nods.

"I'm not running."

"She's not French," continues Grant. "She's from California."

"Hold it—you two know each other?" asks Ernest.

"I pulled her over this evening. She came cruising into town at fifty-seven miles per hour. License and plates both Golden State."

"You never drive slower than seventy," says Johannes, although he's gazing off into the mirrors.

"Reckless driving. There were kids playing..." Grant looks away into far corners of the bar, his gaze similarly swallowed up by reflections.

"...had ambitions of becoming a writer, but it was all hack stuff, he couldn't string a sensible run of words together to save his life, not on paper..."

"What are you running from?" Johannes slips gracelessly out of his reverie.

"I said I'm not running."

"Leave her alone, John," Grant laughs. "She's on the lam. I didn't even call in to run her registration. The car's probably stolen. I know you aren't used to women and all, but don't get involved with this type. Advice from the learned. You should see this hunk of metal, John. Brand new. Very West Coast drug trade kind of ride."

Caryn attempts to maintain her composure and stiff glare, but her grin gradually cracks. Laughter takes over and her limbs relax.

"...a Lennonesque bastard, I always said, heh, never saw him again after that, heh heh heh..." Amondale's eyes come floating out from the mirrors as he finishes his story. The others all stare at him.

"What in the hell are you talking about?" says Grant.

Amondale smiles at Grant and then at each of the others in turn. "Theo, my friend," he slaps the counter, "four cubes of ice drowned in that sweet, sweet Carnival, if you don't mind."

"The Carnival?" Ernest is stunned. "You're drinking again? Scotch? Thank Christ..." He swallows a gulp himself before grabbing a glass for Amondale.

"That mirror right there," Grant points with his beer bottle, "you two maniacs tossed Oscar right off his seat and into the swamp with the rest of us derelicts. I'm telling you, bad luck is afoot."

Ernest fills a glass with ice. Amondale feigns a coughing fit. Ernest looks up to see Amondale holding up four fingers, so he dumps out the ice, pours the Scotch, and drops in four new cubes.

Amondale takes a sip at once and then noisily sucks a mouthful of air through pursed lips. "*Aiiee! Muito bonita!* Mr. Piano Man, this silence isn't right. It's unnerving. Kindly give us the suave tones of that Chico Buarque. *Brasilia, Brasilia!*" Amondale's face is lax with an uncharacteristic ease that is not at all compatible with his heightened bombast.

"You'll have to go downstairs and look for it, Oscar. I retired that record when you quit drinking."

"Blast it all," Amondale pounds on the counter, but the grin splitting his face betrays his pleasure as he bounces toward the cellar door, glass in hand.

A series of meager thuds resounds at long intervals, but no one can tell where they're coming from. Johannes gazes at the broken glass. Ernest stands erect and searches the room for the source of the noise. Grant shrugs and sips his beer. Eventually, Caryn gets up and follows the sound to the entrance.

"Was it French?" Johannes demands.

"No," says Ernest. "She said she's divorced."

"Not her. The melody. The one you kept repeating, your second set..."

"That? You don't remember it? But you have to. I'm certain. I figured it out...you helped...you chose it yourself..."

"Certain of what? Chose what?"

Caryn holds the door open as a motorized wheelchair rolls in, conveying a shrunken elderly gentleman. The man stares straight ahead and demonstrates no thanks to Caryn. A waft of wind and dust follows him in.

"Oh shit," mutters Ernest. He pats Johannes on the shoulder. "Later. I'll have to show you later..."

The old man wheels himself up to the bar and comes to rest behind Grant, who has become absorbed in his thoughts. With imperceptible movements of his fingers upon the controls, the man moves his chair erratically forward and back as he searches for a place to park it. The malcontent carved into the man's face tells of a long, draining life that has taken its toll and left him paralyzingly apathetic. Ernest has maintained an uncomfortable smile the whole time, and only after the old man grumbles at him does he finally run out from behind the bar to rearrange the barstools. The chair buzzes as the man wheels it backward three feet and then swings it up to the far end of the bar. He removes his tattered fedora to reveal a head of perfectly set, thin white hair and hangs the hat from his machine's handle.

"Your finest bourbon, Hemmings." The man's voice is low, slow, and commanding. Ernest encourages the man to take up one of the recently vacated tables, indicating the height of the bar, but the old man will have none of it, and he drinks his first shot off at once. Ernest offers him the bottle, but he refuses, offended, and demands Ernest's full attention. Ernest moves around the bar and takes the stool beside the man, refilling both shot glasses. They're already deep into intimate conversation, their voices concealed from the others. Wheels turn, events take shape, all veiled by a smoky shroud. Ernest bears his usual contented grin, though he's constantly peering sideways, seeking to avoid eavesdroppers. The elder doesn't make eye contact with anyone, not even with Ernest. He has a cynical, lazy expression, one that assumes superiority over Ernest, over the bar, over the town, over the whole damn planet.

Johannes's thumb is bleeding again because he has just unwittingly pulled back the flap of skin. He can't stop himself from touching the incision, not too deep, but just deep enough. The wound on his palm is nearly healed, having left behind a spectacular scar. As he applies pressure to his thumb, unwelcome memories begin to clot, and soon the scar is pulsating. Shutting his eyes, he sees not the black of eyelids but rather—

The landslide is focused, directed at him. He can sense it as he watches, as he cowers against Knecht's great trunk. He is marked, and as he reflects on this, on everything he is, on everything he has lost, he enters a deep, unwilled, meditative state. A void surrounds him, voices within and without, this, a technique he has perfected over many long hours here on the mountain, hours spent feeling out the intricacies and loopholes of his internal terrain, but it has never been this complete, this suffocating. There is no peace here, with one hand bleeding, weak, the other shredded by the tree's bark as he clings on for dear life. He can see neither his hands nor the trunk, though he feels them with intense sensitivity as a wide pit gapes inside of him, its cracks leaking caustic fluid, a reeking, toxic sludge, the congealed remains of his life, of his soul, all that's leftover of something he hid away when he came to the mountain, though he can't identify it anymore. This could be death, it's possible that he did not avoid that mass of earth as it came rumbling, groaning down the mountainside, and for the briefest flicker of a moment there's a sense of relief. But as that moment bends and stretches, his relief becomes indistinguishable from the pain. The pain is alive, encapsulating his entire being. If this is death, then it is incomplete. This death requires action to bring about finality, but it is too much to ask as the void comes crashing down, a swarm of bats hunting in the twilight, the colorless pieces of a united organic entity in jagged, mesmerizing paths, introducing hints of the glowering moonlight behind. Though they dance ever outward, they appear to be bursting upon him, and then they have gone. Finally, a return to his physical self. Once again, pelted by needle-like raindrops. Cold, dripping, bloody, and now homeless, overrun by physical pain and despair, wanting only to throw himself into the river, to follow his home cascading down the mountainside, buried and lost and forgotten, but for this obstruction standing in his way—it is he alone, he himself.

With sleep in his eyes, Grant swirls his beer bottle around like a toy. The woman, Caryn, stirs her drink religiously to melt the ice, water it down, mellow the taste. Her gaze roves about the bar, her interest proudly on display, now and then stealing glances toward Johannes and the others. Talk from the tables is constant but wavering, as though riding in upon winds from a great distance. Ernest and his friend share silent words and unspeakable ideas while Ernest leans forward on the barstool, hanging precariously above the old man and nodding along, wrinkling his brow at regular conversational intervals.

Smoke hovers around Johannes's face, creeps into his nostrils. Caryn offers him a cigarette. She holds it out in front of him, and he looks into her beautiful but dark and strangely cavernous eyes, then around the bar. He's mistrustful of everything and everyone. Next to Caryn, Grant sips his beer. An indistinct sound wafts up from the cellar. Ernest and his immobile friend lift their wrists to clink their shot glasses yet again. Healthy, full-bodied laughter swells at one table, shouting and pounding at another. Excited voices spout their individual nonsense. An endless, reflective repetition all around. Each event emerges separate, distinct from the rest yet bound together, these walls of glass.

Amondale emerges from the cellar, breathing asthmatically and huffing enormous gulps of air. Still, he somehow manages to whistle an off-key melody as he readies the record player. Laughter rises and falls from this corner and that. Jostling at one of the tables evolves into a loving struggle. A bear-like man lights a cigar, his face an advertisement for bliss as a thick cloud plumes around his face, spreading into a gray sheen across an entire row of tables. The middle-aged woman sitting next to him watches with repugnance while her younger, more attractive companion looks on with admiration. Grant has said something to Caryn, and she's answering him, though he seems uninterested in her reply. Sleep has extended beyond his eyes, his lids puffed up, and his complexion gone pale.

The crackle of the record precedes a gently strummed guitar, accompanied by a soothing male tenor crooning in Portuguese. Soon, the soft, steady rhythm of percussion joins in. Music settles over the room like a blanket, collecting the various bits of life occurring independently of one another and imparting cohesion, breadth, and form—the illusion, perhaps, of meaning.

"Don't think so hard, Jack," Amondale wraps an arm around Johannes. "It's all in the body." His breath reeks of The Carnival and honest joviality.

"Sorry?" says Johannes. "What?"

Caryn is still holding out the cigarette. Johannes takes it from her, looks it over, and lets her light it for him. He inhales, exhales, watches as the smoke mingles with the smoke from Caryn's mouth.

"You a smoker, Johnson?" Amondale's hips sway left to right to left. "Never would've guessed it." He pulls Johannes close, trying to conduce participation. Caryn smiles, encouraging them, and Grant seems to be actively ignoring the scene. Amondale gives up, exchanges Johannes for the new bottle of The Carnival that he brought up from the cellar, and refills his glass after swapping out the ice, four cubes. He eyes Caryn as he pours, "How about you? A quick samba? If you can move at all, you'll be better than this block of wood," nudging Johannes.

Caryn stands up without even answering. She and Amondale swivel past Ernest and his friend into the narrow floor space beside the bar. Johannes and Grant both watch as they try to get started.

Johannes leans toward Grant. "Why didn't you tell me?"

"Tell you what?" says Grant, glaring at the reflections of Amondale and Caryn.

"About Ernest."

"What? What about him?"

"About his playing. He's incredible. You really missed something special tonight."

"I don't...I never thought about it. It's not something that's talked about around here. The way he likes it, I think."

"Yeah..." Johannes refills his glass with The Carnival and offers to pour a glass for Grant, who recoils at the mere thought of it. "What took you so long?"

"Huh?"

"What took so long? Getting here?"

"I stopped by the house. To change and shower."

"Tonight? But you missed the whole performance."

Grant stares at Johannes, shakes his head, and then looks away again. "I've seen it before," he says as he focuses on the samba dancers.

Caryn and Amondale each dance their own type of samba. They have begun to give each other pointers, advice, critiques. They're laughing, nodding, accepting suggestions, and trying out their partner's techniques until, eventually, they realize there's no fun in this analytical deconstruction of the samba. Caryn returns to her barstool. Worked to a fervor by alcohol and dance, Amondale continues with furious albeit stiff steps, a dumb grin spread wide below his glistening mustache and The Carnival spilling over the rim of his glass.

"So, is your name John or Johannes?" Caryn leans forward so she can speak without shouting over the music.

John, just a whisper at first, *John*, an echo, *John*, and he recognizes it instinctively, this single pronunciation stretched out indefinitely and acquiring a fullness, *John*, the murky thickness of many voices, *John*, of all the voices he's ever known combined into one overbearing chorus, *John,* a boozy voice, softly critical and sharply cynical, suggesting loneliness as a key, *John,* the non-voice of hermits and monks in cogitation, *John,* a voice commanding, ordering, telling him what to do, how to remember what is true, *John,* a voice beckoning him home, wondering where he's gone, *John,* the voices of children shouting, their harmless games and their noise, *John,* a voice asking why, why, *John,* voice of the landslide calling him out of hiding, *John,* another voice resounding on its own, distinguishing itself from the flock, renouncing the others, renouncing—

This common name, it's just not you. What would make you ignore your given name all these years? Some trauma as a boy? Well, what then? Your true name fits so much better—it is you. How about this, Johannes the Curious Drifter? Johannes the Solitary Soul? Johannes the Lonely Wanderer? Yeah, that's it. What do you think? A name that implies secrets, tight lips, selfish ambition. Believe me. Trust me. You're not alone anymore, and you don't have to wander. You'll stay. We'll kill him together. Once and for all. Chase him out tonight, and that'll be the end of it, forever. We will, we'll end it now, and then start again on our own. Where else have you to go? Back to him? No. Tight lips, secrets. Remember? So let's do it, let's get rid of him. And of John, too. Both of them, forever. Turn out the lights...and keep humming...please...that beautiful melody...but get off the floor...come back to bed...Johannes...Johannes...

The voice is as real as the repetitious notes he's been hearing on and off all night, as sweet and resplendent as the waterfall directing him home, as intimate and tempting as Eve in all her supposed purity, but faceless, nameless, without form.

Johannes spins around and meets only himself in the mirrors. He catches sight of Caryn through the cracks, and she returns a thoughtful, fractured smirk. Johannes glances at Grant. Caryn follows his eyes.

Grant drowsily examines his beer between mouthfuls.

"It's Johannes." He feels heat on his fingertips and quickly smothers the butt.

"Don't let this pretentious little shit fool you, Ms. Pridieux," Grant intrudes. "I've known him all my life and never once called him by that name. We've called him John since—"

"We who?" Caryn interrupts.

"We, us, everyone. Except for—" Grant cuts himself short, staring at Johannes with something like fury. "There have been a select few who insisted, despite...everything. Our old, drunken pastor, for one. But way back when we were just idiot kids, his family, my family, every kid in the neighborhood, every teacher at every goddamn school. In those days, he insisted upon it. Wouldn't let us mention his real name." Grant produces a lurching nostalgic chuckle as his eyes glaze over with the past. "Whenever someone used to call him by his full given name, he would lash out as if he'd been attacked. The first day of middle school was a sight to see. Imagine it, coming into this new world, a new teacher every hour of the day, each and every one of them fucking up his name without fail because that's what the paperwork says. And then the realization slowly sinking in that that's how it's going to be for the rest of his goddamn life. By the end of that first week, he was a grouchy, nervous wreck. We could smell the tension and defiance built up inside of him. All because of the stupidity of the teachers who couldn't get his goddamn name right or his parents' lack of foresight, giving him one name and then chickening out to call him by another. The stupidity of God for such a crooked, mismatched life. John, John...and now, with him like this, refusing to remember anything...without me... Without me, he really is just some John Doe. That's all. Nothing more."

Johannes's eyes rove around their sockets like those of a child comprehending the world's dark secrets for the first time. Reverberations of that infinite voice echo still, a lone feminine whisper, his false name, his true name, though he doesn't have any recollection either way, the things Grant is relating, a maze and a dream.

"Now that I think of it," Grant says, "that was the first time he ever ran away, a week into middle school. First of many. Only three days in the woods, that time. Nearly killed his folks with worry. But, somehow, we all knew he'd just gone off to be alone. It wasn't that surprising, even then."

Caryn searches Johannes's doubtful expression as she finishes her Scotch. She looks at Grant, about to speak, but only nods toward Ernest.

Grant's lingering smile turns grim. "Ernest barely knows him."

"So, you two aren't from here?"

"Nobody's from Creek's Ridge. You haven't picked up on that yet? So you see, you fit right in."

The slow drone of Ernest and the old man continues, backed by the chants of a call-and-response pulsing from the speakers. Amondale's feet pound on the floor in the corner. Vibrations run along the bar top, jingling the ice in empty glasses. Grant tilts his beer bottle vertically above his mouth, lets the final drops trickle in, and then slides the bottle across to Johannes.

"Look," Grant says to Caryn, "I don't give a shit what you call him. Ernest is just as much a pretentious bastard as John is. Same shitty taste in music and booze and everything." He reaches over the bar and grasps Johannes's shoulder with brotherly compassion. "And for all I know, hell, you seem like a showy type of woman yourself. You know, just call him whatever you damn well please. Call him Barry or Larry or Constantine the founder of Roman Christianity for all I care. You call him whatever you want, and I will call him John, just as I always have. Because that's what he is, and there's nothing he can do, nothing any goddamn mountain or natural disaster can do that will change who he is to me. There is history to compete with. Thirty-some-odd years of friendship and collusion, of adventures and fuck-ups, all right here," tapping on his forehead. "Those sorts of memories don't just up and vanish. That takes effort, stubbornness, constipation of the brain. And I still don't understand why anyone would want to do that. He'll never make me understand. Hopeless. He's John. He's hopeless. And I'm exhausted. I'm going to bed."

Grant starts to walk away but stops and half-turns. "You found the motel? No problems?"

Caryn nods. "Got a room before I came here."

Grant gives them each a final heavy look before disappearing into the back passage. Caryn slouches onto her arms and toys with her glass. Johannes reaches for the bottle to refill her, but she waves him off. The sound of something falling and breaking comes from the back, followed by a grating sound just before the door slams.

"Why doesn't he use the main entrance?" she asks.

"Superstition?" Johannes shrugs. "Entry and exit through back doors and windows exclusively."

"Is that true?"

"I'm living at his house. See it every day, with my own eyes."

"I meant all that stuff he said. About you."

"We're old friends. I trust him." He tops off his own glass and then twists the bottle in his hands. Mysterious and illegible, the words of the label spin past like freight containers transporting questionable loads to far-off destinations.

"You don't seem very certain."

"It's...cloudy."

"I see. Well, anyhow, I like Johannes better. It suits you. But I can understand his point."

Johannes nods, looks up. "What would you know about names?"

They share a smile, and Caryn's lips crack with stunted laughter.

"My mother's doing, not my own," she says. "Except my mother stuck by her decision. Lots of people call me Karen. It doesn't bother me. They don't know any better."

The record hisses in the silence between songs. Johannes avoids Caryn's eyes. He feels exposed, unprotected. A male harmony gently lifts them to a more delicate height. In the corner, Amondale has calmed down and stands still, staring into the mirrors and talking to himself. The reflected Amondale has bright, youthful excitement in his eyes as he shouts, "*Câlice!*" with his eyes swiveling across the bar in secret. Dual vocalists begin, repeating the word, *Câlice, Câlice*. Before long, a guitar joins, subtle and melancholy. A few more of the late-night stragglers stumble out. It has reached that crucial crux of the night when the world's progress seems to have halted, when one can only lie back to wonder and wait for the morrow.

"I always wondered about places like this..." starts Caryn. "How people wind up here, and why. There must be so many interesting stories."

Johannes gazes into his glass. "I'm sure there are."

"But I mean, don't you want to know? Why here? This town, of all places? It's so cut off from everything."

"Is that bad?"

"Not at all. I just mean, well, like you. How did you end up here?"

"That's something I've been asking myself ever since I arrived."

"And still no idea? I don't buy that." Caryn reaches for her cigarettes.

"How about you?"

"I was just passing through..." She puts one between her lips but can't find the matches.

"On the way to where?"

"Not to where, but to what. I'm searching," she says as she looks through her bag, beneath the ashtray and napkins, on the floor beside her barstool.

"Maybe that's what we're all doing," says Johannes. "Searching for our own things in our own ways. But there's something about this place that stalls the search. Or makes people feel that the end is near."

"The end? Death?"

"End of the search. Or else they're the same thing. The search just continues on and on, until one day..."

"It stops."

"Maybe that's not so bad."

"Where were you before?"

"At home."

"Where is home?"

"The mountains..." Johannes sees his shack, built with his own hands and sweat, manicured every spring, winterized every autumn. Cozy, sturdy, and perfect—the comfort and solitude of home. Knecht is nearby, casting its cool shade, its leaves trembling in the breeze. Above, the stars and their chatter come out by night. "It was...in the mountains."

"Mountains, huh? That's it?"

"I miss it."

"Is everyone else so reluctant to tell their stories? Explains why everybody seems so lonely, I guess."

"Lonely..."

"Have you seen the matches?"

"I wouldn't call it that." Johannes hands her a new book of matches. "I might say the same about you, though."

"Sure, you could. I know I look it. But I also know what I am."

"What are you?"

"Fed up with people."

"So that's what you're running from..."

"That's not what I meant," she shakes her head, her smile laden with sadness and longing as she lights her cigarette. "I want to be near people, close to them, emotionally. I want the chance to really get to know the people around me. In most places, there's no longer intimacy. It's no longer possible. There comes a point when you stop knowing people and know only types of people. Like being part of a machine. A component. I couldn't live that way anymore. Life shouldn't be that complicated. Figuring people out, guessing, decoding who is who and what is what. The industry I was in was destroying me from the inside. But an interesting, unique night like tonight has been—this is why I left." Her face lights up as she points at the pile of shattered glass behind Johannes. "I'm not running from people. I'm running toward them."

"How will you know when you've found it?"

"Patience, awareness. I'm not in a hurry. I was planning to settle in the mountains, too, actually. Spent a few weeks hanging around small communities in Colorado. Drove down through Arizona and New Mexico. I'd heard rumors of Creek's Ridge but never gave it much thought until I found myself driving through it, the sheriff on my tail. What do you know of its history?"

"Not much."

"The prophet? The Spaniard?"

Johannes shakes his head. "I've heard people talk, but that's about it."

"How about the Saint? The church is named after her, isn't it? It's a gorgeous building."

"Never been there."

"There's little curiosity in you."

"There used to be. I may have spent it all in the mountains. Or lost it."

"You see, I love stories like that. Most people do. And what little I know about this town fascinates me. The noble nature of it all. The bravery to take something you believe in and implement it into the breathing world, to really, truly leave your mark."

"You seem to know a lot for a newcomer."

"I've been talking with the people here all night," Caryn laughs. "The prophet and the Spaniard wandered and tripped along their separate paths through life, only to unite and create a refuge for others like them. A perimeter of safety and certainty in uncertain times. A bond amongst the people that no other place could provide. All sprung from the seeds of ideas. Collectivism, generosity, love. That's true freedom."

"Until the Native Americans came through to crush it all?"

"From what I understand, the raids were essential. An unfortunate but necessary bridge connecting the past to the future. Allowing the Saint to become who she would become and validate the founder's original vision." Caryn places her hand on Johannes's and lets it rest there a moment, her eyes bright with wonder, but something else is hidden there, too. "Now, tell me, what happened to you? I can see it was something big. Something important. That look you've had in your eyes all night...you're lost here, aren't you?"

"Tonight, I heard music as if for the first time. But it sounded... almost like voices, or memories...or both."

"What did the sheriff mean? About...what? A natural disaster?"

Shadowy, sympathetic horns and strings blare an enigmatic climax expounding Brazilian misfortunes. Johannes shifts his weight, longing for a chair or a bed—no, no more beds, no more sofas.

"Yes, a disaster. At the time, I didn't believe it was natural. I thought it was personal. That's why I came here, like you, searching for something, for answers. But that was only because I didn't know where else to go. There was a notion, or more like instinct, that Grant could help me figure things out. Now, I'm not so sure. Possibly. I'm glad he's still here. But, in a way, it has only made things more difficult. Sometimes, I think I should have kept moving. Stayed on the road or stayed in the mountains. Either way, I'd probably be dead by now. A nomad, hiking from one disaster to the next. How else could it end?"

"So why don't you? Keep moving, I mean." Her arm brushes against his as she reaches to put out her cigarette. "You can take my car if you want. Drive it out to LA and then bring it back after the place chews you up and shows you nothing. It won't take long."

"Something is holding me here. In part, it's Grant and this project we've begun. And, some unnamable languid charm that seeps in and makes the passing of time feel like it's worth something. Or, maybe you're right. Maybe it's the people, their loneliness and their stories. The town's history, or even just the landscape. All this space is certainly freeing. Something of a relief after the mountains. You can get lost here, but maybe that's okay. Let the kids roam free and they always find their way back home. But the breadth and beauty of the Smoky Mountains... it never ends. Sometimes that can be suffocating."

"The Great Smokies? I've never been. I'd like to..."

"Living there..." Johannes shakes his head. "It requires extraordinary strength and willpower to stay put, to ignore the way it both encroaches in on you and seductively beckons you out at all times. And if you remain strong, staunch, and secure, then you become a king. And as a king, you eventually become worthless. Invisible. The so-called king that's trapped in his own castle while his kingdom continues beyond the reach of his influence. In what sense, then, is he really a king? And actually, that might be why I went there in the first place. Ultimate solitude. Out of reach. But Grant's right. It doesn't make sense. Who would imagine that to be healthy or beneficial in any way? I wasn't out of reach. We never are. An illusion, a deception fed back to us, the mirror of the self. Better to hide in plain sight. Maybe not here, in the bar, but in Creek's Ridge. There's something about life here that makes things not matter so much. No pressing weight with each rising and setting of the sun. Lives can just coast along, perhaps as they're supposed to. This is where people come to inhabit their own skin after everything else has failed them. It's where people come to die in peace. But maybe it's actually where we should have come first. Maybe it's not about dying in peace but living in it, alone and together at the same time. Grant had it right. I should have listened to him from the beginning. Or to Pa Sonny..."

"Your father?"

"Not exactly."

"So, alright, and then what? Allow yourself to get lost in a long, protracted death? Is that really any better?"

"But that's what all of life is. Here, if I get lost, I can always find my way back to death. In the mountains, it sometimes felt as if I could get lost for longer—longer than the span of a lifetime. And I almost did. Here, there's an invisible hold, something to show me the way. Seems that way, at least. That's a reassuring feeling."

"This is a place not just to be shared but embraced together. That's the peace I felt about this town the moment I passed by that church, when the sheriff pulled me over for no reason other than to talk to me.

All that macho stuff—he was faking it for you boys, I guess. He was a sweetheart. Didn't write me a ticket, just introduced himself and invited me into town. And then, checking into the motel and dinner at that diner. I love the diner's name. The Borderlands. So charming. And finally, the entire night here at the bar. What's the name of the bar?"

"I don't..." Johannes thinks it over and then looks at Ernest. "Hey, Ern? What's the name of the bar? Ern?"

Amondale pauses his dance and glares at Ernest, still huddled over the old man. "The bar's got no name," Amondale shouts. "Reasons unknown, even to those in the know. Used to be called Jo's. Jo's Last Stand. Perfectly good name if you ask me..."

"You see?" says Caryn, satisfied by Amondale's answer. "I feel like I'll wake up tomorrow and this will all have been a dream. I hope it's not because I'm already looking forward to getting to know everyone better and learning more about the founder and the frontier days. The Community of Man, I think, wasn't it?"

"Yeah, I think so. I've heard that..."

"Created to be a kind of commune, or paradise."

"I wonder what went wrong..."

"Wrong?" Caryn laughs. "Maybe nothing went wrong. Maybe this is exactly what he envisioned. What about you?"

"What?"

"The project you mentioned."

"What about it?"

"I love interesting projects as much as interesting stories. What is it?"

"It's nothing."

"I see. But I can count on you not leaving overnight?"

"I didn't say that. Everything I've said might be wrong. You and I both, everyone here, we could all be forcibly ejected at any moment. An ending that just pops up out of nowhere, sealing you off from something beautiful. No more continuity, no more value. An end, even if you're not ready for it. That's the one thing I remember. At times, necessity is fierce. Fear and uncertainty creep up and sink their teeth in without warning. Same thing that brought both of us here, I assume."

"Do you really believe that?"

Johannes nods, then shrugs.

"You don't want to tell me what happened to you, and that's okay. But whatever it was, it brought you here, into the arms of people. And I hope that you'll be able to tell me someday. I look forward to it."

"With people, I feel further from myself than ever. It's not the me I know. It won't last. You place too much hope in the potential of intimacy. Sometimes it's better to tear it all down and start over. And sometimes you have to do it again and again, forever."

"Perhaps..." Caryn drifts momentarily, trapped and wandering the strange foggy corollary worlds behind the mirrors, imposters and replicas alike. "But other people are mirrors into the soul. We use them as we use these mirrors to check our hair and cover our blemishes. That's the only way to see inward. To truly discover yourself."

A subtle glow peeks through the frosted windows. A cloud of smoke hangs near the ceiling, filtering the yellow lights above into a soft brown and gray luminance that stretches into the mirrors' infinite expanse, perpetuating a delusive lightheadedness compounded by fatigue.

Caryn has long since gone back to her motel room. Amondale must have left, too. No one else around but Ernest and the old man in the electric wheelchair, still conversing with the subdued voices of criminals. Johannes wobbles on his feet to the accompaniment of glass crunching beneath his shoes. He looks at the floor, his mind and body both begging for sleep. The floor is covered in a fresh layer of sticky spilled alcohol, tiny glimmering fragments of broken glass and broken mirror that he missed with his hasty sweeping.

He senses the stream's constant gurgle, a song that lulled him gently off to sleep and woke him each morning, the caresses of a lover, but he can no longer remember what it sounded like. He only hears the crash of the rapids, the rush of the torrent.

Voices twist through a hazy past, the confused present, a reflective future, forever on display. As a final thought, an asterisk on the night, the coming morning, the last articulation of desire, Johannes decides that this time he will sleep on the floor...

"It's been a mighty pleasure...hope you...stop by again...before you're gone..."

No, not on the sofa anymore. No comfort there, no rest. Only sore muscles, a crooked back, terror on repeat, and repeat, and repeat...

"Nonsense...think about stocking some decent bourbon...come winter...more from the heart of the matter...others involved...the heart of the matter...must stay informed...be careful...things can fall apart... don't always drive the track straight...the heart of the matter...you'll see..."

From now on, it'll be on the cold, hard ground...

"Almost forgot...great friend...here, wait, but where's he gone?...an inspiration...be careful, watch your...sent from above...let me get that for you...come again...must have left...just, just, this way, yes...or gone to the john...yes, okay, okay, yes...this way...come again...yes, good night, Mr. Wilms...and thanks again...always..."

If he can just get back...

"Johannes...? Johannes...?"

Listlessly, Johannes fades into a dreamscape where all that exists is sound, beautiful weeping sounds reflected off mirrors, the simple sibylline voice of the stream singing its hushed song, forgotten days, forgotten faces, forgotten places wiped sheer from the face of the earth...

He must find the faceless...

John...John...

Nothing alive now but the music, a sprinkling array of notes dancing through the darkness, strings wafting round and round, these vagrant angels wrapping him in silken waves, the silk moist and clinging to his skin, drawing out his essence as drizzling melodic droplets pelt him, merge with him, fill him heavy, sponge-like, and vaporous horns float in from a distance inconceivable, surrounding him on all sides, vibrations like miniature landslides preparing him for sacrifice to the altar of sleep. He must lie down. The floor...dig...in the ground. Make amends. Protect himself, and the mountain. Grab hold...hear and see...through to...the nameless...

Johannes...Johannes...

Here it is again, just before he drifts off, the melody Ernest stole from the record and played, played, played, repetitive and never-ending, played, played, Johannes suckling off its simple splendor, the Babe sucking at the Virgin's chafed nipples, all over Oedipal and cringing from his heretical insanity, trying to re-enter the womb in which he was once safeguarded from the world, from his God, from himself.

Chapter 16

Paradise

The Great Spirit, Mishe Moneto, conceived the universe, the stars, and the earth. Many distinct races of people were spread across the earth, but they were not allowed to tread upon the land—not until they proved their worthiness to the Great Spirit. The land was reserved solely for the animals, beasts of all kinds nesting and raising their young, foraging for food, hunting and being hunted, free to roam and mate with all the ignorant purity of their species' humble existence. Men and women lived at sea, floating atop giant sea creatures that protected them and kept them separate from other tribes. The Shawnees lived on the back of an enormous turtle. The Creeks lived on the mountainous back of a giant alligator. The Iroquois, a frog. The Cherokees, a duck that occasionally took flight. The Potawatomis, a beaver. Dark-skinned folk rode on the back of a whale. And white men resided on the slick scales of a water snake.

For thousands of years, people of all races drifted around the oceans, eating only fish and sea-fowl and drinking only rainwater. They knew nothing other than the kindness of their kinsmen and the generosity of their animal guides. Sometimes, when conditions at sea were right, fortune shone upon them, allowing them hazy glimpses of distant stationary lands rising impossibly high above the sea and lush with colorful plant life. Lands that contained everything men could ever desire, where men could settle and not be ferried on an endless voyage. Lands where life itself diversified and thrived as a result of its own elegant and complex functions. Paradise.

"Paradise indeed," the Great Turtle once told its inhabitants, the Shawnees.

The Great Turtle had never spoken to the Shawnees before and did not speak again for hundreds of years after that. Over time, those words became nothing more than a myth.

So it was, until one day, when the Shawnees noticed one of their old women sitting atop the Great Turtle's head, precariously leaning and bobbing with the waves. She appeared to be talking to someone, but no one else was out there with her. They were certain she would fall off and be lost at sea. The strongest and most courageous men were called forth to journey off the shell and along the Turtle's long neck so they could lead the old woman back to safety. However, no man amongst them was brave enough to climb down from the shell. So they waited and watched for many days, knowing she must eventually fall asleep and tumble into open water. But even in stormy waters, she never lost her balance, and she never ceased nodding her head as though she were engrossed in conversation. It was assumed that she had lost her senses. Finally, the day came, with the entire Shawnee Nation congregated along the forward rim of the Great Turtle's shell and watching her, that the old woman leaned down to kiss the Turtle between the eyes. She then stood and walked the long, treacherous path back along the Turtle's neck. When she reached them, she called for help mounting the shell, and all the men rushed forward to help her. Her name was Kokumthena.

As the oldest living Shawnee, Kokumthena alone remembered the last time the Great Turtle had spoken to them, and she had often pondered the meaning of those words—*Paradise indeed*. She explained to the others that she too had been afraid of descending onto the neck and of slipping into the water, but that she had also become weary of the sea, that she had no reason to distrust the Great Turtle, and that she thought it likely that the Turtle was just as lonely as she was. Kokumthena was of an old generation that had long since died off, so she had been largely ignored by the younger Shawnees.

She told how she had walked out along the neck, the Great Turtle sometimes twisting its head around to glance at her but never addressing her. When she reached its head, she had trouble catching her breath, not because of the trek from the shell, which had actually been quite pleasant, but because the view from there was different somehow —startling and astonishing. In all her many years, it was the first time she had gotten a sense of just how fast they cruised over the water and of the immense peril the sea imposed. It was a terrifying position to occupy, standing there alone with only the fear of death as a companion. But it was also thrilling and inspiring. It was life-affirming and also the perfect finale. She was overcome with both sadness and envy for the Great Turtle's vantage.

Kokumthena greeted the Turtle and sat down. The Turtle responded at once.

"Hello," it said.

"Why do you not speak to us anymore?" she asked.

The Turtle told her that the Shawnees had not said anything important in many years and that it only spoke when there was something worth saying.

"It is a great distance from here to my shell," added the Turtle. "I prefer not to shout. It is much easier to converse when you are here with me. But no one has ever come before. You are the first."

They spoke intimately for many days, getting to know each other and enjoying the rare company. After Kokumthena had become comfortable in the presence of the great animal and the great ocean, when the fear of death had lifted like a fog, then she asked the Turtle about paradise.

Kokumthena spoke to her people, repeating everything the Great Turtle had told her—that those distant, luscious lands were rich with useful materials and generous beyond the most fertile stretches of fishing waters; that there were certain unpredictable dangers, but there were also the means for continuous warmth and shelter; that their enormity and their dramatic landscapes dwarfed even the most virile bouts of imagination; that they were home to an infinite array of beasts and creatures and critters in every shape, size, and color; that they produced copious food and collected water enough not merely for the Shawnee Nation, but for all of mankind; that, in fact, those lands had been created for the use of mankind. They were the Great Spirit's masterpiece. And yes, other people like them floated around the oceans on their own gigantic swimming animals. Some were similar to the Shawnees, while others were very different. Some were noble and honest, like the Shawnees, others cruel and deceptive. And even though the Great Spirit created those stationary lands for men, man had yet to set foot upon them. As the Great Spirit's masterpiece, those lands were not to be despoiled. When Kokumthena expressed her desire to make landfall, to be the first to set her feet on solid ground, the Great Turtle told her, "Yes, you may do so, but it is not easy."

"Will you not take us there?" she asked.

"It is forbidden," said the Great Turtle. "Man must earn his place in that wilderness by proving his purity, his strength of spirit, and his respect for all the Great Spirit's creations."

"How may I prove this?" asked Kokumthena.

"You must swim to shore," responded the Great Turtle.

"But that is impossible," said Kokumthena as she gaped around her at the endless sea.

"And not just you," continued the Great Turtle. "It must be all Shawnees. Together. If you go alone, you will die at sea. If one of you stays behind, then you will all perish. You must all work together. And we, too, must work together. You cannot complete the journey without my assistance. You must trust in me completely. And know this—should you make it safely to land, I too will be allowed to retreat to my paradise below the sea, for all eternity. You can never return to my shell."

By the time Kokumthena finished relating the Great Turtle's words, the Shawnees were staring out to sea, sick with fear and nausea.

It took many more years and many more discussions, but eventually, Kokumthena convinced a few others to venture out upon the Turtle's neck so they could speak with the Great Turtle themselves. As the number of Shawnees who placed their trust in Kokumthena and the Great Turtle grew, so did the quantity and variety of stories they created about paradise.

One day, the gathered Shawnees, carrying their children on their backs, came to Kokumthena. They gazed out at the water, no longer nauseous and afraid but hopeful and optimistic. And they said, "Grandmother, we too are weary of life at sea. We believe in you, and we trust in the Great Turtle. We are prepared to swim to paradise."

Kokumthena smiled. She reminded them that if even one amongst them harbored secret reservations, then they would all drown at sea. Even if their intentions were sincere—every single one of them—some would not survive the journey. One by one, they vowed the sincerity of their desires, their loyalty to her, their love for the Great Turtle, and their humility before the Great Spirit.

The following morning, they entered the water. It was cold, the waves were taller than three men standing on top of one another, there was no current, and the distant lands were but ghostly silhouettes on the horizon. Kokumthena called out encouragements and promises for the future. Women swam with their small children on their backs or held out in front of them. The strongest men held on to elders who were too weak to swim. They swam for many hours. Still, their destination rested on the distant horizon, no closer than when they had begun. Sharks appeared and started pulling some of them below the surface, staining the sea with their blood. Others were caught under freak waves and dragged deep below the water.

While the Shawnees watched their friends and relatives disappearing beneath the waves, they suddenly felt a change. They were being propelled forward by a strong current, a current so strong that it flattened the waves, so swift that a few moments rest for their limbs would not break their momentum. Their destination grew in size as they came nearer. It stepped out from the spectral realm of dreams and obtained the opaque textures of reality. Someone glanced back and saw the Great Turtle still floating behind them and whipping its tail in the water to create the current that carried them toward the land. Word of this spread throughout the Shawnee Nation, and they looked back to see the Great Turtle's enormous tail rising above the water and splashing down with boundless force again and again and again. They cheered and cried from happiness. They forgot their sore muscles and their doubts. They channeled all their energy and thoughts into their limbs, swimming all the harder.

When they reached land, they fell upon the beach, laughing and running their fingers through the sand. They stood and practiced walking on solid ground. They raised their hands to the sky to thank the Great Spirit. They hugged each other, all of them bellowing with joy. They searched for Kokumthena, but no one seemed to be able to find her. Some of them worried that she had been lost to the sea, but those who had swum alongside her spoke up, insisting that she had been whispering encouragements right up to the shoreline. They searched further inland, up and down the beach. They shouted her name but received no response. Finally, someone spotted a lone swimmer far out at sea. "It is her," said another, "it is our Grandmother, Kokumthena." But she was swimming against the current, fighting the waves, paddling her way back toward the Great Turtle. The entire Shawnee Nation gathered at the water's edge. As the frothy surf sprayed around their ankles, their feet sank into the wet sand. They stood there for a long time, watching her become smaller, wondering what she was doing. When Kokumthena had swum so far that she appeared to them as no more than a speck, the Turtle disappeared below the waves, then slowly rose again, lifting Kokumthena up from beneath. The Shawnees were breathless. She was as small as a single grain of sand, but they could see her clearly all the same. She raised her arm and waved. Then, she walked along the shell and out along the entire length of the Great Turtle's tail, just as she had once walked along its neck. When she reached the end, she did not stop. She plunged into the water, holding on to the tip of the tail as the Great Turtle dove into the depths, never to resurface.

Chapter 17

Repetition

Neighbor, my limbs, massive and sturdy as they are, quiver in these gusts, yet that owl flits downstream, don't you see it? Following the river's bends and curves, graceful as an angel sent to counsel you in this time of need. Can't you see?

Johannes...Johannes...turn out the light...

Neighbor, the mountain has finished its work, but it is not yet settled, not content, still it grumbles now and again. Do you hear it?

Johannes...Johannes...hum for me...that melody...

Man of Flesh, just as all men of worth lie down to dream come nightfall, I embark to herd the oxen that spin the earth round. And though each night must come to an end, a new night always settles again. I alone, your friend, Boötes the herdsman, am charged with this task, to maintain the balance of day and night, giving rise to life and death for all creatures, plants and animals, united, as one, dependent upon the surety of my step, the regularity of my pace, the fixity of my gaze...

Johannes...Johannes...I know it's hot...just open the window...but get off the floor...and lie with me...

My Mortal Brother, as you must know, a woman's pearl is both a gift and a curse from the gods...

Neighbor, rain and river combine to form a compelling couple. A chaos of motion surrounds us in this generally tranquil glade, your home for some time, and mine. I have lost more than a few leaves this day. A hearty number of wooden friends as well. The ground is soiled with debris and tears, our Mother's and yours. I have drunk my fill. Hydrated beyond content. In league with the gluttons, perhaps. That owl, now perched upon my longest branch, suffers none from the storm, the wind, the crumbling of the mountain ridge. But she is curious about you. Watching, wondering why. The man is a little worse for wear, she says to me. A trace of concern. And also disapproval. Disgust, I sense. Don't you understand yet, young protégé?

Man of Flesh, the agèd ones placed me heavenward in honor and recognition of my perseverance, my patience, my determination, my faith. The stasis of your world is fixed, at once temporal and timeless. From time immemorial, the giant staff of the agèd ones—piercing the heart of the earth north-to-south, through the chilled and fiery wilds where no men tread—has held your world steady on its course amidst the chaos and desolation of the unknown realms...

Johannes...your humming...it's grown on me so...that melody...a bittersweet dream...just like you and me...just turn out the light...keep humming...but get off the floor and come back to bed...come back to me...

My Mortal Brother, I, too, have loved. I, Orion, son of Poseidon, Oh! How I have loved and lusted a thousand beautiful maidens! Woman, she sets our souls aflame. Her sweet musk draws the animal from us, sets us on the hunt. Possession, ownership, we want. To strike with our bronze club, the force of our manhood, the drip of her blood, to father our godly sons and daughters, pride of our conquered bride and fruit of our sticky mingled loins. But I am no stranger to defeat and loss, time and again, for daring to touch what never was mine. For failing to restrain my desires, drunken on wine and lifted by lust...

Neighbor, the owl has taken flight again, straight and steady as a ray of light, and she has implored me to speak with you, to be blunt—no, wait, don't do that, I advise against it, do not attempt to follow the bird, do not watch her any longer than is appropriate—Ouch! That must have hurt. I would apologize for the exposure of my roots, but I was trying to warn you, advising you, at the moment, to stay put. Our lessons of these seven short years, have they been washed out, too? By these rains? Blown away in the wind? Crushed and taken into the river along with that little wooden structure where you slept? Is that where you kept your thoughts, your dreams, your memories, your intellect? I am afraid I must admit, I do not understand how men live...

Man of Flesh, your rightful place is right there, where you are, amidst Her lush mid-regions. Sow your seed in Her, your Mother Earth, Her green overgrowth, Her flowers, the birds that sing to you and the bees that pollinate Her continued growth. Flora and fauna of innumerable designs, colors, shapes, and sizes, all twisting and twining with Her pleasured, lustrous, erotic sighs. Each night, whisper into Her ear, inhale Her perspiration, drink the sweet juices dripping from Her flowing spring of life, sow your seed upon Her flower...

Johannes...they're only dreams...nightmares...the heat...whatever... they won't harm you...it's not his voice you heard...I promise you...he's not here...far away, God-knows-where...gone from my life...or from ours, if you want...same as John is gone from you now...far away from us...far and forever...we sent him off...killed him together...please remember...

My Mortal Brother, each night I rise with one thought upon my mind, or rather seven—seven thoughts begging, pleading, calling, demanding that I follow, that I take them in my stride. Those seven lovely, graceful, coy, and teasing sisters, the Pleiades, offering themselves to my every whim and manly desire. I rise and move upon them, answering their Sirens' wails. But they run, hidden and protected within the shadow of the bull of the north, offering me only glimpses and visions of skin, their undress reserved for Taurus, each of the seven riding astride that great horned beast into orgasmic midnight heights and laughing back over their bared shoulders at my pathetic chase...

Neighbor, you should not have chased that bird. Always better, I have found in my many years, to stay put. Everything you need, you have right there inside yourself. Sit still. Focus. Search. Your hand, incidentally, is bleeding quite badly. I recommend staunching the wound. A tourniquet, perhaps. Oh dear, look at the ground—your blood—it is everywhere. I suppose I'll have to drink that as well...

Why, then, Man of Flesh, do you strive so to reach beyond? When you have held Her in your grasp? When you hear Her still, Her mounting cries of lust, acceptance, approval, and love? Why chance to traverse the empty loneliness of a timeless mist in which nothing ahead nor behind can reach out to touch your hallowed flesh?

John...John...John is gone...that name is dead...that's not you...never was...who told you you were not you...don't think about it...that name or that man...he's gone, and now you are who you're supposed to be... Johannes...Johannes...we got rid of John...and of him too...the other one...the moment we laid down, embraced, we chased him out...sent him packing...killed him with our screams...our howls of passion...your melody...no one else but you and me...Johannes and I...come now...back to me...we'll chase him out again and again...we've done nothing wrong...nothing but take what we want for ourselves...come back to bed...

And later, My Mortal Brother, I found my sweet princess, my one true love. Oh, fair Merope! Never have I loved another as I love her still. My guilt is built as high and solid as your mountain, my young human friend, for I failed her. I failed myself. My strength, my will, my moral compass clouded and hazy with Dionysus' spirits...

Neighbor, since you cannot see, you must know that night has fallen. This is the pitch black of a stormy, cloud-covered night. The moon and the stars, your friends, will not reveal themselves in this light, but they speak to you still. I know you can hear them. I can, too. True friends always speak with honesty and force enough to shred away the shrouds that sometimes fall to veil one from another, to separate and discomfit, to throw men, such as yourself, off the mindful path. The voices of friends will never fail. But are they reliable? That, perhaps, is a different story. Confirmation falls to you, your judgment, your will, your resilience, your strength...

Man of Flesh, the place you seek is for us, not for you. It is meant for we who have already fought our battles, struggled with loss and troubles, worked the earth and been one amongst its creatures, loved and been loved, admitted our faults and transgressions, accepted our rightful prizes, cherished our gifts of fortune, and laughed over our own graceless folly...

Johannes...what more can you ask...what more can you want...

My Mortal Brother! How I tried to woo her! How I strove to bring her honorably and faithfully into my bed! To make her love me. I hunted and killed the finest beasts for her, brought her the most luxurious pelts and furs, the strongest leathers, bone-work made for queens. Bears and mountain cats, majestically antlered deer, fearless boar with tusks of granite, exotic beasts from wild shores unseen, lizards and reptilian monsters, precious ivories and priceless horns, feathers plucked from the most majestic and illusive birds, the succulent untainted flesh of rare and unknown fish...

Neighbor, wrap your arms around me, hold on tight, the only corporeal friend you have here—don't you understand yet? Feed off my stability, absorb it while they speak to you, telling you what you need to hear in this perilous moment, this trial of trials. I see all that is inside you, your flimsy mortality and mental strength waning, the force of the mountain having hollowed out a void within, the cavity of this loss, and now you too are beginning to cave in, little by little, but just enough...

Man of Flesh, should you succeed upon the earth, should you leave a worthy mark, the reward is only more responsibility. You have got it wrong. There is no reprieve, no escape, only the loneliness of the gods. Trust me, what you seek is something else entirely...

But she would not have me! She rejected me, scorned me, abhorred me! With elegant ease and bountiful freedom, she strolled the sumptuous hills and forests of her father's kingdom, the island of Chios, destined one day to be hers. With eyes for none but her, swaying and unsteady from her father's famous casks, I set myself to task. I resolved to taste her sweetest fruit by force, to take what I desired for my own...

Admittedly, I am not alone in driving the oxen. Were it not for my loyal hounds, I could not coerce—night after night, until the end of time itself—the oxen to start, to struggle, to bite down on their bits and pull upon the reins attached to the staff that the agèd ones left. Asterion and Chara! My little star! My joy! My loves!

I followed her until I caught her alone, undefended, and I groped and drooled, licked and pawed, called her names—my love, sweet thing, bitch, strumpet, star of my eye, my angel, my whore—Oh, to have had her for my own! I might have been a happy man. But, drunken as I was, I failed to pierce her maidenhead, failed even to raise my manhood aloft, though I did not fail to raise her father's spite and ire. And I, Orion, son of Poseidon, expert hunter blessed to walk upon water, was blinded when her bastard father, the King Oenopion, took my eyes!

It's dark...I can't see...where are you...where did you go...hum for me again...that melody you always bring...but get up...get off the floor...open the window and let in the breeze...God knows it's hot tonight...get off the floor...no...I'll join you there...cooler down below...then later we'll come back to bed...or stay right where we are...on the floor...but please remember...and don't leave...

Good God, Neighbor, am I glad I do not share in your mortal lot...

Man of Flesh, you have been, during your habitation of this mountain, a pleasant companion with whom to pass the time. I have heard your moans of discontent, shared your awe at nature's torment, and watched as you have slipped away from what you are. You are temporary, merely passing through. You know this now, but this is no reason to hasten the end of your sojourn, to disregard the gifts or the time you have left. You are but a fleeting memory of the forest, a bursting bubble upon the sea, a single falling raindrop in this torrent...

My Mortal Brother, with a servant guide to lead me—Hephaestus's pity, his charity to the blind—I traveled to the east, where Helios rose and blessed me, returning to me my ability to appreciate all things that contain beauty. Fortuitously, he bestowed upon me my sight, my life, my love for the hunt. But, finally, it was the Huntress herself, Artemis, and her sultry mother Leto who would undo me...

Johannes...the Lonely Wanderer...yes...I like that one best...but you're not alone...not anymore...you don't have to be...and neither do I...your wandering days are done...he doesn't deserve what we have...never did...he doesn't need you...not like I do...stay here...stay with me...

in the morning...you can cook again...for me...by my side...always...
maybe as it was meant to be...as it always should have been...

Neighbor, these friends of yours from above, from within, they speak sense, do they not? Just as I, in these seven short mortal years, have tried to converse with you, to guide you, to strengthen and balance your infirm steps. Providing shade beneath which you might contemplate. Offering fallen limbs as strong as granite for your own mysterious projects. My acorns have filled your belly when animal prey was scarce or when your hunting techniques failed you. You have scaled me and my kindred as ladders, collected our sap for your various uses, carved your human symbols into our trunks, **Cm** for one, so you can remember. I support you still and cherish your presence—I do. Believe me, I do. But you must understand. You must see what is clearly set before you...

For beings such as I, Boötes the herdsman, and your other heavenly friends, your earthly wooden guardian as well, the oak around whom even now you clutch and wrap your hands, expending what little energy you still have—beings such as we require companions who straddle the eternal, who survive centuries as you live a day. My dogs, Asterion and Chara, have never failed me once in all these thousands of years, never fled my approach or bared their teeth, never shirked from their duty, same as mine—Drive the oxen onward, always, continually, reined to the staff that the agèd ones left, trundling round the world's edge, giving the earth to spin for the benefit of you, young friend, and all your kind...

Nothing more than a boast, a jest, another mere conquest. I meant it only as a show of my strength, the manliness of my bones, and the godliness in my blood. I could, if I chose, hunt every last creature inhabiting the earth—and I would, for her, for Artemis, my newest love. As I wooed her, we hunted together, honoring the sacred traditions of the forest and the mastery of man over beast, always biding my time, waiting for my chance to pounce, visualizing our affair in my mind's eye, only a matter of time before we would be making love beneath branches and frolicking naked in cool streams. Her mother, observing all the while from her unnatural perch, felt besmirched, betrayed, forgotten. And so she unleashed the scorpion...

Johannes...I have suffered too...not just him...nobody believes it...my loss as well as his...he is not innocent...I deserve a chance as much as he does...to be happy again...your humming and your cooking, please...the breakfast you made...sincerely mouth-watering...I need it just as much as you do...and you as much as I...together, we are...happiness...you don't have to go...we'll chase him out again...the John of your mind... history destroyed...every night...right here...in my bed...John is dead... Johannes reborn...or on the floor if you like...just you and me...and every morning again...you can cook...to make an omelet you must break... again...and again...and again...

And, My Mortal Brother, fearing the sting of its enormous venomous tail, I fled...

No, Neighbor, the river is not the way out. You delude yourself. You ignore the pleas of friends, the prospects of a worthy and fruitful life. You owe it to yourself, to us, the friends you have made here, and to those you left behind. Betrayal is a bitter juice, which I prefer not to sup. But you, my friend, you brought it upon yourself. This cowering, hiding, forgetting, and running that you do—what is it worth? What is its value if you fail to retain the lessons that nature has graciously provided? I, in particular, and all my ilk, in all our tempestuous, unpredictable, plentiful, competitive, and instinctual chaos, have at least discovered and maintained a balance amongst ourselves...

Man of Flesh, daylight will come again, as will the darkness. They must. You have my word, dear friend. My honor is as dependable as the stars in which I reside. On the lives of my fierce and able hounds, the loves of my life, I swear to never let you down. Fear not the strength of the oxen, fear not my abilities as a herdsman—but fear my dogs. As long as my hounds remain loyal, the earth will spin round. But should they tire, stray, or rebel—should they come unbound—then, my friend, you will be on your own. And then you must fear only yourself. Fear your capacity and willingness to remember, your desire to forget. Your ability to honor the fruits of this life, the womb and the seed from which you spring...

Johannes...Johannes...we can start again...a chance for something... both of us...together...we're fortunate...don't you see...we've found something magical...he and I never had it...only an illusion...don't you feel it...this is real...can't you understand...just open the window...that salty night air...the cool breeze upon our shared skin...that melody...the light...don't you see it...yes, stay on the floor...I'll stay here with you... together down below...we were meant...for this...and this...for us...

And still, I flee, My Mortal Brother, to the west, night after night, from the scorpion's approach as it crawls above the darkened east, stalking me round the earth...

Man of Flesh, these winding mountain paths you traverse continue down into the lowlands, leading back to the place from which you have come or onward to where you are going. Is there a difference? Are they, by chance, the same?

Neighbor, we wish you no ill. We want you to thrive. But not here. You must go now, on your way, down to join those of your kind. To laugh and love and enjoy their musical voices, the warmth of their flesh.

Dispel of this loneliness, give rise to what is owed you, rightfully yours, at least for what time you may find you have left...

Johannes...no...we can...we must...we'll tell him...tell everyone...open and honest...no, here, take my hand, take it now...hold on tight...all things good start with trust...our own willingness to admit who we are...who we love...what we want...you and me...that melody...the light...hold me...hold me tight...

I understand your disquiet, My Mortal Brother, young son of the earth, virile man of flesh and blood. I share your misery, your failure, your weak will and broken heart. Habitation in these mountains suits you well. But always look to the east, as once I did. Look to Helios, look and see, and free yourself, young friend! But beware the segmented species! Those vessels of poison, lies, and jealousy! Be free of their sting!

Man of Flesh, your time, too, will come. As it does for everyone. But this search is futile. You do not belong here with us. Look elsewhere for what you seek. Be content in my gift to you, your day and night. Live your life.

Neighbor, the time has come. Do not forget us—your friends here and everything we have shared, the lessons, the light, the night, the revelations held in the shadows of the forest. But now you must go. Go to them.

Johannes...Johannes...where is the melody...where has it gone...

Chapter 18

Miracles

December 25, 1817
St. Johns River, La Florida

FATHER JIMENEZ DELIVERED A GRAND SERMON THIS CHRISTMAS morning in which he likened the birth of our Savior to the birth of each one of us—Seminoles and Spaniards, Africans and island folk, slaves and runaways—every person enters this world in possession of the same qualities with which Christ was endowed. Every child that survives beyond the womb has already performed a miracle. But time distorts all things. Appearance, strength, family, faith, ambition, memory, perception, morality, mortality—all those tightly wound threads of the soul. Without constant loving attention, life itself can break into pieces under the strain. It can devolve into a living death in which we, the innumerable former miracles, suffer and revile the time that distances us from our one true death.

Addressing his humble congregation more somberly than usual, the Father then related news that threatens to undo our peaceful habitation of this land.

Two months ago, a delegation from Spain arrived unannounced, including a leading official of the King's colonial affairs. The entirety of San Agustín erupted in hasty celebration after they learned who the ships had carried in. The townsfolk received the delegates with a festive welcome. The best rooms in town were prepared, and feasts arranged for each day of the week. Over the next few days, the governor himself, José María Coppinger, led those distinguished gentlemen through the town and along the coast, including a short expedition into the wetlands. At the Castillo de San Marcos, they were privileged to a presentation of regional defense tactics, with groomed soldiers on high alert, choreographed musket salvos and cannon discharges, as well as a rare execution. Later, they were led on horseback to a Seminole village south of the town, where they were warmly received. During long, riotous nights, they enjoyed copious quantities of wine, rum, and women. To crown their tour, the townsfolk held an extravagant parade that terminated inside the Cathedral Basilica.

The King's men seemed pleased with all they had seen, but at a private council with Coppinger the following day, they revealed the purpose of their visit.

Coppinger's secretary was first alarmed by the delegates' curt manner as they filed out of the parlor at the governor's estate. They wished to be ferried to their ships post-haste. Before the secretary arranged their carriages, he asked after the governor, who had not accompanied the delegates out from the parlor. One man remarked without humor that if Coppinger had any brains in his head, then he was already packing for a return to his home in Havana, to which another delegate added that Cuba would soon follow suit and that the governor would be better off trying his luck back in the motherland with the rest of them.

Soon thereafter, Coppinger summoned his closest allies from around the colony, among them our own Chief Kinheja and Father Jimenez, as well as the primary Seminole leader from the interior, Chief Bolek. Dramatically gathering his friends within the fortified walls of the Castillo de San Marcos, the governor briefed them on these sorrowful circumstances.

Although a symbolic piece of land for Spain, La Florida has failed to remain strategic in the wake of the United States' expansionist ambitions. King Ferdinand has lost all hope and interest in swamplands that have become nothing more than a troublesome and contentious dispute between the two nations. With other more useful colonies also struggling, as well as deteriorating conditions back in Spain, the King no longer finds it prudent to provide supplies, monetary aid, or garrisons to fend off an unspecified, looming invasion. Therefore, Coppinger has been ordered to proceed with the preliminary stages of dismantling the colony. When the delegates left San Agustín, they were headed directly for the US capital to initiate negotiations.

Governor Coppinger proved his allegiance to the colony with colorful language lambasting the King. However, he ultimately admitted that he is powerless. The United States is certain to jump at any offer for ownership over the peninsula, and everything that we Spaniards and Seminoles have worked toward will be lost.

After the governor finished, Chief Bolek took the opportunity to shed light upon recent events along the Georgia border that will undoubtedly stoke the coming turmoil.

One month ago, a tribe of Miccosukee Creeks were driven from Fowltown, their village in southern Georgia, by a United States Army regiment. The tribe retaliated a week later by attacking a supply boat headed for Fort Scott in the vicinity of what had been Fowltown. The Miccosukee overtook the vessel and slaughtered the soldiers, along with the wives and children who accompanied them. Word of the massacre spread quickly and garnered a swift reaction from the United States garrisons. Even though those Georgia Creeks have never conspired with the Seminoles and have distanced themselves from the Florida Creeks, they now have nowhere to flee but south across the border to join their estranged brethren.

Ignoring Chief Bolek's pleas for transparency, the Miccosukee are currently dispersing throughout Spanish territory, hiding out in swamps, and deceiving any tribes that will offer them sanctuary. Although he has scouts tracking their whereabouts, he is convinced that the huge force gathering at the border under the command of General Andrew Jackson has little intention of hunting down a few bad Miccosukee. He expects a full invasion within weeks, and without additional Spanish troops to defend our sovereignty, the territory will be ceded.

Chief Bolek says the future of the Seminoles is drenched in blood.

When the Father concluded, he took me aside to deliver the last bit of troubling news in private.

While the delegates were here, they made several inquiries around town about El Soldado Agraciado. I betrayed a smile, assuming it was me they were after. But the Father shook his head and grasped my shoulder. Following its departure from San Agustín, the ship never arrived in Cuba. They have not yet received word from Buenos Aires, but seeing as it has been more than a year with no account for the ship's delinquency, little hope remains. The Father told me of a rumor that Captain Vasquez's ship was often targeted by vengeful pirates because the Captain himself used to be one. He was surprised to learn that I was unaware of the Captain's past.

Since morning, my thoughts and prayers have not once drifted from those dear friends of mine. Though I am surrounded by warm and friendly faces, this holiday has left me grappling with a sense of loneliness I assumed I had left behind.

Chapter 19

The Scrap

The discourse of voices wanders through a fog, lost travelers gone astray and then remarkably come together in an unanticipated destination. Light trappings of music settle the confusion into calm understanding as they mingle, getting to know each other again after all this time elapsed and the distance of untold adventures. But once they realize they're actually all on the same journey, the music becomes livelier, upbeat, festive, staccato piano, hand claps and rhythmic foot stomps, splashing cymbals and the continuous soft thud of a bass drum beneath a melody flying into distant reaches, dreams unraveling and the fog dispersing, footsteps shuffling past, dishes clinking-clattering overhead, water dripping, someone huffing arduous breaths.

Rising onto an elbow, a quick look around, low to the ground.

"Thought I heard you stirring down there..."

A new voice, this. It comes and goes, interrupted by a noisy mechanical whirring, repeated starts and stops that drown the music out.

"About time, too," the voice shouts over the noise. "It's near eleven. Never knew a man to sleep so soundly on the floor. You looked almost happy..."

The facts of location gradually arrange themselves. The air is thick with a damp, indistinct odor and difficult to breathe. Trash cans, empty liquor and beer bottles overflowing from wooden and plastic crates, dual buzzes from the fridge and the ice maker, fat electrical cords, the sickly sweet scent of old alcohol and mixers, stacks of coasters and packets of cocktail napkins, a pair of legs, and worn out shoes.

"I figured Chick would wake you. He writes music to live by, not to sleep with. And this album, in particular, makes me want to spend my dying days in Barcelona, surrounded by pretty señoritas and buena fiestas and bullfights." The whirring sound has stopped, but he's still shouting as he pours the contents of the blender into a tall glass. "Can you imagine it? The running of the bulls? The pulse of life stampeding through those Spanish streets. Run and live, or be trampled, skewered upon the horns and flung away like last night's whore. The matador winks and flashes red, and we are born anew!"

"What?"

"You were talking in your sleep, by the way. Do you always do that? Must drive Grant nuts..."

Johannes gasps as he lifts himself up, a sharp sting on the fleshy part of his palm. A tiny shard protrudes, drawing out a faint red stain within the puncture.

"Be careful," Ernest scolds him. "Bound to be plenty more glass down there. You did an awful job sweeping up last night. Not bad on the take, though. You made a killing behind the bar."

"That was you, not me."

"Nah, we were like a jazz trio, you and Oscar and I. If you can't pull that out, you'd better dig it out. Here," he hands Johannes a fruit knife. "Just washed it."

The shard is slick with blood, so he jabs the point of the knife underneath to wedge it out, drawing more blood and a wince of pain. Ernest breaks a raw egg into the glass and begins to stir. When it's sufficiently mixed, he sets the glass on the bar and walks around to the other side, where he settles onto a barstool to observe Johannes's struggle.

"Got it? Here, drink this when you're finished." Ernest sniffs the cloudy pink contents of the glass and then slides it toward Johannes. "Works every time."

"Maybe just water, thanks..." Johannes finally pulls out the shard and examines it before dropping it into the wastebasket.

Ernest reaches over the bar, grabs a couple of ice cubes, and drops them in. "Goes down easier if it's chilled."

"What is it?" Johannes sniffs and recoils. "It smells like sweat."

"Better to just drink it. I tell you, it'll clear your head."

The drink tastes mostly of citrus, with a sharp aftertaste. Johannes gulps quickly. It's so viscous he can feel it slide down his throat and settle in his stomach.

"Not bad, huh?" says Ernest.

Johannes shakes his head. He swallows a second gulp and peers at particles floating in the liquid. "So what is it?"

Ernest leans forward and rests his elbows on the bar. "Had to make you try it first. No one will give it a chance once they know the ingredients," he says with a lonesome smile. "Whole grapefruit, garlic, ground pepper, lemon juice, shot of vodka, and a splash of tomato juice. The egg goes in last. Sometimes I'll add spinach, but I wasn't about to go shopping for no greens. Still feeling the effects of last night myself..."

Johannes swallows another mouthful.

"Hemingway used to drink one every morning. Or so the legend goes. Glad you like it. So? What the hell?"

"What the hell what?"

"What the hell were you sleeping down there for? On the floor? I don't mind, of course. Slept in the booths over there myself. Just glad you're not dead. Gave me quite a scare when I found you, early morning. But you seemed to be sleeping peacefully. Comfortably even. Figured I'd just let you get on with it."

"I was dreaming...I think..."

"No kidding. All that talking, a constant murmur. Nonsense, as far as I could tell, but almost happily so. Must have been a good one."

"It was only...voices. Different voices. Like old friends, all talking at the same time. Telling me...something..."

Ernest bobs his head to the music, occasionally tapping his fingers on the bar top. The song has grown intense and chaotic. Multiple rhythms layer atop one another, shifting wild and fast, now aggressive, now tender, now vanished. The piano changes mood in a seemingly arbitrary manner. No foothold, no anchor. Ernest's eyes lose focus every few measures as he's drawn out of himself, captivated.

A small globule of blood has collected on Johannes's palm. He can't take his eyes off it. Ernest gets up to flip the record on the turntable, side four of four.

"Here it is," Ernest slaps the bar top and hops back onto his stool. "An intense and novel testament, a quad of songs, highlight of the album, I dare say of Chick's career. Listen to this, will you?"

"Chick?" Memories of the night before crop up, but they're scattered, fragmentary. "This is the same record Amondale played? And...danced to?"

"When? Last night?" Ernest's eyes wander over to the record player haranguing this slick Spanish emotion. "Right, it was still spinning there this morning. I was too far gone last night to even bother. Just let it crackle on all night until it drove me nuts in the early hours. And then I trip over you sprawled across the floor back there. No, no, not the same, not even close. You nearly pierced your entire body with glass, you dope. Why didn't you sweep up better? At least go and lie somewhere safe, like me. I couldn't care less if you sleep here, but I don't intend on mopping up your blood and guts. The booths are plenty wide. Only, not every night, okay? Don't go making a habit of it. Grant's place is only a ten-minute walk. I just don't see why you chose this filthy floor, of all places. And no, this is not Oscar's choice from last night. Whenever Oscar drinks The Carnival, he starts on about that record. Claims he fell in love with Chico Buarque's subversive brand of fighting the man. But that is a vast difference, worlds apart, like saying The Carnival is comparable to the finest single malt. A Bowmore or something. You have a lot to learn. Are you up for it? This is Chick Corea, master pianist. Innovator and accomplice to the modern age of jazz. Quiet down now. Just drink that and listen."

"Ernest, you were...last night was...you were amazing."

"That piano's in worse shape than I am. Like walking with your shoes on the wrong feet. And ten broken toes." He's smiling sadly, looking into the mirrors behind Johannes, or into the music itself.

"You should be playing every night. Everyone loved it."

Ernest groans. "I spent my life traveling around this country, playing every night. Nothing anybody could offer would convince me to do it all over again. And I still do. Get offers, I mean. Last night, as a matter of fact. That old man, Mr. Wilms...but no, I can't. Will you shut up and listen already?"

An obtrusive explosion of percussion, maniacal banging and splashing, bass line roving into the high octaves, accented by fat piano chords and Ernest slapping the bar top. Johannes listens. He hears the sounds but finds no sense in it. It's outlandish, intrusive, pushy. His preferred music consists of a gentle breeze and the gurgle of a stream, or that softly swelling piano melody, sly and addictive, propelling and following him into his dreams. As he finishes the drink, a dime-sized chunk of fuming garlic momentarily lodges in his throat. The music fades suddenly.

"Mornings," says Ernest, "this album's good for peaceful mornings. It's a proclamation, you know, of a coming day and a purposeful existence. Oh, my Spanish heart! Chick has mastered many of humanity's struggles through his music. What do you think?"

"I've heard a lot of music in here with you, but I wouldn't say I understand any of it. Or that it's done anything for me. I don't even notice it most of the time. Except...last night...that one short phrase. Ernest, you played for almost three hours, and that phrase recurred throughout the second set. You kept returning to it, toying with it. It felt like you were toying with me directly."

"Thought you'd never notice."

"And then, after you stopped playing, I kept hearing it all night long.

For the entire night. Even in my dreams. That's the last thing I remember. I don't remember lying down on the floor back here, but I remember that musical phrase sending me to sleep. And it never left...it was there, the whole time, behind them...accompanying those voices... as they spoke...and they told me...what was it...?"

"That right?" Ernest looks up, an odd smile twisting his face. "Good. I thought it might."

"That woman, too, Caryn, she...wait, you thought it might what?"

Ernest points to the carton of record sleeves beside the turntable. "Bring it over here, that one."

"What?"

"That record."

"Which one?"

"Same one you—no, not that one—the other one. Don't you...? Flip back through them. There. There, right there, yeah, that one. That's it, that one. Bring it here. Good lord, how did you ever manage last night..."

Johannes picks up the record sleeve, flips it over.

"That Caryn," Ernest continues, "nice gal. Pretty, too. Like I said, I had no idea you were still here until I tripped over you this morning. I was in quite a state myself last night. Old man Wilms with his thirst for bourbon and respect. Thought you'd left with her, in fact. Gone back to her motel. Walked her home, at least, like a proper gentleman. You two were talking intimately for a long while. Something in her eyes, and in yours, too. But who am I to talk about snagging a good woman? Just another old bachelor, married to and divorced from music, but still bedding her every goddamn night, Christ..."

"But Ern, I don't understand," Johannes hands the record over to Ernest. "You're a real musician? A professional?"

"Not quite the same thing. I was a touring jazz pianist. But, like I told you, I've never been able to write a convincing story."

"You played a story last night."

"You think so? It takes a special type of man. Easier to let yourself go crazy. I know you know what I mean. But you're lucky. You're still young enough to figure it all out. I'm going to show you something that changed my life, and I think it'll change yours, too. Again. I only hope you take advantage of it this time. Just wait till you see this."

Ernest's eyes light up as he looks the record over. The sleeve is scratched, worn to shambles, barely held together. Discoloration and fading render parts of the white script unreadable. Dents distort the symphonic scene spread across the cover. Flakes fall from the edges when he flips it over in his hands once, twice, three times. Adoration and love pour forth, a grandfather holding his grandchild for the hundredth time, and not without pride as he passes the sleeve back to Johannes.

"Last night, I was lost in a maze. Didn't know what I was playing half the time. It's like that sometimes. Gotta let the music lead you wherever it happens to go. But I'd be willing to put down my savings and my bar in wager that we're on the same page with this."

"With what?"

Bold letters stretch across the top of the sleeve. *Sergei Rachmaninoff performed by Campfeld Rimonov and the Vienna Philharmonic, February 1963.* Beneath the text is a photo of an empty stage set for an orchestra, chairs and instruments ready and waiting. A monstrous, sleek, and shining grand piano stands front and center. Johannes's fingers fall into impressions on the sides of the sleeve formed by human hands.

"Don't you recognize it?" asks Ernest.

Johannes looks up and shakes his head.

Ernest's complexion reddens as he shifts on the barstool, his expression souring as though he has actually laid down his property in a bet of dangerous probabilities.

"Is this...what is it? I put this on? Last night? During your break?"

"The intermission..." Ernest exhales, chuckles nervously, wipes the perspiration from his brow. "Yeah, and...?"

"That phrase," continues Johannes, "the phrase you kept repeating." He shakes the sleeve. "It came from this record, didn't it?"

"And..."

"And? And what?"

"You think that's all? That it's just some random record you chose last night? I promise you, it was no accident you chose that record. Let's see those digging skills of yours, boy."

Johannes examines the cover again, flipping the sleeve senselessly. It's only a matter of seconds before Ernest's impatience gets the better of him.

"I obtained this gem years ago. What? Four? Five? It was already well-worn and excessively listened to. I had just moved here and taken over the bar. One day, this fella walks in—I barely knew him at the time —and he's trying to unload a box of old records. I had been planning to keep the bar quiet, no radio, no nothing. Just talk. Stories. Leaving the circuit was...it was like going through a divorce. I didn't want anything to do with music. But I was new here, eager to make friends. So I took the records. Still, it was a couple of months in a quiet, empty bar before I even bothered to look through them. Now, you must understand, I've been a jazz snob since I was thirteen years old. And these records he gave me were mostly classic rock, so they weren't going to be spinning in my bar any time soon. But this one was in there, too. I flipped right past it, and it wasn't until I got to the end of the stack that it registered. Sergei Rachmaninoff. A composer I hadn't listened to since I was a kid, since before jazz took my life hostage. Anything ringing a bell yet?"

Johannes shrugs, then shakes his head. His stomach rumbles. He belches garlic and citrus.

"Anyway, one lethargic, peaceful morning, not unlike this one, I threw the record on, same as you did last night, with no idea what to expect. Musically, I knew what to expect, of course. But not to where that particular piece of music would take me. Disc One, Side One, Track One. Same as you. Rachmaninoff's Second Piano Concerto in C-minor slowly dragging me back through the years. A disconcerting sensation more than anything. Hesitation, mostly. On the verge of fear. Like falling off the wagon. But then that phrase of yours knocked me straight back to the beginning of it all, the blow of a hammer. I was seven years old again, falling in love with magic all over again, as Rachmaninoff whispered into my ears."

"C-minor...whispered...Second Piano Concerto...? Those voices last night...nothing but voices...whispering, speaking to me. For the entire dream, I saw nothing. Just darkness and voices. But that melody, your melody, was always somewhere behind them...with them...tying them together..."

"That very melody delivered something back to me, too, Johannes. A sense of being alive and well that I had lost somewhere along life's trajectory. Helped me rediscover all the things I'd forgotten, about music, about myself. All the memories I'd left scattered in jazz clubs around the country, on the grimy floors of dives like this one. I remembered where I came from and why I landed on the decisions I'd made over the years. I gained a new appreciation for the things I'd accomplished and no longer regretted any of it. Never in a thousand years would I have gone back to do it again. But then, here comes Mr. Rachmaninoff to knock some sense into me with those monster hands of his. To show me my life, with its ups and downs, same as everyone else's. And I saw that there was never another option for me. The life I was given was the only life I could have led. So, I got back into bed with music, and for the first time in a long time, I enjoyed it. Been that way ever since. Which is why I don't want to push my luck. From here on out, I'd rather just appreciate music. I'm too old to overdose. Too old to be miserable all the time."

"But Ern, in the time I've been here, I haven't seen you happier than you were last night. You were a different man behind that piano. Youthful, energized. What makes you think that playing regularly would be so bad? Now that you've found your passion again, just hold onto it. Use it —for yourself and for others. Everyone, they loved it. And me, too. Honestly."

"Misery is a curious thing, isn't it?" Ernest sighs. "Like a cold fire. A walking fish. Have you ever been north of the Arctic Circle in the winter? We used to travel to northern Alaska every couple of years to play the oddest little music festival you can imagine. Two weeks with no sunlight and you start to think you've gotten pretty familiar with misery. But then you come south again and find it's the sunlight that's really making you miserable. You never recognize it when it's upon you, and if you think you do, then chances are you've got it all wrong. You'll know what I mean when you crawl out of your funk."

"I'm not...what funk? I'm not miserable."

"You know, I'm jealous," Ernest laughs. "You've got this unique opportunity, and you're going into it totally clueless. Just how it oughta be. I look at you, and I'm reminded of myself from that time. I call them my deaf years. Instead of a vow of silence, I took a vow of deafness." Ernest is thoughtful for a minute, sweating profusely. Droplets fall from his chin and off his arms onto the bar top. He reaches out and flicks the Rachmaninoff sleeve with his index finger. "Come on then, what have you got for me?"

"What else could there be? It's a record. A tune I happen to like, I guess..."

"But you have seen it before?" says Ernest in a rhetorical tone, certain he's speaking from the right side of a conspiracy. "Heard it before?"

And Johannes, "I don't know. Maybe. You know I don't remember..."

"Didn't want to spoil the surprise, but it could take ages at this rate. What's it been, three weeks you've been here? Four? You've been to the bar damn near every night, and ever since that first day, I'd swear I knew you somehow. It was a damned puzzle, and all the pieces were there, I just couldn't arrange them. Sometimes, our hanging, unfinished conversations contained hints, but never enough. Always the simplest things that are easiest to overlook, huh? That's a double album. Open it up. Look inside."

The gatefold's yellowish interior is covered with tiny black print giving musicians' names and engineers' details. The liner notes praise Rachmaninoff, the Vienna Philharmonic, the Musikverein Theater, and Campfeld Rimonov, the Soviet deserter and piano prodigy. The tracks are listed on the far right, sidled by faint pencil markings, minuscule notes faded to nothing over time, visible only by the imprint they've left behind.

"The young man who gave me that batch of records..." Ernest lets it hang mysteriously, "...was Grant."

Johannes shifts his gaze between Ernest and the sleeve.

"Most of them are still in the same box he brought them in," Ernest continues, "untouched, down in the cellar with the rest of my collection. They were mostly his or his dad's, except for this one and a few others which had belonged to a friend of his, or so he told me. The friend had left them behind some time ago and who knows whether he'll ever be back to collect them, he'd probably forgotten about them, don't worry, he won't miss them. That's all he said. No big deal, right? But for me, it was the goddamned birth of Christ. Sixty years old and born again. Thanks to you."

"What?"

"Oh, for God's sake, how much clearer can I make it? Look closely. The notes in the margin. There, at the bottom."

"They're faded...," says Johannes. "Almost invisible."

"Just look for the sign-off. All the rest will come back to you."

"You sound like Grant..."

Johannes tilts the sleeve to catch the light just right, brings it closer to his face, and squints. There, in the lower right-hand corner, are the faintly visible initials—JM.

"You see?" Ernest's fingers tap frantically on the counter. He's leaning over, almost standing, and watching for Johannes's reaction. "It took me hours to decipher those chicken scratches. Here, I'll save you the trouble. You seem to have had a love affair with this album, and with the Second Piano Concerto in particular. You wrote here about various aspects of the composition, but here you express obvious admiration for that scrap, as you refer to it—there, in your notes, right there—that short piano and string phrase in the first movement. And your thoughts echoed my own. It was stuck in my head for days, like a bad pop song. Only, this was perfect, ingenious. Think of the effort it must take to create a melody like that and then hold back. To play with fire for a stinted instant and then leave it alone forever. That theme holds the entire concerto together, and yet it's like a single magical syllable, a coded spell buried in a thirty-minute speech. In jazz, it would be repeated over and over again, variations to infinity, as our addictive souls desire it, as I couldn't help but play it last night. But, in fact, that ruins it. The clever twists and turns of jazz do not always provide the sensible path. But that's all I was ever any good at, and everything I ever hated about myself, about my music. What sort of man has that kind of strength? The willpower to hold back like that?"

"But Ernest, are you sure? I mean..."

"Then again, what is Rachmaninoff remembered for? Not his symphonies, not his concertos, but his preludes. The pop songs of the day. That goddamn Prelude in C-sharp minor..."

"But how can you be so sure?"

"Proof's right there." Ernest stabs a fat finger at the initials on the corner of the sleeve.

"This could be anyone. JM...I don't remember this...writing this..."

"Nope," shaking his head, smiling. "I took a walk this morning. Over to Grant's. Asked him myself."

"Asked him what?"

"Whether the record is yours or not. And sure as shit. 'Who else?' he says, as though I should've known all along. Then he went back to his digging."

"Digging? Alone?"

Ernest shrugs. "Just left it at that. He seemed to be in a mood."

Visibly pleased with himself, Ernest reaches over the counter for a glass. Then he reaches further, lays his hand on a bottle of The Carnival. But he hesitates, checks his watch, and finally leaves the bottle where it is.

Johannes looks over the penciled notes but can't make them out. They don't reveal anything. They don't mean anything. There's no discernible reflection of past or present, no revelation about the writer or the writer's world. Is this, then, the inevitable culmination of self-discovery? Stupid coincidences? Ridiculous misconceptions about the meaningless objects that link one person to another? Or one person to himself? All things leading back to an inescapable past?

Resist all he wants, there's no denying that this record is, or at some point was, his possession. And therefore, his attraction to the scrap had not been spontaneous. It had not bloomed with the purity of love at first sight, but rather as the reawakening of some-John, a Johannes that used to be, god knows how long ago. But what can he rightfully expect to receive now from this single remnant of the past? Energy surging from the crumbling cardboard? Vibrations from the smooth vinyl entering through his fingertips? An aura of sacredness emanating from within, filling him with himself? With a lifetime of memories? With the holy spirit? The secrets of happiness? In truth, each of these might describe how he felt the previous night as that melody penetrated his heart, mingling and reacquainting itself with his soul.

And it's already in progress. The voices speaking to him through the medium of sleep had done so with a melodic twist to their words, pleasant and soothing, the same mysterious, undulating tones of the melody itself, this *scrap*. Under the conductor's command, the voices were remembering for him, threatening to expose him and also confront him with all that he had run from, not once, but twice.

"So?" says Ernest. "What do you think?"

Johannes feels dizzy, his head detached and desiring to float away, a balloon at the mercy of wind and weather. When he looks up, he's still clutching the record sleeve, but Ernest is gone. Johannes swivels around to find Ernest behind him, pouring himself an orange and cream soda. And those Johanneses in the mirrors, still hanging around, hounding him with demands, threats that he had better pull himself together lest he wind up cracked and shattered and lethally sharp, for he is no less fragile than they are. Better to just lie down again, back to dream and the council of voices. But the floor beneath him is filthy and treacherous. It's certainly no place to run and hide, let alone to seek a peaceful slumber.

"Look..." Ernest makes his way back around the bar. He settles himself onto the barstool with his soda and a book. The carbonation fizzes and pops. "You've helped me, and now I intend to return the favor. Just go with it, alright?"

"What did I do? I tended your bar for a night. That was just part of our bargain..."

"This record came to me from you through the usual channels of chance. As fortune would have it, it rejuvenated my love for music and, therefore, my appreciation for life. It reminded me that my life has always revolved around one thing and one thing only—Mistress Music. It was stupid of me to want to escape that. I can stop playing, I can stop touring, I can change every element of my surroundings, but I can't change who I am. That Rachmaninoff was a slap in the face for me, the wake-up call I needed. I'm old. I've got no woman. I was never going to be famous. And there was no joy left in doing what I was doing. So I chose this place. The owners were an old couple, too old to manage anymore. It was called Jo's Last Stand, after that saint, you know, and the church. A lot of folks wanted me to keep the name. The historical import of it meant something to them, I guess. But I had to assert myself for once in my pathetic life. I bought the bar so I could fulfill the one and only dream I had left, and I even regretted that decision at the time—until this. This record showed me who I was, who I am. Gave me back a sense of pride I had lost in the dark corners of all those jazz clubs. And now, I'm in close contact with my family again, closer than I've been since I dropped out of school. I've met more honorable, trustworthy friends here in Creek's Ridge than I ever did in the business, and I can actually get close to them. Get to know them as they really are. That's impossible to do on the road. But here, I'm not merely content, I have everything I could possibly want, and it's right under my nose. If it weren't for this record, I never would have known it. This here record saved me from myself. From my loneliness. So, sincerely, I must thank you. And I'd like to do so with a nudge in the right direction. Now you got your music back, the same music you gave me, as it happens. I want to help you follow through, to rebuild yourself, starting now, with this single piece of, well...of yourself."

Johannes closes the sleeve and holds it over the bar, passing it back to Ernest, who leans away and raises his hands dramatically, spilling his soda. "It's yours," Ernest says. "I insist. This is how I help you. By returning something you've lost. Piece by piece, if such is the case. One piece at a time, it'll all come together. Don't you worry."

"I'm not worried." Johannes sets it down and reaches for a rag to wipe the spilled soda. "Everyone else is..."

"Maybe you oughta be, is what I'm trying to say." Ernest sighs as he watches Johannes clean up. "Starting to get the hang of the job, eh?"

Johannes picks up the sleeve again, the initials on the inner corner still taunting him. His eyes rove over the copious information inside. He can no longer hear the scrap lilting tenderly between his ears, only *JM, John, John M, Man of Flesh, John Metternich, come on, let's do it again, My Mortal Brother, that melody, get rid of him, of John M, Neighbor, and the other, Second Piano Concerto, Johannes the Lonely Wanderer, again and again, bad luck brother, in C-minor, forever, and ever,* all different voices fused into one and devoid of melody. He drops the sleeve on the bar, opens the cooler, and pulls out an orange and cream.

"You know I stock that for the kids, don't you?" Ernest's voice is severe, but he looks up with playful scorn from his book, an old volume of Hemingway's short works. "Before I forget, because you probably will..." He slides a considerable stack of small bills across the bar. Then, he pulls two fifties from his pocket and tosses them on the stack. "Your tips."

"And these?" Johannes lifts up the fifties and looks at them with something like wonder and contempt.

"I always follow through on my bets. You were right. I concede defeat."

Johannes leans against the counter, shutting his eyes. Though it calls out to him, the melody refuses to return, demanding instead that he come and fetch it himself.

This album, this concerto, this scrap, he doesn't know what they once meant to him. He doesn't want to skim importance from faded pencil marks, nor does he want to fill them in again. An abused mutt, he bares his teeth, slits his eyes, backs away low to the ground. But he's trapped, shackled, noosed, like the herdsman's hounds, tightness around the neck, difficulty breathing, consciousness beginning to fade, those penciled notes in the margins, the names—Asterion and Chara, John and Johannes, Knecht and Boötes and Orion and...who was the other?

"Oh, and by the way," Ernest tugs on the leash, "you still owe me that story."

The usual fever dreams that terrify him night after night are not just dreams but memories that reign over his sleep, sending him back to those days and nights on the mountain, the simultaneous certainty and uncertainty of death, the pain as he idled away the days, the guilt of failure and cowardice, the disappointment of facing each and every day with no end in sight. But last night's dream of voices was something else. The voices were trying to help him, reminding him, showing him the necessary steps, the essential facets of himself, their haunting but friendly words hinting at who he was, who he is, why he was there on the mountain, and why he is here now, in Creek's Ridge. Johannes the Lonely Wanderer, straddling the bridge between life and death.

The piano scrap, a necessary morsel, provides nourishment, allows for survival, quenches thirst, distracts from trouble howling over a distant ridge.

"Hey Ern..." Johannes clears his throat. "Do you think you could..." nodding at the piano. "Would you mind? Just once?"

"No can do. I've told you, never without people. A personal motto I gotta hold to. Otherwise, what else has a man got?" Ernest conceals his grin by bringing the glass to his lips, slurping his soda. "Feel free to spin the record, though. Anytime you want. But beware. If you stick around here too long, I'll put you to work. Best part of last night for me was not having to pour drinks..."

Johannes removes Chick Corea from the record player and prepares the Rachmaninoff.

With his eyes closed, he allows the music to drag him along, listening without truly paying attention. He cannot determine how tightly the music holds him, how entirely it surrounds him. To distract himself, he meditates on other things, anything to fend off the void that swallowed him on the mountain and now repetitively in his dreams—Knecht's protective canopy, a flowing transparent stream, putrid animal carcasses rotting in the sunlight, flies and maggots feasting, the fragrant aroma of the natural world, and also the stink of death. All is well; all things balanced and as they should be. Other thoughts creep in, shadows passing overhead, parents, sister, city streets, forest trails, sorrow and denial, friends and lovers, appease this lot and disappoint the others, eat this scrap and receive the stick, get in the way and get trampled and kicked, wander too far astray and lose track of breath, choked and gasping, repeat, repeat, repeat...

The scrap begins, and all these knotted thoughts are released as the music floods in. With the first note, he knows the rest, the melody complete and alive in his mind, not an arrangement of notes linked by time but a united, cohesive whole—piano, strings, and timpani. Soon, woodwinds and brass return, preparing to propel onward toward the finale.

"Now I remember," says Johannes.

Ernest looks up from his book.

"The voices...they were telling me to stay...and also to go..."

Before the concerto has finished, Johannes lifts the needle, halting the song's progress. He slips the record back into its sleeve and returns it to the carton beside the turntable. Without another word to Ernest, who has been watching with interest and perhaps also with disappointment, Johannes grabs the stack of bills and walks out.

Chapter 20

Sweet Everlasting

The progression of stories had advanced into recent history, his grandfather's generation, when the white man's presence had made its first indelible impressions upon the Shawnee people. After dusk fell, the head of the cave no longer shone so blindingly. Lalawethika approached the cave entrance. He peered beyond without passing the threshold, but he inhaled his first breaths of fresh air in as long as he could remember. His lips were cracked and bleeding, his throat ached from the strain of constant speech, and pleas for water had become a natural inclusion into his orations. After checking each jug and wooden bowl in the cave and praying to the Great Spirit for one solitary drop, Lalawethika checked them again, expecting a miracle, but he found them to be just as dry as his parched throat. He began begging Penagashea for water, for a single drop of saliva, prostrating himself, reaching to grasp hold of the medicine man's legs, to kiss his feet and lick off the sweat. But Penagashea had not yet returned, so Lalawethika had only tongued the few remaining logs for the fire, his delusions clear and real as the flames. Provided with no water, he struggled with a loss of faith in all that he had learned to hold dear. He considered slipping out of the cave, down to the stream, just to wet his lips, to put something into his stomach. Temptation loomed over him, the cave itself trying to spit him out. But he remembered Kokumthena and the Shawnees' exhausting swim, so he slunk back into the shadows and firelight, his voice roaring.

A thick darkness settled over the forest. Lalawethika had finished detailing a prosperous future for the Shawnee Nation, and just as he began reciting preparations for various herbal and root-based remedies, Penagashea trudged into the cave. Lalawethika's voice fizzled out. Penagashea announced that there was no moon that night, so he had lost his way in the forest. However, those were the precise conditions they required. They could not delay. The ritual must be completed. Their time in the cave had come to an end.

Lalawethika asked if Penagashea had drunk the last of the water and firewater, but his voice was so hoarse it was hardly audible. Penagashea set down the pouches he had carried back and told Lalawethika to grab two empty jugs and follow him, for they would need much water.

Terror struck as Lalawethika stepped beyond the cave's entrance, rooting him to the soil beneath the archway.

"There is no moon," Penagashea called back to him. "I have explained this. It means you are safe. Unseen. Hurry."

But Lalawethika could not move. His breaths grew short and heavy, his expression contorted, his limbs trembled. Penagashea gazed curiously into his subject's vacant eyes. When Lalawethika came out of his trance, all he could see was Penagashea's scarred and wrinkled face, masked by the dark of night.

And Lalawethika screamed.

"What did you see?" asked Penagashea.

Lalawethika stared at his mentor without recognition. "I don't remember," he said. "There were many voices."

"They speak to you? Now? That is a good sign. And what did you hear?"

"One voice said, *'Stay in the cave, never leave the cave.'* It showed me what would happen...but I...do not...remember..."

"Nonsense," Penagashea grumbled. "It is a trap. Come, we must start soon. We need water."

"What trap?"

"The Serpent," spat Penagashea. "Ignore the Great Serpent."

Still, Lalawethika did not move.

"Open your eyes," Penagashea screamed and came at him with an empty jug in his raised hand, prepared to unleash a blow, but for once, he did not strike. For once, Lalawethika stood erect, not hunched over and submissive, but towering over the old medicine man. "The night is pitch dark," Penagashea tried to compose himself. "Not a sliver of light. You must move like a wolf, swift and agile, slunk low to the ground, at home on the run. Always like the noble wolf gnawing on the Serpent as a snack. Then you will be safe on nights like this. Will you give in now? To cowardice? Have we wasted all this time?"

"No," answered Lalawethika. "I am weary of this pitiful life. It must be done."

They made two trips to the stream. When they had fetched enough water, Penagashea told Lalawethika to grind the cottonwood buds. Then they pulled down the strange plants with the undying white petals, the Sweet Everlasting that they had hung around the cave walls. Penagashea went to work plucking and crushing the dried leaves and petals. They refrained from speech while their hands reduced plants to dust, the fire crackling nearby. After a while, they began to sing together—traditional Shawnee songs that all Shawnees were taught as children, medicine songs that few remembered anymore, and prayer songs meant to entice the weather, the animals, and the crops into fruitful cooperation. Then Penagashea began to chant in an unfamiliar language and strange rhythms.

Penagashea threw a handful of crushed Sweet Everlasting onto the fire. Immediately, pungent smoke filled the cave. He gave Lalawethika a pouch filled with birch bark, instructing him to moisten it and rub out the white pigment without watering it down, collecting it on a broad, curled leaf. While he did this, Penagashea prepared the powder from the cottonwood buds. When Penagashea had a thick yellow paste ready, he applied it to Lalawethika's face as he sang death laments, calling on representatives of the afterlife to lead away a lost soul. The cave was shrouded in a constant haze from the handfuls of Sweet Everlasting, which Penagashea continued to drop into the fire.

Lalawethika's entire face was painted yellow, with white streaks stretching down his cheeks and up his forehead from his eyes. His maimed right eye was coated with black soot, and his hair was plastered with yellow and white. Upon his body, Penagashea painted intricate yellow designs over his vital organs, and long strokes of white stretched along each of his limbs, his ribcage, and spine—all his bones framed for a peaceful eternal rest.

Before they left the cave for the final time, Penagashea turned to Lalawethika. He stared solemnly at his bepainted subject for a long while.

"From now on, you must not speak. Not a sound. You must not fight this. Your destiny unfurls before you. Are you prepared to meet it?"

Lalawethika nodded.

They brought only one jug of water and the rest of the Sweet Everlasting. They sat in darkness, no longer singing or chanting or speaking, only smoking the Sweet Everlasting from Penagashea's pipe, holding it in their lungs and giving in to its peculiar effects, utterly calming except for an internal tingle, the sensation of tiny pinpricks radiating throughout their bodies, prodding their spirits awake in ever-increasing increments, rendering each gland and organ apprehensible, muscles and tissue bloated with barely containable energy—energy contained only by the desire to store it until a final chaotic eruption, the calm of life revealed as nothing more than the patient waiting and pleasurable anticipation of an explosive and memorable death.

Dawn sleepily awoke above the eastern skyline, casting its first pale hues over the sky, adding texture and depth to the forest.

"It is time," whispered Penagashea. "Lie down. There, beside the stream."

Lalawethika did as he was instructed.

Penagashea used his medicine staff to lift himself onto his feet, but then he dropped the staff, taking up a stone ax in its place. He stared at the sky for a few minutes as it gathered color and came alive. Then, without warning, he lifted the ax above his head and bellowed a horrific war cry. Growling and cursing, he fell upon Lalawethika, straddling his midsection. His arms flailed, delivering blows with his free hand. Lalawethika squirmed beneath his master, his head bouncing this way and that, dance of the struggle, but he did not resist. He understood now. He knew there was no other way. Penagashea, overcome with the fury of a madman, spat and drooled upon his subject's chest, neck, and face. He emitted sounds linked to no recognizable language. His eyeballs rolled back in their sockets as the ax struck repeatedly, an awful thud sounding with each blow as it smacked the saturated mud of the riverbank. Birds exploded out from the treetops. Coyotes howled from over hills and crouched barking amidst their bushes and dens, acknowledging the irresistible brutality of survival. Early risers far off in the village heard the frightening cries and stood rigid with worry and concerns of an imminent raid.

With two hands, Penagashea raised the ax and leaned back, moaning from aches in his tired old joints. With one final blow, he let go of the weapon. The ax head stuck into the muddy bank, but his bare hands continued to pummel Lalawethika's body until the last of his strength gave out. With raspy, labored breaths, Penagashea collapsed over the body. Finally, he placed one hand over Lalawethika's heart and the other over Lalawethika's lips. He bent forward and whispered into Lalawethika's ear.

"Shh, shh, it is done. Sleep now, son of the earth. Rest eternal. Sleep...sleep...sleep forever...upon this barren ground...for now you are nothing...you are nothing...you are..."

Satisfied, Penagashea dragged the heavy, limp body down the bank and into the shallow stream. Crouching on his knees, he rinsed the colored pigments from his subject's flesh, all the while howling the Shawnee death laments loud enough to rouse the Dream Spirits from their deepest slumbers.

Part Three

Illusive Ills and Delusive Illusions

Chapter 21

The Closed Door

"Christ, wake up already. Just listen to yourself, John. Maybe it only seems like a couple of months for you, but Jesus, it's going on eight years for them. Eight years. Without so much as hearing your voice. Do you know that my mom still gives me hell if I go more than two days without calling? You have to let them know you're alive. You have to."

Johannes continues staring out the window over Grant's shoulder. He doesn't respond, only shakes his head again.

"There was a time when you were closer to your sister than anyone else. Don't you want that back? You only have to hear her voice and it'll be the most natural thing in the world. Like when you showed up here, totally unexpected, how you and I...you know? Same thing."

"Are you trying to get rid of me? I've been here too long?"

"No, no, it's..." Grant looks away. "Nothing like that..."

"What then? Do you even want me here? You can tell me to go if you—"

"Are you kidding? It's been great having you around again. You're like a brother, you know? We have to look out for each other. Only I would never...but it's not that, that's nothing now... Look, if one of us is down and out, we prop each other up. Simple as that. Otherwise, what else have we got?"

"Who's down and out?"

"What? Do you think you're flying high? Riding the winds of success and respectability? Contentment? All that meditation is getting to your head."

"And how about you?"

"Me? What about me? I have a house, a job, more than one change of clothes. I'm passionate about things and respectful to those around me. I embrace my past, the memories that have made me. Most importantly, I have a family and actually communicate with them. They care about me, and believe it or not, they care about you, too. So stay here forever if you need to, I don't care. I didn't mean you have to go. But I need you to try. Your family, John, they need you, too. Right? I mean, brothers would never...and so, brothers and sisters...same thing...you know?"

"It's too late," counters Johannes.

"That doesn't make any goddamn sense," Grant, with an irritated sigh. "I wouldn't mind seeing her myself. It's been years. Your sis, and you and I, the shit we used to get up to. Good-natured trouble and mischief and just...goddamn good times. Maybe we should get her to come down for a few days. Or make a trip home ourselves."

Johannes watches Grant abjectly for a moment before shifting his muted stare to the window again, beyond which there are mounds of dirt and pits of all shapes and sizes dug into the ground, the shovel and pickax strewn carelessly where they last worked, and a small cluster of horse bones piled somewhere in the midst of it all.

"Ever since Ernest showed me that record," Johannes speaks in a dampened tone, saturated and deflated, "things have started to come back to me. But it's not happening like you all think it is. It's not a seed sprouting and blooming into a flower. There's no one pinpoint, no guiding star—there are thousands of them. All these doors have opened, all at the same time, but nothing's coming out. And I'm left to tiptoe around, gathering little scraps here and there. That's all I get. A chaos of hints and clues, all meaningless on their own. I can't organize them into sensible memories. Maybe I can interpret it through meditation, come to terms with some of it. But that'll take forever, and I'm not even sure I want to. And then, with you talking about it all the time, forcing all these events and people from the past down my throat, there's this suffocating pressure. I don't know how to cope with it. I don't."

"I shouldn't have thrown out all that stuff you left here. Honestly, I didn't think you'd ever be back. Needed the extra space. I just didn't want to look at it anymore. And I didn't trash most of it. Gave a good portion away—donations, I mean. Good thing Ernest still had that record of yours..."

"No, you don't get it. I don't care about the record or any of those things. They don't mean anything to me. You have to understand, Grant, I can't keep up with your pace of living in the past. Nor do I have any desire to. It's good to hear you talk. It's interesting sometimes—hearing about all those things, people and places I don't remember. But that's it, it's just interesting. No different than listening to Ernest or Caryn or Amondale, it's just somebody's stories. And it's not helping me to remember. Anybody from my past that I might meet, the first thing they'll ask is why, why did I go into the mountains? And I still don't know the answer to that myself. You know, even here, I wake up every morning with this feeling, deep down, that I need to leave as quickly as possible, keep moving, go somewhere, anywhere but here. I don't know where the urge comes from, let alone why I left last time or why I came back. The only things that help me ignore all these nagging thoughts have been digging and drinking. I can't even get myself to approach Pa Sonny. Not even to say hello and thanks, even with everything you and Amondale have told me about him. It won't work. Anyone I meet, it doesn't matter who, it couldn't possibly live up to your expectations. Disappointment all around."

"No," Grant looks down at the floor, whispering, "that's not how the world...not how people work..." Wrinkles of severe rationale spread over his face. His gaze alternates between piercing and pleading. Then, suddenly, he jumps out of his chair. "Alright, fine. Come on, then. Let's dig for a while before you have to meet Amondale. I've got some paperwork to finish up, but it can wait."

"We're meeting Amondale?"

"You are." Grant is distracted, searching the cupboards. "Something about your musical tastes. Music of the forest, music of the soul, or some shit like that, I don't know. He must have been talking to Ernest. Plus, you know, he's on the juice again."

Johannes groans. "Just once, I'd like to meet Oscar without a predetermined agenda. And why didn't he ask me himself?"

"He did. Last night. But he called this morning to make sure I reminded you. You forget things, John. Especially with all that whisky. What does it matter, anyway? What else have you got going on? Finally made a move on Caryn?" Grant's glare softens as he drops to his knees and rummages through the lower cupboards. "She wants it, you know. Christ. You're the only dummy who can't see it. Fuck—" Pots tumble out. Grant yanks his hand out of the way, falling back onto his ass. He stands up and slams the cabinet shut. "Don't worry. Amondale's harmless. The least the son of a bitch can do is make you famous. Thou shalt rejoice in he that cometh to aid thy journey." Grant laughs softly to himself. "Goddamn, I've been begging him to make me famous for years."

"Oscar doesn't want to aid anybody. His entire world is just marks on a page."

"That's his best quality. He makes a point of knowing everybody's business, but he never sticks his foot in it. Just take him with a glass of that shitty whisky you all drink and swallow. He'll grow on you."

Grant and Johannes have little to say while digging, but regular grunts of satisfaction tell all tales. Having lost the original sense of expectation and anxiety, the dig has taken on a more leisurely, mind-numbing quality. The grit and sweat of muscular toil force them into a conscious connection with their bodies, away from the harrowing, offbeat pursuits of the mind. Conjecture and theory have lost all import, and they're left with the undeniable truths of a daily grind—darkened skin, burning muscles, teeth and tongues and throats coated with dirt, and a lackluster collection of bones. Life simplified into pure bodily exertion, a daily prehistoric orgy beneath the scalding sun. Sweat and blood, gasps and moans, the pursuit of death.

The bones haven't disappeared, exactly. They've managed to dig up roughly a quarter of the skeleton. The problem is that the bones are no longer united in a single grave, as a lifeless body is wont to do. After the first few weeks of constant aimless defeat and spreading outward from their initial pit, Grant had finally admitted that the wooden cross marking the grave had often moved around the yard over the past eight years. He would sometimes find it lying on the ground covered in teeth marks and then be forced to replace it at best-guess locations. Other times, he'd find it inexplicably stuck into different parts of the yard. One Halloween, he'd found it sturdily planted in front of the house beneath the living room window. There had been storms and near-miss tornados that had either carried the cross away or destroyed it completely, so it had also been replaced numerous times over. Not to mention drunken nights when Grant himself had smashed the forsaken thing.

The point being—a lot happens in eight years. So the fact had emerged that Grant had no idea precisely where the grave had been. They had found that first femur in the original pit, but no other bones. And once they began digging other areas of the lot, the situation became clearer, or more clearly incomprehensible, because over the ensuing weeks they had gone on to unearth bones all over the yard. Some were buried deep and some just below the surface, but none were buried together. A cracked rib here, a couple of vertebrae there, a fractured shin bone over there, a piece of a hoof somewhere else, no sign yet of a skull. The largest bone they'd found had been a hip bone, buried particularly deep at the furthest corner of the lot. Most days, they found nothing, but this no longer bothered them after a while. They found their solace in the digging, not in the discovery of bones. And as they grew to accept this as truth, their fervor increased. They set into a routine with every ounce of energy and every spare moment. As a result, Grant's yard has been carved up to no small extreme. It's an enormous lot, with great swaths of space still untouched. But to the casual observer, it looks as though a hydraulic excavator has run through on a senseless, meandering path, guided by whim and not by objective. No one in town believes that the two men, all by themselves, have managed to move all that earth with only a shovel and a pickax. Excited whispers and tales of conspiracy abound—undocumented Mexican laborers, secretive underground military operations, Native Americans come to revenge their failed raids of more than a century ago. In a town like Creek's Ridge, such theories are nothing more than playful imaginings induced by boredom or, perhaps, hope.

The mystery has settled around them like low-lying cloud cover, both a comfort and a burden. And they refrain from mentioning it. They never discuss the fact that lifeless bones have no business being scattered about of their own accord. External forces are at play, obviously. But if the mystery speaks to them at all, then it's the hesitant stammer of compounded heartbreak, Grant's reasons for locating the remains in the first place, bulky saturated storm clouds, these, ready to burst and fill the trenches with dirtied pools, muddling the whole process beyond salvation. However, whether through ignorance or denial, Grant and Johannes have reformed the salient intimacy of youth, the bond of repair being the very futility of the dirt they dig.

After those first few weeks, once they'd established a routine, the hunt exposed an inner peace, and each of them went through transitions that were evident to everyone except themselves. Grant evolved into a man of poise and purpose. His internal compass stopped spinning, his course emerged as an unimpeachable reality, and he leashed his magnetism right around Johannes's neck. A tug on the leash, and to this, Johannes has followed willingly.

Each day when Grant is at work, either patrolling the desolate county roads or lounging around town chatting with the residents, Johannes walks the streets on a patrol of his own, during which he receives fawning attention from the people of Creek's Ridge. The residents have become more familiar with Johannes, and they include him in their daily lives. They ask him about Grant, the progress of the dig, and his possibly bartending full-time at the bar so that Ernest can play piano more often. They question him about survival tactics, plants and wildlife, solitude and loneliness, simple construction methods, severe weather, and the purpose of his meditation. They bring him into conversations regarding the development or lack thereof in their static, isolated tract of land here in the heart of the country. He came to Creek's Ridge searching for one friend, and now he has more than he knows what to do with. They are all fine, kind people, but Johannes senses that they like him a lot more than perhaps they ought, a lot more than he cares to know them. And yet, all he has for comparison are his friends on the mountain. Inanimate Knecht. The condescending owl. The traitorous stream. The herdsman and his dogs. The bedeviling hunter. The husband and wife running their quiet little shop at the base of the neighboring mountain. Wildlife, for the most part, fled from his approach, and he had grown fond of watching the mountain creatures from a distance, remaining motionless for hours at a time so they wouldn't notice him. Although there had been one animal—a coyote—that had sardonically mastered complete indifference. Johannes often found it rummaging around his shack early in the morning. It would crank its neck around to stare at him for a few beats and then go on with its snooping, totally impervious.

Amondale reminds Johannes of that coyote. Oscar Amondale, a purely objective floater-about, nurtures the hapless inability to conform. He is invariably either one step ahead or one step behind the human race, and his dexterous self-amputation from the world around him has left him perpetually alone. In this sense, Johannes relates to Amondale better than anyone else, yet he cannot understand the man. Unlike Johannes, Amondale exists as a solitary unit in a strictly social context. Amondale would vanish without his innumerable social connections, whereas all these newfound acquaintances only tear Johannes further away from himself. Whatever aims he harbored on the mountain have slipped into a smoky, imperceptible past. He's still grasping at something, only he doesn't know what it is anymore.

"Grant," Johannes calls out. "Where did you meet Amondale?"

"What?"

It takes a moment for Grant's response to float over the wall that separates them. Although they often work side by side, they sometimes dig in different spots, and the decision always comes down to a roll of the instinctual dice. A few days earlier, they had agreed on the necessity of a trench off one of the main pits, but they had also agreed to disagree on the direction of the trench. For lack of communication, as well as a misunderstanding of the disagreement, they had wordlessly begun digging in separate spots right beside each other, then proceeded to dig parallel trenches snaking southeast, occasionally swapping places to share each other's earthly burdens.

"How did you meet Amondale?"

"Through Pa Sonny." Sounds of exertion cease from Grant's side of the wall. "Amondale hunted him down, tracked him to Creek's Ridge."

"Why?" Johannes rests the pickax on his shoulder. They have to speak loudly for their voices to carry over the wall, and neither finds it odd to hold a conversation in this way.

"He wanted to write a book. About Sonny. Somehow, he heard about that whole ordeal with the Easter service and decided it was a story that needed to be told."

"Did he ever write it?"

"No," Grant laughs and resumes digging.

"I'd like to read that..."

"You don't need to. You already know it all. Besides, he got to Sonny too late. I had written to Sonny and told him that no one would know him in Creek's Ridge, that he could live however the hell he wanted and no one would bother him here. He took my advice at face value. Back home, he drank, but he was never a drunk. When he arrived here, he thrust it into high gear. That's when he turned sloppy. Amondale showed up soon after that, right on his tail. Sonny was furious. He never wanted anything to do with Amondale's book. Didn't appreciate the attention. If Amondale got anything out of him at all, they were barefaced lies. A lost cause. But by the time Oscar gave the idea up for dead, he'd already fallen in love with Creek's Ridge. Origins, that's his obsession. He's always working on a hell of a lot of projects. The meat and bones of his career, he does here. Travels the country gathering stories and facts, then comes here to compile his notes into articles and earn a living. Except he's always distracted, trying to document the history of this wasteland. Researching the guy who founded the place and his friend, some sort of Indian magician or something. Those Indian raids that damn near wiped the town off the map. Strange times. But so are these. I don't know what's the point..."

A breeze funnels through their trenches, wheezing as it passes.

"Hey—" Grant rams his shovel into the dirt. "Do you remember when Sonny punched you in the neck? When you were here, just before you ran for the hills? You two were at the bar. That was before Ernest's time. It was still called Jo's Last Stand. I showed up after my shift at the warehouse, and you were both piss-assed drunk. Falling over in your chairs."

"We had a fight?"

"You two used to bicker all the time. Sometimes it took a turn for the worse. Aggressive, obnoxious. That night, you told Sonny that you had been to some Buddhist temple in Asia that was more, uh...spiritually relevant than our old church had been. He took offense to that. You two had already been arguing for over an hour when I intervened. Nothing I could do. You shouted at each other until he took a swing at you. Hit you right in the windpipe. And then, immediately after that, with you bent over gasping and coughing, he told us he once pissed in the vestibule at our church because a devil told him it would keep the damned devils out. You had trouble speaking for the next week."

A moment of silence passes as they each reflect on the memory, one more efficiently than the other.

"I never understood that about you. You always had to push Pa Sonny's buttons over religious shit, ever since we were kids. I never cared. I like Sonny as a man. I never worried about what he does or doesn't believe in. And I think Amondale felt the same once he actually got to know him, so it was easy for him to respect Pa's wishes about the book. I wish you remembered him that way. That Sonny, the Pa Sonny you knew, he's gone. Since he quit drinking, he keeps clear of people. Comes to see me, but less frequently. Usually, I have to go find him. If he's even around..."

"I don't think I've seen him around more than once or twice. Just a glimpse."

"Yeah, he works a lot, making those small deliveries between towns. Helping out farmers and small businesses. It's wild, isn't it? That shitty diner, the one where he found you, he went out of his way to stop there, constantly going off his routes, extending deadlines. He always told me it was because of their coffee. What crap. No coffee is that good. I knew you had something to do with it. Always had a suspicion you were maybe living around there, not so far afield, and that you didn't want me to know. Either way, he prefers to stick to the road these days."

"Why would I have hid something like that from you?"

"Why would anyone hide anything from anyone? I don't know... because, you know...it's hard sometimes..."

"I wasn't. I remember that."

"Yeah, well..."

Johannes slams the pickax into the wall, dislodging a heavy load. He swings again to break up a giant brick of solid dirt at his feet, but the point of the ax deflects off something within. The ricochet just misses his face. The ax slips from his hands as he falls over. Gazing up at an endearing sky, Johannes dusts himself off.

"Sometimes closed doors are more illuminating than open doors," says Johannes. It's not a bone embedded in the dirt but a rock about the size of a fist. Grant mumbles something in response, but it reaches Johannes as an inaudible whisper. Johannes uses the flat end of the pickax to pry out the rock. As he brushes it off, he notices a deep crack through its center.

"I said, what can you see through a closed door?" Grant repeats, louder this time.

"What?"

"That's idiotic."

"Why?" Johannes grunts as he tries to break the rock apart at the crack.

"Does the door have a window?"

"A what?"

"A window!"

"No..."

"Is it made of balsa wood?"

"Huh?"

"Can we break it down with little to no effort?"

"No...I think you're...missing the point..."

A purple shimmer tints sections of the rock, an odd translucence barely concealed by dirt that seems to trap sunlight within the fissure, hoarding it away. Intrigued, Johannes throws the rock at the ground with as much force as he can muster.

"Did you find something?" Grant calls out. "A bone? The skull?"

"No...I'm not sure what..."

"Because the door is closed." Grant resumes his shoveling, cutting violently into the earth. "Idiot..."

"Grant? What would we do if we found the rest of the bones right now, in this wall?"

"Do you think they are?" Grant's strenuous labor ceases once more. "Right here?"

A gust of wind whirls above their heads.

"No, I don't...but I meant *if* we found her right now..." Johannes grabs the pickax again and drops it swiftly down on the rock like a jackhammer—a swift grinding crack, then silence. Johannes picks up two equal fragments.

"What are you...? What was that...?"

"*If* we found all of her, right here, right now, in this wall between us, then what?" Inside, beyond the fissure, the rock has crystallized to a dull cloudiness, jagged and ugly, solid and yet shapeless. Seeing these disappointing halves, their internal secrets exposed, Johannes's fascination wavers. "What's next?"

"Then nothing. Nothing's next. That's what we want. That's the point. Should we try it? Knock down the wall? Connect the trenches?"

"You stay out of my territory. There's treasure over here." Johannes tosses one of the halves over the wall. It lands with a soft thud.

"What is it?" another whisper skirting across a seemingly infinite divide.

"Some worthless mineral. I figured you would know."

"Me? You were the geology major."

"Geology? No, I wasn't...was I?"

"I think so...weren't you?"

The two men stand on opposite sides of a wall, in opposing worlds, gazing into the split halves of a poor man's crystal.

"No," says Grant, finally. "It wasn't you. Geology was Amondale's game."

"Then what's he doing as a crass guerrilla journalist?"

"Oscar studied everything. That's why he's good at what he does."

"What about me?"

"What?"

"What did I study?"

"What do you think? Philosophy. Sci-phi, we always said, me and... you know who."

"Who?"

"You know."

"I don't."

"But you were actually studying escapism, running off. You never finished. Dropped out. Disappeared. Think it's worth anything?"

"Philosophy?"

"No, this rock."

"I doubt it."

"Of course you do. You asshole. I thought you'd found something. All that talk about doors..."

"Forget I mentioned it." Johannes tries to clean the rock on his shirt, hoping to bring out some illusive shine. "But I want to know, seriously, what do you plan to do if we find all the bones?"

"I told you, we won't do anything. That's the point. Peace of mind and nothing else." Grant's rock tumbles, rolls, and bounces along the ground opposite the wall. "If we find it, then we can stop."

"Stop?"

With each load they displace, Johannes develops a deeper connection to Grant, to the earth beneath his feet, to himself. And that's all they do, really—they displace dirt. They don't remove any of it or refill the holes. When they do uncover a bone, they simply throw it onto the pile, take a quick acknowledging breath, and then continue the dig. No revelations, no usurping or restructuring of life's order, no landslides to alter the shape of the world as they know it.

But to stop?

The rock will not shine, the crystal tainted from the inside. A smudge has formed on Johannes's shirt, but it's a smudge of cleanliness, the surface of the crystal having wiped clear the layers of dirt collected there.

"I think I'll keep it," says Johannes.

He hears movement from the other side of the wall and, a moment later, Grant's voice. "Me too. I'll have to ask Amondale."

"Ask him what?"

"If it's worth anything."

Chapter 22

Into the River

January 26, 1818
St. Johns River, La Florida

MESSENGERS ARRIVE EVERY FEW DAYS WITH NEWS OF MILITARY movements across the border. American forces have yet to breach Spanish territory, but their numbers continue to increase, and trackers have already been spotted scouring the western regions. There is no longer doubt that an invasion is imminent. Although our village is far from the area of immediate concern, our daily routines now revolve around preparedness.

The two northern Creeks who showed up some months ago were, through tricks of language and well-devised questions, confirmed to be runaways from the Miccosukee tribe of Fowltown who began all this trouble. Though Chief Kinheja has expelled them from the village, several tribesmen would have preferred to detain them as prisoners to be later turned over to the Americans, and a few frustrated voices called for their swift execution. In troubled times, the hearts of good men are easily infected.

Our warriors are constantly engaged in drills to build their stamina and sharpen their awareness. Scouts and lookouts have secured a wide perimeter around the village. Food is being rationed, weapons mended, and chores delegated to the children, who in recent days enjoy little time for pleasure. I try to lift their young spirits with impromptu games whenever the opportunity arises. Should we be forced to abandon the village, each family has prepared a bundle packed with essential items and heirlooms. Several days' travel to the south is a tract of swampland where the families are to convene. Conditions there are said to be unbearably sultry. Our Spanish lessons have been on hiatus while the students occupy themselves with more pressing tasks. However, the most dedicated students still manage to spend a few spare moments with me and the Father, soothing their hearts with lighthearted talk.

January 27, 1818
St. Johns River, La Florida

Father Jimenez's health has suffered recently. He finds it increasingly difficult to sleep, and his energy is quickly spent. A few nights ago, while on voluntary watch, I checked on him throughout the night, and each time I passed by his hut, I saw him knelt in prayer.

January 28, 1818
St. Johns River, La Florida

The Father appreciates that I assist with the tribe's preparations in every possible way, but most of the time, he keeps me engaged in more personal matters. He trusts my instincts and acknowledges my intentions to remain with the tribe through hell and back, though he warns me repeatedly that the world's great upheavals rarely align with our personal hopes and fears. The future, he says, becomes increasingly uncertain.

In the heat of the afternoon, when we would typically oversee the Spanish lessons, the Father has been teaching me English. Also, whenever I go to collect water or take up a sentry duty, he encourages me to accompany one of the aged traders, all of whom speak English due to their former dealings with the British. Unless I flee the peninsula, I will inevitably encounter the American garrisons. At some point, I will have to decide whether to remain on the peninsula after governance has transferred to the United States. The Father believes the time for renowned Spaniards in this land has passed. The ability to blend in and pass amongst the Americans unseen will prove invaluable.

Ever since Christmas, I have continued to lead the morning prayer. Morning sermons provide a time of communal serenity in the village, a shining light that illuminates a bleak and nebulous future. To their great regret, the scouts cannot attend our daily services as they are scattered throughout the surrounding swamplands. Most days, Father Jimenez manages to summon enough energy to carry him through, but on certain mornings, he requests my help concluding the service. He will sit amongst the families, take a child in his arms, and listen attentively as I reflect on his sermon or read a few verses of Scripture.

———

February 1, 1818
St. Johns River, La Florida

Today is the Sabbath, the first true Sabbath we've allowed ourselves in many weeks. Heightened anxieties have taken our spiritual endeavors hostage, but Father Jimenez temporarily removed those bonds today, allowing our spirits to breathe and roam free.

When I met the Father walking the trails at dawn, I was startled by a strange gleam deep within his eyes. A barely concealed madness. Assuming he had not slept again, I suggested he return to his hut and rest, which he summarily rejected. Contrary to his wild visage, his voice beamed with infectious bliss and pleasure. It sent shivers through my body, reminiscent of the excitement caused by a first kiss, and it propelled me, against my will, along the pleasant trails of memory all the way back to Spain and into the arms of many fair- and dark-skinned young beauties. I must have flushed with color because the Father regarded me with curiosity. At once, I admitted that I was thinking of women, their touch, their bodies. He shushed me as I began to apologize, reminding me that, as yet, I have taken no vows and that such desires are perfectly natural, indeed even for men of the cloth. He reasoned that love, as a human action, should not strike like a projectile. It is meant to radiate, like heat from a fire, warming all within its reach. This includes God inherently, and man-woman relations directly. God is no buffoon, and he would never intend a level of chastity out of his flock that left an earth populated only by monks and nuns.

As we walked toward the village center, he spoke very much out of his custom, expounding on the act of sexual relations, not as a function of Roman Catholic reproductive duty but as a pleasure granted us by birthright. Intrigued, I wondered aloud whether he had ever been with a woman, to which he replied that he very nearly abandoned his calling for his love of a woman. While he had not emerged without scars, he has always suspected that his courage in those days spared many innocent people an enormous amount of suffering. No matter how I prodded, he would not divulge more.

When we arrived, the Father hastily corralled the tribe into the shallow depression that is our chapel. Bypassing the morning prayer, he shared a revelation he had come to during his—I had guessed correctly—sleepless night.

He spoke to them heatedly in their own tongue, not in the tone of a sermon but rather that of a confession. Only a short while later, he was leading us to the shores of the St. Johns. As we walked, the Father directed his confession unto me. In plain Spanish, he systematically explained his failures as a missionary, his straying nature always leaving the Lord's work unfinished while the pleasures of simple mortality distracted and placated his motives. For more than thirty years, ever since his one and only encounter with romantic love, he has been passive, assuming the Seminoles would come to him of their own accord to embrace his Christian God. He believes wholeheartedly in the importance of their traditional beliefs, the core of their identity as a unique people, and he has always presented the facets of Christianity as a framework with which they should integrate their beliefs, not supersede them. Therefore, he has always maintained that they should request holy baptism when they are ready, by their own will and desire. Then, forever after, they will be free to embrace God in any manner they see fit.

In fact, in his three decades here, few of the tribespeople have done this. A handful of the aging generation converted many years ago, but few have expressed interest since then.

Today, in a matter of minutes, he convinced them to march down to the river, not a soul left behind, where they were to receive the holy sacrament under his hands, thereby granting him the privilege of serving his duty, with the added advantage of spit-shining their image in the eyes of Americans soon to breach these borders.

While he and I walked ahead, I leaned in close and whispered to him frantically, asking whether he truly believed the tribespeople were sincere in their faith. Did they truly understand what he was asking of them? Could an aging Spanish Catholic missionary convince the Americans that the entire tribe had converted to Christianity?

A degree of wildness crept back into his expression. "Recently deceased Spanish Catholic missionary," he corrected. And then, "I shall not survive that long, Emedio. You must accept this truth, as they have. Embrace it."

He then asked whether I had been baptized. From our previous conversations, he knows that I escaped the orphanage too young and careless to have known of such matters, so I have never known with certainty whether I received the sacrament or not. At that moment, we came upon the river. The children ran past us, jumping and splashing through the shallows. The families spread themselves along the grassy bank, seeking cool berths sheltered beneath the shade cast by the tree line.

I became acutely aware of the happiness that descended on the tribe as they began to unwind from these troubled days. The elderly joked and laughed, adults played games generally reserved for the children, and with their joyous cries, the children reawakened the youthful, carefree spirit we have all lost track of recently. Even Chief Kinheja washed the paint from his face while the warriors commenced with practical jokes and stalked the area for alligators and snakes, not for hunt but for play.

Mere months ago, such simple delights made up the normal countenance of the tribe, but it seems more distant than that. Two years, two decades—the full breadth of my life. Isn't it odd how the good life can spoil without warning? Like a fruit you save for later, only for it to rot away unseen, putrefying overnight. But the seeds are protected by something powerful, patiently outlasting decomposition and anxious to flourish anew.

Realizing I had fallen behind, Father Jimenez motioned to hurry me along. We watched the tribe at play. After a while, he pointed to the river and told me that wherever I am headed, whatever my future might hold, this is no time for indecision—even in trivial matters.

"Is baptism such a trivial matter?" I asked.

"It is for them," he answered with a glance toward the tribe. Then, he took my arm and led me onward.

The water was cool and refreshing. We situated ourselves to face the sun rising above the tree line, as traditional Seminole beliefs dictate that all matters of even moderate significance be performed facing eastward, lest bad luck befall our gilded intentions.

One after another, they came forward without the slightest hesitation, as though this were a ritual they had performed hundreds of times. The children came first. I supported their backs and cradled their tiny heads, easing them to the water's surface while the Father attended to the sacrament, blessing their brows with handfuls of water and a steady stream of Latin. Though the children understood the solemnity of the occasion, they still tittered when the water tickled their noses and ears, and their smiles were bright as I propped them onto their feet, their eyes bouncing between the Father and myself as though it were all a part of the games that occupied them on the shore. The elders came next, and then the adult population, by which time the sun's full intensity blazed above us. My arms and back ached from balancing so many bodies at the water's surface, holding them steady in the gentle current. Latin words flowed from the Father's tongue, filling me with an unidentifiable confusion.

Finally, Chief Kinheja knelt before us and plunged his head into the water, holding our hands to maintain his balance while the Father recited the rites. Once finished, the Chief knelt and splashed his face with a handful of water, leaving behind a grin—rare for this grave man. A short, joyous bellow escaped his lips as he stood and swept his hands across all that is ours. Then, he directed me to kneel.

And I froze. My mind and body grew stiff and numb. I was nothing more than a stony pillar rising out of the river while the water flowed around me, unhindered by the obstruction.

On the shore, the entire tribe had likewise ceased their play and chatter. They stood at the water's edge, patient and attentive with the same elevated spirit of joy that had overtaken their Chief. They watched us, expectant for me to have my turn.

I felt the weight of Father Jimenez's hand upon my shoulder.

"I hope you have been paying attention," he spoke to me in the Seminole tongue. "Someday, you will find this useful."

Under the combined pressure of his hands, his words, and the hopeful eyes of all those I hold dear, I held my breath and knelt, submerging my head. But, as I did so, I felt guilt. I allowed the water to cover my ears, dampening the sound of the Father's voice as he blessed me. I felt like a betrayer to some sacred belief, though I knew not what. A herald of deceit, a stranger to myself.

Why on earth should I have harbored such reservations about my own baptism? Do I not love and fear God? Do I not intend to live a long and pure life as one of his flock? Such are the repetitious and unsettling thoughts that flood my mind during quiet, solitary moments.

Chapter 23

The Dogs

Branches protrude from every direction, hundreds of massive arms stacked high into the canopy, bending and creaking, effects of an imperceptible breeze or their own innate striving. Navigation in the pine grove presents a frustrating riddle, weaving a path between identical trunks, the forest floor devoid of all but the most persistent weeds and covered by several layers of brown needles shifting beneath muffled footsteps, the cardinal directions melted away, and sunlight is but a dream. A constant whisper asserts that this is, in some way, the most sacred of places.

He had at one time carved two large letters onto the trunk of the tallest pine—**Cm**—just so he could find the damn thing again if ever he wanted, or needed, to climb.

The creature had chased him around the mountain, along the stream that feeds into the river, and finally down into the valley. He waded the stream, slipping twice, and now his saturated clothing weighs him down, slowing this attempt at escape. In the chill of dawn, he shivers no matter how much nor how fast he runs. The prowler has not yet shown itself, but it's there all the same. No creature has ever pursued him with such hostility, the growling, snarling, snapping of teeth, deep within the pines, unconcealed and far from the safety of his shack, the protection of Knecht. The oak is not as tall but more difficult to ascend than the natural spindle-ladder of a pine. And anyway, black bears scale trees he could never manage, mountain cats are known for their prowess, while coyotes will simply wait.

This aromatic blend of fresh and dead pine is magically soothing.

He regularly comes to collect dry pine needles in a boar hide, hauls them along trails and up steep slopes to be spread over the ground inside his shack, followed by another two or three trips to fetch branches full and green that he will hang from the eaves. Some night at dusk, when all is quiet and still and the smoky aroma will leap from the flames to hang around through the long dark night, that's when he'll throw them onto the fire. They ignite like rockets and fizzle out like true love. The pine sap, too, has been essential in maintaining his shack over the years. He has waterproofed the roof with it, sealed off gaps in the walls, repaired the door countless times. He uses it to mend and hang his meager decorations, chews it as gum, fashions torches that last for days. And of all the trees in the grove, that particular tree, **Cm**, the tallest of the pines, has always provided the most copious quantities of the sweetest, stickiest sap.

With legs weakened and lungs gasping for lost breath, he leans against the nearest trunk, feeling the gnarled and jagged bark beneath his fingertips, chewed or scratched perhaps, sticky with dripping sap. He gives an instinctual glance to admire the tree, just a moment of reprieve, and there, on the trunk, beneath his touch, his scarred palm, unbelievable, what are the chances, those two large letters, **Cm**—

The Second Piano Concerto. In the key of C-minor, naturally—

The limbs above sway and groan, a chilling, ghostly rustle, in which he can almost recognize the Scrap from the Concerto's first movement. He joins in, humming the melody in somber accompaniment, seeking stillness, peace, serenity, bliss. A throbbing sea of green and shadow blots out the sky. Even raindrops are hard-pressed to penetrate that bloated canopy. He has waited out torrential storms for hours at a time beneath these pines and always emerged dry. The spiral ladder of C-minor's branches twists upwards, an inviting yet treacherous gateway to heights unnatural.

The first time he climbed it, with no consideration for his actions, he had followed whim and fancy from one branch to the next, never realizing how far off the ground he'd risen until he was perched at the top. A curious sensation, that; latched to the fifteen-foot stalk crowning the tree's peak, wind-swept back and forth with frightening ease high above the forest's canopy. Strong gusts would bend the treetop near to horizontal, and he, clinging on all the tighter, somehow never recognized a sense of danger up there, floating in the sky, nestled amongst the mists of a summer morning settling over the valley, cradled safely in the up-stretched arms of the earth. Who ever imagined ascension to such heights could come so effortlessly? So devoid of fear?

A branch snaps, and then another, the underbrush trampled here and there. His stalker hunts him down and sniffs him out, the religion of the natural world. But the scent of pine overwhelms the scent of flesh, of sweat, of terror. His hands are wrapped around C-minor's lowest branch, ready to hoist his body up into a darkness that leads toward the light.

It was not just whim and fancy. No, something more had propelled him upwards into the trees. Something from within. Thrill-seeking? Loneliness? Curiosity stoked by boredom? Another escape? Even enshrined in the mountain's constant solitude, one still needs to be alone once in a while. Meditation is not always enough. At times, meditation becomes suffocating, dangerous even, to wrap so tightly around one's self. A mantra, a song, no different than drowning or falling from a great height, when all of life's vast breadth is compressed, compacted down into a single thought, a single breath.

Sometimes, having reached the top, he'll spy a golden eagle perched atop a nearby pine. The bird, almost as large as he is, likewise spots this odd, out-of-place creature, blinks a few times as it stares, not with wonder but disdain, and then returns to its watch over the valley—indifferent, just like the owl that once intruded upon his destitution and unwittingly saved his life.

He has not been completely alone anyhow. That young Native American couple residing at the base of the neighboring mountain—what are their names?—down the steep southern slope where the mountain stream empties into the river, with their Siberian husky and their roadside general store. They had given him the cat. She had. Anne...Anne...Anne Ross. That's it, the Rosses. Will and Anne Ross. Will claims to be descended from a Cherokee chief and says he has a duty to occupy this land, though he doesn't even attempt to conceal the fact that he hates it here. And Anne has turned up at the shack on numerous occasions. She never told him how she found it or why, only that she was seeking companionship she could not find at home.

What is the cat's name?

Every time he ever scaled C-minor's branches, he recognized—but did not fear—the danger. Falling from the top would end this life. A misplaced foot, a weak grip from just a third of the way up, and he'd be lying at the bottom with broken bones, injuries severe enough to render him immobile and helpless. A treat for the coyotes that scour the valley floor.

The cat? Was it in the shack? Is it safe? Could it have survived?

A warm breath radiates along the nape of his neck, an intonation of fear. He remembers his hunter and hears Knecht calling from high above. Something tugs, a leash—he refuses to die here as a predator's helpless catch. If death is unavoidable, it's better to grab ahold of the hunter, to hold on tight as they tumble into the stream above the waterfall, dragging it along with him as they plummet to an identical fate. Or else to die nobly, defending his home with spears and bone knives, weapons of his own design, drawing blood from this persecutor, with Knecht, his neighbor, his truest friend on the mountain, watching over him in battle, and then, forever, in death.

The cat, it was, it was in the shack. Anne Ross's eternal excuse, perhaps his as well. And, but, the shack...

What of his friends of the night? The constellations, Orion and Boötes, who step forward when the world has gone dark, passing on their eternal wisdom and listening as he shares his human plights. They tell him not to scale the heights, but to flee.

The pine grove is already far behind, a distant memory undefined. Winding trails lead him up along the mountain's demanding slopes, the grade rising near to vertical. Brambles and briars complicate the ascent, and fog wafts through the trees, obscuring paths ahead and behind. The forest is damp with the heaviness of rain-soaked days. The ground is slick with mud. He inhales and longs for the scent of pine, but there's no going back there now, maybe not ever. The sound of crashing water grows deafening as he races past the foot of the falls, noting the rocks, slick and sharp. The stream seems bloated from a downpour, and the sky has grown dark, night settling earlier than it ought. By the time he reaches the top, he smells nothing but his own blood as it drips from his fingertips, his knees, and his lips, but he continues alongside the stream, the sound of the falls fading behind but still loud enough to cover the sound of the hunters bearing down. Hunters? Yes, he realizes that there is more than one creature on his tail. No animal should have been able to follow him up those rocks, steep and treacherous as they are, but without looking back, he senses them closing in, and he ignores the burning in his limbs, just continues onward as fast as he can. Then again, they might not be on his tail at all but rather surrounding him, corralling him into a trap.

Knecht's huge outline greets him as he struggles up the final thirty yards. He barrels up the grassy slope, flies into his shack, slams the door shut, and leans against it with all his weight, breathing as though he has just emerged from the ocean's murky depths.

But the shack? It was taken. Destroyed in the landslide. This he remembers. So he turns around and creeps forward, inward, towards these uncertain truths, these fictions—this is not his shack—it's Ernest's bar. Dimly lit, as usual, empty, eerily quiet. And something's off, something odd about the mirrors. He rests his ear against the door, hearing no sound from the other side. Leaning his back against it, wary and afraid, he snuffs out the desire to open it for just a quick peek, comforted by this sudden change, these dual illusions—protection and familiarity.

There's movement, not in the bar but inside each of the mirrors. It draws him out of himself to act, to take part. The danger has gone, trapped beyond these reflective walls. Or is he himself trapped within? These are not reflections but scenes of someone's life, one mirror to the next, a succession of recognitions, rounding the perimeter, a voyeur unable to turn his eyes away from the inevitable progression, the individual ticks of time, one patiently after another, for all eternity, until, naturally, reaching the end, the newest broken mirror, victim of a dance, friendly projectiles of the Carnival glass, something lurking beyond the cracks and walking circles at a distance. It stops, trots closer, all teeth and fur, black sprinkled through with brown, barking now, snarling, snapping jaws, fragments of glass tremble and fall and jangle to the ground, then a howl, cut short by a menacing growl, just before the dog jumps, crashes through, claws and teeth and shards of glass and murderous rage, all of them raining down all at once—

Dripping sweat, flailing, every muscle in his body sore and cramped, Johannes opens his eyes to the darkness of the living room. Dust hangs in the air, shimmering in the soft yellowish moonlight. The damp chaos of bed sheets pins him down. He grunts and his limbs go momentarily wild as he untangles himself. Three days since Grant got fed up with Johannes sleeping on the floor. Grant had cussed up a storm and opened the sofa bed, demanding that Johannes use it or else he'd have to sleep out in the yard. Each night, Johannes had eventually moved down onto the floor again, same as he's doing now, aching and rattled with unpleasant dreams, visions, screams.

Johannes positions himself near the window, watching the moonlit clouds skate by overhead. A breeze bumbles through in sporadic gusts. In quick succession, it cools him, dries his sweat, and sends him into a fit of shivers. He reaches for the sheet but changes his mind. Eventually, his cramped muscles soften and relax, and just as sleep is returning, he hears an animal, somewhere out there, howling in the night.

———

"Why are you on the floor again?" Grant kicks Johannes on the hip.

"What?" He raises himself onto an elbow and looks up at Grant. He's sweating again, this time from the heat, not from the dreams. Sunlight floods the house.

"Why do you keep moving down onto the floor?"

"I told you why. I can't do it. I can't sleep on a mattress."

"You have to give it a chance." Grant is shirtless, still dripping from his shower. He heads for the kitchen. "Need to get used to it, that's all. That's a high-quality mattress pad. Real feathers. Heron, I think. It'll grow on you. And what the hell were you screaming about all night? I thought you were getting over that."

The scent of coffee drifts through the house. Johannes leans over the windowsill and breathes in the dewy morning air. A few cars pass by. Kids are walking to school. The sky is a brilliant blue, a blue hardly natural in its vividness. He leans further out the window and gazes down the road toward the house where the German shepherd lives. There's something sitting in the middle of the street, but it could be anything—a bicycle, a trash can, a child, Charlie the postman, or the German shepherd itself.

He pulls himself back inside, gets up, and follows Grant into the kitchen. "I did try," he says. "But with my muscles sore from digging and these dreams, I'm hardly getting any sleep lately. I'm exhausted."

"Still with the dreams?" Grant's full concentration has turned to a carving knife as he shaves fat slices from a chunk of cold ham. Cutting with minute care, each slice equal in thickness, he piles them on the bare counter, rewraps the ham, and puts it back in the fridge. "I paid a fortune for that sofa bed, you jerk. It's real heron feathers, for Christ's sake. When will you get the chance to sleep on heron feathers again? Or was it ibis...?" Grant leans against the sink, facing the table. He squints, searching Johannes as he exhales a warm sigh of concern. "Almost three months and you still look like hell."

Johannes shrugs and sits down at the table. "You know that German shepherd? From the house down the road?"

"Sure. Doctor Mengele."

"Mengele? It's called Mengele?"

"No," Grant sneers. "Just a personal joke. You've met the owner, haven't you? Vu?"

"Maybe at Ernest's. But how would I—"

"Little Asian guy. Vietnamese, I think. He stays in a lot. Take the time someday. He's interesting. I saw him carrying around a dead coyote pup once."

"The Asian guy?"

"No, Mengele. Carried it up and down the street for hours, displaying it like a trophy. No eyes. Gruesome."

"What?"

"They were gone, the coyote's eyes. Why on earth he mutilated one of his own kind, I haven't a clue. And just a pup. Hence the name—Doctor Mengele. But others around town, they still call him Hero for that, I think. He has several names, I guess. I don't think anyone knows his real name, if he even has one..."

"So the dog's not particularly friendly?"

"Who said that? He's great. With people, at least. I kill time with him a lot, as a matter of fact. Even bring him along on my rounds sometimes. He'll just follow me around for hours or hop into the cruiser with me. Sits right up front, Deputy Mengele. I think Vu beats him. Maybe that's why he seeks attention from everyone else. Seeking out affection he doesn't get at home."

"What?"

"What?"

"Why did you say that?"

"Because that's what I meant."

"In my dream..."

"What?"

"No, never mind. So why don't you do something about it?"

"Why should I?" Grant pulls a frying pan from the cupboard, sets it on the range.

"You're the sheriff."

"Vu's not eating the mutt. It's his business. Why do you care? What? You trying to pull some hippy bullshit on me now? Is that what you picked up living in the mountains? Animals are just the same as people? Flowers, insects, rocks, and trees, too, right? What's next? You'll want me to help you plant the Great Creek's Ridge Bamboo Forest? Or we start taking in all the local coyotes? Nurture them like our own little babies? How about some rattlers and scorpions to round it out? The desert's just a few borders away. All of them, Mother Nature's precious creatures, that it?"

"That's not what I meant. It's just...when I was out walking yesterday, I...crossed paths with that dog. Again."

"And what? Fell in love?" Grant smiles as he looks over his shoulder. "Jesus. What? You're white as a ghost."

"It was stalking me."

"Get the fuck out of here," Grant laughs. "He wanted to play."

Johannes shakes his head. "It kept at a distance, sometimes out of sight. But I could feel it there. Everywhere I went. I must have walked ten miles yesterday trying to shake it. When I first passed by that house, it was sitting on the porch, calm but alert. It watched me all the way down the road. At first, I didn't think anything of it. But after walking a while, I felt this nagging discomfort. That feeling you get when you're being watched."

"You probably were being watched. In a town of this size, we're all being watched. People notice everything."

"Not like that. Not people. By something...threatening. I was at the edge of town, way out by the church. Just me and this dog and this church. No one else was around except for a construction truck parked out front. It wasn't a question of whether it was following me, but why."

"I just told you, he follows me around too," Grant scoffs. "And not just me. Everybody. Like the town stray that everyone looks after. Or, who knows, maybe he looks after us."

"I walked around the church grounds, thinking I could lose it in the field out back, talked with the workers for a bit—"

"Workers? What workers?"

"They said they were surveyors. Taking measurements of the building and the grounds, the cemetery."

"Why? Who for?"

"I asked, but they didn't know. Just said they were sent to take the measurements. They suggested I consult the Lord about it. First time I've laughed in a while."

"I may have to do just that..."

"After that, I headed for The Borderlands and got something to eat. I talked with Ruthie for an hour or more, but whenever I looked out the window, I saw that German shepherd pacing in the street. I had another coffee and left when the dog was gone. I made a break for the creek, following it south until I was almost to the church again. There's that grassy grove of trees and bushes, you know? Where I've been going to meditate. I told you—"

"Yeah, I know, and I told you I know every nook and cranny of this town."

"I tried to calm myself and admire the grove, just drifting and humming the Scrap, but I couldn't focus. My eyes were constantly drawn away, searching for that dog, certain it had followed me. Discomfort became full-blown paranoia. When I finally sat down to meditate— the reason I had gone out walking to begin with—it felt as though the dog was breathing down my neck."

"Plants and meditation," Grant repeats with abhorrence and turns back to his breakfast preparations.

"Meditation wouldn't take. Not even close. There was only one thing left to do."

"What's that?"

"Dig."

"Alone?"

"I had no choice. The only thing I could think of was to have the pickax in my hands when the dog reappeared. So I followed the creek back, and I was almost here, just at the edge of the yard, when the dog stepped out from behind the bushes. It had something in its mouth—"

"A dead animal, right?"

"And it blocked my path, like it knew I'd be coming, had been waiting for me. I couldn't stop. I was so close, the mounds and pits just a few steps away."

"An opossum? Another coyote?"

"I could see the pickax lying on the ground. So I couldn't turn around and couldn't veer away. My mind was bent on avoiding the dog while my body was drawing me right through it."

"So what happened?" Grant drops the ham into the frying pan and adjusts the burner to low.

"I was pure perception, no thought or reason, legs acting of their own accord, only following instructions to get me home, to find the pickax. And I heard growling. An imposing, menacing snarl. It was staring at me, directly into my eyes. A piercing, animal stare, the thing still hanging from its mouth. As I approached, the dog suddenly came toward me. Then I felt it. Here, on my hand."

"Felt what?"

"Right here. The dog. It was licking my hand. And I screamed. I screamed loud enough to drive the growls away."

"What? The hand you jerk off with?"

"No, my scar, from the mountain—"

"Dogs sniff at our crotches. Same thing. Meditation, mental masturbation, why else would he lick your hand?"

"But, no, that's not the point. Why was I so scared of a dog? I was mortally frightened. My neck was in the guillotine."

"You're hardly a French monarch, John." Grant flips the slices of ham and slides them around as they sizzle in the pan. "Maybe you were a Pope once, in a former life. There've been a few Pope Johns. So, I guess you'd fit right in with that church and Del Bosque..."

"The scream worked. It scared the dog away. It jumped back and then just wandered off, finally leaving me alone. And when I looked down, I saw the thing it had been holding in its mouth."

"A rabbit? Weasel? What?"

"A bone."

"One of our bones?"

"I think so. But I didn't recognize it, so..."

"That son of a bitch..."

"And last night, too..."

"Wait... That scream? Yesterday? Everybody in Creek's Ridge heard that. Pestered me about it for hours. I was investigating that scream all fucking day. You asshole, that was you? You're trying to tell me that that's why you were screaming through the night? Hunted by a dog in your dreams now, too?"

"Yes. The dog finally got me in the dream. Only it wasn't a dream. Not really. More like memories of something that happened on the mountain and... It's usually the landslide that gets me in my dreams, but not this time. Something else, something chasing me, and these German shepherds...two of them...but I don't know if anything like that ever actually happened..."

Grant stares curiously at Johannes. He sits down in his chair. "I'm all ears," Grant mutters, a sly grin as he glances at the range.

"The dream ended inside Ernest's. I was alone. And the mirrors... they weren't mirrors but more like windows, each one looking over a different time and place, projecting moments from someone's life. They were so real, like I could reach out and touch them, play a part in them. One image was...it was a little boy and a dog, playing together in a large backyard, with a few other people milling about. I suddenly lost my breath, not because I recognized anything, but because I remembered the dog that had been chasing me. I was still being hunted, and I panicked, but it only lasted a moment before I was engrossed in the mirror again. There was something infinitely serene about it. A faultless innocence embodied in the way they played. Like you say, what is it? The harmless games of youth. An absolutely perfect vision, a slap in the face that leaves a pristine handprint, fingerprints and all. It was a German shepherd in the mirror, but not the same one. Not Mengele. It seemed like I was getting closer to the action inside the mirror, floating toward it from above, drifting around it, my soul longing to be there, to be inside that simple existence. As soon as I realized that the little boy was actually me, I remembered everything. Time, place, circumstances. An honest-to-god childhood memory. I was six years old. It was summer, and I was playing in the backyard. The backyard our families shared."

Grant nods, his brow folded over in thick creases.

"You were there, stuffing your face from your mom's raspberry bushes, and your mom was working on the other side of the garden. Two girls were playing together in the grass. Your sisters, I think. I slipped back in time, swallowed by the memory, led on by the peacefulness of that day, unbounded and carefree. Like meditation. But the more I became a part of it, the more I remembered, and then the fear returned. Because I *was* bound, entirely. By the dream, by the mirrors, by the walls of the bar, and by the knowledge of what was about to occur. I knew what was going to happen. I felt it coming, and I couldn't escape it."

"Shit, that's a first."

"The German shepherd, in the mirror, it was your dog..."

"Cannon..." Grant looks up with sudden interest.

And Johannes, nodding, "Cannon bit me on the leg that day for no reason at all. I kept looking back at the door, expecting Cannon or Mengele or both to bust it down, to burst through, baring teeth through a knowing grin. Terror washed over me. My leg began to throb, anticipating the inevitable attack. The game between Cannon and the boy-Johannes became strained and treacherous. I raised my fists to smash the mirror but couldn't because I knew Ernest wouldn't allow it. So, instead, I struggled to move away. In the next mirror, where I expected to meet another different scene, it was the same vision, still playing, still approaching the moment I'd be bitten. So I continued, from mirror to mirror, frantic, and it was always the same, closer and closer to being bitten. But by following the mirrors, I only ended up trapped behind the bar. As I came to the last mirror, the one that Ernest and I broke that night, that's exactly when Cannon should have bitten me, but the memory ended there. The vision, gone. Something different stalked behind the cracked mirror."

"Mengele..." says Grant, awe in his voice.

"It was waiting for me. It burst through the glass. And it got me."

Grant inhales slowly, holding a long, deep breath that he exhales even more slowly. He waves his hand as if swatting at a fly. "It's beautiful. Perfectly balanced. My dreams are never so succinct, so symmetrical."

"What?"

"I mean, I'm jealous. Mine are maddening. They're like acid trips. Nothing makes sense in them. I never know what they're about."

"You can have mine if you want. Take them."

"Wait, but what about yesterday? Did you end up digging?"

"No. I couldn't. I went to Ernest's."

"Of course you did," Grant sighs. "You see? It all makes perfect sense, like puzzle pieces. What was the rest of the dream about? Before you were in the bar?"

"On the mountain. I was being chased by the German shepherd, by Mengele, all through the forest, everywhere I used to go near my home. Nothing dreamlike about it. Every tree and slope was accurate, down to the smells, the textures. My sweat and burning muscles and fatigue. Even my thoughts flowed just as I really would have thought them. And the tension of being pursued. But I never even saw the German shepherd, not until it jumped through the mirror."

"Then how do you know it was Mengele chasing you?"

"No...it may have been...Asterion and Chara..."

"Who?"

"The hunter's hounds."

"But you didn't see them?"

"I just...felt them..."

"Just felt them..." Grant shakes his head, laughs a little. "Like you felt Mengele licking your hand. Anyway, you see? I told you things would start coming back."

"If this is how my future is going to play out, with bastard memories that terrorize me every night and bleed into my waking hours, then I don't want anything to do with it."

"Of course you do. Like I said, you just need to get used to it. Same as that mattress pad. Real heron feathers. Memories are healthy. They're reminders of who we are, where we come from."

"But then why is a bite on the leg the only thing that's come back to me? In all this time? It's no different than that Rachmaninoff record. The Scrap haunts me day and night. I sense its weight, dragging me along...drifting, disappearing, discovering, I don't know what. That record, maybe it was mine a long time ago. And the music must have meant something to me. But, ultimately, it's meaningless."

"Scrap of what?"

"From the Second Piano Concerto."

"What?"

"Nothing. It doesn't matter."

"I used to think there was only one way to work through a messy situation."

"How's that?"

"It only makes things messier." Grant shakes his head. "But life's supposed to be messy. If it's not complicated, then you're doing it wrong. That's a bit of wisdom I picked up from you-know-who. By now, you should be able to see that your preferred method of escape—literally escaping—isn't doing the trick. Your memories will come back whether you like it or not. That's all there is to it. It doesn't matter if you like who you are or who you were. You don't have the power to wipe the slate. That's what was so damned silly about cutting yourself off from everything and everyone. Most of us assumed you were never coming back."

"What do you mean?"

"Dead. People thought you were dead."

"Who?"

"Who do you think? Old friends. Your mom, my parents. Your sister. Inez. I still keep in touch with everyone, John, almost everyone, and, you know, word gets around. Can you imagine how it was for me? I was the go-to. All of them always asking me about how you were, where you were, what sort of fucking adventure you were off on this time. Never curious about me, about how I was doing, recently separated and all, trying to find my feet, alone, in a new place I'd never been before. Only, always—*Heard from John yet? What's John up to? You think John's okay? Aren't you worried about John?* For Christ's sake, what could I tell them other than 'He's gone'? Not to mention that everyone knew you were here with me before you disappeared. It was unspoken, but I know they all blamed me. Still do. When really, you know, it wasn't even my fault. How can it be my job to stop you from doing the same thing you've always done? After a few years and no word from you, even I had to entertain the idea that this time it was permanent. The only person who always believed you were still alive was Pa Sonny, but even that was just blind hope. What little remains of his faith. Jesus Christ, man, I mean, take a vacation. Take a couple weeks. Go camping or whoring or something. But disappearing won't change anything. Only made it worse, as far as I can tell. But, look, forget about all that now. You're back. We're mending things, putting them right, maybe. And memories are the essential tools of life. They're how we give value and worth to what's around us, to what's to come, to the good or bad that falls in our laps. They're tools in the garage, photos hanging on the wall. I have a lot of painful memories, too, you know? But I would never want to be without them. Not totally."

"But these memories, these dreams and nightmares and visions, the sensation of imperceptible fear, they're all connected. All coming from the same place. After-effects of the same event. And it follows me even now. I'm chained to that wall of photos, only my head's turned the wrong way round and I can't see anything but shadows, the assumption that they're there. Like Plato and his goddamned cave..."

"Let me guess—the landslide. That's one memory you're better off forgetting. At least for a while."

"The landslide? Yeah, but, no, not this—"

"Then what?" Grant interrupts. "Finally going to admit it?"

"Admit what? I'm talking about Cannon. Don't you remember when Cannon bit my leg?"

"No," Grant smirks and looks away. "That dog was a mean shit. He bit everyone at one point or another."

Johannes stares over Grant's shoulder, out the window. They've grown silent, words and thoughts sucked out or sealed in, or both.

"But I don't understand..." says Johannes. "This fear of dogs..."

Without expression, Grant focuses on Johannes, his stare frozen with a thousand silent questions. He tries to look away, but only his head turns. His eyes are nailed to Johannes. His jaw twitches, then he slumps in the chair and scratches his shoulder.

"No, John. You love dogs. You've always loved them. Your family had a dog that damn near lived forever. Sometimes you would come over to our house just to play with our dogs, not even with me or my sisters. You used to walk peoples' dogs for extra cash. Hung out at shelters, volunteered... How can you not...?"

An unsettling silence. Strangers meeting for the first time, each disliking the other's gait. Grant rises, rigid, cautious. He walks out of the kitchen and down the hall. A commotion erupts from the spare room, things being shifted around, thrown, other things falling. Grant returns with a few loose photographs. He's wearing his sheriff's shirt now, though it's still unbuttoned. The badge glints from sunlight glaring through the window. He flips through the photos, but then he glances up, cursing, and throws them on the table.

"Damnit, John, why didn't you—"

Sooty black smoke is rising from the frying pan. The odor of scorched meat fills the room.

Johannes reaches for the photos while Grant runs the pan under hot water and scrapes off the charred ham.

The First: Johannes, Grant, and two small girls sit side by side, all of them wearing swimsuits. Johannes and Grant appear to be ten or eleven, the girls younger. A summer day. Sweat. Laughter. One of the girls is looking at Johannes, in whose lap rests Cannon's oversized angular head, happily oblivious and soaking wet. Grant's smile is aimed at the girl who is looking at Johannes, and the other girl is distracted by something out of frame.

Johannes shudders at the thought that the dream never ended and that he's been dragged into one of those mirrors in the empty bar.

The Second: A teenage Johannes, crouching on the grass between two full-grown English bulldogs. The white dog on the left crowds against Johannes's side. The brown dog on the right stares up at Johannes, panting as Johannes scratches beneath its chin. An open-mouthed smile laden with laughter splits Johannes's face.

He flips to the third and final photo. In all three, the young Johannes stares directly into the camera, meeting the eyes and reflecting the wonder of the present day.

The Third: Johannes, barely an adult, has an aged and sickly springer spaniel lying in his lap, staring up at him with weepy cataract eyes. An equally youthful Grant is beside them, turned and walking out of the photograph, the top of his head chopped out of frame. This Johannes grins a forced smile, incapable of concealing the mournful pain and regret that has brought him there.

"Queen Maj..." he whispers.

"I don't have many photos of you." Grant is standing over him, buttoning his shirt. "We never felt the need for pictures. But there you go. Three for three. Not a single picture without a dog. What more proof do you need? Do you remember her?"

"I didn't," says Johannes. "But I do now." A flurry of ghostly images arises and quickly fades, a deck of cards being shuffled. He looks down at the picture again. Queen Maj, his dog, was old. She looked at the younger Johannes with longing in her eyes, the reluctant acceptance of peace just over a nearby horizon.

"Do you remember when that photo was taken?"

"This was..." Johannes nods, searching for the words, "...the night before we put her down. I came back from school for this. Skipped classes for a week. I had to see her. Had to say goodbye..."

"Keep the pictures," says Grant. "They're yours now. Hang them on your wall."

"I still don't understand." Johannes sets the pictures on the table. "If I've had this affection for dogs, then what was that yesterday? Why would I react like that to a harmless German shepherd?"

Grant sits down, rubbing his forehead.

"There was no reason for me to fear that dog. None at all. But because of that, I found myself hunted in a nightmare, chased directly to the memory of Cannon biting me."

"No..." Grant shuts his eyes and pinches the bridge of his nose. "No, you're thinking too much into it, making it more complicated than it is. It's just mental association, that's all. That's how the brain works. This is how you begin to familiarize yourself with...with yourself. You see a German shepherd, and you recall another German shepherd. I say rock, you say roll. I say birds, you say bees. Ali, Foreman, dig, pickax, Doctor Mengele, Nazi psychopath. Halloween, and we're going into haunted houses. A broken mirror, and we're cleaning up shattered fucking relationships. I say Sammy, and even if you haven't spoken with her in years, you visualize her, you remember all the good times. We had so much fun together as kids, the three of us, playing our stupid games. You're supposed to want to see her, to do it all over again. Hell, you ought to be on the phone in a heartbeat. There it is," nodding toward the receiver, "call her right now."

"Sammy?"

Grant leans forward, looking at the floor. He's rubbing his forehead again, now his cheeks, pressing his temples to suppress the agonized expression that has formed there.

"You're kidding, right?" But Grant knows the truth and cannot bear to look at Johannes. Instead, he grabs the photo of the four children and Cannon. He slides it between them on the table and points out the little girl whose gaze is latched onto the younger Johannes.

Johannes leans over the photo. "Is that...she's your sister?"

They stare at each other for what seems like a long time, but in truth, it's not. Grant gets up and opens the fridge. He takes out the ham and begins his breakfast preparations all over again. After struggling to cut a single slice, he slams his fist down on the countertop. Dishes clatter, he drops the knife, and it clangs to the floor. A glass falls and breaks in the sink. He repeats the violent gesture, letting out a tirade of barely stifled curse words.

"No, no, no..." growls Grant. "That's Sammy. *Sammy*. She's *your* sister."

Johannes gets up and walks out the door, into the yard, past mounds and pits. Nervous and guarded, on the lookout for the German shepherd, he keeps walking until he reaches the grove at the edge of town, where he sits down and folds his legs beneath him. The Scrap already emanates from his throat, a low and repetitive moan, his jaw tense, clenched shut for just one more attempt at simultaneously losing and finding himself.

Chapter 24

To Scale a Mountain

"It is all in appearances. Constructing belief. Theatrics. If we can fool the Great Spirit, then even the sharpest of white men are but infants to our guile, and we can convince the staunchest Shawnee of anything."

Penagashea's strenuous breathing rasped as they tried to maintain a decent pace. They were halfway through the long journey, but Penagashea's frail body had gone into decline since their weeks at the cave. Lalawethika did not think the old man could manage the journey, but it promised a spiritual significance that Penagashea said neither of them could afford to miss, so he would not be deterred. Before they left their village on the Tippecanoe River, Lalawethika had gone around trying to convince one of their tribesmen to lend them a horse. None of the Shawnees had even considered his request, vocal with their assumptions that the two drunkards would only trade the animal for firewater. Yet their tribesmen did not hesitate to load the pair down with goods to be bartered, as they were also reluctant to make the journey themselves.

This gesture, Penagashea reasoned, was a sure sign that the ritualistic pseudo-sacrifice had succeeded. Only a few weeks prior, the tribe would not have trusted Lalawethika with piles of animal shit any more than with their tradable goods. Penagashea insisted that Lalawethika was no longer recognizable as a Shawnee misfit, that his historical essence had been lifted from his body, sent on to death's fields, and all that remained of him now was an innocence, pure Shawnee medicine bound in human flesh.

Lalawethika was not so confident. The tribe's treatment of him had not noticeably improved. His humble claims that he had given up the firewater were met only with skepticism. For the most part, his tribesmen continued to avoid him, children gawked with aversion, and his wife's sighs had grown louder. Whispers floated around the village, questioning the nature of his relationship with the medicine man. But, true to his word, Lalawethika had not once drunk of the firewater in the weeks since leaving the cave. If anything in the village had changed, it appeared to be he, himself.

Lalawethika carried their satchels, weighed down with their meager provisions and the medicine man's wares. And though he dragged the pelts meant for trading on a grass mat behind him, he still outpaced Penagashea, who hobbled along with support from his medicine staff.

"Time is yet plentiful for you," Penagashea warned. "All things grow. Patience is the acceptance of time. It is the participation in and the experience of time. But time is a luxury not granted to everyone. In your first childhood, you were robbed of time. Your patience could not flourish. Be grateful for this, your second infancy. Allow yourself to blossom naturally, with patience. You will be the next Shawnee medicine man—I have deemed it so—but now you understand that a medicine man bears a challenging responsibility. Even more so for you, a medicine man charged with rebuilding the Shawnees' faith in us, in our art. Not only must you perfect the methods and the presentation—which are superficial elements, nothing more than costumes to our true role—but you must also fortify those elements with honest spirituality. You must forge a closer link to the Great Spirit than any Shawnee of our time. Nothing can be allowed to sever the bonds you share with the Great Spirit and our Grandmother. You must commune with the Cyclone Spirits and the Dream Spirits. Not only must you know the great bear monster, Yakwawi, but you must also tame her. You must befriend the little people of the forest and share Cheekitha's lucky intuition. You shall summon Nenimkee the Thunderfowl with a whistle, perch upon its back, and fly high above distant lands. Even the Great Serpent must be in your confidence, though never in your trust. That is why we travel to the white man's city."

As they navigated a steep slope, Lalawethika held Penagashea's elbow and asked, "What good is communion with the spirits if the Shawnee people fail to hold the spirits in high regard?"

"That will change," Penagashea said. "Haven't you noticed? Why has our people's faith in tradition waned?"

"Because of the white man," answered Lalawethika.

"It began when I was still a young warrior," Penagashea said, nodding. "The white men approached, their arms outstretched and bearing gifts. Calculated deceit, the work of the Great Serpent. White men know the red man's path is richer than theirs. They covet our land, our knowledge, our harmonious balance with nature. Their gifts were a poison to us. And then they fought their wars—here, on our lands—staining our fields with their stinking blood and filth. With false promises, they enlisted our help. With their strength, they established a rogue nation in the lands of our fathers. Now, instead of gifts, they bring us papers filled with ink marks scratched by other white men, papers that claim their legal right to these lands. By whose laws? Not ours! Their God-given right? Not our gods! And to distract us when we grumble, they offer still more gifts, their firewater the most potent and destructive gift of all. But you can only dig a hole so deep. Red men are becoming aware of the white man's tricks and schemes."

"You believe red men will rebel?" Lalawethika stopped walking, but Penagashea tugged him onward.

"Red men have never stopped rebelling. You have heard the stories. Battles still occur. Conflicts in our own river valleys become more common with each passing year. They have increased tenfold since the year of your birth. At that time, I was still under Three Stones' wing and the white man's nation was just being formed. Since founding their nation, they have become bolder. They ride into our lands not as explorers and emissaries, but as surveyors and poachers. And the Tippecanoe River, the fields and forests where we now dwell, these are not our true lands. They are lands the white man has designated to us. The Treaty of Greenville? That paper was best suited to wipe a hog's filthy asshole. The southern lands become bloodier by the day, even though many of those tribes have betrayed the Great Spirit by acknowledging the white man's god. And what is the white man's god? What, but the Great Serpent in disguise? But the battles are short and decisive. White men have traded their own weapons to us, and still we cannot prevail. Why is that? Tell me."

A long swath of dark blue appeared as the great lake came into view over the ridge.

"Their numbers are too great," said Lalawethika.

"Greater than ours?" spat Penagashea. "Red men have not disappeared. They cower, they hide. Red men reside in every hidden corner of this land. For thousands of years, that arrangement has served us well. We were given to flourish on our own, thriving within the intimacy of our families and dying in homes we cultivated ourselves. But the coming of the white man destroyed that careful balance. We can return to that. We can reclaim what is ours. We must."

"If red men unite..." Lalawethika was wistful, staring north at the bulging purple clouds rolling in over the great lake.

"And why has that not yet occurred?" continued Penagashea. "Because who are our leaders? Who commands the posture of red men? Who do white men seek out when they approach our villages? Who falls for the white man's tricks again and again?"

"The warriors," answered Lalawethika.

"Only a man who communicates with the Great Spirit can be a true leader." Penagashea's eyes were glassy and feverish. "Many years ago, the chiefs looked to the medicine men for counsel in every decision. When we fail to consult with the Great Spirit through our medicine men, we are no better than those who have forsaken the Great Spirit altogether. Warriors may lead battle charges and hunting parties, but they are not fit to be true leaders. They garner strength from their pride, but it is that same pride that keeps them from joining hands with their fellow red men across this land and pushing the white man back into the sea from which he crawled. Do you understand?"

Lalawethika stared at his mentor, uncertain of how to respond.

"It is a mountain you must climb, a mountain where you must reside, with all Shawnees looking up to you for guidance. Your feet must be planted in the soil, your hands clasped in theirs, but your eyes, ears, heart, and soul will be raised above, on a higher plane, in constant communication with the Great Spirit, privileged to all the secrets of our world. When the other tribes see how you have united the Shawnee Nation, they will embrace the slopes of your mountain. They will follow and support you. And when the time is right, they will help as you topple that mountain onto the heads of our enemies. But first, you must scale its treacherous slopes. To do so, you must learn to utilize the tools available to you, even if those tools are crafted by the white man. When the enemy is strong, we must expose his weaknesses and turn his strength against him. To stand erect alongside the Great Spirit, one must also, at times, lie down with the Great Serpent."

The old man jerked a finger toward troublesome clouds gathered over the lake, towering billowy cumuli with lightning play near the tops and carved out by cavernous shadows.

"Come now," he grabbed hold of Lalawethika's arm. "The storm will break soon. The great lake awaits us. I know of a place, a hermit along its shores. She will provide us shelter and food. And pleasures. We shall rest through the storm and continue when the clouds part. I am eager to introduce you to my good friend, a great man amongst scoundrels in the white man's city."

Chapter 25

Seduction

The barstools are all occupied, so they take the bottle and a bucket of ice to a table instead. Johannes crumples into the bench seat below the mirrors, and Caryn settles in beside him. Giving her a sidewise glance, he starts to move to the chair across from her.

"Stay," she says and rests her hand on his arm before pouring out The Carnival. For a few minutes she remains leaned forward, her elbows on the table, taking sparse sips and swaying her shoulders as they listen to the music. Lately, Ernest has been spinning nothing but a vintage album of Rachmaninoff's preludes and short orchestral works, played by Rachmaninoff himself in some great hall of Boston back in the Thirties. He recently acquired the rare recording from the old man in the motorized chair, Mr. Conrad Wilms. On the night it arrived, he persuaded Johannes to stay late after closing to privilege him with a private listening. The quality was horrendous, as expected from such an old recording, and Johannes had fallen asleep shortly after it began.

Johannes has already finished his first glass. Caryn refills him and takes another small sip of her own. She falls back against the wall, nestling against Johannes's arm. "These benches are so comfy."

Johannes nods. "Not too soft, not too hard."

"The upholstery is perfect. Almost magical. Why do we always sit at the bar? I wonder where Ernest found all these furnishings. The mirrors, the piano, even the tables—they're old but charming. And sturdy. The perfect height. Only one problem..."

"What's that?"

"It's you. You stink."

"We've been digging since before noon."
They lean against each other, slumped and propping one another up.
"All day?"
Johannes nods, drinks.
"And you do that every day?"
"Just about. We missed yesterday."
"Why?"
He points at The Carnival, raises his glass, smiles, shrugs.
"You still haven't told me what you're digging for."
"Mm...you know. The thrill."
"That's a lot of digging for no ends."
"Just digging."
"I've heard the stories."
"About what?"
"About the hippies and anthropologists who used to come through here. Looking for the true burial sites."
"What burial sites?"
"The founders, Tenskwatawa and Emedio del Bosque. You really think they're in Grant's yard?"
"I don't...maybe...could be..." He takes a drink, considering. "Why not?"
"What a fascinating time that must have been, don't you think? Imagine the attention you'd attract if you actually found something. It would stir up the pot around here. The pilgrimages would start again, bringing a new influx of people. All sorts, I'm sure."
"I don't think attention is what we're after..."
"Isn't Grant supposed to be policing or something?"
"He caught you, didn't he?" Johannes lifts his glass to his mouth. "Technically, he's always on duty. He usually wears his uniform when we dig. Ready for anything. But he says he doesn't need to patrol because nothing ever happens, and if anything does happen, everyone knows where to find him." Another sip. "He's right."
"But couldn't you have managed a quick shower?"
"I did. This morning."
She laughs and slaps his thigh, her smile radiant as she searches his face. "You could clean yourself up, though. For a nice relaxing night out. Your skin is getting dark."
"Is it?"
"Maybe just filthy."
"Your hair, too. Lighter, I mean. It looks lighter. Like you dyed it?"
"Just the sun, I guess. I've been spending a lot of time at—"
"Well, goddamnit! Look at the two of you all cuddly as bunnies."

Amondale drops heavily into the chair opposite and winks. "Huff, what a scorcher out there today, huh? Dropped more sweat onto the pages than ink. The air conditioner at the office has been on the fritz, and I busted one of the fan blades with my shoe. Works for shit now."

"You kicked it?" says Johannes.

"Heh. No. My shoe. I threw it."

Caryn is laughing, "Why?"

"What do you mean? I was taking it off—my shoe! Thelonious, old man, bring us a glass, will you? Been spending more'n a bit of time together, I see."

Johannes and Caryn look at each other.

"Guess we have," says Johannes.

"Two lost souls wandering the land and, well, here you are..."

Ernest sets a glass in front of Amondale and retreats without a word.

"Ah-ha, and here we are." Amondale fills his glass and raises it. "*Geonbae.*"

They raise their glasses and drink.

"What did you say?" asks Caryn.

"For a pair of wanderers, you don't come off very worldly."

"It means *Cheers,*" says Johannes.

"That'a boy. Not such a dimwit after all."

"I figured that," Caryn says, sitting up and scrutinizing Johannes. "But what language is it? And how do you know it?"

"It just...I don't..." Johannes shrugs. "It's Korean. *Cheers.*"

"Humpty-frickin-Dumpty over here. And you," Amondale turns to Caryn, "give us the phrase in French."

"I don't know it. I never learned much."

Amondale cringes in mock heartbreak, recoiling with a hand over his chest. "Must have been a helluva dull marriage." He raises his glass again. "À votre santé! Commit that to memory, darling. And to the thirst for knowledge as well, how about it?"

"Thanks, Oscar," she says, raising her glass and blushing.

Caryn takes another small sip while Johannes and Amondale empty their glasses. Amondale immediately reaches for the bottle.

"I suppose it makes sense," Amondale peers at them as he refills. "Two floaters-about naturally drift together. Run and run until you find another. It's not even as if you two aren't busy. That's what impresses me. Flee the scene of the crime and you still can't bear to be without some nonsensical project. I like it. Romanticism at its finest."

"What's her project?" says Johannes. Amondale's eyebrows arch high above a secretive grin as he reaches across the table to refill Johannes's glass. Johannes turns to Caryn, "What project?"

"Just a little something."

"Not so little..." chuckles Amondale.

"What is it?"

"What are you digging for?" she counters.

Johannes grunts through an amused smirk.

"How adorable..." Amondale blushes as he slowly broils with laughter. "You two make me miss my woman, Rosa, from Rio. Haven't I told you about her? I stayed with her in Manhattan last summer. We have her to thank for this perfect liquor. It's the only thing she stocked, not to mention a stash of the finest ganja, heh heh. Helluva woman. Take your head out of the dirt, Johnnies. You've got it buried too deep. She's right here next to you—"

The music stops suddenly. Amondale cringes and shakes his head as he watches Ernest fiddle with the record player.

"Good heavens," ejects Amondale. "Barman, old boy, if you insist on poking the needle right through this priceless record, at least have the decency not to skip over the only track of any merit. It's your fault, Jonathon. He told me he skips it to protect you from musical Bolshevism. What a real A-hole."

"Skips what?" says Johannes.

"Prelude in C-sharp minor. Haven't you noticed? The single most famous piece Rachi ever composed, and our Ernie shuts it off every time it comes around."

"C-sharp minor? How would I know?"

"That's what I'm saying! The song is famous for a reason, but Hemingway over there keeps feeding you his bizarre biases when he ought to let you decide on your own. It's bollocks. I mean, when I prod into your past, it's journalistic curiosity at work. And you can quote me on that. I would never try to rebuild you the way you were or how I think you ought to be. If Mr. E really wants to protect you, then he shouldn't expose you to that sleazy rat, Wilms. Not even indirectly. Ho-*ly* shit, there's a creep for you. That money-grubber single-handedly ruined our man's career. Hemmy will deny it to the grave, of course. But believe you me, I know far more than Ern would like anyone to know. And for the life of me, I cannot comprehend how a person develops that scope of loyalty for such scum. The only reason I don't expose the whole story is because Ernie is such a goddamned nice guy. I'll wait till he's dead."

"It's the small kindnesses that count," laughs Caryn.

"Indeed it is, indeed it is." Amondale nods and slaps the table. "Let the track play, Ernesto," he shouts. "You prick."

Ernest looks up from behind the bar where he's drying glasses. "Screw off, Oscar."

Amondale smiles and bobs his head at Johannes and Caryn. "Speaking of deceits large and small," Amondale barks at Caryn, "I'm curious about the paperwork and regulations. You'll have to fill me in on how it all worked out and such."

"Gladly," Caryn nods. "Another time."

"Of course, of course. Business and pleasure, a motto to live and die by."

"Paperwork?" says Johannes.

"Oh, you know," Amondale sips his drink, "since the church land is technically within Oklahoma territory. Technicality of a technicality."

"The church? So what?"

"You've noticed, of course, how far it is from the town center. Our little Creek's Ridge sits on the border with Oklahoma. The state line is down the way there. You know where. Kansas land ends right there at that grove where you waste all the rest of your time soul-digging, contemplating these beautiful days away at that bit of greenery by the creek, which, by the way, grows so lush like that because it was a mass burial in the old days, the Native American raids, don't you know. Just a little theory of mine. You can dig that up if you like. Help me prove it, heh heh. Anyhow, that's the border, but the grounds of St. Jo's are another four-hundred-twelve-and-a-half meters on, clear across the state line. Only, the land itself is still registered as part of Creek's Ridge. Kansas land, that. Been that way ever since statehood was granted back in 1861. No official on either side of the border has ever given two shits about it, so it's just remained that way. St. Josephine's is our own personal desert island, heh heh heh."

For about a minute, they all three stare at each other and consider this oddity.

"So what?" repeats Johannes.

And Caryn, "It all seems to be working out fine. No big roadblocks yet. I guess that's what happens in isolated places like this."

"Damn right," croons Amondale. "Cut yourself off from the world and you develop these quirks. Ain't that right, Johnnie boy? No one around to mend them, set you straight. Because after a while, nobody cares anymore."

"I did discover some interesting documents, though," adds Caryn. "About the construction."

"1850, if I recall," says Amondale.

"That's just it. The building was finished in 1850, but construction had been stalled for three or four years. The tribal leaders never approved of the plan to begin with, but Del Bosque went ahead with it anyway. And the men he'd hired to build it were using slave labor. When the tribes realized that, they took a stand and eventually chased them out of the territory. Del Bosque tried to finish what they'd started using local laborers, but without the technical know-how, it couldn't be completed. He had no choice but to bring the same builders back again, paying them more than double the original fee because of the risk involved."

"And the tribes knew about it, of course..."

"I assume they must have."

"And they never forgave him... How have I never stumbled across these documents?"

"The place is a mess. No organization whatsoever, almost intentionally so. Father Marover has tried, but I think he's afraid he'll find himself lost down a rabbit hole if he commits to it. So, I'm trying to rectify it little by little."

"Sharp eyes, Pridieux. A regular gold mine in there. And who knows, if this fellow next to you ever gets his hands out of the dirt, maybe he can help you sort it all out. Heh heh. I envy this. Cute little couple, all innocent and dumb..."

Amondale gets up and claps Johannes on the shoulder before heading to the bar, shouting at Ernest about Rachmaninoff's preludes.

"What's he talking about?" says Johannes.

"Nothing," Caryn smiles and rests her hand on his shoulder. "You'll find out sooner or later."

Johannes and Caryn are taken in by the melancholic music. They sit for a while, sipping their Carnival. Caryn speaks of a wild run of tornadoes that killed sixty people in eastern Oklahoma. She tells him of recent international incidents and social upheavals twisting distant countries inside-out—all signs that tides are turning one way or another. Johannes gets lost in her eyes as she speaks. She has beautiful eyes, but they radiate a deep, powerful sadness. She mentions the founders again, the prophet and the priest, and a collection of journals telling a story of escape, of leaving homes behind, not by choice but by force, and then finding a home in the comfort of like-minded folk. They laid the town's foundations together, making promises to everyone involved, but they had trouble allowing the concept to flourish naturally, like a tree's branches reaching out to catch sunlight while always remaining at one with the trunk. Instead, they manipulated each other for their own secret ends. Was it power? Ownership? Possessiveness? And finally, when death and greed made their inevitable appearance, everything changed. First, the prophet, aged and ill, but not before the priest's wife, a more sinister end, never forgotten, never forgiven. Curses and oaths, borders and loyalties, blood ties and ideologies—the trust they had so carefully planted and sown together began to wither and decay before their eyes.

Her voice is soothing, an elixir, an intoxicant. With Grant, he's compelled to talk and defend principles he's unsure of himself, which always leaves him feeling deflated afterward. Without fail, Grant forgets that Johannes doesn't remember—a person, an event, a shared experience, a trivial mistake, a lucky break—and, not one for patience, he invariably resorts to bullying Johannes with facts. But with Caryn, Johannes can just listen and they both cull enjoyment from it. So much so that her voice mingles with the Rachmaninoff and works as a lullaby.

"Don't worry," she says, running her hand through his hair as he nestles against her shoulder. "Just rest for a bit."

"Maybe I should go back. To the house."

"You can hardly even sleep there, you said so yourself. Why bother?"

"No, I have been...I can't sleep on the sofa...but on the floor...I can..."

"What do you mean?"

"Sleeping on the floor. I sleep much better there..."

"Just rest here. You can't leave me alone with Oscar. He'll keep me here until morning with his talk. And later on, you can, you know..."

"What?"

"Walk me back...maybe more..."

Amondale and Ernest argue amiably at the bar. Their voices, their laughter, rising and falling, mingling with bar chatter and piano tones from another time, reflected off mirrors, emitting from a tricky realm of unverifiable realities, like voices in a fog, the truthful unreality of a dream, simply trust and believe as those voices swell, recede, repeat, but one stands out amongst them, a command pulling you back, inherent commitment, this voice is no reflection, but the source of it all—

It's Grant. He stands in the entryway with a strikingly beautiful woman. She's tall, slender, and dressed in a fashionable pantsuit with tapered legs. The delicate navy fabric shimmers. Her bone-white heels are dirtied from the dust of the streets. Her dark, frizzy hair is pulled back from the sides and clipped high behind her head, with Grant's sheriff's hat balanced lightly atop. The healthy pale of her skin sits in unsettling contrast against her dark hair. And her sharp, bright eyes, framed by heavy mascara, are trained on Johannes.

Grant's gaze passes over Johannes and Caryn as he scans the bar, taking account of the customers. Finally, he leads the woman toward their table. Amondale moves in to intercept them, but Grant just sweeps him along in the current.

"John," Grant is staring into the mirrors above Johannes, "someone I want you to meet." His uniform is still dirty from digging. When he turns to introduce the woman, he notices his hat and snatches it from her head. "An old friend. Lani Vals. Lani, John Metternich."

Johannes glances at Caryn, and they both stand up.

The woman has stepped closer, her hand outstretched.

"Say something, you twerp," Grant scolds him.

Johannes shakes her hand. "Hello."

"I feel like I already know everything about you," Lani's face glows when she smiles. "I've been here nearly an hour and Grant has done nothing but talk about you. He hasn't even asked about me yet." She smacks Grant's arm and then takes the hat back. "What are we drinking? I've been on the move all day."

They crowd around the small table as Grant introduces Lani to Caryn and Amondale, but Amondale leaves to fetch his glass and finish his argument with Ernest.

"How do you two know each other?" Caryn asks.

Lani sits close by Grant's side. They stare at each other, doing their best but failing to conceal their grins.

"Oh, it's been forever," says Lani. "Since childhood. Our parents were friends. So, you see, forced into it, really."

Amondale wanders back, pulls another chair over, and reaches for The Carnival.

"Same as Grant and Johannes," says Caryn.

Johannes's gaze swivels around the table, the faces, the mirrors, more faces. Amondale fills his glass and curses the melted ice, then nudges Johannes in the ribs, smiling and nodding as he prods Johannes to join him. Another drink.

"Johannes..." Lani scrutinizes him. "That name...you would think I'd recall a name like that. I suppose we may have met in passing, somewhere, sometime."

"She would have know him as John anyhow," Grant says, shifting around and struggling to find comfort in the chair as he waves to Ernest for a beer. "Same as most everyone else..."

"Hey, Hemmy," Amondale calls out. "More ice, too, if you don't mind."

Lani looks over Grant's hat in wonder. "My old Grant, a sheriff," she laughs as she places the hat on her head again. "It's the perfect job for you. You reek of command and leadership, always have. I hated seeing you runt around under those construction big shots. You were always better than that. But I suppose we all start out as babies in a big bad world, don't we? God, that was ages ago. If you'd stayed in Chicago, you'd be running that company by now. Imagine that, yeah? Biggest firm in the Midwest. What was it called? But then, with those Cubans in Miami, you were killing yourself for nothing. Getting out of that city was the smartest move you ever made. And now this. This perfect little town. So quiet, so peaceful. It's charming, really. I can't wait to see it in the daylight. Oh god, look at how old we all are. I wanted to come sooner, really, I did."

"You're not old," says Grant. "You're all grown up, is all. Life is unavoidable and immediate, right in your face. Got its filthy paws wrapped around you. Purity and the world's bullshit are the same thing. Dreams are only dreams, and time is only ticking."

"You sound like someone I used to know..." Lani glances around at the others. "But you're the sheriff. It's surreal, you nit. There's nothing pure about it." She reaches out to caress Grant's cheek before pinching it. "An entire place, an entire people under your control. It must be exhilarating to be responsible for an entire town."

"Correction, responsible for an entire county. But, really, it's more thrilling to own a car. Creek's Ridge is standing on weak legs, about to tumble into the grave."

"Yeah," coughs Amondale, "and guess who's digging it."

"Thanks, Ern." Grant takes his beer and the ice bucket from Ernest. "Peaceful, yes. But thrilling? It's approximately as exciting as watching a lawn grow and then realizing the grass has been dead all along. Too much peace and contentment can drive a person up the wall. Ask anyone, they'll tell you. Except Caryn." Grant smiles across the table. "She's just a newcomer."

"Is that right?" Lani glances at Caryn, but her gaze shifts to Johannes. She looks him over as though searching for something.

"I wouldn't know about it either," says Johannes.

"Why? How long have you been here?" Lani asks.

"Going on two months, I think." Johannes looks at Grant. "That sound right?"

"Damned if I know."

"Eighty-nine days," announces Amondale. "Almost three." Amondale appears aloof, hardly interested in the little group at all. He abruptly stands and heads over to help Ernest with a sudden rush of customers.

"Friendly fellow," says Lani. "What did you say his name was?"

"Oscar Amondale," Grant sighs. "You were asking about the church and its name before, right? Well, he's the one to ask. He'll tell you everything you want to know about the Saint and her father, the Indian raids, and the church. But also a lot you won't care to know about—his wild theories and hunches, delusions of the past..."

"So what, he's a local history buff? Or some kind of nut?"

"Yes and no to both," laughs Grant. "He's a writer. An oddball, but a great guy if you can get on his good side."

"It's not easy," sniggers Caryn. "But it can be done."

"How about you, sweetie?" Lani says to Caryn.

"Me? About a month in, and I think I've fallen in love."

Lani's eyebrows arch high as her gaze wanders over Caryn and Johannes.

"With the town," Caryn laughs.

"Sweetie?" blurts Grant. "How old do you think she is?"

"She must be under twenty-five. Not older than that. Never."

"Ridiculous," Caryn laughs.

"I'll say," Grant chokes on his beer. "Caryn is your elder by four or five years at least. Be respectful, you little frog. And give me my hat." Grant reaches his arm around Lani's neck and grabs the hat, taking a handful of hair with it. Lani yelps, slapping and scratching at Grant's bare forearm with nails painted a deep violet, almost black in the dim light. Grant gently fights back, and Lani relishes every second of it. Lonely eyes around the bar stare at their table.

"And how do you all know each other?" Lani's cheeks are flushed. She heaves for air as she rests her arm on Grant's shoulder.

"What do you mean?" says Grant. "You've seen the size of this town."

"But it seems like, except for you, everyone is temporary here."

"Horseshit." Grant points toward Ernest and Amondale, who are running back and forth behind the bar. "I've known Amondale nearly ten years. Ernest is a good friend as well. John here, well, I've known him damn near forever, though he doesn't recall much of it. He's here on a sort of...rehab retreat. Progress is slow-coming. And Caryn is a felonious drifter. I think she's a drug mule, waiting on a delivery of grass and powder from the border that never came through, and now she means to disappear." Grant looks sharply at Caryn. "Did I nail it? Is that why you're still in my town? They'll blame you, right? Put a price on your neck out west. I guess you picked the right place to disappear in. The prairie is less conspicuous than the mountains. No one expects it. Been working out for John so far. Don't worry, *sweetie*. No one will track you here, to our little forgotten heart of the country. Though, I'll admit, I sort of hope they do." Grant pats the pistol holstered at his side, rests his hand there. "Finally bring some action to Creek's Ridge." He fingers the gun, sliding it out, its weight audible as he sets it on the table, cutting through Rachmaninoff's preludes.

"Jeez-*us* Christ..." Amondale is watching from the bar. "Hey, John-the-John, don't you let him have any whisky, you hear? Not with his little buddy making its grand entrance, my god..."

"Wouldn't dream of it," mumbles Grant.

"Sorry to disappoint you," says Caryn, "but I'm free and clear. *That's* why I'm here. You've got me all wrong, Detective."

"Dreams all out of whack," says Johannes.

"Besides," Grant continues through his laughter as he holsters his weapon, "I still keep in touch with everyone back home."

"Back home, huh?" says Lani. "Everyone?"

"I talk to my mom every other day. My sisters' kids are growing like weeds. Friends are all either married or addicts. Everything's changed, but that place is still important to me. I can't move back, though. John. Hey John? What's wrong?"

Johannes is unresponsive, sitting up straight and staring over Grant's shoulder toward the entryway where Pa Sonny has just walked in. Pa Sonny nods solemnly at Ernest and Amondale but does not step beyond the doorway.

"What is it?" Grant repeats and then turns around. "Oh shit—" he hisses, jumping up and rushing to the door.

Grant gives Pa Sonny a hug and whispers into his ear. Pa Sonny nods thoughtfully and glances around the bar. Johannes can't take his eyes away. Amondale walks over to join them, but Grant leads Pa Sonny outside, pushing Amondale back in through the door when he tries to follow. Amondale looks around the bar, then shrugs before opening the door an imperceptible crack and placing his ear against it.

Lani and Caryn continue talking and laughing together, but Johannes is blank-faced and distant. Amondale returns alone and sits down beside Lani with a goofy grin plastered across his face. He slams his glass down on the table and whistles.

"*Whew-ee*, sure as hell glad to be drinking again. Not the night to be without it. *Oh, Rosalita...*" With one smooth, uninterrupted motion, he refills his glass and Johannes's with ice and Scotch.

"What's going on out there?" asks Caryn.

"A lot of foolishness if you ask me." Amondale smiles so severely that he has difficulty getting the booze from the glass into his mouth.

"Yeah..." agrees Johannes.

Bewildered, Amondale looks at Johannes before exploding with a howl of laughter. The Carnival sprays across the table. "Oh, John Boy, you are something else. I'll be writing about you long before you croak, you can count on that. There's two whole volumes right here."

Lani is smiling, shifting glances between them. "Oh, they were right about you."

"Who, me?" says Amondale. "So, the peanut gallery's been trying to crack nuts again, eh? Cheers, babe." He raises his glass to Lani. "Or should I say—damn, this is a tough one...give me a minute...*Proost!* Heh heh, knew I had it filed away in there somewhere. You see, John-nee, memories are just files in the office filing cabinet. Get yourself a reliable secretary and arrange them for immediate ease of access, nudge nudge, wink wink, drink up."

"Grant the Sheriff says you're the one to ask about the saint," says Lani.

"And what the sheriff says must be gospel. In a perfect world, heh heh. But that's the first thing you'll learn from the most fleeting foray into the history of this town—it's anything but a perfect world. So, who would you like to know about? Josephine the Innocent? The Cunning? The Vengeful? Or Josephine the Silent?"

"There was more than one?" asks Lani.

"The Cunning?" says Caryn.

"All one and the same, but time changes everyone, don't you know. Time and the trying circumstances that befall us can twist us into the most unrecognizable versions of ourselves. Ain't that right, John of the mountain?"

"How can a saint be vengeful?" questions Johannes.

"I know about that," says Caryn. "Her vengeance was the town's salvation. But why cunning?"

"Simple," Amondale drinks. "No Josephine, no Native American raids."

"What?" scoffs Caryn. "Because of her beauty? Because none of the men, none of the tribes, could stand to see her with anyone but themselves."

"It's a tad more complicated than that," says Amondale.

"I'm sorry I asked..." Lani says, smiling across to Johannes.

Johannes drinks from his glass and averts his eyes toward the entryway, but the door is still closed.

"Believe it or not," continues Amondale, "there was honor in those days. That's what the town was founded on, after all. Some stood by it as sacred and divine, while others flaunted it. But when the code of honor is breached, the truly honorable don't stand idly by."

"What do you mean?" says Caryn as she slides closer to the table.

"You have unearthed your documents, but I have a head start on you of several years. And I have sources, too."

A sudden clamor fills the bar. Things falling, bouncing, and rolling across the floor. Everyone looks at Ernest, assuming he has dropped something, but he only glances up from the cocktail he's pouring.

"So, but what are you saying?" Caryn demands.

"I admit there's some credence to what you've found. I never believed Del Bosque to be free of blame. That said, I always thought his condition affected his judgment. But Josephine almost certainly made certain promises. Plural."

"Promises?" Lani is enthralled. "What promises?"

"To several tribes, several suitors. Not only do we have a conflict of interest, but honesty and motive necessarily come into question."

Suddenly, Caryn jerks in surprise, bumping Johannes's arm and spilling his drink. "Where did you come from? You creep..."

Grant is hovering over them, annoyed and watching them all. Discovered, he makes his way around the table, taps Amondale on the shoulder, and motions for him to move over. He sits down with a sigh, patting Lani on the knee.

"What was that about?" she asks.

"That was our old pastor, Pastor Judson."

Lani stares back at Grant, her glass held still just in front of her lips, hiding a twitch.

"His name is Judson?" says Johannes. "What's he doing? Looking for a drink?"

"Huh?" Grant looks up. "No, no...nothing like that."

"He's off it, right?"

"What? Yeah...yeah, but I guess you never know..."

"Willpower gives out sooner or later," says Amondale. "Always does."

"What did he want then?" presses Johannes.

"Oh, you know, just needed some advice. Trouble with...coyotes."

"Coyotes?"

"Pa Sonny?" says Lani.

"That's right..." Grant tears his gaze away from Johannes, squinting toward Lani. "The man who baptized John and I."

"Blasphemy," says Lani. "No righteous, God-fearing man possesses the nerve to baptize you." She takes a large gulp from her glass and winces. "What is this shit? Some kind of dumpster whisky?"

Grant reaches for his beer and leans back. "I've been baptized hundreds of times. Women flock to me. They beg for the privilege to bathe me."

"I said *man*, sweetheart."

"Man, woman, caravan—I don't discriminate."

"Horse," adds Johannes.

"Aye," affirms Amondale.

"What?" echo Caryn and Lani.

"She haunts his dreams," says Johannes, his gaze lost in the mirrors. "He wakes screaming in the night, scaring them off with his desperate wails and howls."

"That's...no..." Grant's irritation shines as bright as the badge on his chest. "That's not me screaming..."

"Who?" asks Caryn.

"The crooked Lady of his heart..." says Johannes.

"You stupid bastard," Lani slaps Grant on the arm. "What is it going to take for you to get over her? What has that bitch done now?"

"You know about Lil?" asks Johannes.

Lani glances at Johannes, but she's burning into Grant with a fierce glare.

"She didn't...didn't do anything. He's...he doesn't...he's full of shit... doesn't understand...doesn't even remember...you don't know..." Grant's protestations pop in bursts of breath. He doesn't look at anyone, but only at his knees, his feet, his beer bottle, his pistol, into the mirrors. "He doesn't know what he's talking about. It's not like that. That doesn't happen. We're not talking about her. We're not...it's him who screams all night...not me...it's *him*..."

"The last time I saw you—" Lani cuts herself off, lowering her eyes and voice to avoid the others. "Did you sign?" she whispers, but her agitation negates the effect, and they all hear it. "You did, right? You signed?"

"Of course I did," Grant grunts and looks away.

Caryn's confusion is evident. Lani's rage momentarily subsides as she murmurs to Caryn, "His ex-wife."

"Inez?" says Johannes. "No, I meant—"

"John, don't," Grant raises his hands to cut Johannes off. "Just don't..."

"But haven't you been separated for years?" asks Caryn.

Grant nods.

"You must understand what it's like, Pridieux," says Amondale, trying to smooth the tension. "A divorcee yourself. Much more recent than Señor Sheriff, too, I imagine. We all have our hang-ups, our stories of heartache."

Caryn is shaking her head and peering at all of them. And they're all watching her, if only not to look at Grant.

"Mine was a sham marriage," Caryn says finally. "My husband, he was trying to make it in Hollywood and thought the visa restrictions were holding him back. He married me for residency. And connections. And for my money. Turned out he's just a shitty actor."

"Did you know?" gasps Lani.

"I knew," Caryn nods and smiles. "Part of me always hoped it would turn into the real thing. The blind little girl I used to be."

"It's not just you," Lani scowls. "Grant and Inez never had the real thing either, no matter how much he tries to believe it." Lani pokes Grant in the ribs. He jerks and twists but doesn't look up from his beer.

"I think it's sweet," adds Caryn, successfully ending the conversation with this questionable truth that none of the others have the strength or wiles to refute. "Excuse me," Caryn stands up. "Ladies' room."

"I'll join you," says Lani. "Grant, be a darling and order me something decent. This whisky is awful." She grabs Caryn's arm as they head off to the restroom.

"Glad you dislike it," mutters Amondale. "More for the rest of us, am I right, Don John?"

A long Rachmaninoff piece finishes with a protracted fade toward silence, toward death, where nothing grows and no future peeks over an empty horizon. But it is true that death produces life, allowing that which is fledgling to flourish, maintaining the balance of one form against another, the past versus the future. Johannes closes his eyes to grapple with that fate and is swept to a distant place. The oak tree, Knecht, towers above him, day after day, having weathered a thousand years of difficulties with sturdy curtness, offering wisdom and hope in a cruel, animal world. Endurance, survival, balance, and stability—Knecht, created to last, had instructed Johannes in these arts for more than seven years, its roots reaching deep into the earth and its mystifying array of branches always quivering, breathing, and stretching in the wind. Knecht would never flee the mountain, would never abandon the creatures that depend upon it, but at the moment of duress, as the mountain fell, Johannes had failed to implement the lessons he had spent those years striving to perfect.

A low, menacing *A* rings from the speakers, followed by *B*, and finally *C-sharp* just as the music cuts off. Amondale curses Ernest, and Ernest curses him back. Grant orders another beer for himself and a mojito for Lani.

Ernest laughs. "What makes you think I have fresh mint leaves?"

"Right, I didn't... A Long Island, then. And Ern, use the good stuff. Make it strong."

Each day, Johannes struggles with the desire to return to Knecht's safety, to sit lotus beneath that canopy and await diffusion. Instead, he makes do with what's available, meditation in a grove that may flourish because it shelters the bodies of the dead. Were they the victims or the aggressors? In the wild, there is little difference, but not so in the world of men, with its stories of the past, justifications for the present, and selfish aims for what will be. People themselves, the way they are seen, handled, and used by one another. If Amondale is right and there are indeed bodies buried beneath the grove, then the stink and rot of their corpses must have long since faded, but their influence remains, allowing life to flourish where desolation reigns. And if so, perhaps there is no peace to be found by mining the trenches of the past, but rather in leaving it be. The threads of time, of cause and effect, they're all around us. But what's the point in manhandling them every step of the way? Breathing the air of rebirth is so much sweeter under the auspices of mystery...

"John. Hey, John!" Grant shouts and pounds on the table. Those seated nearby stare at their seemingly enraged sheriff. "John, snap out of it. You should take it easy. Lay off the booze, alright? Go home and get some rest."

"Nonsense," Amondale laughs. "Fill him up."

"I've had enough..." says Johannes.

"For Christ's sake, I know," Grant is restless, fidgeting. "I just said that. Why don't you just head home? Go now. We'll catch up. Sleep it off, okay?"

"Thinking..." continues Johannes, ignoring or not hearing Grant, "everything and nothing, mountain and landslide... Their voices... The horse, a good friend... The forest, the woods, a prophet... Knecht said something's wrong... Nothing makes sense...everywhere the dead... I can't sleep there...not like them... The Saint caused them...the cunning? Only on the floor... I think Orion is stung... The herdsman's hounds have strayed, rotation of the earth, fallen off... No growth except at the grove...Native Americans...the scorpion...the raids...on the floor... Walk her home...on the floor..."

"Sex, I'd say." Amondale glances over his shoulder and slides closer to the table, lowering his voice. "About time, too. Pridieux's been hanging on him all night. And he's been visually feasting on your friend ever since you two walked in. Been a while, yeah? Too long, I should say. Let him drink himself back into the real world if that's what it takes. All that time out there fondling nature's titties and he's forgotten what real knockers feel like."

Grant squirms in his chair. With compulsive regularity, he keeps glancing toward the bathroom door. "Oscar, let it go. Not tonight."

"What for? It's the perfect time. No regrets."

"What?" Johannes looks up as if he's just noticed them.

"Never mind, John. We'll sort it out tomorrow, alright? Go home and get some rest."

"Home is...gone..."

"The house. I meant the house. Go back to my house."

"Okay, yes, tomorrow...digging, tomorrow..."

"Ah, no, actually, I forgot to mention... We might have to take a few days off...no digging..." Grant searches the mirrors, spying on the other customers, checking on the bathroom door again.

"No more digging?"

"With...with Lani here, you know...and I'm swamped at work. Yearly evaluations and statements. Budget plans. Just a couple of days. You'll have to show her around, if you don't mind. That's why, you know...just go home and get some real rest...tomorrow, it'll all make sense tomorrow...I promise...it will...it has to..."

"Show who around?" asks Johannes, looking up with eyes half-closed. "Who's here? Who is it? Where?"

Grant holds his breath involuntarily, his complexion tinting reddish-purple, eyes boring into Johannes.

"Lil?"

"Give me that bottle," Amondale screeches. "If you're going to break a man to pieces, it's only common courtesy to get him drunk first. He'll sleep it off, like usual. And, if you're lucky, it'll all fall into place. Lucky like a shark attack. That once-in-a-lifetime jackpot. A goddamned lightning rod." Amondale reaches for the bottle and then slides onto the bench, wrapping an arm around Johannes's shoulders. "Play with fire and what do you expect..."

"Seriously, drop it," says Grant. "He's losing a grip."

"You're losing a grip," spits Amondale. He tilts the bottle into Johannes's glass and forces the glass into Johannes's hand. "There we go, bud, one order of the ol' kidney cheap shot. Bloody piss and all that good stuff. Sometimes that's what it takes, heh heh, to get a fresh outlook on all this madness."

Chapter 26

Giant Dog Sickness

February 17, 1818
St. Johns River, La Florida

ALTHOUGH THE VILLAGE REMAINS ALERT AND OCCUPIED WITH preparations, we suffer less anxiety over the future with each passing day. Our worries have been replaced with a sense of duty and honor, the obligation to hold our heads high, our gazes steady, to welcome our fate.

The Father has undergone a lengthy period of rest. Following the ceremonial afternoon at the river, I learned that I was not alone in noticing his wayward stare. Though the tribe's faith in him has never flagged, they had become concerned. That very night, Chief Kinheja brought the medicine man, Long Grass, to the Father's hut. Of course, I had noticed the Father's diminishing appetite and seen his sleeping habits suffer, but such symptoms I interpreted as effects of his own heartache in light of the coming confrontations, his long days and nights occupied with constant contemplation over life's nasty tricks. However, it only required a brief conversation with the Father for Long Grass to attribute his strange behavior to something I can only roughly translate as Giant Dog Sickness.

The medicine man discovered that not only had Father Jimenez been experiencing stomach pains, which had kept him from eating, but he had also been kept awake by visions and waking dreams, which had, in turn, propelled him along dangerous solitary treks through the forest, further draining his energy and concentration. Our scouts often spotted and followed him on these aimless walks, only to find him unresponsive and mumbling to himself when they tried to steer him back toward the village.

Long Grass remained by the Father's bedside for five days. Whenever I passed by the hut, I heard them speaking. During that time, I gave the sermons and led the prayers. In the afternoons, I trekked to a grove in the forest where a certain pale yellow flower grows in abundance. Long Grass required these plants, roots and all, to aid the Father's recovery. He would grind down the petals and boil the roots with bay leaves, and he allowed the Father to consume only this broth, along with a small amount of snakeroot. By the third day, the Father had regained some strength and was eating fruit and fish again. They also smoked tobacco throughout the day. Father Jimenez never took to this habit in the past, but he has developed a continued fondness for it since recovering from his infirmity.

In my spare moments, I would slip into the Father's hut and listen to them talk, or if the Father had drifted off to sleep, I would speak with the medicine man. Long Grass is thought to be even older than Father Jimenez, although no one, not even Long Grass himself, is certain of the year of his birth. He knows only that he was born in Creek mountain country far to the north of here, in lands his people were driven from when he was still crawling naked amongst the forest weeds. His tribe relocated to the coast, near the British settlement of Savannah. After bargaining with British, French, and Spanish colonialists, they were granted free reign over the land stretching from the Altamaha River to the St. Johns River. After the Americans succeeded in their revolution, Long Grass and his people deserted Georgia along with the British, whence they retreated south, here, to the St. Johns.

More than anything else, Long Grass regrets that he will leave this world with his people still bound to colonialists. When he dies, his people will still be fighting the same wars he was compelled to fight as a young warrior, wars that never ended but have only been handed down through each successive generation. He has long nurtured the dream that his people, along with all the Natives of this land, will one day stand as equals with the nations of Europe that have staked claims here, putting an end to the bloodshed that has tainted this ground.

Though the British have been more regularly upon our shores in recent weeks, their aid has been minimal, limited to secretive deals and transactions that hinge upon verbal pledges for future cooperation. The British do not wish to have their involvement known or to become embroiled in another extended confrontation with the Americans, like their failed war of six years ago. Nothing is written anymore, nothing signed. Therefore, nothing is guaranteed. The threads of faith stretch ever thinner.

Long Grass and the Father often speak of the coming troubles and the inevitable changes that await us. They each express remorse that they won't be here to lend the spiritual support they have both dedicated their lives to providing. But they are also tired, almost anxious to transition to the calmer, sweeter pastures beyond this life.

February 20, 1818
St. Johns River, La Florida

Last night, while Long Grass and Father Jimenez reminisced over past conflicts, they spoke of an encounter that incited the tribe's involvement and misfortunes during the 1812 War. In the year preceding that war, word arrived that a Shawnee leader by the name of Tecumseh had ridden south from the Indiana Territory with a band of blood-thirsty warriors. They visited tribes throughout the mountain country to the north of here before descending into the swamps of La Florida. They did not come to spill blood but rather to recruit followers for a conglomeration of native people meant to defy the aggressive expansion of the United States. Intrigued by the stories they heard, Long Grass and the Father traveled west to Tallahassee. There, along with many others, they met the Shawnee leader at the decimated site of a former Franciscan Mission called San Luis de Apalachee.

Father Jimenez described Tecumseh as an intelligent man imbibed with fierce and infectious energy. Surrounded by his loyal warriors, he gave the impression of an impenetrable fortress. One felt that simply standing beside him would mean never again fearing for one's life. Tecumseh preached peaceful but complete resistance against white men by spreading the word of his brother, a great prophet known as Tenskwatawa. Explicitly, he extended invitations to all Creeks and Seminoles who wished to join them at their flourishing utopia in the Indiana Territory, upon the sacred ground where the Wabash and Tippecanoe Rivers meet. However, he also maintained that no tribe should ever completely abandon their tribal lands. Therefore, pilgrimages to visit the Prophet would suffice. The Prophet's word was deemed infallible, but words, unlike bodies, are easily transported from place to place. Most importantly, feuds between neighboring tribes were to be forgotten and forgiven so that all tribes might one day be united. There could be no more warring amongst tribes, no more running as the gluttonous, infantile United States fattened its borders, and no more tolerating the white man's poisonous, deceptive treaties. For what person, anywhere in the world, would suffer the presence of a venomous snake in his own bed?

However, over the course of the Shawnees' brief stay, it became increasingly evident that Tecumseh's true intentions were at odds with the Prophet's teachings. While he was friendly with the medicine men and the chiefs, it was the warriors who received his flattery and deepest confidences. Ultimately, he convinced half of our tribe's noblest warriors to accompany him back to the Tippecanoe, proclaiming that those chosen would meet the Prophet and return bearing his teachings and blessings.

When a few of those warriors returned six months later, they did not come bearing the promised teachings. Instead, they related that the United States had declared war against the British. Tecumseh had long been indebted to the British armies, and he had compelled some of the Seminole warriors to follow him into the British colony of Upper Canada. As for the Prophet, the warriors who returned had scarcely laid eyes upon him, but they described him as a horribly ugly man, missing one eye, rife with burn scars, and extravagantly made up with paints, feathers, bones, and intricately stitched animal skins. They said his voice rolled and clapped like thunder, blinding flashes of speech that struck like lightning, the shocks of which caused tremors throughout the body, forbidding disobedience. And it was this Prophet, Tenskwatawa, not Tecumseh, who had commanded them to return to La Florida, to gather their allies along the gulf coast, and to attack the United States from the south in league with the British.

Two years later, when the war ended, only a single Seminole warrior returned from the north. The others had all died in battle, along with Tecumseh. To this day there has been no word as to the fate of the Prophet. Only rumors exist—his flight, his escape, his capture, rebuilding an army, living the life of a hermit, a seer crafting the future —all of them nothing more than speculation. Dreams, fears, or possibly prayers.

Long Grass and Father Jimenez speak of years past with precision and clarity. Considering their long, eventful, and sometimes strife-laden lives, they possess a remarkable talent for retaining memories and reviving them as though those events occurred only yesterday. As they stoke the flames of memory, the heat of emotion rises, radiating outward and giving warmth to the present. In the case of the 1812 War, their emotion is contempt. Long Grass and the Father believe much of the blame for our current conflict falls upon the aggressive missteps of those two Shawnee brothers, Tecumseh and Tenskwatawa. But although the Shawnee brothers may have stumbled in their haste, their purpose was noble. Men of various and opposing beliefs should stray from what they know to explore the earth together and stand up for what they believe in. Solitary exiles, such as the Father and myself, will never be strong enough to solve the problems of our world. That task requires the unity of entire populations for many generations to come.

February 21, 1818
St. Johns River, La Florida

The story of the Shawnee brothers has charmed my soul, elevating my every thought with a sense of forlorn admiration. I am struck with insatiable curiosity over what became of this Tenskwatawa in the aftermath of those events. I find myself hoping that he emerged with his bold ambitions unscathed.

Likewise, I am forced to consider which state of affairs represents the anomaly—is it our stable, uneventful life here along the St. Johns or the turmoil that appears to reign everywhere else?

Chapter 27

The Labyrinth

She sits on the sofa, watching over him from above, with her legs folded beneath her and a tender smile. He has a vision of her and Grant arm-in-arm up ahead as they all walked home from the bar. Caryn's arm had been wrapped around Johannes's waist, her strength alone supporting him, whispering in his ear as she compelled him to keep going, to fight off his sheer exhaustion a little longer, at least until they made it to the house, to the floor, to a dreamless sleep. And though he may have dreamed—of the mountain, of the dogs, of a woman, of the mirrors, of a church and a raid and a saint—the dreams have now delivered him into the inviting hands of daylight.

"Good morning." She looks different than the night before. Her hair is frayed and wild, her face without makeup, her posture loose and relaxed.

Johannes blinks.

"Do you remember me?"

"Of course I do." Johannes sits up. "Last night, I was...I remember... I was there."

"You sure?" Lani's smile fades as she falls back into the cushions, her eyes searching the room.

"Where's Grant?" says Johannes.

"At work. He left a while ago. Do you always sleep this late?"

"No. Usually we... No."

"Do you always sleep on the floor?"

"When Grant lets me."

She gets up and walks over to a bulky leather handbag lying against the wall beside the giant mirror—that purveyor of images and memories. "He said to tell you he'll be busy all day." As she rummages through the bag, her reflection glances up at him. "And that you're not allowed to dig."

"He mentioned that," Johannes yawns, "last night."

She faces him, a small leather case dangling from her finger. "Make me breakfast?"

"Me?"

"Omelets."

"What omelets?"

"I'm told you're good with omelets."

"You're told?"

Lani shrugs. "Grant, I guess." She stares at him before heading down the hall toward the bathroom.

Johannes lies back down until he feels tremors in the floorboards. Whenever the shower runs, the water pipes shake and vibrations rattle the floors throughout the old house.

There is plenty in the fridge, but nothing for omelets. He rinses his face and wets his hair at the kitchen sink. Then he grabs a stack of crumpled bills from the nightstand in Grant's bedroom and shoves them into his pocket.

Following a path through town that he walks nearly every day, he notes objects, faces, yards and facades, cars and toys scattered about, the searing blue ceiling and the interminable flat expanse, St. Josephine's spire penetrating skyward, so near and yet so far. On certain days, he becomes fixated, numbed by an absentminded stare as he strolls south on the main street or along the creek, unconsciously admiring the church's form as it looms over the town, growing larger and more real with proximity. By focusing on the immediate present, the shape and organization of the world as it's set before him, he is able to disregard the complex pathways of thought that often leave one stranded, lost. All these hints and allusions to the founders of the town and the Native Americans who nearly tore the place down. Still, it remains, its validity ever questioned instead of simply enacted. He had attended to a similar regimen of calibration on the mountain, sitting to observe and be a part of the stability, the balance inherent in the natural world, always keeping a network of landmarks within carefully accessible reach—treetops, mountain peaks, constellations, letters carved into trees. He had constantly checked in on his emotional highs and lows, and he'd been a frequent visitor to the fringes of consciousness. But such personal chores have been neglected since he fled the mountain. His thoughts always seem to wander through the pits and holes they dig, the flat prairie, back toward the mountain to evade the landslide again and again, then drawn right back here, to Grant and Creek's Ridge, with the melodic trails of the Scrap and any other confounding music Ernest tries to convince him to adore. The allure of Caryn's affections. Amondale's pursuits of histories and truths. And now, Lani's potent pull.

The German shepherd watches Johannes from the porch, and Johannes notices that the dog stays put today, leashed perhaps, but he doesn't notice how the dog lifts its head off its paws or the suppressed wag of its tail. He doesn't consider where he's going or why, doesn't know why he has to look after Grant's long-lost friend or why they aren't digging right now. But he does recognize the landmark up ahead, St. Josephine's arrow-like spire, and he knows he won't look up to find himself irretrievably lost, not today. Unless today turns out to be the day that the steeple itself should fall under the impetus of age, weakness, or the forgotten past.

Few residents speak of the church, except for Oscar Amondale, of course, who is known to embark on long-winded descriptions of its eventful history. Throughout the blood-drenched months of the Native American raids, the church had served as a fort, withstanding a constant barrage of projectiles, impervious to flame, and saving the lives of many of the townsfolk. Amondale, in his unimpeachable curiosity, claims to have identified all but two of the battle wounds scarring the edifice and even documented a handful yet unaccounted for in the town records.

While Johannes may have absorbed these obscure historical facts, what he does not remember is whether he knows how to make an omelet. If he strives, pushes himself, bypasses the grocery store and the diner, ignores the church's spire and the border, if he focuses and attends to his desires, then this same path will lead him to his meditation grove, where all these odd sensations might melt away if he sits and sheds them, washing them off along with the Scrap and everything else. Swept downstream. But he still hears Lani's voice, sees the changes that came over her face during the night—

Their shoulders collide, neither one aware of the other until it's too late—Charlie the postman distracted by the contents of his bag, and Johannes locked onto the spire, overwhelmed by the barrage of impressions it draws out. The sides of their foreheads barely miss each other, bringing all those reflections to an abrupt halt.

"Oh...yeah, yeah, hi, hello there..." Charlie glances up, though he's still rifling through his satchel. "So sorry 'bout that, sir. Running late this morning, I am. Sometimes that durned alarm clock has a mind of its own, you see, gone haywire for a day, a night, electromagnetic fields, and interference, all sorts...but the next day tomorra it'll all go back to normal..."

"Don't worry about it, Charlie. I wasn't paying attention either."

"Sure is a nice day there, though, ain't it?" Charlie nods up at the sky, but his attention is strangled by the contents of his bag. "How's the sheriff? You two been busy, ain't ya? Digging your tunnels. Bomb shelters, is it? A mighty charity. Someday, someday we'll need them, won't we? I bet on it..." He takes a step back and scans the empty street. "Well, I sup-pose I'd better keep moving along here. Lotsa letters today, bills and cards, a few good magazines in here, too. Wouldn't mind having a look myself... Well, I better, you know... Have a good one there, today, sir..."

Johannes watches as he shuffles away. "You too, Charlie."

Charlie is one of the few residents who was born in Creek's Ridge and never left. He's old and slow, but he never makes a mistake with the mail. Johannes has met him multiple times, but Charlie can never remember Johannes's name because Johannes doesn't receive mail. And Johannes admires that simplicity, feels a kinship with it. Charlie walks away, swaying unsteadily while he searches through the bag that weighs him down day after day. Watching him go, Johannes suddenly sees him with utter clarity—Charlie had no say in the matter. He had not chosen this dull, perennial path for himself, yet he is pleased to play his part.

At the grocery store, he grabs a basket from beside the register and nods to Cassandra, cashier on permanent duty. She's the owner's daughter and is supposed to be heading off to college come fall. But, apparently, she and her father, George, had told that same story the previous two summers, yet here she was, still working the register at Daddy's grocery.

Johannes sets off to wander the aisles, quickly getting lost.

He only comes into contact with people like Charlie and Cassandra sparsely, once a week at most, but it's no trouble for him to retain their names or recognize the facets of their personalities. He doesn't need to read their names on the mail every day, doesn't have to keep them categorized by address in order to match a face to its name. But when he hears Cassandra calling out to someone and laughing, he wonders whether he would recognize her if he ever ran into her outside the store, without her apron and forced smile, and he can't recall whether he ever has.

After these few months amongst the people of Creek's Ridge, Johannes assumes that he's establishing a new life for himself, building something to replace that which has been demolished. He is cordoning off a space of his own in which to flourish, working with and adapting to new surroundings, new acquaintances, and asserting his individuality amongst them. All this time, he has believed that, and Grant's heavy-handed assertions have constantly reminded him of it, demanding more and more participation. Ever since Johannes arrived, Grant has been directing his friend's perception toward the departed past, even though Johannes still flounders in the present. And there they are, every morning, noon, and generally well into the evening, digging through the same dirt, for the same bones, though possibly not for the same reasons.

And now, here he is amidst aisles and shelves of immediate satiation. Lumpy mounds of vegetables, the chill from the coolers, neat rows of boxes, jars, cans, and containers. Refreshing beverages, scented bars of soap, packages of prophylactics. Nonperishables to last him years on the mountain. The Liquor Corner brandishes bottles of courage and mixers to make it palatable. But at the moment, he's only after immediate essentials—a clove of garlic, a tomato and an eggplant, a chili or two— each of them into the basket. Don't forget the eggs. Maybe orange juice to balance it out. And what of the basic ingredients? Johannes should've made note of that before he ran out, escaped, pulled a Metternich. Black pepper? Salt? Butter? Cooking oil? Why, of all things, must he dwell on the contents of Grant's cupboards? Are there no more pressing concerns than these?

When Johannes and Grant do eat at the house, Grant generally handles the shopping and the cooking. He is particular about the way things are done. Though Johannes earns a bit of cash from helping out at Ernest's now and again, Grant encourages him to take whatever money he needs whenever he needs it, especially for food or general necessities. However, this defined and exacting errand—*Make me omelets*—is something new.

In the woods, he'd taken from the land. He'd taken from that generous young couple, the Rosses, his only human contact for those seven years. Once or twice a year, he would hike down for toothpaste or materials to repair his shack, and she would send him back up with more supplies than he could comfortably carry. And then, one day, she surprised him with the cat. The cat...its name...that's it...Rozinante. That was its name. Rozinante, the knight errant's noble steed, by some accounts. The husband, Will, with his cold stare and gruff manner, and she, Anne, whispering to Johannes when Will's back was turned, *Please come down more often...don't be so surprised...if you see me up there...we worry about you so...I mean, I do...no, not Will...he calls...Mister...no...never mind... forget I said it...I'm not supposed to...I forget...what it all means...to you and...it's so admirable what you do...but is it safe?...are you running from something?...*

hiding out?...by the way, how's Rozinante?...does he get enough to eat?...and you, anything you need, just ask, please...

Now it's Grant, Ernest, Amondale, Caryn, and Ruthie at the diner. They give and Johannes takes. Even Pa Sonny carried him across an entire state. If Johannes is on a path at all, is it really a path of his own? And if he trudges along this path, is it even by the strength of his own bones? Limping Lady is Grant's project, yet those bones supply every ounce of Johannes's fortitude and feed off it, too.

Of course the cat's name was Rozinante. Scrawny and bony, but loyal. It was inside the shack, wasn't it? What else could he expect?

And now, ever since Grant led Lani into the bar, Johannes has thought of little else. Even Caryn's calming voice and hesitant caresses have faded. *Walk me home,* she'd said. He remembers that now, but that's not what happened. She had propped him up, walked him home, laid him down, and then she'd gone again to leave on her own.

Johannes is staring out the windows as Cassandra finishes ringing everything up. "It's fifteen seventy-two."

He pulls the bills out of his pocket. Bits of dirt and tiny pebbles emerge as well, sprinkling across the counter. Cassandra giggles as she flips through the bills and brushes the dirt onto the floor. She pushes some of the bills back.

"Johannes."

"Huh?"

"You gave me too much."

"Oh." He looks at the bills, then at her. "Thanks."

"Johannes, wait. Your change."

"What?"

"Here. Twenty-eight cents. Hey, you alright?"

"Sure. Yeah. Thanks, Cassandra."

"Tell the sheriff I said hi."

"Yeah, okay."

Outside, the drone of heavy machinery rumbles in the distance, a sound that's out of place, out of character in Creek's Ridge, not unlike Johannes himself. He gazes down the road toward St. Josephine's, but then, choking down the urge to investigate, he turns back toward the house. Lani will have long since finished her shower. She'll be waiting, hungry, impatient, and alone, wondering where he has disappeared to.

Grant's friend, not his. Grant's house, Grant's shower, Grant's horse, not his. The shovel and the pickax, the dirt they dig, the chair where he sits and the floor where he sleeps, photographs and memories, everything, all of it, Grant's and not his. Except for the Scrap, the Rachmaninoff record, perhaps, if only he could get himself to look at it like that.

Still, here he is, hurrying back to Grant's house, to Lani and the breakfast he is bound to cook, acting on a promise he made as soon as Lani looked his way. Grant tells him what to do every day, but always with an unspoken resistance, never such razor efficiency.

"Johannes? Johannes, what are you doing?" Caryn seems confused as she blocks his path.

"Oh, I didn't see you. I'm just...I was...going home...breakfast..."

She squeezes his arm and peeks into the grocery bag. "Do you remember anything?"

"Last night? Of course."

"Did you talk to her yet?"

"She's waiting for me. For breakfast."

"I see. I'm in a hurry, too." She leans in, wrapping an arm around him, pressing against his side. "I was supposed to be at St. Josephine's an hour ago. All that whisky and I overslept."

"Electromagnetic fields, interference..."

"What?"

"Nothing. The church? Why?"

"Come with me. Come have a look?"

"I would, but...omelets..."

"Well, I'll be there all day. Bring her with you. It'll be fun."

"Yeah, maybe..."

"What else are you going to do?"

"I don't know..."

"No digging, remember?" she smiles and squeezes his arm again.

"Yeah, so I hear..."

"Okay. See you later on?"

"Yeah...yeah, sure."

Caryn smiles and hurries off in the opposite direction, maintaining her relaxed gait even in haste, her body swaying rhythmically, shoulders taut, arms loose, her whole form springing with a limber jaunt. She glances back just once, and their eyes meet. Even from a distance, he is struck by her barren eyes, as sad as the flat, dusty prairie all around them, but intoxicating all the same. He's familiar with those eyes, knows them because they reflect his own, the emptiness and experience of roving the earth alone, without the warmth meant to radiate from the conjoining of two lives into one. They contain the secrets of sealed-off doorways to massive underground caverns, shuttered and inaccessible to the outside world, plunged into an inky subterranean darkness that blots out inner treasures, revealing nothing of dreams, heartaches, desires, fears, or pleasures. And though Caryn's words and her touch spring forth like cool bubbling streams, her eyes lack the human warmth that bleeds from those who love, those who covet, a beacon projected to announce where you stand, what you are, summoning and warning and existing, something which Lani displays in abundance and which has already startled Johannes with its potency, contorted him with its force—for when the sailor hears the Sirens' pleas, he straps himself to the mast. Thus, he wanders in search of the knowledge, the singular event, the person or the place that can shed light upon the dark without poisoning the spirit, who can sweep aside the shrouds he's woven to veil himself or to veil the world around him, and finally expose the unexceptional truth—no sailor at all is he—a farce, an illusion, just a dream and a joke.

"Where's my omelet?" The soft, demanding tone of Lani's voice hovers behind him.

Without any clue about how he got here, Johannes stands above the pits at the far end of the yard, cradling the groceries in his right arm as he stares into a vacant trench. He turns to look at her, met by her eyes, sunlight after dark, rain after the thaw.

"Right here," he says, glancing at the groceries and then off at the sharp, level line of the horizon.

"What are you doing out here?" The warmth is not just in her eyes but also in her voice. "No digging, remember?"

"No, I know. No digging. I was just...thinking."

"Yeah? About me? Or about digging these holes?"

"About how to make an omelet, actually."

They walk back to the house, Lani hanging close by his side. She opens the door for him and then sits down at the table. They stare at each other before Johannes begins arranging the ingredients on the counter.

"Aren't you curious about me?" she asks. "You've hardly said a thing."

Johannes glances back but doesn't respond.

"That look in your eyes..."

"You have a look in your eyes, too."

"I suppose we all do."

"There's a lot on my mind."

"Yeah?" Lani laughs. "You've got it real tough living here, huh? Grant's charity causing you too much grief? You ought to come back to Chicago with me. Ten minutes in that city injects a healthy dose of anxiety. But it's like a drug. Consume it long enough and you can't function without it."

"Then, I think it's something else I need. The other extreme, maybe. I'm not ready for a place like that. I'm hardly ready for this, for Creek's Ridge, and whatever it means."

"Well, when you are ready, you come and find me, alright? I'll always be there."

"Always..." Johannes begins chopping vegetables, his back turned to Lani.

"So, you like it here?" she continues.

"I like it fine."

"I only ask because...you don't seem entirely...fulfilled."

"I'm searching."

"For what?"

"Fulfillment."

"Where? In those holes out back? What makes you think you'll find anything here? Is that garlic?"

"It's not that I think I will. This is just where I'm looking for now."

"To be honest, I can't see much difference between living alone on a mountain and living in a place like this. Seven years as a hermit wasn't enough?"

Johannes sets down the knife and faces her. "You know about that?"

"Grant told me," she shrugs and smiles.

Johannes resumes his chopping. "I ended up getting myself lost out there. Sometimes it's hard to believe I found my way out at all. And I needed someone...just...someone. So I came to the last place I had been before the mountain, the only place I had any real recollection of. Here, to Grant. He helps. But...it's difficult to truly leave a place when you're lost."

"You really don't remember anything from before? Nothing? That's such a scary thought—and kind of unbelievable."

Johannes breaks the eggs into a bowl and starts to beat them. "Like I said, Grant helps."

"It doesn't sound like it. Not really. Maybe I can offer something better."

"Like what?"

"Give me a chance. Anyway, you've got no choice today or tomorrow. You're engaged to entertain me. Sheriff's orders." She smiles as she gets up and heads into the living room. "Think of something fun for us to do. We've got two days. I'll be in the bathroom finishing my makeup, but give a shout when it's ready, alright? You've kept me waiting long enough."

Chapter 28

The White Serpents

SAINTE ANNE DE DETROIT, A STONE AND WOOD STRUCTURE UNLIKE any Lalawethika had ever seen, was enough to distract him entirely from the madness of Detroit bustling around them. The size and variety of buildings unsettled him, and the people's urgency intimidated him. Men of all colors lounged about, led horses, laughed and howled while conducting their business. At least ten different languages could be heard as they strolled through the town center—English, French, a mishmash of Algonquin dialects, several Iroquoian languages, and a few that were utterly foreign. The crowd became more solemn when they turned onto a broad tree-lined boulevard. Then, the enormous bulk of the building rose into view.

"What is this place?" Lalawethika said as they trod along the manicured dirt road leading toward the structure. "Its beauty is immense, its strength boundless..."

"And so must you be," replied Penagashea.

The throng still swelled and croaked behind them, but the noise diminished with each step they took. A few people mulled idly around the grounds. They were reticent, displaying none of the brashness of the people in the town square. From above, a melodious thunderclap struck. Lalawethika jumped back in fright, and Penagashea laughed, leading him onward and pointing up at the bell tower. "That is how they signal one another and impose order upon the passing of days. For the white man, time is invaluable."

Beneath the arched doorway stood two white men, one speaking boisterously with frantic gestures and the other laughing quietly along.

The second man noticed them waiting at the foot of the stairs and smiled. He hushed his companion, spoke into the man's ear, and then descended the steps. The man embraced Penagashea as they shared a few words in English. Smiling, the man held out his hand.

Lalawethika recoiled.

"This is their custom," Penagashea told Lalawethika. "You must become familiar with their ways. Give him your hand."

Lalawethika remained silent and stubborn. The white man retracted his hand and laughed, cautiously observing the two Shawnees.

The man, Penagashea explained later, was Father Gabriel Richard, presiding priest at Sainte Anne de Detroit. Dressed simply all in black, Father Gabe—as Penagashea addressed him—was a tall, gaunt figure. He tended to hunch forward and lower his eyes when listening to someone speak, as though out of respect for the speaker. But when he spoke, he stood at full height and maintained eye contact with his listeners. Born in France, he was fluent in French and English. He was also confident with several native languages, though he knew little of the Shawnee tongue. His features were comparable to the church over which he presided. The weathering of age had given them each a delicate perfection that seemed slightly out of place, intended for a more perfect world but caught up in the mix of our own. A bald spot was forming at his hairline. His cheeks were clean-shaven, his eyes sunken far into an otherwise flat face. And they were constantly moist, as if he had just woken from a heavy sleep, or had been weeping.

After a brief tour of the grounds, they parted from the Father and headed back into the mayhem of the town square. Many of their tribesmen feared the white towns and were yet dependent upon the white man's luxuries, so Lalawethika and Penagashea had been entrusted with pelts, beadwork, moccasins, and other such handiwork to be traded in the city. It had been a heavy load but manageable enough for Lalawethika to drag through the woodlands at the sedate pace with which Penagashea walked. However, they were to trade these items for sacks of sugar, salt, tobacco, whiskey, ammunition, and powder —all much weightier items that would prove impossible to convey back to the Tippecanoe River without a horse and carriage. Penagashea wished to complete their trading straight away so they might enjoy their time with Father Gabe. Throughout the afternoon, they traded and bargained, gathering their accumulations near a corner of the square where Lalawethika spent the next couple of hours lounging, continuously filling a pipe with tobacco from the acquired sacks, and watching Penagashea hobble from group to group in search of a friendly party with a carriage they could join for at least a portion of the return journey.

Eventually, a scrawny horse towing a small cart pulled up nearby. The man who dismounted was the same man who had earlier been speaking with Father Gabriel beneath the arches of the church. His name was Darius, a businessman from Baltimore and an old friend of the Father's. Most other traders had already packed up for the evening, so he spotted Lalawethika without much trouble. Speaking loudly in English, he gestured with broad sweeps of the arms and headed straight for the Shawnees' haul. Lalawethika stepped into the white man's path, protecting their goods. The stout man's thick mustache twitched and curled over a wide grin as he extended his hand. Lalawethika grunted and waved the man off. Darius's cheeks jiggled when he laughed, and he laughed throughout, still speaking but with less haste now and more emphasis, all the while calmly inching forward. When he noticed the scarred flesh of Lalawethika's mutilated eye, he stopped to stare and point, asking questions without waiting for answers or even considering whether the Shawnee could understand him. Without warning, he thrust his hand toward Lalawethika's face in an apparent attempt to touch the sunken, knotted flesh of the eye socket, to which Lalawethika reacted with a shout as he reached for his stone ax. Darius backed away with raised hands, but his laughter and rate of speech only increased. A crowd closed in around them, drawn to the stand-off—always when the dogs are barking—and with the crowd came Penagashea, who had first to calm Lalawethika and then to convince him to help load their goods onto the cart, as Darius had volunteered to collect them and bring them back to Father Gabe's farm for the night.

Father Gabriel welcomed them into his home with a feast of several pheasants and a cask of sweetened firewater he had recently received from his family's orchard in France. Lalawethika would not leave their goods unattended. He refused both Father Gabriel's and Penagashea's appeals to join them inside, as well as Darius's apology for the incident at the town square. That night, he slept on the open ground, shivering and guarding the cart loaded with their acquired goods.

Penagashea came to Lalawethika the next morning.

"You must befriend these people. Men like Father Gabe must be your allies."

"These are not men," grunted Lalawethika. "They are creatures of the Great Serpent's wiles."

"Fine, you may not trust them any more than the horse riders who ride through and destroy our crops, but you must instill in them the illusion that they own your trust. They should believe that they have your cooperation. They do not trust us either. Father Gabe is an old and dear friend, but I would never claim to share mutual trust with him. Respect, yes. Trust, we pretend. This is the true way of the world. There is an endless frontier out there teeming with native peoples that white men do not trust. Father Gabe has stepped into those wilds anyhow, his hands extended in friendship. And so, trust cannot determine our relations with the white race. It is a mutual understanding. An agreement, like the balance in the stars. Imagine a night sky in which all the stars shine only in the east, but the western sky is an empty, black, unrelenting darkness that refuses to share the burden. A sky at war. No peace to be found there, no certainty, no comfort. It is better to distribute your efforts evenly."

"This devil you call friend," Lalawethika scoffed and gestured at Father Gabriel's meager house, "he is a bearer of their religion. No different from the missionaries we chase from our lands, those who come with their lies and orders from the white government to silence our beliefs, replace our values, and extinguish our wisdom. To take our land from beneath our sleeping heads."

"Fool! Open your eyes, not your mouth! The bearers of their religion are nothing more than their medicine men. Hardly different from me and you. And yet they possess the power we seek. Have you not noticed? Father Gabe and his church are the center of this city. All decisions pass through him. He has fingers in the United States government and the British royalty, who control the lands beyond the lake. He has friends within every major tribe from here to the sea. And Darius, the man you almost scalped yesterday, is one of the wealthiest businessmen in their nation. That man can order up a white militia quicker than their government or summon an army of Iroquois that would destroy the Shawnee Nation overnight."

They were both heaving silently, each fraught with concealed anger when, without cause or provocation, Penagashea collapsed.

Lalawethika stared at his mentor for a few moments, pacifying and caressing his rage as best he could before finally moving to help the old man back to his feet. He supported Penagashea, leading him to the carriage and helping him to sit on the wheel.

"What was it? A spirit took you?"

"No, no, it was nothing, nothing," Penagashea wheezed. "I felt dizzy, that is all. You are right to be cautious. But you must never forget that we are weaker than our enemy. At this moment, you are small, smaller than a fly. Someday you will be a medicine man, but for now, you are nothing. You have a colossal mountain to scale. Take the time to learn about the world as it exists, not as you wish to shape it. You are not yet ready for that task. The world as we know it may not yet be ready. It may not be ready in your lifetime, but your role will be crucial. Tomorrow is their holy day. You will see for yourself the loyalty and love that Father Gabe receives from his people, a great many people, including red men. He is only a medicine man, like me. But he wields true power. When I am dead, you will want Father Gabe and his kind to hold you in their good graces. Eventually, as a Shawnee medicine man, you must remain unseen, consulted by the chiefs in the shadows. Even the mightiest counselor must seek advice at times. Who is it you will call out to? The Great Spirit does not always answer our pleas for guidance."

Penagashea pointed with a weak and trembling hand at the few jugs they had collected, which were still loaded on the cart and destined for their war chief.

"But these are concerns for a later time. To build a fire, one must first gather wood. That is why I brought you here. Remember where you are. Remember what you are. You have been admirably firm in your resistance to the firewater. Here, you are away from the prying, critical watch of our people, and your old medicine man asks you to accompany him. You must drink of the firewater today, not only with me but with your future allies as well."

They sat with Darius that afternoon, drinking from their war chief's casks. Penagashea told stories in his broken English, and Darius's laughter grew more uninhibited with each drop they consumed. In the evening, the servants brought them dinner. Father Gabriel returned late, and his foul mood instantly improved when he saw Lalawethika sitting at his table. He ordered his servants to bring more of the sweetened firewater, and they drank beside the fireplace late into the night. Lalawethika did not care for the taste of wine. He sipped the liquid moderately, listening to the others rollicking in English, especially Penagashea, who became more animated as the night wore on. Firelight played hell with the shadows, drawing exaggerated expressions across the faces of Lalawethika's companions, never more severe than when they laughed, laughter which he noticed was not drawn from the conversation but directed at Penagashea's increasingly foolish antics.

The following morning, they returned to Sainte Anne's for Mass. The two Shawnees stood in back along with the other red men who, to Lalawethika's astonishment, were not there to observe, as he was, but to worship. The cavernous, vaulted ceiling amplified Lalawethika's unease. Although every seat in the pews was occupied, people continued to push their way in from behind. There was something eerie about the subdued voices of such a large, gathered people. And there was an odor, too, like a barely contained illness gaining in vigor.

Penagashea got hold of one of the books that the white folk were clutching to their breasts. He flipped through it, explaining briefly to Lalawethika the facets of the white man's religion and pointing out similarities with Shawnee beliefs. Kokumthena, grandmother to the Shawnee people, might well stand beside Mary, the virgin mother to the human son of God. He pointed out a small wooden structure called the confessional, where worshippers met privately with the Father to confess their guilt, secret deeds, and wicked thoughts, not unlike how Lalawethika had sought counsel from his medicine man. And there was something called the Eucharist, akin to a medicine man supplying his subjects with herbs and concoctions to aid their communion with the Great Spirit.

Soon, a figure appeared in the pulpit. A hush filled the nave, as though everyone present had held their breath. Lalawethika was, in fact, holding his breath. Before the figure had even spoken a word, he dominated the congregation. And when he did speak, their attention never swayed. He trolled them through shallow waters, intermittently lifting them and thrashing them with lofty demands. His voice was that of a man capable of taming wolves, effortlessly exploiting the weaknesses of their human flaws and temporal pettiness.

Though it should have been obvious, it took a long time for Lalawethika to recognize the speaker as Father Gabriel. Nothing in the speaker's mannerisms bespoke the sensitive, generous man he had been introduced to. From their vantage at the rear of the nave, any distinguishing features were lost amidst the flowing white robe and colorful sashes that adorned his body. He delivered his words with a boldness that would set war chiefs on their toes, and an echo hung about the room like it was part of the building's construction. Not until later in the sermon, at a point where the speaker's tone mellowed into a tranquil murmur and his phrases lilted upwards as he questioned an intimate unseen partner, only then did Lalawethika recognize his host.

After the service ended, they spent some time strolling about the grounds and talking with the other red men. Darius was also wandering the grounds, and each time he crossed paths with the two Shawnees, he would slap one of them on the back and mutter through his thick, throaty laughter.

Later in the afternoon, when only a few silent individuals still hung idly about the cathedral, they went back inside. They looked around for a while, examining statues and adornments before finally resting in the pews nearest the altar.

"You are at peace today," said Penagashea, "more willing to absorb your experiences. Was it yesterday's firewater? Or possibly Father Gabe's fiery oration?"

"Perhaps both," admitted Lalawethika. "You were right about Father Gabriel's power. I could not understand his speech, but his hold upon the people was inescapable. He possesses a careful, intentional equilibrium to his conduct within these walls. He treats us with respect. Those red men, on the other hand, do not. The red men we spoke with—they are scabs. They neither speak nor look upon us with sincerity. They are cowards who have abandoned their people and soiled their history. You once called me a dog. I, at least, will not bow my head in shame. I will never again lower my tail between my legs. I will not be leashed and dragged from my land. I will never lie prostrate at their feet nor submit to their whip. Not without baring my fangs."

"No..." Penagashea was thoughtful. "That has never been your problem, has it? But, son, your fangs have not served you well. They have been aimed no straighter than the arrow that took your eye. Another error like that might well cost you your life. Your tribesmen dislike you precisely for your bite, for the acidity of your breath as you cluck and boast. With what fangs, then, shall you strike?"

"With my brother, Tecumseh. He shall be my weapon."

"And how will you compel him to follow your lead? He is a warrior with a chief's blood coursing through his veins, and you are but his deformed, drunkard little brother."

"Not me. I shall not convince him." Lalawethika had a vacant expression, pale and unfocused as though he were seeing through his mangled eye, seeing beyond the walls of the church, the walls of time. "As a warrior, he perceives in quantities and strength. The multitude of my followers shall convince him. I will first unite the Shawnee people, then all the Natives of this land."

"And your followers? How will you earn their loyalty?"

"Through fear."

"Fear of what?" Penagashea was nodding along, speaking through a grin of pleasure. "Fear of your stone ax? As you nearly converted our friend Darius at the town center? In the white man's towns, the sentence for such an outrageous act is execution."

"Fear of the unseen and the unknowable. Fear of the white man, his so-called justice and punishments. Fear of the Great Spirit and the Great Serpent alike. They will bow before their fear. They will embrace it as they would a lover at the moment of ecstasy. Copulation with their own fear shall give birth to anger and malice. The rebellion you have spoken of shall rise from the heat and passion of them coupling with their fear."

Penagashea struggled to stand. He leaned heavily on his medicine staff and gazed around the chapel. "I am afraid you will have to do better than that. Do you know what these people fear? They fear Father Gabe. No abstractions, just the Father himself. He is the voice of their god, a manifestation they can look upon, flesh they can touch. And they love him because they fear him. Father Gabe is an influential man who wields his power with infinite care and is admired by a great many people. And yet, he is a lonely man. For friendship, he gravitates toward men like us, the staunchest and most stubborn of red men, those who will never abandon their traditions or beliefs. It is because we do not venerate him. We do not bow before him. We do not fear him. He also befriends men like Darius, men who believe in no god, who fear nothing less permanent than death, because in death their wealth will be without value. Come now. It is a long walk back to the Father's farm. And you have many more miles to walk, with many more years to contemplate these ambitions."

"They shall feel fear and awe in my presence because I shall reveal the wicked truths of this world." Lalawethika stood and followed his medicine man down the aisle.

Penagashea chuckled and glanced back. "What do you know of wicked truths?"

"I am eager to return to the Tippecanoe. It must begin at once. I will not sit idle. Great change must occur within my lifetime."

"Suffocate those thoughts," Penagashea scolded. "That is the path to failure. We will leave for home in a few days, but you will begin nothing. You are yet but a child in this rebirth. Do not forget that. Dogs may grow into adulthood in a single year, but they can also be felled with a single strike of the ax. You must grow to be the sturdiest oak in the forest, your roots planted deep below the surface of what you think you know."

Chapter 29

The Summer Blossom

"It's been years since I saw the Rockies." Lani is glowing, almost bouncing in the driver's seat. The grasslands of eastern Colorado stretch on as they push west on US-160. Nearly three hours cooped up in her rental car and they have barely noticed a variation in the grass's monotone shade, the unchanging pastel sky, the unblemished concrete with its measured white and yellow lines, their own hesitant conversation tempered by a voiceless unease. "Not since I was a kid. I still remember the trails, always getting lost..."

"That's part of the fun," says Johannes. "As long as you can find it again."

"Find what?" Lani gives him a stern glance.

"The trail."

"Naturally." Lani smiles and looks up into the rearview, slowing as a sports car passes on their left.

"It's best to keep visual landmarks," adds Johannes. "Trees or boulders you can remember. Distant peaks. Sometimes leaving your mark."

"No, I know. Bread crumbs... But it wasn't me getting lost. Not me, my brother...he..."

Johannes reins his gaze in from the sea of grass.

"We don't speak much, not anymore. I don't even know where he is. He would always tell us he hadn't gotten lost, that he meant to, just wanted to look at the stars, undisturbed."

"Me too."

"Is that right?"

"I used to sit with the stars every night, contemplating and communicating with them. These days, I only get a glance...now and again."

"We can, you know. Wouldn't it be great if we had a tent and some sleeping bags? We could stop. I could buy some. We could spend the night in the mountains. Stargazing, talking. What do you think, John? Or, you know, maybe just look for a short trail? We don't have to go in too deep or stay the night. We'll just stay on the outskirts. No harm in that, is there?"

"Go ahead. Drop me off and pick me up on your way back. I'll be okay here."

"Don't be ridiculous," she says, her stare lingering. "What happened to you on that mountain?"

"Grant already told you."

"He didn't tell me much. Just that something happened, not what it was."

"I'd rather not talk about it."

"What then? We took a drive to get to know each other, didn't we?"

"I thought you wanted to see the summer blossom?"

"You can't tell me anything about where you came from? Your life before? Nothing's coming back to you?"

"You're just like him. Like Grant. If you're so curious, then you should go into the mountains. Alone. The answers are all there. Maybe. At least I thought they were."

"Doesn't Grant tell you about people? Things from the past? Drag out memories? Photographs? Anything?"

"We dig up the past every day."

"Dig? What, those bones? Are you joking?"

"No."

"That's not what I meant."

"I know. But that's what we're concerned with right now. That's all that matters. The bones. Everything else is incidental. I could be anybody. You could be anybody. Creek's Ridge could be any place. And Grant does, he brings up things from the past all the time, memories he believes we must share. But they rarely provide me more than a glimpse, a hint. Like barely audible whispers. Wind through the leaves, moonless nights. I think he does it more for his own benefit than mine. And then he only winds up more frustrated than I do. The bones, though, they're real. We can touch them. We can put them together again. If only we could find them..."

"But don't you want to remember?"

"When I went into the mountains, I was either searching for something or running. I don't remember which, but as far as I can tell, I'm better off not remembering. I tried to stop life from moving forward, but it didn't work out as I'd hoped. I would love to try again. I would love to do it right...but I don't think it's possible. A lesson learned the hard way."

"So, you realized your mistake and then you came back. Sort of. You came back to Grant."

"I didn't realize any mistake. If anything, I buried my mistakes."

"But...why to Grant and not your family? Your home?"

"The mountain was my home. And the storm, the landslide, they destroyed it. I was a part of that place. I lost myself out there...on the verge of death, one foot firmly in the door. Sometimes it feels like I still am. I needed to start somewhere. Something to hold on to. That something was Grant."

"You sound like a wounded lover. If you're going to start over, then start over. Reinvent yourself. If you're trying to find something, go ahead and look for it, but then come back. You don't just harm yourself, you also hurt those around you, the people who care about you. Take Grant—I haven't seen him for a few years either, but he's changed, too. He's in pieces. That bitch Inez ruined his life. And the only thing that carries him through is his family, people like you and Sonny, who he cares about more than he cares about himself. You're helping him more than he's helping you."

Johannes stares out the passenger window. "I've done nothing for Grant."

"Don't be stupid. He's like a brother to you. The bond you two share is only possible through childhood—discovering the ups and downs of the world together, making sense of it, and knowing you're not alone. Sometimes, that's all a person needs. It was obvious the moment I saw you two in that bar last night. This thing you two share, that's a direct result of your past."

"What is he to you, exactly?"

Lani looks at Johannes and smiles. The road has been perfectly flat and straight for most of the drive, but now they're driving on a subtle incline.

"You're more than just old friends," Johannes insists.

"We're good friends," her smile lingers momentarily, then fades. "I've always felt something strong for Grant. Let's call it...an emotional bond. But it's always been...something that could never fully bloom. Not like with you and Caryn. You two have a real chance, I can tell. An exciting time, the early days of new love."

"I don't love Caryn."

"But you see what I mean. Anyway, why not? She's wonderful. Beautiful, kind, and supportive. You could learn a lot from her. Help each other. She's reinventing herself just like you. Completely upended her former life."

"What do you mean?"

"Don't you know what she did back in California?"

"No."

"Jesus. Don't you want to know?"

They both glance at each other, their eyes meeting and latching, the clasping of clammy hands.

Johannes nods. "I do."

"Well, that's not my place. You can hear it from her someday when you figure out how to talk to people. All that matters is that she wanted out and she got out. All on her own. But unlike you, she cherishes her past. Everything she's been through has made her stronger, and she knows it. She acknowledges it. So she's not afraid to accept a little help along the way. All the people who are important to her know where she is and why she left. It took me one night to learn all that about her. Open your window, will you? I need some air." Lani switches off the air conditioner and lowers her window. Air blasts into the car, noisy and crisp and warm.

After a few minutes, Lani says, "I think I loved Grant once, a long time ago. Before he was with Inez. Maybe even while he was with her, but... Do you smell that? The air? It's so fresh. I would love to live out here."

"No dust."

"No smog. Freedom. I do admire that about what you've done, that connection to the natural world. And Grant, too. But it's not for me. I'm content with changing apartments every couple of years. I could never leave Chicago."

"Why not?"

"The city is a part of me. Friends and family. I look after mom since dad died. I have a career, a dog, friends, hobbies. I'm happy, mostly."

"Mostly?"

"There are things, people I miss. Just because I stay put doesn't mean the world around me stays the same. You said it yourself, life moves on. Things change, get left behind, forgotten, usually against our will. I understand that, about what happened to you, but... But everyone has certain things they miss." She stares at him, her eyes prying, questions implied but left unsaid, the car drifting slightly to the right. "I find it very hard to believe that you don't."

"That mountain, it nearly killed me. Somehow, I stepped out of death's path, but I was reaching out to it. As I tried to make sense of what I wanted, who I was, and what I was really doing there, it occurred to me, plain as day, that the forest didn't want me there at all, live or dead, and maybe it never did. That's when I knew I had lost everything. But still, I miss that. My life there."

"You would go back?"

"I can never go back."

"Why not?"

"I can't. No matter how much I want to, I can't."

"But you can."

"..."

"That's just an arbitrary limitation you're placing on yourself. No different from you locking yourself up in the mountains to begin with, telling yourself you could never leave, no contact allowed with the real world. Says who? It's just the same thing all over again. Or how you and Grant say you have to find those dumb bones. You have to? How stupid, how pointless, and so easily swept aside. If you could just see that. What's it going to take to make you see before the same thing happens again? It's already happening again. You're doing it right now, the same thing. So, I guess I should tell you to change your ways before it's too late."

"Our personal limitations are all we have. It's the quality that separates us from animals, defines us as individuals, provides form and order where otherwise there would be none."

"Okay," Lani laughs lightly but with a serious grin. "At least you believe in something."

She lets off the accelerator and reaches out to caress his cheek. Her touch communicates that she understands, that everything will be okay, will always be okay, but her eyes speak a foreign language. They possess heat, the sparks that ignite wildfires, the essence devoid from Caryn's eyes, the knowledge missing from his own. But it's nothing that can be given or taken, taught or learned. The source and the meaning of life—each one burns from spontaneous combustion. We, merely the witnesses.

Lani gasps. "Look..."

Johannes is looking at her, but she cradles his chin and directs his gaze forward, out the windshield. The Rockies protrude over the horizon, piercing the land's spacious monotony. Though still distant and ghostly, the outlines of their angular peaks are brilliantly lit by a sun slowly approaching and highlighting great swaths of blue and yellow upon their slopes, the summer blossom in full swing. Lani accelerates without intending to, driven on by pure excitement, her eyes sparkling and childlike, beacons aflame and begging Johannes, *Please, see how beau-*

tiful the world is, please, let's embrace it together, please, hold on tight, we're going in, we're climbing the slopes, please, the peaks call to us and laugh, the farce of this life is a joke like all the rest, but the beauty, please, John, please, it's real—

However, as her gaze shifts between mountain majesty and human tragedy, she is overwhelmed by the change coming over Johannes. Without another appeal, she pulls onto the shoulder, waits as a semi and a few cars speed past, and then swings the car around in a tight U-turn.

As they drive back to Creek's Ridge, her eyes rarely leave the rearview mirror. The windows remain open, letting the wind batter their cheeks and whip their hair. After a while, Lani starts talking again, casually, as though nothing had happened. She speaks on general affairs, about Chicago and the trivialities of her life there, about a recently failed relationship and a vacation to the Caribbean she'd had to cancel so she could come to Creek's Ridge for a couple days. About taking care of her mom and her dog. About feeling old, the disappearance of youth, the gradual increase of pressure and responsibilities. She mentions again how much she had wanted to take a short hike into the mountains, just a quick one, not to get lost, not to stay, only to smell the flowers, to gaze at the stars, but that she's content just to have seen the mountains from afar, that iconic, stout backbone of the country. Then, as they cross back over the Kansas state line, she is reminded of Saint Josephine and the fascinating controversy addressed by Amondale and Caryn, a town like Creek's Ridge still surviving and attracting people with its historical lure. Who was right? Who wrong? Who at fault and who deserving of reverence? As far as she saw it, all parties were to blame, all of them just separate cogs spinning on the same wheel. But she and Caryn continued talking last night after Amondale suddenly left, with Johannes dead asleep on Caryn's shoulder and Grant lost in his own agitated thoughts. Caryn had told her that she suspected Amondale was correct about the Saint's tricks and manipulations. However, she didn't want to give in just yet because she knew the most effective way to pry information out of Oscar Amondale, and it was not through concessions. And also, Caryn thought there was still more to it, as there was no other way to account for the unlikely coincidence that both the Saint and her aging father had gone crazy before dying of no apparent cause except, perhaps, broken hearts. But who doesn't catch a broken heart once in a while? Once in a lifetime, at least? Like that song...days going by, and the water. And where was Josephine's mother in all of this? That's what Lani wanted to know. And who was this prophet? Some kind of Native American witch doctor or something? It all sounds rather dubious, to be honest. My God, what have I...

Johannes listens. He watches her smooth mannerisms, the way she uses her hands to add emphasis, even while in control of the car. He admires her confidence and her beauty, but the image of those mountain peaks lingers, etched into the windshield. All he sees are mountains ahead and mountains behind, landslides lying in wait.

When they pull up to the house that evening, Grant is still out. Lani asks Johannes to show her around the backyard and provide an explanation. Gladly, he shows her the pile of bones they've already collected. He takes her to the pit where it all started, recounting Grant's paranoid confusion and the discovery of that very first bone. He offers to let her hold the pickax and have a few whacks with it, but she declines, and so it sways, a pendulum by his side as he leads her through the maze. Lani gives him her complete attention. And while she points out the absurdity in what they're doing, she also claims to understand, as though she has something invested in their discoveries.

Afterward, Lani decides to bring Grant dinner. She prepares a salad and asks Johannes to make a couple sandwiches. Johannes walks her out to the street and points her in the direction of the two-story brick building that houses Amondale's office and also serves as the sheriff's office and jail. He waits until she's out of sight before returning to the backyard, and just like after a night of too much Carnival, the bitter taste of betrayal lingers in his mouth like it will never rinse away.

"What's this? I already ate..."

"Just an excuse to come and see you. Alone. There's something wrong with this, what we're doing..."

"We'll figure it out. Come here..."

"Stop it, Grant! That's not what I meant—"

"What then?"

"I didn't come here for this. That's not why you asked me to come to this fucking stupid town, is it? Is it?"

"But it's just so good to see you. Isn't it? It's been so long. I think about you every day. Do you know that? Don't you miss what we had?"

"What did we ever have? You gave it all to her, that bitch, for nothing. And you still do, you're still..."

"No...I don't...she's nothing..."

"..."

"I swear."

"You're full of so much shit."

"No, I mean it."

"Then why didn't you come back when it ended with her? Why? You knew I was..."

"I—"

"Look at yourself. Wasting away in this pointless, pissant, nothing town. Fucking Kansas? Are you serious? You've been here almost ten fucking years."

"It's not so bad...once you get used to it..."

"You're no different than him. You're just as bad. No, you're worse."

"..."

"This was such a bad idea. I should never have come. I shouldn't have listened to you. This is bad for all three of us. And what am I supposed to tell—"

"But on the phone...we agreed, nothing wrong with having a bit of fun. Right? Right? Just a bit of fun, like old times, and he'll snap out—"

"It wasn't real on the phone! None of this was real. I didn't even believe you until I got here and saw him. Now, this is real life slapping me in the fucking face. And it hurts, Grant. It hurts. He's so far gone. I don't even know him anymore. And he has no idea, not a fucking clue. I feel like...I should leave. Right now. Without saying anything."

"But wait, just...come here...don't you want to...I mean...?"

"I said don't touch me—"

"Wait...wait..."

"What?"

"Just give it another day, alright? He'll come around. He has to."

"..."

"And me, too. We'll go slow. I know it's been a long time, but as soon as I saw you last night I—"

"Stop it, this isn't right—"

"..."

"Where can I find Caryn? Where does she live?"

"What? Why?"

"I need to talk to somebody who's not out of their fucking mind."

"She's been at St. Josephine's all day."

"How do I get there?"

"You saw it. Just follow the road south to the edge of town. Look for the steeple, you can't miss it. They're doing something down there. God knows what. She's probably still there. But just wait though...wait... where are you going?"

"Not now, Grant. Get your hands off me—"

Johannes takes up the pickax again. He weaves through the trenches, pits, and mounds, retracing the path he'd led Lani along. Descriptions and explanations echo through his head. It had been so easy to put it all into words for her, but now that he's rehearing it as an observer, he recognizes that what he and Grant are doing here cannot be expressed adequately in words. There's no way to convey the inseparable bond they've developed, to describe the mystery's seductive influence, to elucidate precisely what it is they're seeking.

He remembers having books with him up on the mountain. Remembers reading and reciting every day, keeping his intellect as active as his body. But proactive ideas of his own had been confined to physical ingenuities and problem-solving. How best to insulate the shack for the winter months. Masking his human scent for the hunt while maintaining an acceptable level of hygiene. Proper dismemberment and disposal of animal carcasses in the vicinity of his shack, efficiently using as much of the animal as possible, and then removing the stink of innards and death from his hands, his clothes, his hair. Existential justifications, relegated as they are to the valleys of the mind, had naturally taken a backseat to survival. Meditation and contemplation became more of an emptying, an unburdening of redundancies, and finally, the introduction of simplicity by necessity. Every thought, concern, limit, and unconscious projection had been eliminated. Survival became its own justification. And where there is no beginning, there is no conflict. No conflict allows peace to bloom. But if there is no end, no reason, no validation, then the blossom radiates no color, no fragrance, no beauty upon the world. Instead of enlightenment, life darkens into a featureless range of shadows, its separate paths extending outward in each cardinal direction, stepping around unseen ridges and crevices, colliding with formless obstacles, nothing seen, nothing verifiable, impossible to get lost and impossible to find your way. Therefore, stasis. Oneness, in a sense. The solemn tranquility he had achieved in his time on the mountain and the balance he has found digging up horse bones in Creek's Ridge—they are one and the same, springing from the same well, bringing the same cool, moist, serendipitous relief to his parched skin, easing the pain of life. But that mountain serenity had become an entombment. Here in the lowlands, unobstructed by undulating landscapes or mystifying canopies, where mind and body have entered into a shared understanding, a mutual respect, and an impulse toward ultimate balance—here, enlightenment might just be at hand.

Johannes understands this, but inherent knowledge doesn't always hold water against the pragmatism of daily life. And when finally backed up against the wall and told to justify himself—not to an image in a mirror, but to a real, live woman—what else could he have told her?

He stares into a trench and follows the day's memories even farther back, the car driving in reverse toward the terror and nausea of the burgeoning Rockies. Wading through their conversation, he remembers the curves and angles of Lani's legs, the sly smirking glances she constantly sent his way, unspoken words always on the tip of her tongue. She, too, has suffered. He hears it now in the reverberations of her voice, evident as an admission of guilt. She was reaffirming herself through the power of conversation, a touch on the cheek. She had probed his life so she could validate her own past without confronting the decisions and actions that have shaped her. But she had also maintained her distance. She moved in close, seeming to offer herself up to him without ever removing the cloak that obscures her inner thoughts. A barrage of thinly disguised suggestions had strung Johannes ever closer, and he'd nibbled throughout the day. He'd followed as Lani simultaneously dropped her hints and crept back into her hiding place, distracting him as she led him into danger.

Finally, now, here he is, right where he wants to be, standing above the pits, pickax in hand and ready to tear into the earth, needing now more than ever to melt into this new form of meditation, his mind harnessed by physical exertion, then forced out with the energy he exerts and leaves lying around the yard buried in mounds of dirt. But the sudden intrusive presence of Lani has thrown up a dust cloud, obscuring the simplicity he has worked so hard to retrieve after watching it disappear in the mountain's wrath, flushed down the river into the endless surrounding wilderness, exiled from his exile and introduced to the inevitable chaos of successive moments stacking higher and higher, always threatening to topple—the mountain and the burden of its own weight.

Standing above the pits, pickax in hand and ready to tear into the earth, he finds himself incapable of digging—because he's alone. Fending off a wave of anger, he turns his back on the bones and the dirt. Watering at the mouth, Johannes stomps away.

The seedlings of disloyalty deteriorate the moment he steps out of the yard. The dig has bound Johannes and Grant so tightly together that they cannot help but gaze into the design of the other and share each other's unhinged emotions. Fundamentally, they disagree on life itself. But with the search for the horse, there has been no acidic rejection of beliefs, no spewing forth volcanic-and-ashy of personalities, no allergic reactions of conscience. Only natural assimilation, partnership, and fascination—the highest compliment, the peak of love—and Johannes, swallowed whole by Grant's established though rickety life.

"Caryn? Caryn..."
"Oh, hi. Hi...what are you doing here? Where's Johannes?"
"I needed to...to get away for a while. To talk to someone. Really talk, I mean. Or I needed a distraction, I don't know. I don't even know why I came, what I'm doing here, this place. What are you...what's going on here?"
"Just some renovations."
"You're...?"
"Yeah."
"Wow...I didn't realize you...I mean, it's not what I thought you..."
"So how did it go today?"
"..."
"Not so good?"
"I never should have come here."
"Don't say that. You had to. But you and Grant, this whole—"
"I know, I know. Now I know. I should have listened to you last night. But Grant...he..."
"Shh, shh. Come on. Let's walk. Shh..."
"I don't know what to do..."
"You have to tell him. There might be no other way."
"I'm afraid. What if... He's so...vacant. It's like he's obsessed...with something. I don't know what. What if he really doesn't..."
"You have changed for him, too."
"How would you know?"
"..."
"I'm sorry..."
"Everyone, everything changes."
"No...I haven't, though. Not like that. This is unnatural. I want them back. Both of them. I do. But after today..."
"..."
"Not like this. This isn't right. None of this is right. I don't know if I want either of them like this. This fucking town...neither of them belongs here. What are they doing? What is anyone doing here?"
"Shh..."
"I'm sorry, again. I just..."
"Don't worry. I understand. There's something about this place. It's gotten into me just like it got into them. Johannes once told me that he

finds a significance to life here that doesn't matter so much. That this is the type of place where people come to live out their days in peace. At the time, I didn't know what he meant. But the longer I'm here, the more I think he might be on to something. He's still shaky, still struggles with himself, but I believe he's doing the right things, the things he truly needs to get himself straightened out. He'll get there eventually. He'll get somewhere. But he may need some help, whether he wants it or not. You could be the one to give it. In fact, maybe it should be you. I'm not sure whether Grant is..."

"Caryn...you're so good for him. I wish he could see that. It should be you. Not me."

"..."

"He doesn't need me. He never did."

"He does, though. But it takes time. And honesty. These games... they're not helping anybody."

"But it's the same! It's the same! We always...these games...even the name...he should remember...he has to, he has to..."

"Shh, shh... Come on, come with me..."

"I can't stay here. I can't wait anymore. There's nothing I can do for him."

"I know, I know, but he doesn't remember. I don't think he wants to. And he's not faking that."

"I have a life to get back to. I could never live like this, in this place, this stupid fucking nowhere...no place...and I don't know how to get them out..."

"Shh, shh... This way..."

"Where are we going?"

"Just inside for a bit. It'll take your mind off things. Trust me, it will. It does for me."

"Why are you the only one who gets it?"

"Do you remember what we were talking about last night? What Amondale said?"

"About the Saint?"

"Josephine making promises..."

"Several promises, to several suitors..."

"Well, I found something this afternoon. Are you still curious? It might even change your perspective on things. With him. With both of them. Some promises are meant to be pliable."

"Show me..."

"This way...down here...in the library..."

"I don't think I'll ever get either of them back. They're trapped here...the middle of fucking nowhere and nothing... And how will I..."

"Shh, forget them for now. Let time do its work. Just allow yourself to be receptive..."

Ernest stares at Johannes, unbelieving, like he's lost his mind, or both of them have. Amondale twists around and nearly falls off his barstool with laughter.

"What in the hell did you bring that in here for?" Ernest points at Johannes's hand, which hangs heavily by his side.

Johannes never even thought to set the pickax down before he left the yard. He holds the tool out in front of him, gazing at it fondly, and then peeks around the bar at a handful of familiar faces watching with keen and surprised interest, the faces in the mirrors mocking him as well, all those other Johanneses pointing out his mania, demanding answers he cannot provide. Ernest and Amondale express their confusion through silent questions, wide eyes, contorted expressions. Johannes shrugs and leans the ax against the wall beside the entrance.

Amondale's eyes are glassy and erratic, an unhindered wildness that Johannes hasn't seen from him before, so he leaves a barstool-wide buffer between them. Ernest explains that when Amondale stumbled in that afternoon, he was still drunk from the night before, and he's kept right on drinking throughout the day, declaring his one self-permitted yearly bender. Before Ernest can finish, Amondale interrupts with a series of one-sided comments until he starts intentionally baiting Johannes.

"She's one hell of an actress, that's what I think," Amondale says into his glass.

"What are you talking about?" asks Johannes.

"Not who she seems to be. Putting on an act. Just like that old maid, Saint Josephine."

"What do you mean?"

"I mean, she's two-faced. Hiding truths. Darkness and light, undefined."

"You only met her once."

"How many times have you met her? If you can remember how to count..."

"I spent all day with her."

Ernest sullenly follows their bickering from across the bar.

"Well? So? How long does it take you to assess a person's character? Anyway, it's my goddamned job. Maybe that's what drove you into that forest. You couldn't deal with people 'cause you're no damn good at reading them. Never read too many books. You hear me, Hem-ing-waste. Don't read books, don't read music. Drive a man mad. Read people. Most important skill there is."

"Oscar," Ernest sighs, "when you get to be my age, reading people ain't enough. Need to get close to them. Arms around shoulders, empathy for their troubles. Not just taking notes. Maybe you should..."

"What? Go on. Maybe I should what?"

"Maybe you should stick to that orange pop after all. Johannes here seems to be capable of cleaning up The Carnival."

Amondale shifts his glare between the two of them and finishes his drink. "Cowards," he growls.

A few tense minutes pass, and then they hear a racket resounding from the back, a string of muffled curses. Johannes watches Grant come around the corner, expecting Lani to follow in tow. Grant sits down, and Ernest immediately hands him a beer.

"I told you to move all that shit out of the way, Ern."

"And put it where? Feel free to move it down into the cellar for me if it's such a nuisance. It's not for anyone else."

"Where's Lani?" asks Johannes. "Isn't she with you?"

Grant gulps away half the bottle. "We ran into Caryn on the way over. They went off together."

"Where?"

"Beats me."

"Haven't seen you looking so clean in some time," says Ernest. "What's it all about? You groom for this lady friend of yours, but not for us everyday folk?"

"No digging today. I've been at the office since morning, catching up on paperwork. Started to pile up. Feels good to get some honest-to-God work done."

"What? The day after your lady friend arrives?"

Grant stares hard at Ernest. "Nothing I could do about it. Shitty draw."

"I understand that," concedes Ernest. "All too well."

Grant turns to Johannes and then faces the mirrors again. "How did it go today?"

"With Lani?" Johannes stares at the reflected Grant in the mirror. "I made breakfast."

"Omelets?"

"How did you know?"

"What else?" Grant says and takes a long drink. "Eggs were always your specialty."

"Cracking eggs," Amondale reaches for the bottle. "Heh heh..."

"Then we took a drive into Colorado to see the flowers in bloom on the slopes. But just seeing the mountains, I couldn't...I couldn't go any further. She wanted to, but I just couldn't. Didn't she tell you?"

Grant glances at him with unuttered questions.

"We came back, and I showed her around the yard. Tried to explain how it works and what we're doing. She says she doesn't get it, but there's something like recognition in her eyes. I think she understands or at least accepts it. She talks a lot, but like you, she reflects too much on the past. She's lively, bright, and thoughtful, though there's a sadness to her, too. And, of course, she's gorgeous..."

Amondale breaks into wild, uncontrollable laughter, burying his head in his arms as his body convulses. Johannes, Grant, and Ernest watch him shudder until Grant finally has enough. He chugs the rest of his beer, slams the bottle down, stands up, and lifts Amondale onto his sailor's feet. Amondale's laughter continues as Grant drags him out through the main entrance. Shouting rises beyond the closed door, followed by a momentary tussle.

Seconds later, Grant is stomping back inside. He stops suddenly when he notices the pickax resting beside the entrance. He picks it up, staring at it, then at Johannes, followed by a slow, frustrated gaze at the mirrors all around the bar. He sets it down and retakes his seat next to Johannes, the bar gone quiet. Grant rests his hand on Johannes's shoulder, leaving it there until Ernest hands him another bottle of beer, which Grant drinks even quicker than the first one.

"What did you do?" Johannes stares at Grant.

"That asshole. He's the worst drunk in this goddamn town. Someone has to teach him a lesson."

"Do you even know what you..."

"What?"

"The door...you just..." Johannes hesitates. "Never mind."

Grant doesn't look at him. He only tilts the bottle to his mouth, finishes it, and signals Ernest for a third.

"I didn't mean anything by it," says Johannes. "I won't touch her."

Ernest, neither expressing his interest nor concealing it, washes Amondale's glass as he peers at Grant and Johannes over the bar. Always the innocent, forgotten observer, privileged to hear what others are not.

Grant looks up into the broken mirror directly across from him. His grin, reflected through the web of cracks, is dodgy and enigmatic. He squints, searching the Johannes behind the glass. He's about to respond, but he stops himself with a grunt. Then, he wrenches the cap off his beer and says, "I can't stand these fucking mirrors."

Chapter 30

Reflections

February 23, 1818
St. Johns River, La Florida

SINCE THE FATHER'S RECOVERY, BOTH HIS PHYSICAL AND MENTAL strength remain weak. Our daily walks are shorter than they used to be, and our lessons are condensed and more formal. I support him by the elbow as he makes his rounds of the village, and when he lacks energy, I attend to them myself. Still, he has found time to teach me basic medical techniques, herbal remedies, and strategies to aid communication when there is no common tongue.

Today, upon waking, he expressed his intentions to instruct me in conducting the Liturgy. When I questioned the necessity of this, he informed me that many of the visions he experienced during his infirmity concerned me, brought on, he believes, by the strong attachment he has developed to me and the sudden unpredictability of the future.

"Unpredictability is to be expected," he said. "But when it arises from continual bad omens, as it does under the full weight of our current predicament, only preparedness and fear will conduct you to safety."

After a moment's contemplation on this thought, he continued with a smirk, explaining that he does not feel he has completed his life's work, that cowardice has condemned him to inhabit the shadow-filled caverns one carries within oneself, to remain wet-footed in this swamp when what his calling demands is diffusion and circulation amongst the variegated peoples of this earth. With this tribe, he has found a true family. By acknowledging them as such, by basking in the safety and unwavering love they have given him all these years, he believes he has spent half his life in idleness.

February 24, 1818
St. Johns River, La Florida

After a light meal this evening, Father Jimenez introduced me to a man who arrived in the village late last night. He rode in on a carriage pulled by several horses and packed with wares. I assumed the man to be merely another trader here on prospective business from the port at San Agustín. He roused from sleep late this afternoon, and for the remainder of the day he sat in private council with the Father and the Chief.

His name is Robert Ambrister. He is an Englishman by blood, but born and raised in the Bahamas. He showed some reluctance to making my acquaintance until the Father vouched for my trustworthiness, after which Mr. Ambrister spoke openly. But his eyes are never still. They wander and swivel in their sockets, flitting like flies trapped and agitated. He is filled with suspicion, and his fingers are never far from his knife's handle. Under neither orders nor protection of the British Crown, he has personal interests and close ties to Spaniards and Seminoles throughout La Florida. When he disclosed the contents of his covered carriage—more than thirty muskets, two barrels of gunpowder, and two small cannons—my skin crawled with unease. I was left utterly speechless, to Mr. Ambrister's endless amusement.

Since our tribe has always been generous to him, Ambrister wished to repay us with equal kindness. The Chief, however, is reluctant to accept the weapons. It would be akin to an open acknowledgment of war, which he still hopes to avoid. The day's discussions consisted of Ambrister and our traders attempting to convince Chief Kinheja that war is already upon us and that these weapons, rather than damning us, shall only serve to protect us. "A blessing from the gods," they claimed, to which both the Father and I shuddered, bowing our heads in prayer.

For my part, I align with the Chief. Mr. Ambrister seems to be a fine, well-intentioned man, though at the mercy of physical urges, bravado, and revenge.

Long Grass, brooding and silent of late, broke his silence with an opinion that surprised us all and persuaded the Chief on the matter.

Speaking with calm confidence, he said, "Martyrs begin wars, but rarely do they end them."

Starting tomorrow, I shall split my time between Father Jimenez and Mr. Ambrister, who has obligingly agreed to take charge of my English lessons, under one condition—Mr. Ambrister has requested that I help him train our men in using these weapons of death. Whatever conflicts the future brings, I would rather serve as an interpreter or a mediator, which is precisely the capacity I shall serve Mr. Ambrister. However, he also insists that I learn to load and fire the muskets myself. Though I retain an intense aversion to firearms, the fervor of the times has relegated certain decisions to fate.

Before I parted from the Father for the night, he left me with a final thought to ease my mind, but it only served to unnerve and confuse me—

"You must love people, Emedio, all people. Love them as you love yourself. But never get too close to even one, including yourself. Your own beliefs, too, can become a poison."

February 26, 1818
St. Johns River, La Florida

Father Jimenez told me this afternoon that he has often envisioned me filling his role with the tribe after he is gone. This dream, he now says, was born of and corrupted by hope. The product of an idle mind. The way he sees it, his illness cleared his head and saved me from being led down a misguided path by an idealistic old fool. Since the Seminoles' future becomes more apparent with each passing day, the Father believes I must choose my every step forward with caution. He sees me as a young man with no nation other than God's nation, no land to call home other than the world itself, a man suited to the lifestyle he himself was not courageous enough to maintain. Long ago, as a young missionary in northern Africa, he had been strong, dedicated, aggressive in his work, at peace with himself and with the voice of the world's people calling out to him. But he strayed from that path. At these memories, he laughed and spread his hands before him, tenderly brushing the cheeks of an apparition visible to none but himself.

While his fingers swept through the air, caressing unseen memories, he mused—

"Incredible, isn't it? How our vocation requires that we become lost in the physical world, but the tiniest deviation from the paths of the spirit will toss us out to sea. Absurd, this life."

I recommended that he lie down for a rest, but he abruptly turned his eyes on me, his gaze both sharp and bright. He dropped his hands, shaking his head. Through a sad smile, he told me that I possess the bravery and strength to do the work he should have done in the Americas, but that it will be more difficult now that we can no longer think of this as a Spanish colony. It could be five years from now or as little as a month, but this will soon become another territory of the United States, and that rising nation is not likely to embrace Seminoles or foreign missionaries with open arms.

He has complete confidence that I will adapt, that I will survive, and that I can unite at least a small portion of the people of this land. It is my calling, as it was his. He has likewise observed that Robert Ambrister will play an instrumental role in my survival.

The Father's advice has become more difficult to interpret. At times, his certitude regarding the mysteries of the future can be unsettling, though I have never told him this.

Chapter 31

On Pain of Debt

"What the hell is wrong with him?" Lani sits at the table with the note in her hand, going over it again. "Did you see this?"

"I did."

Scribbled on a napkin in the dawn hours, the note conveys that Grant has gone to Wichita to register some annual paperwork, and he'll be gone all day.

"I don't understand why he invited you down," says Johannes. "He's never this busy..."

"No, it's...it isn't his fault. This was the only time I could come. My job doesn't give me much wiggle room for vacations or...anything."

"What do you do again?"

"I told you. A green design firm."

"..."

"Landscaping for rich people. Gated communities, parks, and urban rooftops, mostly."

Johannes looks at her and shrugs before turning his attention back to the food. While Johannes prepares omelets again, at Lani's request, she explains how she wishes she could stay longer but that she needs to leave for Oklahoma City early the next morning to catch her eleven o'clock flight back to Chicago. When Johannes asks why she didn't just drive from Chicago, she tells him that she's never found comfort in driving, that she doesn't like to waste time on the roads, that she's afraid to be trapped alone with her thoughts for long periods. If she could, she would love to learn more about St. Josephine's and its namesake, to dig deeper into the tangled history she's been teased with the entire time she's been here. Almost as an afterthought, she bemoans the fact that she didn't get to spend more time with Grant, and then, very much like Grant will often do, she begins to speak of people and places in and around Chicago as though Johannes knows what she's talking about. Eventually, her voice strays into personal reveries, presenting a multi-tiered picture of her life in Chicago, past blessings and misfortunes, and a future becoming more difficult to apprehend with each day she grows older. Johannes, chopping vegetables and frying eggs, listens with his back to her as she slips in and out of youth like she's slipping in and out of a dress, desirous of risqué maturity but attached to the comforts of innocence. At points, he can almost imagine her as a young girl, full of verve and energy, except for this unutterable pain, a loss that haunts her still but that she refuses to mention because, sometimes, it's better to cherish the way things were than to confront the changing world.

The morning is breezy and cool, much more temperate than recent days, which Lani decides is perfect for escaping the stuffy house and eating breakfast beside the creek.

"And now Caryn thinks she was intentionally toying with them."

"Who was toying with who?"

"Saint Josephine. She was baiting the Native Americans. There are letters from each of the major tribes in the area, signed by chiefs and witnesses, saying that she visited them—alone—and offered herself for marriage into their tribes. What a strange tactic, yeah? For what purpose..." Lani tears her omelet apart, inhaling deeply as the steam billows out. "You did it again."

"What?"

"Garlic. You put it in yours but not in mine."

"Sorry I..." He leans over and looks at her plate. "Why didn't you tell me? I didn't even—"

"No," she smiles. "I hate garlic."

"Lucky mistake."

"Luck..." She shakes her head and shoves a bite into her mouth. "It was a test."

"What test?"

"John..."

His fork is stranded in the air, waiting.

"It's delicious. I'm going to miss this, that's all."

"I'll show you how..." Johannes chews and swallows. "It's only an omelet." He tries to grasp the same enjoyment as she does from this simple pleasure. It is a decent omelet, better than what he gets at The

Borderlands, but he's distracted out here among the pits and mounds. Rather than considering his culinary abilities, he's thinking about the pressing need to dig and the arbitrary impossibility of digging alone. Why should it matter? He had spent years alone, without aid or companionship, without the weight of past, present, or future, the demands of time and people.

"If you want to come back to Chicago sometime, anytime, just let me know."

"Maybe someday. But...it's hard."

"Seriously. I'll get you a flight. Don't worry about that."

"I couldn't do that. I don't want to owe you anything."

"Don't be ridiculous. You can cook for me. These omelets are payment enough. And you must know other recipes, all-natural, mountain ingredients..."

They eat silently for a few minutes.

"What about Grant?" she says suddenly.

"What about him?"

"You sort of...owe him, don't you?"

"That's different."

"No, it's not."

Lani is lost in thought, staring beyond the creek, at the fields, farmland, and distant trees, but she's hardly touching her omelet.

"John?"

He looks up. The loss and loneliness she lives with are different from Caryn's, from his own. Caryn's lies deep within her eyes, but Lani's weeps from her pores, a persistent daily struggle that wakes and blooms with each new sunrise. Like Grant's.

"No, nothing..." She takes a large bite and chews appreciatively. "You know, Caryn also says that the town records clearly indicate how tribal representatives began to show up, escorting their tribe's most worthy warriors, the sons of chiefs and medicine men, bearing gifts of all sorts, expecting to leave with her, with Josephine. Of course, her father didn't have a clue what was going on, and she's denying ever having visited the tribes. But these suitors were all showing up at the same time, all thinking the same thing—that they had been chosen for her hand. Which naturally led to quarrels among the tribes..."

"How do you know all of this?"

"I was with Caryn all last night. Talking. You should try it sometime. Don't you find it odd that we've both known Grant so long, but we don't...remember each other?"

"You have to understand, I don't—"

"It's fucked up, John."

"But you don't remember me either, so I don't see what—"

"You have to admit it's hard to believe. That a person could wipe their memory totally blank. That anyone would even want to."

"You're right, I don't deny it. But what makes you think I did it to myself?"

"You don't really believe that a landslide and a river stole your past, do you?"

Johannes's gaze passes over her, wandering the yard through pits and holes and mounds and trenches. He finishes eating and sets his plate on the ground between them.

"Never mind." Lani sets her plate on top of his, half of her omelet untouched. "Just think about it, okay? Come see us in Chicago. I have plenty of floor space and a great view—an urban mountain peak, really. Just like home."

Johannes stretches out on his back and stares at the blue above. He closes his eyes and sees his former home. He visualizes Knecht and the stream, the painted ripples of the surrounding mountain range blanketed in mist, and the empty plot where his shack once stood. This is no memory—by shutting his eyes, he simply bypasses the eight hundred miles separating him from that place. And everything is unchanged. The streams still flow, the trees still grow, and that sanctuary still flourishes without him, alone. Opening his eyes again, he stares straight up to no obstructions, nothing at all to complicate the view, no distractions other than a few scattered wisps of cloud. But tranquility does not travel unaccompanied. Whenever his eyes are closed, the threat remains nearby, the changing terrain, the landslide unflinching and incessant, preparing to smack him in the face at each moment, another handful of mud. The only way to avoid it is to keep his eyes open, observing the blue above and the sun rising through late morning to afternoon heights, an honest and unavoidable truth, a mediator and measure of time that never lets him stare too long or wander too far, just as long as he keeps it in his sight. And when every last mountain has fallen, when there's nothing left to hold it up, the sky itself might be next. Then, there will be nowhere left to run except, possibly, into the holes they have dug up.

"What about your family?" Lani asks. "Don't you wonder about them? Don't you want to see them?"

"Not yet." He lifts himself onto his elbows. "I can't."

"But, I mean...Grant and Pa Sonny. They're basically family. Always have been."

"Pa Sonny?"

"He was always like a father—to both of you."

"How do you..."

"Just...nothing." She lies back to join him gazing at the sky. "From Grant, obviously. He's told me everything. Her father went mad..."

"Caryn's father?"

"Josephine's. They say he started to lose his mind after his wife died, years before all this stuff with the tribes and the marriage. So, by that point, he may have been a complete nut-job already. No one knows for sure, of course. She protected him. The townspeople always thought he was protecting her, but actually, it was the other way around..."

He sits up, looks around, looks at Lani. She appears to have dozed off, so he gets up and walks across the yard to sift through their pile of bones. After a few minutes of arranging and rearranging them, with no answers and no direction, he glances back to check on her, but she's gone. He returns his attention to the bones, the holes in the ground, the loose dirt and packed earth. Lani spends most of the day inside the house while Johannes remains outside trying to make sense of it all, trying to visualize the horse, first the bones themselves, and then adding layers of muscle, flesh, and hair. The braying of life and the lopsided clop-clop of motion. Flies drawn to the smell. The sheen of those huge, dark eyes. Were they dark? Is that right? And her tail bouncing and bobbing as she trots. Powerful, shapely muscles twitching and shivering. But the color? It occurs to him that Grant has never revealed much about Limping Lady's appearance, other than her one leg shorter than the others. What color was she? And why is Johannes so intent on piecing together the bones from a creature he knows so little about?

By evening, Grant still hasn't returned. Johannes tells Lani that he's going out.

"Why? Where?"

"To meditate. I need to...to meditate."

"Meditation? Really? Okay, let me grab my shoes."

"No, but—"

"I'll just be a minute."

"But it...that's not how it works..."

"I'm not going to meditate with you. I just want to get out, too. Get some air and see the town. I'm leaving tomorrow, after all. And that's why I'm here, isn't it? I want to see this grove you told me all about. Witness it for myself, a little bit of beauty in this town, see if it really exists..."

"No, but...it won't work. With you watching me, neither of us will get anything out of it."

"What, you think I'm just going to sit there and stare at you? That would be its own kind of meditation, wouldn't it? Not interested, sorry. I told you, I don't have time for things like that. I'll just keep an eye on you from afar. I want to see how it works, that's all. Don't worry, John. I won't bother you. I'll be nothing but a ghost if that's what you want."

"But..."

"I'm ready. Lead the way."

As they approach the edge of town, Lani stares, fascinated by the striking figure of the church's steeple against the evening sky. She continues asking about the building and its history even after Johannes reminds her that he doesn't know anything about it.

"I wonder what it will look like when she's done..."

"Who? What?"

"Nothing," she laughs. "No one."

The calm and seclusion of the grove strip away Lani's inhibitions, disrobe her unhappiness and loss, and remove the mask she wears, all washed away by the creek's crisp waters. As she splashes at imaginary companions, her hair clumps into thick strands, her clothes cling to her curves, and she laughs like this is her first time away from the city, the first time she has been unshackled from the hindrances of adulthood and responsibility. She explores further downstream and finds something fascinating in every shrub, stone, weed, and insect along the bank, emitting constant gleeful yelps about the way the mud of the streambed slinks between her toes. Whenever she finds a scrap of trash, she picks it up and adds it to a pile near her shoes.

She has kept an eye on Johannes the entire time, clearly not impressed with his struggle for inner peace. She approaches him, hesitantly at first, but before long she's running circles around him, spraying him with droplets from her flailing hair. And the water feels refreshing, same as the cool spray from the waterfall, where he often sat for hours on end during the hottest days of summer, to where he's lifted now, his eyes lightly closed, an illusive realm of truth, the past or the present, or both...

Lani skips away again to fall in attack upon the creek, dropping to her knees with a splash, bending forward to dip her hair and wet her face. She heads downstream, stepping carefully alongside the bank. As he watches her go, the desire to follow tugs at him. But he can't. In order to get up from this stagnant lotus pond he has sunken into, he will have to reach up and allow someone to assist, to peek below the surface and view the tangle of roots and weeds holding him down. To dig him out. Grant has had a glimpse below, but that's because Grant is buried just as deep as Johannes is—their combined weight, an anchor. Someone needs to cut them both free, but that someone needs to know where and how to cut.

"John..." Lani sucks at the air. "I found something..." She huffs labored breaths as she approaches. "Buried in the bank..."

And Johannes, struggling now not for nirvana but only to maintain his composure, stares up at her radiant face. Her athletic exertions have abated. She tilts her head back to ring the water out of her hair, then unexpectedly throws her head forward. Her hair follows and smacks Johannes's cheek before she shakes her head from side to side, spraying Johannes with a refreshing mist in the same way he has seen the neighborhood German shepherd, Mengele, dry its fur after a romp in this same creek.

Lani squeezes the last drops from her hair, but she pauses when she stands upright, stock-still with her gaze following something she has seen. Johannes twists around, but the bushes block his view. When he finally lifts himself up, he sees Pa Sonny walking with someone along the roadside. The street is a long way off, but it's clear that he has seen them, too. He returns their querying gazes as he orates to his attentive companion with sweeping, animated gestures that may or may not be waves of greeting. Lani hesitates, but then she waves back. Johannes watches as she grapples with her thoughts.

"Come and take a look at this," Lani shakes her head, snapping back to herself. "This is serious. You're gonna love it."

She leads him to a shallow point in the creek. Johannes kicks off his shoes and rolls up his pants. He follows her across to the opposite bank, where she takes him by hand and leads him downstream before pointing out an object protruding from the mud.

"What is it?" asks Johannes.

"I figured you would know..."

"Is it...?" Johannes squats down and rubs the object's smooth surface. "It is."

Before another word can escape his lips, he's already digging in the mud along the bank. It's dense and moist, and only a fraction of the bone is exposed. He kneads the mud with his knuckles and digs his fingernails into it, his patience quickly defeated.

"We need a tool. Something to loosen the mud. We can't use our hands."

"We? You want me to help dig up your bones?" The rising pitch of her voice and her defiant smile betray her pleasure at the idea.

"I can't dig by myself."

She drops down into the water at once, splashing and soaking Johannes. "You're not supposed to dig at all..." But her hands are already working the mud as intently as his. "You're really going to owe me after this..."

"We need something to work with," Johannes repeats. "We'll go and get some tools—the pickax and something smaller, more delicate. It might be fragile, being near the water like this. What's it doing way the hell out here?"

"You don't think it's one of yours, do you?"

"Oh..."

"What?"

"Something Amondale said. He thinks this might be a gravesite from those times. The Native American raids. No, but we won't know... not unless we..."

"Can you tell the difference?"

"Of course...I mean, maybe. Once we get them out. I don't know..."

"I think our hands are better," squeals Lani, no more inclined to move from the excavation than Johannes. "The mud is so cool, so smooth..."

"But we should have tools."

"We're here now. Have to make do with what's available while there's still light. Look, it's getting dark."

Verbal communication ceases. Lani's smile grows impossibly wide as they dig. She shifts positions constantly, working from different angles, sitting, kneeling, standing, swiveling up onto the bank and then back down into the water, leaning in to examine their work, leaning back to stretch and take in the surroundings as twilight settles around them. She falls in close beside Johannes, nudging him out of the way and then pulling him near again.

Time goes rogue. Neither of them is aware of how long they're digging, their progress so slow that it might be a single prolonged instant, though the sky maintains its gradual trend toward the absence of color. Lani reiterates her admiration for this absurd project. Johannes curses the Kansas sub-terrain and the cramps forming in his hands. She comments that he has started to talk like Grant. And by the time evening settles in, the reality of Lani's discovery has revealed itself—the elegant arch of linked vertebrae and evidence of so much more.

The thrill infects them equally all the way back to the house. They stand in the kitchen, swallowing enormous quantities of water and laughing over the details of their discovery. They stare at each other with the eyes of children who have been promised a surprise and are consequently strangled by anticipation. A fog of wordless ecstasy blankets the house for the ten minutes they're alone, until headlights flood through the windows and the unmistakable roar of Grant's cruiser announces his return.

Grant drags himself over the windowsill and promptly collapses onto the sofa. He listens to their twin stories, amplified by a duo of restless pacing and expressive gestures. Exhausted and distracted, Grant lacks his usual interest in the bones, but neither Johannes nor Lani notice his indifference.

By and by, Johannes convinces a reluctant Grant to return with him and finish the job by moonlight. But while Johannes searches cabinets and closets for tools, he never notices how Grant's gaze has not once strayed from Lani, nor how Lani has come down, simmered to cool contemplative composure as she returns Grant's stare, accepting and somehow appreciative of that penetrating attention.

Johannes gathers towels, flashlights, spoons, brushes, and screwdrivers, stuffing them all into a canvas bag. While he's filling water bottles, Grant and Lani disappear down the hall. Johannes waits a couple minutes, fidgeting and pacing between the living room and the kitchen. Before long, he shouts down the hall that he's leaving, telling Grant to meet him at the grove by the creek. Lani, too, if she wants to continue their discoveries. He throws everything into the canvas bag and crawls out the window, trying his best to ignore the only response he receives—passions emitting from behind a closed door.

Johannes walks as though the German shepherd were chasing him. He considers calling on Caryn for a digging partner. A wild range of thoughts assails him, twisting his mind into knots, and he reaches the site lacking clarity or understanding.

Within minutes, both flashlights have died. The creek water is frigid. He tries to remain up on the bank but keeps slipping into the water. A thick cumulus covers the moon and will not budge, the outline of the cloud clearly defined by the filtered moonlight, but none of that light completing the long trek to the ground.

Johannes sits alone in the darkness, running his fingers over the exposed bones, afraid of damaging them and also of losing them forever.

Grant shows up a while later, sweaty and fatigued.

They don't speak, they can't see, but still, they dig.

By the time they finish, dawn is only an hour or so away. They gather up the bones, knowing them only by touch and sound, dropping them one by one into the canvas bag, bouncing and rattling as they trudge toward the house through the absolute silence of a Creek's Ridge night. Grant remains silent all through it, restless and ill at ease. But Johannes is pacified, relieved.

"Grant? What color was she?"

"You shit. You motherfucker, you've got nerve..."
"What? Lil, Limping Lady..."
"What?"
"Her coat. You never told me about her. About Lil. What color she was. Or how big. Sometimes I try to, you know...to visualize her..."
"You'll never..." Grant breathes heavily. "Gray. She was gray, flecked with white. Beautiful. Perfect. You'll never know her. Not like me."

Chapter 32

The Voices

Sleep brought with it many terrifying and confounding visions—fear of the cave, of the white man and the spirit world, fear of his own blood and his hideous appearance, fear of his tribe, of his family, of his past and his future—the poison of the firewater had contaminated his body, his dreams, his perception of truths and falsehoods.

As on the other nights, there had been whiskey after dinner. Darius claimed to possess an endless supply. Even the servants were given a glass each to ease their nightly labor. Minding Penagashea's demands, Lalawethika had partaken each night for over a week. Since he still felt uneasy around these white men, he had consumed very little, fighting off the remaining traces of his intense thirst with due pride. However, Penagashea had been in a festive mood on this final night and persuaded Lalawethika to take more than on other nights. Darius had also offered them a horse and carriage at no cost other than their friendship, hinting at a favorable introduction to their tribe, especially the women, should he one day travel in the vicinity of the Tippecanoe River. Lalawethika began to protest, but Penagashea quickly silenced him, assenting to Darius's requests. They were to depart at dawn, so the two Shawnees withdrew early to fall asleep beside the fireplace while Darius and the Father continued their discourse into the night.

But now Lalawethika woke alone, covered in sweat and yet chilled. The room was dark, the fire reduced to a few glowing coals. Dawn was still several hours off, but Penagashea no longer lay beside him. Owl calls and the chirping of crickets drifted in through open windows, along with a soft, wheezing wind. Sporadic sounds sometimes broke the calm, like the distant voices of loggers or soldiers working recklessly in the midnight hours, similar to how the voices that once controlled him would murmur at all times, night or day, sleeping or awake.

His body felt rested, and though the hour was still early, he wished to rise and sit in silent contemplation before the others awoke. He also meant to prepare energizing herbs for the return journey. The pressure in his lower abdomen reminded him of the whiskey and wine he had consumed, so he rose and found his way outside, following a winding path into the garden at the rear of the house. He limited his voice to a hoarse whisper as he called out in search of Penagashea.

The moon shone full and ghostly, veiled behind static wisps of cloud. The sound of his piss spraying the hedge died out and was replaced by the unmistakable roar of a massive fire. His eyes attained balance with the blackened landscape, allowing the glow of a blaze to show itself emanating above a distant tree line. The sound of voices rose again, carried to him on a faint breeze. They did not seem so distant now, nor were they the voices of men at work, but of men engaged in revelry, debauchery, and mayhem. Back at the house, there was no sound, nothing but a flicker of candlelight inside what Lalawethika assumed to be Father Gabriel's bedroom.

Bent low to the ground, he made for the woods through the cow pasture. He stayed clear of the well-worn trails and kept his eyes sharp, though he encountered no trace of life along the way. However, the closer he came to the fire's glow and crackle, the more its accompanying din saturated the moist night air. It soon became apparent that the voices were not delusions. The fire was every bit as large as fires they built in their village following a successful harvest, the ascension of a new chief, or annual ceremonies intended to summon plentiful game and crops. He could approach within a few meters of the flames and still remain concealed within the shadows cast by the dense trees. Although stealth had never been a trait that Lalawethika possessed in excess, he had plenty of experience sneaking along the outskirts of fires such as this, selfishly clutching a stolen jug of firewater, avoiding discovery even from the prying curiosity of his own children.

Lalawethika counted nearly forty men sitting, standing, carousing about the flames. Most of their faces were familiar, men he had seen either at Sainte Anne de Detroit or in the town square. A few were red men, the type of red men who had gone to great lengths to alter their appearance and resemble the white man, and yet these red men were now decked out in mockeries of their traditional garb. A couple of black men were present as well—servants, most likely. They stood off to the side, motionless as statues and without the slightest sign of emotion.

None of the white men ever strayed far from a jug of firewater. Some were hopping around in circles, swinging off the arms of their mates, patting and slapping backs. Others slopped whiskey over their faces between obnoxious, nonsensical shouts. Many of them sucked religiously on tobacco pipes. And Darius, the rowdiest of them all, led the revelry. He rarely stood still, bouncing from one companion to the next, whispering into their ears and speaking with exaggerated gestures, his arm draped over their shoulders as he shared their whiskey and exhaled plumes of smoke. They added logs to the fire indiscriminately. Sometimes, one of their party would collapse, then the others would drag him away from the reach of the flames, only to leave him sprawled amidst the underbrush with vomit dribbling down his chin.

And at the center of it all stood Penagashea.

Two other red men stood with him, a father and son they had briefly conversed with on the grounds of Sainte Anne de Detroit. The family had left their Delaware tribe before the boy could even walk, and they had been running a modest general store in Detroit ever since. The boy was twelve years old and had spent his entire life amongst white men.

The father and son were both dancing around the fire and made-up in full face and body paint. Long strands of beans and corn jangled around their necks. Feathers hung from holes in their earlobes and mingled with their dark hair. Penagashea wore his personal headdress, reserved for Shawnee medicine men and donned only during important rituals. The two Delawares wore crude crowns of branches, the boy's headpiece resembling a bird's nest. They danced to a strange rhythm dictated by something the white men were chanting. Penagashea held his medicine staff in one hand and his stone ax in the other. His medicine pack—a sacred heirloom in Shawnee culture, the medicine man's most of all—lay strewn across the ground, unprotected and trampled by careless feet. He shouted sacred Shawnee words, blending them into senseless phrases meant only for the reaction they elicited from the white men. Whenever one of the Natives let out a war cry, the entire gathering would howl in imitation.

The white men laughed constantly, not laughter born of merriment or intoxication, but of derision, of superiority over the red men flailing naked, slurring drunken chants, tripping over their own feet.

Darius supported those who displayed signs of exhaustion and drunkenness. He propped them up and coerced them to continue. He poured whiskey into tin cups and distributed them to Penagashea and the Delawares, coercing the reluctant young boy to drink. At one point, Darius dropped his trousers to piss into the fire and left them down around his ankles, taking his flaccid member in his hand and swinging it around.

It didn't take long for others to follow his lead. Men removed their clothing and came closer to the fire, dancing with abandon and mimicking the pseudo-ritualistic behavior of the Natives, which had devolved to resemble nothing like traditional medicine dances. A disheveled, hairy man discovered the paint bucket and ran around slopping it over naked bodies as the mob acquired a more devious, unhinged quality.

But when Lalawethika first noticed the women, something churned inside of him. It churned, then snapped and splintered, tearing through all that he had come to know of the world and perforating his soul, which he had worked so hard to save.

The rest of the Delaware family—the wife and two daughters—sat on the trunk of a felled tree opposite the fire. They were wide-eyed and visibly trembling, yet incapable of taking their eyes off the shocking scene. One of the girls was a few years older than the boy, and the other was a year or two younger than him. The mother buried her face in her hands as two of the white men staggered toward them, and the younger of the two girls screamed through her tears when they forcefully dragged her elder sister into the thick of the woods. The father watched, looking ill and broken, but Darius stood between them, staring the father down with a wicked grin. The pained red man made no attempt to stop what was to come. His eyes drooped with a sadness risen from regret and helplessness, and his son, surrounded by a group of cheering, howling white men, began to vomit on the edge of the fire pit.

Penagashea was speaking with Darius. They had both stopped prancing around and shared a jug as they watched over the scene, their heads swiveling in admiration of this chaos. When four more men approached the Delaware mother and her youngest daughter, Penagashea and Darius nodded approvingly, watching as the men dragged them both into the forest's suffocating darkness.

The Lalawethika of old would not have held back in the shadows. However, the reborn Lalawethika could not claim with certainty whether his former self would have attacked these villains or whether he would have joined in this madness. This new Lalawethika had learned much, first and foremost, how to suppress his hatred, his anger, his fear. As he slipped unseen back to the house, his hatred burned as hot and bright as the roaring fire, but he contained it. He held it in his hands and became familiar with it. Then, he hid it away in the safety of his heart, where the blaze would be fed, smoldering for as long as he could keep it. But such soul-stirring emotions can only be stored for so long before they erupt. He knew this, and he would wait for the right moment to release its scorching fury.

In the morning, ten large jugs of whiskey, a barrel of whiskey, and a barrel of wine had been added to the cart Darius had provided them. The horse was an aged, sickly mare, distracted and jumpy, and Lalawethika had to push the cart in order to encourage the animal to start.

As they set off for home, Lalawethika asked Penagashea where the additional firewater had come from.

"Darius is a generous man," Penagashea replied, a trace of red paint still smeared in the creases of his nose, beneath eyelids heavy with fatigue.

Part Four

Skeletons in the Desert

Chapter 33

The Debt Collector

WATER RIPPLES PAST, WASHES OVER, WASHES THROUGH, RIPPLE RIPPLE splash gurgle ripple ripple. Water washes clean, purity. Beyond the body, water flows forever onward, towards eternity, the current, smooth, steady, a linked infinitude, molecules moving organically, as one, same as this body. Obstacles appear, and water slips around, redirected, fluid, tranquil, slow, flow, slow. Breathe. Breathe. Slow. Removed from time. Only motion, only the flow, picking up speed now uncomprehendingly fast faster still now, but smooth. Peaceful. As one, moving swiftly away, shores unseen, destinations out of reach, beyond time. Nowhere. Everywhere. Eternal past within the present of an eternal future. Water cleanses, infuses, becomes a part, leads within and away, distances indescribable. In the water. Of the water. Breathe. Breathe. Breathe. Slow. Breathe, through the water. Water settles. Motionless. Serene. A singular-plural dispersal, an event ongoing and forever. Oneness. Separateness. Floating outward, all separate, all together, out and away, always linked, and detached, forever bound, forever free, always, never, forever, now, eternity, nothingness, this—

An engine growls, slowly at first, a kitten purring. Kitten becomes cat becomes lynx, and then mountain lion. Growl becomes roar, agitated breaths, noxious and warm—

Nothingness? Eternal bliss and all of that—

The engine dies, a door creaks, then slams—

Goddamnit—

Water still ripples past. Footsteps drag through the dirt and grass. Johannes lifts his eyelids and calmly watches the creek. He notes the warm breeze rinsing over his sweat-beaded skin. A large figure momentarily blocks the sun. Within the shade, a flush of coolness plunges inward. His muscles grow tense, constricting the temporary peace he has found, forcing it out. The man steps around Johannes and squats down. A recognizable face, old and slack. Bushy mustache, thin hair framing a furrowed brow, sleepy eyes, all of them different shades of gray.

"Walk with me, Johannes."

Johannes prays that he has not been disturbed, that these are the hallucinations of an altered state. But the sensations of the world swiftly flood his senses. So he uncurls his legs and stretches before reluctantly following downstream.

The old man strolls at a relaxed pace. No sooner has Johannes trampled the man's shadow when a voice is upon him.

"Still trying to escape this life, I see."

Johannes hasn't yet sufficiently collected himself for words. He answers with a guttural grunt.

"Been, what? Five months or so since I picked you up? I have to admit...I questioned my own perceptions and memory when I saw you there. Even after I coerced you into the truck. Whether it could possibly be you or not. Certainty can be impossible to seize at times. Heart and senses working in opposition." His eyes sit deep in his melon face, bleeding kindness, surrounded by creases engraved into his weathered skin. "Seven years...that's a long time. Seven and a half? Didn't really believe you had it in you. Figured you'd have given up long before that and, I don't know, found another road. Leading someplace else, I suppose. I would have."

"I didn't recognize you," says Johannes. "Didn't remember you."

"I know you didn't." Pa Sonny looks at him thoughtfully. "After so long, I'd nearly forgotten why I started going there in the first place. The No-Show No-Go. Spent a lot of downtime there, made a lot of good friends. Nice folks around there. That'll happen when you visit a place often enough, return again and again. Waiting for something. Though I suppose everyone is. I knew you'd come round eventually, but I'm not sure I truly believed we'd cross paths. Just looking out for a word, a sign. A spotting of the illusive creature. That time, it was different, of course—"

"I still don't," Johannes interrupts. "Not completely."

"Scary thought, isn't it?" Pa Sonny smiles. "Two grown, intelligent men such as ourselves. Although, I wasn't in a proper state of mind before you disappeared, either. And, there was something about you that day at the diner. Something in your eyes, or more precisely, nothing. They were cavernous. Impossibly empty. That's why I was cautious...to approach. Or to come clean with the truth. You understand. And then, after I got you here, I had Grant coming around every day, badgering me about the ragged state of your clothing, the dirt and mud about your body, animal hair and wounds, your memories scattered and vague. But I hadn't made much of those things. I'd seen only the chaotic state of your being. You resembled a certain lost soul, a self-destructive mannequin I once coaxed into health."

"I thought of it."

"Suicide..." muses Pa Sonny. "I don't blame you. Years ago, I may have been more critical. Not anymore."

"Good. I don't want you trying to fix me. I've got enough people working on that already."

"No, no..." Pa Sonny smiles again as he looks Johannes over. "I have more respect for you than that."

"You do? Then why couldn't you let me meditate in peace?" An uncharacteristic curtness sharpens Johannes's tone. Intuition tells him this man is safe, trustworthy, yet resistance is irresistible.

"Don't insulate yourself now," says Pa Sonny. "It won't work in a place like this. Believe me. Trust in history. Besides, you know as well as I do that if you'd been meditating properly, nothing could have disturbed you—not me, not a woman's aromatic flower, not a deluge from above."

Their footsteps grind in the dirt beside the creek. The steeple of St. Josephine's seems to stand taller and prouder as they approach it. Vans and trucks are parked out front and minor construction equipment is strewn about the lot, but there's no sign of any workmen. Pa Sonny and Johannes both notice each other staring at the church.

"I haven't been able to truly meditate since then...since the mountain," Johannes admits. "I've tried. Every day, I try. And today, right now, was the first time I've even come close."

"Grant told me."

"Told you what?"

"What happened to you out there, those mountains."

"He told me what happened to you, too."

"Games are pointless."

"What games? You came to me."

"Hostilities, for a start. And those bones. You'll never mend that way."

"Not trying to mend. I'm not broken."

"Believe it or not, I've got troubles of my own that need mending. Same as everyone. I don't want anything to do with your problems, or

Grant's, or anybody else's. That part of my life is gone. Better if you put your life back together on your own, anyhow. Though, I am curious... what were you meditating on? Just now."

"Some Eastern yogis meditate on rotting flesh and feces to fend off the primal urges."

"I taught you that, you thankless little twerp," Pa Sonny laughs. "Practiced that method myself for many years. But after a while, it begins to darken the bearing of a man's soul. There's a reason that such foul things exist in the world, and it's not to suppress our urges. Although I suppose it is appropriate, given your choice of landscape."

"Why?"

"Why do you think this is the only healthy green in town? It's the nutrients. Lasts for ages."

"I've heard Amondale's theories."

"Theories, are they? Suit yourself. You know, a man can spend his entire life denying the truth of who he is, but when the Reaper comes a'sowin', it's the inner glow that gives the man away, the unique markings of his soul. Through and through, you are who you are. All of us are. It was you who taught me that. Helped me to snag my first woman, in fact. Do you recall?"

"How do you mean, your first woman?"

Pa Sonny's pace slows, his expression joyful as his gaze wanders the landscape, lingering ever-so-briefly on the creek and the clouds, on St. Josephine's and Johannes. Then, he stops suddenly and grabs Johannes by the hand.

"I've had many more since then."

"And is it better than a decaying corpse?"

"Sometimes..." Pa Sonny's attention drifts to an unreachable vista. "Sometimes."

Johannes steps away and kneels beside the stream. He dips his hands into the water and wets his face. "I was meditating over a babbling brook," he says over his shoulder. "All of life, immersed in a calming water-artery like this one." Johannes cups his hands and sips the water, but it tastes like dirt. He lets it dribble back into the creek, spitting to clear the taste. Behind him, he hears grinding and scraping.

"This here..." says Pa Sonny as he carves a deep line into the dirt and dead grass with his foot. "This is the state line. Right here, where Oklahoma begins." He waves to swat at a fly, then steps over the line and back again. "It's that simple." Again, he crosses the border, but this time he continues on a few strides before turning around.

Johannes approaches. Clouds roll in, covering the sun and rendering Pa Sonny distant, shrunken, almost shadow-like and ethereal. Johannes forces his eyes away. He looks to the creek, but when he shuts his eyes, the water still flows, bloated and threatening, the mountain river carrying away the last of his possessions as the fractured walls of his shack bob helplessly in the current.

Johannes opens his eyes and treads on the line in the dirt, brushing the boundary clean away. "A mental construction. An arbitrary wall we're compelled to recognize. No foundation in reality."

"Is that so?" asks Pa Sonny. The sun peeks out from behind the clouds and splashes his face. "And when this illusion is universally accepted by people the country over? On your side of the line, liquor sales are legal. On this side, illegal. On that side, our friend, the sheriff, can arrest you at no one's discretion but his own, gun you down if he wants to. And why shouldn't he? But, over here, on this side, he's powerless. Who are you to decide what's real and what's not? Only revolutionaries and extremists ignore established boundaries."

Johannes glances at St. Josephine's. "What about that place?"

Pa Sonny looks over his shoulder and grimaces. Nodding, he says, "There are always anomalies."

"The sunlight makes you look younger," says Johannes.

"If only it made me feel younger." Pa Sonny pats Johannes on the shoulder, directing him toward the red pickup. "Or better yet, if it actually made me younger. I wonder—why do you choose to meditate on water after what the water has done to you?"

"Why did you quit the Church?"

"So...you're asking the questions now, are you?"

"Was it the women?"

"I could have had a woman if I'd wanted, a good lady wife. No such rules to hold me back. The Catholics are prudes. We were not."

"This water has done nothing to me," Johannes sighs. "This town... this life...it's not what I know. Right now, I'm figuring out how to adjust my perspective, trying to enjoy the view while I float along with the current, at least until I wind up where I need to be."

"And is this what the search for those bones is all about? Seems more like rebuilding yourself from the ground up, if you ask me. Lost is lost. No point in going to all this trouble. In that case, why not just rebuild that hovel of yours in the mountains? Build it right here, or in Grant's yard, anywhere. Perhaps because you learned some invaluable insight out there? That no matter what you do, freedom is never free?" Pa Sonny's jocular laughter slowly layers upon itself, becoming thicker, more devious. "That lesson slaps all of us in the face several times over the course of a life. Don't let it bother you."

"Who said I'm bothered?" Johannes, poised on the defensive. "I'm doing just fine on my own."

"Yes...still all on your own. Well, I hope you're strong because these people are certain to stuff you full with all sorts of compelling nonsense. Valuable lessons are hard to come by around here." Pa Sonny laughs again as he opens the passenger door and groans when he lifts himself into the truck. The door creaks, then slams shut. Pa Sonny sits for a moment, never taking his eyes off Johannes.

Johannes stares back through the filthy windshield. He's overcome by the strangest sensation, like he's suddenly alone again after a long spell, but with the knowledge that he's being watched. It's reminiscent of those few stubborn weeks he remained on the mountain after the landslide, sleeping in caves and bushes, sick and weak and terrified, wishing he could summon the strength, take flight, disappear, even if that meant flinging his body into the river and being carried away, drowned and crushed upon the jagged rocks at the bottom of the waterfall, buried in sediment—

The horn blares. Johannes looks up.

"Best not to stand around," shouts Pa Sonny, his impatience loud and clear. "There may not be landslides here, but this is tornado country. And the coyotes, you know, they emerge at dusk. Sun's on its way down, as always. Better just get in."

Glancing at the stream, Johannes steps around to the passenger door, his mind racing, searching for an excuse—the dig, another go at meditation, Grant waiting back home, bartending tonight at Ernest's, the Carnival, the pickax, an appointment with Amondale, a date with Caryn, with the bones or with Rachmaninoff and the Scrap, the half-promised trip to Lani in Chicago, or back to the mountain once and for all...

"Over there," Pa Sonny shakes his head and indicates the driver's seat. "You're driving."

The creek flows gently beside them, though it sounds uncharacteristically loud. Johannes is suddenly overcome by the sensation that he's still settled deep in his meditations, that he's under some influence other than his own, that the Pa Sonny beckoning to him now, ordering him around, is nothing more than an unconscious representation of... what?

His desire to flee?

He opens the door and lifts himself onto the seat.

To hide?

Turns the key in the ignition.

To confess?

"Well?" says Pa Sonny. "What are you waiting for?"

The truck bounces along the rigid, bumpy ground back to the road. Through the spotty windshield, the world appears confused, rejecting, content with its fill and unwilling to accept another morsel. As they reach the pavement, Caryn's convertible blows past, heading into town. Her long, auburn hair is strewn wildly behind her, her tanned caramel skin a perfect match for the sleek shine of her car.

Johannes begins turning the wheel to follow her.

"Other way. Directly across that border, the one you have no faith in."

Johannes pauses, then steps on the accelerator and turns south.

"Don't take this place too seriously, Johannes. Don't ever take any place too seriously. You always did."

"And you will try to change me now? A formless block of clay, you will give me shape?"

"You did it to yourself. You're the artist. Whether it's to be a masterpiece or a dung heap, that's up to you, but you might as well pay attention to it. Float along or run all you want; you still must take heed of the things around you. For there lie the artist's tools. But there's a difference between utilizing elements and depending upon them."

Johannes sighs. "Where are we going?"

"Due south, about five hours."

Johannes takes his foot off the gas and lets the truck coast, his jaw agape.

"Got a delivery to make," adds Pa Sonny, pointing out the full load of unmarked sacks in the back of the truck. "Texas. A little ranch outside of a town called Gail. I'm tired of driving, desperately in need of a rest. But I must make my deliveries still. Responsibility is a growling god of wrath, and it has reared its ugly head. Lucky for me, it doesn't mind if an old man seeks some help now and again. You owe me a lift, and I've come to collect."

Oklahoma's panhandle differs little from the land surrounding Creek's Ridge. Browning grasses extend far into the distance, a haze of dust hovers low to the ground, and trees grow at distances impossible to gauge. They've only been driving for forty minutes when a small rectangular sign crops up announcing that they've passed through the panhandle and are now entering Texas. No structures appear other than distant farmhouses, barns, and silos. They pass no more than a few cars and a semi-trailer resting on the shoulder at a crossroads. Pa Sonny seems to be sleeping, except that his head is held upright, unsupported by the headrest.

A warm, dry wind funnels through the cab, making the air dense and difficult to breathe. Johannes toys with the air conditioner, but the vents emit hot air. The truck's radio has been torn out. The gap in the dashboard now serves as a trash receptacle, colored veins exposed in wiry, chaotic disarray. Untenanted grazing land stretches out in all directions. The endless untrimmed fields beneath the pink sky of a setting sun are paradoxically the loneliest place on earth and also the most suffocatingly swarming.

The truck rattles. Rachmaninoff's stream of notes drifts on, sad beneath the dimming sky layered with clouds. The breeze cools slightly, an imperceptible refreshment. A herd of cattle stands just beyond a barbed wire fence, the first sign of life Johannes remembers seeing since crossing the second of the day's borders, Pa Sonny's line in the dirt looming in his memory as a noncommittal choice. Pass over it or destroy it altogether. The emptiness of decision versus the formality of action. Eventually, he assumes, they will return to Creek's Ridge, crossing effortlessly over those two unmoved borders. America is sturdy and daunting and oppressive, and its borders are not so easily erased, yet the fluid passage between them is almost too easy, inevitable. So, too, is the spiritual realm segregated from the social, the individual never free to reside entirely within himself. Freedom elusively slinks amidst the folds of time, in and out of the mouths of men, the shadows of the forest, the depths of the mountains, where Johannes never had cause to consider freedom, as though he had escaped even the concept itself, broken free of the attachments that give rise to such questions until he came face to face with immortal Death knocking down his door —*There's only one way to escape the trials of this life. You might have come to me first and saved yourself the trouble and the time.* The voice cackles and trills along to the melancholic piano notes of the Scrap.

From the moment Johannes entered Creek's Ridge, he'd begun to understand that the concept of freedom is itself bound. It can flourish, reaching deep into the firmament, stretching itself beyond its humble beginnings, but not on its own. It is dependent upon the world, contained, connected, a chain slung around the necks of all things. Freedom is the striving of those who strive for it. Such was Knecht, the mighty oak that would never move an inch from its place of birth. And that was how Knecht earned—and maintained—its freedom.

And so, here is Knecht's loyal pupil, slaved and driving a spiritual destitute, Pastor Sonny, this diviner of spontaneous self-denial, who hasn't uttered a word since they crossed not one but two so-called borders. If Johannes had but the strength to resist, then he might have remained behind in Creek's Ridge, digging for bones under Grant's command, avoiding Caryn because he still can't stop thinking about Lani, perpetually on the lookout for a dog that's never done him any harm, dodging Amondale's endless inquisition, or listening to Ernest unravel the world of music when all Johannes really cares about is this single brief motif from Rachmaninoff's Second Piano Concerto in C-minor. And then, finally, day after day, lying down to sleep on the floor in Grant's living room beneath the continued weight of the mountain.

And Johannes craves a glass of The Carnival. He doesn't recall the last time he spent an evening someplace other than Ernest's bar. If he turns onto one of these side roads, maybe he'll find a little dive, some hole in the wall no different from Ernest's. Pa Sonny, inert and unresponsive, won't even realize what's happened until the sweet juice wets his tongue. After a playful binge and a bit more friction, Johannes can really get to know him, unlike their cryptic conversation by the creek or this stubborn silence of the road. Destroy the ghost and get to know the man by that easiest of routes—Highball Highway.

Gail: 228 miles.

They arrive around midnight. The rancher is still awake, sitting sleepy-eyed on the front porch with a bottle of bourbon by his side and a shotgun balanced on the railing. He doesn't bother to get up from his chair when they mount the steps. Pa Sonny shakes his hand and asks what he's doing out here this time of night.

"Who in hell's this young fella?" the man responds.

"This here is my protégé from another time," Pa Sonny grasps Johannes's shoulder. "Johannes, Old Man Sumner welcomes you to Texas. He's been ranching these parts longer than anybody. Started when he was a boy. Damn near a century now."

Johannes nods to the old man and looks around the weathered porch, his eyes lingering on the bourbon.

Old Man Sumner stares at Johannes as he refills his glass with slow, measured motions.

"Well?" says Old Man Sumner. "Best get to work. Been sittin' here a'waitin since sundown."

Johannes looks to Pa Sunny, who only stares back, grinning.

"My boys're inside, gatherin' their rest for the morn. And expect'n them sacks you brought, too. Be up well before dawn, eager to work."

"I think what he means, Johannes," says Pa Sonny as he settles onto a wooden stool beside Old Man Sumner, "is that you're going to have to unload all that feed and fertilizer with those strong young arms of yours."

"Twigs. Them're twigs. Barn's over thatta way, through that gate and down a ways. You'll see it. Don't run over the chickens, but if that bastard mutt gives you trouble, you feel free to hit that sum'bitch now. Just stack ever'thing up in the barn, next to Miss Audrey there. And close up tight when yer done. Coyotes round these parts're ruthless."

"Miss Audrey?"

"My filly. And don't you spook her now."

Johannes descends the steps, but he looks back at Pa Sonny. "All of it?"

"All of it," nods Pa Sonny. "Try not to take too long."

"We're heading back tonight?"

"One more stop."

After struggling with the rusted latch on the gate, Johannes brings the truck through and then gets out to close the gate behind him. Roosters are sleeping alongside the dirt road leading to the barn. The rumble of the engine wakes them and sends them dashing in front of the truck. Johannes slams on the brakes several times until one enormous, dark-feathered bird, unperturbed by the noise or the headlights or the size of the vehicle, takes to walking down the center of the path, leading Johannes past the hen house and all the way to the barn at a temperate pace.

Johannes remains hesitant at first, his eyes constantly searching the darkness inside the barn, his ears picking up every little sound. If ever there was a moment he needed the pickax, it's now, though he sees no trace of coyotes or a dog. Nor is there any indication of a horse through the thick shadows.

The sacks are heavy and unwieldy, but the work gets his blood flowing. It rejuvenates his energy and wakes him up some. Thirty sacks in all. One of the sacks slips off the pile, so he squats down to adjust it, hoping it hasn't torn and spilled. And when he stands up again, he hears a moan straight ahead. A shimmering black orb floats in the darkness. Johannes freezes as his stomach drops. He notes the pounding of his heart, a familiar accompaniment from recurrent dreams—landslides, predators, storms, or fear in the form of immediate and present unknowns. He hears heavy breaths, not his own, and then the sound of animals stirring all throughout the barn.

Miss Audrey steps forward and hangs her head over the railing of her enclosure. Her eyes and black coat shimmer in the sparse light from the truck's headlights. She brays gently, enticing Johannes to approach. The other animals around the barn settle back into their silent slumbers. Johannes's fear is still there with him. He can taste it. He wonders what he's doing here, flinching at all these unanswered questions. But as he stares at Miss Audrey's beautiful, droopy eyelids and long, thick eyelashes, he thinks of Limping Lady, a horse he's never seen but cares about beyond all bounds. He reaches out slowly, steps closer, and Miss Audrey reciprocates. He rests his hand on her forelock. The fur tickles his palm as he pets her. She brays again. Johannes steps up to the rail and reaches out to run his fingers through her mane, soft and silky as anything he remembers ever having felt. He finishes the work, but before he goes, he reaches up with both hands for one last touch, feeling her, absorbing what he can, the shape of her skull beneath that soft, soothing fur...

"G'ddamn, Judson," says Old Man Sumner. "Yer boy sure took his sweet-ass time."

"You all done, Johannes?" Pa Sonny laughs. "No trouble?"

Johannes shakes his head. "I met Miss Audrey. She's beautiful."

"Sure is," says Old Man Sumner. "Finest filly I ever raised. All the stallions think so, too. Give her a few years and she'll bear us some dollars, boy. Gon'be the highest earnin' whore in all the South."

Old Man Sumner and Pa Sonny both roll with the calm laughter of old men.

"Head inside and grab something to eat," says Pa Sonny. "We've already had a bite."

"A'course, help yerself," adds Old Man Sumner. "Ain't much, no fine dinin', but if it's good enough fer me and m'boys, it's damn well good enough fer you. In there, thatta way, just there."

The food is plain but filling. Johannes eats quickly, leaning against the counter and looking around the kitchen. They live a simple life. Nothing hung on the walls, not even window curtains. All the furniture is made of wood, not too old and not new, but practical. The kitchen is orderly and clean without being spotless. It reminds him of Grant's house.

As soon as he returns to the porch, Pa Sonny stands up and begins his farewells. He thanks Old Man Sumner for his hospitality, apologizes for the delay, and reminds him to call should he need anything, anything at all. Then, he nods at the whiskey.

"Think you might spare a shot for Johannes here? He saved our old bones a lot of pain and hassle."

"Same as I tell m'boys," grunts Old Man Sumner. "When the work's done, get up to anything you please. Just so's the work gets done tomorra, too. And as long as you don't spook, shoot, or screw the animals."

He pours the bourbon into his own glass and hands it to Johannes.

Johannes drinks it in one shot and hands the glass back. Old Man Sumner finally stands up to stretch and see them off, and when Johannes starts the engine, the old man retakes his seat on the porch, drinking as he watches them go.

"How do you feel?" says Pa Sonny.

"I was getting tired, but those sacks got my blood flowing. The food and the drink, too. Thanks for that."

"That's good. I was hoping a bite and a quick shot of booze would give you a jolt. Need to be alert."

"Where are we stopping?"

"Still a ways to go. When you get back to the main road, head west and just keep going. You'll start seeing the signs for El Paso soon enough."

"How far?"

Pa Sonny leans his head against the headrest, tilted away from Johannes.

"Sonny?"

"Just follow the signs."

It's not long before the soft sound of intermittent snores fills the silence. Pa Sonny's breath reeks of bourbon. After half an hour they pass the first sign.

El Paso: 282 miles.

Pa Sonny's face is tranquil and relaxed as he watches Johannes through the dark. "Any trouble recalling the fine art of driving?"

"I'm falling asleep, that's all. We need to stop for a while. I have to rest my eyes. Unless you want to take over."

"Sorry. Got to keep on. An appointment is an appointment."

"What sort of appointment needs us driving through the middle of the night?"

"The secret kind." Pa Sonny grins. "You're only the driver. Just drive and concern yourself with naught else. Pay your debt. And for God's sake, if you must pose questions, do try to make them interesting. Or else you'll never get anything close to an honest reply. Our world is built on falsehoods."

"Were you meditating earlier?" says Johannes. "On the way to the ranch?"

"Of course. Always."

Johannes rubs his eyes and rests his arm on the windowsill, his forehead jammed against a closed fist, his hair splashed by the wind.

"It'll be morning by the time we arrive," adds Pa Sonny. "I hope you've appreciated the scenery. The grazing lands and the desert are perfect for self-discovery, especially by night. Contemplation free-and-clear. Solitude is bliss."

"This isn't solitude."

"Speak for yourself," Pa Sonny murmurs, staring out his window. After a while, he repeats his question. "So, you're comfortable commanding this ancient machine?"

Johannes peers at him.

"From the vague and incomplete stories I've been hearing about you, I had to assume you'd forgotten basic skills as well as memories. You know, like tying your shoes, writing your name, or wiping the steam from the bathroom mirror. Driving and following road signs. You haven't bothered me once with that nonsense. Impressive. Illuminates this crisis of yours from an entirely different angle, doesn't it? Have you been helping yourself to the coffee?" Pa Sonny picks up the thermos that's been rolling around on the seat between them. "Doesn't feel like it. Here. Might be a day old, but it's strong."

"Great. Thanks. Were you drinking with him? With Old Man Sumner?"

"I don't drink anymore. Not like I used to. But Sumner, he's from a different time. Doesn't understand. Men like him insist on certain forms of respect. I think you impressed him. Few can."

"So you do drink."

"When circumstances require it..." Pa Sonny gazes out his window, his voice almost inaudible amidst the roar of wind and engine. "Or allow it. Certainly not like we used to, you and I. I have to say, I'm intrigued by your habits. You can't have had much booze all that time. Unless, what? Making your own out there, were you? Neighborly with the local moonshining hillbillies? I doubt it. And yet, still, you return and sink right back down into that swamp without a moment's resistance. That too...it's illuminating..."

Johannes wants to slam on the brakes, give the man back his truck, dash into the prairie, and lose himself in this unsheltered wilderness. To return to the simple splendor of Miss Audrey's eyes, the blanketing black of her soft flowing mane. But there's so much wisdom evident just on the surface of Pa Sonny. All the steadiness, confidence, experience, and history he'd expected to find in Grant. Pa Sonny must have a lifetime of stories to tell, and Johannes has a thousand questions to ask, but his thoughts are stunted, incapable of forming cohesively without his usual nighttime fuel of The Carnival.

"Sorry about the radio. Some rotten son of a bitch stole it months ago, and our sheriff never did a thing about it." Pa Sonny laughs softly and shrugs. "All for the better. Forces me to let my thoughts roam the landscape during these long, lonesome drives. A healthy dose of what's good for us. And don't worry, no more borders to cross tonight. Only the big one to approach. We'll come right up to it. Have to face the truth sooner or later."

The Scrap fled into the night some time ago. Johannes tries to summon it now, but it won't come, not when he needs it. He keeps his eyes trained firmly on the road, though he can sense Pa Sonny watching him. Eventually, he reaches for the thermos and takes advantage of the proffered cold coffee.

The air wafting through the cab continues to cool, diluting the odor of sweat. Occasional lights shine at great distances from the main road, cattle ranches and farmhouses. The flickering light of a giant blaze appears behind distant trees, its smoke rising in a perfectly straight, undisrupted line, white against the black of night. High above, a breeze swirls the smoke trail tip, dissipating it into the infinite, consuming it.

El Paso: 145 miles.

———

"Sonny...what's this all about?"

"I told you. A delivery and a pickup. An old fogey who needs some help. What? You don't trust me?"

"Not particularly, no. I have no reason to."

"I found you, didn't I? Saved your ass. Got you back to Creek's Ridge, right where you wanted to be? Didn't I?"

"But you didn't tell me who you were."

"Or who *you* were," Pa Sonny chuckles. "Well, now you've had several hours to consider it. What do you think we're doing here? Way out in the middle of nowhere, more remote even than Creek's Ridge. You must have come up with a few ideas. So? Let's hear them."

"I think Grant's been telling you about me over the past few months and that he's sick of trying to help me. He finally asked you to give it a shot? You two got together and planned this little trip?"

"That's what you think? I assure you, Grant knows nothing about this. I imagine he's just as confused as you are right about now. Worried sick. Swearing and cussing up a storm. That's his way. Although...it is just possible that he's glad you've disappeared. Hasn't that crossed your mind?"

"I..." Johannes turns his head to glance at Pa Sonny, but his eyes strain against his will. He can't bear to look at the man, so he searches the pitch-black prairie beyond the window instead. "Yes. It has."

"Grant developed more than a few unsavory habits while you were up in those mountains. But those wild habits kept him grounded. A lot of folks around Creek's Ridge, they thought he was losing his mind. What a load of horseshit. I know Grant better than anybody, so believe me when I say it's happening now. That boy's got something brewing inside of him that even I can't put my finger on. Inez is nothing more than his pity card. You know her, of course, so you know that she's one of the sweetest, most generous people on this earth. People like that do not transform into beasts of pain, not even in our wildest nightmares. It's only since your return, all happy and perfect on the surface, that Grant's been trapped in a maze of memories. He longs for the past, the entire past, wrapped up like a Christmas gift. He wishes for a future that repeats that past, that resurrects it. A dangerous wish, that."

"You're saying it's my fault?"

"It's no one's fault," Pa Sonny shrugs. "Everybody's complicit, and everybody's responsible for their own hardiness, their own well-being. This is just what happens sometimes. The human mind takes on more than it can handle. When walking the tightrope between past and present, some people are sensitive to the tension, others never feel it. But those who fall are the ones who can't stop trying to shift the anchored ends of the rope. Great men—be they leaders, scientists, intellectuals, or visionaries—they don't see the future any clearer than laymen or lunatics. They don't anticipate or create a future. They don't commune with God. They live not for the present, the past, or the future. Instead, they become intimately familiar with and totally separated from every moment, the woven threads of their life. They know where each and every memory begins and the precise path taken to their present circumstances, all the overlaps. They know the exact shades, all the frays acquired along the way, the truths and implications of the patterns created. Most importantly, they can feel the strength of the twine at any given moment, sensing precisely how much weight it can support before it gives out. Immersion, in anything, can be perilous. The ghosts of our pasts either fortify our resolve to live or break us. When I'm in town, Grant comes to see me every day. You didn't know that, did you? And he talks a lot, tells me everything, because he claims you're not really there. That it's not you, the real you, who's living with him. He says that the man who came out of those mountains is not the same person we knew, but elementally changed. He thinks you're only somewhat like yourself when you're digging. And he may not be wrong, but he places too much weight on it. He's obsessed with his past. He feels that life is not worth the trouble unless he can return to the way things were. Why else do you think he's got you digging up a bunch of lifeless bones? And the others, too, you know. A lot of folks come by to talk. They seek me out no matter how I strive to avoid them. Never was too good at hiding, or escaping, like you. So I've learned all about you from several different sources."

"Who? Amondale? Goddamnit, that asshole wants to write a book about me now. I keep telling him to forget it, to finish his book on you instead."

"I know," laughs Pa Sonny. "Oscar does enjoy hearing himself talk."

"Who else? Caryn? What has she told you?"

"Ahh," Pa Sonny groans. "What happens in the confessional must remain there. I took a vow to keep certain secrets between myself and God."

"You renounced your vows."

"You know this? Were you present when I renounced them? Standing as God's witness while I spoke the words, yet absent from everything else? Is your memory of this event intact, but your memories of life itself shattered and scattered? Be careful whom you trust. Anyway, vows are for the weak. They're the flashing neon signs above your head, burnt out in places and attracting the moths."

"Like those borders...flimsy...pointless..."

"Yes, well, some are less sturdy than others. Still, some can bear the weight. They must. Johannes, Creek's Ridge was built on rumors and lies. It has congealed over time into mystique, a belief that there is some special means for discovery to be found there, some secret inscrutable history that will spew timeless revelations, the rote for living a saintly life without lifting your fingers, without manning the torment. It has attracted all kinds of people over the years and also created its own unique breed. A dying breed, but then all such creations face extinction. And rightly so. The formation of Creek's Ridge is documented quite well. A cursory scan of the available material will show you one glaring pattern. Every major player in the town's history left by the same route. Death, the only way out."

"That's not so uncommon, is it? Home is a part of the person. People are attached to the places they were born or settled in."

"Other than the Saint herself, none of them were born there. Her entire existence took place in Creek's Ridge, and it was all pain and suffering. Lived into her nineties. That's something most folks don't realize because they forgot about her. Imagine the hypocrisy, at once idolizing her and also forgetting about her while she was still living amongst them. But they idolized what she once was, what she came to represent for them. And people now, they still do. Buffoons, the lot of them. Many thought she finally found the courage to leave, and others believed she had long since passed away. And some assumed she befell the same fate as her father, a mind twisted in upon itself by her peculiar plight. Madness, they call it. I, for one, believe she was of sound mind until the very end. And you?"

"I wouldn't know."

"You should. You should know more than you appear to."

"So I'm told."

"You used to. I'm sure of it. And so the enigmas begin to emerge. Who could have known that this is what it would take..."

"What enigmas?"

"Yours, all of them." Pa Sonny heaves a sigh and shrugs. "The journals are all housed in St. Jo's. Some of them nobody's seen, not permitted. But it's mostly crap. History is full of examples, just more of the same crap. Once the people rally around an idea and come together to implement it, the idea itself takes on the qualities of the people. Ideas, too, can grow old, sick, feeble. They decay. And it's only the highest grade of person, those impeccably balanced few, who can fully grasp an idea and whole-heartedly nurture it, like a child. When you raise a child, you acknowledge your own mortality. You take the entirety of your being, all those sheltered memories, the heartaches, the embarrassments, the pride and regret, and you grab them with your grimy fingers and reach into the unseen future. It's the ultimate selfless act of faith. Still, all that we know eventually starts to rot, and it becomes impossible to sift through the shit. When truth and fiction are all muddled together, who can you believe? Who does one trust? Until you find your footing—until you know and accept what you are—why should you believe a word anyone says? I can tell you everything you want to know about the Johannes I once knew. John Metternich, his family, his education, his beliefs. His strengths and his faults. But I won't. It's not as easy as that. It would ruin you. And we are not unalike, you and I, except that I know where I stand. I know to be cautious. I've heard a lot about what happened to you in the mountains and also the nonsense you've been up to recently. My curiosity was sparked, but I couldn't believe any of it. I had to see for myself. And that was the easy part. You've already answered all my questions. I could have learned these things about you during a thirty-minute stroll through Creek's Ridge. Now, here we are, damn near into Mexico, on a trip far too long for simply catching up with an old comrade-in-arms. This is exhausting for both of us, believe me. I never intended to bring you along with me today. A knee-jerk reaction after talking to you by that creek and seeing for myself what's become of Johannes Metternich. Turns out he's just the man I was looking for. It's selfish, but I want you to see me for what I am, too. I need somebody to know what I've been hiding."

"Where are we going?" Johannes eases off the gas and examines the shadowy figure beside him. "There's no pickup, is there?"

"The air here is invigorating, isn't it? Breathe deeply, my friend. Maintaining a healthy mind is a strenuous task with no foreseeable end."

The truck drifts over the center line. Several seconds pass before Johannes notices the headlights coming at them. He panics and pulls the steering wheel to the right, sending the passenger-side tires spilling onto the shoulder. They grind and slip in the gravel as Johannes slows to regain control. The oncoming car passes them with an arm extended out the driver's side window, a coarse and angry finger.

Johannes's heart pounds. Pa Sonny remains motionless, staring out his window into the all-consuming darkness. The scent of cattle enters the cab, and their lowing momentarily sounds impossibly near, as if they've surrounded the truck.

The air has chilled considerably, but neither Johannes nor Pa Sonny roll up their windows. Pa Sonny descends into contemplation again. Bovine musk and the odor of manure come and go. Armadillos scurry along the shoulder, occasionally braving fate when they dart across the road as the truck speeds toward them. The Scrap is a distant voice, a whisper hardly distinguishable from the wind and the engine. Johannes is no longer sleepy. He's alert, bristling with the cautious edginess of waking in an unfamiliar place. The course of events that led him here poses a frustrating riddle, a disorienting staircase that would be simpler to negotiate with his thoughts numbed by The Carnival, with a companion who doesn't sprawl so completely, so heavily across his mind. Someone like Amondale or Ernest.

El Paso: 33 miles.

As the El Paso city lights frisk the dark horizon, they are promptly swallowed by coming daylight.

"Why does Grant think you quit drinking?"

"Because other than on rare occasions, I have. It wasn't fun anymore. After you left, I was mostly drinking alone. That, or on the road in different places, with different people every day. And I had a car wreck. Damn well should have died, but I didn't. Wasn't even injured. Something backward about it, something unjust about how such things turn out. Extinguished the peace I had always found in it."

"Why did you quit the Church?"

"Why'd you disappear into the mountains of Tennessee?" Pa Sonny rejoins as though he'd anticipated the question. "I thought not. Better to leave well enough alone, then, yes?"

"Did I tell you anything? Before I went away?"

"Plenty. But as I said, what is divulged in confidence must remain there."

"Even when the confessor is the same?"

"Do you consider yourself to be the same man you were?"

"No," says Johannes. "I don't. I'm not."

"Then I swallow the knowledge I'm privileged to."

"How did you find me? At that diner?"

"The storage lockers of the subconscious, I assume."

"What?"

"We talked about it before you left. Talked about it at length. Your plan was to never return—not very well thought out, in my humble opinion. But I bore a certain amount of responsibility. Felt it in my heart. I insisted on a backup plan, and you resisted. We finally agreed on The No-Show No-Go as a rendezvous, just in case mountain life should ever flip sideways on you. Your only safety line. I assume you'll thank me for it someday."

"But how? How did you know I'd be there?"

"Who said I knew? I didn't. Let's just say I bet on it all the same. Gambler's instinct." Pa Sonny's voice barely rises above the low moan of the wind. "I drive out that way once a week at least, sometimes going out of my way. Their coffee really is something special. And the people...they're good people there. Johannes, we are not the same men we once were. Neither of us is. But that's no cause for lament. It's the natural state of existence. From moment to moment, time tramples forward. That elusive Father of all experience renews our sojourn. Time is the creator, the destroyer. There is no static state. Most people struggle their entire lives just trying to catch a glimpse of their own true self, to understand it, to accept and embrace it. But that's no struggle. That's humanity's dream, isn't it? To embrace the answer to the one unanswerable question. The struggle only comes after that. It's a magic trick that few can pull off—being able to recognize your own self in this ever-shifting maze, keeping one eye firmly locked onto the only truth you can ever really know with any certainty while always keeping pace with the speed of time. The deciding factor, in every circumstance, is loss. Loss in all its myriad forms is, ultimately, one-half of the human condition. Potholes and inconsistencies on an uneven road, and the shock of each one rattles our bones. Sometimes it's enough to knock you right onto your ass, to overturn you when you're zipping along at full speed. The available choices are but few. You right your vehicle and keep going as fast as you can without looking back. Or, you remain where you've fallen, knowing only the pain and despair of that moment while staring back along the road already traveled. Or, finally, ideally, you embrace the change and allow it to inform your further travels, continuing, not cautious, but prepared. Almost expectant, looking forward to the next jolt and the changes it might bring. Like Christmas morning when you were just a sprouting shit. The people of Creek's Ridge fear failure and upheaval, so they shelter themselves. In attempting to sidestep the potholes and debris, they fight against the progress of time. A losing battle. It will catch up with them in the end. Always does. The prophet loses his prophecies and disappears along with them. The missionary loses his prophet, his wife, everyone who ever mattered to him, and finally his faith. The Saint loses her way but still cannot find her way out, and she wallows forever in a life of misery. Repeat ad infinitum. The most recent example is none other than Creek's Ridge's latest addition. Your sweetheart."

"Sweetheart? She's not...she was Grant's...no...Lani was only visiting...visiting Grant..."

"Lani?" Pa Sonny sighs. "Johannes, you fool. This is exactly why I'm concerned about you. You've been infected by their disease and you haven't a clue. Lani. There is no Lani. You said it yourself—only a mysterious visitor, and now she's gone. I'm talking about Caryn. Ms. Pridieux seeks to escape the misfortunes of her past by, what? Squandering her money, her talents, her life? She spends most of her time in a forgotten cathedral in a town that stinks only of the past. And that church is the festering shit-hole that started it all. How many more lives will it snuff out before someone finally razes it to the fucking ground?"

Pa Sonny's breaths grow labored. Eleven hours on the road, and this is the first time his unyielding composure has staggered.

"It's a miserable place," Pa Sonny finally utters. "Built for the damned."

"You are too, aren't you?" asks Johannes. "Diseased? Damned? Stuck in Creek's Ridge with everyone else?"

"Of course. Even worse than the others. Creek's Ridge is my hell. That's why I keep to the road, which I prefer only because it keeps me away from the town. And, the town is ideally situated for my work. A cyclical punishment, my Sisyphean nightmare. And that's why we're going to El Paso, the very edge of our country, the uncrossable border. For smoke and women. For respite."

"What women?"

"There." Pa Sonny points at the approaching intersection. "Turn right."

"Prostitutes?"

Pa Sonny only laughs as Johannes makes the turn.

The outskirts of El Paso are still at rest. No longer cruising at highway speeds, the sticky air of early morning attaches to their skin. The first street lights in hundreds of miles are still glowing but rendered ineffective as the day advances.

"If I were going to tell you why we came," says Pa Sonny, "then I would have told you back in Creek's Ridge. And I would have left you there."

They pass through the center of a military base that's cut in two by a public road, giving them no choice but to proceed through the heart of this prison-like austerity. Tall fences erected along both sides of the road stand twenty feet proud and capped with razor wire, pronouncing blatant remonstrance of the natural order. In pairs, rifle-clad guards march down the silent street. Each uniformed soldier keeps his head trained forward as their repetition stomps menacingly onward. Each time the truck overtakes a pair of guards, another pair approaches from the opposite direction, their eyes lazily examining both driver and passenger, and the whole system repeating itself every few seconds. Johannes and Pa Sonny have entered an oppressive labyrinth, an endless fortified road, the demands of conformity. By attempting escape, they will only be selling themselves off as willing participants, moving targets begging to be gunned down. A distant sound rises, startling in the early morning, a low rumbling that gains in intensity and then plateaus. The sky has acquired the blue sheen of dawn, but the sun still hasn't presented itself. Ghostly shadows beyond the fence manifest into vaguely solid structures through the subtle glow of morning. Tall, dew-splashed grasses tremble like ripples on a pond. The rumbling of a moment before returns—boot campers in separate packs of thirty or forty, jogging and barking mechanically.

Johannes eases on the gas, and the truck crawls along the empty road. The new recruits sway together in waves. They disappear behind regularly spaced pillars and watchtowers and then organically re-emerge. When the groups pass one another, their collective voices swell and recede like the surf while shadowy blurs explode silently in the shimmering grass.

"Jackrabbits," explains Pa Sonny, "the little shits are everywhere. They keep to the base because the coyotes stay out." He nods toward a pair of guards who have slowed their step and are watching the truck, their hands gripping the rifles slung over their shoulders. Pa Sonny waves and smiles and nudges Johannes. "Keep us moving."

The rabbits burst up and out and race away from the droning mobs, an eternal chase, never a victor and never a rest.

Soon, the chants subside behind them, and they pull up to a desolate intersection. Mom-and-pop shops and seedy motels line the opposite side of the street.

Pa Sonny thrusts his hand out his window, directing Johannes's attention toward the hazy skyline of downtown El Paso. "No reason to enter the jungle," he says, then nods to the left. "That way. Almost there."

Johannes steps hard on the gas and turns the wheel without looking to see whether the light has changed.

Still driving alongside the rear of the base, they pass silent storage structures and single-engine airplane hangars, squat buildings lining the fence, and the uninterested actions of half-asleep officers smoking cigarettes. The base seems to stretch on forever, and before they reach the end of it, Pa Sonny motions Johannes onto an inconspicuous gravel road hidden among the lush foliage to their right. The narrow, winding lane leads through an alley of weepy trees. Their branches brush and scrape against the truck's roof. The trees open upon a clearing with a tiny house sheltered by still more trees at the far end.

Pa Sonny watches the house with deep concentration. After sucking in a breath, he carefully, noiselessly opens his door.

Even with a conscious effort to mimic Pa Sonny's hushed motions, Johannes comes off like a horse in a house. The driver's side door creaks and won't latch. He has to lift and slam it. His footsteps on the gravel scratch and grind in the ears of silent morning.

Quivers of discomfort and uncertainty course through Johannes's muscles. He observes Pa Sonny but doesn't dare move another step or announce his growing list of questions.

As he stands there, having reached the end of an endless drive, interrupted for Old Man Sumner and Miss Audrey, for gasoline, road snacks, and piss breaks, an immense fatigue finally catches up with him. He thinks of Creek's Ridge, the solid, motionless floor of Grant's living room, swept clean and waiting for him, but it's so far removed now, an impossibility, a dream, a memory—

"Ah, hell," Pa Sonny kills the silence. "We forgot the smoke. Back in the truck. Come on, load in."

Pa Sonny retreats, but Johannes looks toward the house again, silently pleading for a floor to lie down on. Standing in the doorway is a woman. She's broad-bodied and firm, the sort of commanding figure that one can't help but admire. She steps down from the porch and moves briskly toward them, a dubious hint of pleasure spread across her face.

"Why all the commotion?" she says, her voice carrying across the clearing without difficulty.

"Any grass left?" shouts Pa Sonny.

"Picked some up a few days ago. Figured you'd be paying us a visit. Long overdue, but so it's true..." The woman's voice is smooth and articulate, all the vowels strung together by silk, like a singer's voice tuned to perfection with age. As she approaches, she pauses to look at Johannes.

"Long time," she says, nodding at him without expression, her eyes locked on his as she moves toward Pa Sonny.

"Wait until you try this smoke," Pa Sonny tells Johannes. "Take you to the highest point in all of Texas. Don't look so surprised. The hard part's finished. We made it safe and sound. Now, try to enjoy yourself. Here we are, secret exposed. This life is for idle pleasures, not idle suffering. I told you we were coming for smoke." He smiles as he reaches out and wraps his arm around the woman, affectionately planting a kiss on her cheek. "And women."

Chapter 34

Resident of Nowhere

February 28, 1818
St. Johns River, La Florida

AMBRISTER INSISTS THAT I ADDRESS HIM BY HIS ADOPTED SPANISH name, Roberto Horacio Nuñez, as his given name is that of a well-known fugitive. In jest, I asked whether he is himself the fugitive, to which he responded only with laughter. Many years under the tropical sun have darkened his skin. He speaks Spanish naturally. In fact, the only time he speaks in his native tongue is during our English lessons. Only a select few of the tribesmen know that he is, in truth, an Englishman, and he finds it particularly pleasing, a sort of personal game, to conceal his origins from fellow Englishmen. As for the Americans, he says they are easily fooled, which is why he believes he can make a passable English speaker of me.

Despite his warm feelings and high regard for Roberto, Father Jimenez dislikes the idea of giving up one's Christian name to hide behind a false identity. The ultimate goal for any man or nation, he says, is harmonious coexistence with our neighbors around the world. Reaching that apex by means of cheap trickery and deception can only serve to complicate, if not destroy, that achievement. Therefore, the Father refuses to waver and still addresses him simply as Ambrister.

Roberto fearlessly and adeptly negotiates the swamps, equal to any Seminole warrior born and raised here. His body is rife with scars, many of which were laid upon him during the 1812-14 campaign against the Americans in West Florida. Each scar comes with a story that he is always glad to retell. He harbors great hatred for the Americans, balanced by an equally powerful fondness for the Seminoles. After completing his service with the British Royal Marines, he relocated permanently and secretly to La Florida, where he began preparing the Natives and the Spaniards for an invasion he has always believed to be inevitable. For the past four years, he has funneled weapons through the Caribbean so the tribes of the peninsula might have a fighting chance at pushing back when the Americans advance. He has entered the United States numerous times, under both his given and presumed identities, seeking out fellow conspirators and a particular type of businessman, those with no qualms selling arms and provisions to the enemy—a type that is surprisingly common there, he claims. He has traveled from the Georgia border to the frozen wilds of Quebec, from New York in the east and as far west as the Mississippi River, where large populations of Natives continue to be herded. And though the Natives have tried to build new lives, they merely bide their time while waiting for the Americans to expand their reach once more. Roberto says America is a beautiful land, and so it is unfortunate that it has been claimed by such scoundrels and brigands.

Every day, along with many budding young Seminole warriors, we spend several hours practicing with the weapons. Roberto praises me as a natural with a musket. The positive nature of his character is well-versed in reinforcement, but he does not provide an accurate portrait of my skills, for my aim and confidence are sorely lacking. Nor does his enthusiasm for weapons feed my desire to participate in such barbarities.

———

March 1, 1818
St. Johns River, La Florida

To conclude our English lesson today, Roberto asked me to speak of my past. As I struggled to make sense of the years of my life, he corrected my mistakes in conjugation, taught me to flatten my accent into an almost monotonic drawl, and replaced unnatural expressions with more commonplace parlance. But when my story reached the point of my sea voyage from Spain, he stopped me short, asking me with curious urgency to repeat the ship's name and the dates of our voyage.

"El Soldado Agraciado," I repeated. "The autumn before last."

The ship he knew well and had even sailed with them on occasion.

He had considered Captain Vasquez a good friend and a reliable business partner. Then he expressed his condolences.

It has been some time since I last thought about my friends aboard El Soldado Agraciado, so his comments caught me by surprise. The world, rendered impossibly expansive by that very voyage, suddenly contracted. It squeezed tighter around me, approaching the more manageable size of former days.

Last spring, while in Cuba bartering for a shipment of weapons, Roberto was present when a local fisherman returned to port with a small collection of sea wreckage—a few damaged planks and bits of a mast. Soon, a veritable militia of fishermen were venturing onto the choppy waters in search of valuables for salvage. Just as night fell, the first boats returned bearing the floating remains of unknown cargo. It could have been any of several ships thought to have been lost during the storm season, but when another boat returned to harbor with the cover from a ship's log, as well as fragments of inventory books and personal journals, everyone's fears were confirmed. It had been a Spanish ship. And as the only Spanish ship unaccounted for in recent memory, it could only have been El Soldado Agraciado. If there was still any doubt, it was cleared up in the days that followed when they found a drinking vessel with the Vasquez family seal and navigational tools inscribed with the Captain's name.

The next time he visits the island, Roberto has promised to track down a piece of the wreckage for me as a keepsake. He also made it known that he would welcome my assistance and companionship on any of his future journeys. He offered to give me a full tour of the Caribbean while providing me with work. Uncertain of how to respond, I said simply, "My work is here." To this, he laughed heartily for several uninterrupted minutes. Then, to conclude this disheartening lesson, he taught me a new English expression—*One lucky bastard.*

March 5, 1818
St. Johns River, La Florida

Father Jimenez continues to struggle, still recuperating as he is from his recent illness. What little energy he commands each day, he gives to the families who seek counsel and reassurance in these worrisome times.

Since hearing of my troubled past and the providential circumstances surrounding my desertion of El Soldado Agraciado, Roberto, who was at first guarded and difficult to get along with, has become more open with me. He and I spend a great deal more time together, both in training and leisure, and it has become easier for me to judge his stony character. He is generous and likable to those he trusts, but those he trusts are few. He is honest to a fault and quick of tongue, traits which he tells me have at times served to sour trading transactions and raise problems with his business associate, a Scotsman named George Arbuthnot. And I have learned, to my surprise, that though he is of solid build, heavily whiskered, deep of voice, and with sharp creases already wrinkling his face, he is but a few years older than I am.

Though Roberto has visited Europe, he prefers the colonies of the Caribbean and the Americas, and his deepest wish is for them to one day blossom as independent nations, free from Europe's strife and more respectable than the brash and greedy United States. It is not uncommon for him to dream of his home islands. The Bahamas offered him a glowing, happy childhood, a life that he never intended to leave. But after following his father's path into serving with the British Royal Marines, he became aware of humanity's darker shades, including the continued installation of slavery in certain British territories. Slavery was abolished in the Bahamas when he was still a child. The islands have become a haven for runaways from the United States and Africans rescued from slave ships, so he had been under the naive misapprehension that slavery no longer existed in the British realms—a falsehood, he later discovered, not only widespread throughout the British colonies but also reinforced by his own father's lies.

The war against the Americans in 1812 changed the course of Roberto's life. He developed a profound respect for America's indigenous tribes, formed a lasting friendship with Arbuthnot, and grew to despise the misleading historical narrative of his heritage. He prefers the peaceful reassurance of his own mind and morals, and he is determined to use them to affect change in a heartless world where so many others choose to sit back and watch or, even worse, to mindlessly partake. By his own proud admission, he is a resident of nowhere, a subject of no one, a believer and a dreamer, a pirate of idealism who will not lay anchor until he discovers utopia, or at least helps to bring it about. And for this, he has earned my admiration.

March 10, 1818
St. Johns River, La Florida

Roberto and I have just returned from an excursion that took us three days trekking around the entire perimeter of the village and assessing the integrity of our borders. Along the way, he spoke of his explorations and various connections within the ever-expanding United States. He described the inhumane cruelty of Southern landowners, bewailing the wretched lot of the Africans who must endure hopelessness in service of those idle rich. The foundation of that country, he says, is built upon the sweat and suffering of those unwilling slaves while white men sit behind closed doors, plotting the eradication of a native population that has maintained this continent's natural purity for thousands of years. And though there are pockets of resistance, neither the tribes nor the slaves have recourse to the resources or the soulless greed of the Americans.

With wit and a sharp memory, he recounted numerous experiences with the native people he has encountered there. As he spoke, he happened to mention a name I recognized—Tenskwatawa, the Shawnee prophet. With my interest piqued, I asked for more details. The tale, he related gladly, though it was not something he had experienced himself. Rather, he had heard the story from his friend and associate, George Arbuthnot.

Roughly a year ago, Roberto and Arbuthnot passed through a Cherokee settlement in the mountains to the north. Arbuthnot, who is considerably older than Roberto and has been drifting around the colonies since 1803, was speaking with a Cherokee trader he had known since he first landed in the Americas. As the three drank, ate, smoked, and laughed, Arbuthnot and the Cherokee recollected a trip they had taken together in the year 1806 through the Indiana Territory, an expansive and flat piece of land shored up against several enormous lakes and claimed by the United States. At the time, the territory served as a place of relocation for tribes from the east. They traveled the territory for several weeks, and as they went from village to village, they could not ignore the whispered tales of a prophet having risen from ashes. At first, they thought nothing of it, but soon enough, they began crossing paths with groups of Natives from across the region, all migrating in the same direction. After a few troublesome inquiries, in which the Natives either refused to communicate with Arbuthnot or were blatantly hostile, his Cherokee companion managed to learn that all those Natives from various tribes were indeed on their way to join a so-called prophet called Tenskwatawa, located in a Shawnee village along the

Tippecanoe River. The Cherokee received assurance of the prophet's great power and vision and was encouraged to join the other Natives, for the prophet and his brother Tecumseh were uniting all the tribes of the land. However, he was also warned that his white companion, Arbuthnot, would not be welcomed there and would most certainly be killed upon arrival.

Both Arbuthnot and his Cherokee friend were young, curious, and adventurous, so they accepted this threat as a challenge. Through various tricks of the forest, they disguised Arbuthnot as a Cherokee and headed for the Tippecanoe River. They entered the Shawnee settlement under cover of night, keeping to themselves and merely observing the strange energy that had delivered all those disparate peoples to the unassuming, innocuous shores of the Tippecanoe. Over the following days, they watched from the shadows, waiting to catch a glimpse of the prophet, but they only ever saw his warrior brother. Tecumseh, the war chief, prowled through the throng, which had grown to over a thousand Natives of different backgrounds. The modest Shawnee village did not possess the resources to support such a massive influx of inhabitants, and seeds of discontent sprouted like weeds. Tecumseh and his warriors stalked through the scores of people, handing out meager, insufficient rations of cornmeal, barking commands and promises, ensuring one and all that a new paradise was just over the horizon.

After a week, only a select few individuals had been chosen to meet with the prophet. By then, the food shortage had become severe, and disagreements between opposing tribes began to resurface. Finally, the entire gathered company was summoned to a large, nondescript wood cabin at the height of the afternoon. People clambered over one another to get closer. Disorder spread amongst them until Tecumseh, fierce as a hungry wolf, commanded his warriors to implement order. They surrounded the enormous gathering, taming them with force when necessary. In the light of day, and after so many days of waiting, Arbuthnot's disguise had begun to wear off, and a few curious strangers surrounded Arbuthnot and the Cherokee. They touched, poked, and prodded, asking unintelligible questions in their unknown languages. And then, just as they seemed to have discovered the white devil in their midst, the prophet himself emerged from the wooden hut.

Arbuthnot and his Cherokee companion quickly pushed through the crowd to evade their pursuers. However, there was no need, for the entire gathering had turned their attention to the sight of the prophet hobbling into the open, surrounded by numerous terrifyingly decorated warriors and bedecked Shawnee squaws. While the other Shawnees wore plain, simple outfits, the prophet was covered in shawls, feathers, beads, and gems of every color. He was an imposing, heavy figure, who displayed several ritual piercings through his nose, ears, and cheeks. Swirls of different pigments covered his scarred skin, bright and lively colors all of them, with the exception of his eyes, which were darkened to black to conceal the puckered flesh of a bad eye.

An eerie silence fell upon them as the prophet began to chant words that no one appeared to understand but which Arbuthnot swore resembled the solemn rhythms of a Catholic Mass. The prophet then summoned his brother, Tecumseh, and they held a short, private council in front of all the gathered. Finally, Tecumseh stepped forward and spoke to the crowd on behalf of the prophet. At that moment, several individuals stepped forward. They had been chosen as interpreters for their various languages and dialects, though there was no representative for the Cherokee tongue. Just as Tecumseh finished, Tenskwatawa rose and dramatically stepped forward. He said something in anger to his brother, and then, raising his medicine staff skyward, he spoke to the crowd for the first time, his voice deep, gravelly, and uncommonly loud. In response to his words, the other Shawnees began to howl like dogs, weeping and cowering with their families, while Tecumseh tried to no avail to stop his brother from continuing so.

Both Arbuthnot and his Cherokee companion knew it was in their best interest to leave the village. However, neither could resist the opportunity to witness the following day's events. After the two brothers' pronouncements, the Cherokee eventually found an Iroquois trader with whom he could communicate, and the trader relayed the basics of what had been said.

Tecumseh had first spoken at length about the evil of white men and their poisonous contamination of these pure lands. He promised that the white man would one day be defeated and sent back to the hell from which he had slithered. He then reproached everyone present for their lack of perseverance while living in the white man's shadow, for their overbearing pride and inability to sacrifice their comforts, for failing to bring about the white man's apocalypse, for their weak faith in the Great Spirit and in the words of their prophet. It was at this point that Tenskwatawa had stepped forward to berate his elder brother for being too soft, for allowing the confused and ignorant Natives off too easily. When he raised his medicine staff, he aimed it at the sun and announced that he would force all the Natives of the land to follow him. Together, they would reclaim the traditions of their past and live as they had for thousands of years before the white man's hideous visage rose in the east to cast its foul shade and stench across this land. And he announced that the white man's power and tricks would not go unmatched, that he too possessed the ability to communicate with the spirits, the strength to alter the course of the heavens, the will and knowledge to manipulate the future and the past. To prove this, and to gain their loyalty, he would bring about a miracle—he would threaten the earth and all of mankind with extinction. He promised that, on the following afternoon, he would render the sun impotent. All its warmth and light, all the blessedness and beauty it bestows upon the earth, he would snuff it out as simply as one pisses to extinguish a stray flame in the grass. And at that time, if all these frightened, faithless, and spineless mortal travelers still did not acknowledge and fear his will as one and the same with that of the Great Spirit, then he prayed that they relish their final day as creatures of this world.

The following afternoon, a solemn and silent crowd gathered in the same place around the prophet's wooden hut without being summoned. The prophet emerged but did not speak. He only glared menacingly at the crowd and then turned his attention toward the sun. Closing his one good eye, he performed a series of exaggerated gestures that once again reminded Arbuthnot of the Holy Benediction. Surrounded by his largest warriors, Tecumseh stood at the head of the crowd, ordering one and all to look skyward, where the moon was on course to collide with the sun. All the while, he roared at them, demanding allegiance and obedience, strength and community. The prophet finished his prayers as though awakening from a trance and stepped beside his brother, suggesting to one and all that they repent—though this was a word that none of the interpreters seemed to understand and Arbuthnot only inferred later.

Arbuthnot alone recognized the approaching event as a solar eclipse, natural and beautiful in its rarity, but he hardly paid any attention. He was more interested in the Natives' reactions, for as the moment approached, they were suffocated by panic. When the sky began to darken and an unnatural night descended over them, chaos erupted. Their choking silence broke into wails of terror. The Natives ran in all directions, covering their eyes and ears, shaking one another, and bemoaning the frail flesh and bones of their bodies. Some sat on the ground in contemplation of their lives, the villages and families they had left behind, while others tripped over them as they scattered and fled. Tecumseh's warriors trudged amongst the crowd, persuading them to heed the prophet's will and his word, and when the horrid cries of fear began to subside, the prophet demanded proof of their allegiance. The entire gathered mass prostrated themselves. After a few moments of uneasy silence, the prophet announced that he would forgive them their faults and spare their lives, that they had been reborn, no longer as members of their respective tribes, but as the first true inhabitants of the new earth, a community of the Great Spirit's elect. He proclaimed with grand gestures directed skyward that he would bring back the light and allow the world to survive another day. The moon passed across the sun, and daylight returned to the earth.

For the remainder of that day, Arbuthnot and his friend observed the new and terrifying aspect of the collected Natives, who spoke only of war and death, of reclaiming the lands where their fathers were born, of skinning white men from head to toe. That evening, Arbuthnot and his Cherokee friend made a silent, fortunate retreat from which they did not stop to rest for two full days.

By the time the two men had finished relating this tale to Roberto, they were each trembling at the real and present fear brought on by the voice of their memories. But as Roberto came to the end of the tale, he laughed without restraint.

Reluctantly, I joined Roberto's laughter and delight. But in truth, this tale of the Shawnee prophet has shaken my soul, just as it must have shaken Arbuthnot and his Cherokee friend in reality.

Chapter 35

The Disciples

Lawn chairs, picnic tables, stone and wooden statues. Gardening tools and manicured tree stumps. Half-painted canvases, tarps, huge empty flower pots. All of it lies indiscriminately around the gravel hamlet, as though overflowing through the house's front door, yet still protected by a perimeter of thick foliage. Parked beside the house is a second truck, almost identical to Pa Sonny's, the pair of them lending a homeliness that both Pa Sonny and the woman, Ms. Fairy Faystone, naturally embrace. It reminds Johannes of the grassy area surrounding his shack, soft and gently inclined toward Knecht, stretching down the bank to the stream, abundant with natural growth and deliberately arranged stones, time and space enough for anything, everything. Home.

Pa Sonny and Fairy speak warmly with each other, all the while smoking aromatic tobacco mixed with trace amounts of skunky marijuana. Pa Sonny smokes from a pipe while Fairy rolls fat cigarettes for herself, occasionally handing one to Johannes.

Fairy is younger than Pa Sonny, though she looks older. Years spent beneath this desert sun have weathered her skin, its copper tone complimented by the ashen red of her hair, hair of middling length and greasy with several days' sweat, changing shape whenever she runs her hands through it. Her wrinkles are, at a glance, the carefully carved lines of aesthetically advancing age, but upon closer inspection, they more closely resemble deep, hard-earned ridges of wisdom, the type of feature etched suddenly, dramatically, by way of unexpected and often unwanted experiences. She's every bit as large as Pa Sonny but even sturdier, with broad shoulders and thick arms accustomed to labor, her posture more confident and assured. The effects of the weed have draped Pa Sonny over the lawn chair, dough-like and immobile, set his vocal drawl at a slow crawl, but Fairy remains a pillar.

The passage of time has become incomprehensible since leaving Creek's Ridge. At certain moments, Johannes catches himself in a daze, scanning the featureless blue above the trees. He'll think he sees something slipping across the sky, and then he'll realize that his line of sight has trickled hazardously close to a midday sun that is several clicks farther west than the last time he checked. Johannes has, in fact, been dozing in and out of a light sleep all morning. Even when an enormous tattered parasol mysteriously materializes, blanketing the three of them with cool shade, its center pole rammed into the gravel and steadied between three polished rocks, it never occurs to Johannes that he must have drifted off. Their low, calming voices make it difficult for him to focus on anything other than the scope of his fatigue, an entirely alien tiredness that has nothing to do with swinging a pickax for hours on end.

As the day grows hotter and more arid, and Johannes floats higher into a hazy realm of lethargic sleeplessness, he's drawn toward the weepy, tangled greenery enclosing them. Several times, he stands to stretch his legs and finds himself wandering off, plunging into the bushes and trees, scratching his arms all to hell, and getting himself entwined amongst the branches. The moist scent permeating from the leaves catapults him back to the Smoky Mountains, those humid summers, his daily descent down the jagged side of the waterfall to soak in the lavish, cool spray at the bottom, long hikes foraging for anything edible that always deposited him in some unexplored cranny of the surrounding wilderness. Only when sorrow and longing grow more potent than the illusion does he dare to retreat into the sunlight, dragging his feet toward the theater of lawn chairs, smoke, and voices.

The lawn chair squeaks and bends as Johannes tries to make himself comfortable. His iced tea has been refilled and now bears the sharp aftertaste of bourbon. Fairy hands him a lit cigarette. He coughs as he inhales the thick, unfiltered smoke. As their voices rise and fall, his drowsiness follows their vocal tones to peaks and depressions, and these transitions deny him access to true sleep. A raucous noise sounds from inside the house—his mind is lost amidst the trees, mountains, highways, and trails, time a drenching torrent, rapids thrashing and splashing over a mountain ridge—and then he notices movement behind one of the windows.

His gaze lingers there. Pa Sonny and Fairy show no indication of having heard anything. A curtain flaps on the other side of the window frame, and Johannes wants to accept the warm breeze as a satisfactory explanation, except for the nagging feeling of being watched. But, having been staring at the house for this incalculable time, he finally perceives that if anyone is watching, it's he himself. Just then, as though dictated by his thoughts, a young woman steps soundlessly out the front door and descends the porch steps. She's holding something with outstretched arms. Her eyes sweep past them, betraying no interest in the lazy trio, and she rounds the corner to the backyard. Pa Sonny and Fairy speak of dead sheep and cattle found on nearby grazing lands, decapitated rabbits and the vibrant colors of blood-stained grass in the morning dew, the inevitable trickle of migrants hopping the border, the dreams and casualties linked to such ventures, the peculiarities and habits of their neighbors on the military base. As they prattle on, they occasionally glance at Johannes, their eyes shining, speech unbroken, until their conversation gradually slows, spaces between words stretch longer, and the words themselves become mere interjections with no identifiable subject. But when Johannes looks at them with dumbfounded curiosity, they are focused on him, grinning identical grins of mysterious complicity.

Without any words for his lips to form, his breath escapes, formless.

The young woman returns to the porch and leans on the railing, her gaze resting in their direction. Even from a distance, it's clear that her eyes are unfocused, gazing arbitrarily upon a familiar scene, easily veiled by passing thoughts.

"Ionia," Fairy sings, and the sound rings out in the air, the magic of her melodic voice. "Come and sit for a while. Rest a minute away with us. A little idleness will do you good."

The woman disappears into the house again.

"The young sprite doesn't rest, not ever," Fairy goes on.

"Takes after you," Pa Sonny smiles and nods happily, "once upon a time. You're not quite as energetic and active as you once were. A great relief to me. Makes these little visits almost bearable."

Johannes is alert, truly absorbing their conversation for the first time, and thoroughly confounded by it. He recalls the difficulty he had in following Pa Sonny's speech at the diner, a time so distant now—not exactly a lifetime ago, but not so different either.

"Not all of us can attain the mastery over sloth that you have managed," says Fairy. "The Master Idler, in all his indolent glory. You could write volumes, preaching non-action and passive carousing to the masses, if only you had a motivated bone in your body."

"You very nearly infected me once." Pa Sonny finishes his iced tea and looks into the glass as he swirls the ice around. "It's your way of speaking. Even now, in our autumn years, worn out and approaching death as we are, you can still convince anyone of damn near anything. You should have been a lawyer, like your father. Or a cult leader like the Spaniard."

Fairy's laughter swells, an interlaced blend of highs and lows that tickles the earlobes and resonates in the inner ear long after it has faded. "Late-autumn years, more like. At least it's warm here in this desert. I was never one for cold autumn days. Rather die in the heat with my cult-of-one. Too bad my only other devotee is the Master Idler himself, whose armor has petrified too thick to pierce."

"You helped construct this armor, m'lady. I'm forever in your debt."

"Heh. The last words of any decent swindler."

"Don't bother yourself with an old sap like me. Better to assess your remaining influence on someone like Johannes here. Why do you think I brought him along? He's unnaturally lazy, except that he cares far too deeply for himself. Something of a dreamer, in the purely selfish sense. You could do wonders sculpting something out of him. If you keep working away at this one like you've been, there won't be anything left but a replica of yourself." Pa Sonny waves his glass at the young woman, who is now approaching. "Self-portraits are for the sick, the neurotic. What kind of maniac needs a copy of what they already have too much of?"

"Ionia, sit, sit, sit down. Save me, will you please?" Fairy beckons to the young woman, gesturing toward a short stool nearby. "Your ceaseless moving about has got my nerves on edge again, and this derelict ghost-of-a-man has me halfway convinced that I'd be better off living with those coyotes."

"She's acquired the habit of claiming nervous fits," Ionia tells Pa Sonny. She strolls toward him, although she's curiously examining Johannes. "Anxiety attacks. But she's as calm as a desert sunset. She wants to make everyone else nervous. And it works, too. Like a sickness. An aging genius with a child-like mischievous streak."

"The goal is to make an idling genius of her before it's too late," says Pa Sonny. "But her genius never shines through because she's always working too hard. She has already ruined you. Got to you too young. Now you're lost to the world of the industrious and the zestful. The uptight and fastidious who get nauseous at the mention of being alone for any amount of time. I mourn your loss."

Suppressed laughter barely escapes Ionia's lips as she leans down to give Pa Sonny a casual, unaffectionate embrace. A short, tight ponytail lifts the hair at the back of her head, exposing her tanned neck. Strands of short, sandy hair cling sweat-plastered to her cheeks and forehead. Her jeans are tight, dirty, and torn in places. She's wearing a black tank top and flip-flops. All of her exposed flesh is evenly bronzed.

"Where've you been, old man?" she says. "We haven't seen you in weeks. You could die out there some night and we'd never know the better."

"Ionia..." Fairy tut-tuts.

"What? If we heard news of his death at all, it would be six weeks too late."

"What's the difference?" Pa Sonny shrugs and glances toward Johannes. "Death reigns king o're us all."

"She's right, you know," Fairy is stern. "You haven't even notified us of your dying wishes. What are we to do with the body? Surely, you have no remaining wish for a Christian burial. What then? Voodoo resurrection? Mummification followed by an endless tour of backwoods curiosity museums? We can't prepare a corpse for the display case after six weeks, and we certainly can't bring it back to life."

"Decomposition will have left you beyond recognition," says Ionia.

"Your soul will unravel," says Fairy. "You'll be trapped piecemeal in the firmament for all eternity..."

Pa Sonny's expression grows serious. "Better if you just dump me in a ditch on the side of the highway. Up north someplace. Interstate 80 is a decent stretch. The calm of the plains. Them Nebraskans have interesting imaginations. You can count on them to build a compelling story around a mystery corpse. Prop my dead ass up against a milage marker for maximum effect, outstretched thumb and all."

"Don't bet on it," laughs Ionia. "When your life ends, so does the grand joke. We'll have you spruced up and ready for the next incarnation before you can enjoy a single moment in limbo."

"In your case, waiting to return in the body of a camel," howls Fairy.

"A camel!" guffaws Pa Sonny. Amusement and contentedness color his laughter and shape his features, and Johannes realizes it has been there all along, ever since the day at the diner. The rock-solid solemnity Pa Sonny projected while they were cooped up together in the truck was nothing more than a front, his attempt to assert some sort of power over Johannes.

"I was thinking he'd make a fine ostrich," says Ionia.

"Bah," barks Pa Sonny, "ostriches are good for one thing only."

"What's that?" asks Ionia.

"This creepy old man," Fairy sighs, "is alluding to their long legs and fat asses, I assume."

"Burgers!" laughs Pa Sonny. "On my mother's grave, I meant only burgers."

"There was this black bear..." Johannes speaks softly, and they each stop to stare at him. "It used to watch me from a distance. It never approached. Never fled either. Big, soft eyes. The resemblance is uncanny." Johannes can only glance at Pa Sonny because he finds it difficult to look away from Ionia.

"Who invited these young folk and their terrible ideas?" Pa Sonny shakes his head in disappointment. "A camel, though—that's wonderful. I'll fill one hump with Cognac, one hump with water, and wander from the Punjab to French Algiers."

"Algeria hasn't been French in years, you camel's ass," Fairy scolds him.

"Who said reincarnation has to occur chronologically?" Pa Sonny closes his eyes, already dreaming the expansive plains of spiritual immortality. "And cyclical time is as real as my ten fingers and eleven toes. We land wherever we deserve to land. I have a right to revisit the past and make my own terrible decisions. False youth, new hope. My reward for having grown old and banal."

"Oh, but your blessed idleness would suffer," says Ionia. "You'd be forever walking."

"Nonsense," says Pa Sonny. "The camel is the paradigm of idle animals. That droopy face, that slow chaw, the filthy coat. And they hardly walk. More of a bankrupt, encumbered trot. Cripples move more efficiently. It's the camel's conservation of energy and resilience against adverse conditions that creates the illusion. Strong, like yours truly."

"Still," states Ionia, "endless wandering on foot is not your game."

"Of course I won't wander without end. To hell with Algiers. After a brief, pointless rest and refill along the shores of the Mediterranean, I shall lazily head south, into the desert, with two humps full of the finest Italian wine. A long desert drunk until I've passed out, exhausted, and am swallowed, idly, by the Sahara."

Each time Johannes manages to tear his eyes away from Ionia, they are drawn back to her. And each time, she notices. Her bemusement disappears, shifting to wonder as she stares back at him, and her expression takes on the strained look of someone who never stops observing the world with critical scrutiny.

"I know," announces Johannes.

"You know nothing..." snorts Pa Sonny.

"They are...in danger. You could be their savior."

The others watch him, waiting for the complete thought.

Ionia takes a step closer.

"What's in danger?" croons Fairy.

Johannes looks from one to the other, uncertain of himself. "The Giant Panda."

Pa Sonny roars with laughter. "Now that's the sort of idea I expect out of you. Grand, majestic, fierce, and supremely inactive. From here on out, it's all bamboo wine and fucking the species back from the brink of extinction."

Ionia's stoicism cracks. Her small mouth extends in a smile as her laughter gradually loses its initial restraint. "Who the hell is this?" She's looking at Fairy as she nods in Johannes's direction. "He's cute. Where'd you scrounge him up from? Not the base again...he doesn't look it..."

"Born of sand and dust," says Fairy, this time in a distinct attempt at song, a brooding, sibylline melody. "While you worked the morning away, a sand twister rose and danced, spun its hymn, and deposited him right there, in that rusty chair."

"This one's all wild," adds Pa Sonny. "Not a tame bone in his body, nor a pure thought in his mind. Runs on instinct alone." His tone is pleasant, but he eyes Johannes severely. "Like them coyotes that scavenge around the barren wasteland out back, what's it called again? Oh, right—Mexico. This might be my last chance to warn you before I'm dead and gone. Beware the shifty creatures of dusk and dawn, Ionia, dear."

"Oh—" Ionia, extending the vowel sensuously, "no need for warnings. You've been away too long, old man. I've taken them in, embraced them within my small bosom. Those are my coyotes." She approaches Johannes and extends her hand as she stares, a mocking grin on her lips. "I'm tired of those pawns across the street. They're not men, they're insects. Hardened exteriors, but their insides gone all soft. Manipulated and molded. So easily stomped flat."

Fairy giggles in the background. Pa Sonny sucks on his pipe and exhales a cloud of smoke that obscures his features.

The Scrap struggles to reach Johannes from a great distance, its tempo stunted, its structure fragmented and reshaped by the force of the winds that propel it, the resistance encountered along the way.

Lifted, grasping for the individual notes, Johannes rises from his lawn chair lethargy and takes Ionia's hand, her palm soft and slick with perspiration. However, he doesn't shake her hand; he only holds it.

"I'm Johannes."

"Johannes?" Ionia smiles as she turns to Pa Sonny and Fairy with unspoken questions. "Nice to finally meet you, Johannes. I'm Ionia Josephina."

Dinner brings the four of them into the shade of the porch. They sit on cured tree stumps with their plates in their laps. After spending the entire afternoon lounging in the sun, and even now still reeling from the effects of the weed, they are all four broke for words, their focus entirely given over to huge portions of ribs drenched in Fairy's home-made sauce and tongue-numbingly spicy Spanish rice, Pa Sonny's favorite. Johannes and Pa Sonny are each given second helpings, which they devour. Afterward, Pa Sonny disappears into the house with Fairy. Ionia leads Johannes to a shallow pit in the backyard to deliver a gift for the coyotes, all thirteen of which she has named after the twelve disciples.

"But there were only twelve..." wonders Johannes.

"Twelve what?"

"Disciples."

"I know, of course." She hands him the plate of bones, observing him before she inclines her head toward the pit. He tilts the plate, and they watch as the bones fall and scatter in the dirt. While contemplating the resulting arrangement, Ionia asks, "Do you know them?"

"Who?"

"Christ's merry band of hoodlums. The Apostles."

Johannes looks at her and shakes his head, but her eyes are still locked onto the bones.

"Can't say I do," he says.

"Sonny raised you in the Church, confirmed you into the flock. Think."

"How do you know that?"

"Should we make a game of it?" Ionia turns a stern glare on Johannes. "For each of the twelve whose names you can dredge up, I'll... remove an article of clothing. How's that?" She lifts her right arm straight above her head, her wrist angled sharply, and her left hand on her hip, which she juts out in an exaggerated pose. "Well?"

Noticing that she lost her flip-flops at some point, Johannes points at her bare feet. "You're not wearing much."

"Exactly." She gives him a coy smile and swivels her hip to the opposite position. "You manage just four names and I'll be bare-assed. Get more than that, and I'll have to start taking yours."

"Sounds fun," smiles Johannes. "But you don't understand. I don't remember anything. Really, nothing at all."

"Oh, I understand just fine." Ionia drops her arm and steps toward

Johannes. "Those two, they talk a lot. I've heard all about you and your little mishap. Actually, in a way, I envy you."

"My mishap?"

"What? I suppose you blame the mountain for coming down on you? Just God's displeasure with a wayward soul..."

"No...but..."

"It was your fault, of course. Come on," Ionia says, motioning for him to follow her back to the house. "If we don't wash the dishes before the sauce dries, I'll be scrubbing them for the next week."

"How my fault?" He watches as she walks away and then hurries after her.

"For starters, what were you doing on that mountain? Waiting there, like you expected something to happen. Wanted it to happen. Don't pretend you haven't thought about this."

"I wasn't waiting, I was living. And you're right, I have thought about it. But I don't remember. I was just there, living my life."

"That's living? Well, only one way to remember."

"How? Washing dishes?"

"You see?" she laughs. "You are more than just some mountain hermit. You're a regular prophet."

As they gather the dishes from the porch, Pa Sonny and Fairy can be heard inside the house talking and laughing. Johannes peers through the window while Ionia dumps the utensils and glasses into the empty rice bowl. She stacks the four plates and hands them to Johannes, setting the bowl on top. Then, she takes the glass platter they'd served the ribs on, but instead of bringing Johannes into the house, she shoves him down the steps and leads him back into the yard.

"So? Have you remembered yet?" Ionia runs her index finger through the remains of barbecue sauce thick upon the platter. "The names?"

"Yes," lies Johannes. "All of them, actually."

"Are you going to tell me?"

"Not just now."

"What's wrong?" Ionia smiles as she sucks barbecue sauce from her fingertip. "You seem rattled. Worried. Lost."

"I am. And I haven't really slept."

Ionia laughs. "You were sleeping out there all afternoon."

"Barely. I was in and out, but never in a deep sleep. I need a floor and ten uninterrupted hours of rest. But now, with this talk of coyotes, I don't know if I'll be able to sleep at all. What have you named the thirteenth?"

"Jesus, naturally."

"The leader..."

"Oh, Johannes...you make Tenskwatawa sad."

"Who is Tenskwatawa?"

"And so the truth reveals itself. You're no prophet after all, are you?"

A water pump sprouts from the ground, a tall iron weed in the far corner of the lot. Ionia fetches a discolored dishrag from a clothesline strung between two emaciated, leafless tree trunks.

"And I had such high hopes. You probably don't remember how to do dishes either, huh? You pump and I'll wash. Give me water."

The pump resists, it squeaks, it pushes back against Johannes's efforts. He has to put his full body weight into it before it loosens up and starts spitting water. Ionia rinses the rice bowl first and then fills it with water for the rest of the dishes. Johannes is breathing heavily, but his limbs have come alive, his muscles tense and burning, like he's been digging.

"So Jesus isn't the leader?" he asks between gulps of air.

"He's the thirteenth," Ionia shakes her head and looks up from the plate she's scrubbing. "The unlucky one. Hand me another."

He hands her another plate, and she trades him the clean one. He holds it up, watching the water drip from the edge, unsure of what to do with it. Suddenly, "Judas?"

"Shall I begin?" Ionia asks with a flirtatious flick of the eyes. "Top first? Or straight for the bottom half?"

They finish the dishes and spread them out to dry on a log bench. Ionia teases Johannes by toying with the hem of her tank top, dropping and lifting the shoulder straps, letting her hair down so it curls around her ears and splashes across her face, then pulling it back again. A muffled scream comes from the house, and they both turn in that direction. Ionia grabs Johannes's hand, leading him back to the pit where they dumped the bones. The haphazard array reminds Johannes of Lil's bones, which he and Grant had brought into the house and similarly dumped onto the kitchen table the day after Lani left Creek's Ridge. Only a few hours earlier—exhausted in the noon sun and stoned and regretting that he'd given in to Pa Sonny's whims—Johannes had yearned for the horse bones, dreamt of them in those fuzzy transitions between wakefulness and sleep. But now, he doesn't miss them at all. Life's treasures, so easily forgotten, so readily replaced.

Ionia squats down beside the depression to inspect the lay of the bones. "They've already been here," she whispers. "So close..."

"What?"

"Just look. Can't you see it? The arrangement...it's all different..."

Johannes steps around the pit, viewing the bones from various angles until he lands upon the same perspective as when he dropped them in.

Ionia reaches down to pick up a long, curved rib bone. "See? Here, look at these marks. They're from teeth. Canines." She examines it a moment longer before handing it to Johannes. "Feel it..."

Tiny, jagged nicks and scratches cover the bone's surface, slick and slimy with saliva, inducing a sudden disgust that travels through Johannes's body like the unexpected heat of a flame, and yet this warm disgust ends in a chill that constricts his limbs, renders him motionless. Ionia is speaking, "And you can smell them," she's saying, "I think it was Bartholomew. Bartholomew's a she, a bitch, I think she's in heat..." Behind clenched eyelids, the images of dogs manifest as specters. The German shepherds—Cannon of old and his local persecutor, Mengele. The prowlers that run him down and tear his throat open in dreams, feasting upon his organs. Queen Maj, the light of his youth. The hunting hounds bound to Boötes, their master, chasing the oxen around the earth's axis in constant rotation, loyal repetition. And finally, the coyotes themselves, Twelve Disciples and the Unlucky One, so close, so quiet, stalking through the chaotic untamed growth of the field not five yards distant, the desert stretching on forever. Predators sniffing out their prey, surrounding them, watching them, waiting for an opportunity to pounce.

"There," Ionia grabs his arm. Johannes jumps and exhales an enormous breath. She's pointing at an isolated grove of bulky bushes and spindly trees out in the field. A tail flashes and disappears amongst them as the branches tremble.

"Johannes? What is it?"

He glances at her and shakes his head, but his gaze returns at once to the trees, their branches now at rest.

"Oh my god...you really are afraid? Of the coyotes?" She squeezes his arm. "You're stiff as a post. And trembling. I'm so sorry...I didn't think you were serious..."

"No, it's... Don't worry, it's nothing... I just..."

She's taken his hand, massaging it to ease his death grip on the bone. She slips the bone free from his fingers, drops it into the pit, and tugs on his wrist.

They walk away from the house, across a vast stretch of uncultivated farmland to the northwest. She maintains space and silence between them, peering at him in secret, noting that his eyes are squinted and that he keeps stumbling over clumps of dirt he doesn't seem to notice. Still, he continues to walk alongside her, mindlessly following, unconsciously aware of his precarious position in this unfamiliar wilderness, an unutterable distance from the wilds he knows so well. After a while he stops, looks around, looks at her.

"Sorry, I—"

"Don't be," Ionia cuts him off and jerks her head to convey that they should keep walking. After a few steps, she says, "It was Judas." Happiness colors the simple statement, bliss even. She watches Johannes, waiting for his reaction and wishing he could join her reverie.

"How could you tell?" He stares back at her just as intently, trying to compel his fear to recede faster than it is.

"He's bigger than the others. A lot bigger. And his coat is fuller, more vibrant. Cleaner. His stride and posture are nobler, almost regal. Haven't you ever had a pet? An animal you knew through and through?"

"Queen Maj..."

"A dog?"

Johannes nods and then looks away. "It was a long time ago."

"And you remember her? But nothing else?"

"Not exactly. I was reminded of her. A photograph, just one. But I only remember the emotions associated with...with the moment shown in the photo. Loss, guilt, fear—they were a part of that picture. Someone gave me the photo and it opened a door...released a kind of recognition of those feelings. But not a true memory. Not of her, not really."

"Something more, too," says Ionia. "Attachment. Loneliness. You miss her. That tone in your voice, the lilt of your words."

"Maybe you're right, but dogs, they..." Johannes shakes his head. "Somehow, I've developed a fear of dogs."

"Strong emotions are like scars," says Ionia. "You might forget how you got them, but they never leave you. Imagine having thirteen of them—pets, I mean. Thirteen animals scarring you right here," pressing her hand to her heart, "with their teeth and claws, the intensity of their glowing eyes, their devotion. Except they're independent, self-reliant, intelligent, and you rarely get to see them. But when you do, it's... remarkable."

"And what if you never see them?"

"Then you go and find them. Seek them out. Like a lover."

"With Queen Maj, it's different. Adoration of this sort comes to us by chance and circumstance, along with all the warmth and hurt attached to it. When the connection is gone—or even the memory—the emotions remain, dug in. Permanent. Pain still hurts, even if you can't identify it."

"But even when it's right in front of you, slapping you in the face, you still have to participate. You need to reach out and touch it. Hold tight, a passionate embrace. Let's call it what it is." She stares past Johannes, out into the vast field, sweeping her eyes across the desert.

"Love..." he says. "Have you ever embraced your coyotes?"

Ionia smirks. "Sometimes I wonder why I stay here with Fairy. Do I stay for her? For our work? Do I stay for The Disciples? Or am I just afraid? Fairy tries to teach me patience. She does. But her life has been extraordinary. She has done everything, been everywhere, learned everything she ever wanted to know, and touched everything she has ever wanted to touch. And she has emerged from it not simply content but happier than anyone you'll ever meet. Blissful, you could say. Because of that, her spirit has not aged. She's eternally young, so she has no true concept of time. For her, time is infinite. How do you learn patience from someone like that? I don't want that kind of life for myself, nor does she wish me to follow in her steps."

They stop at the base of a steep incline. When Ionia notices the coming sunset, a change comes over her, captivating Johannes. She turns to him, just a quick glance, and her eyes flicker like a bird in perpetual flight, its wings held wide and steady for immense distances, propelled by calm, powerful sweeps, a creature enamored with the entire world and yet—due to either mistrust or boundless curiosity—averse to perching for even a moment's rest upon any stationary object. Johannes catches only the briefest glimpse before Ionia flushes red. Barely perceptible creases appear around her eyes, her forehead twitches, and her lips close in a tight pout of unutterable secrets. Abruptly, she turns and flees, bounding up the incline that marks the far edge of the farmland. From the top, she looks down at him, beckoning him to scale the ridge and gesturing with excitement toward the setting sun.

The incline is steeper than it looks, so Johannes really has to dig in. He pulls himself up with his hands, leaping to scale the top. From the crest of the hill, they are given an extensive view of the field that stretches out behind the house and a wide river separating the field from the desert, its barrenness and desolation.

"I've explored most of it," she says when he's standing beside her. "Everything you can see from this point."

"That river..."

"The Rio Grande."

"Then all that, the desert...that's..."

"Yes. That's Mexico."

"But how do you...?"

"Same as the coyotes. I cross the river." Ionia smiles and rests her hand on Johannes's arm. "Sometimes, when I go out to walk and think and plan out a future without Fairy, I'll see one or two of The Disciples.

Usually, I'm not so lucky. No, I have never embraced them. But I've given them gifts, things that were extremely important to me. Things that were given to me. They take them, they always take them. Beyond this, beyond what you can see, it continues. The desert goes on and on and on. There is nothing. And it all belongs to the coyotes. Absolutely nothing. Except for what I've given them."

"Bones?"

"My love."

Their eyes meet briefly, then return to their watch over the field and the desert beyond. From a distance, these two unmoving figures perched upon the ridge are indistinguishable from the withered cacti dropping long shadows across the desert floor. Only their peculiar odor would alert a coyote to their presence.

"Looking out over the land like this..." Johannes pauses to clear his throat. "It reminds me of how I used to look out over the mountains. And I've had this feeling before, like everything I do is just a different way of doing things I used to do in my old life. Is that how it is for people who remember, too? Is it normal for everything you encounter to seem vaguely familiar, but strange and foreign at the same time?"

"Almost sounds like a case of reincarnation. Recalling life in a former vessel."

"Pa Sonny, he said something to me. He asked why I would meditate on the notion of water after what it did to me. But water is one of the few things that still makes sense to me. Since he said it, though, I can't help but wonder if I've got it all backwards."

"Water, yes. I can see that. There's something innate in that. A fear of something so necessary, something upon which our very existence hinges. Powerful enough to wipe us out, and absolutely without feeling. It's the dogs I'm curious about. We can figure it out, I'm sure. If you want to."

"You're the first person who gets it..." Johannes gazes at her in wonder. "Thinking about water, I feel a fear so powerful that it becomes awe, admiration, and subservience. But with Pa Sonny, it's like everything he says is carrying some concealed secret that I'm supposed to figure out. I don't understand him. Makes me wonder if I ever did."

"Do you know that you're the first person he's ever brought here?"

"But why?"

"He didn't do it just for you. It's for him, mostly. To justify his choices or to break the spell. I haven't decided which yet."

"Back in Creek's Ridge, everyone is trying to help me. To fix me. But I have this feeling that Sonny is the only one who can. And yet, there's this impulse to...push back. I can't help it. Maybe I really do want help. Or need it. But nothing anyone has done has helped so far—until now. Being here seems right. Maybe this is what I needed, not Creek's Ridge, and Sonny knew it all along."

"Give it time. And your full attention. Like the sunset. Really look at it."

"If he didn't bring me to help me, then why? What's the point?"

"He needs help, too. And he's just like you—there are few he will accept it from. He brought you so you could help him. Just like he has shoved you and so many others in the right direction, sometimes the wrong direction, he's hoping you can do the same for him now. Right or wrong, he just needs a push. All the same in the end."

"But help him with what?"

"Haven't you figured it out yet?"

After a moment's thought, Johannes pushes it out with a dearth of breath. "Fairy..."

"You're the only one who can."

"Is she the reason he left the Church?"

Ionia smirks and then looks toward the sunset again. "Blessings are not sent shimmering and obvious on the wings of angels. True blessings are disguised, requiring that you act. You must not only sift through the dirt but also embrace it. Consume it. What better way to requite your love than to heap it upon the impartial acts of the universe. No lover will ever meet you eye to eye. No soulmate can ever inform you of your past or correct the mistakes you're guilty of. But the universe can if you allow it. If you caress it with the hands of a lover. If you give yourself over to it instead of trying to force your will upon it. The universe will destroy you before it's coerced by you. That town you came from, Creek's Ridge, Emil Wood struggled his entire life searching for such a place. Instead of searching forever, he took it into his own hands and created the place himself. Put every bit of who he was into it, so others would be poised to discover what he had always sought."

"The founder? From what I've heard, it didn't go so smoothly."

"And yet the town is still there. Still drawing people like you to it."

"Where'd you pick up all this tough wisdom? That come from Fairy, too?"

"From the coyotes." She smiles and raises her index finger to his lips. "No more questions. You must witness it. Embrace it. Words cannot compare to this, the desert, at sunset."

Chapter 36

The Medicine Man

"The Chief will not see you," Tecumseh averted his eyes. "He says you have no claim to Changing Feathers' sacred position, and he cannot understand why you left the body behind."

"We were along the shores of Erie Lake," replied Lalawethika, "still many days ride from the Tippecanoe. The season's heat is intense. The corpse would have putrefied before I arrived."

"But he was our medicine man." Tecumseh eyed his younger brother suspiciously. "You had a horse. You should've ridden with all haste."

"And with haste would I have ridden were it not for the load I was obligated to transport. The useless, vulgar wares of white men, requested by our own tribesmen. I am no wagon driver. I have no oxen in my charge. That poor horse could barely pull the cart. The weight of a dead body would have snapped the animal's frail legs."

"Yet you failed to acquire the war chief's firewater," Tecumseh mused. "He and the Chief...they do not trust you. They believe you drank it yourself."

"And you? What do you believe? You know I have given up that disgraceful habit."

"I..." Tecumseh looked away, focusing, strategizing as always. He glanced out through the wigwam's flap, his gaze roaming in every direction except at his brother. He squatted down, rubbing his temples in deep concentration. "I do not know."

"It was Changing Feathers' dying wish," Lalawethika continued, "to be carried away by the waves of that majestic lake. He was not highly regarded by our people. He knew that and had no desire to burden them with the task of preparing his body, a body they did not care to behold even in life, nor of asking them to send off a soul they did not respect. He was a fiend, a pervert, and a drunkard, but a skilled medicine man nonetheless. He has done us a favor. Slipping away silently and gracefully was his final expression of gratitude, an acknowledgment of his guilt." Lalawethika suddenly jumped to his feet and approached, towering over Tecumseh. "Brother! Do you not believe me? Have you, too, lost all faith in me? If so, I might as well return to Erie Lake and join my mentor beneath the waves of that watery grave. I have received his guidance and instruction. I have acquired his knowledge. I alone have heard his deepest secrets. I shared his pain, and he has decreed that I replace him in this sacred post. Although his unexpected death is heartbreaking, it is so. I will not falter in my first steps as a Shawnee medicine man by ignoring the dying requests of my predecessor. Nor will I taint the memory of our noble father and mother with failure. I have spent my life in your shadow. Now is my time."

Tecumseh stood to match his brother's height. His expression was somber, fraught with apprehension, but his eyes conveyed brotherly compassion. He placed his hand on Lalawethika's shoulder and led him out of the wigwam.

"It is not me you must convince, brother, but the Chief," said Tecumseh. "Much of what you say is correct. For many years, there has been little faith in Changing Feathers as an influential elder. The wretch neglected his people and his duties. The Chief knows you were under the old man's wing, but he does not trust that the old man taught you to fly straight. Or to fly at all. Our medicine man was incompetent and unreliable. Besides, medicine men are not created overnight. It requires years and years, half of your life devoted to perfecting those skills."

They walked to the fire pit where Tecumseh's youngest daughter sat roasting a strip of skunk meat. The rest of Tecumseh's children were chasing each other in the field beside the longhouse along with several other village children, including one of Lalawethika's boys. They watched the children at play for a long time, listening to their joyful, innocent cries.

"As your brother, I advise against this path," Tecumseh spoke gravely. "However, it would please me beyond measure to see you pick yourself up from the filth and realign your life with the honorable history of our tribe and our family. I will speak once more with the Chief. Do you hear me? I hold sway with the Chief, and I will speak on your behalf. But the Chief will not be easily convinced. The Chief, like most Shawnees, has distanced himself from spiritual matters. And he despises you. But also, Noisemaker, remember this—if your desires are heard and you are permitted the honor of serving as our medicine man, you will be lifted beyond my reach. I will no longer be able to protect you."

"I do not need your protection," growled Lalawethika, glancing at the fire. Then, as he glared back at Tecumseh, he stepped forward. His bare feet crunched atop the burning coals and flames licked his thighs. Tecumseh's daughter shrieked, dropping her strip of meat as she backed away. Glowing embers jumped in every direction. Smoke billowed outward as Lalawethika emerged unharmed on the other side. The girl stared at her uncle and retreated until she was hidden behind her father, clinging to his muscular leg, concealing her fright.

Lalawethika faced his brother over the flames. "Go. Speak with your Chief. But I will not wait. It has already begun."

Nor could the village wait. A strain of white man's disease had been ravaging the Indiana Territory and rapidly growing into an epidemic. Out of desperation, the Chief sent for white doctors, but the messengers returned alone, bearing reports of villages across the countryside crippled by the illness. Every doctor for hundreds of miles was entrenched in the struggle. The white men's towns were stricken just as severely as the native settlements. Their medications ran low, their doctors' horses were run to exhaustion, and so they grew less willing to spare their services or supplies. No one came, and the red men's remedies were proving ineffective.

A few of the oldest Shawnee women took the tribe's fate into their own hands. These were fearless women, immune to fatigue, danger, loneliness, to death itself. Women who gathered herbs and roots from the forest in all weather, during all seasons, who worked ceaselessly behind their toothless grimaces, never a complaint escaping their lips.

These old women rubbed down every man, woman, and child in the village with various preventative concoctions and healing ointments. Amazingly, they avoided the contagion altogether. Though, in truth, most of the villagers would have found it more unbelievable had those particular women succumbed to the disease and deserted this earth.

Lalawethika worked alongside these women, witnessing firsthand how easily the infection spread and how quickly it could attack a healthy body, rendering one helpless. While the women administered their cures, he loomed behind them, adorned in one of Penagashea's ornate headpieces and giving off the airs of a leader, of a war chief deploying his men onto the battlefield. In truth, he was studying their every move, memorizing the names, ingredients, and applications for their unique remedies, each a delicate balance of herbs and roots far more complex than those that Penagashea had taught him.

The Chief fell ill, and Lalawethika himself soon displayed the telltale symptoms, though he admitted nothing to those who questioned his glassy eyes, croaking voice, and lack of strength. It laid him out for a few days, and most assumed he had disappeared into a jug of the firewater. However, on the fourth day, he struggled along a meandering path through the village, attending the sickbeds of his ailing tribesmen while seeking his own remedy from the old women in secret. He believed it to be the force of his will alone—his stubborn refusal to face defeat at the mercy of a white man's illness—which contributed to the resilience of his body. Against the advice of the old women, he would not be confined to rest at a time when he should be out showcasing his worth and value to the tribe. He took to wandering, staggering from wigwam to wigwam, poking his head into every shadowy hiding spot, sometimes standing delirious beneath the blistering sun for hours at a time. Throughout those feverish days, he was persecuted by the strangest visions he had ever known. He was said to have approached his confused tribesmen on numerous occasions, claiming sightings of Penagashea, of his mother, and of illusive representatives of the spirit realm.

By the time Lalawethika's health returned, the humid season had neared an end, and the disease's hold had begun to wane. It claimed more than thirty lives in their village alone and more than a hundred amongst nearby tribes. Every family felt the effects of loss—men and boys unable to hunt or work the fields, women unable to prepare clothing and food stores for a quickly approaching winter, children minding their siblings but falling behind in essential lessons. The Chief had come perilously close to death, and he finally reappeared in the foulest of moods, furious with his tribe's weakness and a quarter of the year lost to the scourge. After assessing the damage incurred, he laid full responsibility for the loss of life upon the acting medicine man, though he still refused to bestow that title upon Lalawethika.

Despite this, in the months following the epidemic, relations between the two brothers gradually improved, due in no small part to Lalawethika's strict abstinence from the white man's firewater. Tecumseh also noted his brother's newfound restraint over his tongue. Where once there had been only curses and lies, Lalawethika had begun to utter thoughtful, intelligent, almost profound insights. His skill with words had evolved beyond compare, best demonstrated by his ability to persuade and manipulate others. The elder sibling developed a previously unknown appreciation for his wayward baby brother, watching him develop into an active member of the tribe, if not yet respected, then at least looked upon with interest, as opposed to the revulsion of only a year prior. And while Tecumseh did wish to help Lalawethika take on a more productive role within the tribe, he also wanted to snuff out his brother's wild dreams of becoming a healer, a mystic, a medicine man.

One cool day in late autumn, Lalawethika compelled a boy of no more than eight years old to leap from the highest branch of a beech tree, over the water, and onto the protruding branch of a beech on the opposite bank. Several other boys were present, and they ran back to the village, proclaiming that they had witnessed a miracle. When the story reached Tecumseh, he sought out and scolded his brother for irresponsibly taking advantage of innocent young boys in such a reckless manner. Lalawethika listened to his brother's remonstrances without protest before calmly leading Tecumseh to the sight of the alleged jump. Standing upriver on the bank, he pointed out the two beech trees and asked Tecumseh whether he thought such a jump was possible. Viewing the immense distance that separated the two beeches, Tecumseh admitted, with much relief, that no, it was not possible. No sooner had he begun to apologize for believing the fantastic tales of children than Lalawethika interrupted him, offering to repeat the feat with any Shawnee that Tecumseh might choose. He promised to convince all disbelievers. Infuriated by his brother's presumptuousness, Tecumseh returned to the village and called upon one of his weakest, most inexperienced, and uncoordinated hunters, with whom he returned to the river. Lalawethika had not moved from his spot, and as soon as they arrived, he took the young hunter aside and began to spin his words masterfully around the youngster's head. Disbelief shifted to fear, fear to wariness, wariness to acceptance, and acceptance finally became duty. The elemental timidity that had always defined that hunter's fledgling capabilities had disappeared. And after he completed the jump—witnessed by Tecumseh himself—that timidity never returned. From that moment on, the hunter exhibited admirable courage and confidence. Not long after that, he was elevated to the rank of warrior. Tecumseh recognized that his brother's talent for persuasion was not to be understated. However, he also knew that it could be put to better use in bargaining with their red and white neighbors.

Lalawethika understood that he was slowly winning Tecumseh over. His influential brother's high opinion was indispensable—Tecumseh had earned immeasurable respect, not only within their tribe but throughout the entire Shawnee Nation and with all the various tribes spread across the region. But Tecumseh still harbored his doubts. Lalawethika's qualifications were questionable, and his unreliability was infamous. Tecumseh regularly chided Lalawethika for spending too many idle hours in contemplation, for fussing over herbs, roots, and his appearance. He constantly reminded Lalawethika that he had not yet been designated as Penagashea's replacement and that it would be better not to get his hopes up. Through these frequent denouncements, Lalawethika began to recognize Tecumseh's ulterior motives. At Tecumseh's insistence, Lalawethika had already conceded and spent several months acquainting himself with the French and English languages. But he had no desire to act as a tool for his brother's rise through the tribal hierarchy, a mere middleman for the tribe's dealings with white men. White men had destroyed his life once already, and Penagashea, wearing the guise of a savior, had very nearly led him down a disastrous path to ruin and madness. After miraculously prying his true-self from Penagashea's death grip, Lalawethika would no longer allow others to mold him or impart their influence. Only the Great Spirit would indoctrinate him. And soon, it would be he alone—Lalawethika, Shawnee medicine man and vessel of the Great Spirit—who would extend his reach and give rise to a new order throughout the wilds of this vast land.

Chapter 37

The Hunters

Walking amongst the trees, entangled, lost, on the verge of panic—that might as well have been a different day, the invented memories of an imagined life. Because now, following Ionia as she faultlessly winds her way through the darkness, he has the feeling he's trailing a butterfly through spacious caverns that will lead to the center of the earth, the warmth and complete shelter of which might offer some respite, might cradle and nurture him, allowing him to accept and embrace somnolence as it returns with the night.

They emerge on the far side of the trees to a sky being gradually pricked by stars. Ionia lowers herself down, and a confused couple of seconds pass as Johannes wonders how she's floating. Ionia pats the bench of a picnic table shrouded in branches and shadow. Johannes takes up beside her. The night is windless, but the air has cooled, and they can feel each other shiver every now and again.

Stars continue to dot the sky, simultaneously adding light and intensifying the darkness, bringing texture to the featureless face of dusk. But only after the final beauty mark has settled into its designated position does Johannes notice an unsettling lack of depth. Layers upon layers missing and a sickly pallor strewn all across it, the yellow-gray of nausea and infirmity originating over the city skyline to the north. By shutting his eyes, he can fill in gaps between the brightest stars to flesh out a more populated and familiar sky, one that almost feels like home—the same sky he observed every clear night, stretched out beside the mountain stream or upon the rocks at the peak, the comfort of always knowing exactly how Orion's arrow would fly.

"I've never looked at the night sky in Creek's Ridge." Neither of them has said a word since watching that breathtaking sunset, so his voice, though soft, startles them both. "I may have looked, but I've never really seen it."

"Why not?"

"Because...I'm always looking at the ground, I guess."

She tilts her head to scan above, then raises her hand to trace a line with her index finger. "There. Do they have anything to do with it?"

Johannes leans into her shoulder to stare along her outstretched arm. He immediately recognizes the constellation. "Asterion and Chara," he whispers. "The herdsman's hounds. You know the stars?"

"Mmm... Isn't it funny? How the things that hold us together are often so far away? So fragmentary?"

"Your coyotes?"

"Sonny, too. He's like a ghost, for Fairy and me both. And then there's the life I've never known, not as my own..."

"This seems like a pleasant enough life."

"Pleasant, sure. It is. With what we do, it's even thrilling at times. But...there must be more."

"It's not the herdsman's hounds that keep my head down. They were my friends. And you said it, they did, they held me together. But in Creek's Ridge, we're looking for something. Digging."

"For what?"

"A skeleton."

"A horse?"

"How did you know that? Everyone assumes we're looking for the founders or for burials from the Native American raids. Relics from those days."

"Just a hunch," she says. "Sonny, he has...never mind. Maybe the hounds can help. If you let them."

"The digging was only meant as a time filler. A way to dust off the past and await whatever's next. I guess I never noticed how completely the project has taken over. It's good that Pa Sonny dragged me away from that, if only for a few days. It might give me some perspective. I wonder what you would think if you actually saw it...our mounds and pits, hours and hours of dirt removed, nothing but a couple of lifeless bones to show for it."

"Who are you digging with?" she asks. "Not Sonny..."

"No. A friend. Grant. My...host."

Ionia glances at him, searches the shadows obscuring his face.

"You don't know him, too, do you?" says Johannes.

"Never met him," she shakes her head. "But like I said, Fairy and

Sonny talk a lot. I guess I know him just as well as I knew you before today. Suddenly, I feel like I know you a lot better than I did a moment ago."

"Grant...he's more like a brother. He's all I have, really. There's no one else. Pa Sonny...I haven't figured out what he is to me yet."

"When I first saw you this afternoon, I assumed you were a soldier. Or a new driver."

"Driver? For Sonny?"

"No, for us," Ionia says as she looks toward the stars again. "Do you want to know what I do when Fairy sets me up on dates? With the young officers from the base? I go along with it. I let them take me out. It's always into the city. Downtown for an expensive but mediocre dinner. I make nice and listen to them talk all night long about their mommas and papas and the exotically wholesome towns they reigned over with their buddies during high school. And if they've been stationed overseas, then they're sure to inform me of what a big, dangerous world it is out there and how fortunate I am to be an American, safe behind our impenetrable borders, with big, brave soldiers like them perpetually watching over me. Then, when the food and wine are gone, when they've finally run out of things to brag about, that's when I ask them to take me to the desert. By the time we get there, they might as well already have their pants down around their ankles, so certain are they that I'm just dying to blow them or ride them in the back seat like we're fucking sixteen. But instead, I get out of the car, lie down on the hood, and tell them about the constellations. Star names, mythology, and history. Planetary alignments. Even navigational techniques, which they should know about as soldiers. But they don't. A sort of game I like to play to see how long they can stand to listen. And if they try to feel me up while I'm talking, it's game over. On occasion, they impress me by paying attention or at least feigning an interest. Other times, they fall asleep. Then, I drive them back to the base and drop them off at the front gate so their superiors think they're drunk."

"And Fairy sets you up with them?"

"She gets flustered when I come home the same night," Ionia laughs. "She even warns them beforehand, *'Don't let her take you out to the desert.'* But they've all got their dicks in their hands, so it only fuels the fire, and she knows it. She knows my game, and I think she likes to play just as much as I do. She's the matron of that base, been working over there twenty years now, ever since we came here. She flirts with them constantly, and they eat it up. She dishes out her advice, and they eat that up, too."

"What? She's a cook?"

"No," Ionia's laugh cracks through the night's silence. "The handywoman. Imagine that. A small city's worth of supposedly hardened men, and they need her to fix their plumbing, repair their roofs, patch up their potholes."

"So she...what? It's some kind of competition? A wager?"

"She's not trying to marry me off to some military lackey. But, let me see if I can put it in her words—*'Ionia, dear,'*" she sings in a perfect, somewhat cleaner replication of Fairy's voice, *"'you must explore your body to release your soul and discover your passions. You cannot know the things that will truly move you in this life until you know the limits of your body, inside and out. The soul resides amidst waves of ecstasy.'* How was that?"

"Then...it's just for sex?"

"Most things in life begin and end with sex, don't they? We're not the local cattle ranch. It's nothing like that. Just the pleasures of life. Always the pleasures..."

"Cattle ranch?"

"You know, men slip between the cracks to kill some time, loosen up in the heat, then slip out and disappear before morning, leaving their lunch money behind. She knows more about every officer and new recruit than the generals they serve. And she also knows that my romantic options are limited way out here on the edge of nowhere. Before she even considers setting me up, she puts them through a more rigorous screening than they go through at boot camp. But you're not wrong—sex and the body have always been paramount for Fairy. She and Sonny both, as you heard. Age hasn't slowed them down, them and their pleasures."

"Pa Sonny and pleasure...hard to imagine..."

"I think what she wants is for me to discover those secrets, too. To be self-reliant. To be able to sniff out and take hold of the things I want or need, anything, whether it's sexual gratification or self-defense. A roof over my head or spiritual enlightenment. But Fairy is still mentally and emotionally a young woman, and she will be eternally. All that she observes attains the blinding gloss of youth. Surely, she assumes you are stranded in infancy, just like she does with me. But, really, that's a compliment. It means she likes you. I appreciate what she does for me, I do. She just wants me to enjoy life like she has. The thing is, the deeper I get, the more I realize that all of this is more her idea of the pleasures than it is mine. But I think that's what she's trying to show me. Anyhow—*Welcome ta Texas, hun. Ya wanna ride?*"

"Infancy..." Johannes reflects, scouring the sky, watching as Boötes and his dogs patiently drive the great oxen. "She might not be too far off. Ever since the landslide, I've been plagued by emptiness, an unwillingness to attend to life because this life has already abandoned me, left me stranded. Thrown me from my paradise to be devoured by the demands and wills of others. I survive only by *friends* stuffing me full of what they believe I lack. Breastfed by a dozen different mothers of questionable sterility."

"All people need guidance at times. Young and old. Oblivious and wise. Not everyone accepts the guiding hand, and some grab hold of hands that are not of man. But any person is lost without something to guide them. The truly unfortunate are those who grasp too fiercely, those who forget that it's only a guiding hand and that even guidance can sometimes lead us astray. Fairy has taught me a lot. She's shown me incredible things that I couldn't have learned with anyone else. I'm lucky and grateful to have had her in my life, but I sense it's coming time to sever myself from her guidance. Cut the kite string and watch it fly."

"And eventually crash."

"The most exciting part. Isn't that what everyone secretly wishes for?"

A sudden rustling of leaves startles Johannes, but Ionia doesn't stir even when a bulbous shadowy form approaches from within the trees.

"Is she teaching you all her hard-earned life lessons, Johannes?" Fairy's soothing voice calms Johannes instantly. She and Pa Sonny step out from the shadows, their arms wrapped around each other and their steps in perfect sync.

"She does have a unique outlook," Johannes breathes deeply. "Might be better off in a circus or something."

"I've been telling them that for years," groans Pa Sonny. "She'd make a marvelous lion tamer."

"Rather be the lion..." says Ionia.

"Nope, that'd never work," Pa Sonny objects. "They could never tame you. You'd end up mauling the lot of them. Think of the poor children."

"Oh!" chimes Fairy. "What a horrendous circus."

"That's the point," says Ionia. "Scare the wits out of the kiddies and scar them with an experience they'll never forget. Besides, what scars them must certainly scar me, too."

"I was thinking more like a fortune teller," says Johannes. "Or a healer."

"Oh, for God's sake," huffs Pa Sonny. "Loosen up already. Look at where we are." He disengages from Fairy's side. As he steps around the picnic table, he is focused on the starry above, his shoulders bouncing in a sort of continuous shrug. "Edge of the country. The known world.

Haven't you realized yet? That this trip is for the pleasures and nothing else?"

"The pleasures, again..."

"What? You know, idle leisure? The emptying of the self? Unburden your mind. Give everything over in offering to the desert. The sand... the stars..."

"But I was...I am..."

"Wound too damn tight, that's what you are."

The four of them seem to be floating, drifting nearer and farther from one another with the regularity of breaths. The stars drop down to meet them halfway, mingling, adding populace to this small gathering of what? Of strangers? In truth, they're no more like strangers than the blanket of stars above, a constant that has always been a part of Johannes's life, unshakeable and dependable, honest, true to themselves, pregnant with stories and brimming with answers, but as tight-lipped as the most devoted voyeur. Not unlike stumbling upon Grant all those months ago, amidst a confusion of body odors, aches and pains, utter exhaustion and half-recognition, but then realizing with all the certainty of instinct—or perhaps Descartes' pineal gland—that Grant Cagniss, remembered or not, is the most stable and persistent element of Johannes's fragmented world. On hazy nights, when the herdsman's hounds lose their sight in the fog, Boötes is left alone to keep the oxen on task. But his loyal hounds never fail to return home.

"I would see that circus," says Johannes.

"You've already seen it." Pa Sonny stops spinning and plops down on the opposite bench. "They've dismantled the tent and moved along to the next town, my friend. No use returning to the site to sweep up the crumbs. Move on yourself. Got to move on."

Fairy sits down beside Pa Sonny. Her mirthful tittering accompanies the creaks and squeaks of the wood shifting beneath their combined weight. "He's told us about what happened to you, Johannes. A terrible thing. I stay out of the mountains."

"She hasn't left this desert since we came here," says Ionia.

"I've experienced the world as much as I need to," says Fairy. "I've been simply everywhere."

"But you don't go anywhere anymore," says Ionia. "And that has affected me."

"Aye," affirms Pa Sonny.

"Soon, child. Soon. Is our desert monasticism no longer good enough? We have our work, don't we? Noble, important. Who else is going to do it? But, I suppose the world calls still. Never stops, does it?"

"Your work on the base?" asks Johannes.

"Humanitarian dirty work," answers Fairy.

"Coyote Samaritanism," huffs Pa Sonny.

"Ionia told me you're the handywoman," says Johannes, straining to see Fairy's face. "I don't understand."

"No, of course you don't," says Fairy. "But no bother. It's just where I've ended up. One place leads to another. I know what you go through, Johannes, that wandering life, never settled, never at ease. There's charm in it, certainly. Stimulation. A lot of unpleasantness along the way, sure...but plenty of blessings, too."

"Same as your cooking," mutters Pa Sonny, drawing a smart smack from Fairy.

"The perfect balance," she continues. "That's how I knew it was right and proper to settle down. There is an end to it, you know. Whether you're looking for it or not, there is. Always."

"There's a man back in Creek's Ridge who's said something similar," says Johannes.

"Creek's Ridge..." groans Pa Sonny. "The whole of that damned town has settled down, but none of them knows why. Dust in an abandoned house."

"You and me included," says Johannes. "But I was talking about Ernest."

"Worst offender of them all," says Pa Sonny. "That son of a bitch has ruined more lives than just his own for his stupidity."

"And what's so wrong with this Ernest?" asks Fairy.

"Anybody can sling beer and whisky and peanuts," Pa Sonny grumbles.

"Ernest was beaten down—" says Johannes.

"By an abstraction—" Pa Sonny interrupts.

"Defeated by his name—"

"Harvested by prowlers—"

"Rejected by his dreams—"

"A slave on the run—"

"Victim to all the unwanted experience that his name served him, in all the places he visited—"

"A man needs to own up to what he is—"

"In the end, I think it's only insecurity," Johannes finishes. "He's not comfortable in his own skin."

"Just another old fool," Pa Sonny moans violently, "except he's the finest damned pianist alive."

"We all fault and misstep on our way," Fairy's voice dances softly around them, bells struck by the wind alone. "You two certainly have, with your names, your homes, among other blunders. It's not exactly sporting to judge his pain as you would your own. Just look at where you've both wound up, along with this Ernest the pianist. A place named by misfortune herself. More than a century has passed, and the folks who built it are still misunderstood, their motives misconstrued. But by us no more than by themselves. Until the day he died, Tenskwatawa always claimed that he had no memory of his former name, no recollection of a former life. Not unlike you, Johannes. And the gallant founder himself, never fond of his adopted name, forced upon him, he believed, by circumstance, necessity, yet he abided by it anyway, for thirty-some-odd years. Who, the false prophet indeed? And when did he shed this name he had supposedly despised? When did his will grow strong enough to embrace who he believed himself to be? Only after his wife died. Mother of their daughter, the blessed Saint of Creek's Ridge."

"Tell them how she died," chuckles Pa Sonny.

"Oh, Ionia knows..." whispers Fairy.

"A thousand times over..." confirms Ionia.

"Our own name-disoriented friend here, it seems, may not. Lost, is he?"

"How did she die?" Johannes takes the bait.

"Official town records list the cause as consumption. A bad case of tuberculosis. Although, since there were few other cases in or around Creek's Ridge at that time, this claim is suspect. The truth was not as easy to accept. A shotgun. One shot to the stomach and one to the chest as she marched down Main Street, raving and foaming at the mouth, so they say. Rabies, you see. A danger to others. Especially to her young, innocent daughter, who was there, running towards her mother when the fatal shots were fired."

"Tell him who..."

"I love this story, your sing-song voice..."

"By who?"

"Why, her loving husband, of course. Who else? Who else would dare to shoot the wife of the great founder, the mother of the town's daughter, a Cherokee princess with deep connections to all the tribes, most of all to her own people. But she was ill, it is told. Bitten by a coyote while trying to save a fawn. Infected with that horrible disease, a slowly encroaching madness. She had to be put down like a disloyal mutt. Her husband would not have had the wherewithal, but he saw their daughter running towards her. At that moment, he was gifted the strength by God's own hand, or so he claimed. Then he hung up his name, became Emedio del Bosque once again, and dedicated what time he had left to something else he had left behind, forgotten about."

"What?" asks Johannes. "His name?"

"Tell him," says Pa Sonny, "to what the man dedicated his remaining years..."

"To God. Or so it is said." Fairy sighs. "But only one thing is certain. He was never the same after that. Who would be?"

"But was it God that brought this change? Or killing his own wife?" Pa Sonny, feigning concern.

"Or was it the shame of his name?" wonders Johannes.

"I like how this one thinks," Fairy nudges Pa Sonny. "All of the above, I'd wager. And a whole lot more besides..."

"And who remembers his wife's name?" adds Pa Sonny.

"No one...not a soul..."

"There's not so much weight in a name," says Ionia.

"Oh, sweetie, them boys over there," Fairy half-turns and gestures toward the base. Her voice has dropped a register and become deeper, more somber and serious. "They all hear about you. Eventually, they hear. Word of mouth. Military gossip, you know, can be just as bad as church widows. And when they do, they come looking for me, strutting their feathers, trying to find their angle, looking for my approval. The first thing they ask is always the same. Your name, child. I can read them boys better than a gas gauge. If they've got nothing good to offer, or even if they simply ain't your type, then I tell them your name is Bertie. Or Griselda. Turns their rigid peckers soft real quick. That's all they need to hear and they've already forgotten all about you. You're sitting here with three people who've struggled long and hard for their names, dear. Don't take yours for granted." Fairy breathes a heavy sigh, more of a collective moan for the four of them. "Perhaps *John* here will tell you about it someday."

Johannes juts upright, jerked unexpectedly into wakefulness. He shifts around in discomfort.

"John?" says Ionia.

The whole picnic table shakes under Pa Sonny's low, slow chuckle. The chirps of crickets, the calls of toads, the rustle of grass and leaves—all swell and recede in the silence. Their bodies shift imperceptibly on the creaky wood while contented yawns and sighs complete the night calm. No cars drive the nearby lonely road, but headlights occasionally crawl along beyond the military fence. Muffled slams of car doors and sporadic shouts carry over from the base. After a while, the moon appears, peeking around the tree line and granting them to observe each other's faces. But this warm blanket of idle tranquility withdraws abruptly, commanded into hiding, every audible note driven away—by the calls of coyotes.

Howls take possession of the night, three distinct cries in quick succession, overlapping before they blend into one penetrating wail that slices the darkness into individual seconds. This is not the sorrowful, lonesome whine of thoughtless nights on the edge of nowhere, drifting over the landscape and playing off the moonlight like a fog. No, this is a call to arms, the biting urgency of survival and domination as proclaimed by the bloodthirsty, the vengeful. One by one, the howls drop off, the last one fading gradually, incompletely, leaving a maddening silence that Johannes has heard once before and still hears in dreams, an absence preparing for something dread and unseen. Johannes and the others are no longer floating in the night. They are suspended over it by a single thin ligament...

"The danger is not ours," sings Fairy.

"It's absolutely ours," says Pa Sonny. "Listen, they are near. They surround our every living breath."

"Oh, let's go to them," Ionia's tone sounds very much like a young girl's. "They're calling to us. Please, can't we go and watch? We could... join them..."

Dizziness lifts Johannes to his feet, dizziness that might be the lucidity of dreams or the trailing away of consciousness, pursued by fear into a blooming paradise or a barren hell. Same as during the landslide, Johannes, as he knows himself, is buried away, hidden and wrapped amongst folds of perception, sheltered from the terrifying realities of the physical world. The sound of attack reaches them as though it has always been underway. The coyotes mount their chase through bushes and low-lying desert grass, barking and snarling like mad, communicating strategy in their frenzied language—the whole band of thirteen, it sounds like—converging, bloodthirsty, manic. The intensity rises as they approach and pass near the house, circling round and round their prey to corner it, Boötes and his hounds and the German shepherds come fiercely to life right here in this Texan desolation. Ionia has risen from her seat, stretching to see what she can see, clutching at Johannes's shoulder, squeezing when she thinks she has seen a blur of silhouettes. When they pin their prey, she trembles, from pride or from fear, or only a chill in the air, and she lowers herself down again as the noise grows horrific...

"Bertie, sweetie, you did leave Emil in the house, I pray?"

"Jesus-on-the-cross, is that what you two nuts named that goat? Emil?"

"Emil Capricornus is safe and sound. But coyotes, they always find a way..."

"Capricornus? The sea goat of the south?"

Even the moon, unwilling to bear witness to the massacre, has taken refuge behind the clouds. As Johannes squirms, sweat drips down his temple, his back. His limbs shiver, but not from the cold. The evening chill has been sucked out of the air, replaced by the moist warmth of their collective determined breaths. He searches for signs of unease or restlessness from the others, but their expressions are hidden as their faces turn toward the field—this, their television screen—a happy little family huddled together and anticipating the appearance of this week's monster. Judas and Jesus and Josef Mengele, Cannon, Queen Maj, the herdsman's hounds, the landslide itself—they're all here, huffing, wheezing, teeth snapping, jaws taut like compressed springs, the hunters' perimeter drawing inward, tightening concentrically around their prey...

"This is the world's song."

"This, the death and the birth."

"One day soon, I shall join them when they cry. For sorrow and for joy."

"Can't you make it stop...?"

Johannes senses movement at his side before anything has touched him. A prolonged and cautious presence moving closer, an open jaw ready to clamp down on unprotected flesh, dig in and tear out the bones, clean them of meat and discard them in a pile, forgotten and then fawned over later, the memory of a lean, succulent meal, leaving only a skeleton rearranged and imbued with reflective importance, fantasies of the past.

But it's only a hand. Her hand—soft, steady, and reassuring. Ionia pets his arm, gently clasps his wrist, and eases him back down protectively by her side.

Her fingers seek his, graze and caress them, interlacing as their two hands become one. She squeezes and releases, communicating that she understands his pain, that she wishes to ease his fear, to share it. Vicious noises fade into obscurity as piano notes return, the string section not far behind, wafting delicately in upon a breeze and washing over his flesh, bones safeguarded, Rachmaninoff and his Scrap, the ease and calm of a time when all was set in order. Someone hums in harmony, it must be Fairy. He squeezes Ionia's hand, absorbs her warmth, and understands, without thinking it, that underneath her flesh, too, there are bones. The melody continues with its vocal accompaniment, but when he looks up, Fairy and Pa Sonny have gone. Only Ionia's skin, soft and dampened with sweat from his grasp, and all he sees are bones dancing and bouncing and clinking about before his eyes, rearranging into unrecognizable configurations, not woman, not human. However, when he turns to look at her, he recognizes just that, an outline, a silhouette.

Of human, of woman. Unlocking his hand from hers, he lifts it to graze her cheek, not gentle, not rough...

The shape of your cheekbone is enough, it confirms that your bones are truly there, close beside my own, just below this surface of flesh. Together, we placed the bones from dinner into the pit, for the coyotes, Jesus does not lead, but Judas, while Limping Lady's bones remain unaccountably scattered, and Grant is all alone, waiting for me to return, again, so we can finish digging her up, if only we can recover the trail. Patterns emerge even in disorder—repetitions, similarities, delineations, duplicates, kindred spirits, guides, persecutors, and saviors alike —as long as one knows how to look, how to really see. But one cannot learn to see through emptiness, the opposite of chaos, the abrupt expulsion of all form and shape and light, like Caryn's eyes. Her hair, always worn down, swings and plays about her cheeks to conceal her eyes, the emptiness therein. I will return to Creek's Ridge, I must, and Caryn will still be there with her beauty, her perfect body, her playful yet serious mind, and I cannot deny a desire for her, though access is barred, it is currently out there being devoured by the coyotes. I can never lay my hands on her, I can never embrace her because of those eyes, hidden yet intimately familiar, treacherous. Reaching out to them will only cause them to collapse like dust, dissipate like smoke. Or perhaps me, myself, disappeared again. If Caryn finds the strength that Pa Sonny and Grant and everyone else lacks, then she will leave Creek's Ridge. And so will I, someday, won't I? I must. Then why not just remain here? Edge of the country, of the known world. A border with implications, severity, and consequences. No trick of the mind, this, no mental construction, only hard truths. With you and Fairy and the Twelve Disciples under Judas, leader, out there in the desert, it could be so much simpler to disappear, no worries of water or land crashing down from above, no one to witness me go, no one else to impose their will or request my help, no one to harm but myself. So why bother to return? What calls me there? What debts owed? To whom? And for what? Why not? Why not here and now? Your thumb is pulsing, I'm squeezing too hard, but still, I won't ease off. I can't. Extraordinary—to handle bones and also apprehend the flow of blood as it courses its channels and tributaries. Pa Sonny and Fairy have gone, dragged their aged, idle, euphoric bodies back into the house to fuck whenever Pa Sonny is around, always maybe for the last time, and when he's away, Fairy screws sergeants and colonels and generals because the pleasures are forever and her voice is a music that no one can resist, while Ernest tickles mentally upon the ivories but refuses to sit still on his bench. Why the hell doesn't Pa Sonny stay here? Like the great horned owl with its jaundiced eyes relaying that my home, my shack, my entire existence has gone rushing downstream even as the bird itself announces its own unshakable permanence, its strength and will to endure. No different was Knecht, tall and thick and rooted firmly to its home through a thousand such storms, that tremendous command over Being, certainty in the face of bedlam, the stubbornness to never abandon its rightful place in the world. The sea captain going down with his vessel. The loyal mutt starving itself as it finishes off its days beside its master's grave. Boötes and his hounds, on their eternal chase, never betraying their fatigue or their mission to keep the world balanced upon its axis. Orion's lust, the rigid shaft of his pointed arrow aimed straight but missing target after target, yet still the hunter stalks his prey, his one true love. The sun and moon show up every day, exactly when and where they're meant to. And what of Inez? Once upon a time, Inez convinced Grant to relocate to a tropical paradise, and nearly me, too, where she identified a part of herself that had always been missing or had perhaps been taken hostage by Grant when they married, just as Grant took Limping Lady hostage upon arrival in Creek's Ridge, though now, in death, she holds him accountable, a debt extending beyond the borders segregating life from death, a burden he cannot toss away, a hostage to his own actions, to his memories, just as much as I am to my forgetting. But Inez knew to stay put, to become what she had to be. She was Grant's storm, hardly different from my landslide. And someone has done something unforgivable, but Grant cannot let go, and therefore neither can I, preferring instead to dig up what's been buried. Creek's Ridge itself is calling me back. Can you hear it, too? The prophecies of prophets, the howling of America's Natives, the laments of the people, the silence of the Saint. Limping Lady's lifeless form begs respect, honor, cohesion—the freedom to gallop Elysian fields unbound and sacrosanct. Forgiveness—that must be what we seek. All of us. Or is it a form of revenge? Merely a return to the way things were? Is there a difference? The debts are all the same. To Grant, for an unanswerable breach of faith. To the faces in the mirrors, for penance, reconciliation with myself. Lani had been like a voice from the past, but the wrong past. No matter what drew me to Lani, I did not touch her. I knew that she was not really the person I sought, only a distraction, a detour through the woods serving little purpose other than to kill time, to vary the scenery, to glimpse the unseeable, if only for a moment—all valid endeavors, when time is plentiful. Though she had touched me, reaching out from an incomprehensible divide, the abnormal intensity of our connection creating that divide, she trusted me, confided in me, and when the allure of sin rose like the beckoning, shapely forms teased by the heart of a fire, I wanted her only because she was Grant's, same as Lil, the Limping Lady, and the bird tattooed in the leaves. But that massive collection of bones Lani discovered near the creek—are those even horse bones? We hoped they were and assumed it on pretense, but the bones from the creek do not correlate with the other bones we have found. So what have we done? According to some, my sacred grove along the creek is, in actuality, a mass grave. But for who? What history have we desecrated? What past have we trudged into and destroyed? And then Grant and Lani, in the bedroom, sounding just like the coyotes sounded only seconds ago. Or was it minutes? Hours ago? Is there a difference? Is there? The beautiful, reassuring piano tones have returned to steal away the coyotes' voices. A scrap of meat, of satiation, of lustful appetites served. And Ionia, you have stolen my fear, sent me careening into the past, the future. Is there a difference? You are fastened to Fairy just as I am garrisoned with Grant. We owe eternally, we will never live down life's debts. Lani had pleaded with me to go with her to Chicago. Home, apparently. Offered me the opportunity, an easy out, to escape Creek's Ridge when it still might have been an option, all that before helping me dig up the bones in the creek bed. All these debts, adding up. Bones feel different when held through the snug warmth of flesh, blood pumping laboriously beneath, between, an equal part of the arrangement. Maybe that's it? The two of us could leave, bail on our debts and start from scratch—the desert, perhaps. Seven and some years in my shack and a blur of weeks on the earthen floor. Where are father, mother, sister? Where is the home I left behind? Even if I don't belong there, couldn't I at least start the process afresh? From scratch? Using the Scrap that I have left? For Christians, it's called rebirth. Reborn in Christ, one prospers. Or perhaps in following Judas, leader. Is there a difference? But for me, it is only a repetition, a repetition. I almost died in those final weeks, but I would have had to see the act through myself, the force of my own hands offering myself to the river, ensuring it, ensuring an end, a repetition. At least now I have what is possibly a father figure in Pa Sonny. And I always have Grant, a brother, and the comfort of Grant's floor, a repetition. But not tonight—why am I here? How have I strayed so far to the outskirts? Edge of the country, of the known world, an unfamiliar place, a strange floor, strange faces somehow just so. No mountains in sight, but instead a river raging nearby. Is it a protection or a threat? Is there a difference? And outside, just beyond the door, coyotes lie in wait, preparing to claim the bones as their own. Is there any chance at all that we make it out alive...

It's okay, you're safe, just stay there, stay on the floor, yes, to sleep, it's okay, okay, to rest, to dream, stay, don't go wandering, out there, not out there, not now, not tonight, no, not tonight, the Disciples are active, love and a curse, you've nothing to fear, you've nothing but just to rest, to sleep, to stay, are you sure, just here, on the floor, but you can, I'll be here when you wake, don't go out, not out there, don't go outside, not tonight, just stay there, sleep, sleep now, remain, with us, you're safe...

Chapter 38

The Tide

March 13, 1818
St. Johns River, La Florida

THE TRIBE HAS BEEN BLESSED WITH A SENSE OF RELIEF. NOT BECAUSE we have avoided war, as we have repeatedly prayed for, but rather because the waiting has finally come to an end.

We received word this morning that three days ago, some three thousand American troops crossed into Spanish territory. Nearly a third of them are said to be Georgian Creeks allied to General Jackson. They were headed toward Tallahassee, the center of Seminole activity in West Florida. Women and children have fled the area while the warriors prepare to defend their villages.

Roberto has numerous friends and associates in West Florida. Only with careful reasoning did the Father and I convince him to remain here with us and await news of further developments. As a wanted man known to be a primary weapons supplier to the Seminoles, he must refrain from brash decisions and leave displays of bravado on the front lines to men less recognizable than himself—to this, he eyed me curiously, uncomfortably.

He has conceded to our pleas for the time being, but it will not be long before his emotions overrule our logic.

In the meantime, Roberto continues to work toward strengthening our village's defenses. He has also been making arrangements for the Father's safe removal to the Bahamas or some other remote island, a paradise where he might live out his final days basking in the sunlight with a refreshing sea breeze instead of entwined amongst this fickle bloodletting in the world of men. Still, the Father remains firmly opposed to abandoning his people.

March 19, 1818
St. Johns River, La Florida

I remember spending the evening at the beach on the day following El Soldado Agraciado's landfall at San Agustín. I had already agreed to accompany Father Jimenez inland, but my heart required a moment of solitude. I was alone, overwhelmed by new memories that hardly seemed my own, and fretful of the unrecognizable shape the future was taking. Dolphins played in the sea as the sky slipped beneath its heavy blanket. The dolphins swam off, and I began to laugh as I thought about the quantity of water separating me from Spain. From home. The ocean's sheer size only becomes more incomprehensible after one has placed his life in its mercy, and the very act of remembering only exaggerates that unreality. Such memories play out like bad stage performances, a contradiction of reality and imagination in which actors slip in and out of character, the audience wanders onto the stage at will, stagehands are sprawled about in full view, smoking their pipes and drinking from wineskins. Lying there in the sand, I drifted off to the lapping of the surf, mesmerized by the haunting spectacle of moonlight glinting off the crests of the waves. And it was a deep sleep, from which I woke coughing and spluttering as the sand shifted beneath my body, slowly dragging me into the watery darkness.

The tide had come up, and I never noticed until saltwater and sea foam filled my mouth. It was at that moment that I first considered the possibility that I might never return to Spain. The tides of life are constantly at work. They never stop. And although they may be imperceptible, their influence is immense.

Four days ago, Father Jimenez collapsed while delivering his morning sermon. Roberto and I carried him back to his hut, with Long Grass and Chief Kinheja trailing close behind. An endless hour passed before the Father regained consciousness. He stared up at us, startled as though we were specters. Long Grass knelt beside the bed, clasping the Father's hand. They spoke in whispers for a long time. When the medicine man stood, he turned to us and announced that death would claim Father Jimenez before sunset that same day, and if anyone had peace to make with the man, they should do so quickly.

The entire tribe stood breathless outside the Father's hut. Roberto and the Chief made brief business of their eternal farewells and then went out to comfort and disperse the tribespeople. Long Grass had been chanting softly all the while, and he continued to do so when I took my place beside the Father.

I gave him water. At his request, I filled his pipe with a special blend of weeds that he and Long Grass often distributed to ease the pain of the ailing. But I possessed no words. I had lost the ability for language. After a few pulls from his pipe, the Father asked whether I intended to administer his last rites.

"I cannot," I told him. "I do not know how...it is not proper...I am no priest."

"You shall learn now," he muttered breathlessly. "You are ready."

I found the vial of oil in his trunk. It was already blessed, of course, but he guided me through the blessing and explained how I was to anoint him. I followed his instructions precisely and was careful to speak in a voice that hid my grief. For his penance, he began by commending the admirable way I handled all matters of the Church. He knew of the doubts I harbored—in my faith, in myself, in the ethics of carrying out God's work without having been ordained, in the injustices of this world—and he said that such misgivings are necessary for the pursuits of a healthy spiritual existence. There must be friction to bring about fire, he added. And then he made his confession.

When he was a young priest in North Africa, he fell in love with the daughter of a wealthy merchant from a neighboring village. His love for her was powerful, outdone only by the intensity of his internal struggle after he learned that she shared his feelings. But the battle was short-lived, for when he next set eyes on her, he did not see her beauty, grace, and kindness—he saw God. And when he looked away from her, expecting to see only the desolate hell of the desert, he saw God there, too, and he understood that God was of-the-earth and also of-the-people-of-the-earth, and that the human love he felt, a love that renders two individuals inseparable from one another, this was God's intention. It was not a test meant to torture his loyal servants—this was God's Love, God's manifest desire. At that moment, the Father apprehended that the test of humankind is to attend to our natural passions honestly and honorably, not to suppress them. Man must respect the gifts of the earth by exploring and embracing them, not by building temples or shuttering ourselves within walls. From that moment on, he decided he would no longer preach and convert. Instead, he would marry and procreate. He would continue to love and help all people, for that was right and proper—it was his calling, his life's dedication. But it was his love for that woman—his future wife and their future children—that would elevate him to the saintly heights he had always labored towards. And so, he retracted his clerical vows. But the girl's family were devout Muslims. Her father distrusted Father Jimenez and the entire network of European missionaries, and now he also distrusted his daughter. Even if Father Jimenez had converted to Islam, the merchant would not have allowed the union. So Father Jimenez and the girl ran off together. They survived the desert and arrived in Tangier, where they remained for several happy weeks until the merchant's men tracked them down. Friends helped them to escape, securing their secretive passage through Gibraltar. They entered Spain safely, but the strain of the long journey had taken its toll on the girl. Having been pursued across half the Sahara by her own father over a transgression for which he would not have hesitated to execute the both of them, she lapsed into an unspecified illness that took her swiftly and quietly as Father Jimenez held her one final time amidst the hills of Andalucía.

He and the girl never married. Since they were on the run for the full scope of their courtship, they never had the chance. But they had slept together every night of their flight, embracing beneath the stars or hidden in back rooms at the homes of considerate strangers who were envious of their bold love. Only the girl and God had borne witness to the renunciation of his vows. Therefore, from the moment of her death, it became a secret between him and God alone.

Upon return to his home in Valencia, he told his superiors only that he had been chased from his post by a murderous merchant. However, the details of the escapade did not concern them because they had recently received news that the colony of La Florida had been released from British control and returned to Spain. Both the monarchy and the Church were eager to saturate the peninsula with emissaries who would implement amongst the Natives a deep and thorough love for Christ, a hallowed reverence for the Virgin Mother, and loyalty to the Spanish King. God's message was clear. Father Jimenez allowed the tides of life to take him where they would. He was aboard the next ship headed for the Americas, and to his dying day, he never retook his vows to the Lord. In the eyes of the Church, he remained an honorable cleric, but in the eyes of God, he had been, all that time, merely a man.

As the Father related this story, he seemed to be asking my forgiveness rather than God's. He wanted me to remember him not as the flawless, holy medium I had come to view him as, but only as an honorable man of the earth. Having admitted this, he would not ask God's forgiveness for the events of the past. God had never left him, he said. There were no explanations left and no requests. The Father's years with the Seminoles demonstrated that if God had ever disapproved of his actions, then forgiveness had long since been granted.

When the Father finished his story, Long Grass paused his chanting and said, "Amen." Then, the Father asked me to perform the Eucharist. He nodded at Long Grass, who removed a small bottle of rum from his medicine bag and handed it to me without breaking the rhythm of his chants. I poured the rum into a wooden bowl and, following the Father's instructions, blessed it as the blood of Christ. The Father and I both drank from the bowl. Long Grass drank from the bottle.

Here, I must record the Father's last words. I wish to remember them always, exactly as he spoke them.

"Emedio, every day of my life, I have felt her loss. Not a day has passed when I did not chastise my inability to save her or regret that it was not I who was sacrificed in her stead. But I do know this—if we had not spent those few short months together, then we would have had no time together at all, and many more people than just her would have died. Nothing short of death could have kept me apart from her, and there is nothing I would not have done to defend her. Likewise, I would not have become the man I became, nor would I have found a place in this world, here, with these wonderful people. In all these years, I have shared these memories with no one, but they have encapsulated my soul with their warm embrace, propelling me through the duty of this life. Her memory has provided me strength, and I have cherished and loved those memories with every moment I have walked this earth. For to spurn those memories, to disregard my own continued existence, would be a dishonor both to God and to her, the two great loves of my life. God's gift to us is not His love but our ability to love. And so, you see, there are no vows you need to take. Your training comes with each day that you survive, each day that you plant the seeds of your love in the freshly tilled earth, earth which you have worked with the strength of your own hands. Your training is born of experience and the life you choose to lead. I have spent my love, I have paid my debts to God, and so shall you. Ambrister will not remain here any longer. My passing will inflame his anger with the world. He will go west to fight, and he will ask you to join him...it will be a difficult decision for you...the recent voyage I endured to our motherland...was not so I might look upon Spain's beauty one last time...nor to tread upon her soil...but to visit the grave of my beloved...so I could ask...and tell her...I have always wondered...whether...she was with child..."

The Father's strength gave out. I took his pipe and set it on the ground. I focused on Long Grass's repetitive, melancholic chanting, and when I had listened long enough to learn the words, I joined in. Occasionally, the Father hummed along with us, but his eyes remained closed. Many hours passed in this manner before he died. It was dark outside when we left the Father's hut for the final time.

Over these past three days, all activity in the village has ceased. Scouts do not venture into the forest, traders do not go into town, and hunters do not hunt. The women do no cooking or mending, and the children neither play nor study. We still gather in the mornings to pray silently, but I deliver no sermons and read from no books. Thus we stand, vulnerable, but together.

March 20, 1818
St. Johns River, La Florida

I realize now that I never truly believed the invasion would breach the barrier from conjecture to reality. Now that it has, I find myself repulsed by thoughts of battle, blood, weaponry, and vengeance. I have no place in this war. But, had I not come to this land through my own free will and attached myself to these good people along the St. Johns, then I would have continued upon the wavering seas. I would have served out my sentence and met my end along with my compatriots aboard El Soldado Agraciado.

All those good men, the Captain with his stern countenance but kind demeanor, my peaceful fear aboard her decks, my absolute acceptance and prostration in the presence of an inescapable blue fate—these memories haunt me still. I feel that I will never be free of them, these ghosts that will follow for a lifetime, the burden of a thousand crosses weighing upon a weak man's shoulders. And I have begun to contemplate whether I deserve the happy life that I have discovered here. Both in my dreams and waking hours, I hear Father Jimenez's calm utterances, Captain Vasquez's coarse commands, and the crew sarcastically plying for my loyalty, demanding that I sacrifice my pittance and demonstrate thanks for unintentionally skirting fate's will. They shout orders to this lowly deckhand. I hear them day and night, commanding me to stand tall and face the surge, ordering me to serve honestly the natural momentum of winds and currents, insisting that I pay my due tax for this port of call.

Strike, Stay Your Hand

March 21, 1818
St. Johns River, La Florida

The mourning period has now passed. Come the morrow, the tribespeople will resume their daily lives, readying themselves for a possible attack. However, I will not be here to aid them. With the befuddled temperament and despondency of a lost soul, I have agreed to Roberto's persuasive calls to action. I have already gathered my few meager possessions, mementos of my time with these hospitable Seminoles—Father Jimenez's family and my own. My horse, Lucia Roja, has been fed and groomed. Tomorrow, we go west. We set out for Tallahassee at dawn.

Chapter 39

The Betrayer

The pickax, awkward and unwieldy, offers no control. No two blows land the same. A sense of defeat boils into full-on rage as he launches the ax out of the trench with every ounce of his strength, a bit overzealous, perhaps, as a sharp ache now sears through his shoulder.

But the shovel—the shovel rests naturally in his hands. Calluses in all the right places, not a tinge of discomfort. Each and every motion executed smoothly and with ease, even when chipping away high above on a wall. He thrusts in with the shovel again and again, first loosening the dirt, and when a mound has formed at his feet, he tosses it to the side and then stabs at the wall some more. His shoulder throbs whenever he stops, so in lieu of the pain, he just keeps on.

Since the day John inexplicably turned up, every bit looking the part of the zombies from those horror flicks they used to watch together as kids, this is the first time Grant has dug alone.

Digging alone is quiet. Not that he and John speak a great deal while digging, but there are other sounds. The thud of the pickax landing and grating against the earth. High-pitched *chinks* as the ax-head ricochets off buried rocks. Moans of exhaustion, whimpers of pain, grunts of satisfaction. Slurping, gulping, gargling of water to mask the taste of dirt. Sometimes John will pause in his work to retch up the previous night's liter of The Carnival, covering it discreetly beneath a pile of freshly dug-up earth. He'll hum or whistle without being aware of it, always the same repetitive melody—something he calls *the Scrap*. And when they're working beside each other, Grant swears he can hear a heartbeat. Although, who's to say it's not his own?

The shovel runs into the wall. He has learned to be gentle and not push it in too far, or else it gets stuck. He doesn't need to waste energy getting hung up on tricky retractions, better to save it for the attack.

Solitude—probably how it should have been from the start. Why had he bothered to include John in this project at all? It was his horse. His yard, his memories, his pain. Inez was his wife, his life. His world that he's been trying to normalize all these years, seeking out stability and responsibility piece by piece. And he almost had it. He was so close. How does John fit into any of this anymore? Just because of a bit of hearsay? Never any proof, only allusions, bad feelings, intuitions, wanting and not wanting it to be true. But never a spoken word, never an admission of guilt.

Did you...?

Without explanation, John extricates himself from people's lives on his own whims, and when he bothers to come back, he brings only the world's mysteries as translated through his own skewed and selfish experiences. No, this project should be completed without assistance. And if help were necessary, then John Metternich is the last person who should have a part in it. There are dozens of others languishing away in the boredom of Creek's Ridge who would love to spend some quality time with their sheriff.

More than once, Grant has fantasized about turning the shovel on John, same as he'd done with Lil eight years ago. One swift blow to the head, a bit of gruesome handiwork later, and there you go, he's got himself a skeleton. No more of this groping in the dark. Every single bone accounted for, a handled entity, a completed form. And then set it on display...as what? A scientific model? A vanity piece? A warning? No one would even miss John. They would only assume he'd disappeared for another spell. But in reality, that would be the worst sentence he could serve his friend—John Metternich would never be able to run off again.

John, John. John Metternich. Going to the John. Probably simpler and more reasonable to just throw him in jail. Why the hell else did he fight for this goddamned position? Sheriff? Sheriff of what? The dull, the tired, and the wasted? Western Kansas-Oklahoma's drunken breeding grounds? America's forgotten hamlet of shame? How does that joke go? A prophet, a priest, and a saint all walk into a bar. The bartender asks what do they want?

The first of them asks for a peek into the future...

Before long, John will be off again, on some personal crusade to discover God-knows-what and peripherally ruin more lives without the slightest clue. This time it will be Caryn Pridieux. Grant could have had Caryn—easy, no problem—except John had swooped in. What is it about him? The blasé attitude? The wear and tear? The mystery? Yesterday, when he was searching for John and eager to start the day's digging, he discovered that John and Caryn were both nowhere to be found. Probably holed up somewhere, fucking like dogs. And, if he hasn't already, John will drag her off on some misadventure, to some Third World rut where he'll eventually abandon her, and she won't ever know what went wrong because nothing did. It was just him all along. She's already put down the dough for the renovations—her pet project—unloaded her guilt money and found a man to fill her emptiness, the voids in her eyes, the arid region of her soul. And John, well, John never has a reason to be anywhere, does he?

Did you...?
Unless he's gone again.
Did you...?
Gone to her.

A man without memories, without acknowledgment of his past deeds, lessons learned, influence given or influence received—is this even a man? Without a past to inform and temper his actions, can he be trusted with future decisions? Heave that shovel once more—

Is this truly a friend at all?

Even if John isn't present in the fullest sense, it has been nice to have him around again, as long as Grant can ignore, just this once, that unbearable aspect of the past. For the first few weeks after John showed up, Grant had experienced the same resurgence of vitality he'd felt when he first moved to Creek's Ridge himself. John had always had that effect. As if John, without realizing it, carries around all the freedom and innocent antics of their shared childhood, dishes it out like candy at a parade, and here's Grant to scoop it all up, gorging himself on the sweet past, a time when pain meant scraping your knee or breaking your arm. Superficial wounds that built character instead of tearing it down.

This time, however, those feelings had been short-lived. Grant's emotional landscape has become a battleground, the Creek's Ridge of more than a century ago, when the Native Americans—rational, experienced, capable, and ruthless—were nevertheless out-maneuvered by a rag-tag bunch of hillbillies and a nun. One manic nutcase is all it takes to shift the tides.

Grant always assumed John to be that nutcase, even during their playground days. Now, he's not so sure. Even the past moves along, shifts gears, speeds up and slows down, slams on the brakes, crashes, and is left to rust and ruin on the roadside.

Almost two months now since John speculated Lil's presence in the wall here between these two trenches, and Grant has become obsessed, convinced of its truth. All the bones still unaccounted for, they must be here. Because, really, he doesn't want to do this anymore. The dig is leading them nowhere but into themselves. He's sick of it. Sick of John. Sick of himself. He's been digging with half a heart, always dreaming of the moment when he could break off on his own and demolish this wall, proving John both right and wrong at the same time, ending this nonsense once and for all.

Why would you go there...? After I had left...?

And now that John has finally given him the opportunity, a very real nervous expectation tickles his abdomen with every shovelful of dirt. The bones might be exposed at any moment. Yet he can't ignore the facts—when the bones tumble out, any second now, John won't be here to see them, to believe in them, to confirm the truth.

Did you...?

Isn't there someone else who can validate the hard reality of bones? Why does it have to be John? What about Pa Sonny? Pa Sonny doesn't give a shit about the skeleton. Most likely he doesn't even remember the incident—that night, with Lil, the shovel, in the dark, and the booze. He's probably off on a delivery anyhow. So, how about Oscar Amondale? Ernest? Maybe Claire Young could come by to tell him he's not crazy and massage this tightness right out of him. She's anything but young, though you'd never guess it. Four kids and Grant's senior by at least ten years. He's never asked her age, or her husband's. Why should he? She's the one who came on to him. Her flirtations are the type you cannot refuse, and she bends and moves with the agility of a much younger woman. Excitable, wild. Although, he had touched her first. A moth to a light bulb. But it's been months since he's been with Claire. It's been months since he's done a lot of things.

So then, no one is good enough. Might as well take the bones straight to where they belong, where they were always meant to go. Own up to the facts. Accept the purpose and intent lurking behind all of this. Take them straight to her, straight to Inez. Go crawling back, a loyal, miserable mutt bringing bones to its master. *Here, look at what I've got. Look what I've done for you. This is proof. Proof that I could never betray you, not again. They're not just bones. It's a sacrifice. This has all been for you. Everything has always, always been for you...*

No, no, no, who is he kidding? A blatant untruth—he has dug alone. The last time Johannes didn't come home. He'd slept on the floor of the bar, apparently. A likely story. Almost certainly he'd gone off with Caryn, fucked her through the night, and then sent Ernest over here to smooth things over, distract him from the truth, asking some bullshit about LPs, whose is whose and what from where and when. He'd been working on Caryn all evening, and John hardly said a thing. Caryn should have been his.

When Grant lashes out with the shovel, the pain in his shoulder extends down his arm. His shoulder is killing him. John has dug alone, too—once—only one time that Grant knows of. But John was waiting for him that night. That night. With her...

What kind of a fucking name was that, anyway? Lani Vals? What had they been thinking? She said it was a name he would know, a game he would recognize immediately from their childhood, kids playacting under the guise of mysterious foreign identities. But John remained blind all the way through it. That, or he recognized their bluff and was heartless enough to take it one step further. Take it all the way. And then, on her final night in Creek's Ridge, with John impatient in the kitchen and calling for help, Grant had instead taken her into the bedroom with the weed and the coke he'd tracked down in Wichita, and he fucked her like it was the end of the world, both of them high as goddamn satellites while John went on ahead and knelt down in the wet of the stream to dig alone in the dark. How long had he waited in the kitchen before he went off into the night? Had he heard her moaning? Her screams of ecstasy? And then, after they were finished, had he heard her cry? Not for him, but for John. Or was it for herself? Had he heard them talking? And what they said? He left her there and went to the john, and then he went to John, sniffing down the drip as he walked through the night. Those bones they found weren't Lil's bones. Grant knew it the moment he saw them. They weren't even fucking horse bones. But he helped John unearth them anyhow, out of guilt, or because he felt sorry, he still doesn't know which, both of them blind on that dark night, the moon cloud-covered, flashlights dead. He helped to carry the bones back to the house, expecting rounds three-four-five with her in the bedroom. But she'd long since fallen asleep, so he smoked the rest of the grass and passed out at the desk, watching her but terrified to go near her again. Same as it always was between them— because he was not without guilt, and neither was she. When he woke in the morning, she was already gone, and John was still none the wiser.

Holding hands and...that's what I heard...how long were you...?

He's always liked fucking her because she fucks like Inez. Unhinged, assertive. She even looks like Inez, he always thought. Paler skin, sure. Thinner, with a more defined bone structure. But they have that same dark, unruly hair. Same height and body type. And the curves, oh, the curves. Others must have noticed the resemblance. The most obvious difference, though, was the tattoo. Inez's oasis, he'd always called it. Clothes on the floor to reveal the lush rainforest greens draped around her left flank and fanning out across her back, with long dewy stalks bent down and framing her ass, the flowers under her arm and left breast reaching down, cradling her navel, and the bright tropical bird hidden in the folds of leaves and petals, constantly peering out. Sometimes, he swore he could hear that bird laughing.

Did you...? Hear it, too...?

Nothing left anymore but betrayal on all sides. Life itself has become one great betrayal. Everyone, guilty.

Grant has been chipping away at this wall for what seems like hours, days, a lifetime. The sun has gone, abandoned him here, pathetically alone. He drags his aching body through the yard, avoiding all the dangerous pitfalls and mounds. Back at the house, he flips the switch for the porch light and gazes through the screen door upon the vaguely threatening shadows cast across the lot. No beer in the house, no rum, no tequila. Only a half-empty bottle of The Carnival on the coffee table in the living room, beside the space on the floor where John sleeps.

The fucking Carnival. Jesus Christ, he hates this shit.

Stupid asshole, sleeping on the floor every night when the sofa bed is right there. Like some kind of rangy mutt. The least he could do is show some loyalty.

Did you...?

He grabs a handful of ice from the freezer, paying no attention to the filth covering his hands. When he sits down in his usual chair, John's chair taunts him, grotesque in its vacancy. He glances at the bones arrayed across the table, then again at the empty chair. The whisky's scent reminds him of old paint thinner in his dad's garage, the canister cap disappeared and a nauseating stench free to permeate. He quickly drains the glass.

The aches in his body are a sign that he should stop for the night and maybe try to get some honest sleep. But his thoughts are pistons hammering in an engine. Better to keep up the momentum. He hopes to find a few lines worth of leftover coke in the bedroom. He'd paid exorbitantly for the eight-ball, and the quality was good, but she'd only reluctantly snorted two small lines, saying she'd moved past that stage in her life. Well, fuck, so had he—but wasn't that stage of life so much better than all this? He brings the baggie into the kitchen and dumps it onto the table, where it mixes with bone dust and dirt. He uses an unopened envelope—a bill, junk mail, a card from mom, he doesn't bother to check—and sweeps it into a couple of tight lines, then leans in and snorts them in rapid succession.

As he walks through the yard, swigging The Carnival straight from the bottle now, he gazes at the night sky. The longer he stares at any one point, the more stars grow faintly visible, revealed like whispers. And as soon as he shifts his eyes away, they slink back into the oily blackness. They'll hide there for time immeasurable, waiting for someone to stare with the longing it requires, waiting for someone to need them.

He doesn't hear movement from the trenches but senses it nearby. That eerie premonition of another living presence just beyond reach, too close for comfort, too far for confirmation. Oh, for fuck's sake—that's just the kind of abstract horseshit John would come up with. He retreats a few steps to fetch the pickax from where he just stepped over it. Cautiously forward, down the ramp leading into the trench, the sound clearly audible now. Someone is there, just around the bend, scratching in the dirt, digging.

"John?"

Did you...?

"John!" His voice peaks, a burst of gunfire through the silence.

The stillness after a good shout like that is unnerving. Crickets hush, fireflies blink out, the wind freezes in attention. He pulls from the bottle and steadies the ax on his shoulder, gripping it tightly as he scrapes his boots through the dirt, knowing that he'll find no one there, nothing but another of the realistic visions that plague him. Which will it be this time? John the mountain man, grizzled and filthy and rail-thin? Limping Lady, alive and kicking? His father shaking his head in disappointment? Pa Sonny back on the booze? Inez blowing kisses? It's not beyond him to hallucinate any of these. He regularly dreams and daydreams these memories, static encounters that haunt his days and nights, too close for comfort, too emblematic of real life. He wishes that just once he could be haunted by the kinds of terrors that tend to John in the night.

But there, crouched low to the ground, motionless near a mound of dirt, its head twisted back, two small eyes glimmer at him, reflecting some imperceptible light. It jerks around suddenly and then jaunts toward him. He drops the bottle and squeezes the handle of the pickax, mounted to swing, prepared to kill, and at the final instant—with his heart up in his throat—he recognizes Doctor Mengele.

The dog hesitates, waits for him to lower the weapon, then bounds forward. Grant grabs hold and scratches around Mengele's ears, clutching the dog close. Mengele licks Grant's hands before disengaging and trotting back to the mound from which he came. After another glance back at Grant, the dog crouches low again and continues digging.

Grant picks up the bottle and walks to the mound. He stands over Mengele as the dog wades through loose dirt, precise and thorough, sniffing every grain.

"You bastard. Why didn't I think of you? My deputy, the Doctor Mengele. Every bit as good a digging partner as any one of those assholes. Better, I bet."

Grant can't remember the last time he laughed. It feels good. Together, he and John have little to laugh about. They work, they talk, they dig as the dog is digging now, but they don't laugh. He is suddenly pricked by the sensation that he hasn't seen John in years. He saw him a day ago, of course. But John never came home last night. Yesterday morning was the last time. It doesn't seem that way. Seems like it's been ages and ages cozying up to this loneliness. He wonders—if they are able to finish the dig, will they ever be able to look out over the yard and laugh about all this?

Another swig, The Carnival roars, and then he trades the bottle for the shovel and resumes his own digging, wailing on the wall, regularly checking to see whether Mengele has abandoned him. He grunts, growls, and swears aloud, sweat pouring out. This time, he doesn't bother to toss away the mound growing beneath his feet. He just stands on top of it, sinking into it as he works ferociously at the wall. There will be no bones in here. Deep down, he knows that, but he still can't stop. The allure of proving John wrong, of finishing the dig without John's help, becomes a drug coursing through his veins, never a thought of turning his back on hope.

After a while, he notices Mengele standing nearby, watching him dig. He serves the wall a barrage of solid hits, then backs off, heaving harsh, raspy breaths. Mengele wags his tail as if in approval, and then Grant sees something sticking out of the dog's mouth.

"Come here, boy," Grant says, huffing for air and patting his thigh.

Mengele trots forward, and Grant kneels down. He cradles the dog's head, rubbing and scratching as though it were his own best friend. After a brief playful resistance, Mengele releases the object into Grant's hand.

And, yes, of course it is. It wouldn't really have made sense to expect anything else. Small and unbroken, it's about the size of his index finger, and unlike any other bone they've found. One end is hollow, the other pointed, a slender, elegant cone slick with saliva. The last tail vertebra, he assumes. He wipes it on his pants and holds it up again so he and Mengele can get a good look.

"Thatta boy, thatta boy..." He pats Mengele on the head and slips the bone into his pocket as he stands up. "This is it. The perfect gift..."

With this bone...forgive me...please take me back...

Sensing that his work is done for the night, Mengele wanders off.

The thought of the bone weighs heavily upon Grant, this tiny brick of gold, payment for a hard night's labor when honesty is the furthest thing from his mind. Grant looks at the pickax lying on the ground, at the shovel leaning against the wall of the trench. Mengele's absence gradually fills the pits with a thick, suffocating fog of isolation and doubt. The whisky bottle lies on its side, empty now. Good. He could use a real drink anyhow. Up the ramp and out of the trench, he looks around for Mengele, but the dog is gone, back to its home, back to its master, or slipping secretly through the town on some other adventure, free to roam as it pleases.

Grant starts the car and speeds to George's Grocery, which also serves as the only liquor store within about a hundred-mile radius, more in some directions. Dry counties all around. The only thing that's kept Creek's Ridge afloat for the past fifty years is the booze. No, longer than fifty years—all the way back to the start of it, more like.

The second one asks for remembrance of the past...

That's what Miami was supposed to have been, paradise on the edge of nothingness. Drive the road as far as it goes to a spacious, airy house on the beach with three or four kids laughing and causing their innocent havoc. Jumping on the sofa, toys scattered about, sand and towels and beach gear trailed throughout the halls, stray balls bursting through windows. And when the kids are grown, then it's just him and her listening to an endless surf, watching their shared life reflect off the water's dancing surface, the tide coming in and out. But here, in Creek's Ridge, where he's ended up, this is the actual end of the earth. As far as you can get, in any direction you choose, from the sea.

Did you...?

He parks the car in front of George's, gets out, and marches toward the entrance, never noticing the empty parking lot or the inside of the building all dark. A dead end, the store locked up for the night. He shields his eyes from the red-blue globe spinning on top of his cruiser, shining, glaring, bouncing, and glittering, laughing in his face, painting the concrete and the brick walls of the building, though he doesn't even recall switching the police lights into motion. Goddamnit, just like John again—his memory as fragile as porcelain all of a sudden. It must be late, and Ernest's bar would still be open, but the thought of sitting still with the stale odor of sweat and cigarettes and spilled drinks, the thought of speaking with anyone inside the bar right now, repulses him. He's the sheriff, for Christ's sake. The time of night doesn't matter. He can always call George to let him in and make a sale. George is a drinker himself, with troubles all his own, alimony to two or three ex-wives, estranged kids, behind on his taxes. Grant has let the guy slide on his driving habits a number of times—weaving over the center line, up the curb, an open bottle right there on the passenger seat. George understands hopelessness, too. He would let Grant in at a moment's notice. He would have to.

The lights, he remembers now, were only meant to give George a fright. Drive up with the cherries and berries spinning just as George is about to close up. But instead, it's Grant's patience being harangued by red and blue careening up and down the street, reflected off signs and shop windows. It feels like someone's watching him, the sheriff on his tail. Good thing he hadn't turned the siren on, too. Last thing he needs is the whole damn town stumbling sleepy-eyed into the street in their robes and pajamas and bare feet, coming up to him with their slurred midnight concerns and asking what can they do to help?

Just a few long strides back to the car. He pops the trunk and finds the tire iron, slick with grease, lying in the corner beside the shotgun. One swift blow to the roof cuts off the obnoxious lighting effects and spills glass all over the hood. The mechanism slowly stops spinning as the current dies out. He admires this trite death before stomping back to the store's entrance and smashing the old glass doors with less effort than he would've liked, his craving for destruction suddenly stronger than his thirst for booze. Once inside, he can't help but indulge. He bypasses the liquor counter and takes a lap around the store, indiscriminately wrecking things as he courses amongst the canned goods, toiletries, snacks, and condiments. One lap is enough, as satisfaction is not for sale in any of the aisles, frozen, or produce. There's a new sign above the liquor counter, The Liquor Corner, it says. Clever. A cheap wooden sign that looks like it was glued together by school kids. One whack with the iron breaks it in two. He busts the lock on the quality liquor cabinet. Everything is so fragile. Nothing in this fucking town can stand the slightest bit of pressure. What luck has allowed them to stay out of tornado paths all these years? He's never even seen a tornado, not in his whole life. Hadn't that been part of the reason he came to Kansas to begin with? Tornado Alley. To witness a real monster, an F-5 with a grudge and a hard-on for demolition. The only building that would stand a chance is St. Josephine's. Maybe that's where he ought to be holed up, just like Saint Josephine herself, straight through until the end of her days. The woman behind the legends was inseparable from her sanctuary, even while her reputation amongst the good people of Creek's Ridge gradually shifted from reverence to fear and then, finally, to ridicule.

Two pints of spiced rum should be enough.

The car is still running. He drops one bottle onto the passenger seat and opens the other, taking a huge slug before putting the car into gear.

As he pulls around to the street, the headlights fall upon two teenagers with bikes standing on the corner. They're watching him and whispering to each other as the car approaches.

Grant pulls up beside them, rolls down the passenger-side window, and stares at them for a long time. He knows both of them, knows their names, but he can't remember which is which, who is who.

"Hey."

"Hey, Grant," answers one of the boys.

The longer he stares at them, the more fidgety and anxious they become.

"You tell anybody about this and I'll fucking kill you."

He waits a beat to let it sink in and then steps on the gas.

Just about two miles separate Pa Sonny's house from St. Josephine's, the northern and southernmost borders of town. Grant drives from one to the other, the same as if he were running his daily patrol, only now he stops in front of each of the two buildings to drink his rum and stare the structures down, those two sanctums and the suffocating dark of the endless road beyond, then he turns the cruiser around and heads back in the other direction. The first bottle is half empty when he finally chucks what remains of his compromised concern for the law and just drives with the bottle to his lips. As he suspected, Pa Sonny's truck is gone, off on a job in some goddamn backwoods place. At the northern border, he's compelled to keep driving north, and when he comes to St. Jo's, he wants to floor it south. But at each lap, something like loyalty or responsibility stops him. He curses himself out, pulling hard on the rum and telling himself that by the next turn he'll be drunk enough to break these bonds.

The gas gauge lights up, so he pulls into the gas station down the street from Pa Sonny's place. A local down-and-out AA graduate named Len works the night shift. Len watches through the window as Grant fills up and then simply waves when Grant flips him off. Soon enough, nature calls, so Grant drives down to Tarrow Street and pulls into the parking lot at the warehouse where he wasted so many years. He means only to piss on the outer walls, but temptation overcomes him. Next thing he knows, he has broken in and is pissing on various merchandise. Before he leaves, he knocks over some shelving units for good measure.

Did you....?

The car seems to be moving in circles, spinning out of control, although he's only driving the arrow-straight main stretch up and down, down and up. But he soon tires of this repetition, of his inability to escape.

Coming upon his house, the tangy sweetness of the rum rises into his nasal cavity. He pulls in and drives right past the house into the backyard. It's only luck that he avoids driving into one of the pits. No, no, no—it's only luck that he has a home at all. And not even truly his, not his name on the paperwork. It's only luck that his parents aren't as disappointed in their son as he is in himself. Luck that he has maintained a close relationship with his family, earned their loyalty, trust, and love. Is that luck? No, that's the way of the world, or at least how it's supposed to work. But it hadn't worked that way with Inez, nor with Lil. And John would never understand. John, Inez, and the Limping Lady—his Trinity, his failure.

Did you....?

He opens the other pint of rum, takes it with him down into the trenches, and picks up the first tool he sees—the pickax. With just one swing at the wall, a swing for the fences, the ax is stuck. Home run. Growls, roars, snarls of rage. He tugs and pushes on the handle, fuck this and fuck that and fuck you and fuck me and fuck her and fuck everything until his throat hurts and his face slams into the wall as though someone has shoved him forward. There is no other, no one there but him. He's alone. He gathers himself, steadies his feet, and searches for the pickax, but now it has disappeared, abandoned him like everything, everyone else, everyone but mom and dad. The sharp flavor of rum rises from his stomach. He gags, clenching his fist and punching the dirt wall over and over again. Finally, he manages to swallow it down. And then he sees the hole.

He touches the dirt around the edge, feels it crumble in his fingertips, then sticks his hand through. He did it. He broke through with his bare hands. He stumbles around the trench, searching for the shovel, and when he finds it, he attacks the wall, knocking dirt away from the rim of the hole until he has opened a passage wide enough to walk through. As soon as he's finished, he drops the shovel and vomits beside it.

No bones are buried here. Both he and John, both right and wrong.

He walks through the doorway a few times, staring at the archway in awe, and then trips over the pickax protruding from the loose dirt piled on the ground. He digs it out and uses it as a crutch as he tries to find his way back to the house, following the porch light through eyes half-closed—two porch lights, in fact—but he knows instinctually that only one is real, the other a false hope. He chooses one, barely able to keep it in his sights. Though the mere notion of sleep terrifies him, he approaches that natural vista, as we all do, at times against our deepest wishes, and the best we can ask for is a safe place to lay our weary bones.

Did you...?
When he looks up again, he's at the house but barred at the gate. The door won't open. He pounds on it, grasping the handle, but it doesn't budge. He backs away, finds his balance with the aid of the pickax, looks up, focuses. When it hits him that he has come around to the front of the house, he loses his mind. He raises the ax and charges the door, giving it hell. How, why would he walk around to the front, for Christ's sake? Bad luck, brother. The locks rattle as tiny chips of wood bounce off his face and cling to his shirt. His shoulder trembles with weakness. Though he feels no pain, he can barely lift the ax anymore. So, he relents, sidles over the few steps to the window, and drops the pickax over the sill, letting it crash noisily on the floorboards inside. After several failed attempts to lift himself up over the windowsill, he walks around to the back door, defeated and supporting himself against the walls.

At the kitchen table he sifts mindlessly through the bones, shifting them around, an impossible puzzle, infuriating yet addictive. He remembers the tail bone Mengele found and fishes it out of his pocket, drops it onto the table with the others before retreating into the living room. His eyes immediately dart to the swath of floor beside the sofa, where John always sleeps.

Did you...?
Where John should be right now.
Did you fuck her?
Grant retrieves the pickax, groans as he lifts it above his head, and brings it rushing down onto the floor directly where John's head would be, but it's not. The blunt end of the ax bounces off the floorboards. Grant loses his balance and falls, falls, falls, safely cradled by the sofa, the cushions offering him peace, promising him soft, deep, blissful sleep...

Jolted up, startled by movement in the house, there in the room with him, a presence that doesn't belong but will never leave him be, not now, not in sleep, not while he lives and breathes. He channels his concentration, remains patient, searching, believing he is steady, firm, and capable. But he wobbles and tilts as he clumsily leans forward for the pickax once more. Rising from the sofa, with the ax raised and ready, he discovers the movement of the Other. It is found, checked, pinned down in the corner of his eye. He channels all the energy and balance he has left and charges across the room, at the arched opening into the kitchen, where the movement comes from, beyond which the bones are displayed on the table, awaiting life and form and purpose—but he stops himself just in time, his double vision wavers, wobbles, settles into the frame of the giant mirror leaned up against the wall, right where it's supposed to be, right where it has always been.

And it's her. Of course it's her. She, the motion in the mirror, the mirror that has always hung over his bed, in every place he has ever lived except here. Her image, captured there, hidden behind it, forever within the vast world of reflections. He can't shatter the mirror, not this mirror. It has seen so much. Witness to the best moments of his life. It carries them and keeps them safe while he falters and slips. He must protect this relic, protect her, save her from what's to come, because after all, just look at what became of the horse. This mirror might be all he has left. Of her. Of himself.

And the third says, "You fools! The town is burning! We need a savior right now!"

Chapter 40

Penance and Reconciliation

Just before winter, Lalawethika accepted his brother's invitation to join a small party journeying north to the British colony of Upper Canada. The ravages of the outbreak had left the Shawnees' winter stores sorely understocked, so Tecumseh was tasked with securing extra provisions to get them through the winter. The British, although further afield, were always more generous with their aid and less aggressive seekers of recompense than the Americans. Initially, Lalawethika rejected his brother's request, but upon overhearing that they would pass through Detroit, he expressed a change of heart.

Along with twenty young warriors, they spent a pleasant, easy week on horseback. Conversing about the tribe's future, they discussed unjust treaties bartered with the United States government, the shifting hands of traditional plots of land, and the introduction of new farming methods. Lalawethika honored his brother with his full attention, leading Tecumseh to believe that Lalawethika had finally accepted a more productive means of participation in tribal affairs. But as they rode onto Detroit's main thoroughfare, Lalawethika revealed that he would not be continuing north. Instead, he would pass the time there in Detroit and rejoin them for the return journey. Tecumseh's fury rarely overtook his good sense, but on this occasion he ordered his warriors to seize Lalawethika and, if necessary, to force him along to meet the Britons bound in chains. To Tecumseh's chagrin and wonder, Lalawethika met little resistance in convincing the young warriors to let him go free.

As Lalawethika strolled along Detroit's main avenue, beneath maple and pine trees lining the parkway, he was attentive to the faces passing around him. Some, he recognized from his previous visit and a few from the midnight gathering in the woods behind Father Gabriel's farm. However, he was on the lookout for one man's unattractive features—a face he would never forget—but he did not see Darius, merchant of poison and master of that dark ceremony.

Father Gabriel was surprised and delighted when Lalawethika stepped through Sainte Anne de Detroit's grand entryway. However, he was also aggrieved to learn of Penagashea's death and then visibly shaken to hear that it had occurred mere days after they last parted company. He led Lalawethika into the church with a somber smile and a firm grasp of the shoulder, and then he knelt before the altar, reciting what was to Lalawethika's ears a haunting prayer. This concentrated display of the full scope of human emotion riveted Lalawethika. From the priest's patient, regal way of advancing down the aisle to the all-consuming silence after he had finished his prayer, and then the graceful, nigh imperceptible way he smoothed his robes, his eyes gleaming with actual calm and blissfulness, conveying that those words, that the very act of prayer itself, could be as powerfully transformative an elixir as any firewater or medicine man's trick.

After Lalawethika managed to convey the circumstances of his visit, Father Gabriel hesitated briefly before inviting the Shawnee to stay at his house. Although the Father exhibited extreme kindness, he had little to say at first. But Lalawethika made a point of expressing his gratitude and showing an interest in the Father's life. Lalawethika curtly rejected repeated offers of wine and whiskey, which mystified the Father. A day or so passed before Lalawethika sensed the Father truly warming to him, at which point he appealed to the Father's heart. He expounded honestly about his continuing troubles within his tribe, the obstacles of his past complicating his ascendancy to the role of medicine man, and his own brother's lack of faith. He spoke in simple truths, his rudimentary grasp of the English language demanding simplicity, and he overplayed only the loss of his mentor, this feigned mourning having long since become habit.

As the days wore on, these cheerless subjects shifted toward more lighthearted tales. The Father related humorous adventures of his youth and his initial encounters with America's Natives, and he listened intently to Lalawethika's childhood recollections. Father Gabriel was the only person Lalawethika had ever met who did not cringe when he looked at the scarred and puckered eyelid, who commented on it without revulsion, demonstrating an honest curiosity and empathy for the difficulties Lalawethika faced as a result of his scar. Lalawethika asked the Father about biblical stories and sought clarification for everything he could not comprehend of the white man's religion. He examined the Father's holy garments with minute scrutiny and fascination. Following a Sunday Mass, they spent an entire evening discussing the Father's vocal inflections, hand gestures, eye contact, and spontaneous impulses while sermonizing.

The more that Lalawethika learned about Roman Catholicism, the more he questioned Father Gabriel, who delighted in the challenge of stripping away the entanglements of language to more accurately portray the tenets of his life's devotion. He turned it into a sort of game in which he would attempt to adequately explain the Eucharist, for instance, in the simplest words possible, and then propose a similar challenge to Lalawethika about some curious aspect of the Shawnee beliefs.

Father Gabriel also noted Lalawethika's apparent fascination with Sainte Anne de Detroit, including the various religious objects and icons housed within. The crucifix, the chalice, the holy water fonts and colored tapestries, images of the Holy Virgin, even the pews—but in particular, the confessional booth. As such, after Tecumseh and the others had returned from Upper Canada and rested for a few days, the Father invited Lalawethika to perform the sacrament of Penance and Reconciliation as a parting gift. He explained how the repentant individual enters the confessional in order to privately expose his wrongdoings and immoral thoughts. No one but God would be given to judge the confessor. Step into the box, shut the door, kneel on the cushioned kneeler, lean toward the grated wall panel, and speak your truths. Simple as that.

"Forgiveness could not be easier to come by if it were free," laughed the Father.

The booth was dark and cramped, the air stuffy with moisture and a scent of ash and mildew. It was cozier and more welcoming than Penagashea's cave, but also suffocating. He knelt and bowed in the same posture he had seen the Christians adopt in the pews, which he now realized was a posture that Penagashea had often ordered him to take.

At first, Lalawethika began to hum one of the medicine chants he had learned during his time in the cave, finding comfort in the familiar, undulating tones until he heard a heavy breath very near to his face, almost like a sigh of longing. Peering at the grated panel gave rise to the super-sensory awareness of another presence, which then bloated into a sense of utter loneliness.

"Where is the Great Spirit?" Lalawethika muttered in his own language. "Why am I alone in a place such as this?"

Another barely audible sigh followed, like a subtle breeze emitted from the wooden panels themselves. Lalawethika lifted his gaze to the grating again and held his breath. He was silent for a long time, his fingertips running along the walls. His wandering hands discovered the small crucifix hung on the rear wall, reminding him of what the Father had told him of its significance—one man, condemned for seeking and preaching peace, tortured and bled and displayed as a victory, as a warning, but instead serving ever after as a reminder of sacrifice, duty, and strength. He removed the crucifix from the wall and wrapped his hand around it, squeezing tighter until that tiny effigy of man dug into the flesh of his hand. How ridiculous—that one man should imagine it feasible to unite all men under harmony and equality, that one man could ever desire to carry the weight of such immense responsibility. Ridiculous and unbelievable—and yet, a stirring and powerful idea. Their Savior had not been an amalgamated beast of fancy or a group of ethereal spirits spinning tricks and miracles, but only a lone man. How had that man found the strength and courage to shoulder the burden? Had he erred? Suffered? Bluffed it all? His blood had been shed in the end, but had he shed the blood of others? Had he killed?

Lalawethika remembered the brilliant, sickening color of his blood. He saw it still, painting his entire existence, everything he perceived covered in red. But life had not ended with the spilling of his blood that day. The stink of death had followed him ever since, persecuting his every move, sprouting pain and hatred, producing the fruit of fear, rotting and festering and fermenting, lying in wait for its noxious fumes to erupt into the world.

Suddenly, Lalawethika could neither breathe nor move. It was stifling inside the booth, as though a fire smoldered in there with him, smoking him out. All the injustice and betrayal and blood and disease and death spread wide across the plains and mountains and seas of this and distant lands descended upon him at once, squeezing the breath from his lungs. If only he could push the door open and tumble out onto the cold stone floor, where perhaps this creeping suffocation would dissipate to be shared, suffered equally by one and all—because it wasn't his fault. The arrow had left him half-blind, but it wasn't his fault. The medicine man, the firewater, avarice and jealousy, all had led him astray, but it wasn't his fault. His mother had abandoned him, and it wasn't his fault. The Great Spirit had singled him out, chosen him, but it wasn't, it wasn't his...

His breath returned in heavy gasps punctuated by words spoken in the same direct and simplistic English he had grown accustomed to with Father Gabriel, bracketed only by interjections in his native tongue. Hardly aware of where he was or what he was saying, he spoke of the despicable acts he had witnessed that night in the woods behind the Father's house, the hatred he had worked so hard to shed rekindled by that chorus of mockery and the cries of those poor Delaware girls as they were defiled in the darkness. Their mother, more knowledgeable of the horrors befalling her daughters, had screamed louder even than they. And their father had done nothing to stop it. He had almost certainly accepted payment in return for his wife's and daughters' honor, just like Penagashea—and by extension, Lalawethika and Father Gabriel as well—had been complicit. He and Penagashea had hauled off a year's worth of whiskey for desecrating the heart of Shawnee culture. Then, he told of walking for two days, south along the shore of Erie Lake, all the while with this reawakened hatred boiling ferociously, frothing and spitting more scaldingly than he had ever endured before. That old drunkard, Penagashea, had slept upon the lanky horse for the entire first day, a dead weight no different from the sacks of sugar and tobacco on the cart. And then, on the second day, half asleep and mumbling, Penagashea proposed an unrealistic future for the Shawnee Nation. While Lalawethika walked alongside the encumbered animal, he measured his own countless faults against Penagashea's abhorrent behavior during a single night's depravity, a single night's betrayal to all red men who ever tread this earth, a night illuminated by the moon and lit by flame, set on display for the Great Spirit, whose infinitely intricate threads of existence must still be unraveling from the shock. Lalawethika's fingers had remained clamped around his stone ax while war cries collected in his throat, but they never issued forth because he was helpless. Ever since the day he lost his eye—when he first saw the world through the red sheen of his own blood—it had always been blood that frightened him more than anything. And he told, too, of that blood. As a blooming young hunter, under his brother's tutelage, the arrowhead pierced his eye, penetrating painlessly and without resistance deep into his skull, and he suffered that endless stream of blood running down his face. The pain would not come until later, after he regained consciousness, but a deafening high-pitched sound screeched in his ears as the pointed stone tip entered, so loud he had assumed the forest and the sky were collapsing around him. The blood would not stop running from his eye socket, its metallic thickness seeping in at the corners of his mouth, coating his tongue and his throat as he heaved for air, its slick opacity flowing in streams down the length of his body, staining the stones and dirt and weeds below. At that moment, a moment he could never wipe from his memory, he underwent the peculiar horror of an out-of-body experience, his one good eye seeming to gaze back in shame at the lumbering idiot who had tripped over an exposed root with the arrow held out in front of him like a stone ax. But it was not his fault. *No!* It was not his fault that no one had shown him how to hold his arrows as he scampered through the forest. It was not his fault, but they blamed him just as they had blamed him for his mother's desertion. Before he had even lost consciousness, he already believed he was dead. No one could suffer a razor-sharp arrowhead embedded in the eye socket, lose that much blood, and survive it. And he had felt a happy release then, glad that he would die because only death would provide a quick and welcome respite. The immediate cessation of life. Total disappearance from this earthly plane would promise a more blessed future than facing the humiliation and disgrace of a failed Shawnee hunter who had profaned the noble warrior's blood passed down from his father, like some lowly wretch contaminating the tribal water supply with his feces. They had carried him back to the village, and when he regained consciousness, he was left with only one eye and a staggering headache that would not subside for the next three years. The first thing he saw with his remaining eye was the blood, its indescribably dark heaviness covering his body, dried in places yet slick and shining in others. Then the vomit came all at once, spraying everywhere, staining all that wasn't blood-drenched already and emitting the foulest of odors. And after he had expelled every last drop, he had looked up with his one good eye to see his kinsmen, their disappointment and disgust bearing down on him heavier than the headache ever would. The blood that spilled from his eye in his youth was the reason he could not lay his stone ax into Penagashea's skull as they trod along the calming shoreline of Erie Lake. Even though he desired it with his whole heart, even though he recognized it as a duty to his people and to the Great Spirit, blood was a reminder of the monstrous fear that had shoved him off the path of an honorable life—not the fear of death itself, but the fear of pain and the unbearable passage from life to death.

Lalawethika's voice grew louder and the air inside the stall reeked of sweat. He clutched the crucifix so tightly that his skin broke. Blood trickled down the length of the cross, slid down his wrist and forearm, dripped onto the kneeler, but he did not notice. He did not feel it because he began to tell of how, on the second night along Erie Lake, as he observed the undeserved rise and fall of Penagashea's chest, the voices returned, voices that had long persecuted him, along with haunting new voices he had never heard before, voices he barely understood. They kept him awake throughout the night, not whispering but shouting, not appealing to his vices but invoking the pride of the Shawnee people. Visions arose, giving form to the voices—first, his father and mother, demanding he make amends with the Great Spirit by answering this just call for vengeance. Then, he saw Cheekitha, the clever woodland spirit, hopping through the trees and dancing atop the waters of Erie Lake as he sang accusingly that a medicine man without command over death is no medicine man at all, but only a man like any other, at the mercy of death.

His voice grew firmer. It flowed assertively like the great western river as he told of how he stood above Penagashea and recited the Shawnee death prayer, his voice rising until the old man woke. Seeing his disciple thus posed, he asked in a hoarse whisper, "What's happening? What is this...?"

At the sound of Penagashea's voice, Lalawethika fell onto his mentor's body, crushing the old man's chest with his knees to the sound of ribs snapping. He covered Penagashea's mouth and nose with one hand and leaned his full weight onto Penagashea's frail neck with the other, squeezing maliciously. In a few moments, it was over. Penagashea's breath had stopped, his body gone limp. It was not Lalawethika's fault! Not his fault, but his duty! The old medicine man had done this to himself. All treachery receives its due punishment. Lalawethika was only the carrier, a trader on these ephemeral shores.

And he told of cleansing the body with water from the lake, his first true act as medicine man, and of chanting the Shawnee songs of death to the rhythm of the waves lapping the shore, of dragging the corpse out into the lake and then dumping every last drop of Darius's sullied firewater. Once and for all, he turned his back on that unworthy traitor and also on the sun rising in the east—the same horizon that had turned white men loose upon their shores.

"I come, now, to Detroit," Lalawethika concluded. "I seek, Darius. Darius Devil, will meet, one day, reckoning. Red man blood, no more. Enemy, one enemy, white man, all. Darius, die first. Father Gabriel, has forgiveness, but not, without, guilt."

The wood inside the confessional creaked. The structure shook as the Father stepped out from the adjacent booth. The air inside was no longer stifling or rife with death. Lalawethika had brought it into the booth and expelled it through the grated panel to where Father Gabriel sat listening.

After a quiet moment with his thoughts, Lalawethika pushed the door open. It swung hard, the slam of the wood echoing high above in the rafters. All those sitting in the pews and immersed in their silent meditations looked up, startled and staring as Lalawethika stepped down. The Father was pale, swiveling his gaze uncertainly about the nave. After fixing his sights on the effigy of the Virgin Mary, he made the sign of the cross and cleared his throat.

"Your confession has been heard," he said. "Now...you must...you may not...you are no longer welcome here..."

The Father glanced down and saw the crucifix in Lalawethika's hand, along with the red streams trailing down his forearm. He recoiled as the blood splattered the stone tiles at their feet. With a gasp, he looked into Lalawethika's face, looking somehow both deeper than anyone ever had and also not looking at all, his focus unspeakably distant and hazy with fear as he murmured to himself, a prayer or a curse, and then he turned in retreat, rushing up to the altar where he prostrated himself below the likeness of his Savior.

A unfamiliar lightness and buoyancy lifted Lalawethika. Walking outside to face the Great Spirit in all its natural glory, he felt justified and validated. He had received forgiveness; he felt it in his heart. It was the first time in his memory that he had been free of his burning hatred. The sight of his own blood dripping from his fingertips and coating the crucifix did not render him sick. And even those worshipers hanging about the church would have sworn that Lalawethika did not walk out the doors, but that he floated—so light and graceful were his steps.

"How have you befriended that priest?" Tecumseh asked. Their horses were trotting at a relaxed pace. The rest of their party had fallen behind, towing the minimal provisions the British agents had provided.

Lalawethika reflected on the question. "He was a close friend of Changing Feathers."

"Is he not a missionary of the white religion?"

"He once was, but no longer. Now, he is just a priest. He has spent much time with red men, and he has a high opinion of our cultures and beliefs. He does not wish to meddle."

"And is he not also a representative of their government? It is a marvel that you have managed such a feat. He trusts you completely. Friendships with such men will serve to benefit us immensely. You should have been with us to bargain with the Britons. Be careful, though. Always keep them at an arm's distance."

"I intend to." Lalawethika regarded his brother seriously. "Never shall I return to that city. Father Gabriel possesses great knowledge, but he and I have shared all we have to share with one another."

Tecumseh seemed surprised by this answer. "And your ambition to become medicine man? Has it flagged since the epidemic?"

"Why would you ask that?"

"You have changed since the illness was upon us. I have never seen you as reserved and contemplative as you have been on this journey."

"I have many sins to atone for, brother. But my ambitions have not wavered. Rather, they have become focused, intense as the heart of a fire."

Tecumseh stared at Lalawethika and sighed. "Though your heart is set, I entreat you to think rationally. The Chief will not support you. You will toil away what strong years you have left, only to suffer misery and exile in old age. Same as that old fool, Changing Feathers. Once you step into that pit, you will be without a guide, lost."

"You show less loyalty than a wild dog," Lalawethika scoffed. "Perhaps I should keep a pack of mutts for my family instead."

Tecumseh smiled. "Since you gave up the white man's firewater, you have also developed a scathing way with words, brother. I admit, I was impressed with how you negotiated amongst the white men in Detroit. When you master their language, you will become an invaluable asset on future excursions. And if their government continues with current trends, you stand to be one of the most important members of our tribe. A voice like yours is better suited to crafty manipulations of emotion, appealing to foreign sensibilities, securing the means for the Shawnee people to survive."

"Blasphemer!" Lalawethika struck his horse and it leapt forward, spooking Tecumseh's horse to a halt. Lalawethika steadied and turned his animal so that he and his brother were face to face. "Coward! Snake! You are the dirt that stains the soles of my feet. You are the stench that clings to a whore's genitals." He reared his horse, its forelegs climbing high, nearly vertical, and its squeal startling birds out of the nearby treetops. "I will not use my gifts to befriend the white man. I will not follow you or the Chief into the white man's bed any sooner than I will allow fear to tear me from the path of righteousness as dictated to me by the Great Spirit. What warrior speaks as you have spoken? Of fears and doubts and of surrender? Of bargaining our courage away for the few rotted scraps of food that the white man will toss at our feet? Of crouching in the dirt and begging permission to occupy our own homes? If you insult me again with such suggestions, you can ride away from me now certain of one thing—you will be the first to be destroyed in the Great Spirit's wrath. My will is also the Great Spirit's will. And the flames of our world burn a thousand times hotter in the afterlife."

Chapter 41

The Horned Goat

THE TENDER NUDGING SENSATION RUBS GENTLY AT HIS MIDSECTION, a variable pressure moving here and there. Something had occurred in the night, but for once, there had been no Carnival. He wakes with a clear head, rested but languorous in an extended sleep that could just keep on truckin', as they say. Keep right on truckin' toward eternity's horizon and never a complaint, especially should this pleasant massaging sensation continue along the way. The scent of incense permeates the room, a hint of grapefruit and mint, too. The floor is not uncomfortable, though he can tell his alignment is all wrong. He needs to identify true north, adjust east-to-west, the mayhem of the night before never having offered him the chance. And he has only the vaguest memory of returning to the house, lying down or collapsing, or both. The howls had sounded from every direction while a hand led him on and away, or astray...

The sunlight becomes stronger and more apparent, easing him closer to wakefulness as the nudging and the pressure shift thigh-ward, a constant swiveling touch—Ionia, Ionia Josephina, her hand leading him on, now a moan, her bones, leading him away, beginning to stiffen, it shifts this way slightly, then that way, and now the pressure moves up toward the hip, works along pelvis and flesh, fleeting sensory-visions of women, their bodies all different, writhing beneath a blooming chaos of flowers and greens, concealed feathers and an eye watching from within the leaves. But their faces are all the same—Ionia, Ionia Josephina—it sure would be nice if this lazy foreplay stretched on indefinitely, all the way to eternity's horizon. This is the budding pleasure of life, not a death knell nor a coma of the flesh. The vague, translucent memory of Ionia's hand ripples across these last vestiges of sleep, the heat of her flesh, the flow of her blood, the sturdiness of her bones wrapped together with his.

Incapable of ignoring it any longer, he gives in and opens his eyes, expecting her face hanging over his, but—

A goat? Sniffing, prodding, horns protruding.

Johannes jerks away. Sliding back, he hits his head on an ornate antique trunk. No less startled, the goat jumps back, watching Johannes with its eyes wide and head tilted in...is that...recognition?

Wisps of memory rise like noxious exhaust fumes from an old pickup truck or the dust of the road kicked up. The same goat Pa Sonny tried to pass off to him all those months ago, kicking him out at the Creek's Ridge service station, telling him he looked like he needed a friend, offering him this companion to soften the solitude. But how, why does he recognize this goat, surely identical to a million-strong throng of other goats, when he barely knows the mentor who morally raised him? When he doesn't recall the family that literally raised him? When he can't apprehend the facets of a life that led him here? To the edge of the country, the known world.

The animal's gaze is warm and steady, if not a bit confused. Its head bobs to a human rhythm, the rhythms of speech, intonation, implication, telling him that yes, it's true, they know each other, they do, they have met before, the eyes alone capable of communicating as much. No need to ever speak again. Is that not how he got by in the mountains? Exchanging nonverbal information and quips with squirrels, foxes, songbirds, and Rozinante the cat. Although, with Knecht and Orion and Boötes, it had been different. With them, he spoke aloud and listened when they shared.

The goat trots forward, sniffs at Johannes's crotch, and then bites into the hem of his shirt. Johannes doesn't have a chance to dodge or resist. All it takes is one-two stiff tugs to tear a chunk right off. Two inches lower and it might've found and looted the treasures of manhood. The goat clops noisily to the opposite corner of the living room and lies down to gnaw on the fabric.

Someone laughs. Johannes looks up to see Ionia Josephina leaning against the doorframe, her arms crossed and a bored grin stretched across her lips.

"Sonny said you two knew each other, but I didn't believe him. The exciting and romantic adventures of Johannes Metternich and Emil Capricornus. Or is it John? John and the Horned Goat..." She laughs again and waves Johannes into the kitchen. "Get up. Lunch is ready."

Lunch consists of an enormous and colorful salad with boiled eggs. Before they start eating, Ionia tells him the vegetables are fresh from the garden and the eggs straight from the chicken coop. Johannes never saw a garden or a chicken coop, but he doesn't ask. He merely digs in, chewing his food in appreciative silence. They watch each other as they wade through the communal salad bowl. Though they communicate with eyes alone, they share more than he's shared with anyone in the past four months. They confirm with one another that everything is okay. The canine terror of the night before has passed, retreating into the desert. She was there for him, to witness his elevated fear and temper it, bring him down again. And she's still here for him now.

"What was that you were humming?" she asks.

"Humming? I wasn't..."

"Sure you were. On the floor. I thought you were awake. That's what drew Emil to you...your voice, the melody, it hypnotized him. He was chewing on your shirt for an hour before you woke..."

"I don't remember..."

"You were humming the same thing last night, I think. Weren't you? When the coyotes...and you talking..."

"It must have been..."

"You talked and talked. You said so much, I don't even know what. But it helped, it calmed you down a lot..."

"The Scrap..."

"It was beautiful, whatever it was."

"Rachmaninoff..."

Johannes offers to do the dishes and Ionia happily accepts, directing him to the kitchen sink. A little while later, he finishes and returns to the living room. Pa Sonny and Fairy are sprawled out on the sofa, but Ionia is nowhere to be found. Johannes stares at them, apologizing and backing out, but they stop him. They explain how they've just returned from the temple, and Ionia took Fairy's truck to run a few errands and meet a friend.

Their eyes had expressed many things during lunch, but they never got around to saying goodbye. He wonders whether she has gone to meet another officer from the base, whether he'll ever see her again. But all he says is, "What temple?"

"Oh, more of a personal sanctuary," Fairy croons. "Prayer and meditation, you'd think it gets easier as you get older. But I've expended every last trace of energy. And I still have dinner to prepare. The Master Idler here couldn't even lift himself off his haunches. Can you believe I had to lift him myself? Right under the armpits, like a toddler. Imagine it!"

"Looks like you're fully rested, though," Pa Sonny says to Johannes. "Good thing, too. I won't make it driving a single mile like this."

"I had to drive us home," Fairy nods along.

"Then we should get started, I guess." Johannes gazes at the truck through the front window.

"What's the hurry?" asks Pa Sonny. "Plenty of this Texan daylight left. A pity to waste it. And besides, wouldn't you like to give Ionia a proper farewell?"

"She'll be back by dinner time, Johannes," says Fairy. Both she and Pa Sonny grin between cryptic glances.

Johannes peers around the room uncertainly. From the corner where he slept, Emil Capricornus lifts its head and watches him, inquiring after the soul's deepest concerns.

"For the love of God," shouts Pa Sonny. "Relax and enjoy yourself. I've given you your freedom. Isn't that what you wanted? What do you need to get back there for? Those bones will always be there, most of them, anyway. Grant will always be there. Everyone and everything will always be there. If you need something to do so badly, why don't you take the truck? Drive into the city and get a taste of the modern age. Or try to cross your imaginary border out there and see if you can get into Mexico so easily, across the Grand River, you and your precious water. Ionia manages it, somehow. But freedom has its limits, too, boy. If you make it, though, then good on you. Try to befriend Ionia's coyotes while you're out there. An entire desert to explore following Coyote Man, your guide."

"It's not as difficult as he makes it sound." Fairy's laughter is melodious and punctuated by the slap she lands on Pa Sonny's arm. "You really can get over there if you're careful. And leave him alone, you nag. Have you completely lost touch with the world as the young see it? There's nothing wrong with keeping busy. If you want to, Johannes, you can give me a hand with dinner. Just allow me an hour more of this sofa-death."

Emil Capricornus sits up, cranking its head to look around the room.

"Do you mind if I...take the goat outside for a bit?"

"Best not," sings Fairy. "With those coyotes so hyperactive recently, it might not be safe. They become more and more comfortable around us by the day, coming nearer to the house than ever before. No fear anymore. We've lost ten chickens and four cats to them in the past year alone. That Ionia and her kindnesses, you see. Sooner or later—I keep telling her—sooner or later, they'll bite the hand that feeds them."

"Same thing I've been telling you," says Pa Sonny. "So this is what it takes for old Fairy to draw from her own lessons..."

"Freedom..." mumbles Johannes as he walks out the door to the sound of fresh laughter behind him.

The screen door slams as he descends the porch steps. He unfolds one of the lawn chairs, but as he looks around, at Pa Sonny's truck parked askew on the gravel, at the hearty green of the trees, at the sky tinged pastel blue through thin cloud cover, he knows he doesn't want to sit down right now. He doesn't desire solitude, calm, or silent contemplation. What he wants is Ionia. Barring that, he wants to dig. Instead, he is forced to wander, first into the trees and back to the picnic table, revisiting last night's scene of terror. Then he's off again, through fields of dried grass and clumps of dirt, rows where crops haven't been planted in several seasons, past the ridge where he'd chased after Ionia and witnessed a sunset to rival those he once called his own. Eventually, he circles back and finds himself deposited in the yard again, standing over the small pit dug out at the rear of the property. A puzzling minute passes with Johannes staring into the hole, knowing something is off but unable to identify what. And then he remembers—the rib bones. Every last one of them, they're gone. There's a paw print clearly embedded in a spot of dirt beside the pit. He is alone with the sensation of coyotes circling around him, thirteen sets of legs, that's fifty-two paws ripping silently through the grass, mingling and rubbing fur against fur, aggressive and affectionate, in complex coverage of the desert and the yard, stalking the house, surrounding it with the hungry eyes of addicts as he attempts to steady the noticeable trembling of his hands. He follows all these imperceptible tracks to the edge of the field where browning stalks reach up to his chest and extend as far as he can see, patches of bushes and short trees, with bland flowers spread throughout. The Disciples have slunk back into the field, coursing deftly through this sea of concealing grass, without concern for the intimidating border of the Rio Grande, and finally disappearing into the desert beyond, for now.

"What can I do?"

The kitchen is already in disarray. Barbecue sauce simmers on the stove. Vegetables and spices litter the countertop. Music drifts through the house, a neurotic orchestral piece. Fairy tosses an onion at him from across the room and nods at the cutting board.

"Do you enjoy Stravinsky?" she says as she pulls a cleaver from a hook on the wall and hacks into the rack of ribs. "I've been introducing him to music for years—anything at all, really—Chopin, Tchaikovsky, Coltrane, Dylan, Ravi Shankar, The Mothers of Invention. But he has the attention span of a two-year-old when it comes to culture."

"How about Rachmaninoff?"

Fairy is looking over Johannes's shoulder. "Don't chop them so finely," she nudges him. "You only need to break them apart. They should be big, thick, like fingers. Rachmaninoff's symphonies are spellbinding. His concertos, too." She watches him briefly before moving to the stove to stir her barbecue sauce. "I sure hope you don't turn out like Dunmore later on in life. He's a wonderful man, in his way, but the world does not need another."

"Dunmore?"

Fairy grins and nods. "Don't you even remember that? My, my, and you never thought to ask, did you? Oh, Johannes. Pastor Dunmore Judson. Sonny, of course, to you, to most."

"He hasn't given me much to work with. Not about himself or about me."

"No, of course he hasn't," Fairy laughs. "That's where you get it from. He's toying with you, Johannes, pushing, testing for stress points. He's still trying to figure out...oh, how can I say it?"

"Just how broken I am?" Johannes sets down the knife and wipes tears from his cheeks.

"More like how broken he is. Don't get the wrong idea. This trip has not been for you, even if he does trust you more than most." She takes the onions from him and drops them into a frying pan. After they begin to sizzle, she removes the pan from the burner. "I always make men chop the onions," as she dumps them into a large bowl with the rice. "Love to see men cry. The first time he ever met you, you don't remember the story? Knowing your folks, perhaps no one's ever told you..."

"You knew my parents?"

Fairy winks. "It was your baptism, of course. You'd been sleeping the entire service, not a peep or a complaint, not even when your parents brought you forward and handed you over. Dunmore held you in his arms, rocking you and bouncing on the balls of his feet as he often did, blessing you with the same scripted speech he recited for every baptism he ever performed. Then, suddenly, he stopped. Stopped bobbing, stopped speaking, and only stared—at you. When he lifted his eyes to the congregation, his fright was as evident as a thunderstorm. The true word of the Lord. You, young man, had stopped breathing in his arms. A full minute passed, maybe even two, with him frozen stiff as the crucifix, incapable of calling for help or even announcing the problem. Claimed he couldn't even pray during those endless seconds, that he was spiritually stunted, in holy shock. Toughest trial of his life, he often says. After a while, your eyes shot open and your gasp for breath was such that it echoed throughout the chapel's silence. The relief delivered upon him at that moment was unlike anything I've ever witnessed. And I've seen plenty. You initiated an honest-to-goodness metamorphosis in him, obvious to even the most stubborn of skeptics. It was all he could do to collect himself and complete the ceremony without—I don't know what—bursting into song or something. Hasn't been the same since."

"You were there?"

She glances at him, then smiles as she shoves her bare hands into the rice bowl. "Unfortunately for him, the members of that church were blind to the nature of the spirit. They chalked his change up to alcohol and never looked back. He never bobs anymore. Stationary as a two-ton boulder."

"But what were you...why were you...how did the two of you meet?"

"Personal sanctuary," she says, winks again. "Come now, Johannes. Is it really so difficult to believe that we've crossed paths before, you and I? The world is large, but our personal realms are not. No matter how thin you try to spread yourself, overlaps are unavoidable. The strands that link you to others are the very same strands that wrap so tightly around you and keep you from dissipating completely into nothingness. Sometimes they squeeze too tight, but that's what strengthens you, gives you form, defines your essence. Pass me the wine, dear. There, next to the habaneros."

"So you weren't a member of the church?"

"My hands are a mess. Pour a bit in for me, will you? Here, in the bowl. A little more. I used that church for many years, but not as others do. You'll have to stir the sauce."

"What do you mean by personal sanctuary?"

"You know exactly what I mean," she pauses and glares at Johannes. "Don't play dumb. If you want to ask something, it's better to just ask it."

Tiny eruptions explode in the sauce pot. Johannes yelps when the boiling, oily splatter lands on his forearm. "When we first arrived, I thought maybe you two were...brother and sister?"

"Oh dear," laughs Fairy, "just imagine it..."

"Then I thought you might be old friends, grown close over the years, through business or..."

"Nothing so noble, I'm afraid. We're lovers, Johannes. In the truest and most honest sense, unfortunately."

"Then, I'm wondering..." Johannes stirs and stares, mesmerized as the oil separates from the sauce, the trail left in the spoon's wake as he drags it around. "How you ended up here? And Pa Sonny in Creek's Ridge?"

"You want life stories, is that it? I suppose you bookish types prefer to have it all in one shot, don't you? Since I respect you, and since you're leaving tonight, I'll give you the condensed version. But I told you to stir that sauce, not to pet it."

By the time Fairy was twenty-five, she had set foot on each of the populated continents several times over, but her travels came to an abrupt halt with an extended sojourn in India, where she studied Hinduism, sitar, yoga, and the Kama Sutra. Upon learning this, her strict Roman Catholic parents, Mr. and Mrs. Adamire Faystone, threatened to cut her off. A ceaseless tour of the world's cultural landmarks and capital cities was one thing, but this heathenistic personal investment into the Third World was unacceptable. Fairy had settled in a village to the north of Varanasi, living simply, off the land, and never once touching the American dollars that continued to flow into her bank account. After two years of this, the Faystones demanded with one final roar that she return to New England at once, finish her education, and begin leading a respectable life. She replied with a long letter informing them that she was getting more of an education than they could imagine and that they themselves might benefit heroically by following her lead. They responded by cutting off her funds and publicly disowning her.

Although Fairy had long been at odds with her parents, she had always loved them. In fact, love was one of the prickliest subjects of contention between them. Fairy's outpourings of love stood in stark contrast to her parents' cold indifference to the world beyond their social circle, which Fairy first perceived at the age of five while visiting relatives in the south of Scotland, near Edinburgh. Meeting distant relations for the first time drew up powerful waves of affection and emotion, which she doled out without discretion. Her parents' bitterness during that trip, their short tempers and condescending manner toward their relatives, and finally their rebukes of young Fairy's unsuitably tender behavior—all this distressed their daughter and perhaps opened her eyes. But it turned out to be the issue of her name that would jab like a lance for many years to come. Until that point, her birth name, Fredericka Faystone, had been her only name. Without exception, her parents introduced her as Fredericka, and they had never used so much as a pet name with her. Not sweetie, darling, pumpkin, princess, not even Freddie. But an older cousin in Scotland, with whom young Fredericka had immediately formed a strong bond, took to calling her by the name Fairy, due in part to a speech impediment but also in acknowledgment of Fairy's graceful, flighty, almost magical charm. The very moment young Fredericka heard the nickname uttered from her cousin's lips, she knew she had been misnamed, that her one true name—the identity of her soul—was Fairy. From that moment on, she began introducing herself as Fairy, and the only people who ever refused to accept the name were her parents.

After India, she studied Buddhism in various Eastern religious epicenters, then slowly wandered west, revisiting favorite locations and people across the Middle East and Europe until she found herself back on the American side of the Atlantic, volunteering and organizing charity work in Chicago. But for a city as diverse and energetic as Chicago, it proved sorely lacking in places that might provide personal sanctuary. Very nearly resolved to continue her westward momentum, her restlessness was wrested by a dashing young pastor with a heart as light as a feather whom she happened to meet during a charity march along the shore of Lake Michigan. Pastor Dunmore 'Sonny' Judson invited her to his church on the city's outskirts, and when she finally paid a visit a few weeks later, she discovered her sanctuary. Though she rarely attended the services, she was amused by Pastor Sonny's passionate sermons and enthusiastic but cynical worldview. This man was nearly free, and he helped ground her in this strange country where she now felt so alien. But her connection to the religion he preached differed vastly from the congregation's understanding of it. She visited the church mostly during off hours, often late at night, to exercise her soul with a meditation routine she had perfected in India. It had proven difficult to adapt this strict practice to life in a bustling modern city, but she found that contemplation and meditation came easily in Pastor Sonny's church. She could melt into time itself, with an assurance of silence and safety, drowning herself in her inner world for hours at a time without fear of interruption, approaching that peculiar, indescribable emptiness-of-self where secrets and revelations dwell. She continued to live, work, and volunteer in the city, and as the years went on, she spent more and more time at the church, eventually taking charge of their fledgling volunteer and donations program. She practiced yoga there, played sitar, cooked spicy curry dishes in the kitchen, painted occasionally, and spent countless hours immersed in conversation with Pastor Sonny.

As Fairy finishes preparing the rice, she's motionless, gazing into the living room. Johannes leans over to see what she's looking at—Pa Sonny, just beyond the window, sitting in a rocking chair on the front porch and sipping bourbon on the rocks with Fairy's approval.

"It was indeed rare," Fairy continues, "and purely by chance, that I was present for your baptism. And it was only after that service that Dunmore and I realized the true intensity of our feelings. There were no longer any barriers, no longer any doubt. You freed him." She turns toward Johannes with a sad smile, then laughs nostalgically. "Not long after that, I introduced him to the Kama Sutra. I suppose we ought to thank you."

"Too bad we're not staying longer," says Johannes. "I'd like to hear the long version."

Fairy laughs, swooning at the thought of divulging more. "My dear, not even Dunmore knows the full story. And besides, you should be more interested in Ionia's story than mine."

"Ionia's story is still unfolding. It's a story to pay attention to as it evolves. And I would...I would like to be able to. To pay attention, I mean. But I can barely manage that much with my own story. Your life, though...your life is brimming with knowledge and lessons and experience. She's lucky to have you."

"Already intending to stay in touch, are we? Or, perhaps, to stick around?"

"I've thought of it..."

"You're welcome to. We could use the help. We're all fortunate, Johannes. We're all mystics if we choose to be. Fate doesn't spin positively or negatively for anybody. It's a catapult, and each of us gets only one ride. Dreamers, philosophers, and soldiers alike. Fanatics, lunatics, and everyday folk. Anyone can learn to see beyond the catapult's trajectory. If you think any notion of fate controls or restricts you, then you're a fool. I cleansed my hands of that when I untangled myself from my parents' net. Our conscious decisions and actions define our fates, embellish them. But we all land in the same nasty pool. There's nothing so spectacular about my life. I have found a balance with my place in the world, as a breathing creature of this earth. That's all."

"What about Ionia?" Johannes watches as Fairy picks up the wine bottle, adds a few more drops to the rice bowl, and then takes a huge swig herself. "If you found your balance out in the world, then wouldn't she be better off...I mean...out in the world?"

"Ionia may yet be young, but she is a grown woman, after all. Her own woman, free to leave whenever she likes. I don't know what she's told you, but she may have spun you a web. Takes after her father in that regard, I'm afraid. No, she stays here because she is invested in our work. She's a part of it. She believes in it."

"What work? On the base?"

"On the border, Johannes. We run a sort of halfway house here. Undocumented migrants. We help them cross the border safely and then shelter them until time and circumstance ensure they can reach their final destination. And if they have no destination, we inform them of their options. Without people like us to help them charitably, at no cost, they would either die crossing the desert, indenture themselves to the coyotes, incurring debts they can never pay off and endangering their families, or else wind up in a detention center, forgotten by the world. But they will never stop trying. We just help them to do it safely. Do you see now? Understand? Don't worry, there's no one hiding out here at the moment."

"Isn't it risky? Doesn't that put you both in danger?"

"Certainly. But it's no different from the danger you got yourself into on that mountain, is it? Ionia loves what we do, and she's good at it. I noted certain qualities in her when she was still quite young, and I nurtured them. Perhaps that is the paradox of fate. Fate and freedom—they are cages. We are bound the moment we are born. But what else is a parent to do? There was never a question of raising her otherwise. At least not with Dunmore off on his mission from God, or whatever he's calling it these days. But at some point, perhaps when we two are dead and gone, she will be forced to find a new road, her own sanctuary. Like you did."

"Wait, you mean...Pa Sonny is...her father?"

"Oh my, Johannes..." Fairy says with a furrowed brow and a disappointed shake of the head. "What did you think was going on here? Some kind of make-believe playhouse? I take back what I said. You are broken. How would you like to have a real surprise?" She hands Johannes the wine bottle with a nod, a wink, a secretive grin. "As you got older, you and I often crossed paths at the church. Your parents didn't care much for me, but you were always a little sweetheart. And you have also met Ionia once before. If you'd brought your senses down off that mountain with you, you might be able to recall the day yourself. Ionia had only just been born, so we decided to have a sort of baptismal ceremony at the church. We called it a baptism for the sake of appearances, but it was really just our way of introducing her into the Community of Man."

"The Community of Man? You mean like...?"

"Indeed. You're living in it, up there in Creek's Ridge. You would have been eight or nine years old, I suppose. You were seated front and center with your family. Grant and his family sat directly behind you, as usual. And Dunmore was, well, he was drunk that morning, but he was so beloved by his congregation that they let it slide, and so did I. He and I had agreed to perform the ceremony as we saw proper, and it was...unconventional. He never told them, of course, that it was his child. As far as I know, he's never told anyone. Believing Ionia to be my child alone, with no father in the picture, those in attendance were confused at the least and offended at the most. But they were also curious. They sat through the ceremony, every one of them except for your parents, who grabbed you and your sister—Sammy, isn't it?—and stormed out, cursing openly as they did so. But you, young John Metternich, you were fixated on the ceremony, on Dunmore's baffling words and mannerisms, and on our little angel. You argued with your parents right there in the aisle, in front of everyone, and finally flat-out defied them when you went to sit out the service with the Cagnisses. I can still recall the look in your eyes as you gazed at our darling Ionia. How's that for your precious fate?" Fairy belts out a harsh laughter, lacking any form of melodiousness. "Memory can be a wonderful thing at times."

"I don't usually yearn to remember..." Johannes sips from the wine bottle. "Sometimes I wish I would. Why didn't my parents like you?"

"Because, at your baptism, I overheard them calling you John. The moment they had you christened as Johannes—such a lovely name—there they were, taking the cheap way out and calling you by another name. I pointed this flippancy out to them. It was ludicrous, and I told them so. They did not appreciate my meddling, and they never forgot it, to say nothing of forgiveness. Or admitting their own fault."

"Wow... Thanks for that."

"But their decision wormed its way into you anyhow, didn't it? A fully grown adult before you claimed your identity for yourself, only to promptly mishandle it. Your mistakes, not theirs. I could never have raised Ionia as my parents raised me. I never expected Dunmore to be active, or even present in her life. A part of me hoped he would be, but our differences would have compromised her upbringing. Better to have aborted her than to bring her up trapped between two immovable walls like Dunmore and myself. Freedom is all-important, Johannes. You're right about that. I found it in India with the help of several yogis and monks, but as soon as I touched it, I knew it had been with me all along. The very cage I had always been bound by. Ionia will discover something similar when she's ready. I've guided her and shown her many things about the world, about herself. But the world around you means nothing until you've discovered freedom for yourself. Surely, one day, Ionia will find herself in India or someplace equally illuminating.

Perhaps the Smoky Mountains? Any place on earth has the potential to illuminate. And she will take far more away from her special place than I ever could have. Because she won't be starting over, as I was. You know what I mean."

"You think my time in the mountains was good for me? Necessary?"

"Neither good nor bad. Your time there simultaneously created you and was created by you. *It is you,* Johannes. Caged and freed at the same time, a tragicomedy of reversals."

"But—"

"But nothing. It is, so it is. That's it."

The screen door creaks and slams. They hear Pa Sonny curse in pain and then a momentary tussle. Johannes sips from the wine bottle again while Fairy casually glances behind her.

"That damned animal charged at me!" Pa Sonny's face is red as he limps into the kitchen, grabbing his crotch. "Soon as I opened the door! Rammed its nub-of-a-horn right into my machinery..."

"Trying to repair it for you, I reckon," Fairy smiles. "Give it a jump start."

"Nastiest goat I've ever come across." Pa Sonny hands his empty glass to Fairy.

"How many is this now? Three or four?" Fairy glances from Sonny to Johannes as she refills the glass with ice and bourbon.

Behind Fairy's back, Pa Sonny silently, vigorously holds up three fingers to Johannes.

"I make it four," says Johannes.

"My, my, we sure are burning through our allowance today, aren't we?" She fills the glass and hands it back to Sonny, then gives his cheek a pinch and a slap. "Johannes, have you ever seen him with a drink in his hand up in that little town of yours?"

"Summer is my busiest time of year," Pa Sonny objects. "And the harvest is right around the corner."

"I've never—" Johannes is shaking his head, watching Pa Sonny, remembering certain chance sightings. "I rarely see him."

"I'm on the road every day."

"Never stopped you before." Fairy scrutinizes each of them in turn. "I'm not sure whether either one of you is trustworthy."

"Grant swears that he's been sober for years," adds Johannes.

"Ah yes, from the mouths of prophets," Fairy scoffs. "Grant the almighty. Grant the honorable leader, heir apparent to the noble Emil Wood."

"Emil?" says Johannes. "The goat?"

"The founder of Creek's Ridge..." Fairy looks curiously at Johannes and then turns sharply to Pa Sonny. "He's been living there for almost half a year and you haven't even given him a clue to the place's significance?"

"Emil the Blunderer, more like," Pa Sonny shrugs as he sips his bourbon. "I'm not his caretaker. And I know he knew something about Creek's Ridge before his mountain hermitage. Johannes the Vagrant, no different from Emil the Vagabond."

"If he had known, perhaps he would not have gone to the mountains."

"Or maybe that's exactly why he went."

"When you get home, Johannes, take the time to visit that wonderful library beneath St. Josephine's and learn the history of Creek's Ridge—or relearn it, if you will. No shame in that. A fascinating story. Just the sort of thing people like us appreciate."

Pa Sonny jumps forward with a wild shout, spilling the entire contents of his glass. "The bastard just bit me on the ass!"

Emil Capricornus runs circles in the living room, hooves clopping on the floorboards.

"Tough shit," says Fairy. "That's your last one. And clean up the mess."

Pa Sonny groans and grabs a rag off the counter. "If I was young and limber...I'd bend down to lick it up."

"It would suit you, too," Fairy laughs.

Pa Sonny sets down his glass. He examines the rag and the puddle on the floor.

"A treasure trove of valuable religious works down there," continues Fairy, "along with Emil Wood's original journals. He documented most everything, from his arrival in Florida all the way through to the approach of death. How's your Spanish?"

"I'm not sure..." says Johannes.

"Of course you aren't," mumbles Pa Sonny.

"There were only partial translations the last time I visited, far from complete. I would hope someone has done something about it by now. I nearly took it upon myself, but...the writing becomes trickier to navigate once he started to lose a grip."

"Lose a grip...on the town?" asks Johannes.

Pa Sonny laughs.

Fairy's lips curve into a smile, ready to join Sonny's laughter until she notes Johannes's earnest bewilderment. "On reality, Johannes."

Johannes trades glances with each of them. "But why?"

"Weren't you listening to the story last night?" Pa Sonny is irritated, still glaring at the spilled liquor.

"I was...but the coyotes..."

"Local tensions," says Fairy.

"The Native American raids?"

"So you do know something," says Pa Sonny.

"More like the cause of the raids," Fairy shakes her head. "Emil Wood's wife and their daughter...such a tragic story, it really is. What we told you last night were only bits and pieces. The good pastor and I exercising our dramatic bones. Visit the library."

"I remember that. He shot his wife? Rabies? A coyote?"

"Well, yes. That's one version of the story, for those who have dipped their toes in it. But dig a little further and you find it's a bit more complicated than that. Everything is. It may not have been a mercy killing at all, but calculated. Planned. Followed by these layers of deception to cover up the truth. Their daughter, Josephine, you see, was by all accounts angelic in every sense. Beautiful, pure, generous, and honest. Qualities which shone through from the moment she was born on the very day they founded the settlement."

"The original settlement? And that was the Community of Man?"

"That's right. Both of them being born on the same day was considered the best of omens. What could possibly go wrong? Throughout her childhood, she was adored by everyone who lived there and all who passed through. She became the symbol of what the town was meant to be and the principles upon which it was founded. For a time, it was just that—a free, open, and accepting community, where people of all backgrounds came together to worship the Earth and the solidarity they'd built. All sorts came through, families heading west, journeymen and explorers, traders, and religious zealots. Even criminals on the run were welcomed, the roughest of individuals. Whoever it was, just half a day with the Community pacified them, showing them there were better uses for their energy. While Josephine was a child, the town was exactly what they had intended it to be. But no one remains a child for very long."

"Have you lived in Creek's Ridge, too?"

"Oh my, no. Passed through..."

"Tell him the truth, you scamp," mutters Pa Sonny.

Fairy smiles and nods. "I did intend to settle there, but things changed. In the end, I only visited."

"Visited?" bursts Pa Sonny. "For two years!"

"That's a long visit," agrees Johannes.

"A year and a half," says Fairy. "Nothing to your seven years, is it?" And then turning on Pa Sonny, "Or your nine." She sighs. "I had visited before that and have returned a few times since, though it has been ages. Nearly fifteen years, I'd say. Ionia, too, she was with me. Back then, when I still had ambitions to change the world, I studied the great free-thinkers. Social innovators, spiritual idealists, that sort of thing. I visited Creek's Ridge for one reason and then promptly got the hell out of there."

"Why?"

"Once I learned the true history, I smelled something...call it failure. Call it a peat bog of untruths. A festering hive of unethical codes, dubious doctrine. Emil Wood decided to call it The Community of Man after befriending that ornery old prophet and laying the groundwork. The whole thing was built on fond reminiscences, a flimsy foundation at best. Both Wood and his new friend, the prophet, were trying to recreate the most peaceful, happy times of their lives. They claimed to be creating something truly for the people, the modern age, the forward momentum of life itself, but in the end, their wills faltered and gave way to weak-willed longing. They were cowards wishing to relive the past, nothing more. Such a letdown..."

"The prophet? Is that Tens-kwa-ta-wa?"

"Look at him go today," Pa Sonny nods admiringly. "Putting pieces together, recalling fragments and whispers. That Ionia's magic touch? Or them coyotes scared you straight? In any case, this is your national history, boy. The least a forager like you ought to be up on."

"The infamous Shawnee rogue," continues Fairy. "He hid his dual motives from his new friend, Wood. For one, a deep-seated desire to rebuild Prophetstown, his utopia on the Tippecanoe River. But also, he still harbored the fiercest hatred for white men. Though he had been saved by them countless times since his failures as a revolutionary—in fact, Emil Wood proved to be his final savior—he always intended to have his revenge. If he couldn't rid the country of white men, then he would at least make as many of them as miserable as he possibly could."

"How?"

"In their hearts, the people believed in the ideals of the Community. They wanted so badly for it to be real."

"Hogwash..." says Pa Sonny.

"Tenskwatawa had always been a master of playing off people's emotions. He knew how to draw out their deepest desires and fears and then turn those qualities against them. Even as a little girl, Josephine loomed over them. In their eyes, she actually became something she was only ever meant to represent. Their projections of her faultlessness obscured their wishes and dreams. But behind closed doors is where people confront their doubts. And the prophet remained behind those doors with them, speaking to them in private, setting them up for failure. He set them against each other. A word here, a suggestion there—sowing the seeds that he knew would one day overtake the Community and be their downfall. Poisoning their beliefs while leaving his own hands clean. The most wicked trick of his life, planted and sowed for so many years, tendrils wrapped right around Josephine, though she likely never knew it. Throughout her old age, she had only fond recollections of her 'Shawnee Grandfather,' as she called him."

"How do you know that?" interrupts Pa Sonny. "You've never seen her journals."

"There were some who had. And when I was there, a few elderly residents were still alive, those who had been children during her final years."

"More hogwash. She was a recluse. Nobody saw her in those years."

"What did the prophet do to her?" asks Johannes.

"He merely pointed out to his fellow red men within and around the Community that Josephine's blood was half red. Her mother was a Cherokee. Her eyes conveyed the heavy sadness of the natural world, and her skin was dark, even darker than her mother's, which was an effect of her father's Moorish heritage. The Natives would not have understood that complicated genealogy. As an orphan, Wood himself didn't even understand it. But, oh my, what a shame if young Josephine's pure, innocent, indigenous beauty were to be claimed, taken, mishandled, and corrupted by the greed of white men. Over the years, his rhetoric shifted until he finally convinced each tribe that it was their sacred duty to protect Josephine by marrying her into their tribe. Under a veil of secrecy that would not become apparent until Josephine came of age, he had pitted the tribes against the town and against themselves. The masterstroke, however, was her mother. He appealed to her heritage and convinced her that she must not allow her daughter or the town to fall into the grasp of evil. The only way to ensure that was to see her daughter enter into a tribal union. And so she took up the mantle and began her campaign. But since she did so with less skill and subtlety than Tenskwatawa, her assertions only managed to draw a line in the sand. Her claims were illogical, against the entire belief system of the Community she had helped to create, so her voice only sounded all the more divisive. The debate became public, rifts were formed, and the peoples' true beliefs and allegiances were exposed. And all of this before poor Josephine was even ten years old."

"So Emil Wood didn't shoot his wife because she was sick? He did it to stop his daughter from being married off?"

"Or perhaps she did have rabies. Perhaps he or some other member of the Community caused her to contract the disease, to cover their need to be rid of her. And again, perhaps he was not protecting his daughter but the Community of Man, his creation disintegrating before his very eyes."

"Wood was more twisted than we give him credit for," says Pa Sonny. "He left all the nasty bits out of his journals, always trying to make a saint of himself. But it's all there, between the lines—his thievery and vagabond life, his training under the Seminoles, his loose principles when it came to faith and the law. He was recognized as a sharp-shooter by none other than Robert Ambrister. I don't trust Wood for a minute."

"Indeed. The problem with the clergy. The point of the story, Johannes, is that no matter how many stones you overturn, there is always something more to be revealed. Always a new angle to view and approach from. As you know."

"I do?"

"What else are mountaintops for? Still, one must eventually ascertain the terrain from up close, no? Some paths provide for wonderful explorations, others not so."

"How do you know which is which?"

"Or who's a witch?" Pa Sonny laughs.

"Only after it's too late, I'm afraid." Fairy smiles sadly. "We can stand around here conjecturing about the beliefs and motives of those people a hundred-and-fifty years on. But for them, for Josephine and her parents, and even Tenskwatawa, it was just life happening to them, speeding by and leaving them behind while they reacted in real time. Therefore, how can we observe them through the distorting bifocals of time and expect to understand their trials any better than we understand our own? It requires but a glance at your own reflection in the mirror to remind yourself of the difficult task before you. How are we to grasp the essence? How are we to truly understand what we see reflected back at us? Within the mirror and beyond it. But, most importantly, you must know when it's time to look away."

"That's why you left Creek's Ridge?"

"It simply wasn't what I thought it would be, what I'd hoped. Or maybe it was, but seeing it like that, up close, I only saw the blemishes. Those sorts of grand schemes and ideas, the great coming-togethers of humanity, they may end well in theory, but in this unpredictable world, it's a gamble that rarely pays out. I recognized that time was passing me by too quickly for me to ever apprehend. So, yes, I stopped trying. I left and did what I needed to do to give Ionia and myself the best chance to seek the truth. No point in trying to force something that's no longer there and possibly never was to begin with."

"And yet here you are," Pa Sonny grumbles, "in the midst of it.

Setting up your very own Creek's Ridge. Faystone's Chasm, shall we call it?"

"Says the man who wallows in Emil's Shame. Adopted it as his own. Gambled away even the crumbs. Even your mountain, Johannes, couldn't have taken from you as unforgivingly."

"You'd be surprised," says Johannes.

"No. I wouldn't. I've lost things, too. Been lost myself. Even when it seems you are all alone, it's rare that you truly are. Anyway, when I was last there, Wood's original journals were the only copies, and they were in tatters. I do hope someone has remedied that, along with some translations. The resident priest at that time was an asshole of special breeding. A few locals told me that Josephine also kept extensive journals throughout her life. But that son-of-a-bitch-of-a-priest had them hidden. Wouldn't even admit their existence. A lying clergyman is always easy to spot."

"Because we're all liars," says Pa Sonny.

"I hope he's dead," says Fairy. "And I do not wish that upon most folks."

"He is," says Pa Sonny, "but the current priest isn't much better. And he looks like a muskrat." Pa Sonny tosses the rag to Johannes. "My back and knees...would you mind, kid?"

Johannes looks at the rag and the puddle at Pa Sonny's feet. "So you named the goat after the founder? And Capricornus...the horned sea goat..."

"Emil, yes," says Fairy. "Emil Capricornus. So glad you're familiar with the stars. Maybe you can teach old Dunny here a thing or two after all. I told you, Johannes, it's a small, small world, this. And deception is God's favorite pastime."

Pa Sonny chuckles as he gazes wistfully into his empty glass.

Johannes says nothing as he lowers himself onto his knees.

Fairy sighs. "Dunmore, leave him here. We can help him."

"Sweetheart," Pa Sonny laughs, "you can't even clean up the mess you've created in your own home. How can I trust you with him? Creek's Ridge won't break him. He can rest there. Collect his wits before moving on to someplace...more suitable."

"That's what he said about himself nine years ago," says Fairy, looking down at Johannes, "on his way here to join us for good."

Johannes lets the cloth soak up the spilled bourbon, wiping over the floor again and again until the streaks of alcohol begin to evaporate. He stands up and rings out the rag over the sink. He washes his hands and dries them on his pants, and when he turns around again, they're both watching him.

"Sonny might be right," Johannes says to Fairy. "I still feel too fragile...or lost...or incomplete. And I have unfinished work in Creek's Ridge. But I'll visit. I do want to come back. Truly, everything here, you and Ionia, the food and the desert, the stars, everything has been incredible. Peaceful. The perfect escape. Everything, except the coyotes..."

Fairy accepts Johannes's decision with her customary warm smile and a firm pat on the back before she begins preparing the ribs for the grill. After stealing a few drops of bourbon, Pa Sonny walks through the living room to the front porch, mumbling curses at the goat.

"But Fairy," says Johannes. "How did you leave Creek's Ridge? Why does it seem so difficult for everyone?"

"Admitted the truth. No matter how disappointing, I had to admit the truth. Then I just caught the next ride out."

"I tried that. I've already done that..."

"Yes, but then you went back. And now you're heading back again. No telling what might happen."

"I'm glad he brought me. I wasn't at first, but I am now. I never expected...any of this."

"You'll come again?"

"I will, I'll..."

"You're welcome here anytime, you know. You could help us, our work..."

"Crossing the border...yes, maybe, I could learn. These two days have been... You... You've given me a sense of stability that I haven't felt in..."

"Shh. The fewer words for now, the better. Just leave me with the memory of your humming, that haunting melody..."

"The concerto, you can listen to it yourself, it's—"

"Shh, no. I don't want to know. I prefer to hear it from you, the slippery calm in your voice. The way you make peace, comfort, loneliness, and fear all hang from the melody by a thread."

"Do I?"

"You do. But if you're anything like him, you won't be back for a long while. Anything can happen in that time. Anything. Best not to force form upon the formless. I'll try to remember the tune, your voice. You will, too."

"..."

"I hope you're nothing like him."

"Me too. And you...if you ever need to...get away...you can always come to see us. In Creek's Ridge. You've been there?"

"Only when I was a child. I would love to, though. To go back again. I've heard so much... I want to see the church, St. Josephine's. You know, my name is...I was named after her, the Saint, in part..."

"No, I didn't realize... From everything Fairy told me about Josephine and her family, what she thinks about them, she might regret that now..."

"Not at all. I don't know what she told you, but she didn't tell you what she truly thinks. She told you what she thought you needed to hear. That's her way. You get used to it..."

"But it's such a disheartening story..."

"She hasn't told you everything—and me neither. She seems to have given us different jumping points. The Josephine I know was the bravest, strongest, and most honest woman. A survivor. A true saint."

"She wants us to discover it on our own..."

"Yes. But perhaps we can help each other. Someday. Someday, I'll visit. I'd like to visit the library there. Learn more about her, about Josephine. But Fairy, you know, she won't go...and our work is...unpredictable...important...we can't just leave..."

"She can stay. You can go alone. You don't have to bring her along."

"Shall I bring the coyotes instead?"

"..."

"Keep you on your toes? But will you still be there?"

"I don't know..."

"You'd better be going..."

"No. Yes. I should...good—"

"Don't. Don't say that. Whenever we get someone safely across the border, help them get set up, and finally set them loose in the country, we never say goodbye. Goodbyes are for the end. Right now, it's only getting late. You have a long drive ahead. Don't say anything. Not yet."

"Yes, right, I do, okay..."

"And Johannes. Try to remember their names. The Disciples. For next time."

"I will, I'll...try..."

"But no cheating..."

"Cheating?"

"You have to really remember..."

As they get further from the city, the stars multiply exponentially until everything about the sky recalls Johannes's final morning in the woods, the storm and the landslide already weeks past as he woke from a mind-numbing rest to a crystal clear pleasure dome swelling overhead, twinkling pin-points spread all throughout a deep blue pre-morning, fading and then replaced by a heavy silence as fear crept in from every dark corner of the forest, fear that had never inhabited that place before but now dominated every aspect of life there, shoving him into a sudden terror-fueled stealing from the woods.

"A fine sky this evening..." Pa Sonny has noticed Johannes's lack of concentration on the road. "Your precious constellations."

"Is she your wife?"

"No. No..."

Johannes contorts himself for a better view of the sky, trying to see upward through the windshield, shoving head and shoulders out his window and setting his focus to infinity, desperately searching for Boötes and his hounds working the oxen, for Orion lost in his simultaneous pursuit and escape. Failing that, Johannes retreats somewhat, widening his gaze in search of any grounding star to locate his bearings, all while in control of this vehicle, their two lives, linked and limited here together, the entire barely-controlled system momentarily gone haywire as the truck veers one way and the other.

"But, Ionia?"

"Be careful," says Pa Sonny, reaching over to steady the steering wheel after a few stomach-churning swerves. "That's my advice. Be careful."

"Of what?"

"Shouldn't have brought you along... I forget sometimes..."

"Forget what?" Johannes waits. "I forget, too, you know. At least tell me if I'm headed in the right direction."

The thermos rests in Pa Sonny's lap, both hands wrapped securely around it. Since they left—almost an hour ago now—Pa Sonny has been mostly tight-lipped, refusing to help Johannes navigate toward Creek's Ridge. Johannes has had to rely on memory to retrace their route, but the further they go, the less sure he becomes. Road signs announce places like Odessa, Grandfalls, San Angelo, Carlsbad, Roswell. Every so often, there's a larger sign with San Antonio, Austin, or Dallas-Fort Worth in bold letters. But it's the billboards promising Mexican getaways that get his mind churning, the suggestion that they turn south and hop the border together, crossing that Grand River to disappear in the sand of pristine beaches or the chaotic jungles of Mayan history. But jumping the border would have been easier with Fairy and Ionia's help, as with everything else, apparently.

"Goddamnit, Sonny," Johannes blurts. "I don't know where I'm going."

"You're doing just fine," says Pa Sonny. "What's crawled up your ass?"

"Nothing. I just don't know what I'm doing here."

"Just itching to get home? Creek's Ridge...has it become that for you yet? Home? Its wide golden boulevards bubbling over with life and culture. The friendly faces of happy, ordinary folk. The pleasant comforts of rugged Americana. Narcotically content, stoically dreamless. Stained with blood and the grim reality of a coffin."

"And where is your home?"

"What's the saying? Home is...where the heart is..." Pa Sonny finally looks at Johannes, his lips clenched tight by something like pain. "Normally, an apology would be in order. But you would have made it to this point eventually. Sometimes we need a shove. Those two girls...they really dig their claws into a fella, don't they? Nobody can teach a man better than those two can, that men like us have no home."

"I don't understand. They care for you. They want you there, with them. You can finish your life with all the attention and loving devotion anyone can ask for. And they suggested I stay, too. Both of them."

"Is that what you're searching for? Your deepest desire? If that's the case, you just drop me off in Creek's Ridge and take the truck. Free of charge. Go ahead. Consider your debt paid. Freedom is yours for the taking. Flee back to them and all their doting attention. Is that how you wish to spend your life? Taking lessons and directions from a woman who is never wrong? Screwing my daughter in the desert while the coyotes howl along? Well?"

A car or a semi passes every couple of minutes. A cool draft blasts into the cab, so Johannes rolls up his window. Pa Sonny is cradling the thermos containing his final allotment of bourbon like the valuable artifact that it is, Fairy's reservoir of generosity. Johannes knows he should have stopped for coffee before they entered the grazing lands. At a crossroads, Johannes contemplates his three options, yielding the stop sign to five cars and two pickups before Pa Sonny finally directs him to the left.

"It may have been a mistake, bringing you along," says Pa Sonny. "But then...on the grand scale of things, what's one more mistake?"

"Well...but...why then? Why bring me?"

The pain contorting Pa Sonny's features subsides. As they get further from El Paso, he transitions back to the pure, arrogant fortitude he'd displayed before they left Creek's Ridge. Still, he doesn't answer. He only twists the thermos around in his hands.

"Why?" Johannes repeats.

"So you could see them. So that you could understand. I wanted you to know. I won't be around much longer, Johannes. I needed someone to know. About them. And believe it."

"No one else knows?"

"There is one. But those lips are sealed."

"Grant?"

The truck veers and dips onto the shoulder.

"No...no..." Pa Sonny shakes his head. "Grant doesn't know."

"But why? Why can't anyone know? Your friends, Sonny?"

Pa Sonny grunts, "Friends...what friends?"

"But then, why me? You and I...we didn't even recognize each other at that diner. We're basically strangers."

"Do you remember the story of your baptism?"

"Fairy told me..."

"Of course she did. So you know, then, that we are nothing like strangers. Since that day, you've been a beacon in a dark cave, the crack that admits sunlight. But what she didn't tell you, because she doesn't know, is that I've never forgiven myself."

"But you didn't do anything wrong."

"Didn't I? I stood there frightened and numb like a fool. I should have done something, anything, to help you in that moment. You were literally in my hands. I failed. I failed you, failed myself, failed my congregation. It was either sheer dumb luck or God's good grace that brought you back in that moment...but it should have been me. So I've always felt the need to...make up for it."

"Why did you leave the church?"

"The truth? Or what I tell people?"

"The truth."

"It was an Easter Sunday. I stood in the pulpit, gazing upon my congregation and sermonizing once again on the metaphorical value to be gleaned from the Resurrection. It hit me like a bullet. Immediate. Decisive. As my eyes fell upon each of their faces, I realized that I did not love a single one of them."

"Were you drunk?"

"May have acted like it. The shock of it made for a disorienting moment, certainly. It's no picnic, stumbling upon the knowledge that your entire life has been misdirected by your own hands. That it has become a farce and a mockery of everything a man should be. And at such a late stage on life's way. But the weight is staggering. I couldn't continue. You understand this now, I can tell you do. You brought something down with you from those mountains, even if you don't realize it yet. I could not be the man telling those good people how to live and what to believe because I had failed so spectacularly."

"It had nothing to do with Fairy?"

"It had everything to do with Fairy. Although you initiated the cascade, my first independent step was toward Fairy's exotic charm and the haunting sound of sitar from the altar when no one else was around. By that time, we had already become quite close. We spoke at length every day, on any topic two people can conjure. Prayed together, often late into the night. Occasionally, we met outside of the church. But after your infantile brush with death, the rules that governed my world began to crumble. Fairy was the hand that led me through the wreckage. She helped me to make sense of it. And those years were the best of my life. Because of my newfound appreciation for all things, I could relate to my congregation better than ever before. With the exception of my relations with Fairy, I hid nothing from them. And, in turn, they hid nothing from me. The spiritual chasms that cropped up in our community became badges on our sleeves. Medals of honor. Shame and regret disappeared...until Ionia Josephina surprised us. Fairy left with Ionia soon after she was born. They traveled the country for a few years, coming through Chicago every few months to say hello. But then they left permanently. Settled in Creek's Ridge for a bit. She lied to you. It was two and a half years. I was counting. Then, they came here, to Texas. She wanted me to come with them and help with her humanitarian schemes. I couldn't do it. I don't strictly believe in what they do here. Or I don't have the stomach for it. I don't know. But the next twelve years were a torturous hell."

"Because you missed them?"

"Because I had convinced myself that it was my duty to love all people equally, that the nature of my vocation prohibited me from straying, lest I lead others astray. But it was all a life's great lie."

"You loved only Fairy and Ionia."

"No. I loved myself—only myself. If I had loved them, I would have gone to them. Even now, each time I visit, I pray for the sort of epiphany that struck me that day in the church. Or else for a lightning bolt to strike me down."

Out of the pitch-black road ahead, a single stationary headlight switches on. Johannes and Pa Sonny look at each other, and then Pa Sonny tucks the thermos tightly between his legs. As they approach, Johannes slows the truck. They pass an unmarked sheriff's motorcycle with a giant-of-a-man straddling it, uniformed in brown and sucking continuous drags from a cigarette. Johannes continues to watch in the rearview long after they've passed, but before it's out of view, the tail lights switch off again.

Johannes yawns, once, twice. "That doesn't make any sense," he says finally. "They love you. You have nothing to lose with them, and everything to gain."

"Makes as much sense as you holing up in the mountains all those years or pointlessly digging up bones that aren't even there. A man can have the best possible guide to navigate this life, but the only place to find sense in any of it is within himself."

"What do you know about the bones?" The truck veers toward the shoulder, but Johannes corrects it in time. "Or why I went into the mountains? You know, don't you?"

Pa Sonny nods.

"Tell me."

"It's not worth it. Some things truly are best forgotten. You knew that before you went. Your success, in that respect, may prove to be your saving grace. If only I could forget those two girls back there...then my life would be much simpler..." Pa Sonny trails off and scans the long road ahead, the endless fields to each side. "When you were up there," Pa Sonny starts suddenly, "in the mountains, and your very existence had been swiped out from under your feet, was it the loneliness? Missing her? Missing him? What brought you to contemplate taking your own life?"

Johannes glances at him but manages to hold the wheel straight.

"Why didn't you?" Sonny adds.

"Missing who?"

Pa Sonny looks away, out the window.

Johannes shrugs. "Cowardice, I guess. Fear."

"No, Johannes. Don't delude yourself. That's the reason a man kills himself, not why he refrains from it. You know, Fairy's tale for you this afternoon, the tragic history of Creek's Ridge, she left out a crucial chapter. After he murdered his wife, Emil Wood did indeed revert to his true name, Emedio del Bosque. He did indeed re-establish his faith, devoting himself to God's work and instilling that holy reverence into his daughter. But the question of his madness...that is, in my opinion, a subjective view that gained traction on its romanticism alone. A myth based purely on the fact that, following the raids, after witnessing his own daughter single-handedly save the people who were left, he spent those last ten years trying to end his life. No less than fifteen attempts at suicide in those years, probably more. Because he was a coward. He was terrified of what he'd created, what it had become."

"He wanted the raids to succeed? To wipe out the town?"

"Perhaps, in part. I doubt he knew what he wanted. And that's exactly it. The indecision, the uncertainty in himself. Who he was or why, what his daughter had become, and why—that's what he was afraid of."

"But what...? Too cowardly to pull it off successfully?"

"No, in that his hand was firm. But once again, his daughter stepped in. Every time he tried, she was there to stop him or bring him back from the brink in the nick of time. And he grew to despise her for it. She took from him the one thing he believed in anymore. And that's what they call madness."

"You're no different. I don't understand how you think you can help me. You bemoan the stagnant idleness of Creek's Ridge, yet you share it with them completely. The Master Idler. You're their leader. Not Grant, not really. You've not left your position with the church at all. You've just had Grant standing out front, exposed in the pulpit this whole time, while you direct from behind a curtain."

"I'm not helping you. I'm using you." Pa Sonny sighs as he unscrews the top from the thermos and takes a sip, which brings on a subdued, rolling laughter that he only derails by taking another sip. "You're correct, in a way. I have reverted completely into myself. I've shunned everything I once was. Escaped the desirable tracks of life and found a kind of solace on the outskirts, but without taking my hands off the wheel. Grant is...he's a good man. And I do, I use him, too, but for different purposes. I have used you both to serve myself. Once, I had myself convinced I loved you both like sons. A mistake, that."

"What about Ionia?"

"What about her?"

"Don't you love her?"

"You know, when they left for El Paso, I packed a bag. Every morning, the first thing I saw when I woke up was that suitcase, just sitting there, unmoving, staring back at me, waiting for me to pick it up and follow them. I struggled with an unbearable uncertainty for those twelve years, the thought that I might wake up any morning prepared to leave my life behind, to leave you and Grant behind, and run to them. I knew I should love Ionia, and I shut my eyes every night wondering if I would wake to find love had blossomed. A volcanic island that appears overnight amidst an ocean of doubt. It never did. Although I cannot love them, I do need them. Both of them. Because I cannot forget them. That is my failure."

"But does Ionia love you?"

"Sure as hell hope she doesn't."

"What if she does? Couldn't you sacrifice yourself for that now? Give over the rest of your meager existence so she can have a father?"

"Ionia is no longer a child. And blood be damned, she has never been my child. She doesn't need me."

"Let her decide that for herself."

"It is done. Fairy has fed Ionia her freedom from birth, and that's something nobody but Fairy could have succeeded at. But it's dangerous. Ionia hasn't earned her freedom. She will be a saintly woman someday, no doubt. Others will love her, but she'll never be able to relate to regular people. Like the Saint of Creek's Ridge, her namesake. Unbelievable, isn't it? The power of a name. Like everyone else, Fairy has her madness. And so will Ionia."

"As her father, isn't it your responsibility to right that? To offer her balance and stability?"

"I tried that once before," Pa Sonny sighs. "But you and Grant...did not turn out as I expected. As I'd hoped. No, Johannes, I can offer her no more than what I offer you now, the same as I've tried to explain to Grant time and again. It's something I should have taught you both a long time ago, if only I had known it myself. Freedom is not what it seems."

"What the hell is that supposed to mean?"

"I always knew."

"Knew what?"

"Where you were."

"What?"

"How did you think I knew to be at that diner? The very same week you turned up?"

"You said you...passed through there...regularly..."

"I always knew. Hell, it was me who gave you the idea, I suppose. Years ago. As a kid, probably. Forgetting, losing yourself, cutting off, cutting out. Solitude as a cure to our transgressions against ourselves. Mountaintops for the view. What crap, all of it. So I followed you. Never far behind as you hitched east. Followed because I no longer believed the horseshit I used to believe. But you did, and you wouldn't listen to me anymore. I couldn't stop you. I tried, but I couldn't. So, instead, I had to know where you would be. Had to know you'd be okay. I felt a responsibility. I met the Rosses and got to know them quite well over a few days. Gave them my phone number, in case...just in case. I asked them to keep an eye on you, and Anne called with updates every few months—for all seven years. They never let it slip, huh? Yeah, they're good folks. Well, she called to tell me about that storm. It scared them. Said they'd never seen one like it. I asked her to check in on you, but a month went by and I still hadn't heard from her. Until one day, what do you know? A message. To inform me that your shack was gone, that you were nowhere to be found, and...I don't know what I thought. Then she called again when you showed up in front of their store, looking like death. They tried to help you, to take you in. But you only said one thing, and then you left that place. So I knew where you'd be headed. Because in all my pleading, I convinced you to agree to only one thing. A single safety line. And it stuck. I always had faith."

"You..."

"The No-Show No-Go. That's what you said to them. What a perfect name, a perfect escape. Prophetic."

"But..."

"I'm tired, Johannes. I must sleep."

"Me too."

Pa Sonny only chuckles.

"What's the other one?" asks Johannes.

"Other what?"

"The lie you tell people. For why you left the church."

"I tell them..." Pa Sonny closes his eyes and leans his head against his window. "I tell them I left to be with my lover and our daughter. No one has ever believed it."

For the rest of the drive back, Johannes dwells on their conversation. He gets lost five separate times, but Pa Sonny does not respond to nudging, shaking, or name-calling. His sleep is absolute and impenetrable. Backroad filling station attendants help to redirect Johannes, but their directions to the Oklahoma panhandle are vague and confusing. Occasionally, he thinks about the horse bones and the labyrinthine trenches awaiting him, the pleasure of the dig soon to be resumed, but also its interminable and fruitless nature. Ionia and The Disciples never wholly leave his mind's periphery. Clouds move in overhead, allowing Boötes and the hounds, Orion, Capricornus the horned sea goat of the south, and all the others to slip behind the night's heavy shroud and cavort in secrecy, together in collusion, should they please. Fairy's melodious voice is gone, and Johannes can no longer recall its sweet tones. And the Scrap, too, stubbornly refuses to come and ease the disconcerting silence of thought, the revolving repetition of all that has happened on this brief getaway, and the uncertainty of what's to come.

There was Simon, who was called Peter.

At long last they cross over those several anomalous borders, past St. Josephine's and onto the main drag of Creek's Ridge. The new day is already more than half spent, and the only conclusion Johannes has reached is that he hates riddles. At least Grant speaks without mystery.

Chapter 42

The Cost of Loyalty

March 28, 1818
La Chua, La Florida

We left our horses with a friendly tribe near Moon Lake at La Chua. From here on, we travel by foot. A splendid animal, my sweet, dependable Lucia Roja. A gift, so many months ago, from Chief Kinheja himself. Though I regret the loss of my animal, my transport, my friend, it was inevitable. Scouts of all loyalties traverse these forests. We must not invite danger. We build no fires at night. We speak only in whispers and only when necessary. In return for our beloved beasts, the Seminoles at La Chua provided us with food for several days and saw us off with a resplendent feast, more than enough to replenish our energy for the long trek ahead.

Our destination is Tallahassee, where George Arbuthnot is said to be supporting the resistance. Arbuthnot is Roberto's friend, partner, and mentor of many years, and Roberto intends to do battle alongside no other. The rations we carry should see us through to that city as long as we are not diverted, captured, or killed—as Roberto often jokes. I find his rugged humor repellent. But he only laughs all the hardier at my distaste, claiming such is the lot of life even in times of harmony. In truth, I have found little to laugh about in these trying days, especially concerning the subject of our mortality. Father Jimenez's death remains at the forefront of my thoughts. But I do make an effort to smile whenever Roberto does. He shows remarkable resilience of spirit, which has helped to steady my nerves through several difficult tests.

Roberto insists that the American soldiers pose no threat. He says we will hear them—and likely smell them—from hundreds of yards off. It is, rather, the Georgian Creeks in their recruit that cause him worry. Roberto has never enjoyed amiable or honest dealings with those bands of brigands and thieves, whose loyalties, he says, are bought as easily as wheat and broken down into excrement just as quickly. His penchant for curses and insults has become more pronounced of late, and he does not hesitate to explain these phrases to me. This has become the new tone for our English lessons. Under cover of darkness, he often struggles to stifle his laughter after hearing me repeat the lines he feeds me. A bitch in the bushes, seven Marys and a steer, bloody pigeon-livered sod...

During idle moments, he froths with rage at the mere notion of losing La Florida to the Americans. He laments equally the changes this will bring upon his established life, his trade, and the loss of all those years devoted to a cause so dear to his heart. When I chanced to point out that his cause has involved the supply of weaponry to opposing factions without discrimination and that our current circumstances were the inevitable result of such actions, he denied the suggestion outright. Some men, it seems, prefer the world to remain unchanged, straddling ethical boundaries and forever on the verge of war.

Despite this, his wits are as sharp as they have been since I met him. Given that my pace and stamina are far inferior to his, he shows considerable patience with me. Each day, he teaches me more about these swamps and marshlands than even the Seminoles at the St. Johns could do.

All of Father Jimenez's final predictions have occurred with startling precision. His instincts were inspired until the very moment death claimed him.

April 3, 1818
Gulf Coast, West Florida

After being trailed for two full days, we were left with no choice but to abandon our course and take refuge in the coastal swamplands. Navigating the swamp has tested my patience. Without Roberto's guidance, I would have turned back to surrender. As it turns out, our detour, though costing us much time and trouble, befell us by the grace of fortune's fingertips. Not only did we lose our pursuers, but the release from the swamps unto the coast offered a most welcome respite from the weariness of constant movement and concealment. The splendor of the sea and the salty clarity of the air were enough to freshen our constitutions, and the definitiveness of this impassable obstacle has focused our agitated senses. The mud flats provided us our first taste of blue crab since we left the St. Johns, and Roberto has taught me how to dive for scallops, of which I brought up three to his thirty. We later faced a frighteningly tense encounter with a group of Seminoles that had encroached upon us, seemingly out of thin air.

Though our small fire was carefully concealed, the savory scent of roasting scallops alerted them to our presence. A series of pointed questions was volleyed through the darkness while we all held our weapons at the ready, whence Roberto learned that they came from a tribe near Tallahassee with whom he and Arbuthnot have often done business. However, a long time passed before they felt assured of our identities. They knew of Roberto, but his long absence from the region had birthed rumors of his capture. Naturally, this greatly amused Roberto. Through a mixture of who's who and local lore, they finally accepted Roberto's claims and approached. All that time, we had only been trading words with two distinct voices, but four warriors bled out from the darkness. They remained reluctant to lay down their guns until Roberto showed them that their muskets had, in fact, been provided by himself and Arbuthnot, which he proved by the most ingeniously contrived means. He bears on his right thigh a branding scar that corresponds to the discreet marking he and his partner engrave upon every weapon they handle. Arbuthnot, he says, has an identical scar branded upon his left thigh. The Seminoles laughed heartily at the thought of this light-skinned man branding himself in the traditional style. They gladly accepted our invitation to share our meal of scallops and crab, and after tensions had subsided, two more warriors stepped out from their cover. We had been surrounded without knowing it.

While we ate, the Seminoles divulged the details of their flight. Five days ago, General Jackson's army overtook Tallahassee and burned it. Nothing remains. The surrounding tribes have scattered, disrupting the resistance. Several American regiments have already begun advancing on St. Marks, while the remaining troops are encamped strategically around the ruins of Tallahassee with the intent to intercept rebels unaware. Rebels—this, the title we have earned for defending our rightful lands.

Of the six Seminoles, two of them are colored. One is a former slave who escaped his Georgia plantation some years ago. He has a Seminole wife and three children whose whereabouts and safety are unknown to him. The other is roughly my age and was born into the tribe. He bears the mixed features of his colored father and native mother, culminating in perhaps the most attractive person of any gender I have ever beheld. The women of mixed blood, they say, are absolutely angelic, to which Roberto concurred.

These wanderers have not merely fled their destroyed homes, they have made it their mission to hunt down their enemies. In an effort to disrupt the chain of scouts that transmits reconnaissance to the American General, they have been collecting scalps from the Georgian Creeks who have penetrated the interior. With subdued, angry pride, they showed us their grim trophies—nearly twenty blood-encrusted skins already—the knotted hair tangled together in ugly masses reminiscent of monstrous rabid rodents. At the sight of this gruesome collection, Roberto laughed and congratulated them while I did my best to swallow down the sickness that had risen in my throat.

On their recommendation, we shall follow the coast north to St. Marks, where Arbuthnot will have fled following the fall of Tallahassee. We must travel from here on without rest if we are to reach St. Marks before the Americans do.

Though I try to suppress such urges in these dire times, I have developed a fervid desire to gaze upon the young women of mixed blood.

———

April 7, 1818
St. Marks, West Florida

American scouts had already begun to surround St. Marks by the time we arrived. Had we shown up half a day later, we would at this moment be bound in chains. As it is, we have been hiding in the broom closet of a local inn while American soldiers patrol the town day and night in search of Seminole sympathizers. We have not had so much as a breath of fresh air in these two days. At times, we can hear them marching the streets and calling out—

Ambrister! Ambrister! Robert Ambrister! Information leading to the capture of Bahaman Englishman and merchant Robert Ambrister will be generously rewarded! General Andrew Jackson himself guarantees full pardon and an eternal place in God's good graces, in exchange for knowledge pertaining to the whereabouts of Ambrister! Ambrister! Robert Ambrister!...

An associate of Roberto's named Dan Bull has been looking after us. Although Dan Bull was raised by Georgian Creeks, he claims Cherokee heritage and has long since lost all filial feelings for those Creeks now in league with our enemies. He has worked alongside Roberto and Arbuthnot for many years, mainly functioning as an intermediary between them and tribes north of the border. He brings us scraps of food when he can, generally shrimp or oysters. They tell me I am free to walk through town if I dare to chance it, but that my lack of papers might raise suspicions. And the troops are not exactly impartial in their festive use of ammunition. Dan Bull has also been busy trying to find us more permanent, comfortable, and secure lodgings. Roberto has countless friends and associates in and around St. Marks. However, no one will take us in. The events of yesterday have set the populace on edge.

Around noontime yesterday, George Arbuthnot was discovered hiding in a barrel at the blacksmith's workshop. When the soldier tipped the lid, Arbuthnot extended a cutlass into the man's throat, killing him outright. The assembled soldiers promptly overpowered him. The blacksmith was publicly whipped before being sent to the town prison, whereas Arbuthnot was paraded around town with a crier announcing his long list of unlawful activities, as well as his impending execution, after which they carted him off to their camp near the ruins of Tallahassee.

Dan Bull informs us that a great many people seek Roberto's assistance during this difficult time. Those who wish to fight request his leadership. Those who want only to stand armed and ready request his weapons and ammunition. Those who wish to flee request passage aboard one of his vessels. Still, thus far, it is Dan Bull alone who risks his life for our safety. Roberto is confounded by the frigid reception we have received. The residents of this once open-armed, happy community have become miserly and selfish in the face of danger. They blame people like Roberto and Arbuthnot for the sudden rise in tensions, yet they have the gall to request unreciprocated assistance. Fear, it seems, disorients people in the most treacherous of ways.

We can be thankful, at least, that no one has yet discovered us or revealed our whereabouts. Though our circumstances are not optimistic, for the present moment, we are safe.

April 8, 1818
St. Marks, West Florida

During long silent moments such as these, cooped in the damp dark of a broom cupboard, with unseen dangers stalking the streets on all sides of us and at all times of the day, I am reminded of my voyage aboard El

Soldado Agraciado. I feel as though I have been reacquainted with the fleeting, fragile nature of life that I came to venerate during those weeks, the ability to cull an eternity's worth of love and blessedness from a fleeting instant, to stop the flow of time and sit hand-in-hand with providence, to absorb it until I overflow with the Divine Light and accept the always immediate approach of God, and of death. At peace with myself and with God's earth as it stands, flaws and blemishes and all. Grateful to have been a recipient of His will, if only for a short time. These are sensations I have lost hold of, loosed from my grip and swept away in the pleasant current of the St. Johns River, no different from Father Jimenez basking in the idle longevity of that life. Finally, I understand the Father's sorrows. Although I do not regret the time I spent with that kind and generous tribe, I presently find myself here, encased in this broom cupboard, and feeling truly alive once again because I am prepared to die. I expect it. I accept my helplessness. I prostrate myself at its feet.

Chapter 43

The Weight

"Where in the hell have you been?"

Grant sits on the floor, leaning against the sofa, his arms limp and resting on his knees. Dust particles float lazily about the dim room, glowing in what little daylight seeps in, casting a wavering haze of unreality.

After dropping off Pa Sonny and the truck, Johannes's walk back to the house was a drowsy, daze-filled trudge that seemed to take even longer than the drive. He wants only to lie down, but Grant is occupying the square meter of floor space he needs right now.

"Texas..." Johannes says, fighting to hold his eyes open.

"What?"

"Pa Sonny...he tracked me down. A few days ago. Asked me to...drive him...to Texas..."

Grant grunts. "Why?"

"He—" The truth pools onto Johannes's tongue, trickles out, evaporates. "Just a delivery. He was sick of driving. Wanted to reconnect."

"I thought you'd gone again. Gone for good. You've been different ever since..."

"Since what?"

"What? Since she left."

"Who?"

"First thing I did was check to see if anything was missing. If you'd taken anything with you. But you don't have anything to take."

"Sure don't." Johannes glances around as he walks past Grant. Something is off in the room, something missing. He pokes his head into the kitchen, sees the bones still spread over the tabletop, and then glances down the hall. Finally, his gaze settles upon the empty space against the wall. "Where is it?" he mutters.

Grant lifts his head to look at Johannes.

"The mirror," Johannes says as he leans against the wall where the mirror had always rested.

"I moved it. It was... It almost broke."

"Moved it where?"

"What does it feel like?"

"What does what feel like?"

"No possessions. No burdens."

Johannes's eyes sweep over the room, but they're consistently drawn back to the floor beneath Grant. Outside, a short burst of voices erupts from a group of kids running down the street—Jared, Carl, Mallory, and Conner. Johannes watches them, surprised that he remembers their names.

"I wouldn't say I have no burdens. But it is sort of...freeing. Now that the shock has passed. Almost weightless."

"You can have anything you like around here, you know. Most of it, anyway. What's mine is as good as yours."

"What would I do with it?"

"You know that, right?"

"What?"

"That they're as good as yours."

"Your floor is enough for now."

It takes only a few seconds of silence for Johannes's vision to grow blurry, his eyelids anything but weightless. And, too, there was James, son of Alphaeus.

"Grant, I need to sleep. For a day."

"Yeah." Grant shoots up onto his feet. "What? You drive the whole way up?"

"There and back."

"Where?"

"El Paso."

"Jesus Christ, that's almost what? Ten, eleven hours each way?" Grant steps away from the sofa. He stretches and paces aimlessly around the room. "He doesn't usually do deliveries that far away. What an asshole. Must have had a night's rest down there, huh? Been gone what? Three days?"

"Yeah. And I found out how he knew I'd be there. At that diner. Did you know?"

Grant shakes his head. "Sonny does like to play his games. He's not the only one."

"What do you mean?"

"No. Nothing."

Johannes slips past Grant to take his place on the floor, but as he's lowering himself, Grant switches on the lamp. The sudden flood of light jolts Johannes upright. He notices layers of exhaustion upon Grant's face that must equal his own. Grant is unshaven and pale, with dark circles cradling his eyes, smudges of dirt here and there. He's not wearing his uniform, just shorts and an old, worn T-shirt that Johannes thinks he should probably recognize. Then, just as Johannes is about to lie down, he notices a gash in the floor, a deep chip in the wood right where he always lays his head.

"What's this? What happened?"

"What? Oh, that. Nothing. I told you, almost broke."

Johannes studies Grant for a moment. He reaches down to touch the chipped wood but then gives in to his body's demands, collapsing and stretching out along the floorboards.

"Anyhow," says Grant, his voice so hoarse it's almost inaudible. "Good thing you didn't stay away much longer. I need to leave town myself. A few days."

"Why?" Johannes adjusts his position, aligning himself precisely east-to-west. "Where are you going?"

"It's nothing. Nowhere."

Johannes tilts his head back, looking up at the fuzzy, inverted outline of his friend.

"Just some business," adds Grant. "Out east."

"Business?"

"..."

"When?"

"Don't know. Leave this weekend, I suppose."

"Weekend? What's today?"

"Thursday."

"When will you be back?"

"I don't know."

A cramp attacks Johannes's neck. He relaxes his muscles and lies flat. Staring at the ceiling, he lets his eyelids blanket him as he melts into sleep. Grant remains stranded in thought for a moment before shutting off the light. The last thing Johannes hears is the musical handling of horse bones around the kitchen table.

―――

A warm breeze drifts through the window. His limbs are stiff as he props himself up, hanging his arm over the edge of the coffee table. The house is dark and silent. Beyond the window, the street is gray and yellow. None of the neighboring houses are lit up. No one is out for a walk or hanging about, no friendly chatter or neighborhood din. He's still drowsy, but his throat is dry, so he gets up and heads into the kitchen. The weak yellowish glow of the rear porch light filters in through the screen door and the window. All the glasses and dishes in the house are dirty and stacked around the sink. He opens the faucet, slurps tepid water from cupped hands until he's out of breath, and then leans back against the counter. The bones are vaguely organized on the table, along with a half-empty pint of spiced rum and a few open cans of Coca-Cola. He rinses a dirty glass and grabs a handful of ice from the freezer. For a few minutes, he stands over the table, sipping his drink and admiring their collection of bones. The rum is strong and aromatic, like too much cinnamon.

The silence draped over the house becomes unnerving. Even the roving thoughts of the long drive home have fallen quiet. He handles a few bones just to hear the sound, and when he peers out the window, he sees a figure standing motionless among the trenches, the silhouette sharp against silvery moonlit clouds.

Grant's head jerks up at the sound of Johannes's approach. "I was wondering if you'd ever wake up."

"I don't think I'm really awake. Feels like I need more, but there was a dream...I don't remember what. Maybe I just needed to stretch. Wet my throat. Still feels like a dream."

"Too much sleep, I'd bet." Grant's head drops down again, staring into the deep recess of the pit before him. "The imbalance. Correcting it can be hard work. I know."

"How long have I been out?"

"Long time."

Johannes stands beside his friend at the lip of the pit. "What is that? Who's down there?"

"Nothing. No one."

"Is that...? Jesus, Grant. The mirror? There? That scared the shit out of me. So much for pleasant dreams...just another nightmare..."

"Another one, huh?"

"Why would you move it out here?"

"When tornadoes come. In times of war. Where do we go? Where do we flee?" Grant looks up slowly, not at Johannes but toward distant, indistinct points in the field, the sky, the clouds, the few sparse stars peering down on the two of them. "An impressive network of trenches and holes we've made here, isn't it?"

"It'll break."

"Ernest's mirrors break," Grant's voice is no more than a whisper. "Not this one. Here...it's safe."

"What? Like Lil was?"

Grant's head falls at an angle. "Have you eaten anything?"

Johannes shakes the glass, the ice jingling in reply.

"There's a brick of cheddar in the fridge. Deli meat and bread, too, I think. Maybe a few eggs. Your famous omelets."

"This'll do for now." The rum and the warm air wrap their arms around him, coaxing him again toward dreams. "A drink like this wakes me up and sends me to sleep at the same time. Have you been digging?"

"What? No, not now. I could." Grant half-turns. He considers Johannes with a hesitant, sidewise glance. "Do you want to?"

"Later. Wait till daytime. I should probably get a bit more rest."

"Yeah, you look it."

"That bad?"

"Getting better. You've come a long way in these past few months. How long? Four, five, six? Not a bad run...longest since..." Grant trails off and takes a few deep breaths—not quite sighs, but more like desperate heaves. "Will you dig when I'm gone?"

"I don't know..." Johannes remembers the one occasion he dug alone, blind and shivering in the creek on that moonless night while he waited for Grant. Grant and Lani, in the bedroom. And he remembers the rib bones in Texas, thrown into the pit and then promptly scavenged as soon as they'd turned their backs. He and Ionia Josephina. And later, he by himself, Ionia gone off, and the bones claimed by the Disciples, every last one of them. The Scrap crops up, but at a laughable distance. He knows it's there. He can sense it, wandering the night, concealed behind clouds, floating by on the creek's silky current, trapped within the mirror down below, lurking in the trenches, buried in the mounds. But he can't hear the Scrap, and the more he grasps for it, the more possessively the night claims it. Andrew was a brother of Peter. "That depends," he says finally.

"On what?"

"On..." Johannes isn't sure either. "On how long you're gone, I guess. I was looking forward to it. To digging. What about the sheriff?"

"What about it?"

"Well...it's you. You're the sheriff."

"Yeah?"

"If you're gone, then who does the job? I mean, if anything were to happen?"

"There's a reserve person. A sort of deputy on call. But...come to think of it, I haven't seen Rich around for weeks. He may've skipped town. Probably in jail someplace."

The chirps of crickets swell with the breeze, taking the reins of their conversation. A toad croaks near the creek. An owl calls from some far-flung, directionless perch.

"You want a job?" says Grant.

"Me? No. Not sure I'm the man for that particular type of work."

"You'll keep an eye on things, though. Won't you? Somebody has to."

"Sure. But you won't be gone long, will you?"

"Mm-hmm. Not if things go as planned. Decent pile of bones we've gathered, don't you think?"

"Long way to go yet."

"I figure we made it halfway. Not too bad."

"We've been at it a long time. They didn't just get up and walk off."

"A goddamn mystery. A bit of voodoo."

A low, dark shadow crawls out of one of the pits, lingering briefly before taking off south alongside the creek. It leaps, splashing through the water and heading east, the shadow disappearing instantly into the field.

"Did you see that?" says Johannes.

"I did, yeah."

"What was it?"

"A coyote, maybe. Too big for a fox or a possum."

Johannes finishes the rum in one huge gulp. His heartbeat resonates, someone pounding on an oil drum.

Grant is watching him as though he can hear it, too. "Them dogs still bothering you?"

"There were these coyotes in Texas."

"There are coyotes everywhere. Widest spread predator in the Americas. Panama to the fucking Yukon. Eat anything, fuck anything, live anywhere, thrive everywhere. I saw one in Chicago once. Downtown. A long time ago. When we were...just kids..." The shadows of Grant's face twist in feverish excitement, a sort of unsettling smile just as he turns away. "Those fuckers would attack her. Had to chase them off. Drew blood once."

"From the coyotes?"

"No, they did. Her blood. Limping Lady's..."

"Lil...wasn't she sheltered?"

"And mine, too. My blood. Used to be a small stable and shed, over there." Grant points to the northeast corner of the lot. "Sturdy, too. But they found a way in. A coyote always does."

The glass in Johannes's hand has become immensely heavy. His breath stops. "I've never seen one here."

"I bet you saw them in the mountains. Don't remember, right? Well, they're here, too. Don't you doubt it."

The ice cubes shudder and ring against the sides of Johannes's glass.

"C'mon," Grant pats Johannes on the shoulder and starts back toward the house. "I need to get some rest myself."

Johannes lags behind, his head swiveling and jumpy at the slightest suggestion of motion slinking through the darkness. Grant glances back every couple of steps.

At the back door, Grant ushers Johannes inside. The screen door slams, but then Johannes hears the interior door shut and the hard metallic clank of the deadbolt.

"You've never locked that before," he says.

Traces of a grin remain upon Grant's lips as he steps around Johannes and leans his hands against the table. They can only see by what little light finds its way in from the back porch.

Bones litter the tabletop from edge to edge, jutting over the sides and overlapping to form lumpy mounds. Although individual bones cannot be identified in the low light, the resulting form has a certain cohesion. Contours surge and bulge like something organic, an aesthetic purity instinctually familiar, like commonplace, recognizable objects as arranged by a child, an artistic savant, or a madman.

"What the hell do we do with them?" asks Johannes.

"Piece them together again. All the king's men."

The clumsy noise as Johannes sticks his hand into the pile reminds him of the indiscriminate shuffling of toys, countless varieties spread around a playroom floor, and the slew of impossible decisions ahead. Share or covet. Adore or demolish. Smell, lick, bite, chew, or swallow. Brushing his fingertips over just one bone causes the entire system to shift, revealing hidden treasures and rendering others lost, suffocating beneath the heap. A bone tumbles over the edge and bounces across the floor. Another, this one heavier, falls with a single solid thud, then a third, a fourth.

"Can't be too hard," says Grant. "Same as tuning up a motorcycle or working beneath the hood of a car. Everything has order, especially skeletons. Only one way to arrange them. Next step in the process. That's it." He slides a few around, lays them out in some semblance of order. "See? Nothing to it. It's been fun, anyway. But nothing ever truly ends, does it?"

"I think Pa Sonny knows something about the missing bones," says Johannes.

"Of course he does. Sonny knows something about everything. Always has. I caught him digging out there once. It was a few years ago, back when he still drank, but I never said anything about it. I wonder if he..."

"What?"

"Nothing..."

Johannes continues sifting through them. A few of the bones he recognizes by touch alone. He slides them around, lifts them up, sets them down. Every now and then, Grant will grab a bone that Johannes has just set down and rearrange them again. Johannes picks out a small conical bone, smooth-edged, un-fragmented, hollow. It's thin and no longer than his index finger. He has noticed before that when he's thinking of nothing but the bones, his thoughts obtain clarity—certainly not order or elegance, but at least confidence, recognition, the appreciation of a spit-shined mirror—and as he studies the shape of this bone, tests its mass and balance by rolling it over in his palm, brings it within centimeters of his face to see what he can in this light, he knows with absolute certainty that he has never seen or handled this particular bone before.

"What's this?" Johannes mumbles. "I don't remember this one..."

"No surprise there..."

"You have been digging..."

Grant takes the bone from him. He examines it almost lovingly, saying, "Vertebra. The tip of the tail. That's my guess. Feel free to, you know, conjecture yourself. But you can't worry too much about the smallest bones. We have ours, too. The hammer and the anvil. Carpals and whatever. You'd be lucky to recognize them as bones at all, let alone distinguish them from fucking pebbles. God knows what obscure bones a horse might be hiding. Could spend lifetimes searching and still come up empty-handed, details like that. Gotta learn to let some things slide. Basic requirement of the human condition, right?"

"Yeah. I guess so..."

Grant's words contain an undeniable logic. But logic and sense don't always provide answers, explanations for what they're doing, or reasons to continue unchecked.

Johannes touches something that is not a bone. He picks it up, and though he cannot see it, he recognizes the crystalline rock and relives the struggle of trying to break it open, the disappointment of what lay therein. He holds it out to Grant. "Do you remember this? Did you ever ask Amondale?"

Grant takes it, tests its weight. "No. I don't remember."

"And what about the skull?" says Johannes.

"Could be anywhere."

Johannes sighs, a breathy, panoramic sound, as though Grant had joined him. He wants to believe that Grant sighed as well, that they share this painfully evident observation.

"That dog," says Grant. "The one you're afraid of..."

"Mengele?"

"I think it's been digging, too. Maybe for years. All along. Could be why."

"Why what?"

"Why they're scattered all over the yard. All over town. Who knows."

"But how?"

"I told you, we didn't bury her very deep. No...not deep enough..." Grant picks up the bottle of rum and twists it around before handing it to Johannes. "Finish that off. Help you to get a deep, healthy sleep. Quality booze. Better than that shit-whisky you drink. Straighten you out some, maybe."

Johannes spins the bottle around just as Grant did. Sleep is already prodding him the way it is, so he doesn't need any more liquor. And if he did, he would prefer The Carnival anyhow. Though the promise of a dreamless sleep is tempting.

Grant waits until Johannes refills the glass and swallows a mouthful. Then he sighs, pats Johannes on the back, and shuts off the porch light. Johannes takes another long, slow sip and follows as Grant crosses the threshold into the living room. Grant turns down the hall, Johannes toward the floor.

"See you in the morning," Johannes calls out.

Grant's footsteps pause, followed by a throaty grunt that could be of laughter or could be of pain.

"It is morning."

Johannes wakes at about eleven o'clock. The heat has already grown intense all throughout the house. The bones are in disarray, nothing like he remembers them from the night before. Most of them lie strewn around the kitchen floor, a few in the chairs. The back door is open again, and when he steps into the yard, he discovers a sporadic trail of bones leading out into the pits. He's expecting to dig, his mind and body both craving a session before Grant leaves on his trip. But when he calls out, he receives no response.

So, Johannes goes about his day, walking, meditating, retrieving the scattered bones, appraising and admiring the strategic art piece they've created of the yard. As he weaves his way through holes and mounds and trenches, he notices that the mirror is no longer down in the trench where it had startled him in the night. After he brings the bones back inside and arranges them on the table, he makes a cursory search of the house, but the mirror is nowhere to be found. While he's rubbing down the bones with a dry cloth, it occurs to him that the one bone Grant found on his own—the last tail vertebra—is missing. As he shuffles through the bones in search, he realizes the absurdity of looking for a bone again after it has already once been found. A repetition. His search loses its urgency and peters out with no reward. He cleans the pickax and the shovel, preparing all they'll need for a solid day's digging. Later, he checks in on Pa Sonny and finds him busy preparing to leave for a pickup in Denver. After seeing Sonny off, he stops by the office and persuades Amondale to break for a late lunch at The Borderlands, where they chat with Ruthie over coffee and fresh carrot cake. On their way out, they run into Caryn, who's heading in the opposite direction. They talk with her for a bit, and then they all part ways, making vague plans to meet at Ernest's later on. He watches after her as she heads toward the distant bulk of St. Josephine's, its spire rending through the monotony of land and sky. Johannes considers following her, finally going into the church to have a look around, to see the library so worthy of Fairy's praise and Ionia's curiosity, to learn, once and for all and all on his own, the history of this town that is beginning to seem a lot like home, no matter how much he tries to resist it. But he decides against it and simply walks a while longer, waving and smiling to all and sundry as he wanders through town, casually poking his head into all of Grant's usual hangouts and keenly aware that Grant's cruiser, common and unavoidable as it is on the streets of Creek's Ridge, hasn't made a single appearance all day. He must be out patrolling the vast, empty county roads, perhaps napping in the driver's seat to the sound of the breeze through the cornstalks.

There was a second James, he who was one of the sons of Zebedee.

Drawn back to the house, he's expecting to find Grant's cruiser parked in the driveway and is disappointed when it's not, so he heads for solace in the yard. As the sun sets and the landscape dims, his limbs become restless, anxious to expel the pent-up energy of the past few days, past few months, past few years. Every pit he lowers himself into or lifts himself out of, every corner he rounds, each contour and pile of dirt, the grass torn up and shredded and lost—the entire yard is composed of memories. Shared memories he and Grant have placed here through the act of conscious striving together, reaching for the unattainable, supporting and encouraging one another, grasping and missing but simply loving the push and pull of the ax, the shovel, their calluses, blisters, and sore muscles. The strength of the memories they've carved out leads him on a path, this way and that, recognizing what he's been fortunate enough to have stumbled across in the time he has spent here, as memories seep from the walls and rise from the holes, reinvigorating his need and desire for this camaraderie, all that they've accomplished, all they have shared, all that he has lost and now retrieved, or at least, in part, rebuilt. His weak, pitiful shack on the mountain fell without the slightest resistance. But these walls are solid, built of his and Grant's stubborn refusal to yield to the impossible, their careless perseverance in the face of defeat, the ritual pleasure of their trials and failures. These walls are themselves those harmless, innocent games of youth.

The brother of James, whose name was...

And as Johannes winds his way in and out of these reveries, this happy daze, he stops short, startled by movement in the trench beside him. No, it's behind him now. He passed it by, almost missed it, a confused witness on the periphery. What had Grant said? About Mengele? Not only pursuing Johannes, but the bones as well? He hadn't thought to bring the pickax with him—he's empty-handed, and he hesitates before turning to investigate. A crack, a gap, a break in the wall of the trench. Not much sunlight remains, but as he turns and steps back, a repetition, a déjà vu, a repetition.

John...

It's him. He, himself. Johannes 'John' Metternich. The missing mirror—it's here, upright and embedded like a doorway through the wall. He faces himself, wondering how and why Grant would have installed the mirror here. He said he wanted to protect it—but this? In Grant's mind, *this* was the safest place? Johannes steps toward his reflection. He touches the edge of the mirror, checking it for stress points. The mirror doesn't budge. It's wedged securely in place and wiped clean as well, but the weight of the dirt above, an archway he does not recall having dug out, rests precariously atop this fragile slab of glass. An eerie, distant feeling takes hold, the troubling sensation of staring at yourself, of being alone with yourself, of knowing yourself all too well, and of coming face to face with your guilt.

When the last traces of light have gone, he turns his back and flees, keeping his head to the ground and ignoring everyone he sees. People pass by and call out, yelling *Hello* and *Good evening* and *See you around.* Asking *How's the sheriff?* and *How about them holes?* He stops in at Ernest's for a few glasses of The Carnival and even convinces Ernest to spin the Scrap from the Second Piano Concerto in C-minor, just once. Amondale arrives late and leaves after one quick drink. Caryn never shows up.

Not until Johannes returns to the house, well after midnight, does he finally accept the plain fact that's been staring back at him all day long—Grant has already gone.

Chapter 44

The Visitor

Lalawethika sucked on his pipe. Smoke swarmed upward when he exhaled, hypnotic swirls mingling with the smoke from the fire, rising and funneling through the wigwam's flute into the leaden blues of the coming evening.

Ignoring his wife's fears that they would be ostracized as thieves, Lalawethika had taken the medicine man's stump from beside Penagashea's permanently cool fire pit and brought it into their wigwam as his own. He rarely heeded his wife's concerns, and this was no exception. He claimed rightful ownership over the stump and promised to see it burn rather than allow it to serve any other Shawnee.

Although the fire blazed with intense heat, he had wrapped a thick hide of wolf's fur around his shoulders. Still, it failed to stave off the chill, and he shivered visibly as he crouched over the fire, smoking tobacco from his long pipe and recalling Father Gabriel's descriptions of heaven and hell. The flames showed him the vast vistas of paradise as well as the shadowy crags of the inferno, their pleasures and tortures, eternity's stranglehold on freedom.

His wife sat at the far end of the wigwam, sweating and mending moccasins for their children. She had been casting furious glances his way ever since he turned up in the afternoon with an old whiskey jug. And she had berated him as he tossed log after log onto the fire, quickly bringing it to its current unmanageable size. However, her normally stoic, expressionless face did betray consternation when he reached for the wolf's hide because she was positively roasting from the fire's heat.

After he had been sitting in the same position for several hours without so much as stretching, her fury gradually softened into curiosity. It was not common for him to remain inside the wigwam with her for any length of time. The jug rested on the mat beside him, and he drank from it at regular intervals, though he displayed none of his usual signs of intoxication. No nonsensical rants about the domineering white men with all their frightening and awesome witchery. He had not once profaned his tribesmen or his warrior brother. He had not boasted imagined feats of endurance and strength. He had not insulted or struck her. Nor had he wept over his hideous visage or bemoaned the pointed arrow of fate that had taken his eye, destroyed his life.

"Your idleness will starve your children." His wife avoided the serious, accusing tone she generally used with him and watched him only from the corner of her eye. "And your carelessness with that enormous blaze will burn down our home. We have little food left, and all you will bring us is that white man's poison? Pull yourself from that fire long enough to fulfill a Shawnee's duty."

"I'm waiting..." Lalawethika muttered as he stared intently into the heart of the fire. He drew from his pipe and exhaled a thick, billowing cloud. "Someone important is coming."

A lie. For how could he have told her? She would not have believed him. No one would believe him—that, a curse he had brought upon himself. And why should they? Even after so much time proclaiming and squawking that he was the true and rightful medicine man, Lalawethika was reluctant to believe it himself.

"Who's coming?" She paused from her stitching and looked up. "I hope they bring water and firewood. We're almost out of both."

His wife finished mending the moccasins and attended to other chores around the wigwam. He paid her no attention. He did not look up when his youngest daughter burst through the flap, upsetting the flames with a frigid gust of air that kicked up ash and embers. He did not notice when the wolf's hide slipped off his shoulders or how his teeth began to chatter. He did not feel the throbbing behind his bad eye or the itchy dryness of his good eye, his parched lips or his aching throat.

He was not waiting for anyone. The visitor was already there. It had, in fact, been hovering around their home for many weeks now, during which Lalawethika had been constantly engaged in a one-sided conference, a contest of wills. But it was only Lalawethika's will against the persistence of his fear, for though he pleaded with the visitor, he received no response. The voices that had always persecuted him had vanished. He thought, he hoped, he prayed that the visitor had come for his wife, perhaps for one of his children. But as the truth became apparent, his fear began to disperse, just as fog seeps through a valley. His fear was no longer simple mental tremors; it had become the unifying element of his human fabric. Breathing became difficult, sporadic, and dry. During endless nights, he would lie awake, trembling and feverish with cold sweats, troubled by voices in the night and the tremulous vibrations of an approaching stampede. Fragmentary nightmares straddled the boundary between wakefulness and sleep, following him into the daytime and shifting toward the sinister as the day advanced. They thrived in the illusory vision of his dead eye, burgeoning a haunting, fractured reality just shy of madness. Penagashea's ghost always lingered nearby, but the dead medicine man's spirit was a minor presence, like a whispered word or a hint dropped by the visitor. And he could never be sure whether these whispers intoned friend or foe.

When the visitor finally entered their wigwam that afternoon, Lalawethika's relief was not an expulsion of fear but rather a merging with that fear—for what is there to fear when fear is all that remains? The visitor moved amongst them, emitting a chill that cut through the fire's warmth and a stench like rotting animal carcass that even the richly fragrant tobacco could not overpower. It arrived with the ability to stop time flowing permanently, with the compulsion and sole purpose to ruin lives, to scatter all the earth's creatures with its foreboding approach, to launch souls into the irretrievable reaches of a questionable eternity. And only Lalawethika sensed its presence.

Who are you?

"No, this is my home," Lalawethika replied in a calm, careful, commanding voice. "Who are you?"

"What?" His wife looked up from her work. "What did you say?"

I am scarcity and abundance. I am pestilence and health. I am silence and noise. I am darkness and light. I am ugliness and beauty. I am predator and prey. I am idleness and toil. I am frailty and strength. I am immovable and nomadic. I am everywhere and nowhere.

When Lalawethika walked out of Sainte Anne de Detroit for the final time, he emerged without the enormous guilt that had stunted his steps since childhood. Murdering Penagashea, owning up to that deed, and believing in the justness of his cause—this had freed him. For his confession, he had received pardon, and the fear with which Father Gabriel had uttered those final words of parting, the beads of sweat that had glistened on the cleric's forehead, the way his limbs shook as he knelt before the altar, those were the first rays to illuminate Lalawethika's path, guiding him out from the thorny briars where Penagashea had stranded him. In the months following, Lalawethika meditated on that revelation, exploring the hills and crevices promised by the future. He stopped posing as a medicine man, donned plain outfits, and spoke simply or not at all. For hours at a time, he would watch the children at play or stroll through the village, observing the unhappiness that had recently taken root amongst his people. For the first time in his life, he began offering to help his tribesmen with their daily tasks, not in trade for food or whiskey, but so that he might listen to their sorrows while they worked side by side. And every night, sitting within arm's reach of low flames, he would sit in contemplation, ruminating over what they had told him until the only sound left in the village was the crackle of dying embers. If his good eye stung from the heat and the smoke, he would wander off deep into the fields where he could observe the stars without obstruction, tracing infinite paths from one end of the sky to the other. The voices still came to him at that time, several different voices demanding firewater or beckoning his return to Penagashea's cave, voices castigating his weak position within the tribe, voices comparing his failures against his brother's successes, and also voices urging him on toward prominence and recognition. And, for once, he listened to the voices. All of them. He only listened. He heard what they had to say without fleeing and without confronting them. He suppressed his impulses and his hatred. He stripped away the superfluous, the incoherent, and the dissonant until all that was left was a single word—Nothing.

"Why do you haunt me?"

"That's how you feel, is it?" muttered his wife from behind a scowl. "You might at least pretend to be something better than a cur."

I am guilt and innocence. I am vengeance and justice. I am misfortune and grace. I am poverty and wealth. I am an enemy and a lover. I am swine and nobility. I am north and south and east and west. I am ignorance and knowledge. I am spite and benevolence. I am shame and glory. I am deceit and honesty. I am struggle and triumph. I am the giver and denier of memories. I am the passage of time.

Fires are open mouths. They reveal truths and prophesy the future. They convey the incommunicable. Each phrase, the curl of every flame, is unique, instantaneous, and never to be repeated in any fire pit, candlewick, wildfire, or burning village. Not even in hell itself. They tell stories, they reveal all—

Blood pours forth from the wound where the arrowhead entered his eye. He is condemned to an adolescence of being loathed and loathing himself. Death has inhabited his shadow, and he is plagued by his constant failure to catch it, to grapple and entwine with it, to bring about a conclusive demise, a release from pain unto the soothing pastures of peaceful oblivion. Even death reviles him. He becomes a father, but his children grow up fatherless, just as he had. His father died in battle, leaving behind an honorable legacy that gave rise to songs and legends. Lalawethika's children, on the other hand, are reared in the shadow of a father who lives perpetually drowning inside the white man's bottle. He only crawls his way out by following the village outcast and placing his trust in the one Shawnee who is even lower than himself. Penagashea, the lecher, wheezes his foul breath and struggles to inhale as Lalawethika smothers him, taking what heat remains and stealing this small pleasure from the true executioner, righting his own mistakes with sin and guilt and shame, for he is no warrior. Tribesmen fall dead around him like autumn leaves, forming mounds around this suspect medicine man. They die of a disease he should be competent in curing, but instead, he is himself taken by the sickness. And even then, with his body howling and convulsing and all his thoughts acting as reflections of his own regret, life will not leave him be.

Bloody battles took his father and so many other warriors. Their spirits whisper promises of wars to come, marked by shifting alliances and unfamiliar frontiers, friends and enemies siding together in fields of distrust. And then, from the flames, steps a new medicine man. A guide, a seer, a confessor, a leader—but it is not Lalawethika. Lalawethika is not present in those flames. He has no place in this story.

"What do you want here?"

I am volition, and I am duty. I am swift and disinterested, leisurely and passionate. I am violent and abrupt. I am comforting and gentle. I am pain and loneliness. I am the devotion of loved ones. I inhabit men's bodies, I inhabit men's minds, just as men themselves inhabit their homes, inhabit and contaminate the Earth. But men also inhabit me. The duration of man's existence is but a fleeting speck of dust drifting through my timelessness. I am the dirt and the stars. I am the blood and the memories, the stains upon the ground. When all of the Great Spirit's creatures have been laid to waste, when there is nothing left to torture or release from pain, only then may I rest myself in peace. Who are you?

"I am Nothing," answered Lalawethika.

"What are you saying?" scoffed his wife. "Who are you talking to?"

At that moment, Lalawethika collapsed and fell forward directly into the flames.

His wife stared from across the wigwam in stupefied disbelief. When, after a few seconds, her husband neither rose nor so much as twitched, she called his name, shouted it, and finally began to scream as she struggled to drag him out of the fire. His right arm and shoulder, his neck, and the side of his face were already blistered, and his hair singed.

His good eye was wide open, but he did not respond to her voice or to the wild thrashing as she shook his body. She ran outside for help, where her urgency was met with whispers of resistance—

"Her husband?"

"Lalawethika?"

"Too much firewater."

"He has fallen unconscious again."

"Lost his mind this time."

"Nothing surprising about that."

"Into the fire?"

"Burned by the flames?"

"The drunkard."

"The braggart."

"A parasite upon our tribe."

"If anyone deserves such a fate, it is he."

When she finally returned with a few neighbors, only weak puffs of air escaped Lalawethika's lips. She sent one of her daughters to fetch Tecumseh, and then she cowered and wailed as the neighbors half-heartedly attempted to restore life to her husband. Drawn to the commotion, others soon wandered into the wigwam. Some of them tried to comfort her, some stared in disgust at the bloodied and blistered body, some aided with efforts to revive him. Someone examined the jug nearby, sniffed it, sipped it, and declared with amazement that it contained only water. A crowd formed outside as word rippled through the community, and the crowd segregated into factions, one group of surprised gasps and the other of knowing smirks.

A long time passed before Lalawethika's daughter returned, pulling her uncle Tecumseh by the hand. A stern grimace of irritation contorted his face. He pushed his way through the mob, eyeing them with vehemence as though whatever problem had arisen, they were to be held responsible. Tecumseh stormed into his brother's humble wigwam, bringing a blast of cold wind with him. A hush fell upon those gathered outside as they listened to Tecumseh barking commands within, ejecting gawkers, calling for water, herbs, and ointments in the same harsh tones he utilized on the battlefield.

Finally, silence descended.

When Tecumseh emerged a few minutes later, his expression had been transformed by rage. Everyone was watching him, waiting, but he did not speak. He only returned their stares, intentionally prowling through those gathered, meeting their eyes and expressing his disappointment in each of them individually. With a grunt, he reached his hand back through the flap and dragged Lalawethika's unwilling wife outside. She covered her face and buried herself weeping into Tecumseh's shoulder.

"Prepare the body for the pyre," Tecumseh ordered to everyone present and no one in particular. Then, he wrapped his arm around Lalawethika's wife and led her away through the crowd.

Part Five

Faceless and Nameless

Chapter 45

Loss

The timelessness. The meaninglessness. Of speech. Words of consolation, as fleeting as the truths that require them, rarely dent the armor of emotion—exoskeletons painstakingly formed by the petrified pain of despondence, longing, regret, shame, and defeat—especially not when tossed around willy-nilly by greasy, unwashed hands, coughed up with the reeking alcoholic stench of failed prophets.

> "The heart is never consoled,
> it only grows old,
> collects its dust, congeals,
> until one day, finally,
> it withers away."

Drunken and unsteady atop an ornamental cured-and-coated tree stump, Pa Sonny slings these abstract phrases of pity, a mishmash of holy protocol, spiritual defiance, and under-zealous human fervor. He lacks the appropriate stalwart command for such an occasion, stammering his confusion unto the others instead. His black vestment is dirty and wrinkled, and the sweat stain soaked around his collar adds a clownish aspect to this sacred dress.

The impromptu gathering has unfolded slowly and disorganized, with no one quite sure how, why, or to what purpose it's being carried out this way. But, with one exception, no one has objected either. An event like this has never been rehearsed, not in Creek's Ridge or anywhere else. It has more the spontaneity of drunken revelries than it does of solemn reverence for the dead.

An oppressive heat bears down upon them, one of those mornings when the sun wavers, huge and not at all romantic, posing not as a gracious provider but as a cruel distributor of misery.

The residents of Creek's Ridge, plus a few unfamiliar faces sprinkled throughout, are emotionally withdrawn and staring at the ground. Some have already gone home, having taken offense as soon as Pa Sonny opened his mouth. But then, such behavior is expected at any decent wake. There are always those who, whether from pride or grief or callousness, can only bear to poke their heads into the mourning room in superficial acknowledgment of their loss.

Those who have remained to see the thing through are drenched in sweat and tears, one indistinguishable from the other. The ceremony has only been underway for a short time before they discreetly remove their dark outer layers, unconcerned that their garments hang draping in the dirt and dust. Pa Sonny cuts himself off mid-sentence, openly and vigorously curses the chance weather of mournful days, struggles out of his robe, and drops it to the ground. A cloud of dust rises majestically around him, sending him into an equally majestic coughing fit, which he cures by producing a flask from his rear pocket. With liquor dribbling down his chin, he breathes deeply and continues.

"Ashes to ashes, dust to dust. Wash it away, the coarse, accursed dust covering this coarse and accursed land. Wash it down! Dust be gone!" He laughs gloomily and lifts the flask to his lips again.

His tree stump is coated in several layers of varnish that protect carvings upon the wood. They had haphazardly chosen to set the stump on the flank of the park furthest from the school, nearest to the main street, and the gathered had shown up later to form an uneven semicircle that now spills into the road.

The dust finally settles around Pa Sonny, revealing a wild expression of doubt, the look of a man who has no idea where he is or how he got there. With his robe on the ground, he now sports only a stained white T-shirt, discolored brown work pants held up by suspenders, and work boots, untied. Master of ceremonies, conductor of the circus.

Of course it was Pa Sonny. Under the pretense that it had been the deceased's one dying wish to have no service inside any established place of worship—a bold claim in a time of uncertainty and pain—Pa Sonny had insisted that the ceremony take place outdoors. "About the town," he'd clamored, "just as any fit young man should strike it."

An untruth, naturally. It came down to nothing less than Pa Sonny's unwillingness to set foot inside the church. The only objection had come from Father Marover, priest and caretaker of St. Josephine's. When news of the death first arrived, Pa Sonny got good and drunk. As the days dragged on and he continued to imbibe, his drunkenness rendered him proportionally more and more convinced of the truth in his claim. He finally insisted so aggressively that Father Marover, a meek and passive man, had no choice but to comply. Come the morning, Father Marover showed up bright and early with his Bible in hand, donned in his vestments, and stoically prepared to lead the day's sorrowful events. But Pa Sonny, still reeling from drink, immediately embarked upon open, hurtful criticism of 'the Muskrat,' as he spitefully refers to Marover. The unrestrained manner of Pa Sonny's remarks drew a hush over the mourners, which only goaded him on until Father Marover, uttering no reproach and no defense, quietly retraced his steps for the long walk back to St. Josephine's, where the church's tall spire has stood prominent in the distance throughout the morning, a constant mocking reminder of the farce they are all complicit in.

"We are, all of us, crumbling mountains, chipped down by cancerous winds and rains of lead. Fragility is our one true quality. Mend the wounded? Shepherd the lost? Comfort the sick? Sure, why not? Hardly makes a difference. We are...all of us...we are...flimsy, frail things. Wounded, lost, sick—these are the foundations of our being. Life and death? Brothers in arms. Comrades. We have two hands, don't we? You ought to. Well, what do you think they're for? But...but...could we ply them together? All of our shredded and scarred hands? Is it possible to fuse them together and fend off this intruder, this hypocrite, this malicious weed? Can't we protect just one of our kind? Our friend—our dear, dear, departed friend..."

The crowd quivers with nervous energy, groaning as an expansive valley of ineffaceable anguish forms. Their emotional states follow Pa Sonny's wayward train of thought, flitting about the terrain of life and death, knowing neither direction nor time. Sheep following a drunken shepherd.

A cheery, sociable black woman named Greenah Taylor has taken it upon herself to lead the gathered in song. She hobbles around, hugging people and distributing hymn sheets, which she tells Pa Sonny are nothing but old blues standards. She's trying her best to coerce everyone to sing, acting as chorus director, but those who do participate bring it off horribly. Pa Sonny ignores them and keeps right on rambling. All this tremulous ambiance, accented by sobs and unsynchronized prayers, the corner-store remarks and well-wishings common in the mourning lounge of a stranger, because no one ever knows what to say, how to speak, where to look, or when to cry at a wake. Death, the great taboo until it's in the room with us, and then what? Still, it does appear that the townsfolk are unified in purpose at times, as they are each in turn swept along by the airy undercurrents of Pa Sonny's inebriation.

As Pa Sonny looks over the crowd, his features are tortured by permanent surprise at the sight of them standing there and giving him their fractured attention. His hand slips around to his back pocket and fingers the flask, but he leaves it be for the moment, comforted by its mere presence. One by one, he silently acknowledges the people of Creek's Ridge, but when his gaze passes over Johannes, he stops, spellbound—

"No," Pa Sonny murmurs. "No, we can't. It is a vagrant that lives with each of us. Run all you want, forever if you want. Hide, come out into the open. It matters little. Patience is the highest virtue? Is that so? Then, well, who is the most virtuous? Who? Not me. Not you. Not our friend, certainly. His patience was as long as his...no...don't... Patience is only waiting. Waiting and listening, giving your attention to the distracting sound of the aggressive knocking at your door. That unnecessary knock knock knock. Because it has the key. The only key. It invented the keyhole! It mastered the lo-ha-ha-hock! That's its game. It enters whenever it has the urge. Now or later, doesn't really matter. But the more import we allow it, the more it taunts us. Violates us. This... this...this is the master stroke. Rimbaud's ghost curling our toes. Abraham ascending the mountain. Isaac, the obedient son, following in tow. The Shawnee prophet infecting entire populations with his rhetoric and hatred. Emil of the Forest, the great founder, forsaking his name and the names of others, tripping over the ridges of cowardice, leaving his innocent, unfortunate daughter forever...to the wolves. This is not a deadlock, it's a goddamn checkmate! Day one, day ten-thousand and one, you've already lost."

Johannes has no desire to be here, basking idly in the heat, dodging this-way-and-that Pa Sonny's determined glare, which blankets the mourners with astounded intrigue. However, each time it lands on Johannes, it acquires an antagonistic solemnity. Johannes is torn in several directions at once, knowing that he doesn't truly belong here while also recognizing the reality of what faces him—death has finally tracked him down. And his extended stay in Creek's Ridge has acquired the scent of permanence, smelled on himself and also emanating from these friends whose company has drawn him close, the potent, alluring musk of collected pathos. He is entwined with the daily lives of these people. Slowly, they recreate him, this event just another crack in the mirror. Any suffering they endure, it's certainly right and proper that Johannes suffers it, too.

"If death is out to get us, then this is exactly what it wants. To make us wait, and wait, and wait, and wait...and shiver with terror through it all. To deliver us visions of what awaits us in our turn. To gloat about its methods, its successes, its power over us. Its collusion with life. Black is white. Day is night. Darkness, light. Don't you see? The great trick, like dominoes painstakingly laid out. Did men not invent the wheel? And then the carriage? The locomotive, the car, the fax machine? When we gave birth to the printing press, we became lazy, demanding, idle. Sure, some sorry bastard needs to build the machine, and some other sorry bastard stands by to tend it. But is it not worth it? Look at how our ideas spread, across the globe if we want—words, ideas, and friends. Death, then, is not all that different from men..."

If Johannes is being honest with himself, this is no different than what Pa Sonny told him in the truck—wishing he could somehow forget Fairy and Ionia, wipe them clear from his life—because what Johannes is really experiencing now is closer to relief. It's not relief for the loss of a human life but for all the corollaries, all the hurt and suffering that that person underwent, released. All the pain and worry he caused for loved ones has been swept away. All rifts suddenly mended, misunderstandings corrected, betrayals forgiven.

This is not suffering, not as such. Johannes, as a man on intimate terms with loss, is not now experiencing the swell of suffering as he expects it, as he knows it. But, after all these months of trying to elude suffering through a combination of bodily toil and meditation, does this mean he has succeeded? He looks at the tree stump again, its intricate carvings. When he had helped Sonny carry it out that morning, his thoughts had been elsewhere. He'd been filled with apprehension for what the coming day would bring, bent on trying to straighten Pa Sonny's jagged steps before anyone showed up, reflecting on the desert howls of coyotes and Ionia's calming caress. But now the carvings stand out, seeming to beckon to him. And he recognizes them. Not the images themselves but the method, talent, and artistry involved, identical to the carvings that decorate Ernest's piano. Upon each of the six flattened sides, where the bark has been shaved off, a depiction of the Buddha is carved, each posed in a different asana, their hands leveled in unique mudra. Thick lumps of craggy bark separate them, though they are all six connected by a delicate web of lines that curves around the edges, carved directly into the bark, defying norms of spatial-formational continuity, all linked and unified into one. And yet, the lines are so subtle that nothing but a slight shift to one side changes their form, rendering them nearly imperceptible.

Suffering or not, he currently feels restless, tired of being dogged by Pa Sonny's accusatory eyes. So, he steps back and slips silently through the crowd. He paces around the perimeter of the sullen mob, occasionally halting to stand near one of his company and resting a hesitant hand on their shoulders, each time expecting to feel the surge of body electrics charged with loss. But the conduction is poor. Nothing flowing. Nothing but the unforgiving sun scorching his face, something he's used to and could receive much more efficiently through digging or meditation. Or both.

His meditation in the grove never really took hold. A bit of peace and quiet—sure. On the verge of calmness—perhaps. But he was never able to reproduce what he once had beneath Knecht. After they found their rhythm with the dig, however, meditation and digging were compounded into a single activity that propelled him through the hours, making the days bearable and giving rise to a repetition he could look forward to. This, a pattern akin to his life on the mountain, a solitary existence set against the backdrop of spiritual abandon that must inevitably lead to transcendence—he had believed that. His days spent digging had been buffered by the light social existence of Ernest's bar, after which he would stretch out on the hard floor of the living room to await the dreams and nightmares, his courage plucked up with the help of several glasses of The Carnival. And each sunrise brought a new awakening with purpose and means. The sway of the pickax was a pendulum; the discovery of a bone, a triumph. Life itself had been reduced to a sole pursuit.

But the trip to El Paso had killed that. He'd been alone ever since, and though he had regained the ability to meditate effectively, his meditations had bloomed and flowered with the thorns of an incomprehensible guilt. Judas Iscariot, leader. Regret for some slight, for the pain they had both endured. And on each of those lonely days since, he has spent hours at the glade near the creek, inhaling to embrace an established life and then exhaling the pain and regret, reaching deep and striving for the return of infinite calmness and clarity to his life. But in these past two weeks, meditation has not helped him. He has learned only that calmness and clarity alone cannot set life in order. Knecht's wisdom has been chopped down, its rings of lies exposed. Fairy and Ionia, for all their steady-handed wisdom and allure, had not succeeded in corralling Pa Sonny, keeping him caged. The coyotes rove the desert, unbound.

"Life is not waiting, but searching. A constant search for how to best distribute our wills. And what if? What if... What if it is your will, your one and only desire in this life, to extinguish...ants? To wipe them off the face of the planet. Eradicate them absolutely, once and forever. Do you seek them out? One by one? They're ants, for God's sake!" Pa Sonny curls over in a fit of laughter, wobbles, and falls off the stump. An unknown old man steps forward to help him mount it again.

"Thank you, thank you... But no, no, no, you poison their spirits. Corrode their colonies from the inside. Penetrate their little ant souls until they no longer have the will themselves. Until they no longer care to resist the burden, the terrible pressure of...*the boot!* But there is no boot! Only the thought of the boot. Awareness that at any moment, without forewarning, without cause or reason, the boot may stomp stomp stomp!" Pa Sonny raises his hands above his head to defend himself from the aforementioned boot, but as he looks up, he catches the sun's full glare instead. He shrinks away, shielding his eyes. "Somebody lend me a goddamned hat so I don't go blind. Quick, quick. My face'll peel off in this...someone, help..."

All the men glance down and around at each other. A young boy, too young to fully comprehend the day's events, steps forward and holds out a white baseball cap. Pa Sonny smiles and ruffles the boy's hair as he takes the cap and spends a few moments adjusting the size. Everyone is patient and attentive, watching as though this is the most critical part of the ceremony. The ritual head-dressing. Crowning of the bandit king. After he's got it settled askew atop his thinning hair, he is once again helped up onto the stump by the friendly hand of the unknown old man.

"Thank you, yes, thank you always. You... Your suffering...is the spider's web that connects us all. Our friend, he held onto life's torrents, its monstrous crashing waves, too tightly. Too dear. He swallowed them with the thirst of a desert nomad, of a sober alcoholic. A mistake that many of us make. You...where are you? Me too. We cling to suffering because we must. Man is not meant to, is not capable of attaining pure detachment. The soul's threads are woven into it, adhesive and abrasive. And by sharing it, by treading and consuming these same threads as everyone else, we can begin to understand and accept it. But never— *Never!*—allow it to dictate your path. Never give yourself up. You fight, you climb, you dig so that you are always above it, looking down upon it, quipping sarcastically over it. Alive and dead, one at the same time, now and always. Mark off your perimeter, own your place amidst the chaos, but never try to escape it. To do so is only to play into death's bluff. Loss comes to us, as it does today, an aid and a prop to suffering, a wrecking ball swinging pell-mell for destruction, scattering bones all over God's earth. What then? Will you seek them out? One by one by one? Devote yourself to the reconstruction of what was not strong enough to withstand a blow in the first place? Will you locate the missing bits and attempt to arrange them into some sensible semblance of worth? Will you, goddamnit, waste away in that desperate inertness that is a cyclical roving existence? Happiness and misery are the same goddamned thing... And freedom will never bring about detachment because freedom is born of detachment. And vice versa...ad infinitum... damn you..."

At the outset, Pa Sonny seemed grateful for the attention he received as he relived his glory days, but now, he appears unconcerned with the presence of the others. Johannes is constantly on the move, hanging behind the crowd, hidden at the perimeter, fingering the torn hem of his shirt, its frayed threads. But every time he glances up through the sea of heads, Pa Sonny's unwavering gaze seeks him alone. He and Johannes might as well still be cooped up in the truck on the long drive between Creek's Ridge and Pa Sonny's secrets.

Standing above these people, Pa Sonny denounces detachment, but he exemplifies it in every facet of his existence. Even though he was drawn away from his life's devotion by his loosely defined family, he is defined by his own refusal to join them. He torments himself with self-chastisement, a balking stew of confidence, regret, and selfish endurance that affects Fairy and Ionia Josephina in equal measure. Instead of choosing them, he rises each morning to a duplicitous residence in Creek's Ridge, a town he detests so vilely that his entire existence becomes almost fraudulent. If Johannes were to step forward and reveal the crude, disjointed organization of Pa Sonny's life to everyone gathered here, would they continue to regard him with this level of fascination and loyalty? This reverence? Or, with Pa Sonny waist-deep in fervor and bender, Johannes could just take the truck. Pa Sonny would never notice. In just twelve hours, Johannes could be back in El Paso, basking in the bliss of Ionia's touch, her flesh and bones, learning life's cruel lessons from Fairy, and cooking ribs all day, every day. Doing what Pa Sonny should have done years ago.

And Matthew was a tax collector.

Pa Sonny's shoulders tremble. He's crying, but he doesn't seem to realize it. Johannes searches Pa Sonny for any resemblance to his daughter. Their mouths curve and twist into similar shapes, although he recalls Ionia's mouth being larger, like Fairy's. She shares Pa Sonny's broad forehead and something in the eyes, but it's difficult to say what. Johannes's mental image of Ionia, although still intact, has deteriorated somewhat in the two weeks since El Paso.

Pa Sonny's weeping is enough to distort his features, making it harder for Johannes to see evidence of his daughter there. Many of the mourners have taken this as a cue, and the sound of sobbing spreads among them. Finally, Pa Sonny composes himself and compresses his vocal energy.

"May thou see Me coming, I am Time,
Bearer of doom and death,
Harbinger of beginnings and ends,
None shall remain...
Strike, I say..."

Pa Sonny fades with a sigh and an exaggerated shrug. "A quotation, that," he mumbles, noticing the tears running down his cheeks and wiping them away with his bare forearm. "The holiest of books..."

Johannes can hardly believe Pa Sonny is capable of such sagacity in his current state. As with many of the utterances to pass Pa Sonny's lips over the past week, including a large portion of this raving eulogy, this passage seems to be intended for Johannes. He has read, recited, contemplated those words, and possibly even studied them with Pa Sonny. He has handled them as he handles and recognizes horse bones by touch alone, he's sure of it. Although Johannes's thoughts are clearer and more focused than they've been in months, he is still incapable of dredging up the past on his own. He tries, briefly, but he knows he won't be able to remember the source of an obscure quotation. What a shame, too, because how pleasant this morning could be if he was alone with the Scrap and a book. Sitting beside the creek or beneath Knecht. A cup of coffee or a glass of The Carnival. The pickax lying within reach, just in case.

Ceremony and ritual seem unnecessary, almost contradictory to the swell of life all around them. People cannot cushion the shock of loss if they insist on keeping up with the religious and sentimental loose strings of custom and tradition. And yet, what better way to draw those who remain closer together than the eternal mystery of death? Conjecture as long as you wish, you will never find agreement, there will never be an answer, but there will always be the warm and lively breath of another upon your face. Perhaps the people of Creek's Ridge have got it right. Communal suffering. Loss as a social function rather than a personal burden. Emil Wood's Community of Man rises again, or perhaps it never died.

If such is the case, then there's still a matter of fitting in, of being embraced by the community and embracing it back. Even now,

Johannes drifts listlessly on the fringes while the community unites and every member combines their heartache into a collective heaving mass. But, in all honesty, he doesn't want to share in their pain any more than he wants to unshackle and expose his own.

"Now, a quiet thought for the deceased. Let us take our mortal time and hand it over in offering. Selflessly, give all. What else have you or I to give?"

Pa Sonny bows his head without further instructions, and the crowd follows his lead. The sound of their sobbing fades. Pa Sonny watches over the crowd from beneath the cap's brim. Though sunken low into the depths of self-pity, he's amused and confused as he brings out the flask yet again. He discreetly unscrews the top, lifts it to his nose, and sniffs, a deep inhalation followed by a drunken, self-indulgent gleam in the eyes, an unabashed admission that he is leading his sheep into a pack of wolves.

Once more, his eyes seek out and land overbearingly on Johannes. He holds up the flask and wriggles it enticingly, a gesture meant to beckon Johannes forward. This is followed by a not-so-subtle wink and kink of the head, a grin of deepest understanding and complicity. A few mourners notice and turn around to see who Pa Sonny has singled out.

For the first time all morning, Johannes stares Pa Sonny in the eyes, concealing nothing from this mentor of former days while he considers the options before him. He can stay put and continue feigning active engagement with this rogue ceremony, bending his thoughts to dwell on death and joining the others weeping, praying, remembering—drinking from this flask of loss. Conversely, he can retreat to the calm of his glade and crawl meditatively into himself. Or he can dig, alone. If he prefers to suffer the long silence of the road, he can take Pa Sonny's truck and begin the drive back to the edge of the country, of the known world, safety and solace under Ionia Josephina's tender touch. These last three options are, all of them, thorns in Pa Sonny's side.

But each of these equally attractive choices is whisked away by a hearty puff of breath teeming with rebellion, pure and instantaneous emotion dictating as Johannes catches a whiff and follows a sudden inspiration—an alternative he's sure will infuriate Pa Sonny more than all the rest.

Chapter 46

The Missionary

July 13, 1818
Athens, Georgia

By the grace of God, the orphan I once was has stumbled upon yet another loving home. The Cherokees of northern Georgia have welcomed and accepted me. Nevertheless, I still hear the haunting whispers of former days. They alternately beg my return and snarl stern warnings, sometimes in the same breath. They sing me to sleep with sweet lullabies only to jerk me awake in the night with terrors never shed.

It has been three months since we made our escape from St. Marks. Though American soldiers pursued us for two days, our safety was ensured by Dan Bull's unparalleled familiarity with the surrounding woodlands. Confident and boasting along the way, Dan Bull led the soldiers directly into their own camp at Tallahassee. We watched on from a nearby hillside as they were reprimanded by their officers for losing us, the fugitives. Hundreds of troops occupied their camp, possibly more than a thousand. Roberto wished to halt our progress to rescue Arbuthnot, and he argued passionately, but Dan Bull rejected such recklessness. I sided with Dan Bull, as it seemed nothing more than a glorified death wish. Though we had succeeded in our temporary escape, we remained in danger of being found out, captured, and relieved of our lives. After more than a month on the run, a week in hiding, and a few terrifying nights of scurrying through the woods, I yearned to return to a simple life with a peace-loving people. Yet, try though I might, I could summon neither the courage nor the angst necessary to join the battle for such a privilege. No soldier am I, no warrior. Therefore, I decided to risk it alone and begin the journey back to my Seminole family on the St. Johns. But by that point, the American ranks had already filtered throughout La Florida, and my companions would not hear another word about it. Roberto believed that a Spaniard found wandering the interior without papers would be killed for sport, later adding that he had promised Father Jimenez he would see to my safe passage.

"Safe passage to where?" I asked.

"Anywhere but here," he answered and refused to say more.

Against any logic I could follow, my friends decided my only option was to enter the United States. Dan Bull assured me that due to General Jackson's disproportionate hatred for the Seminoles and his obvious attempts to occupy the peninsula, all hostilities were moving south for the time being. There would be no more opportune time for us to slip north. Once we crossed the Georgia line, assistance would be easier to come by with Dan Bull's innumerable friendly connections and debts owed him across the border. And, should he safely deliver me as far north as Cherokee country, he claimed I would be free as an eagle.

I hesitated to agree, for my thoughts and prayers were at that moment concentrated on the people of our village at the St. Johns—the cheerful times I spent with them, mere days turned into nigh on two years, the warm familial greetings one received each and every new day, be they days of prosperity or of heartache. But on the run, hesitation is dead time. Though life may pause or stop altogether, the world continues its course. And so, before I even had the chance to protest in earnest, we were already northern-bound.

Roberto accompanied us as far as the border. He never said as much, but I believe he always intended to make good on his attempt to save Arbuthnot, his brother-in-arms. Every day, as Dan Bull and I trekked north through Georgian hills and forests on the outskirts of vast plantations, I prayed for them.

Before we parted, Roberto left me with one final offering of advice. To ensure my future well-being and a long, fruitful life, regardless of whether I remain in the United States or eventually return to Spanish territories, I will need papers proving my identity. He suggested I seek the solution to this dilemma with another friend of his, a priest based in Cherokee country named Jeremiah Evarts.

Mr. Evarts is well known amongst the Cherokees. The families and missionaries who offered us shelter along the way told us we would most likely find him here, in Athens. Indeed, when we arrived, we found him sitting on the steps of a modest wooden chapel, contemplating the pleasantly cool weather, almost as though he were waiting for us.

He was delighted to receive the note Roberto had sent along, and even more pleased upon learning of my experiences with Father Jimenez, whom he knew of but had never met. Throughout our initial conversations, he repeatedly expressed admiration at the thought of a young man such as myself—unschooled in the Christian faith, unshackled from society, and free to roam the world with a bit of youth still on my side—showing the interest, talent, and patience for a missionary life. Even as he spoke, I noticed his memory at work, recalling the trials and misadventures of his life as a young missionary. At the time, I found it difficult to accept his compliments. Thinking back, I recalled only moments of indecision. Running away from the orphanage. Boarding El Soldado Agraciado and later failing to honor my word. The ransacking of Friar Ruiz Ruiz's trunk. My hesitation to undertake the tasks of the cloth during Father Jimenez's convalescence, including the act of personally delivering the Father into God's eternal and blessed hands. Thus, I marveled at the unintentional course my life has taken. While I have at times made deliberate decisions, I never made those choices with my current station in mind, nor with any far-flung objective. Even now, as I continue toward a destination becoming more evident, I cannot fathom the certainty or hopes attributed to me by the likes of Father Jimenez and Mr. Evarts.

As an influential member of the American Board of Missionaries, Mr. Evarts set directly to securing my legal status in this country. Already, I have obtained identification papers from his organization. Mr. Evarts assures me that these papers will suffice for any circumstance as long as I am on Cherokee land. Given some time, it will not be difficult to obtain a more permanent standing, allowing me to travel the country with my fellow missionaries.

I have been forced, however, to make one great sacrifice. With Spain's role in the current tensions over La Florida and the nature of our work, it is in my best interest to adopt a new name. Mr. Evarts himself publishes all his writings under the pseudonym William Penn. The day after my identification papers arrived, Mr. Evarts led me into the same small chapel where we first found him, and he introduced me to a congregation of Christian Cherokees by my new moniker, as it appears on my papers—Emil Wood.

Some weeks ago, we received word of Roberto's fate. Mr. Evarts related the news to me with tears rolling down his cheeks. The Americans captured Roberto not long after he left us at the border. Both he and Arbuthnot were hanged at the end of April. The Americans have used them as cautionary examples. Not only have they yet to lower the corpses from the gallows, but they have concocted twisted histories around those two brave men, histories that do not represent the true nature of my friend, Robert Ambrister, but rather reflect all the atrocities of humankind. Even now, they continue to spread these lies throughout the territory.

Dan Bull, too, has returned south. In vain, I tried to persuade him to remain here with us, in the relative safety of Cherokee country, as I do not wish to be burdened by the news of his execution a couple months hence. He was moved by neither reason nor emotion. As he told me, it is fitting that I should stay, for this is not my war. But it is his war, and he would consider it an honor to die defending the Seminole tribes who have repeatedly saved him and reawakened his love for life, an admission that I heard with a surge of acute guilt.

Tomorrow, Mr. Evarts will escort me to Ross's Landing, a rapidly growing Cherokee settlement on the Tennessee River, nestled beneath the lovely peaks of the Blue Ridge Mountains. There, I will assist the residing missionary while I continue to familiarize myself with the Cherokee people, their language, and their customs. The Cherokees are accomplished English speakers, but I will find no one in Ross's Landing with whom to speak my beloved Spanish.

A curious side-effect of my acquaintance with the Cherokees has been the resurrection of my interest in the prophet, Tenskwatawa. This country is more vast than I ever imagined, and the prophet is certainly not to be found in these mountains. But, to my surprise, I have discovered that unverified rumors and sightings abound. It is said that—owing to his divine nature—he escaped the mortal fate that took his brother during the 1812 War, while others claim it was merely his cowardice in the face of battle. Some say he hid in Upper Canada under the protection of the British. However, in recent years, traders and missionaries have begun traveling west of the great Mississippi to the distant territory known as Indian Country. There, several reliable sources claim to have encountered an egotistical individual who dressed in a gaudy style, had only one eye, and was covered in burn scars. They insist this man could have been none other than the Shawnee prophet. It is believed that he lives a reclusive life, still harboring grand ideas for a self-sufficient utopia, something I myself have often dreamt of. I should enjoy beyond measure the opportunity to cross the great river myself one day and confirm these suspicions.

One aspect of my former life in Spain has crept back into my present circumstances. With the sinking of El Soldado Agraciado, the deaths of Roberto and Father Jimenez, leaving my Seminole family, Dan

Bull's return to the war, and now my impending separation from Mr. Evarts, I feel again as the young orphan I once was. Everyone has abandoned me. By fortune and grace, I have been reared by a few generous mentors, but now, again, I must set out to discover my own course, with only God as my guide.

Though life's tribulations must occasionally revive and repeat, they do not weigh like stones upon my chest this time, but rather more like birds in flight. With some small amount of experience on my side, along with the extreme kindness extended by Mr. Evarts and the Cherokees, I am confident I shall persevere. Loneliness functions as a transition and a necessary condition of the human soul, God's means of humbling us, his servants.

I believe Father Jimenez would approve of the path I am setting upon, though he would not deign to accept my new name. And, I admit, I myself do not yet feel perfectly at ease in this new identity.

Emil Wood—it is a fine name, though it is not truly my own.

Alas, I must shoulder this moral burden as I embark into the unknown. No matter what I face or what name I adopt, I shall always know who I am.

After all, is God not both faceless and nameless?

May 31, 1819
Ross's Landing, Tennessee

The unparalleled majesty of these mountains is matched in equal step by the mysteries they conceal. Treading in the footsteps of Father Jimenez, I have attempted to carry out the Lord's noble work, and I continue to settle into my newly assumed place in the kingdom of God. However, every day I am forced to re-evaluate my perceptions of this world, to question all that I have believed and held dear, including the path I currently traverse.

Of all the upheavals I have faced in these months with the Cherokees, none has unsettled my soul as severely as facing death alone in these mountains. Although certain adventuresome encounters with the shadow of death have provided a sort of prideful import to my life in the past, I recognize now that I never faced true mortal danger in the hills of northern Spain, aboard El Soldado Agraciado, or hiding in a broom closet in St. Marks. Nor was I ever alone on such occasions, but supported by friends and allies.

Four weeks ago, or thereabouts, I left our parish on my morning stroll, one of many habits I picked up from Father Jimenez at the St. Johns. The temperate weather at this elevation has made these morning jaunts even more enjoyable, though I long for the Father's company. I have explored and familiarized myself with most of the nearby mountains. Several Cherokee families have built their modest homes upon these slopes, near enough for frequent neighborly niceties but secluded enough to enjoy the blessed solitude of these mountains. That day, I exchanged pleasantries with many of them, even announcing my intentions to venture into areas of the forest I had not yet explored.

I trekked for many hours, my thoughts wandering to and fro, happy and free and unhinged, spilling over with gratitude for the way things have turned out, the fortunate turns life takes, and on this particular day, as I rose higher onto mountain ridges I had only ever viewed from below, I was filled with love and admiration for God and all his creations. The stunning view of the mountains spread out below me, the folds and ripples of our mother earth stretching, yawning, cradling us day and night. I continued on, lost amidst a deep appreciation for all things, and when the sun began to set, I wept at the sight of the vibrant shades the sky acquired and the profound beauty of mists shrouding the valleys below.

And then, all at once, it was dark. I had allowed the entire day to pass me by while I strove to heights unseen, vistas unknown. Knowing I could not retrace my steps at such a late hour, I resolved to seek out a comfortable perch upon which to observe the stars and rest through until dawn. Dark clouds appeared before I found some pleasant nook, as though risen to smite my innocent intentions, covering the night sky and rendering the forest unnavigable. And though I knew myself capable of surviving the wilderness, fear crept into my heart as I questioned my ability to find my way home even after daylight returned, for I had walked throughout the day without considering my direction or whereabouts within those wilds. As I stumbled blindly onward, praying for strength and resolve, attempting to calm my lurking fear, I spotted a shadow—the welcoming silhouette of a great tree stretching its arms against the gray sky. It was as though I could hear it calling to me, offering strength and security under which I might pass the long night. I heard the sound of falling water nearby and took a few cautious steps.

The next instant was both the longest and most compact moment of my life, a contradiction to the passage of time itself, for with my first step into the unseen water, I slipped upon a mossy stone, tumbled into the swiftly flowing stream, and was dragged over a rocky ledge. The drop itself was but a flash, the blink of an eye. The pain upon landing, however, stretched beyond this life. Having landed upon an angular boulder, the full weight of my body snapped my right leg at the shin. Though I could neither penetrate the darkness nor twist my body to see it, I could feel the bone protruding through my flesh. The most I could manage was to drag myself out of the pool at the bottom of the waterfall and onto the muddy bank, where I lost consciousness, a victim of excruciating pain, and never once expecting to wake from the timorous sleep that followed.

I did wake, periodically, both in darkness and daylight, but I harbored no hope for survival. I tried and failed to lift myself. I lacked strength, and I repeatedly lost consciousness, wandering the terrifying realm between waking and dream, between life and death, slowly wasting away whilst at intervals being shocked into consciousness by sharp stings of pain or the nearby calls of wild animals. I dreamt that a coyote or a wolf returned repeatedly, sniffing my face in anticipation of that final dying breath, eyeing my wound and my exposed bone with possessive, gluttonous eyes, only to be startled away by a frightening shriek. I dreamt, too, of Father Jimenez and Roberto warning me to keep away, of a father and mother I have never known calling me home, and of the sea, deafening in its silence.

How much time passed in that state? A day? A week? An eternity, perhaps. Then, I was jolted to by a voice, someone shaking me awake, and I opened my eyes to a hideously ugly, vaguely feminine face grinning down over me. Malnourishment and dehydration left me too weak to speak or enter fully into consciousness, though I sensed my body being conveyed across forest trails, through brush and leaves, beneath branches and thorns, over stones and mud.

I later awoke from a dream in which I was drowning as El Soldado Agraciado broke apart around me, spluttering from my mouth and nostrils, calling out for my fellow deckhands. But it was only the old crone forcing water into my mouth. I drank heartily as she busied herself with preparing a pungent broth, uttering not a word, although often glancing back at me, occasionally clucking and tittering in grotesque mirth.

She fed me and tended to my wounded leg with the skill of a European doctor, though lacking any form of medical equipment. She numbed my leg with an anesthetic herb and persuaded me to drink a foul-tasting liquor she had apparently made herself. Then, she set the bone to the sound of my screams. She wrapped the leg tightly in a splint, murmuring all the while, and when she finished, she sat back to observe the relief in my countenance, cackling with both amusement and interest. Finally, as she offered me another taste of her homemade liquor, she spoke.

In English, but with an unplaceable accent, she asked my name—
"Emil Wood," I answered.
"A good name," she said.
"Thank you, yes."
"Strong, though you are not." Her grin grew wider, and I noticed that her mouth boasted no more than two teeth.
"And may I learn your name?" I asked. "So I may know who it is that I must thank. I shall be grateful always. I wish to include your name, your memory, into each prayer I make, for the rest of my days. Madam, you have saved my life."

To this, she erupted with wild, unkempt, though slightly melodious laughter.

"To save a life," she muttered through her chuckling. "Each day, a life saved. My own, your own. The difference matters none."

"But," I stammered, "I had already entered the valley of shadows. I do not know how many days I lay there incapacitated, out of my mind. I know only that any waking moments I experienced were wrapped in delirium and visions of a world other than this. An afterlife of no pleasant aspect. I always expected more courage from myself in death..."

"Another world," she burst through her swelling laughter. "What world is other than this?"

"Madam, forgive me, but I must..." I hesitated, unsure how to measure my joy with being alive against her terrible wrinkles and creases of dark skin, her thin, mottled hair, her warts and scars, her piercing and disagreeable merriment. "I must," I found my voice again, "I must express my gratitude. How can I ever..."

"No need, lad, no need." Her cackling subsided, settling into a smile at once tender and ghastly. "Rest a few days, then I take you back to where you came from."

"España..."

"What is that?"

"It is nothing. Another world..."

"Indeed," she cackled. "Ross's Landing, then, if I have to guess."

"That is right," I said. "Ross's Landing. I do not know how long I have been gone or how far I have come."

"Long, long way is Ross's Landing. What you're doing way out here, eh? Not many venture this way. Not many, not often."

"I was...out for my morning stroll... I lost my way."

At this, her laughter resumed, and it was several minutes before she could curb its momentum.

"Are you Cherokee?" I asked.

She nodded in affirmation but answered reluctantly. "I once was, suppose I still am."

"Will you, madam... I am so thankful. At this moment, only the weight of my gratitude causes me grief. My incredible debt to you. Truly, I do not know how to express it... Might you be good enough to pray with me?"

"No," she said. "No need, lad."

"But you are a Cherokee? Of these parts? Are you...are you not a Christian?"

"I am not," she said.

"You are a follower of the old beliefs? The Great Spirit?"

"Dear me, no!" Her laughter now tumbled and rollicked so untamed that her voice grew hoarse. She wheezed as she continued. "One being?" she spat. "Only one? To create and care for all things? Our dreams and fears? And all the natural world aside? How? Why? No, no. Ridiculous."

"I am sorry again..." I stuttered through my shock, my wariness, my uncertainty. "But, what then, may I ask, do you follow? In what do you believe?"

"Was it God who found you? Fed you? Mended you? No, it was I. We help each other. We must. The only way. The only thing to believe. Each one to another, and so on, and so on. Until the end."

Graciously, I conceded, accepting this wisdom from the tremulous old hag, burdened by her own laughter and amused by my sternness and trepidation. Once more, I chanced to ask her name.

"It is not important," she said.

"But it is," I begged. "It is to me. This is the last favor I will ask of you, the only favor if you wish, as you have already given me everything a man could ask for."

She snorted through her toothless smile.

"Please, madam?"

"Once upon a time," she said, "I was called Josephine. Suppose I still am."

"Josephine," I marveled. "Beautiful...a lovely name. I shall honor your deeds today, along with your name, for all time. I am bound to you, eternally."

"Eternity," she snorted, coughed. "Absurd."

And then she laughed and laughed and laughed.

Chapter 47

Guilt

Wide, wobbly, crack-plagued stone slabs lead up to enormous twin doors, one bolted securely from the inside, the other requiring an immense exertion of strength, knuckles taut around wrought iron handles, and then the drastic transition from blinding sunlight to unlit interiors. Silence roars, demands veneration—

He followed her up the steps, seeking release from the afternoon's humidity. It's always cold inside churches, she said again. He slowed his advance to get a better view of her ass, and she swung the door open only to disappear inside that gaping entrance, a blast of cool air rushing out as he bounded up the remaining steps in pursuit...

The vestibule is wide but only a few paces deep, with twin doorways leading into the main building and coat closets inlaid along the wall to the right. Elegant tiles of white marble pattern the floor, pristine and perfectly set. Muted light filters through the narrow stained-glass windows high on the three exposed walls. A massive, solid slab of gray marble sprawls between the two interior doorways. At first glance, it resembles a casket, a reminder of the ceremony taking place out in the heat and the dust, of a life reduced to ashes. Deep basins filled with holy water bulge at either end of the marble slab, which displays a number of flower arrangements in ornate vases, each bearing a card with a note and the name of the deceased—

She didn't even lift her head but only looked up at the sound of him bursting in. Her eyes, cloudy with cataracts, gazed at him without recognition. He had flirted with the law, speeding the entire two-hundred-some-odd miles, only to be met by this pitiful sight, the unfortunate remnants of a spent life. Surely, she couldn't know what was in store for her. But would she really mind? No more fight left in this Queen. Get down on the floor with her, not to pray but just to hold her tight, there, on the floor, just for a bit, one last time, before this brief rendezvous with eternity...

The flowers obscure images and text carved onto the length of the marble's surface, Latin phrases that disappear beneath the vases and are only visible around the edges. The crisp, unworn carvings are not historical in the slightest. They stretch around the table's rounded corners, winding and interweaving along the sides of the marble, lines carved so fine, so delicate, nearly imperceptible, disappearing entirely when viewed from certain angles, and therefore giving the table to tremble with life, like a disturbed pond rippling with silent meditations. No patterns emerge from the organic flow of lines, only a style identical to the etchings upon Ernest's piano and Pa Sonny's tree stump. Entrancing intricacy, minute detail, an organically flowing beauty despite, or perhaps because of, the lack of any immediately evident pattern, the illusion of non-existence—

Did you hit it?
I think I did. But then it ran. It got away.
We need something stronger than this piece of shit. We need a real gun.
What's the point of a gun? It'd blast them to bits. Nothing left...
Yeah?
They're just squirrels...
Yeah, so?
Well...what's the point then?
And what's the point in injuring them? They'll only die later, in agony...

Silence in and around Creek's Ridge is normal, but this is altogether disarming, a fabricated silence that drives conscious thought away rather than encouraging it, opening up wounds of the past instead. Stepping through those enormous doors has led into a place removed from time, existence flattening into an everlasting instant blended with the past and the future, a peaceful stasis not unlike meditation in a shaded grove beside a calming creek or upon a solitary mountain peak—

The river swelled and crusaded insistently down the mountainside. Bloated raindrops pummeled from above, like a rapids falling from the sky, too heavy even for the mountain to stand without falter. The crushing mountainside moaned, lunging downward as it forced itself upon the river. They contorted and struggled and eventually became one. The river broke free, tried to flee, but it was only running in place as the earth thrust upon it. The mountain shook and spat itself into the water, creating a sludge that choked the stream, thick, pulsating, lusting after the pleasures of destruction. The man crouched nearby, paralyzed by fear, capable of nothing other than cowering, staring, and groping at the trunk of the great tree...

The enormous stone blocks constructing the walls show no signs of age, holding up the structure without concern for long years past, without fear of many more to come, each block boldly defined, polished, and naturally cradled between its neighbors. The masons may have just packed up and left. Empty candle holders sprout from the walls. The high, cavernous ceiling and its sturdy rafters are concealed in shadow. A gentle breeze raises ripples upon the surface of the holy water, and a distorted reflection, a powerful thirst, a craving for water, running frantically up and down mountain slopes, digging endlessly under a sweltering sun, the long escape from madness and despair, and then the doorway, still unvarnished, the fragrance of oak and the inviting expanse of the room beyond, revolving, twisting, vining, unmanageable and beginning to tangle—

You've been gone a long time, just bumming around, huh? Went to finish school, dropped out again, and now you're putting it all to the wayside. All that time, all that money, flushed it right down the john. Well, then, what's the point? Always wondered that myself. Why I never bothered. I'd rather use my hands anyhow, to make my way...

You always did like to get your hands dirty. So, you're here now, in the middle of nowhere. It's peaceful. I like it. Where are we?

Yeah, yeah, welcome to my new home. Nothing so special. Modest and my own. Go ahead and make it your own, too. What's mine is yours. Same as always, I guess. Same as when we were dumb-shit kids, anyway. So, you're back. Where've you been? Heard you were there, you know, on the coast? Never came when I was there, of course. Only after I left...the tropics, the swamps...but she's still there and...so I guess you...

He steps into an attractive, spacious nave, many times larger than appears possible from the outside. The muskiness is both historical and recent, with traces of incense and fresh-cut timber. A long red rug, fading to orange down the center and frayed along the edges, runs the length of the aisle up to the pulpit. Multicolored illumination emanates from tall, hazy, stained-glass windows, the light falling in long, angled patches across the pews. The ceiling is three times higher than the ceiling in the vestibule, and the shadows at the top are as thick as oil. Neat stacks of lighting fixtures and boxed bulbs lie against the rear wall. The pews are age-worn and plain, but durable and elegant in their simple design. The back rows seat an array of tools, lumber, paint cans and brushes and rollers, bags of cement mix, tubes of caulk, tiles, tarps, and trash. Even buildings seek life everlasting. But for buildings or for men, what appeal is there in living forever? Forgetting and remembering forever?

Inside the vestibule, he closed his eyes and absorbed the cool air. He wanted to stick his face into the large brass stoup, lap up holy water like a dog to relieve this thirst—he'd done it before, as a kid—but she stuck her head around the corner of the inner doorway and kinked her head to ask, Aren't you coming? So he chased her into the nave and matched her steps walking down the aisle. Deep in their solitary prayers, the old women scattered about the pews paid the two of them no attention until she hooked her arm through his and took up a rigid stride, humming the nuptial melody, their hands all over each other as they gazed around at the elaborate ornamentation, the life-sized white crucifix and Christ's wounds, golden trim adorning the altar table and the lectern, the scent of incense, burning candles, melted wax. She wrapped her arm around his waist, leaned in close, and whispered, I have a confession to make...

The center pews seat a thick layer of dust. Old wooden panels cover the lower parts of the walls, many of them termite-eaten. Panels have already been torn off at random points, revealing masonry and cobwebs long since hidden away. Candle holders decorate the walls, just like in the vestibule, except these ones still contain charred wicks and mounds of wax. The disarray, deconstruction, and low lighting recall a drinking parlor, not some specific place, but rather the general atmosphere of an alcoholic's basement rec room or Ernest's bar. Instead of neon beer signs, old advertisements, and mirrors, the walls are hung with tattered draperies. They are aesthetically arranged, filled with Latin phrases and sacred images—lambs, crosses, a baby's shoes, doves, skulls, armor, fish, ferns, children knelt in prayer, olive branches. And upon the altar table, a silver chalice and a decanter, the blood of Christ. The thirst again, suddenly, painfully, but for liquor this time, the contents of Pa Sonny's flask—

He gazed around the small chapel at all the sleepy faces, at the single square skylight above the altar, at the Holy Bible in his hands, at the pastor, his mentor, his friend, discreetly pouring a fifth of 95-proof bourbon into his personal chalice instead of the blood of Christ, and he understood that God was not there with them. With any luck, God could be found somewhere out in the world, amongst the people of the earth or the wilds of nature itself. A lonely island far out at sea, perhaps. Or spied in secret from some remote mountain peak. But luck was a gift of God. Without God's help, it's only chance. A fifty-fifty shot at existence. If those people—those towering adults and their obedient children—if they genuinely believed that God was there with them at that moment, then their souls were already lost. And if they didn't believe, then they were faking it for appearances, allowing their souls to rot out on the curb when they should be nurtured instead. What desperate hankerings they prayed for and what beautiful possibilities were lost in that united sepulchral hum as they mouthed words deemed sacred. But their utterances only exposed them, the actual objects of reverence, for what they truly were—mere melancholic tonics of themselves...

The memory comes and goes, knotted, twisted, confused, and vexing, just another in the steady current. This babel of life is not surfacing all on its own, not risen from the grave through the recitation of cryptic incantations. Give credit where credit is due, to this church, or the day's ceremony, the airy undercurrents of time catching up. Nothing resurrects of its own accord. The Rachmaninoff record and the Scrap. Photographs of a friend, of a sister, of dogs and what they meant. Stories of a shared youth and other more obscure tales from Fairy. Influence of the stars under Ionia Josephina's gentle guiding touch—Simon the Cananean, yet another one. Even the Limping Lady. All of it has been revived only by the graciousness of others.

Sammy, Sammy, come over here. Sammy, hey, Sammy. What are you doing? Why don't you answer me?

Excuse me? Were you talking to me?

I told you to come here.

But you were calling someone named Sammy. Who's that? That's not me.

What are you talking about?

My name. Ask me my name, you jerk. You're so rude.

Okay then...what's your name?

If he is to dig up the past all alone, he's still better off exhuming the rest of Limping Lady's bones from the pits in the yard—assuming they are even there to be found. The bones are as deep a mystery as anything else because they are not where they are supposed to be. At one point, there had been faith in the dig and the completion of a skeleton. But now—

I'm going out. Why? Because you're having my Queen murdered in the morning. Just a few hours from now. That's why. My best friend is here to take me out and get me drunk so I can forget. So I can make sense of it. No, that's not what I meant. To make sense of it all. Of everything. Of life and death. Of having the one thing I love ripped out of my grasp. A picture? No, I...I don't want to remember her like this...or myself...not like this...I don't want to remember...okay, okay, fine...just one...

His footsteps are muffled upon the rug. The front rows of pews sparkle and shine, Bibles and songbooks arranged on the seats, velvet kneelers all tucked in where they belong. A life-sized wooden statue stands off to the right of the pulpit, the woman's name carved onto the base. Her face is small and angular, with a sharp nose, high cheekbones, and narrow, almost Asian eyes. Instead of the sublime expression of ascendancy granted to religious effigies, her features are strained with creases of contemplation, the barely contained struggle of an internally tempestuous existence. Although her head is bare, without coif or veil, and her hair falls long and straight over her shoulders, the gown appears to be a basic nun's habit, flowing smoothly, neatly down to her feet. A long scapular is draped around her neck. It hangs flat and crosses over her chest, tucked in beneath a hemp belt, and it bears a design not at all in keeping with the norms of Catholicism. Tribal rather, more like a Native American garment. Unbelievable, the detail—a mere carving from wood sprung to life. And held out in front of her, her hands are clasped together in a gesture of prayer. No, they're not clasped...they're bound. A rosary wound tightly, completely around them—

What confession?

Nothing more than her form, her essence—a woman, a friend, a lover. But that's not all. There's risk, thrill, and denial as well. The last woman he had been intimate with. When? How? Perhaps there had been love? This stagnant memory has long since been tucked away, no time now to dig things up as guilt blooms and billows, watered by the shame of personal ignorance, spawning a powerful desire to flee, to escape into the bloodthirsty hands of the historic native horde, to chance a gauntlet of arrows and hatchets and war cries on the long-driven path back to a more graspable memory, to Ionia Josephina, Fairy's proffered asylum. Perhaps the coyotes had been judged all wrong. Perhaps The Disciples were not persecutors at all, but were, in fact, the persecuted. Perhaps they only sought the truth.

He dipped cupped hands into the holy water, lifted some to his lips, and slopped it over his chin and cheeks. It entered through his nose, ran down his neck and chest, soaking his T-shirt. It splashed to the floor as he scooped in more, gulping it down through a gluttonous smile, spluttering as he laughed at this mocking proof—it does not burn, it does not choke, it does not drown, nor does it bless. He is alive, and this is water. That's all. Of course it's sacred! Without it, we couldn't survive! None of us! All water is holy! In the shadows stood his sister, faceless and shouting at him, Stop it, asshole! Stop it! What are you doing? What's the point? While the pastor stood by, a father figure shaking his head in forced disapproval but holding back his laughter with an artificial scowl, twisted features making him look ridiculous. And then the crash of footsteps came thundering along outside the church, smashing upon the concrete walkway, his friend fallen behind once again, thoughts eternally split, murky with desire...

The hazy past tingles as living memories flow like blood. Unbalanced, something within him topples and begins to churn, a mixture of the blissful fulfillment of having drawn up these illuminating memories and the harrowing nausea of what lay there. It's not a thirst for water or for whisky—never was—but rather a thirst for ridicule. A deep-set longing to pile weight onto the bridge of faith and test it for stress. To openly offend the blindly faithful and to stab into the hearts of the closet faithless. One man alone in both roles—staring into a mirror, and neither one knowing which is the reflection, which one is real—feeling the intense pressure of the glass as it prepares to burst, battered as it is by these cold opposing stares. Distant cries waft in and the name of the deceased hangs in the air, a shroud of smoke trapped inside St. Josephine's, same as the townspeople of old, under attack, suffocating and starving themselves on their own fear and contempt and self-righteousness.

Look at the branches on these pines. They're like rungs on a giant ladder.
It's like a spiral staircase. Should we?
Up?
Why not?
How high?
All the way...

The Saint stares down at his approach, and behind her is Christ, hung by his flesh, waiting patiently through his pain, questioning the meaning of all this, the immense height, and what it might mean to fall.

Keep going.
Where's the top?
We'll only know if we keep going. Up.
That's what Icarus thought.
Who?
Icarus. His father was Daedalus. Didn't you read that book I gave you?
I looked at the pictures—nymphs and whatnot, right? Maybe there is no top. No end in sight. Just keep on climbing up and up, like Jack.
Jack?
You know, for all your books and smarts, you're kinda dumb sometimes.
We're getting pretty high. Shouldn't we stop?
Or maybe we oughta jump...

Suddenly, he notices movement near the pulpit. A body slowly unfolds from its bent position, stands upright, and then carefully turns to approach. Although he has never met the man before and only caught a brief glimpse of him that morning, he recognizes the figure as Father Marover.

"I am sorry for your loss...John, isn't it?"

"It's Johannes. And you don't have to worry about it."

The mountain stream roars nearby, bloated, gluttonous, and proud, a former brother-in-arms daring him to approach, daring him to test the farce...

"Why have you come?" Father Marover's soft eyes, surrounded by rings of dark, droopy flesh, search Johannes with equal parts confusion and pity. His gaunt face is dry and blotchy, his nose crooked. Wrinkles stretch long and deep around his mouth and eyes, and a scant beard covers the loose skin of his cheeks. "What I mean is, why aren't you out there? Enjoying the ceremony?"

"Enjoying?" scoffs Johannes. "It's a game. Pointless, meaningless. Nothing at all."

"I'll admit, it is a foolish business they've created of death, but were you not close to—"

"Death is a foolish business in itself," Johannes interrupts, but he finds it difficult to look at the priest's face for too long. His eyes drift toward the altar. "They would be hard-pressed to make it more so."

"You've resigned yourself to death," says the Father, nodding in approval. "Accepted the inevitable and placed yourself into the hands of God. That's good."

"Two out of three, Muskrat." Johannes glances at Father Marover but then averts his eyes again toward the statue of the Saint glaring down at him. Thomas was sometimes called Didymus—

Why do I have two names?

You don't have two names. You have only one, like everyone else...

"Mm-hmm...I see. Then, I shall leave you to your thoughts. Make yourself at home..."

The Father takes a step back, and Johannes looks down just in time to glimpse two distressed eyes before the priest turns to shuffle away—

But you don't use it. You don't say my name. Nobody says my name. Why do you, why does everybody call me by a different name? What do I have my name for if no one calls me that way?

Now, now, calm down, son. Don't worry. We've told you before—a name is just a name. It doesn't mean a thing, not really. Your name doesn't tell you who you are.

Then what does?

What does what?

What tells me who I am? How do I know who I am? Who I'm supposed to be...

"Father...wait. I'm sorry I said that. I don't know anything about you. I have no right to call you that." The spice of mockery still flavors his voice, unintentional and killing the taste. So he looks away, drawn again to the statue.

Father Marover stops and scrutinizes Johannes, then he turns to see what has arrested Johannes's attention. They both contemplate the Saint for a long time. Eventually, the Father steps forward again. He doesn't say anything but only looks at Johannes with a probing, sorrowful gaze.

The congregation half-heartedly followed their pastor through scriptural passages that should have been memorized. The monotonic sound of sinners and revelers who didn't care, who directed their faith only generally. Outwardly, they lived in their Sunday best for two hours a week, inwardly never. Surrounded by the towering adults of his life, he shrank away from those haunting chants. He was finally realizing that the words they spoke did not exemplify their supposed Christian sorrow and reverence, but rather their gross and drooling human boredom. They used God only when they needed Him, and while they sat through Sunday's sermon and droned savagely away, they reflected not upon God but on their mistresses and affairs, on their refrigerators full of beer and the afternoon's big game, on the neighbors, customers, regulations, and laws they cheated daily, on their own narcissistic images in the mirror...

"To tell the truth," says Johannes, "it's been a long time since I've been inside a church. And I'm not sure I like it too much."

"May I ask why?"

"There are things, about myself, that I'm discovering here. They're not...the kinds of memories I expected. Or maybe they are. I don't know which is worse."

The priest shifts his feet and clasps his hands behind his back.

Where else have you been?

Everywhere. I've been everywhere. And nowhere, really.

No, doesn't matter, I suppose.

No.

But...what have you done? Did you...you know? Did you...?

What?

See her?

See who?

Johannes nods at the statue. "Can you tell me about Saint Josephina?"

"You mean Josephine? Hers is a long, unfortunate story."

"I've heard some of it, but I'd like to hear it again. I'd like to know more. From the source, if possible."

"The source? Well, to keep it brief, she saved the people of Creek's Ridge and then died a recluse many years later, praying fervently and clutching her rosary, completely weak but for the strength in her hands. It is said that—post-mortem—they could not pry the rosary from her hands at all."

"How did she save the people exactly?"

"Well..." the Father blushes and glances at the statue. "Murder."

My confession...it's always been my deepest desire...the most severe longing...

for as long as I can remember...but he never would...the coward...hijo de puta... but being here...us two together...I can feel it resurfacing...and I want it...I want it now...not with him, but with you...

"Do you know of the raids?" asks the Father.

"Vaguely. From Amondale."

"Oscar? The historian?"

Johannes's laughter echoes throughout the chapel. "Is that what he told you? That he's a historian?"

"You know," the Father smiles, "people rarely laugh in here these days. But you are the third person to do so in recent memory. Oscar is one of the others. He is a fine man. He comes often."

"I know. To examine the church and its battle scars."

Marover turns again toward Johannes, searching his face. "We talk. He's kind."

I have always wanted...to fuck...inside a cathedral...

"So the Saint of Creek's Ridge was also a murderer?"

"Necessary evil, some would term it."

"What happened?"

"Our Josephine was at the heart of the raids. She was desired by many, and her eligibility, or the question of her hand in marriage, nearly brought the entire region to its knees. Tribes from near and far joined together to settle the dispute by first erasing Creek's Ridge and then carrying Josephine off, bound and helpless. The tribes overwhelmed the town. Many lives were lost. The survivors fortified themselves here, in these very walls, where they remained, helpless and starving. One morning, without a word to anyone, Josephine opened the barricade and went out to meet the Natives as they resumed their daily barrage. The townsfolk believed she had given in. That she was finally, bravely, going to offer herself to them, bringing an end to the attacks and saving their lives. And they watched, the townspeople did. They saw as she sought out her primary suitor, a Cherokee warrior chief who had once been highly favored by her Cherokee mother. As Josephine approached him, she withdrew a large blade, stabbed him in the heart, and then removed his scalp. All very gruesome. Very uncharacteristic of her. But the townsfolk, they witnessed it. All of them."

"And the Natives just let her get away with it?"

"Not a shred of resistance, as it is told. She was surrounded, but none of the Natives would touch her after that. Later, the townsfolk who witnessed it claimed that she was protected by an angelic aura. There were apparently few words shared; none, by some accounts. But the tribes got her message loud and clear, and they retreated for good. I've always believed she possessed a commanding, intimidating nature that the Natives would have recognized and honored. A sort of imposing, untouchable reverence for her boldness. Though, that is really just another word for fear. The townsfolk felt it, too. For as grateful as they were, not even they would touch her after she returned, unscathed but covered in blood. For the rest of her life, she would be honored and revered...but also feared."

"Misunderstood."

"Indeed, yes. Many of us are."

He wanted to shake from laughter and howl with delight, expecting a sarcastic, fanciful expression from her. But he turned to find her staring back at him in earnest, flushed red at the mere mention of fantasies come to life. Grasping one another tighter now, their hands pawed at each other's bodies as Christ's gaze fell upon them with his pain, his agony. A few old women were still watching them, stirring uncomfortably in the pews and grumbling in Spanish...

"That can't be right..." murmurs Johannes.

"I'm sorry?"

"No, I mean...I've heard parts of the story before, but never anything like that. Why would they leave that out?"

"Many have studied and conjectured on this town's past. Few have done so objectively."

"Maybe there's a lesson there. That such things cannot be understood objectively. Maybe they aren't supposed to be."

"You seem to have a deeply embedded mistrust. Like Josephine, as a matter of fact."

It had been a couple of hours since they woke up together on the floor, still wrapped around each other from the night before, and it didn't take long for the suggestion to take root. Her confession had been heard, and his blood pumped in response. Her desire became his, and he pulled her by the hand down a hallway off to the side of the pulpit...

"Doesn't the lack of worshipers around here bother you?"

Smiling in response, Father Marover lurches toward the first row of pews and lowers himself onto the bench. "I'm sorry, but I must sit. I get tired. It's this heat. I've never gotten used to the summers here. The heat and the dust, my only complaints." He struggles to force out a chuckle. "Would you care to sit?"

"No, thanks."

"There are plenty who come. They are loyal."

"I just meant..." Johannes trips over his words again, and now he has trouble taking his eyes off the small man. The Father has reclaimed mastery over his gaze and his house, and his stare is unwaveringly locked on Johannes. "I guess...it's just unsettling, this building and its history. Total isolation from the town and the people, its very purpose driven away from what it's supposed to be. I noticed the dust and the tools on the pews as I came in, so I assumed they aren't often used. And...I don't think I know of anyone who comes..."

In the morning, she knew. The look in her eyes, foggy with ignorance the night before, had now become sharp and clear, gazing back with wisdom upon a life lived and toward the approach of an imminent end. She knew where she was going and why. Not an ounce of fight left in this Queen. She knew. She had accepted what was to come. But that look in her eyes expressed something else, too. Fear. Dread. A silent plea for just one more chance...

"Ah, yes, but I can assure you that every one of them knows you. You've earned quite the reputation here in Creek's Ridge. And the dust, well, the dust is everywhere in this town. Can't escape it any more than you can escape your own shadow. Or your reflection in the mirror." Marover sighs, slowly turning his shoulders to scan the empty pews. "In a way, you are correct. The pews are never full. The seats in the back get little use. Recently, though, the construction has provided them a purpose. But there are faithful worshipers. They all sit close," he pats the bench for emphasis. "It's different where I come from. I do miss it."

"Where is that?"

"Far from here. Yourself?"

"Me too—"

They peeked inside open doors, the first a barren meeting room, the second a storage room, the third a broom closet. The priest's study included a small library, too personal to invade, but the next room down the hall was a strange, purposeless room. One wall had been converted into a glass display case containing various religious icons and artworks. Between the two tall, narrow windows stood a beautiful grandfather clock gilded in gold, its huge hanging weights, the regulated aphrodisiac sway of the pendulum, the musk of wood and incense. The only furniture was a low table and an elegantly worn red sofa, above which hung a vivid and gruesome depiction of the crucifixion. She tugged at his arm, and then he pushed her into the room and shut the door...

"You can't escape yourself," Johannes mutters.

"Pardon me?" says the Father.

"What you said a moment ago. It seems important, somehow, given the circumstances of all this. Today's ceremony and the town itself. What it all means."

"Don't you have any faith?" Marover asks, his eyes shifting from Johannes to the statue and finally resting upon the immense crucifix behind the altar.

"Not here. Not with God. I think I do have some, or at least I used to. Only, I've forgotten where it lies."

"You have an illusive way of speaking," the Father muses. "Reminds me of our slippery friend out there, Pastor Judson."

"We have a history."

"So I have heard."

The other forfeited the race—eternally distracted, eternally on edge—when he stopped to flirt with the pretty new neighbor girl. She just moved in down the block, so invite her along, welcome her to town, get her drunk, feel her up. The entrance opened and slammed shut, footsteps stomping, crashing upon the floorboards of the aisle. Here he is! announced the pastor. The prodigal son shows up! The dilly-dallying straggler arrives! The diddling-twiddling ladies' man comes to lend a hand! They laughed, the boys, but not so for sister, enraged again, now cursing out the other, Stop it, asshole! Stop it! What were you doing? What was the point? Don't worry, the other answered, she wouldn't come anyway, she wouldn't come ha ha ha ha ha...

"He taught me my catechism. Confirmed me into the Church and then raised me to shun it."

"Did he?" the Father says softly. "A deep and troubled history, then. That I did not know. In that case, perhaps you can explain something to me. I know that I am getting older and somewhat naive to the ways of the modern world, but can you help me understand why the pastor insisted so adamantly on performing today's ceremony outdoors? And without the involvement of myself or the Church?"

Johannes begins pacing between Father Marover and the steps of the pulpit. A strange sensation, this, as he looks out over the empty pews, he, the preacher—

Okay, okay, enough twaddling about Tweedle Dum and Tweedle Dee, lovers' spats are for married regrets, teenage lust a-whole-nother fuss. The pastor laughed and joked as he directed them through the day's work, a day's labor rearranging and cleaning the chapel, the foyer, the unused back rooms, cobwebs and dust, scrub out the stains, the footprints, the waste. Labor comes at a price, nothing free, this life, he'd taught them that—and all this because they had discovered where the pastor, their father figure, kept his stash, a bottle here, a bottle there. A bargain, a blackmail, a house party at the Lord's house. Of course, the pastor would let them have at it. It was easier than cash. He'd keep those thirty pieces of silver for himself. After all, what are father figures for? But only here, in the safety of the church, supervise them even, join them perhaps, just a taste, but don't take it outside, beyond the doors, and don't overdo it. As long as they don't tell anyone else...but everyone knows about it anyhow, so, sure, why not, drink it, straight up, from the chalice if you want...

"Pa Sonny disentangled himself from his vows," says Johannes, "only to replace them with contradictions. He refuses to enter a church or take part in holy rites. And he's been uncharacteristically affected by this tragedy. Maybe it reminds him that his own death approaches, and maybe, like a poison, that has brought on a form of regret. Pa Sonny has been saved more than once, but not by his own hands. He has constructed a facade of strength, but even that was not by his own devising. He is a troubled and lazy man. The opposition of faithful devotion and human emotion has torn him to pieces. The time has come for his repentance, and I think this is the only way he knows how."

The Father's eyebrows form high arches below his wrinkled brow. "You say he will not step inside a church?"

"Not into any recognized place of worship."

"Interesting…"

"Why?"

"Because sometimes I find him here in the mornings…sleeping in the pews. One time—only once, thankfully—he lay sprawled upon the altar table itself." The Father shudders at the memory.

"Was he drunk?"

"Perhaps. He never explains himself. Just gets up, looks around, and then leaves. He has great contempt for me. And as far as our deceased friend is concerned, wasn't it Pastor Judson's argument that his one dying wish was to not be remembered inside of a church? Wasn't that his rationale for all this…this…this lunacy?"

"Yes, that's right. It's not true, of course."

"Oh, I know it's not true. The sheriff was one of our most devout. He never missed a Sunday service. As a matter of fact," Father Marover scans from side-to-side along the front row of pews and then pats the seat beside him once more, "this is right where he always sat. Right here, right up front."

Johannes stares, stunned, speechless, his eyes linked with the spot on the pew, bound, inseparable. And yet, the urge to flee is as strong as it's been since he entered the church. He can feel their eyes burning through him, all of them, Marover, Josephine, Christ, each of them tearing the layers away to expose the truth—

Holding hands…that's what I heard, is all. And grapevines make wine. I didn't believe it. Couldn't. No, I won't. Not a chance in hell… Because if you… But no, why would you? Not you, you couldn't, you can't…

No, yeah, no, I…that's not…you know…city life is not for me…or the beach, either, the sea…terrifying, in its way…I prefer the wilderness anyhow…mountains and forests, the stars…always have…so I decided, yes, to leave…got the hell out of there…wandered a bit…and then came here to find you…

Yeah, I know. You always did like the woods, the shelter of the trees, and the

shadows. I've been thinking I might go someplace myself. Leave for good, maybe even back there, give it another shot, with her...
    Are you sure that's a good idea? You seem to be doing well here in...where are we, again?
    I told you, on the border...but you did, didn't you? You saw her?
    I did...yes...
    Well, so...I mean...how was she?
    She was...yes, she was doing alright, you know, not bad, I suppose...
    And?
    What?
    Did you...?
    "You didn't know that, did you? About your friend?"
    Johannes shakes his head. "No...I didn't..."
    "He spoke with me about you on numerous occasions, you know. He did like to have his secrets. Are you sure you wouldn't like to sit?"
    The Father's warm, inviting smile reminds Johannes of a younger, thinner, happier Pa Sonny. It's as though that youthful Pa Sonny has risen into the present to speak with him, to spell everything out.
    Repetition, these thoughts had burgeoned forth before. He had acted on the impulse countless times before, turned and fled, to seek a fresh start, a new avenue, a more complete outlook. This time, the desire had been born from another place, an influence more palpable and shameful, a city on the sea, a friend of years past, a rest from the rote monotony of solitary wandering, sharing what you have, what you want, what you love, together for once, bound body-to-body, an embrace worth the wait, with someone who knows who you are, your true name. But nothing truly lasts, names least of all, though the briefest caress leaves a mark deep as caverns stretch, and a scar lasting as long, visible to others, for time everlasting, evidence on display in the anteroom, first thing anyone notices, hard to miss, the decorations of deceit, a choice made is a choice made, no turning back, only looking back for as long as it lasts, and when such a choice poses such pain unto another, no forgiveness to be had...
    "I think I understand," says Johannes. "Pa Sonny doesn't have a problem with entering the church. He has a problem with his ability to cope. He knew. From the moment we received the news, he knew that he would act a drunken fool. He knew that he would make a mockery of this place, of the people's faith. He knew that this whole ordeal was inseparable from his heart and that he wouldn't be able to keep his mouth shut. Today's ceremony is...I think he's acting out of respect for his past life, for you, Father, and for the Christian ideals that still swirl within him, still dictate his behavior, more or less. But he's too proud to admit it, so he used a week's worth of booze to stir a giant bullshit cocktail just to convince everybody to go along with him. He has contempt

for most things, Father, but most of all for himself. Try not to let him get under your skin, too."

"That's not easy," the Father laughs hesitantly. "I live my life for the sake of others. The people of this town first and foremost."

"Think of it as a kind of joke, then. It fits the context."

"The context of what? Morbid self-interest?"

"The context of this town. Of this modern world which you so naively misunderstand. It's a carnival. Everything is."

"Word travels in a place like this. I know of your mountain and your holes. I know of your troubles. Will you tell me that you understand this world we inhabit any better than I do?"

Jesus Christ, the weather here. It's so hot, so humid. How do you stand it year round?

My blood. My heritage. I'm made for this. Sticky and sultry. I love it.

You're crazy. I can't breathe. Let's get away from the beach. Let's go somewhere cool for a minute. Or a day. This is hell for me. I need a temperate breeze, a mountain peak.

I know a place. There's this cathedral. It's so beautiful, and it's always cold inside churches. I want to show you.

Sounds great. Lead the way.

Oh my god. Look. There. Isn't that...? Over there. It's his parents...

What? What are they doing here? Do they see us?

What does it look like? They smiled. They're waving. They're coming this way. What the hell are you doing? Take my hand, you asshole.

They'll see us.

They already have. What does it matter? We're adults. We can hold hands. And we can fuck whoever we want to fuck. He always did. So can I, so can you. His parents don't care. They love you like another son. Take it. Take it. Hold my hand. What are you afraid of? You spineless shit. Hijo de puta. You coward, you're just like him...

"No," admits Johannes. "For a long time, I think, I believed that there is no world other than the internal. Each of us, the world we know, the world we see and traverse, it springs from our own understanding of ourselves. A mental, spiritual existence that has nothing to do with God but rather creates an expression of God within ourselves, implementing the framework and structure best suited to allow us to thrive. No different from tilling the soil, caring for and accumulating the sustenance required for physical survival. A spiritual exercise that requires work, dedication, patience, humility, and perseverance in the face of defeat. But once we discover the truth—the meaning and value at the core, the seed from which we spring—then our path should become clear, illuminated not from without, but from within."

"Might that be what you call your faith?"

"Possibly. But something about Creek's Ridge seems to be tempering that view, putting forth objections. I'll have to write a treatise to see if it holds water. Make changes, additions, redactions. I have a feeling that there may not be anything left by the end. Just an empty page."

"Please do," smiles the Father. "If your empty page is any good, I might just inter it into our library here. Deep in the darkest recesses where no one will ever stumble across it..."

Johannes laughs, marveling at how he has been playfully entrapped by a conversation he'd been so reluctant to enter. "It's true then," he says, "the library? And the town records? Emil Wood's journals?"

"Emil Wood... I'm surprised you know that name," Marover chuckles, squinting at Johannes like he is a puzzle to be solved. "There are few who do anymore. Of course, you mean Emedio del Bosque—of the forest. He was an orphan, discovered as a toddler in a forest outside Madrid. He led a difficult life in America, but on the advice of an infamous Native American prophet, he later founded a haven for lost and wandering souls, people without a home, people seeking collectiveness and togetherness. Help. Love."

"The Community of Man..."

The Father nods. "Which later became the frontier town of Creek's Ridge. Life was still hard. He struggled with his faith for most of his life. After his Cherokee wife left, he was—"

"Left?"

"He...lost her. After which, he was himself lost. And the Cherokees blamed him, naturally. Most of the townsfolk as well. But his daughter," Father Marover smiles and nods toward the statue. "She grew into a beautiful young woman. Sought after by many. Americans, Spaniards, and Native Americans alike. She was also strong and purposeful. She didn't need her father's protection, but he forced it upon her. It is assumed that, in trying to take care of his wife and daughter, Emedio del Bosque himself caused the raids. Emil Wood was an adopted name meant to help him integrate more easily in the early days. It's understood that he abandoned that name once they settled here, though some say it was not until after he lost his wife. I have found evidence that he continued to use both names for different purposes. Cross purposes, perhaps. Eternally indecisive, unable to commit. And it also reinforced a quality he picked up as an orphan and was compelled to develop throughout his life. Some things never leave us, no matter what."

"What quality was that?"

"Slipperiness, cunning, deceit. The ability to twist his identity at will, fitting circumstances as they arose."

My name is Lani Vals, from Copenhagen. I am here on business.

Okay, fine, Ms. Lani Vals of Copenhagen. Come over here. I've got an important business matter to show you.

And who am I doing business with?

What?

I only conduct business with people I can trust.

It's me. John Metternich.

No, you idiot. You have to make a false identity.

Why?

Because that's the game. We're supposed to act like other people. Pretend to be someone we're not.

But what's wrong with my name?

You can't just use your own name. It doesn't work.

Well...how about my real name? No one uses it anyway.

Johannes? Alright, that works for me. So, Mr. Johannes, what sort of business do you have for me today?

"You make it sound like he's the bad guy in all this."

Marover searches Johannes's face carefully, then shrugs. "It's a trait that has certain uses. They're not all wicked, but there is a fine line. I believe he always tried to remain on the right side of that line. Sometimes it just takes a single misstep...but his intentions were honest."

"What makes you so sure?"

"Just my own casual research," Father Marover sighs. "Yes, the library does exist—real as anything. It's not meant to be a secret, although few show an interest anymore. You are free to explore our collection any time you like. Although, I do not allow the items to leave the premises, especially Del Bosque's journals. Their condition is fragile, to say the least."

"What do you know of his suicide attempts?"

"Who?" Father Marover looks at Johannes, startled.

"Wood. Emedio del Bosque."

"I thought you meant... No, why? Why would you say that? He died of malnutrition in the winter of 1875. After his mind began to come undone, he had trouble taking care of himself. Basic needs, washing, feeding himself. Physically, he could manage, but mentally, you see, he was distracted. Josephine did everything for him during the worst years. He lived pleasantly long. Long enough. His final years were difficult. He never attempted suicide. But he did attempt to run away. Several times."

"From what?"

"Not from what, but to where. I suppose he wished to return to where he came from. Spain? Florida? The Smoky Mountains?" Marover shrugs. "The sea?"

"Why didn't he?"

"He couldn't. Or they wouldn't allow him. For his own safety, you understand, his—"

"I know, his mind. But if that's what he truly wanted, why stop him?"

"They needed him just as much as he needed them. His daughter especially, she needed him."

"How could he die of malnutrition if Josephine was feeding him?"

"She tried her best. I assume he was despondent, not always cooperative…"

"Or purposefully starving himself?"

"You're a persistent one, aren't you? Since you brought it up, I am reminded of one letter… It's in the library, though it's kept separate from the main stacks. If I recall correctly, it is part of a correspondence between two residents from those times. It seems to indicate that the writer, a young woman who sometimes helped Josephine, had witnessed or overheard Josephine caring for her father and that it was anything but standard caretaking. It's a short passage, lacking detail, but it alludes to mood swings."

"From Del Bosque?"

"No, from Josephine. At different times, she might enter his room with the airs of a small child seeking protection from her father, as a nun fearful of being in the presence of any man, or as a mistreated woman exacting her revenge."

"So it was Josephine's mind that went?"

"She led a difficult life herself. Different from her father's, but no less tragic. Her mind was…fractured, to be sure…"

That woman, she's a whore. We're leaving.

What's a whore? I don't wanna go.

Don't argue. Put down the book. Grab your coat. Let's go. Now! This minute!

I wanna stay. I wanna see Pa do the thing with the water and the name.

She's unmarried, and bringing a fatherless child here, of all places. Not even a proper member of the church. The nerve. She's a parasite. And a slut. This is sacrilege.

I'm not going.

Get your ass outside.

Pa, Pa! Tell them to let me stay! I wanna stay!

Don't you dare, don't you dare, he is not your father. Don't start with that, not today.

They are your parents. You must obey. Go on now, go. Go on ahead.

No, I won't. I'll stay. I'll sit here, with my friend. I'll stay till the end, with them. I wanna see the thing with the water, and the baby, and the name...and then I'm gonna run away...

"Then what proof is there that Del Bosque went insane?"

"Insane? That is a loaded word. He became lame and incompetent, not crazy. He withdrew, much as Josephine would later in her life. People still came to see him. Old friends would come to spend time with him, to help out in any way they could. But these visits often passed in silence, at times unacknowledged. Del Bosque could still speak, but it seems he chose not to. And on the occasions that he did, he rambled. It wasn't raving but rather a calm, steady stream of words that could go on for hours and hours. Peaceful, soothing tones, but utterly senseless. No logic that anyone could follow, seemingly no grasp on reality as it was. That's how the town acquired its name. Up through the late 1860s, it was still officially called The Community of Man. As the residents grew more concerned, they would quip over the state of their so-called governor, a title he continued to hold, though Josephine had long since taken over the administrative end of things. Someone once likened his manner of speaking to a small creek flowing slow and steady, but insensibly. As though it were flowing uphill or feeding into the wrong reservoir. And another pointed out that he was clearly on a ledge, madness only a step away. A creek on the ridge of madness. A single stone dislodged, and it all spills over the edge. As the analogy became more common, folks naturally abbreviated it. And voilà."

"Is there any chance that he was completely sound of mind?"

"The way he spoke, that constant babble of nonsense, is also precisely what his journals turned into. Pages upon pages of words without break, forming neither coherent ideas nor recognizable patterns. All sorts of people have examined them over the years. Psychologists and shamans. Medicine men, lawyers, and codebreakers. Mystics and fortune tellers, representatives from the Vatican, and from Madrid. Hippies, revolutionaries. Even film producers. No one has come away with any other opinion or idea of what to make of it."

"And you?"

"Me..." Marover looks away, sweeping his eyes around the nave. "I disagree."

"On what basis?"

"No basis. Simply time. I've gone through the available documents thoroughly, more so than most. I am blessed with plenty of free time here in Creek's Ridge. And I have developed a deep interest in the story of this place, of those people. As have you, it appears. I have found something that is difficult to put into words. Perhaps it is personal, subjective. I don't think it can be explained. Either you see it, or you don't. But it takes time and patience. And, as I said, you're free to comb through our documents any time you like. As long as you're careful."

"Isn't it possible that he simply grew tired of this life? The suffering and the unfairness. The guilt. The fear."

"Many people become tired. There is unfairness everywhere. Suffering is inescapable. But guilt..."

"For those who can't bear it, the most welcoming path, sometimes, is to simply end it."

"A mortal sin, which Del Bosque would have shunned at the mention of."

"It could be another explanation for his supposed madness, couldn't it? Repeated attempts at your own life would not sit well with those around you, those who care for you. Cause embarrassment even. One of the unmentionable acts. What better way to get rid of it? Hide it behind a romantic, idealized condition that will explain away every last little quirk and fascinate people just enough to stop them from seeing the disappointing truth."

"You speak like...like Pastor Judson."

"Because it's his theory."

"I might have assumed as much. That's his rational explanation, is it? That Del Bosque was of sound mind because he repeatedly attempted to end his own life? Even if it were so, is that a behavior you would ascribe to a sane mind?"

"I..."

Redeem yourself...grab my hand...hold me...take me...

"I encourage you to read the diaries. I would also suggest—and please don't take offense to this—that your friend out there, the good pastor, may himself struggle with the maintenance of a sound mind."

"Me too."

"So we can agree on one thing at least."

Johannes nods, smiles, and looks away. They sit in silence for a few moments.

What's this?

They're records.

I can see that. What are they doing here? Take them with you.

I can't. I won't be able...to play them. Not where I'm going.

Where are you going?

The mountains.

What? Like, off the grid? So you just leave all your unwanted junk with me now, is that it?

It's not unwanted junk. They're my favorite pieces of music. They're valuable to me.

Then just take them with you.

I can't. I'm leaving them to you.

Leaving me with classical music? It's like you don't even know me. What am I supposed to do with them? I don't even have a record player.

Just...I don't know...I don't have a choice...

Are you asking me to hang onto them for you? Keep them safe? That it? Show them the respect of a true friendship? Really?

I...yeah...no, no. Just do whatever you want with them, but I can't take them.

Thanks a lot. You could at least leave me with something good...

"Maybe you can help me with something," says Johannes.

"That's what I'm here for. Anything you want, faithful or not."

The two men smile awkwardly at one another. Johannes finally sits down beside the Father, and they both gaze up toward the pulpit.

"Sonny recited some words this morning, after you'd already come and gone. They struck me as important. Resonating, humbling, and meaningful in a personal way. As though I had once set them on a pedestal. Honored them, lived by them. I would like to revisit the book, but I don't know the source. And I'd rather not ask Sonny. Not today, not in his current state. Do you mind?"

Father Marover nods approval.

At once, Johannes is overcome with doubt that he will be able to recall the passage. But, when he shuts his eyes, the words return to him. "'May thou see Me coming, I am Time. Bearer of doom and death, harbinger of beginnings and ends. None shall remain, strike, I say. Strike...'" Johannes pauses and opens his eyes as if searching for something. He gazes at the floor, the pulpit, the Saint, and the darkness of the rafters up above. "There's more, I think. He didn't finish it. And I don't know the rest."

"They're very...stirring," says the Father. "They are not of the Christian canon, I promise you that. I'm afraid I do not know where they originate from. If anything comes to mind, I'll come and find you."

"Other than this morning, I don't think I've ever seen you around town. You don't get out much, do you?"

"It is rare, yes. I have my occupations here, my obsessions, my guilty pleasures. Not unlike you, I'm led to understand. There's very little else I require from this life. I have seen you from a distance almost every day since you arrived. The glade across the way? Along the creek? I've often wondered what you've found over there. And on occasion, I've seen, or at least heard you, at The Borderlands. I adore Ruthie's food. But I always sit at the booth in back, if I can help it. Away from the gossip."

"Why is it only the interior of the building that's being renovated?"

"You have rather odd concerns for a day like today." Father Marover wrenches his gaze away from Johannes, almost like he doesn't trust him. "There is a young woman who moved here some months ago. She's only somewhat active in the life of the church, but she's very faithful. And very selfless. I've been helping her come to terms with her past, so she wanted to help us in return. She made a large donation and is personally overseeing the renovations. It was all her idea and charity, of course, but the congregation and I are infinitely grateful. And she prefers the outside of the building the way it is. Charm and history—those are the words she uses. I believe her future aim is to add structural support to the exterior, ensuring preservation and a long life. Ms. Pridieux. I believe you know her?"

"Caryn? Not as well as I thought I did. And that marble slab in the vestibule? Those carvings on it? She's responsible for that, too?"

"She commissioned it, yes. A wonderful addition."

"I've seen carvings like that...around town."

"Of course. All done by the same local artisan who carved our blessed Saint there, another wonderful—"

Father Marover twists around to stare at the entryway. The hum of humanity enters the nave, swells, and recedes. The ceremony approaches, crossing the borders that separate and fortify the church. And Johannes hears other voices as well, even more distant but just as distinct—

John. Hey, John. Why'd you stop?
This is it.
It's what?
The top.
The top? We made it? I didn't think...
You're not going to believe this.
What?
This tree, it's bigger than we thought. We're so high.
What can you see?
Everything. I can see everything...
What's it like?
It's...terrifying...

"Gracious Lord...don't let him do this...I beg you..." Father Marover buries his head in his hands. "I knew it would come to this." Unease and panic distort the sadness in the Father's eyes, as though he has just witnessed the incomprehensible reality of God, shuddering in the afterglow and unfit to cope with the truth of the ceremony's slow but impending approach.

How is a place like that supposed to raise veneration? Or the sense of something higher, mightier than man?

What do you mean? It was perfect, perfectly—

I mean, it was nothing but an eyesore. A bothersome obstruction along the roadside. A small pile of organized rubble. It was pleasing to neither the eyes nor the nose. There was nothing sacred about the place, nothing at all.

A place, a building, has no bearing upon matters of the spirit. You know that...

Please. I've stood below structures, trees even, that elicit more awe-inspiring devotion at a glance than your church inspired in a generation. I have known permanent change and felt its surge within me, sparked by the radiance of such places.

It's all there, inside you, and shared with the people surrounding you...

I'm glad you left that behind. That place, that life. You were the only good thing about that shithole.

You've got it wrong. Personal sanctuary can be anywhere, anyplace...

Even so, there was nothing for the spirit there, in your church. A single stone from the ruins of Borobudur enamored my soul more than a thousand years inside your—Ouch!

You little shit. For all your aimless travels, you haven't picked up a fucking thing about the world, have you? Or about yourself...

"Come on now, Father. Buck up, for God's sake." Johannes shoots off the bench and faces the entrance. "That's your flock out there, bemoaning the lives they have yet to lead. A wave of life about to crash on your doorstep. They made their choice. Today, the ceremony, this is their fault. They allowed Pa Sonny to wrangle and subvert all that you hold dear. Now, make them swallow it. If you want to hold on to them, you need to fight for them. Tough love, Father. They'll appreciate it someday. And so will Sonny. They'll respect you. Go out there and tell them all to get out of here, to go home. Let it be done with. Tell Pa Sonny to fuck right off."

"You talk like him at times, do you know that? Like the sheriff. But you don't understand—I can't. It's impossible. I can't turn them away, not even Pastor Judson. It goes against everything I am, everything I hold dear, against the very principles of the Church and this town. My house is a sanctuary, for all...it is...it must be...as it always has been..."

By sudden inspiration, Johannes thinks about the bones. He sees them, needs them. He wonders whether it's merely a matter of digging deeper to unearth the rest of them, all those bones still unaccounted for. He senses a subtle tug at his loins, a weight pulling him down, the weight of anguish and distress, of fear that if he does dig deeper, he might find himself buried too deep. But if he doesn't—

The injection goes in. Still, her eyes do not close. She must feel a swift pain, as he feels now. The liquor inside him was meant to cope, but instead, it only brings him down to her level. This is it. It's happening. A final shared glance, sharing pain in life and now in...

"Johannes, I can't, I can't, but could you...? Don't let him inside. Please. Not today. Not again." Marover speaks in a soft, hoarse voice, a failed attempt at concealing his weakness, his fear. "Please. I didn't want to tell you this...but Pastor Judson, he...he came by early this morning, before dawn. He sought me out and whispered something to me—I can't even bring myself to repeat it—but he will tarnish this sacred ground. This was his intention all along. I understand that now. He will drive me away from all that I have left. I can't...I can never go back...don't let him in. I know we are not friends, and that you are more of his kind than mine, but please do this. I cannot keep him away on my own. You may not care for Saint Josephine or the church, but do it for a fellow castaway in this forgotten town. I'm asking you—"

Look at him, curled over himself, gasping for what it's worth. There's still a bit of fight left in these old fists. You're lucky I didn't break your goddamn nose, you little shit. But do you two know? Do you want to know what I did? A secret between me and the Big Man, whoever that is. It was a few years ago. I was out to the pub, disguised and juiced-up more than usual, but feeling good. Feeling like myself, for once. I stumbled back to the church, our church...are you listening, you wheezing sack of crap? Our beatific, blessed place of worship. As I walked through the doors, I tripped over someone's foot, flat onto my face. I looked up to see a devil laughing down at me, asking me what kind of priest am I? What sort of priest can't even hold his liquor? Can't even protect his holy house from miscreants and ghouls? Then he offered me a piece of advice. Told me all I had to do was take a piss. Mark my territory. Cover the doors and the entryway and the plants and the rugs and all the vestibule in my stinking holy piss, and that would do the trick. It would keep out all them devils, just like him, keep 'em out for good. Simple as that. So I dropped trousers and let 'er rip. A bladder full of rye whiskey, emptied right there, covered the vestibule, dripping and fuming. And you know what? I never cleaned it up. And I never saw that devil again, never...until just now. Maybe next time, you'll show me some respect and keep your damn mouth shut...

"Two things, Father," says Johannes. "First, tell me two things. No riddles, no mysteries."

Father Marover looks up at him, worry contorting his face.

"What is your guilty pleasure?"

"The Borderlands," the Father sighs. "Ruthie's carrot cake. It's bad for my heart, but each slice is a step in the door to heaven. Whenever the craving arises, I inconspicuously work it into the prayers at Mass. She has never let me down."

"That's it?"

"Just that and the study of this town. I'm a simple man."

"Did Saint Josephina leave journals as well?"

"Josephine?" The Father hesitates, glancing nervously at the entrance. "She did. But they're locked away. We don't show them to anyone."

"Why not?"

"They are not...the conventional words of a sainted personage..."

"But does she address the questions? Settle up the story?"

"The questions? Nothing in life is ever really settled until one meets—"

"Father..."

"She ruminates. On everything. That's what became of her. More sensible than her father's final writings, but difficult to read."

"Rambling?"

"Honest."

"If I help you, then I want you to show me. I want to read them. Full access."

Pa Sonny's voice separates from the cloud of noise, a roar above the rest.

"Okay?"

"Yes, alright," says Father Marover. "But only you...no one else..."

"Don't worry." Johannes pats the Father on his shoulder and promptly retreats down the aisle. "I won't let him in. I do care for Saint Josephina."

"It's Josephine..." Marover calls after him.

What? What happened?

He bit me! Stop laughing! Stop it! Help me! Get him away from me...

Don't worry. It's nothing. The blood, wow, it's so red...

Why did he bite me?

You were...you were bothering him. I saw it. I told you not to.

I didn't do anything. We were just playing...and then...

I told you to leave him alone. I told you so...

It hurts...

I know. He bit me, too, once.

I'm going to...

You're going to what? He'll eat you up. It was your fault, after all. Go on...

Go on what?

Go on and apologize to my dog, or else.

Or else what?

Or else you're not my friend, not anymore...

As Johannes enters the vestibule, he catches sight of his own faint reflection in the holy water. He continues past it, but the echo of his footsteps on the marble tiles and the lingering, rippling reflection of his own countenance remind him of everything he has discovered about himself during this brief escape. His throat is dry. He can already taste the dust outside. The thirst has returned in a different form, incontestable now, the demands of his body after dredging his soul dry, a parched throat preparing for more. So before he pushes open the door, he stops and steps back, unable to resist.

He cups his hands, dips them in, and brings the holy water to his mouth. Droplets fall from his chin and hands, disturbing the placid pool. As the water settles and he heaves for air, his image in the water takes shape again. As it gains clarity, he sees himself, but there's someone else as well—

She pulled him over to the sofa, their mouths tasting each other, their hands prowling aggressively, his hands lifting her top as his tongue sought her midriff, her bellybutton, tracing the outlines of the tattoos that wound sensually round her flank, she squirming and squealing in delight as his saliva drew goosebumps over her ribcage, licking along her spine and the dewy leaves fanned across her back, down to her ass, kneading her tits from behind and shoving one-two fingers into her mouth, her tongue swirling on overdrive, the black orb of the bird's eye watching on, concealed amongst vibrant greens and tropical flower petals. They made quick business of it, each of them staring at the graphic violence of the crucifixion as they failed to stifle their moans, she coming explosively at the fulfillment of fantasy and he feeding off her excitement as well as his own debasement of ideas that he found weak, simplistic, lazy, threatening. And without a doubt, with one-hundred percent faith, he knew that the old ladies in the pews had heard their short religious tryst, the glares they received on their way out, a curse...

He gasps, spinning quickly around and searching, but only to find himself, alone. No one hangs over his shoulder, nobody is in the narrow vestibule with him, nothing but the silence of the church being increasingly violated by voices intruding from beyond the doors. When he looks down again, the other reflection is still there, staring up from the holy water, gradually acquiring light, color, and depth as the ripples diminish, the surface steadies, flattens out, and now two distinct faces stare back at him, her face clear and tangible as the water itself, as his own—

Loyalty before the temporary. History before the present day. Yourself before others, unless the other is your brother, your sister. Now before never. The idea has been with him for years, fed to him as seedlings, hints and visions, notions and allusions, a father's wisdom, to free yourself and leave others to do as they will. To search within until you can bear it no longer. But the decision hits him now as a lightning bolt, an earthquake tremor, the eureka moment of a scientific breakthrough sending him back into a prehistoric age. Life would be pure, simple, and honest, as it was meant to be. Never again would he have to look his betrayal in the face but only avert his gaze over hills and trees and mountaintops forever, allowing the forest to swallow the superficial artifice of emotion, like temples of idol worship buried beneath centuries of overgrowth, the blood of sacrifice having seeped into the dirt and provided nutrients, giving the flora to persist, to thrive, to climb and cover, growing into the very foundations and incorporating this lost relic of history into the folds of the eternal. This is the last time. The last time he'll say goodbye. The last time he'll look behind...

Chapter 48

The Open Door

Nothing.

It had never been a message for Penagashea. No, it was a fundamental truth. A truth that had not appeared out of thin air but had always been the case.

Lalawethika—as the tribe knew him, as the Great Spirit knew him, as he knew himself—could not continue to exist. This was no time for foolish games, body paint, new moons, sleight of hand, or tricks of the light. He had to invite Death up to his soul's doorstep, swing that door wide open, and place his mortality at the mercy of Death's claws. With supreme firmness of spirit, he would need to offer the greatest sacrifice to prove his worth. To remain on this earth as he was, derided at every turn for his insufficiencies, cowed under the white man's thumb, incapable of redirecting the flow of the puniest stream, this was futile. He had to resign this life and then return, unrecognizable.

Unflinchingly, as only a true zealot could, he reminded the visitor whose home they were in. Even as he tore down the walls of his fortress and threw down his weapons, his prayers rang out as battle cries. He was a field mouse willfully entering the snake's gaping maw, its fangs already dripping venom in anticipation. After weeks of clipping his tongue, of funneling his thoughts toward this one action, and of living under the perpetual sway of a fear more potent than any he had ever known, Lalawethika faced his visitor. And he was afraid, but he did not withdraw. He prostrated himself before its wrath.

Who are you?

"I am Nothing."

Finally, after the visitor had spoken its piece and Lalawethika had spoken his, they embraced with the sensuality of lovers. Bound in ecstasy, they tumbled into the fire. And although Lalawethika's mortal body lay scorching in the flames, he had already been lifted free of earthly concerns, sent on to traverse mysterious fields far from this world. Nenimkee the Thunderfowl, clutching him in its huge talons, carried him above the firmamental hinterlands, those far-reaching destinations of the beyond not meant to be breached by the living. They soared at nauseating speeds and precarious heights, but gone were all traces of fear and doubt, humiliation and shame. His soul was woven with threads of joy, and his one all-consuming thought was a prayer of gratitude and faith that this noble-winged creature would conduct him as near as possible to the Great Spirit without dropping him into an irretrievable hereafter. With full vision restored and clarity previously unknown, he witnessed the tremendous vistas where all the potentials of life are produced, nurtured, and prepared for their earthly trials. The landscapes of that place were formed much as those of our world but elementally perfect, devoid of the slightest flaw. Even those places where decay and degeneration were reared contained an innate grandeur. Nenimkee the Thunderfowl swooped down into the canyons where languages are kept, the rocky walls of which were not eroded by wind and water but carved and polished with the art of master craftsmen. Each canyon was the permanent keeper of a language, with elders perched upon stony outcrops and speaking continuously in booming voices that echoed off the canyon walls, keeping their respective languages alive. One canyon for each of the Algonquin dialects— Shawnee, Kickapoo, Fox, Sauk—more still for languages he recognized as Iroquois, Cherokee, Menominee, Delaware, Creek, and a thousand other unfamiliar tongues. The canyons of the white man's languages housed no elders but rather reptiles that clung to the cliffs or slithered along the mud and filth of the canyon bottoms, hissing those foul tongues. Nenimkee flapped its enormous wings and a deafening thunderclap rang out. They were lifted out of the canyons, rising high into a sky that evoked all possible colors at once. Ripples of motion tore through the sky in every direction, mixing and blending the colors in what appeared to be an elaborate form of communication, and Lalawethika knew it was The Four Winds remembering, jesting, defying, and creating. When they glided down again, the canyons had transitioned into mountains, their ice-capped peaks standing tall enough to brush against Nenimkee's wings and sharp enough to impale Lalawethika should he be released from the thunderfowl's talons. There was no sun in the sky, only the glowing colors and pure light of The

Four Winds, but the mountain snows melted all the same, and those pure waters cascaded down the mountainsides, spilling over cliffs to which there were no bottoms, only a drop that took the water down, down, down, far below to the ocean where the Great Serpent reigned. Lalawethika prayed that Nenimkee would not deliver him to that evil region, and Nenimkee immediately screeched in response, the decisive, carefully inflected call of a bird of prey. But Nenimkee's meaning was clear—

"We must. It is not only my duty but a duty we all share. All of the Great Spirit's creatures must do battle with the Great Serpent."

At once, Nenimkee angled into a dive beside the falling waters, and they sped downward for what surely would have been several lifetimes, except there was no time in that place. Before they even reached the surface of the great decrepit sea below, the Great Serpent hove into view, swimming not in the sea but in the rancid, sulfurous fumes above the surface. The beast saw them coming. It snarled and barked and hissed in agitation, twisting its head with its enormous antlers, each with thirteen points as sharp as arrowheads, and thrashing its tail adorned by the colorful feathers of all the holy men and chiefs it had corrupted over the centuries. It evaded Nenimkee's attack and plunged into the sea, disappearing into the muddy, bubbling depths. They glided just above the surface and Lalawethika saw that the sea was polluted with the souls of the wicked, the maimed and gruesome body parts of all the Great Serpent's victims, as well as infants and young virgins, sacrifices to the Serpent's wiles. Upon the shoreline, slaves fished out severed body parts and used them to fashion all the white man's mysterious tools—his ships and carriages, his guns and cannons, his machines and printed books, his firewater. And there were festering cesspits which bred all the white man's diseases. A shadow appeared beneath them. The entire sea receded a few inches, and Nenimkee screeched again, but without meaning this time, only an instinctual submission to terror, half battle cry and half prayer, a plea to the Great Spirit for strength. The Great Serpent broke through the surface directly below them, flying upwards with the speed and accuracy of an arrow. It bit into Nenimkee and coiled around the bird's powerful haunches, slashing with its antlers. As they struggled and battered each other and tumbled across the water's surface, the Serpent's tail was all the while calmly, persistently, trying to pry Lalawethika from the thunderfowl's grasp, not merely tugging but also stroking and massaging him, offering him gifts and sensual pleasures, exotic flavors and comforts of the flesh. Lalawethika chanted every prayer he knew, including those he had learned from Father Gabriel at Sainte Anne de Detroit, the Hail Mary and the Our Father, the Lord's Prayer, anything to stave the temptations. He dug his fingers into Nenimkee's feathers, squeezing until his hands bled, all while the Serpent tried to pull them both below the surface of that black sea. Nenimkee's wings strove like mad to keep them airborne. Thunder crashed around them, and the foul water splashed into Nenimkee's eyes. When the great bird blinked, blinding flashes of lightning struck, sometimes in the distance and sometimes right there upon the Great Serpent's back. Lalawethika felt tired, weary of this struggle, and when he happened to glance down at the water below, he saw that he was being watched by an eyeball floating in the stagnant mire, a pierced and oozing eyeball that he instantly recognized as his own. And he desired it. The irresistible pull of that missing body part was begging to reunite, promising to never abandon him again until eternity itself should be smothered. He reached out to it, unaware of how he was gradually loosening his grip upon Nenimkee. But the great bird sensed this change and summoned its strength. Nenimkee threw the Serpent off its back with one violent jerk, and they drew away from that terrible sea where all wickedness is born. Lalawethika sang praises upon the thunderfowl. He cheered and laughed, embracing its legs and rubbing his face in its feathers, saying, "You have done it! You have defeated the Serpent!"

But Nenimkee screeched, "No."

As they rose higher, they approached a forest. A pair of ravens joined them in flight and flew alongside, speaking to Lalawethika.

"The battle is always..." said the first raven.

"There can be no victor, never, never..." said the other.

"The Serpent stole a stray thought from the Great Spirit..."

"And now the Great Serpent contains a part of the Great Spirit..."

"So it is..."

"So it must be..."

"Always..."

"Always..."

The ravens, cawing and weaving back and forth, accompanied them above the treetops. When the ravens tired from keeping pace with the enormous bird, they would rest by perching upon Nenimkee's talons, nuzzling into Lalawethika's shoulder and observing him with their wise black eyes. The forest below bristled with activity, swarms of insects, herds of wandering beasts, solitary predators, as well as the plants themselves, which seemed to be constantly regenerating, changing color and size and shape, able to take on the form most befitting the creatures surrounding them at any given moment, thus creating the impression that they were spinning and shifting, undulating organically, all the flora and fauna participating in an elaborate dance, not unlike the Shawnee harvest dance. The forest terminated in a perfectly straight, unbroken tree line bordered by a wide river, surely wider than the great western river. The river's current flowed with ferocity, yet the surface was smooth as glass. Waterfowl dove in and fish leapt out without disturbing the water's calm. On the opposite shore, groups of people crowded together on the steep bank, a nondescript race, unadorned by clothing or ornaments, with all their attention turned toward the river and the forest in an apparent show of reverence. The ravens bid Lalawethika farewell and dove to snag jumping fish out of the air, after which they deposited them selectively amongst the people, drawing praises and affection from all at once. The sandy riverbank rose and then leveled out into an unfamiliar landscape, a featureless stretch of sand dotted with tall rock formations and oddly shaped, spiny plants. Creatures scurried about the sand, moving quickly and often disappearing below ground, concealing themselves from the intense heat of the place, heat that rose up and warmed them from below, though there appeared to be no source for the heat—no fires burned on the land and no sun stirred above. Lalawethika twisted to look around and realized there were no clouds either. Behind them, he could glimpse traces of all he had seen already, the river, the forest, the ice-capped mountains, and the endless plummet to the dark depths. Even the languages in the canyons seemed to take on a visible shape. But when he faced forward again and focused on the hazy horizon, he could make out ghostly, half-formed shapes dotting that unreachable distance. When he stared long enough, they revealed themselves to be the same river, forest, mountains, and canyons he had seen behind him. He wondered whether those formations were moving across the sky like the constellations of our world or whether Nenimkee had circled around to take him back. It occurred to him, too, that they might be replications, that the hereafter may boundlessly repeat itself, tweaking towards an ultimate perfection. But Nenimkee, as if reading his thoughts, screeched a warning—

"Do not steep yourself in these tangled perceptions, son. There are no directions here. No front or back. No up or down. No in or out. No before, no after. All things are motion. All things perish and renew. All things are lost and then reoriented. All things are one, and all things are nothing."

As the thunderfowl's screech faded, Lalawethika glanced forward again to see a barrier, like an enormous wall rising out of the ground straight ahead. They approached, and it was not a wall but a field, an expansive prairie, not extending outward from the sand below but rising upward out of the ground and into the air. Nenimkee maintained complete control, never shirking from the responsibility of its charge, and they angled sharply, gracefully upward, passing low over the grasses of the prairie, so low that wheat and flowers brushed against Lalawethika's cheeks and the fragrance filled him with happiness. A peculiar structure, many times larger than Nenimkee, rose out of the prairie, and only as they approached did it become evident that it was no structure at all—it was a woman. She sat with one knee bent and her head tilted forward, her long dark hair spilling down to conceal her naked body. She was braiding her hair and humming a serene melody that filled the prairie with the most wondrous sounds. As they swept past her, near enough that Lalawethika reached out and touched a few silky strands of her hair, she lifted her head and turned to watch them, tossing her braids as she spun around. The force of her hair sent out a gust of wind that flattened every blade of grass in the prairie and nearly knocked Nenimkee out of the sky. She smiled, her eyes bright and twinkling with a deep internal light. When she waved, she looked directly at Lalawethika and nodded, as though offering her approval or confirmation. Lalawethika was instantly overcome with the confusing inner turmoil of love, the upsetting of all known laws, the overturning of the sea itself—for he had never been granted honest acceptance before. Then, he saw people wandering through the field. Only a few, scattered here and there, but more soon appeared, and each one would look up to wave at Lalawethika. They smiled and nodded just as the enormous woman had, beckoning him onward toward the villages that cropped up at the outskirts of the prairie, thousands of villages without divisions or boundaries or defenses, mud huts with thatched roofs, basic teepees and ornate leather wigwams, vast log meeting halls and weathered stone structures, multi-tiered buildings of brick and marble, all of them intermingled and connected by dirt paths and cobblestone roads with no deference to one form or another. Stables and pigsties were communal, and everyone treated the livestock with respect. People moved freely amongst one another, entire communities mingling with their neighbors, smiling, laughing, playing together, and sharing what others lacked, whether it was copious or scarce. And still, as Nenimkee and Lalawethika circled above these towns, each person stopped to look up at Lalawethika, welcoming him with high praises and directing him toward the great mountain beyond their villages. The mountain was unlike any he had ever seen, surrounded by a tumultuous sea and domed, rather more hill-like than mountainous, although every bit as large as any mountain he could imagine. The waves battering the shoreline were as tall as the tallest village structures, and the villages were built right up to the water's edge, but the seawater inflicted no harm upon the structures or the villagers. And although the sea raged so furiously that none of the villagers ventured out in boats and none could have possibly reached the mountain island, they often paused in their work and stood gazing at it across the water, appreciative and filled with awe. The mountain's slopes were a patchwork of colors marked off by perfect geometric squares. There was, however, one person on top of the mountain, all by herself. When Lalawethika saw her there, he forgot about the attention he had received from the people of the villages. He forgot the giant, alluring woman of the prairie. He forgot everything he knew about the world and about himself.

I am Nothing.

His eyes welled with tears of veneration, tears of love, tears of hope, and of fear. At first, his tears fell sporadically, one at a time, but soon they were pouring off his cheeks, spilling down to join the wild sea. Kokumthena, their Grandmother—matriarch of the Shawnee Nation and provider of life—sat atop the peak weaving the blanket that would one day bring the world to its end. It trailed in long folds down the smooth, gradual slope of the Great Turtle's shell, for it was, in fact, no mountain she sat upon, but the Great Turtle itself.

She watched placidly as Nenimkee flew closer. They flew now without the unbridled haste of before, but drifting and circling cautiously above the sea. The Great Serpent appeared again. It burst from the frothing mouth of the sea and coursed through the air, but even the Serpent demonstrated reverence in the presence of their Grandmother. It steered clear of the Great Turtle and ignored Nenimkee the Thunderfowl. Kokumthena's tiny, sharp eyes kept watch over everything all at once. They fell upon all of creation, casting light and darkness. Night fell when she blinked, and when her eyes were open, they gave forth the gifts of the sun. She did not smile or welcome him like the others, nor did she express dissatisfaction or turn him away. Instead, she bore a grin of amusement, expressing her absolute knowledge of all the folly in the world, particularly the absurd plight of this sorry subject. This dejected Shawnee son. This detestable boasting drunkard. This...this...this...

I am Nothing.

He had forgotten his name.

Their Grandmother's hands worked continuously while she observed all that she had created from her high perch, and as she wove her stories into the blanket, it grew longer and slid down to the edge of the shell, where it fell into the waves below. The Great Turtle's gigantic neck swayed back and forth above the waves, occasionally dipping low to pick little white creatures out of the water. For as the

Great Serpent rolled and coiled through the sky, it would curl over on itself, slashing and biting at its own body with its rows of stained teeth and its gnarled antlers, shredding scraps of flesh from its scaly hide and letting them drop into the sea where they obtained life and purpose. They were not fish, but little white serpents with the heads of wolves, and they swarmed around the edge of the Great Turtle's shell, biting and tearing segments from the blanket and then consuming them so that the frayed ends never extended past the shell's rim—growing and shrinking constantly and at the same time. The Great Turtle chewed and swallowed the little white serpents without haste, and by the time it reached down to fetch the next, the Great Serpent was also tearing another hunk of flesh from its body to let loose in the water. This, the perfect balance that permits the world to persist.

The panels of Kokumthena's blanket contained the stories of creation and destruction—the rise and fall of tribes and nations and civilizations, the blessings of the Great Spirit and the curses of the Serpent, invasions and wars and plagues, as well as miracles and destinies and saviors, the will and temperance of nature and also the carelessness and greed of men. As the little white serpents chewed away at the fabric, their Grandmother wove her stories again and again. Sometimes the stories changed, and other times they were exact replicas. They might be more appealing than before or more disheartening, while some panels were simply indecipherable to the eyes of men.

After a while, their Grandmother beckoned them with a sigh that carried the meaning of a thousand words. Nenimkee glided gently towards her. The thunderfowl was gradually easing its grip on the man who had forgotten his name, and the man trembled and clung on all the tighter so as not to plummet downward. Soon, he was face to face with their Grandmother, watching as she wove a simple panel. An open door. The thunderfowl had now completely released him. He hung only by the strength of his hands grasping a single feather, sliding down, down, down, as he watched their Grandmother weave this beautiful door. He knew it was time for him to leave this place, but he was sad. And he was afraid. He no longer remembered where he had come from or where he might return to, nor did he understand why he must leave the domain of the Great Spirit and the presence of their Grandmother.

"You have a question," spoke Kokumthena. "Ask it."

The man who had forgotten his name had many questions, but he knew his time was short. He thought carefully and quickly, trying to condense all his questions into one.

"Before I go," he said, "can I not look upon...can I not just glimpse the Great Spirit? Can I not witness the full scope of the Great Spirit's magnificence?"

"But you have," responded Kokumthena, her grin growing more sardonic. "You have seen the Great Spirit in all that you have witnessed here. Have you not recognized the Great Spirit, then? You will, Tenskwatawa. You must."

While speaking, she finished weaving the panel of the open door. And within the door, she had woven a fire—not a depiction of fire, not another story in the blanket, but a real fire that burned true and produced heat, that curled and crackled and spat smoke and embers. The blanket still slid rapidly down the shell, and their Grandmother moved along without pause to weave her next panel, then another, and another, all while the little white serpents populating the water continued to gnaw and unravel the threads below, maintaining the balance of all things.

The man would be granted only one chance to return, to become. He called out to Nenimkee the Thunderfowl, and so the great bird positioned itself, hovering above as the door receded down the shell, nearing the edge where it would be devoured forever. With tears in his eyes and gratitude weighing achingly upon his heart, he let go of the feather and fell, fell, fell, into the fire within the open door.

A strenuous gasp escaped his lips. His body shot upright, sending the ritual herbs and stones they had painstakingly laid atop his scarred and lifeless flesh to scatter across the ground. His good eye squinted, straining to adjust and see through the dimness of this world. He felt at once exhausted and rejuvenated, as though he had rested for thousands of years. Those standing around him jumped back in fright. Some scrambled out of the wigwam, shouting, "Sorcery! Evil! Possession!" Others entered and looked around curiously. Tentative whispers soon rose. "Piqua. Piqua. Risen from the ashes. Alive out of flame." They offered him water, of which he drank a full bowl and then asked for another. They tried to reapply medicinal herbs to his burns and blisters, but he waved them off. When he attempted to stand, they came to his aid, supporting him as he stepped outside to find the Shawnee tribespeople flocking toward the wigwam, drawn from all corners of the village by rumors of a miracle. As they cautiously approached, he nodded to each of them in acknowledgment, and the smile he produced, stern though it was, shone with strength and calm, with understanding and purpose, intoning that he had not seen them in many years and was glad, blissful to be one amongst their company. They spoke to him, but when they said his name—Lalawethika, Noisemaker—he did not respond. He only trudged a slow path through the village as the others followed behind, their confused, hesitant whispers fluttering, as do the leaves of the forest.

At the village center, he turned and was surprised to find so many of his tribespeople there with him, watching him with both fear and awe. He asked for a fire to be built—a huge, scorching fire—because the air of this world chilled his skin. His request was tended to at once, without protest. And as the flames grew taller and licked the sky, he spoke to his tribespeople. He recounted how he had faced off with Death and was taken to the world beyond. He told of noble Nenimkee's boundless strength and fearlessness as they glided through the narrow canyons where languages are kept, as they witnessed The Four Winds commingling and copulating in the acts of creation, as they engaged in battle with the Great Serpent above that festering sea. He described how the pristine, untainted landscapes, generous and caring with all their abundance, were honored by the united tribes of that paradise. Yearningly, he related their Grandmother's indescribable beauty and calm justness, as well as the ever-present, unseen threat of the Great Serpent, unleashing its poisonous influence and its white devils throughout all things the world over with all the power of the Great Spirit, from which it had stolen a single thought.

He spoke for many hours. Night fell, and his oration continued. There were those who insisted that he had drunk himself into delirium. But most of his tribesmen remained, listening attentively, whispering in admiration, "A prophet, a prophet. We have been sent a prophet."

When he finished speaking, many called his name. They asked for more stories, begged his advice, and sought remedies for their earthly troubles.

"Please, tell us again. Tell us more. Tell us what we must do, Lalawethika."

But he only stared at them in bewilderment.

"Who is Lalawethika?" he said. "I am Tenskwatawa. I am The Open Door."

Chapter 49

Fear

The procession approaches, spread out behind Pa Sonny, who's using his bundled black vestment to dab at the sweat dripping from his face and neck. Half of them sing a mournful melody, glancing at hymn sheets in their hands while their eyes bounce this way and that, a disjointed choir lost from the start. Johannes stands on the top step out front of St. Josephine's, wiping water from his chin and drying his hands on his pants as he trembles imperceptibly from the bitter taste still upon his tongue.

He had been with Pa Sonny when the call came, had witnessed this self-absorbed stoic being crushed by something as ethereal as words through a telephone line, his self-love exposed as either a costumed cop-out or an ignorant misunderstanding. It had been Grant's father on the line, calmly stating facts about the accident while Pa Sonny blubbered uncontrollably, contesting it as a ruse, a lie, a cruel and malicious practical joke. When Pa Sonny mentioned that Johannes was there with him, *Yes, really, right here beside me, I would never lie,* an uneasy silence followed on both ends of the line. Finally, Mr. Cagniss said he planned to arrive in Creek's Ridge in about a week to deal with the property and take care of his son's belongings, and in the meantime, Pa Sonny was free to go to the house and take anything he might want or need for himself. And, he added, Johannes was free to stay at the house as long as he needed. As soon as Pa Sonny hung up the phone, he had a bottle between his lips, and he hadn't stopped suckling since.

Over the ensuing week, the alcohol had inflicted Pa Sonny with a short attention span and recurring dazed reveries during which he would recite strange but poignant passages, passages he would then go on to include in his rambling speech atop his tree stump at the park—

> Death curls like ocean waves,
> And you are swallowed by its flooding waters.
> Ropes from the land of the dead coil around you,
> Setting a trap in your path.
> It looks like a friend, like a lover,
> Like a crumb leading you home—
> But this is deception at its finest.
> Death has destroyed your home, taken your throne,
> And by the time you call out for help,
> Fear and trembling are your only refuge,
> When from the temple comes an answer,
> It's nothing, nothing but a sound,
> Only the wind and the rain.

Pa Sonny stumbles and barely catches himself with an unsteady hand. It takes him a moment to regain his balance even though he's aided by those around him, Ruthie from the diner and Alonso, the blind half-Cherokee. By pure hapless coincidence, the mourners appear to follow Pa Sonny's tumble and the entire party nearly trips crashing to the ground. But, somehow, they all hold each other up. They bump into their neighbors, grab hold of elbows, grasp shoulders and pat backs, blush at their clumsy missteps, but keep moving forward, as one.

Everyone is exhausted. It's the heat, the sorrow, the unwillingness to believe. Amondale is decked out—black suit, black shirt, black tie. George holds his daughter Cassandra by the hand and is surrounded by the rest of his kids, who are visiting for the summer. They have stayed a few extra days to attend this ceremony, glad to miss the first week of school. Claire Young is in a tight, form-fitting black dress, black streaks of mascara staining her cheeks. All four of her kids huddle in close formation around her, each one just as torn up as their mother, even the youngest, who can't be more than five years old. Greenah Taylor leads her few dedicated singers, all holding song sheets and attempting to continue the bluesy hymn. Charlie is trapped in the center of it all, wearing his uniform and, for some reason, carrying his satchel full of envelopes. Several elderly couples are grouped together at the back, slowly trudging along and fanning themselves, looking like they're about to keel over at any moment and join the missing pillar of their community in the afterlife. Further back still, trailing far behind everybody, is a man of about Pa Sonny's age, the same stranger who has remained on the periphery all day, except for earlier at the park when he repeatedly stepped forward to help Pa Sonny back onto his stump. Doctor Mengele runs alongside the procession, jumping and playing in the roadside grass, blissfully unaware, and off to the side, all by himself, is a short Asian man, who Johannes now realizes must be Vu, the dog's owner. There's a group of young men and women Johannes has only ever seen at Ernest's, as well as a group of teenagers that constantly prowls the town, boisterous and mischievous and stoned, but today they are placid, pale, and withdrawn. The younger kids are gathered around their teachers, the entire school having taken the morning off. Ernest holds his jacket in his hand. His wrinkled white shirt is a size too big, and his tie is crooked. He looks taller than usual but also younger and brighter, an effect of the sunlight, to be sure. Caryn is coming up behind Ernest, and she's supporting a hunched-over old woman who, despite her bent frame and infirm steps, is walking with more haste than any of them. Caryn almost has to hold her back.

Several of them look up at the church, shocked and confused to see Johannes standing out front. Others keep looking back toward the town, uncertain about the distance they've walked from their homes in following this drunken lunatic. And for what? To be turned away at the gates of repose? To be let down when they learn that this is all that's here for them? Only and always this endless trek through dust-heavy streets, parched throats and blistered feet, as one by one their companions collapse beside them, and there's nothing to do but leave them behind and continue on while their memory and influence weigh you down. They glance at the steeple, at Johannes on the steps, into the cemetery and the fields out back, in reverse toward the town. They hesitate. They want answers, but they get Pa Sonny's curious recitations and speeches instead. And that's enough. Enough to remind them where they are, what they're doing. To remind them to look to their sides, at their friends and neighbors plodding obliviously onward alongside them, and to persuade them to maintain their pace. To remind them who they are.

> Water provides us life,
> Wind is the source of our thoughts.
> But taken without restraint,
> Only nightmares rise from the waste.
> Cyclones, tornadoes, and sandstorms—Oh my!
> They come to blot out the sky,
> Clouds thick as glaciers, black as ink.
> Waves tall as sequoias, falling like hammers.

The surface foams and froths and churns,
Deafening winds, blinding rains, swirl and pounce,
The cardinal directions are lost, and so are you,
Disorientation reigns now as King.

The shock of loss binds these people. None of them, Johannes included, was allowed a final parting word with Grant. No one had a chance to say goodbye. Hardly anyone even knew that Grant had left town. And so now, as they tread this long road searching for answers, their heads hung down, directed at the dust clouds obscuring their feet, singing a song of regret and sadness shaped by their own heavy sobs, they are, all of them, dwelling on him. Grant J. Cagniss, Sheriff, Morton County, Kansas, USofA—towering figure in the community, in each of their lives; friend, neighbor, confidant; lenient officer or strict enforcer, as circumstance dictated; the eyes and ears that kept them safe; the clown that made them laugh; the unrequited smile that mended their troubled days. At this very moment, Grant is inhabiting their memories. He is as alive in that realm as ever he was in actuality. They see him in their collective mind's eye, hear his voice, feel his breath, and smell his musk. They answer his calls and bicker with his nagging orders. They cradle him in their arms.

And at the hour of death,
Only the man that meditates on Me
Shall become one with My Being,
Of this, doubt not.
In putting off the flesh,
The remains of a man will be enmeshed
With that upon which he has obsessed,
For his Soul will be bent
In death as it was in life.

After Pa Sonny got off the phone with Grant's father, Johannes had tried asking him what they ought to do. How should they tell people? What could they say? Pa Sonny had no answers, wouldn't even respond. He poured bourbon from a bottle he'd had buried deep in a closet and stared out the window as though he could see a thousand miles. Johannes pestered him for a few minutes but eventually gave up and walked to Ernest's. The bar wasn't open yet. Johannes considered breaking in, but he thought better of it and walked around to the rear entrance. Sure enough, the back door had been unlocked, but it was obstructed by the usual stacks of supplies and junk. Squeezing his way through, he had knocked over brooms and mops, an empty trash bin and the various tools and items stacked on top of it, an old sign, a crate of utensils, and a few broken dishes. Then, while he was trying to straighten it all up, he received a nasty bump on the head, a bruised elbow and shin. He finally made it to the bar, grabbed an unopened bottle of The Carnival and a tumbler, and then settled in, staring into the mirrors as he drank.

"What the hell is this?" Ernest said when he turned up. "Your own personal liquor cabinet? Some goddamn drunken buffet? I know I gave you an open tab, but this is pushing it."

Johannes reached for another tumbler. He filled it and handed it to Ernest. "It's Grant..." Johannes swallowed a mouthful, barely holding it down. "He's dead."

Ernest examined Johannes uncertainly. "He's only been gone a week," he said, checking his watch before he allowed himself a sip of the Scotch. "That boy deserves a vacation. Let him have one."

Johannes could think of no other words. How does one convince another to believe the unbelievable?

A little while later, Amondale poked his head in the door. "A bit early in the day, isn't it, fellas? Is today a holiday? Shit. Have I got my dates mixed up? It's not Labor Day already, is it?" He was drawn toward them, his eyes arrested by The Carnival, but checking his watch, too. "What's the celebration, then? Somebody's birthday? I do not like to miss a party, heh heh."

Ernest shrugged and gestured at Johannes, then grabbed a glass for Oscar.

Johannes stared at Amondale, at Ernest, at Amondale again, then at his Scotch, and finally at himself.

"Grant's dead."

And Amondale, watching Johannes through the mirrors, began to laugh. After a few good-natured slaps upon the bar top and enthusiastic stomps on the barstool, he tried to silence his laughter with the whisky but only spluttered it all over his chin and shirt. Ernest had caught the bug as well and stood across from them, chuckling with mirth.

"I just spoke with him," Amondale said once he'd finally managed to swallow his laughter with a mouthful of Scotch.

"When?"

"Oh...when was it? A day or two ago. Well, maybe three or four. He called about...something or other. I was half asleep. Said he was almost home."

"Didn't you say he went out east?" asked Ernest.

Johannes nodded.

"Chicago is...east-northeast," said Amondale.

"If he was going there, he..." Johannes shook his head, "he would have told me. He would have taken me with him. Would've insisted on it. And he wouldn't have said 'out east.'"

"He's a secretive fellow," Amondale rationalized. "Likes to get up to no good sometimes. Can't blame him for that. Let him have his fun, his skeletons in the closet. Everyone deserves to keep their secrets, even from you, Double-Oh-Jonathon."

"And he's a momma's boy," added Ernest.

"If you want to drink during the day, just drink. We're all adults here. Although I suppose that's its own counterargument, isn't it? Heh heh. Anyhow, own up to what you are. No need to concoct an excuse."

"I'm not," stated Johannes. "He's dead."

Ernest and Amondale stared at Johannes, then at each other. Ernest shrugged again.

"Get outta here," Amondale laughed. "These sorts of cons and cock-and-bull stories aren't for you, Johnson. You can't pull them off. Grant can. How do you think he convinced you to go along on this wild goose chase for a bunch of horse bones? He's a master of the practical joke. Stick to what you know, alright? Meditation and mountains and uh... Rachmaninoff, I guess."

> Paradise is an uncharted island,
> Unspoken of and accessible only by boat,
> Your vessel is rickety, leaky,
> A speck of driftwood merely afloat.
> You can battle the storm,
> You can find this place,
> But it's at the eye of the cyclone.
> And who can you share it with
> If everyone that you love
> Has convened, wisely, on the shore?
> With their feet planted firmly on solid ground,
> Their bearings held clear and bright.

The procession has now arrived at the foot of the steps. They're still down on the street, and though their weary, defeated eyes fondle the looming shape and cool shade of the church, only one of them is willing to defy Pa Sonny. The bent old woman on Caryn's arm pushes through them, mumbling and muttering along the way. Everyone else huddles together as Pa Sonny stops and turns to face them. The little old woman plows forward, dragging Caryn through the throng until they emerge out front, where they share a private word before the old woman disengages herself, scowling at Pa Sonny and then hobbling past him up the steps. Caryn brushes her hair away from her face and watches Pa Sonny, unfazed by his absurdity. She scans the faces around her and the field across the street, the nearby glade where Johannes goes to meditate, and the stretching bank of the creek, which from this distance is just an indistinct shallow ridge. Then, she turns toward St. Josephine's and looks directly at Johannes. The old woman's slow progress up the steps is heartbreaking, but the hardened determination upon her face is anything but.

Pa Sonny is on the move, too. Johannes notices, but he is held rapt by Caryn, by her beauty and strength, when all around her are the uncertain, worry-stricken expressions of people in the throes of loss.

Halfway up the stairs, Pa Sonny stops and announces, "This is the place we seek."

Johannes steps down. "You can't go inside, Sonny."

"No desire to. Never a thought of it." Pa Sonny hobbles toward Johannes. They meet a few steps from the top, and Pa Sonny grabs Johannes's shoulder to stabilize himself. "I never go into churches, you idiot." As he gazes at the huge wooden doors, he grasps Johannes's wrist with his other hand. "I despise them."

"Then what are you doing here?"

"I'm looking for a place to end this. I'm done. Can't go on much longer, not in this heat. Why oh why do they always die in the summer, goddamnit..."

"This is hardly an appropriate place to finish the thing. Not after the hell you raised all week."

"Nonsense, nonsense...one place is just as good as the next. Everywhere's the same as everywhere else. You know that."

"If every place is the same, then why don't you head back into town? Take them to Ernest's. Get everyone a drink so they can forget."

"Forget? Who said anything about forgetting? Nope, this is the place. I was looking for a sign—" Pa Sonny wobbles, almost tumbles backward down the steps, but his grip tightens on Johannes's wrist.

"What do you mean? There's nowhere else to go, nothing past the church. Where else could you have been taking them? El Paso?"

"Don't you dare... Taking who?"

"Them." Johannes looks up, directing Pa Sonny's eyes to the people gathered below.

"Who? Oh...them...no, I...I asked for a sign, and a sign I was given. Clear and real as anything."

"What sign?"

"You!" Pa Sonny's laughter rises in pitch until it becomes a howl.

"Come on," Johannes nudges Pa Sonny's elbow. "Let's steer them back into town. I'll come with, help you finish it off." Another nudge, but for the first time all day, Pa Sonny stands firm.

"Gotta do it right here. We'll do it here. This goddamn heat'll make a funeral for us all if we don't end it now."

Pa Sonny sits on the top step and waves to his flock, beckoning their approach. They share worrying glances with one another as they inch forward, few of them willing to mount even the first couple of steps.

"One is lost to us," Pa Sonny begins. He remains seated, hunched over and constantly wiping sweat from his eyebrows, but his voice is deep, thick, roaring. "Our maternal fathers round this earth, help us to honor your seed from which we spring. Help us to grow and set up human kingdoms, so that everyone on earth will remember you, as you are remembered through this godforsaken dust, which is you. For to dance...with this life...is to return...to dust..."

Pa Sonny pauses, but he appears to be whispering to himself. The crowd remains respectful and patient. How easily they bend to his distorted will. And how thoroughly they revere their sheriff despite his abandonment, leaving them without forewarning and without any advice on how to proceed. How warily they flick their guarded eyes toward and away from the church, acknowledging its allure but suppressing the desire to give it their full attention. Johannes is witnessing this immense sense of community amongst the people of Creek's Ridge, thick as the dust they've kicked up and inhaled into their lungs, these pilgrims on the march. They want more than anything to charge up the steps and claim asylum inside, to cool off in the shade of its masonry, to repent their sins before death sneaks up on them as well, to wail and sob and shout the name of their beloved sheriff so loudly that Death itself regrets having taken him. Strength in numbers, their willpower has grown stronger over the course of the day, and their recklessness bolder. They breathe together as one unit, sigh and lament as one entity. They prop one another up, lead one another in the darkness and confusion, protect one another from the fears and dangers of the wider world. These are the same good people who welcomed Johannes and Caryn with open arms, who welcomed Pa Sonny years ago, when he was at his drunkest until today. Grant himself had come here in search of solitude, loneliness, relief from life, but he'd been cradled into their bosom, held and adored, nurtured back to health, and then placed on a pedestal. Almost every one of these people came here seeking a sort of peace or running from some pain of their own.

"It must be said again." Pa Sonny bends his head backward to look at Johannes upside down. The glimmer in his eyes intones mischievousness, but then a tear slides down his forehead, and the glimmer is gone. "This will send them home," he says, nodding and squeezing Johannes's hand. "This will help us to accept what has happened. What has happened to us. It must."

"Selfish bastard..." says Johannes.

"You and I both, friend. All of us."

Johannes hears a sound behind him and glances back in time to see the little old woman finally reach the great doors. She casts back an angry grimace meant for everyone and then enters the church. A wide-eyed Father Marover pokes his head out before gently shutting the door.

Pa Sonny stands up and raises Johannes's hand in his, stretching tall to add emphasis and authority. Johannes resists, but Pa Sonny's strength is greater than should be possible in his current state. Pa Sonny turns to face the town of mourners gathered below, and he roars,

"The worlds, my Son,
Roll back and forth
From Death to Life's unrest.
But those who reach out to Me,
May they taste birth nevermore..."

"All of you, all of us..."

As the saturated mountainside flooded him out of his home—

"Brothers and sisters..."

As his friend's faceless image poured in, instantly recognizable upon his casual approach, the sound of his voice—

"Neighbors and friends..."

As the Scrap from Rachmaninoff's Second Piano Concerto in C-minor drowned him—

"Community of men, women, and children..."

As the names of Christ's disciples have risen to the surface, bloated by lust, and Bartholomew, a bitch in heat—

"Beasts of burden, dogs of the night..."

As the memories flowed through him, an open-mouthed kiss breathing life-giving oxygen from the Saint of Creek's Ridge—

"Grant Cagniss is not taken from us. He remains here with us always, as much as ever he was..." Pa Sonny's jowls and lower lip tremble. He makes a herculean effort to steady them, but the struggle is too much, and soon his entire body is quivering.

"When that endless Dawn finally breaks,
The unknowable is brought into the light.
When that impenetrable Night steps forth,
All things fade again to the One who bore them.
Hark! The Community of all the life-endowed
Falls, falls, expires with the Night,
Only to wake yet again, wrapped in Me,
At the coming of the Dawn..."

Unbelieving, oblivious, and stubborn, Amondale and Ernest had gone on to talk about recent events in the news, about sports, politics, and the economy. Amondale asked Ernest for details regarding a few stories from his days as a touring jazz musician, and Ernest asked Amondale, for the fourth and final time, to get him a copy of one of his books, a history of the Dust Bowl that had been published some years ago.

But when Pa Sonny eventually stumbled in with the nearly empty bottle of bourbon in one hand, a slim unmarked book in the other, and tears running down his cheeks, Ernest and Amondale's expressions took on a more serious aspect. Pa Sonny glanced around the bar like he was searching for someone. He looked right past the three of them, but then they realized Sonny was only averting his eyes because his tears would resume if he looked directly at them. Ernest and Amondale were speechless. As they studied Pa Sonny, who still hadn't said a word, the undeniable truth squeezed the breath from each of them. Ernest's eyes welled up, and Amondale turned beet-red. All four had become men without language, withdrawn so deeply into themselves that all traces of knowledge and reason, the lessons of a lifetime, were swept clean away, back, back, back through the decades until they were but infants, just moments ago released from the womb and in possession of a single voiceless thought—that the only thing they'd ever known, their home, their warmth, their sustenance, their fortress, had evicted them. And now this monstrous world had encircled them instead, wrapped its powerful grasp around them, with its paralyzing scale and its awful truths, its intention to nurture and throttle them in equal turns.

But Johannes, although sorrow weighed on his heart and the words resounded noisily inside his head—*Grant's dead, Grant's dead, Grant's dead* —he had already been living with the reality of loss for months, possibly longer. Therefore, his reflections in the mirrors displayed the casual ease of monks in cogitation, the reassuring comfort in the knowledge that the world had, in fact, grown somewhat less vacillating and uncertain.

Over the course of an hour or so, the steady flow of Scotch brought those infant castaways back to face the music, as it were. Pa Sonny struggled at first, but he soon managed to find the rhythm of his words, and he told them precisely what he'd been told by Mr. Cagniss over the phone, which hadn't been much in the way of particulars—only that there had been some sort of an accident, but the specifics had yet to be released. A tragedy. A terrible tragedy. Near the water. An officer from the Marine Patrol Unit of the Dade County Police Department had phoned the Cagniss household the day before, and Dom had taken the first available flight from O'Hare to Miami International, arrived in the middle of the night when they were still fishing the car out of the water. Yes, Grant had been in Miami. Yes, the car. From the water. That's right, the Atlantic. Yes, yes, it was true. He had seen it himself, yes, with his very own eyes. That was all. He knew nothing else, not yet. Unbelievable, unbelievable. Yes, Miami. Yes, yes. He'd gone to see Inez.

"Inez?" Johannes choked. He looked up, feeling as though she was right there in the bar with them. But there were only mirrors, reflections.

Grant had told Johannes and only Johannes that he was heading out east for some business. But Johannes had never considered what that might mean. Grant had no business dealings that Johannes knew of. Of course he'd been going to see Inez. Even with the dig, the only explanations that Grant had ever been able to provide were nothing more than abstract allusions to her, to Inez, ambiguous connections that only Grant could see between those two ladies of his life. And, too, all that talk of leaving, escaping, following Johannes's lead to somewhere, anywhere away from here, the envy and the regret, going to the john once and for all, and never coming back. But Johannes had allowed his friend to continue unchecked and unquestioned, had helped and become a part of it as though he were not digging for Grant at all, but for his own vested interest.

Johannes set down his glass and stood up, gazing at the reflections in the mirrors. Ernest, Amondale, and Pa Sonny all watched him, gloom and confusion twisting their expressions like wet rags, and Johannes stared back at them as he backed away toward the door.

"I have to go..." he said in response, but only after he answered did he realize that none of the others had spoken first.

He stood with his back to the door, pulling it open slowly from behind as though trying to sneak out undetected. But pairs of eyes watched him from every corner of the bar, from every wall, and his three friends as well.

"Hey, Johannes..." Ernest called out. "You okay?"

As Johannes held the door open, his gaze swiveled around the bar, past each of those friends, silent and waiting, still as a museum or an old photograph, no movement other than the swiveling heads of all those Johanneses in the mirrors.

Then Ernest shook his head and turned away. Pa Sonny slumped further into himself.

And Amondale, "What the hell's wrong with you?" as he slammed his glass down onto the bar, spraying The Carnival all over himself again.

Johannes could think of nothing to say except to repeat his only thought.

"I have to go... I have to dig..."

"Heartless prick," Amondale finished his drink and reached for the bottle.

"May thou see Me coming, I am Time,
Bearer of doom and death,
Harbinger of beginnings and ends,
None shall remain fastened to this mortal plain.
Fight or fight not, your kingdom is Mine,
The strength in your hands and arms, likewise,
For you shall be my instrument.
Strike, I say! Strike or stay your hand!
It matters not! They perish all the same!
At My bidding, never your command,
And there shall be no victor upon this plain,
But One."

The expressions on the faces of the mourners are not unlike their faces in the bar that day—downtrodden, mystified, betrayed, angry, but without the malice of the abused. And these expressions have not been altered by Pa Sonny's obscure quotations. They don't care what Pa Sonny says, they only want him to be the one to say it, to say whatever needs to be said. If he were to stand there cursing out and lambasting their truant sheriff, they would applaud and cheer because he'd be giving vent to their pent-up frustration, angst, and dread for what's ahead. They are here to feed him their collective strength and to savor his, to remind him that if he falls, then they are here to pick him up.

But their support isn't enough. Pa Sonny pulls out his flask and brings it to his lips. He peers back at the doors of St. Josephine's and up at the steeple. With a half-turn, he takes a single step toward the building, his eyes welled with tears. But then he looks at Johannes and stops, dead in his tracks. His strength fails him as he crumples again into a heap on the steps.

"Think not of heaven or hell," Pa Sonny says with barely any strength left in his voice. The mourners lean their heads forward and huddle closer with short, anxious steps.

"Do not attempt to displace our friend from your thoughts. Keep his memory alive here, in your hearts, and here, in your minds. He's with us as long as we need him to be. Do you not feel him here, with us, right now? Death returns us to dust and soil, and here on Earth we remain, a part of something vast beyond our wildest dreams. Our friend is united with the Great Oneness, with God, the Buddha, Vishnu, the Great Spirit, the Great Emptiness—call it what you will. The universe itself. It is the most elemental and basic simplicity. It is every idea and every possibility coalesced into one indisputable truth. And the truth is everything. Our friend has returned to it, is a part of it completely. Do not despair for him. He is fortunate. He is at peace. He has found his true love. But we are alive. And we will suffer this life together until each of our individual turns arrives, our time to pass through, no sooner. Until then, we breathe our friend into our lungs with every breath, we pollute ourselves with him at every passing moment. Dust and memories, embrace them. Hold on with all your strength."

Pa Sonny's head falls into his hands. "This was not predestined to happen..." His voice is so quiet now that only Johannes can hear him, and his shoulders heave with deep breaths. "If any are to blame, we are they. Responsibility falls upon us. Embrace your guilt."

"Sonny, they can't hear you."

"That was for you and I alone..."

Each of the mourners has bowed their heads. Pa Sonny slowly stands up, ignoring Johannes's outstretched hand. He wipes the tears and sweat from his face and stares at Johannes for a long time with a strained, vacant expression. Suddenly, he winks and then steps past Johannes so that he's situated above and behind, his hands resting on Johannes's shoulders as he looks out over the gathered.

> "Lo! I have seen!
> Lord, all is bound with Thee.
> The gods dwell in Your glory,
> As do the creatures of earth, heaven, and hell,
> All come forth and return to You,
> Upon your lotus throne,
> A hundred-thousand arms, breasts, and faces,
> With eyes on every side,

Neither end nor beginning nor center,
Only the all-encompassing,
Wherever my eyes seek,
I see, I see!"

Pa Sonny's voice has regained its full force and volume, and the mourners jerk their heads up in surprise.

"The heart is pulled from Creek's Ridge! Now is no time for weak wills or dark thoughts. Our dead sheriff, Grant Jeffrey Cagniss, he had enough of that to go around and then some. He was a tortured soul who knew how to hide his suffering for the benefit of others. For the benefit of us. All that we undergo—be it favorable or bleak—becomes entangled with the perpetual forward motion of life. We are not meant to escape from people," Pa Sonny pauses to flick his hand back toward the church, "not unless it's an angry horde come to remove our scalps. We escape from our own inner turmoil, from unbalance and disorientation, from the storms that separate us from peace and happiness. But to these aims, we must come together! As galaxies collide and merge, as birds flock in formation, as oil and water stick to their kind. We are drawn together and repelled like magnets, exerting our influence upon one another at all times. We exist only because of one another. Grant would demand that you move past this loss. He would not recognize it as loss, but as opportunity. He would demand that you plant him firmly in your memories but also that you replace him in your lives."

Pa Sonny vigorously pats Johannes's shoulders, kneading and massaging them. Johannes turns to find a devious grin, a gambling man overly confident in his next bet.

"Sonny?"

"Fret not! You want a new sheriff?"

"Pa Sonny, don't—"

"Here he is! Literally sent down from above by an act of God. Need a friend? A spiritual guide? This is your man. How about a boyfriend? A husband? He's single, in a sense. Need a ditch or a well dug out? John can do it, no problem. Your dog missing? John will find it. He both loves and fears them. Do you need a savior? Johannes Metternich has scaled the mountain...and returned to tell about it."

The collective gaze of Creek's Ridge falls upon Johannes. They watch him with wonder, curiosity, with budding excitement. The sorrow and despondency that have congealed over the past week are loosening, liquifying, evaporating into thin air. Johannes is shaking his head, trying to tell them *No, no, no, no! Don't listen to him, this drunk, this lunatic, he's delirious, he's insane,* but it's too late. Their minds are already made up. In their eyes is something akin to desire, greed, ownership. Even if they haven't been listening to a thing Pa Sonny has said all morning, they certainly heard this—and they're in the market to buy.

"Very good," announces Pa Sonny as he steps beside Johannes. "It is done. So then, let us pray. Give us our food, both for mouth and for thought. Let the dust rise and always settle peacefully at our feet. Forgive us for doing wrong as we try to forgive each other. Keep us from being tempted and protect us from evil. Protect us...from ourselves."

A few heads rise from their prayers once they realize Pa Sonny has finished. About half of them collaborate in an awkward, disjointed *Amen*. Pa Sonny sits down again. He's got his flask in his hands and is looking at it as though there's nobody else around, just him and his booze in their own private paradise, lovers in a darkened motel room.

The people of Creek's Ridge shift their weight upon their feet, resembling the undulating waves of dense treetops as seen from above. A few of them wander through the crowd in search of some particular neighbor or friend. They pat each other's backs, shake hands, smile with relief, and whisper brief, meaningless comments. And they keep looking up, too. Not at the church, not at Pa Sonny, but at Johannes. Although no one is saying anything, their unspoken question is clearly voiced—

What now?

They seek an answer, but in a moment such as this, Johannes, too, would look to Grant. And Grant would absolutely have an answer—honest, appropriate, and helpful. His answer would bring everyone together. It would make them stronger. But Johannes is stock-still. Stiff as Saint Josephine inside the church. Motionless as Knecht up the mountain. Static as Limping Lady's lifeless skeleton. The hollow cavern he has endured ever since coming down from the mountain is exposed. Over the past few months, Grant had helped to tear away the layers, but the events of this day have finally left him stripped bare, and Pa Sonny has just offered Johannes up on a platter. None of them know what Johannes did, what brought him here, or what drove Grant away. Though, perhaps, this is precisely Pa Sonny's intent—*You may forget, you may conceal the truth, but eventually your debts come due.*

Pa Sonny is slouched over, giving every ounce of his attention to his flask.

St. Josephine's stands tall and protective behind them, and though there may be some answers to be found inside, none of those answers will help Johannes right now.

Johannes tries coaxing Pa Sonny to get up and head home, to get some rest, and to lay off the booze for a while. He hears Grant's voice in his own, tastes it.

Pa Sonny does not respond.

None of the others have left yet, either. They stand around chatting, waiting, looking up at Johannes, who tries to get Pa Sonny onto his feet one more time. But the stubbornness of a drunk always wins, so Johannes gives in and squats on the next step down.

"Sonny. Sonny, hey, look at me."

"Leave me alone. I've passed it along to you, the figurative torch and map."

"Pa Sonny, I have to ask you something."

"Look, look, they wait for you. *You* take them back. *You* get them drunk, if that's what's to be done. Show them, teach them how to forget. Not me...not me...I can't..."

"Pa, tell me what I told you before I left Creek's Ridge. I need to know. Why did I go into the mountains?"

"Now? Now you want to remember? Now?"

"I think I...I've already remembered. I went inside before, into the church, into St. Josephine's, and I... I started to remember. Things are coming back, but they're not clear. They're not right..."

"No, they are not right...perhaps never were..."

"I need to know."

"No," Pa Sonny screws the cap back onto his flask and finally looks at Johannes. "It doesn't matter anymore. It's over. He's dead, he's gone. You try to forget about it now, as you did once already. Like he tried to forget. Tried and failed. He was a role model for all of us. And forget about her, too. Forget about Inez. Forget about everything. That's something you're good at. Don't remember now. It's too late. It's not worth it. Now is the time for forgetting. Go and live your life. If for nothing else, then for this. For the memory of Grant's death. Out of respect for him, and what he meant to them."

Johannes stands and stares off behind the church, at the cemetery, the distant woodlands, and the tranquil blue sky. He brings his focus in closer, tracing the outline of the building, the cracks in the old stone steps. From here, through the heat and moisture in the air, the town appears distorted and restless, an impressionist's pulsing rendering. His glade along the creek is just across the way, and it calls out to him. But there can be no meditation today, not with his inner and outer worlds as agitated as flames overfed.

"Is that it?" somebody calls out from below. "Is it over?"

Pa Sonny's face is buried in his hands. Johannes looks out over the crowd, scans the sky, catches the sun's glare, and raises a hand to shield his eyes. Then, with his other hand, he points at the sun and waves them off with an ambiguous gesture.

"Go on, live your lives," he says, expecting them to disperse at once. But they stay put, looking up at him, waiting for more. Then, they begin to form small groups, huddling together and chatting about what it all means.

As Johannes descends the steps, a lone figure steps forward to mount them. It's the unknown old man, the one person who'd possessed the courage to help Pa Sonny up onto his stump back at the park, to rein him in and align his words when he fell astray. The man ascends from off to the side of the crowd. He and Johannes don't pass by each other, but they are each watching the other. The man's expression differs from those of everyone else. He is stern and without emotion. He nods at Johannes but continues up the steps, stopping to place his hand on Pa Sonny's shoulder and bending low to speak.

Johannes locates Ernest, Caryn, and Amondale standing nearby. Before he goes to them, he lingers at the bottom of the steps, watching as the old man does something he was incapable of doing—with only a few short words, the man has brought Pa Sonny to his feet. Pa Sonny smiles sadly as they speak, shaking hands repeatedly and hugging each other with the warmth of brothers. Finally, they part ways, the man continuing up to the great doors of St. Josephine's and Pa Sonny wandering off without another word to anyone.

Caryn's dress flutters around her legs in a sudden breeze. Amondale and Ernest are both holding their jackets at their sides. Amondale's sleeves are rolled up, and Ernest's shirt is thoroughly drenched with sweat.

"Who's that old timer?" says Ernest.

"Who do you think?" snorts Amondale.

"That's Dom Cagniss..." says Johannes. "Grant's dad."

They all stare at Johannes.

"You remember him?" asks Caryn.

"Yes, just now I...I remember..."

"Jesus Christ, Johnnies," says Amondale. "Of all the days...today's a helluva day to start remembering."

All four look down at their feet and then around at all the others still hanging about.

"Well," Amondale breaks the silence, "then you might've remembered to ask me to borrow a suit for the day."

They all look at Johannes's clothes.

"Still them same old rags," continues Amondale, "and with a big ol' hunk missing right there. No respect at all for the duds I pass on. Maybe it's time for a change, don't you think?"

"Yeah, maybe it is."

"What did you say it was that tore it?"

"A goat."

"What goat? Here in Creek's Ridge?"

"No, I told you. In Texas."

"Oh, sure, right..."

Johannes rests his hand on Ernest's shoulder. "Hey Ern, let's head back to the bar. I need a drink."

Ernest sighs and immediately starts walking toward town. "We'll each have a bottle."

"Goddamn right," says Amondale, following after Ernest.

Caryn looks at Johannes, forcing a smile before heading in the other direction.

"Aren't you coming?" Johannes calls after her.

She stops walking and looks back.

"You boys go on ahead. I might stop by later on. Some things I need to do first."

"Caryn, I wanted to say, to tell you...that you look beautiful today. Despite all this." He sweeps his arm in a broad, all-encompassing gesture.

"Johannes..." She shakes her head and looks down at a crack in the steps. "You should call your sister."

"I know."

"You know, she was...it was...just a joke..."

"Yes."

"How did you...?"

"I remembered."

"When?"

"Today."

She smiles her usual sad smile and nods as she turns away. Just as she turns, Johannes sees it, finally. A lively shine, the aggressive pursuit of desire he has often wished to see in her eyes, has appeared, brought sparklingly clear to the surface, touching and stirring and entwined with her sadness. The trenchant void that had made her inaccessible to Johannes has been replaced with an endearing adoration for life, the acceptance of and respect for loss. Johannes feels a desperate longing to know everything about her—her failed marriage, why she left California, her interest in Creek's Ridge, and her generosity with the church. But not now. And quite possibly not ever. Because there she goes, walking away, right on up the steps and into St. Josephine's.

He watches her disappear behind the doors, and before he turns to go, he realizes that most of the people who were standing idly around them just moments ago are now walking up those same steps and through those same great wooden doors. He watches until the last of them are safely inside. A couple of others are still talking at the bottom of the stairs. Some have gone to stroll through the church grounds, a few others to walk alongside the creek. Johannes heads back into town, alone.

Chapter 50

The Saint

February 3, 1935
Creek's Ridge, Kansas

I HAVE NOT EATEN IN TWELVE DAYS, I REMEMBER, THE DAY MY mother died, eighteen-hundred and fifty, a day, two, before my birthday, the sun shone, a breeze blew, I remember, the cool air, refreshing but not yet cold, the town had prospered, it showed in the men's waists and the women's fabrics, the groom of our horses, when winter arrived it would bring a biting chill, our prosperity provided protection, fires in every home, quilts and animal pelts, I had a favorite, a wolf's hide, a gift, I can still, smell it, feel it, I remember it, it is gone, many years since returned to those who gave it to me, though still wrapped around my shoulders even now, in old age, the way of things, a comfort and a sense of who I was, its soft hairs, musk of the wild, wrapped within it, knowing I am home, safe, feeling my mother by my side, her caresses as she lifts the wolf and slips beneath, embracing me, as I drift, towards sleep, even now, eternal sleep approaches ever nearer, I sense it, I have lived enough, at times the life I wished, as a child perhaps, desired, cherished, desire is for the wicked, I have not eaten in twelve days, I have not slept in three, the pains will not allow it, this life is a punishment, not a test, all who survive past infancy undergo this penance, in answer to a blatant transgression, the pilfering of life from the living earth, the living universe blanketing her, as the wolf blankets me, weak with infirmity, and poverty, what is this chastisement we receive, the agitations of the people, setting each one against all others from the first, and then one discovers power, power over many, or perhaps over one, tipping the weight of the scales for or against us, the weight of an additional punishment, as they pile higher, the mountain, the mountain, there is a saying, I have heard it uttered, that all of life is suffering, loss and suffering, I have lived this life, far longer than I ought, longer than I might have chosen, had I a choice, I have felt loss but once, just once in nigh on a century, it undid me, it altered me, I do not feel that I have suffered, though I have known punishment, for what, the contours of my face, the desires of others, my Shawnee grandfather's endless stream of falsehoods, his ill-mannered treatment of all who entered his presence, his wiles and crafty manipulations over my father who only and always admired him, unerringly, until the day my father died under my own watch and care, the one belief he always held dear as truth was my Shawnee grandfather's honor and esteem, never did he see behind the facade, that conman's mask, displayed to shroud his fraudulent existence, he, my Shawnee grandfather, he too lived a hellish punishment, his ugliness turned peoples' stomachs, his voice a harsh grating, it rasped, choking and coughing and growling as he spoke, the one thing he did well, his power over others, over us, his stories, he had many to tell, stories of all kinds, they enchanted all who listened, swayed us to believe, if only momentarily, whatever he believed or wished us to believe, my Shawnee grandfather, he knew only vengeance, a twisted, petty form of vengeance, wanting only to prolong the suffering of others, to enlist them in helping to unburden his own punishments, to spread his shame and pain across the country, there were, and are, and always have been, many others like him, the pettiness of mankind, an art form passed down from primitive times, this was everything my father meant to cast doubt upon, to expel when he created this Community, but he was only hiding, his own wolf's hide, covering himself, sheltering away from what he knew to be the truths of the world, as mankind has built it, though the Community of Man was my Shawnee grandfather's suggestion, they developed this future together, my father never once questioned his mentor's sincerity, an actual truth-be-told proven false prophet, still my father showered him with praises, his undying trust, never suspecting hidden motives or wicked intentions, my father often told the story of my name, the old woman was uglier even than my Shawnee grandfather, she groaned and cackled with the most unpleasant voice he had ever known, but she saved his life in more ways than one, set him on the path that led him here, creating and nurturing the Community of Man, a responsibility which caused him to neglect me until it was too late, without her deeds and her wisdom he would have perished on the forest floor, lost in those eastern mountains, and along with him everything that poured forth, the Community of Man, its legacy, its failures, its bloodshed, its role in the westering of this nation and the continued expulsion of the land's natural inhabitants, and also me, I myself, the forgotten matron of Creek's Ridge, wasting away without a bite to eat, without energy enough to lift my face or look upon the sun rising another day, desire is a waste of precious breath, the very notion of me would have died in the wilderness if it were not for that woman, Josephine, Josephine, bless you dear godmother, bless and damn you to hell, in all the years he lived, a life saved, my father claimed, he could speak of the memory of that woman's repulsive features, though when he visualized her, he saw only a pure and resplendent beauty, a beauty unmatched even by my mother and myself, so he said, he meant it, I believe he meant it, and more, I believe it, this truth, there is no beauty here, no honor, not here, not in me, perhaps there once was, beauty, to be found in my outward appearance, the physical deformity of perfection, as my Shawnee grandfather often referred to it, to me, but the inner grace of Josephine, my namesake and spiritual godmother, an inner beauty that shines more brightly from within than any physical attribute ever could, this I have lacked, instead of following in her footsteps, I became the spiritual opposite of that woman, in every sense, my mother however, she, I believe, possessed both, true perfection, though I admit my aged mind is frail, perhaps contorting, disfiguring those fragments of life that I care to recall, and also those I do not, just as my father viewed the woman Josephine as a pure and faultless life-giving angel, I too may trick myself unknowingly into similar misconceptions, the incontestably precious beauty possessed by none but my mother, when I try to see her, in my mind, I do not see a woman, I do not see her human form, rather a glow, an ancient and eternal light encapsulating and distributing all that is good, that was my father's greatest mistake, the blunder that cost us everything, I was there, I remember the blood, a day, two, before my birthday, the sun shone, a breeze blew, I ran to embrace her, for she had been gone, missing since the morning, no one had seen her but me, just before they took her, I saw my father raising the weapon, but I didn't understand, I heard a blast, felt the blood spatter my cheek as she bent over, hunched and writhing in pain, in fear, she looked up, caught me in her glare, her lips moving but making no sound, she told me to run, to leave this place, to run from all those people who had collectively raised me, to run from the very concept into which I had been born, they meant to make my life an impossible hell, I must get out, run back to the place from where she had come, I could not then and I cannot now, I would not leave her, she fell after the second shot struck her shoulder, and I did run, I ran to her, I could not leave her side, in all these years I have never been able to leave the memory of her behind, I remain here, the town itself a living reminder, aggravating this memory that hangs over me, a great shadow bringing darkness where there should be light, cold where there might have been warmth, all this time, this fruitless and lonely life, she died then, with me draped across her body, soaking up her blood, no strength left for further words other than, *Run, Josephine, please escape,* those were her last, her death was painful, yes, and quick, my father died in pain as well, though his was slow and drawn long, I watched over him through it all, his limbs quivering with hurt and regrets, it lasted many months, he rarely slept, just as I rarely sleep now, he rarely ate, though likely more often even than me, in those days the sands had not yet come, money and commerce remained strong, there was still food enough to go around, all mouths fed, people still here to watch out for one another, he fell unconscious in the end, as though under a spell, the medicine man's final trick, or my own perhaps, in his unconscious states I spoke to him, I told of many things, the state of the country as it progressed without him, the failure of his town, the name it had taken, a mockery to him, I made sure he finally recognized his greatest mistake for what it was, so he would go to the grave knowing what he had done, people assume ignorance in children, believing they may safely say or do what they please in the presence of the young, that there can be no comprehension, no harm, no risk, they forget that children are yet but sponges, yet unspoiled by the memories that will haunt their lives and carve out their futures, children are supremely curious, blessed with ample time to sit around considering all that they see, and hear, witnessing and truly appreciating the tricks of perception, tracing the relationships and entanglements among complex issues they do not yet understand, therefore free to discover, that pure and bottomless well, a child's curiosity, reaching deep into their core, as easily sullied as the earthen wells, streams, and rivers from which we subsist, I knew, from a young age, I knew, there were plans for me, my life never to be my own, I knew this because they spoke of it in my presence, I heard everything, over the years it grew darker, more sinister, though I did not fully understand the whys or hows, it started to make sense, my role as a bearer of peace, my body as an offering, my life as a sacrifice, discussions took place behind closed doors, whispers through clenched teeth in the shadows, while my father nurtured his fledgling child, his true child, the Community itself, never me, my Shawnee grandfather extended his foul fingers unobserved, touching upon all who would listen, drawing them in with his fantastic stories, myths and legends and histories, twisted and knotted by his bewitching ways with language, before drawing their attention to me, the adorable half-blood of dark skin who wandered the Community barefooted, sharing the innocence of youth and the fraternity of communal living just the same as her mother did, the woman's role, naturally, to placate, to attend, to cure and to mend, to ease the journeys of others, of men, never their own, for men latch on once they taste power, worms, parasites imparting their will to flesh, there were conversations which took place while I still suckled my mother's breasts, before I could walk or experience the world with sense and rationale, I have not eaten in twelve days, or has it been more, thirteen already, a day for each of the apostles and another for the masquerader who corralled them, I would give anything, I would sin a thousand times more, for a single drop of my mother's milk, desire is for the damned, they have forgotten me, the people of this town, a Community of Men no more, nothing, nothing remains but a pathetic creek flowing at the edge of my father's fever dreams, this mockery of everything he held dear, it is fitting, he deserved it, his missteps were many, now it seems the creek has all but run dry, swallowed by the great clouds of sand and dust that have overtaken this land, the gods will have their way, their vengeance and their fun, most of my long life was spent wishing to be left alone, wishing for them to forget, now they have forgotten me, or perhaps they have all left, I do not know which, I am lonely, I see for the first time, that maybe, although my Shawnee grandfather spread lies amongst the tribes, he always claimed to be a prophet, could it be, is it possible that he prophesied this day, my solitude, my pain, my heavy heart, me, as I am, he spoke first to the women of all the tribes, knowing that their voices and opinions would carry weight in their homes, thereby convincing the men who held sway, the gorgeous half-blood daughter, physical manifestation of everything they wished for, she, a claim of the native peoples, she would perform miracles for their fate in a nation reeling and expanding beyond control, this while I still crawled at their feet and nipped at my mother's teat, with these first seeds sown, he then turned his attention to the medicine men and the chiefs, doubt and mistrust are powerful potions and so easily dispersed, this as I learned to walk upright and came to know the various languages that were spoken in those days, because of who I was, for my childish innocence, I was never turned away or ignored, but welcomed, held and coddled, though I had not yet mastered the languages or the truths behind the words, I learned to follow a change in tone, same as any trusted canine, a lowered voice, conspiratorial assertions, an honest desire cannot be concealed when it rises up, much like panic, it is expressed through the pounding of the heart, the lubrication of sweat glands, the agitation of limbs, roving eyes, and eventually, given time, the tongue spills all, or the heart, I stumbled into countless such councils in my search for attention and puerile pleasures, both of which I was given in abundance, my Shawnee grandfather would at times take me into his arms while he spoke to them, speaking of me and holding me up as a prize to be obtained, passing me off to them for a momentary enticement, the taste of an exotic elixir meant to instill loyalty, after a number of years he had convinced enough of the native peoples to encircle the settlement with their secret complicity, then he turned his attentions unto my mother, appealing to her native blood, her native beliefs, the rich and complex history of her people, the Cherokees, telling her that I was one of her kind, that I must be brought up to believe it, that I must be educated in the ways of the natural world, in the traditions that once made her people honored and revered, admired and feared, as gods implanted in the mountains look down upon all others, he decreed it must be me and no other to hasten this return to the natural way of things, my unique heritage and upbringing, my unquantifiable beauty and goodness of heart, I already showed signs of affinity, he said, for the Great Spirits of this land, an obvious aversion to the bastardized form of the Christian faith my father had instituted here, by this time, during these long talks with my mother, I was old enough to understand what was said about me, but without following the devious conspiracy driving such conversations, intelligent enough to recognize the import and urgency lacing their speech, aware that I must remember their words so that later I might decipher the true meanings carried therein, hopefully before it was too late, I was then at a tender age, fully capable of being left on my own, of carrying on friendships away from home, of helping others, of fending for myself and attending to my own intellectual growth, an age also when I was still emotionally dependent upon my mother, I idolized her and wished to remain in her presence, in her embrace, always, until the end of time, still now, this, my one and only wish, I was often with her during these talks, my Shawnee grandfather's lectures, on her lap, or his, amusing myself with some trivial knickknack, always listening, without fully knowing what it entailed, I knew I was to be groomed for marriage and tribal life, the moment puberty struck I would be married to a warrior or a chieftain's son from one of the leading tribes, it is true, at that time and ever since, I was closer to my mother, I identified with her and wished to emulate her, what my Shawnee grandfather sold off as my affection for her native blood and upbringing was nothing more than another of his lies, I was attached to her soul, not to her heritage but to her, she herself, her caring and devoted ways with all people, her lavishing affections upon me, but my father had become distracted by his creation, the survival of the Community required more governance than he ever wished to bestow, his dream was for it to survive on the collective will and cooperation of the people alone, but he found it difficult to let go the reins when the time came, failure terrified him, it was in this overly cautious, controlling, and mistrustful state of mind that he misread the obvious, I knew, I alone knew, my mother never once faltered, nor did she back down from my Shawnee grandfather or the tribal chiefs already vying for my hand, she sat through those conversations with the so-called prophet, responding and carrying on rationally while he spouted his baseless predictions, she never once considered his plan, she sat with him anyhow, knowing it was her obligation to dissuade him, to assert her power over him by showing that she would not be manipulated, that it was not possible, that she would raise her daughter to know only freedom, freedom of choice and of will, of thought and expression, of amorous devotion and unbreakable loyalty, all qualities the Community of Man was meant to represent, I would never be held down by my heritage because I would grow knowing that I was neither Cherokee nor Spanish nor American, I was a woman who would discover herself, by herself and for herself, as her parents had, my mother believed these things, she had been leading me down those paths since she first held me in her arms, I do not know whether it was my Shawnee grandfather himself or others of the tribes, they recognized my mother as an obstacle, all harbored affectionate feelings toward her, she had at some point directly helped all of them in one form or another, but they had also been convinced of a duty, and they believed that obstacles must be removed, a rumor let loose, that it was she, my mother, who had worked tirelessly to ensure my eventual marriage away from the bosom of the Community, a union meant to crack the foundation of what my father had built, rumors spread as a pestilence, in the strong there is strength to ignore the worst of it, but the weak carry it, pass it unto others, allowing it to seep unseen and widespread through minds and hearts, even this can only sow doubts and mistrust, given time it must enter the realm of the personal, relatable and threatening to each and all, the story as it has been written, to bury the truth alongside my mother, it was consumption, her insides wracked by that vile disease, though the story accepted by most, equally fatuous and unfounded, says that she contracted rabies after being attacked by a coyote, and therefore had to be put down herself, those of vivid imagination have sometimes claimed it was my father who, having discovered her intentions and transgressions, employed those under guidance of my Shawnee grandfather to agitate a rabid beast and set it upon her, such are the tales men and women create to quench their thirst, to tie up loose threads, to avoid staring at the truth, I have carried the truth within me, I have told others, then and after, none would believe me, just a child at the time, naive and innocent and blithe, without experience or guidance, no understanding of the ways in which adults navigate the thorniest of briars, but I do, and I did, I have seen darkness, I watched as they fed it to her, I sensed evil in that room, ominous intentions, the smell of death rose from the concoction they mixed, I tried to stop it and was silenced for the first time, taken out and led away, and she restrained, I cannot say what it was, from time to time there were travelers from the south and the west, they brought with them precious plants, dried slices of certain types of cacti, flowers and wild mushrooms, perhaps it was these or the liquors they had shipped in by the barrels, forced upon my mother, initially sedating her, but when she woke, she was not herself, transformed, as a creature or a demon, some said, though they would later retract these claims, pretending she had been calm, meek as a lamb, that I concede, her soul was indeed meek, but a lamb who senses it is being sent up for the slaughter, this lamb willing to fight back, whatever foul mixture they gave her that morning wrenched and twisted her features, set upon her unnatural visions and horrid sensations palpable to none but her, as her screams and cries grew more horrific, as her frantic mannerisms and labored movements became more grotesque, she was then set loose, into the Community, to the very same people who spread the whispered rumors that led to her downfall, those voices left to dwell and make of it what they would, afraid to approach, afraid to touch, unwilling to comfort or come to the aid of one of their own, of the woman who had once hoisted all the burdens of this town upon her shoulders, alone, in that state she had become a physical representation of their guilt, their willing but underhanded participation in the charade, this they feared, my father would afterward claim that he did not intend to shoot my mother, in his heart he believed she could be cured of whatever ailment had befallen her, instead it was me, my own childish instinct to run to her in that moment, to run to my own mother as she plodded erratically down the main street, when he saw me, he knew he could not allow whatever had infected her to contaminate his flesh and blood, therefore he pulled the trigger, very much as I ran to my mother, without thought or reason, commanded by something deeper, duty, morality, an action pure as life itself, unexplained and unexplainable, as wolves pack together, hunt and howl, gather behind their leader, and yet, in the years following, as he struggled to come to terms with his actions that day, not a single gunshot, but two, a new truth birthed in his mind, a whispered word perhaps, the last of my

Shawnee grandfather's tricks, a way for him to dispel his guilt, to deny his involvement, from then on he placed all blame upon me, I alone had caused this, fate had linked me to his finger on that trigger, but even fate could not be held to blame, it was me, me alone, as I would be forever more, as I am now, as she was then, dying, alone, he forsook me, he loathed me, he wished to be rid of me, it was he who finally pushed to have me married out of the Community, into a tribe that would take me away, further west, he did not hide it, though in his journals he failed to record it, his untruths ran deep, the legacy he meant to make, and so it was I who brought about the disturbance with the tribes, I caused the raids, the deaths, by using the very underhanded treachery they had once eaten from my Shawnee grandfather's filthy fingertips, which I learned by watching and listening to him all those years, I defied my father's intentions whilst feigning willing participation, for while he had placed the blame upon me, I did the same, I blamed him in return, never a trace of forgiveness sown, the day he shot my mother, he set a fire within me, the day he let it be known that he resented me, he stoked that fire into a furious blaze, so I disrupted the trust amongst the tribes and the Community, after which, with his failure secured, his faith, his sanity, his hope, all of him, destroyed, I kept him alive, strive though he did against this life, I ensured he remained shackled to it when the only thought he still possessed was escape, all his ill-fated attempts to evade responsibility, I denied him every opportunity to take flight, though I dangled that tempting fruit before him, this he deserved, as he had done unto me, he would not leave without bearing witness to the hell he had set loose upon the earth, my father, when he killed my mother, he did not feel the surge of power that accompanies the taking of a human life, he did not taste mastery over his humanity, he was born a wanderer, a scavenger, a solitary, he may have been better off to have remained so, lost in the forests, alone, like his savior, Josephine, no leader was he, neither as head of a community nor head of a home, no less fraudulent than the Shawnee prophet, though for me, born here, surrounded by the first residents of the Community and then growing up upon an elevated platform, above them, revered by them as some divine blessing, a gift for them and their frontier wilds, the very success or failure of their lives and livelihoods dependent upon my daily progress and kindnesses, simple folk, each without an idea of their own, no different than the Natives who once followed the word and cause of the Shawnee prophet, those who died fawning over his and his brother's lies, I was indeed raised into and amongst those people, nurtured by them and attended by them while my mother and father busied themselves with the establishment and legitimizing of the settlement, the very circumstances of my birth set me amongst them and demanded I lead, yet as I came of age my own father meant to throw me to the wolves, it was later, when I stabbed through the heart and cut the throat of the Cherokee warrior, organizer and leader of the raids upon us, it was then that I felt my thirst quenched for the first time, the thirst that had arisen from the heat of the fire my father set, I felt power over the Cherokee warrior, over every warrior who stood there gawking, over every member of the Community who cowered behind the walls of this very church, I underwent sensations I had never known, a lightness of the soul, ecstasy, divinity, purpose, peace, it was then that I understood my Shawnee grandfather's unshakable lust for power and control over others, for it fundamentally alters what one's life is and must be thereafter, power becomes the one and only thing that matters, a craving that must be satiated, pleasure of pleasures, I wished for, I sought only a single revenge, I have often been tempted in the many years since, and I have devoured the fruit, gladly have I repeated that sin, though for me it was no such thing, but rather a cool balm, an anesthetic upon an open wound, one that has often required reapplication throughout the years, I made sure that my father knew who I was, knew what he had created, I showed him grim trophies, described their silent agonies, their prayers and last minute repentances, my father was weak, frail of body and of faith, his faith scattered between here and his birthplace, never certain to whom or what he must pray, the Christian father, Christ the son, the holy spirit, the Great Spirit of the Cherokees or the Shawnees, the natural gods of the Seminoles, the furious sea or the alluring mountain, the crone Josephine, or me myself, flesh and blood, I heard him utter confused prayers to each in turn, at times one after another, at times all together, as one, a single contradictory and heretical utterance, representative of all he had become, he feared the life he had constructed for himself, he feared me, he feared an afterlife of such varied divine retribution, I never hurt him, I kept him alive to suffer with his thoughts, his knowledge of me, his memories, a personal torture of truth slowly suffocating his final years on this earth, those, his final thoughts carrying him through into an uncertain hereafter, the weight of his own conscience and all that he had wrought dragged behind him for all eternity, a stench that can never be washed clean, a pain that can never be diminished, memories scorched into the eyes of his soul, as my death nears, I feel it, though unlike him I know who I am, just as many another, once I was misguided, searching, until the moment my blade pierced that Cherokee's chest, as I felt his warm blood soaking through my garments and running over my flesh, I knew who I truly was, I have embraced what I am, I have not followed fraudsters and masqueraders, I have not bowed before unseen spirits or howled to gain the acceptance of higher powers, I have satisfied my urges and buried their bodies along the creek that has given this town its name, desire is all that I am, I have instilled fear and awe into others and they have left me to my devices, forgiven me because they believed me to be their savior, I did not kill the Cherokee war chief for their sake, but for my own, same with each one I have laid hands on since and would do yet, had I the strength, I have not eaten in fifteen, eighteen days, I have never eaten the flesh or drank the blood of Christ, I cannot sleep, cannot release these memories of a life, there is no guilt, I know what I have done, I know who I am, who I was, fear is the price of life, I am resigned to death, I am satisfied with the pleasures inherent in my deeds, my mind is, it is, absolutely clear, though a single regret remains, my cowardice, to leave, the mountains I have long wished to see, the oceans, to believe, now it is too late, my age, my strength, fails me, I have never left this place, not once, nor will I, my end is near, I wish only to leave, as my father wished to do before me, though I would not let him, I kept him here against his deepest instincts to flee, in the end our purest desires were the same, to escape this, to scale the mountains where my mother was raised, to unite with her there, the mountain, the mountaintop, paradise, I have never seen

Chapter 51

Jo's Last Stand

A FEW LONELY INDIVIDUALS ARE SPREAD OUT AMONGST THE TABLES, by themselves or in small groups, and speaking low, if at all. Ernest and Amondale are at the bar as usual, with their personal bottles already opened. Everyone looks up, their low spirits momentarily elevated by surprise as they stare, not at Johannes, but at the pickax resting on his shoulder.

"What'd you bring that thing in here for?" Ernest pulls out another bottle and a glass and hands them to Johannes. "Again..."

"You had to dig?" growls Amondale. "Today?"

Johannes lays the ax on the bar top and sits down beside Amondale. "I just stopped by the house. Picked it up."

"But what for?"

"Comfort," Johannes shrugs. "Peace of mind."

"Lunatic..." Ernest stares at the ax and sighs. "Anyway," he turns to Amondale, "you think there's any truth to it?"

Amondale sips his Scotch. "Both true and not true, I'd say. Gotta give some credence to the rumors. With his history and all, you know, and nothing concrete to discredit them..."

"What's true-not-true?" asks Johannes.

"That vandalism," Ernest takes a drink, "occurred, what? A few weeks ago, down at George's Grocery."

"Hit the warehouse, too," says Amondale. "Same night."

"There've been rumors...that it might've been..."

"Couple'a doped-up adolescents have been saying they saw it. Juvenile delinquents, probably. Could just as easily have been the other way round."

"What? He saw them do it?"

"And then let them go. Why not?"

"I'm sure our resident investigative journalist could dig up some evidence..."

"Damn right, I could. Always thought I'd make for a decent private dick. Not this time, though. No point. Not anymore."

"What about you?" Ernest asks Johannes. "He say anything to you? Before he..."

Johannes shakes his head and pulls the cork from his bottle.

"See what I mean?" says Amondale. "We can't even talk about him openly, so why bother? He did it, he didn't do it. Same thing at this point, far as I can tell. People will believe what they believe."

Ernest shrugs, drinks.

Johannes asks Ernest to play the Scrap on the piano. Ernest refuses. Johannes gets up to put the record on, but by the time he returns to his barstool, Ernest has shut it off, murmuring, "No room for music today." Amondale offers no opinion but only stares reflectively into the mirrors and sips his Scotch. They spend the next hour or so drinking The Carnival, avoiding eye contact, with nothing much to say and no games to play except the solitary games of memory. Johannes attempts to dredge the Scrap from the overflowing bog of his mind, the sludge of past and present commingled and uncooperative. Occasionally, and to the irk of the others, he'll begin humming fragments of the melody.

"Hey, Ern?" says Johannes. "I saw something today that reminded me of your piano."

"What about it?"

"Those carvings, that same style of line or texture...I don't even know what to call it. Static motion. I keep seeing it in different places around town. Sonny's stump is done in the same way. And there's this marble slab inside the church with the same flowing, linear design. Father Marover told me it was done by the same person who made the statue of Saint Josephine."

"All the work of the same fella," nods Ernest. "Local craftsman. I thought you knew him?"

"Who?"

"Mr. Vu."

"Vu? Doctor Mengele's owner?"

"Huh?"

"The German shepherd."

"Hero? Right, yeah, that's his dog. I thought its name was Hero..."

"But those carvings, his work is so delicate, so sensitive, how could he..."

"Master of his craft," says Ernest. "He's internationally renowned. Gets commissioned from all over the globe. You never met him?"

"But how could someone like that...beat his dog?"

"Huh?"

"Goddamnit!" Amondale slams down his glass, splashing its contents all over the bar top. The people seated at the tables gaze toward the bar as Amondale glares at Johannes. "I want a fucking answer."

Ernest grabs a rag to dry himself and wipe down the countertop.

"To what?" says Johannes.

"To my question."

"What question?"

"The question I asked you last week when we all found out, and you just got up and walked out of here like...like you just lost your job...like your goddamn dog just died...like...like...goddamnit!"

Johannes expects a shrug from Ernest, but Ernest only stares at him, serious as all hell. Through the mirrors behind the bar, he can see the others all watching him as well.

"What question?"

"To refresh your Swiss cheese brain then," Amondale gasps, "the question, as uttered by these very lips, was—What in the almighty hell is wrong with you?"

Johannes's reflections in the mirrors possess eyes just as persecutory as Amondale's or anyone else's, and the sudden silence reminds him of the silence inside St. Josephine's.

"I have a question, too," Johannes says into the mirrors. He swivels slowly to look at both Amondale and Ernest. "I tried to tell you. As soon as we heard the news, I came here specifically to tell the two of you. I didn't know what else to do. I had to... So why didn't either of you believe me?"

Ernest looks down at his glass and then at Amondale.

"Well, you see, John the Baptist," starts Amondale, "there's this notion floating around amongst the good people of this town that you're a bit loony. Loose in the screws. No offense, but you get my drift. You wouldn't be the first psychological sacrifice of the place, and certainly not the last. To be blunt, openness is not your finest trait. Which naturally brings trust into question."

"You're probably right..." Johannes nods and takes a drink. "But then why did you believe Pa Sonny?"

"Because Sonny, for all his peculiarities, is morally reliable. He has social tact, when he's sober. And even when he's not, at least he has a motive."

"Didn't you hear him today? Ranting, rambling, quoting this and that?"

"I did," says Amondale. "Listened very carefully. I'm still trying to figure out Dunmore Judson, the man. He's an intriguing question mark. And once I come across a riddle, it's difficult to let go."

"You've been searching in the wrong place," says Johannes.

"What's that supposed to mean? That story he tells people? About a woman and child? It's not true. What? He fooled you with that, too? Nope. All trails end in Creek's Ridge."

"Suit yourself," says Johannes. "But Grant's didn't."

They all three look down into their glasses before taking a drink.

"Asshole..." mumbles Amondale.

"And Pa Sonny's doesn't, either. He was headed south when he came here. You want to solve that mystery, start there."

"Where? Texas?"

Johannes nods.

"Jesus stepped on a fire ant—can't you be any more specific than that?"

"Boys, let's leave Sonny alone for now," says Ernest. "He ain't done nothing wrong except to give an honest voice to his grief. That's more than you can say for any of the rest of us, I'd wager. And not everything he had to say was ranting and rambling. He expressed more than a few heartfelt sentiments, better than we could have. Some odd quotations, to be sure, but appropriate, I thought. Like to know where he gets them."

"Beyond my range of knowledge, Hemmy." Amondale refills his glass. "Some of it sounded Eastern to me. Buddha? Confucius? Sun Tzu? Mao's little red book, for all I know. You might ask Vu. He would—"

"It was Hindu," says Johannes. "The Bhagavad Gita."

"What's this?" says Ernest. "Another memory out of the blue? All on your own?"

"Poor Grant," moans Amondale. "He's dying a thousand deaths himself right about now. Heart attack after heart attack as he listens to us bicker, watching from the afters as Johnny-come-lately remembers every last little thing, and Sonny off in the deep end thrashing about with his esoteric nonsense. You should have heard him babble on after you disappeared from the park. Holy shit, just like a monkey in a library. Complete crap, most of it, but if the man knows one thing, it's public speaking. Christ, he can make anything sound enticing. Wrapped his fingers right around all these buffoons. Talking about...what was it, Thelonious?"

"Oh, let's see," says Ernest, "there were camels. Reincarnation and toxic waste. Something about raising children, stealing from and giving to those we love. Ants and boots. Jackrabbits, I think, and coyotes. Truth and despair, horses running to and fro, skull and bones. Rain and wind and boats. The picking of locks. Theft, responsibility, loyalty, and then a bit about...sexual awakenings, was it? Or failings? Tough to make heads or tails of a lot of it."

"Goddamn, check out the memory on Mr. Monk here. That was impressive. I could use someone like you on my staff. You taking notes, John Schmo?"

Johannes tilts his glass to Ernest.

"It's nothing," Ernest shrugs. "That's what happens when you spend your life shuffling music notes around your head all the damn time."

"And what were you doing all that time anyway?" Amondale barks at Johannes. "Where'd you run off to? Just who in the hell do you think you are?"

"St. Josephine's. I've never been inside before, not in all these months. So I went in, and I..."

"Yeah?"

"I had a chat with Father Marover."

"Huh..." huffs Ernest. "Never pegged you as the religious type."

"I'm not."

"And so when do you think you might get around to answering my question?" spits Amondale.

Johannes holds up his hands as he swallows a mouthful of The Carnival. "Did you hear what Pa Sonny was saying about storms?"

"Cyclones," nods Ernest.

"Paradise in the eye," Amondale groans.

"That's what I was trying to do on the mountain. I was trying to attain the peace of mind that can only be found at the center of a storm. Of myself. I needed to find it because I was running. And Pa Sonny, he knew. I don't know how much he knew, but he knew. He knows. I think Grant did, too."

"Sonny might be a lost cause," says Amondale, "but you're not. We can help you figure it all out. Puzzles beg to be solved."

"Like your horse bones," adds Ernest.

"Exactly," shouts Amondale. "Just like those damn bones. But that is, now, a literal dead venture. Excuse the...damnit Oscarcito...I apologize for that. Just...not today, alright? No bone talk today. I think we all need a rest from that for a while. That waterfall of yours, though..."

"The bones were only a distraction," says Johannes, shaking his head. "Something Grant and I had to work through together before we even considered working out our differences. But the dig...it became something more."

"You're not planning to keep it up, are you?" asks Amondale. "That digging?"

"You and Grant had differences?" says Ernest.

Johannes nods and looks away into the mirrors, expecting to see her face again, clear and real as it appeared in the holy water. "I don't think Grant wanted me here at all."

"Imagine that..." Ernest turns around to see what Johannes is staring at.

Only mirrors, reflections.

"Grant was better off without me. I knew that once..."

"And that's why you went...?" starts Amondale.

"Into the mountains," Johannes nods again. "To release him, and myself, from the anguish of my mistakes. That was supposed to be the end. Not this. Not like this..."

"Solitary life in the mountains, though... That's a funny place to escape to, isn't it?" Amondale stares into his glass as he swirls the ice gently round and round. "A place where the only person is yourself. You ought to have found a new life. With people, I mean. Some urban jungle where there are distractions enough for all the weaknesses and transgressions of man. Escape yourself by disappearing into yourself? What is that? For most people entertaining such convoluted ideas, there's only one way out, you know?"

"Suicide..." reflects Ernest.

"Sure as hell a lot more definitive than this mess you've gotten yourself into," Amondale points accusingly at Johannes through the mirrors.

"I know," Johannes is nodding, remembering. "And I wanted to. During the landslide and after, I wanted to. In the face of failure, we become desperate, we start to reach for things that aren't there. That's what Pa Sonny was talking about. The danger, the torrent, the disorientation—all implied by our perception and participation in the world. Our own reactions to the ups and downs, the highs and lows, successes and defeats. In order to reach the peace and tranquility at the center of it all, you have to fight your way there. Just as when you trek through the mangy, tangled underbrush in the thick of a jungle, you must wield a machete, clear a path, leave your mark. The starting point of all creation is destruction. So, maybe the mountain did me a favor by chucking me off its slopes. Then again, if I'd lasted longer than those seven short years, if I could have persisted in chipping away, little by little, maybe then I would have arrived at the place I sought, emerged as the person I wished to become. Gone on to become faceless, nameless."

"What?" splurts Amondale, The Carnival dribbling down his chin. "Like an animal?"

"Why not?" Johannes shrugs. "At least then I wouldn't have come back here. And Grant wouldn't have...you know. Since the landslide, I have lived with constant fear. A certainty of the unknown. As though someone or something was constantly hovering over me, wherever I was, crouching around every corner, watching from within every shadow and beneath every trunk, stump, and branch. From up in the canopy and below the water's surface, creeping along noiselessly behind me, beside me. Fleeing that fear, I left the mountain. I believed the natural order had turned against me. I was not strong enough to end my life then and there. My fear was too great, and it drove me out. But after just a few days on the road, not knowing where I was going or who I was trying to find, I started to think it was not the finite world of the mountain producing my fear, but the world itself. The entire world, its incomprehensible size and scope, its twists and turns so impossible to navigate. Nothing like a simple, modest life on a mountaintop. But, with Pa Sonny's help, I made my way here, and I found comfort in sticking close to Grant, digging with him, sitting and reminiscing over events and people I had no memory of. He gave me food and shelter, asking nothing in return. He allowed me an easy, moderated transition into this new life. And although he sometimes pushed me to identify the questions and puzzles of my past, he never forced it. At times, I got the feeling that he already knew all the answers but that he enjoyed the game of trying to make me remember on my own. And, as strange as our pursuit for the horse bones was, it was still a healthy pastime that brought us closer together and allowed me some introspection, too. He even got me out and interacting with people again, persuaded me to pursue a fruitless relationship with Caryn and, in a different way, with Sammy."

"Who's Sammy?" blurts Ernest.

"Remembered that too, did you?" says Amondale.

Johannes nods into the mirrors and drinks.

"Wait, what?" Amondale gapes at Johannes. "I meant that as a joke. You mean they never fessed up? Grant never...? And she never...? No one ever told you?"

"What's this about now?" says Ernest.

Johannes looks at them both, shakes his head, and shrugs.

"That was a nasty trick they pulled," continues Amondale. "And not even a very good one. Obvious from the start. Although Grant never admitted it to me either, not until she'd been gone for a week. By then, I already knew, of course."

"How?" asks Johannes.

"It's my profession. Mysteries are my forte. What do you think I do all day, diddle myself? No sir, I find things out."

"How about a few missing horse bones?"

"I am not going to dig with you, if that's what you're getting at. Physical labor is not in my wheelhouse. And I thought I said no goddamn bone talk today? Not today. You got it?"

Johannes looks away and nods. "Yeah, got it."

"Your mountain, on the other hand, that might hold a real key. If we could take a trip out there someday, you and me, you might show me around. I'd like to gather some notes, grab some shots, confirm a hunch or two."

"What hunch?"

"Your waterfall, for one. Been doing some rereading of Del Bosque's journals, you know, and I've begun to suspect that it's one and the same. *The* waterfall, if you follow me. Just imagine the chances of that, huh?"

"Same as what?"

"Why, the start of this. All of this—"

"Who in the hell is Sammy?" yells Ernest in a rare show of frustration.

"Remember Lani Vals?" says Amondale. "Well, there is no Lani Vals. Never was."

"She's Sammy," says Johannes. "She used that alias when we were kids, playing games, fooling people, just goofing around. She's my sister."

"Shit..." says Ernest. "Imagine that..."

"Right..." says Amondale.

All three refill their glasses from their personal bottles and take personal, unacknowledged drinks.

"The most important thing Grant shared with me," Johannes continues, "was the stability of Creek's Ridge and the support he received from its people. He made sure I was a part of it and that I benefitted without being the slightest bit deserving. And I have benefitted. Although the fear has persisted, I have felt as though everyone in Creek's Ridge is witness to it and sharing the burden. And here, where I got to know you all, I have felt safe. I can talk and also disengage, lose myself in the music, the sound of your voices. Drink enough of The Carnival so that I don't think and don't dream, so I don't see the landslide or the dogs chasing me every time I close my eyes. So I don't run screaming from all these faces staring back at me," Johannes swings his hand around the room to indicate the mirrors, "pressuring me for answers."

All three of them, as well as the others seated at the tables, glance apprehensively around the room, at each other, at the faces in the mirrors.

"The day Grant's dad called, I felt dejected and confused. We all did. But loss... I did not feel loss. I knew I was supposed to, but I didn't. I don't. Everyone else feels it, and in their minds I must suffer it more severely because I was his friend. Childhood friends. Those harmless games of youth. Except what no one seems to realize is that we're not young anymore. And I wasn't even a good friend. He didn't need me, didn't want me here. He was so much better off all that time without me."

"He had an enormous heart," says Ernest. "Welcomed you with open arms..."

"His heart was cleaved in two. And the first thing he did when I arrived was unload me. Handed me off to Oscar."

Amondale looks up, remembering, nodding in affirmation. "He did indeed. Damn...I never caught onto that. And then I brought you here..."

"And in the past week, I have had to return to his house every night. Grant's house. I use his shower, his kitchen, his personal items, and the cash he left lying around. I sleep there, not well, not consistently, but I have slept some. Still on the floor. I try to dig, alone, but the enjoyment is gone. All that's left now is something like duty. Responsibility. I miss Grant. I wish to see him again. I need him just as much as I did the day Pa Sonny brought me to Creek's Ridge. But still, I do not feel the excruciating emptiness of loss. Because, without Grant, cruel as it may sound, my entire world has become less convoluted. As though I am bound to nothing, to no one. And I began to think I had shed the haunting presence that pursued me, the fear. Because of everything I've been through in the past few months, because of everything Grant has done for me, I understand myself and the world more clearly. I've touched upon a certain appreciation for life that I never had on the mountain, the desire to absorb it and pamper it and watch it grow...like my own child. To let it reach its arms out. To see and touch and be a part of the world, not to be secluded away, hiding, running. This is, possibly, the freedom that I have always wanted."

"Good on you, then, I guess..."

"Only...the cost is too high. It's not right. It wasn't his debt to pay. We've both fallen, Grant and I, but somehow we've landed the wrong way round."

"A terrible price," says Ernest, nodding. "For all of us. Creek's Ridge'll never be the same."

"Freedom ain't free, pal," Amondale drinks.

"Grant didn't owe me anything. He wanted to turn me out, and he should have. He had every right to."

"What are you getting at?" says Amondale. "What the hell did you do?"

Johannes looks at their faces but avoids their eyes. He peeks over his shoulder and sees that, yes, everyone in the bar is still watching as well. Watching and listening. The countless Johanneses in the mirrors included.

"Today...in St. Josephine's..."

"First-rate building, that," Amondale raises his glass. "An absorbing history. Glad that nutcase Sonny caved in to the demands of propriety..."

Johannes stumbles, his mouth and tongue gone numb. He shuts his eyes and the landslide has ended, the ground and water have settled into the shape of her soft rounded features, sharp cheekbones framing full lips, small nose and ears, the flora of the mountain slopes darkened into wavy black hair, wild in chaotic long strands, and large round eyes full of life and love, glimmers of starlight in the natural spring, her slim neck gracefully curving into angular shoulders and the shallow valley of her backbone and everything beautiful below, her midriff and lower back alive with the vibrant colors of flowers, greens, and feathers tattooed there, the constant sensual gurgle of the stream, her womanhood awash with the clarity and profundity of life itself, the playfully seductive charm in her voice, calling out to him, *Johannes, Johannes...that melody...a bittersweet dream...just like you and me...we sent him off...get off the floor...keep humming...turn out the light...we killed him...together...come back to bed...come back to me...I have a confession...remember...*

"So what was it in there?" says Amondale. "Finally found God? Had your religious epiphany? Woke up and smelled the incense?"

"Something like that," Johannes opens his eyes, evaporating the memory. "I stepped in there thinking about Grant, about everything Pa Sonny had been saying, about life here in Creek's Ridge. About trying to find a way and a means to get out. I actually felt proud and a bit envious of Grant because he did it—he got out. I was glad to be away from everyone for a little while but also comforted by the knowledge that I could return. That I would return. But there I was, trudging up those old steps. And then, once I was inside, memories came to me of their own volition, as naturally as I suppose they are meant to. I remembered bits and pieces of my life. A strained friendship with Grant, with my sister...and with Inez. I knew, intrinsically, about myself and Pa Sonny. How he raised me, in a way. I remembered the names of the Disciples—Philip, Thaddeus, and the one that was missing. I remembered things about myself that had been buried on the mountain. And I suddenly understood that the fear had never left me. The fear was me. Johannes Metternich is made entirely of that fear. John Metternich, me, myself, and all of these others," he points so aggressively at the mirrors that he's drawn onto his feet, startling everyone when his barstool tilts back and crashes to the floor. "These variations on a form, on a theme, variations influenced by and influencing the world, the people and situations...that made me. Grant had a single path through life. He had it mapped out a long time ago, and he could not deviate from it. He sometimes faltered, but he always kept it in his sights, always moving towards it. That was both his strength and his weakness. He wanted—he cared for—only one thing in this life. And I took that from him."

"Took what?" says Amondale.

"The one person he needed for his life to be complete. It didn't even matter whether he could ever have her back. All Grant needed was the thought, the possibility. If it had been anybody other than me, the possibility would have remained alive, the dream of his paradise would have flourished, and everything would have been okay. Sometimes, I guess, that's all we need, our childish fantasies. But not me. It could not be me taking that away from him. And because it was me, that careful balance that governed his one dream was shattered. And I knew it would be. She knew it, too. But we...Inez and I...we went on with it anyway. Behind Grant's back, two thousand miles from here. At the time, we thought it wouldn't matter. So far away, time and people move on, life moves on, and so should we—all the excuses we could come up with. But life moves on differently for some. All people carry the weight of their burdens at their own pace. For Grant, it was pain and jealousy. For me, it was the guilt, more intense than what I ever felt for her. But he...that's all he felt, nothing else. Everything he felt was for Inez. So I left. Just like I always have. But I always came back in the past. This time, I shouldn't have. For Grant, I shouldn't have...and I meant not to. I knew what I had done, what Grant needed and deserved. But I... When the landslide came, I failed him..."

"Grant knew?" says Ernest. "About you and..."

"Inez...?" Amondale finishes what Ernest could not.

"He knew enough," says Johannes. "Enough to confront me...but he wouldn't, he couldn't...he didn't. Grant was too good of a man. Or too afraid of the emotional consequences for himself if he did. He wanted us to remember our youth and innocence so that we could both escape to those days when we were always knee-deep in some project of negligible significance. When the worst we got up to was to steal a bit of booze from Pa Sonny or our parents. He didn't want me to remember everything because of what it would have meant for him, too. Still, he couldn't silence his own memories. So, he went back there. He was only trying to return to the best time in his life. He went back to her, to Inez. Because of me."

Amondale clears his throat. "What will you do now?"

"Just gotta move on," says Ernest. "Nothing else for it, really. Sonny offered you a job. Imagine that, huh? You, sheriff, over all this... You could pay your tab. And people around here, you know, they would love for you to stick around. I mean, if that's what you...to become something more, to fill the void—"

"Not yet," says Johannes. He reaches out and rests his hand on the handle of the pickax.

"What?" Amondale squeals, jutting upright on his barstool. "You want to keep digging for that goddamn horse?"

"I have to finish what we started. I don't know how yet, but the Limping Lady deserves to be put together again. And then put to rest." Johannes lifts the pickax and holds it out before him, gazing at it fondly, twisting it slowly, lovingly in his hands. "*This* is what the digging was always about. Not him, not me, not Inez, but something larger than all of us. Something that both separated us and held us together. Conceptually, I will find every last bone, no matter how much dirt I have to dig. Grant would have done the same. And I think, despite everything, he would expect me to. Any help that either of you or anyone else wants to offer, I will gladly accept. But I don't deserve it. This burden rests on me. It's the only way I can...atone for my errors. But not today. Today, this ax is not for atoning. Today, it's for honoring the dead. And today, you can help me if you want, or you can stand by and watch, but you can't stop me. And you'd better tell them to leave."

"What are you on about, you crazy asshole?" says Amondale.

"Ern," says Johannes, "tell them to go."

"What? Who?"

Johannes looks into the mirrors across from him, directing Ernest's eyes to the other silent drinkers seated at the tables, all of them gawking at the three men by the bar and wondering what's in the works.

"Grant hated these fucking mirrors," says Johannes.

Chapter 52

The Carnival

They're gone, for now, though they wait outside, just beyond the door, shut behind and locking them out, their silhouettes visible opposite frosted glass, muffled grumbles of discontent, the unfairness of it all, shitty days gotten worse with this unreasonable slight and nowhere else to go, so they'll just hang around on the sidewalk and curse, shout and complain to passers-by, the dark curtain of mourning drawn up, dragging along behind them on the ground, Christ, this town...

It takes some convincing, after all, the owner of the bar none too keen for chaos, demolition, or loneliness. The mirrors, a dream he'd nurtured since he was a kid, just starting out and lost in a world of smoke and jazz and echoes of the past, a reflective bar far from home, New Orleans or someplace like that, steeped in tradition and history, down south where it all began, but not where it will end.

And the journalist, the historian, the author, is not quite drunk enough yet, not for this. A little far-fetched, a little beyond the boundaries of decorum, a little unhinged even for the grief-stricken, isn't it? But their drink of choice provides him the courage to be honest—though the drink itself is nothing but a farcical felonious fabrication, not even honest in its representation of itself—and the irony is not lost on a man of letters.

The man without memories remembers, has recognized himself in the mirrors, then and now, though reconciliation and restoration are no longer possible, restitution and forgiveness irretrievable. Still, the possibility remains to regain a hold upon himself, remembered but not yet clenched with utter confidence. He knows what needs to be done, but the others are fickle—just think of the mess, the cleanup, the sharp edges. Imagine the noise, the cost, the potential for spilled blood, and the resulting stains. What will people say, what will they think, how could they ever relate?

By and by, the man without memories convinces the others of what is right, what is fair, an offering, last respects, moving on, payment on demand. The trio prepares to take to the stage, to manage the salvage, the salvation of a man.

For this is Carnival, a sea of heads as far as eyes can reach, costumed, of course, but lacking festive colors and true depth, decked out instead for a celebration of death, to part ways with a life lived, at times lived well, other times not so, but lived nonetheless, never a lost breath, never a missed chance to wish for what has passed.

But just for a moment, a more comprehensive view, a panoramic thought, from the mountaintop, if you will. A town on the fringe and the people therein. A nation, creating means by wresting faith from the naturally ensconced peoples of the land. Several friendships, intertwining paths, unique identities built of glass, filled with shadows, glimmers, shimmers, whispers of hope and a future's sweet repast. A light glints in the cracks, distracts, contracts. Blemishes acquired here and there, distortions of facts, misrepresentations at every step. Fragile worlds and lives sheltered behind, spit-shined and streaked, squeaking and bleak, rap on the pane asking to be let in, or stand by observing, admiring, critiquing, and swooning. A misfit, torn down and reformed by powers other than his own, trapped and molded by his own pathetic lot, controlled by alcoholic diffidence and Sweet Everlasting stasis beneath thumbs of all colors—and yet, reborn, awakened, elevated, and leading the charge. A vagrant, an oceanic crossing, listing and swashing in an element unfamiliar, but a choice all his own, tempestuous risks and demands, the Voice of God braced by gunshots and cannon fire—then led north to safety, foundation, love, and admiration, though misfortunes rarely fade entirely. A runaway who fled once, then fled again, back to the friend with whom it began, the disintegration of respect, the rotting seeds of love and regret, until nothing is left but the bones of the past, not even an end to what they began. Languages blend, friendships bend, mentors transcend, histories contend, and time wears the feathers of suffering eternally upon its head. The shape of the world lies in their control to manipulate as they see fit. Not to be shown or told, not to fall in line and walk the selfsame road, nor to be pigeonholed and buried beneath the history of some self-effacing dot on the map. Not to give in when the mountain falls. Because sacrifice begets absolution, and are they not, each of them, guilty to some extent? So take up arms, declare fealty to the natural order of life and death, loyalty to the discourse between the waters of Lethe and consciousness, humility against the passage of breath.

The man without memories tightens his grip around the handle of his ax.

The barman has an old baseball bat, protection against hoodlums and rats.

The journalist, a chair, held aloft by the backrest.

Blindly we move forward, and blindly, too, shall we look back.

During Carnival, the festival-goers dance, they pound out their rhythms and chant, they revel and debauch the proprieties of life, lives well-rounded but begging temporary escape, to let loose for an hour, for a day, for a week, for a final chance to taste the fruits before the fast, before, at long last, the resurrection comes to pass. Every moral prescript hidden away, buried beneath mountains of last night's trash, to be neither seen nor reflected upon until the festivities cease. They're gone, for now, the ropes that bind wrists, leashes that tug at necks, thorns jabbed into temples, hands, and feet, lances splitting sides below the ribs. The disciples included—all thirteen—the betrayer himself made scarce, and the others scattered into dens of disreputable deeds, houses of flesh and drink, the aromatic scents of different types of weeds, merriment beyond belief. Judgmental friends and relatives, too, out there masquerading as depraved transformations of themselves, along for the ride because even judges must stand trial at times. For once not together, but apart, solo, each alone to mingle and get lost under the groping touch of strange hands, behind the grotesque visages of masks, to forget the scraps of hurt and loss—beware, be careful, they are in the crowd, your flesh and blood, your precious ones—one and all searching for the thoughtless thought, striving to catch hold of their true-selves, ballooning and diminishing all at once, until we are, each of us, faceless, nameless. Perfect versions of ourselves.

The prophet wields his medicine staff, adorned in feathers and beads, shreds of scalps and animal furs, and strung with pouches full of fragrant forest herbs.

The missionary shoulders a musket, a burden and a gift from his fallen Bahaman guide, for protection on the frontier, a prop for the Community he holds dear.

The coyotes require naught but their teeth, their instincts.

A deep breath before they begin, all noise rescinds except for the anticipative roar from the spectators outside, beyond the closed door. The man without memories demands a Scrap for accompaniment. The barman and the journalist assent, so the barman spins a well-worn disc. They each swallow a shot of the drink, their pride and reservations, alight with their weapons and aggressive stances, inhibitions spat upon floorboards, stamped out and dirtied, the moon on cloudy nights.

Who shall begin? How shall they proceed? Speaking respectfully of the deceased? Or swinging for the fences? Meditative and orderly? Or cathartic and passionately?

The barman and the journalist stand back. They wait.

The man without memories sees a shape, framed and blurry behind a layer of dust, cramped, trapped, the memory of a man who tramps through his dreams, trundles across a mountain pass, trips at questions about his past, callow and afraid through tempest and storm, as creatures of the forest hunt and howl, bearing down, he cowers from dogs, coyotes, a dead horse on the run, the rain and the wind, scraps of music whipping round, the Carnival must go on, leaves and branches torn loose, flung dangerously close, shard-like teeth, bones fractured and whole, mud and rock cascading down, a groan sounds from deep within, not from the mountain and not from the storm, but from within the man, the man who reaches, grasps, clutches at his fear, the howl is his own—

Fear of the blood-curdling cries trapping him in nightmares and then bursting through the barrier into waking life. The fear that makes people cry themselves to sleep and coyotes howl in the night. This fear is an accuser telling men they've done wrong without intoning what it is they've done, denying them the opportunity to defend their honor, their rights. It's the same fear that makes the ex-pastor drink, causes cowards to shrink away from pain, and renders the courageous weak from suffering. This, the fear that sent the man without memories into the mountains and the same fear that drew him out. The fear of death, which is also the fear of life, because without one the other cannot be justified. Fear of the world and fear of the unknown, together as one.

He swings his ax. Once is enough. It has begun.

The vitreous scream of glass, a cry as the shattered mass hits the ground and the Other, the one behind the mirror, is on the run, inverse of Kristallnacht, as now Doctor Mengele, the mutt, retreats into the crowd and the chaos of Carnival steps it up a notch.

The barman, his bat, lets loose a crack.

The journalist does not hold back. His chair, flung from afar, brings on a shriek-like crash.

Dual memories spring forth from each effortless swing, smashed and jarred free by the ear-splitting din, resistance at the border, the Sirens' shrill, seductive hymn. A word, a gesture, or an act of the deceased, the friend who's been released from time, stamped out, silenced in brine. And too, a place, a choice, or an intensity felt more than seen, an experience revealed, relived, repeated, from within. Dance steps enmeshed, lost and found again, creating an unstoppable flow, a river's wide grin around rocky bends, banks, and dips, the roar of onlookers ebbs, the tide climbs high, peaks, and then sighs, until all that's left is fragmentary, the coarse rub of bones, granulations of sand, sparkling sharp edges of glass shifting beneath the feet of those who roam still, free to be, to scale to heights unseen or to foul up their lives with clumsy, misguided, selfish aberrations, defections, defecations. Trampled, suffocated, crushed, and ground to dust, ashes, embers pulse and one day fade out.

The song stops.

Spread upon the floor, this offering for the dead, our actions not for him, but for ourselves, to mend.

"And Jesus cracked," the journalist gasps for breath, "so men could follow step..."

"I hope this satisfies you," says the barman, heaving for air. "Helps you find your blessed paradise at the eye of the storm. Because it sure as shit didn't raise paradise in here."

"Didn't erase the past either," observes the journalist.

"No, it didn't," admits the man without memories. "And it wasn't meant to."

The barman, dripping sweat, glances around his establishment, altered now beyond recognition. He winces with each grinding tread atop the glass, careful to keep his balance as he weaves a path toward the hidden rear entrance, a pile of supplies and cleaning apparatus.

The man without memories grabs the journalist by the shoulder, leads him back to the bar. He refills their glasses and the barman's as well.

"But it is nice to know that we have a hand in it," says the man without memories as he picks stray shards off his sleeves.

"In what?" the barman returns and hands the journalist a broom. Then, he sets a short-handled brush-and-dustpan-set on the bar top and slides it toward the man without memories. "Sorry, it's all I got left."

"Have a hand in what?" repeats the journalist.

"In moving out of the past. The passage of time itself."

"Not a day any of us will forget..."

"I ain't gotten up to so much mischief since I was just a little shit..."

"Raise 'em up, boys. To him, one last time..."

"To him..."

"He'd be proud, content, for once..."

"Cheers, fellas. Now let's get this over with."

As they sweep up the pieces, the tranquil sound works to ease their minds. Soft rustles crackle and scratch beneath their feet. Their brooms brush at different pitches, each with bristles made of unique materials—one of corn straw, one of polystyrene, and one of Tampico fiber. Their pitches blend, push, and whisk together, often overlapping, sometimes in sync, calm as the surf on a beach, wind through the leaves. No need for a song when they can compose music of their own. They cross paths, form lanes, communal and personal piles, the gentle trickle and tickle of minuscule shards added to growing mounds. Old hidden bits of trash and food dislodge from crevices and corners. After rounding up the largest shards, out comes an ancient aluminum bin. Placid silence punctuated by bursts of noisy, resounding racket. Heavy loads dance and slide and bounce off the sides, broken into still smaller fragments but contained and quickly filling the bin near to the brim. The floor gradually becomes safer to negotiate. Tables and chairs are moved around, slid away, and then replaced. Every once in a while, a suppressed cry escapes someone's mouth, a minor scream as they reach for an uncooperative jagged piece wedged between floorboards or caught in the sticky remnants of spilled cocktails, forcing them to remove slivers of glass from their flesh, to suck on the blood or wipe it on their pants. Someone suggests gloves and the other two mumble dissent. The three of them share occasional glances, helping one another to push and navigate fragments gone astray. The piano, too, must be shifted and swept clean. The man without memories remains low to the ground, crouched, stuck as he is with the short-handled broom. Invisible splinters cover his pants and pierce his kneecaps, while the barman and the journalist step up to the wall for the hardest part, several dangerous bits still wedged in place, jutting out, knives and teeth begging release. After what they have been through today, the men are adept and confident, maneuvering hands and fingers around precarious razored edges. Sometimes, a screwdriver helps to pry out a problematic piece. Other times, a pair of pliers is required. The shards squeak and whine as they rub against the wooden trim and slip free. Now and then, a piece will fall from their grasp onto the cushioned seat of the wall-side bench, tearing the upholstery. But the barman doesn't curse, doesn't even flinch, just carefully retrieves the stray and drops it into the bin.

They work and work, going over the same spots again and again. Whenever it seems that they are almost done, it is then that nigh imperceptible sparkles and redirections of trapped light catch their eyes, and they know they can never truly complete the task. Destruction of this sort, it lasts. They know it, but they vow to pick up as much as they can. Somber and yet serene, they discuss other methods. Hose the place down. Cover every square inch in duct tape or paint. Raze the entire building to the ground. All viable options, for some later date. But for now, today, they'll simply sweep.

At one point, the man without memories stands up. He stares at the empty wall for a long time. The barman and the journalist cast silent, curious glances. They pause to watch as the man without memories steps forward. The tiny fragments of glass stuck to the bottoms of his shoes scrape across the floor. The room is thick with the scent of dust, disturbed by all this sweeping happening all at once, and the barman sneezes.

"What is it?" says the journalist. "What do you see?"

The man without memories stops where he is, a few steps from the wall. He scans the room, winces, breathes.

"Nothing."

But the Saint of Creek's Ridge sighs, ill at ease. For she has heard this joke before.

A Note on Digging
From the Author

More than any creative work I have produced, this novel deserves the epithet of "a labor of love." Never mind the cliché; there is simply no more apt description if I'm talking about this novel. So much of my time and myself has gone into bringing this story to life. In a way, *Strike, Stay Your Hand* is my Limping Lady. This is my horse skeleton that will never be finished. There will always be more spots to dig, more to uncover, and more to surprise me, but I have reached a point where I feel comfortable putting it on display.

I still remember the curious, emptying feeling I felt upon finishing the first draft. As Johannes says to Grant, it felt "Almost weightless." If only I had known how many more years of my life this story would continue to live with me, I may have felt differently. Then, and for many years after, it was titled *Into the Valley of Dogs*. That title referenced something Josephine wrote in her journals. While I still like that title, it did not have quite the same impact after some heavy restructuring saw the exclusion of those original journal entries.

This novel is a culmination of sixteen years of my life, almost all of which I have been living abroad. To answer a question I have often received—No, Johannes is not based on me. That is, not any more than any of the other characters. I think of these characters as me engaged in a conversation with myself. As a younger man, I formed certain ideas and convictions about life. But, like most young men, I lacked experience of the world. Coming from a background in philosophy, I recognized the importance of testing those notions with resistance. Those sixteen years of editing and rewriting were not happening only on the page but also within the workings of my own mind. I needed that time to grow, gather experience, and dissect those ideas with the rigor they deserved. This came about through traveling the world, getting to know people and their motivations, and a lot of reading. A few books that propelled me through the early drafts were Kafka's *The Castle*, Huxley's *The Doors of Perception*, and Kierkegaard's *Either/Or*. The philosophical concepts explored in these books laid the groundwork, but the evolution of the story and structure was later influenced by the giants of postmodern fiction, such as Gaddis's *The Recognitions*, Gass's *The Tunnel*, Fuentes's *Terra Nostra*, and Vargas Llosa's *The Feast of the Goat*.

Despite the ensuing years and all the myriad changes to the story, the essence of that first draft remains. The ideas and their presentation, however, have grown with me. Returning to the question above, all the characters in the novel stem from a part of me. And they have all been allowed to grow with me over time. Their interactions with each other —both directly and indirectly through the weaving narratives— provided a way for me to investigate every angle of certain beliefs and ethical dilemmas in a sort of Socratic dialogue. For every idea any given character might espouse, there are several counterarguments presented by other characters. Since many of those ideas originated from a young man's perspective of the world, I am also having a conversation with my younger self. Years of re-examining those ideas through (hopefully) wiser eyes resulted in a more balanced viewpoint on what it means to be alive. There is never a right or wrong answer, but only the choices people make and how they react to the consequences of their actions.

The decision to include Emedio Del Bosque and Tenskwatawa in later drafts led to a complete overhaul of the novel's structure. Lalawethika/Tenskwatawa is, of course, based on a real Shawnee prophet of the same name, brother to the famed Shawnee chief, Tecumseh. The tales of those characters, while based on actual events, are entirely fictional. Emedio Del Bosque is not based on a real person, but several of the characters he encounters during his travels were real, including Robert Ambrister and Jeremiah Evarts. The original draft contained only a single chapter outlining Saint Josephine's life. With the inclusion of her father's story and the tripartite structure, I decided to unravel Josephine's story as perceived by the present-day residents of Creek's Ridge. However, the very last chapter added to the novel was Josephine's diary entry in the chapter entitled "The Saint." That character's story is far too important to have left the final word to anyone other than her.

The gradual formation of the finished novel would not have been possible without the invaluable insights I received from countless readers over the years. In no particular order, I would especially like to thank Paul Drydyk for eating up those first draft chapters serially; John Rozumowicz for encouraging me through initial doubts; Jason Then for foreseeing the inevitable reduction of the main story long before I did; PJ Mortenson for taking time out of his busy schedule with a draft that was entirely too long; Adam Sawicki for putting up with several new drafts and always digging into the trenches with me as I worked out new ideas; and Emily Franklin for giving me the confidence to start reframing the story. I would also like to extend my warmest thanks to the team at Deserted Home Press for their support and creative input during the final stages of publication.

Finally, the book in your hands (or on your device) might never have been completed if it weren't for the bottomless well of support I get from my wife. Thank you, Gyubin, for being my constant reader. You have listened to me fret and worry over this novel. You have steadied my nerves as I constantly took one step forward and two steps back. Through all of it, you have encouraged me with your smile, both calming me and urging me onward in a way only you can. Because of you, the next books will be easier. Because of you, everything is easier.

And a genuine thank you to all my readers. If you've made it this far, you've completed quite the dig yourself. I hope you've found a few bones worth hanging on to. Just remember—all things in life must end eventually, but as long as you're still around, there's always a bit of digging to be done.

Anton Brinza, September 2024
Goyang, South Korea

About the Author

Anton Brinza was born in 1983 in Milwaukee, Wisconsin. Though he is primarily an author of horror fiction, *Strike, Stay Your Hand* stands as an outlier, an ambitious literary undertaking bookended by his lifelong interest in weird tales, uncanny creatures, and the things that keep us up at night. This novel is fleshed out by minor elements of horror, but it owes its existence to the immense influence of the greats of post-modern literature: Marcel Proust, William Gaddis, William H Gass, John Barth, Thomas Pynchon, Don DeLillo, Carlos Fuentes, Mario Vargas Llosa, David Foster Wallace, and Roberto Bolaño. While Anton intends to expand his literary repertoire in the future, he is currently hard at work on a series of horror novels entitled *The EORYX Saga*. Anton lives with his wife in South Korea, his home of the past seventeen years.

Also by Anton Brinza

Though this novel is not a work of horror, most of Anton's other writings are set firmly in worlds meant to inspire fear and terror. For information about the author's other works of fiction, including the novels comprising *The EORYX Saga,* please visit:

www.ludovicotreats.com

www.antonbrinza.com

Sign up for the mailing list and keep an eye out for updates on other literary offerings by Deserted Home Press.

Milton Keynes UK
Ingram Content Group UK Ltd.
UKHW030720041024
449263UK00004B/333